Beyond the Masque

Beyond the Masque

by

Kae D. Jacobs

Beyond the Masque
Copyright © 2008 by Kae D. Jacobs
All rights reserved

This is a work of fiction. All characters are fictional and any resemblance to persons living or dead is purely coincidental.

No part of this book may be reproduced in any form whatsoever, whether by graphic, visual, electronic, filming, microfilming, tape recording or any other means, without the written permission of the author, except in the case of a brief passage embodied in critical reviews and articles where the title, author and ISBN accompany such review or article.

Published and Distributed by:

Granite Publishing and Distributions, LLC
868 North 1430 West
Orem, UT 84057
(801) 229-9023 Toll Free (800) 574-5779
www.granitepublishing.biz

Cover Design by Steve Gray
Page Layout and Design by Myrna M. Varga

ISBN: 978-1-59936-032-4
Library of Congress Control Number: 2008939619

First Printing: November 2008

1 3 5 7 9 10 8 6 4 2

Printed in the United States of America

*For all those whose hearts treasure up simple beauties,
in every form.*

*To my husband and family
And. . . dearest Jen*

When dreams connect with our soul, therein resides a place of beauty. This is where my life began... so long ago... where my dreams are at last, my reality.
Erik

Chapter One

His body was bent, legs parted, lungs heaving with unrestrained exertion as he stood, wavering slightly. A sudden, ragged breath forced clarity to glare before his unseeing eyes and slowly the anger, in all its consuming rage, began to recede. He blinked, then his eyes clamped shut, sweat feverishly dotting his brow as the pain and anguish hit.

Eighteen! The years tallied rapidly as he realized it had been eighteen years from the time he had been professionally engaged, since he had lived—if one could call a meager, parasitic subsistence life—and had come to be lodged beneath an opera house in the center of Paris! *And to what purpose might I lay claim? None! That is the tragic, pitiful drama of it all!* His thoughts cut unmercifully in their reproach.

There would be nothing left, of course; he had begun the erasure upon his return from that final, concluding interview with the Persian just hours before; yes, all would play out. The other rooms most likely resembled an unerring reflection of what faced him now. Walls, their black draperies stripped unheeding, bore shamefully the harsh exposure of dignity removed, the rich finery heaped at their base. The canopied, funereal shrine lay smashed, as were the remains of a desk, piled in a twisted heap, ink dripping from a thick-fingered blot against the hardened stone. Then there was the organ, the mangled pipes of *his* organ. He gasped. His panting thinned, his breath more even, as he held an arm out to catch the brunt of his impending weight upon the bench. Yes, here. Here he would complete and bear alone a predetermined appointment with Fate.

"No curse can be as bitter as the one we give ourselves," he spat in sorrowful ire, flinging the masque he forever despised across the room to collide with another unrelenting surface, the explosive contact rendering the molded glass into an array of useless fragments. "No fate could possibly encompass all I wish to blame."

Rounding, he confronted a surge of despair rivaling any remaining sanity and sat, slumped in disheveled evening attire; seams, pulled beyond capacity, burst randomly at the shoulders and down the back of his tailcoat; buttons, having been stretched from their place of repose, loosely managed the now ill fitted waistcoat and neck of his rumpled shirt; and the filth dusted the inky black of his suit to grey. He shifted and his mind went blank, eyes void, mouth empty of words as his fingers gently caressed his lips. They had touched her skin, tasted her tears as she cried over him. He trembled. Had she responded, felt anything at all for him? He was unable to recall more.

"She would have stayed, and later resented. . . the kiss, hers and mine. . ." Reality's door slammed, compelling him to doubt. "But, that was days ago. It was enough, it must be." The lack of confidence gnawed. "To know she will be happy, well cared for. . . that should be enough, should it not?" Again, a finger raised, touching those sweetened spots upon his lips and upon his forehead, and a tear fell. He knew he would not be the one for whom she would reach or respond to, not his voice, nor his touch. A knot cinched in his throat and a sob bellowed from within, begged surrender, only to die behind his parched lips. Then, leaning into the once comforting instrument, he wrapped his arms about his head in the confines of that quietly dim room, and wept.

"She was so good," he whispered, "I have tasted all the happiness the world has to offer."

He lay with his upper body sprawled against the console, wandering through a mental haze of evaporated hopes and plans; it was then that he heard the light voice, a familiar voice, angelic though distantly faint, speak his name.

"Erik?"

With a mind screaming foul his restraint waned, scarcely holding back the ferocity pounding to be released. "Not only is my genius mocked with this accursed face, but what is left of my mental balance, God wishes to rip from me as well! What more?" he spewed heavenward. "I gave her up! I gave back your angel. . . what I longed for. . ." his voice diminished in a pitiful moan, then resounded anew. "How fitting, to be plunged further into insanity by the sound of her voice! It is madness, to be sure!" Vengeful as his temper was, the inevitable doused any remaining spirit, and weariness of heart captured head to arm once again, producing momentary deliverance.

"Erik."

Madness. . . Shaking uncontrollably, his hands rose to block the excruciating pain from his ears; he rocked lightly, for the sound he once relished was now only a gut wrenching twist to mind and body. "Stop!" His fist pummeled mercilessly into the keys. "Stop!" he pleaded, hands clenched. "Please, no more. . . just let me die. . . no. . . more."

She jumped, staying her ground just out of reach. The distance was gauged wise under the circumstances, as ending up a member of any strewn décor could not possibly be the desire. "God does not mock, Erik," she expressed softly, "your ears do not deceive you."

She? Here? An immense feeling of powerlessness threatened Erik's very connection to reason, debilitating his sense of logic to the core. For a man who at one time seemed the epitome of control, he was at a loss, mollified by her very presence into humility. Composing what he could of himself, he turned his exposed face away to the left, leaving his right arm draped unceremoniously upon the keys.

Erik spied her somewhat self-assured movement when she sidestepped into view, he inhaled sharply—it was a feeling not unlike having a burst of ice water flush through his lungs. He did not strain long for lack of self-discipline; the guard so successfully raised had his countenance marked by indifference and thoughts summoning all manner of resources to combat the unexpected. *Does she comprehend? No, she could not possibly. Here, my heart lies open, rent wide within my chest and she has come to rub salt in the wound. Let us watch poor, pitiful, unhappy Erik expand his lungs on her scent, her closeness, then strip them of all hope until he suffocates. No, it cannot be allowed! I shall keep my dignity and writhe in private, thank you. . . give her no satisfaction!*

He struggled with these innermost workings, attempting to regain sufficient poise before uttering a single word, but he rasped out unintentionally. Irritated at the influence she had over him still, he breathed in again and repeated, "Christine."

"Yes?"

She blanched at her eager sounding response, allowing Erik time to evade the extended hand making to smooth several displaced strands of hair—or so he supposed this to be their desire—and draw away to stand; the presumption was unwelcome. In the back of his mind he half expected that infernal Chagny chap to storm into his flat at any moment, demanding Christine's return, and to find himself weakened, for any reason, would be inexcusable and deadly. *Deadly? Why worry now? Why care?*

"Where is your. . . young man?" Erik ventured blindly, not knowing what to expect.

"Gone. . . at my bidding," she said without emotion.

"An explanation then," he lightly demanded, his daring pride allowing his peripheral vision only a derisory glance in her direction. The few candles which had yet to meet their end in a waxen snuff on the floor, were backlighting her innocent form and caught him unaware. Where fright had once shared space in those comforting brown eyes, there was now determined acceptance.

"Inside," she began timidly, pointing to her chest, "in the deepest part of who I am lies a piece of me that was torn between two very different emotions, and decisions were ultimately made in my behalf that I disagreed with."

Erik's brow creased. "You said. . ." Sighing, his mind tried to congeal around such odds, even if it were only for a minuscule duration. "I. . . do not understand."

"I have much to learn about myself, about you, but I find that I desire to learn *from* you, to be taught *by* you. It is where my heart feels connected."

Without warning, all pretense disappeared; there was nothing to hide behind, absolutely nothing! It was that first-time introduction in garish repeat—when she discovered him to be just a man, just Erik. He had played on her vulnerability then, her desire for guidance from an angel of music, her father's promise as he passed from this life to the next, but the moment of truth had revealed the man behind the deception of vocal deity. He was tangible and certainly no angel, this she knew.

Erik sensed weighted touch, Christine had bravely moved in front of him. The shadows engulfing his features dissolved any protest as she gently took hold of the lapels of his tailcoat. His eyes closed to the brief, upward gaze applied before she laid her head against his chest. *Oh! Blessed touch!* He felt it all, indeed he did! She tucked her head, not much, but just enough at the base of his neck that he chanced to lay his chin to the warm invitation; the softness of her hair, the trust in her lean, and his perilous self-worth; he felt every availing particle. He stood there paralyzed to motion, his thoughts lost, sensing that thrumming beat in tune with his.

Christine could not have known what turn of events she had just set in motion. The implications of that long denied touch on the human psyche nor the bearing of their parting affection those days prior, spoke volumes to his soul, and though her naïveté of youth was transparent, the choice seemed to suit. His response was irrefutable but went largely undetected, the subtleties missed, adding to the confused countenance of the young woman. The secure sensation of belonging caused his throat to thicken; the weak glow of candlelight saw a glint against his left cheek as his hands gripped fiercely, his right upon the organ, and his left at his trouser leg, crushing the dark, velvety-like pile of the stripe within his palm.

Fearing the moment would end too soon, he held onto the mental image, refusing to open his eyes. Finally, feeling her warmth dissipate and her narrowed glare fixed upon him, Erik cleared the sweet mist to the back of his mind and straightened; his distant, magnetic eyes repelled her with a piercing glare. *You must maintain the upper hand, at all cost!*

"Would you. . ." Erik hesitated. *What are you about, and what do you mean, would you?* "Perhaps, you would consider accompanying me. There is a place I wish you to see, a place I know."

Christine recovered herself and assented cautiously.

"Come. . . this way." Erik showed her through the chaos to a wall at the rear of his chamber, where slight hand pressure released a counter balance, permitting the stone door to pivot inward. Then, moving in synchronized harmony within a precise amount of time, they slipped through as the barrier rotated to re-engage upon itself. "Wait here," he commanded gently, after leading her a few strides into the darkened passage.

She molded to the solid, unforgiving mass with her back, hugging her body against the fear closing in. Choking, she whispered, "I am really not fond of—"

A sizzling could be heard, followed closely by the light whoosh of a torch being engulfed in flame. "The dark," he said, ending her concern and sentence altogether. "I know." Erik had cautiously watched her as he manipulated the cords, severing one, to secure the mechanism from being tripped. *There, no Daroga, Chagny, or escape. . .* an airy huff of satisfaction exited, *at least until I understand.*

Wary once again, the low blaze dipped against the black as he approached and began to assess under a new perspective. Unsure of who was to become prey to whom, the well-positioned blaze became camouflage in its own right: a masque, hat, cloak, and gloves lay patiently around the bend up ahead, but his curiosity piqued prematurely.

"Who has knowledge of your destination *this* night?" he asked, unwilling to mitigate the menacing edge. "It has been a scant smattering of days, why did you return?" Erik maneuvered Christine to his left, the question burning from those two pools of boiling angst.

"No one knows!" she half growled at the implication. "And. . . and I require a bit more time, if you don't mind, to have a complete grasp of why myself before I attempt any more of an explanation than I have given." Christine nervously twisted one thumbnail under the other and refused to drop her steady examination of him, almost in a challenge of defiance.

A tad mousy, but defiance nonetheless, he smirked inwardly. "Fair enough, Mademoiselle." He directed her forward, making one last stop to gather his things and implement his shackles of distrust.

Christine waited with her back turned, allowing him the respect to do so as the torch rested within a bracket anchored to the wall. After a moment, she rounded slightly. "Erik?"

His name surprised him and he took a step backward, leaning to brace himself against the rise of heat her tone elicited. Instinctively, she reached out and their forearms clasped together. They froze. A light tug brought Erik upright, though neither relinquished the other from that position of support. Tenderly, and ever so slowly, Christine led each of his hands to her waist in turn. As he watched, Erik fought mentally, feeling his emotional overdrive supersede all control as she gradually coaxed his extremities into motion. He beheld those traitorous appendages; they were his most assuredly, and they were gaining acquisition of surface, despite the insulative properties of the leather gloves. Each time he felt the transfer of pressure to his hands and arms, his breath caught. Years of debilitating inhibition crumbled from malleable joints, and fingers stretched, drawing her against his chest. The sensation, its magic, washed over and through his timorous, vulnerable body, heart throbbing within the ribs of his mortal cage.

An eternity has passed by in seconds. . . to wrap my arms. . . the distribution of weight I hold near. No! Erik cannot. . . it is forbidden! He sighed, heeding the repressed voice to gently move Christine away, avoiding her eyes. "We should go. We have quite a distance to travel, come. . . this way."

Christine's perplexed look spoke two-fold in disbelief, the first, he figured came as discomfort, and the second, registered wonder, most likely at the depth one could attain below the Opera House. But as to this mysterious *where,* he took pride in withholding the specifics. "Not to worry, I would never resign beauty to a life of moling. Even *I* have my limits." His jocularity won him a light smile, made answer to the unasked, and so they traversed onward.

Penetrating the way ahead, a low, nearly inaudible whistle warned and alerted as they emerged into the galley. It was a wide section of angled, interconnected maze, the juncture where the stable ramps led up to the stage; here, a soft whicker hailed in salutation toward the two of them. The horse snorted at the reacquainting mention of "Cesar" by a feminine register, the generous patting and scratching of muzzle and forehead setting apprehension aside.

Erik considered the interaction with no more than a disinterested grunt while he quickly readied the stallion for their departure then offered his hand. By torchlight, the spectral streams, from small crevices in the masonry walls, hung as jagged shards, casting eerie blue ripples upon the glowing white of Cesar's coat. Such a majestic, beautifully formed animal was now beneath her as she was lifted with ease atop the saddle. Erik mounted and wrapped them both under the settling wing of his cloak; a protection offered against the night above.

"Please, forgive me for seeming crass, it is not my intention," he explained, "but I should think because of the distance we shall negotiate, it may be more preferable to sit astride."

Complying in silence, Christine readjusted to the sensible request and Erik surrounded her lithe waist, securely holding her against the jarring grasp of reins before wheeling Cesar. The horse moved swiftly under the hand of his master, leaving the cellars behind to make their way through the underground labyrinth. So many twists and turns had Erik wondering whether Christine owned a goodly amount of directional faculty about her, but his thoughts dissipated along with a small, frustrated sigh from her. Perhaps she had decided that their whereabouts were best left to those with the instincts, to whom she now entrusted her safety.

The air gradually cooled during their ascent, sending a chill over Christine's bare neck. Erik felt her shiver and pulled the edges of the cloak in tighter about them. They were at ground level, looking down on an obscured section of fencing near the Cour de l'Administration. Erik moved their darkened shadow parallel and quietly released the ordinate features of a hidden gate, enabling horse and riders to blend through the well-constructed design.

Cesar could feel the electricity and his ears immediately pricked at the sound of his master's command, "Away, my friend." In response, they were off, gliding in a northwesterly direction through the narrow cobbled streets, their low, concealed cloud of misty silence floating effortlessly out into the countryside.

NOTHING PENETRATED THE world of either rider as they flew to their undisclosed destination. Erik's muscles would expand and contract in harmony with the horse's gait as his undeviating focus placed distance between them and all probable interruptions. Disjointed thoughts and comparisons led out next when Cesar slowed to a more melodious sway; and though neither would dare openly confess impetuosity nor allow Prudence an attack on any front based on their limited knowledge of the other, Erik's mind raced on furiously. All was internal assessment, but when his mind could no longer remain quiet the questions began: *What have I done? What must she think? Too impulsive an act, too headstrong, for sure! Then again, it is who I am.*

And what of her? Did the things she knew have her emotions upended? Would she compare and contrast his ruthless behavior with inspirational genius and irrational calm? He was filled with so many opposites; so much of who he was conflicted with the good, dependable, and sound, as well as the abilities, experiences and talents professed beyond what any single man could rationally attain. Ah, but being shunned from the world, alone, had perhaps afforded him many lifetimes. *And she returned because a part of her is irrevocably attached to me.* Was there a reason? Pushing these reflections, and more, to reside upon a little-used shelf in his mind for the time being, he concentrated on the warmth radiating from inside his heart. . . or was it hers?

Time ticked on and Erik's consciousness was once again employed, becoming alert to any and all sensations. Gone were the unresolved queries under the tender hands of Christine. He could feel her periodically stop along his arm, to soothe and caress the apprehension from each resting place, lulling him, and the tingle had such a tranquil effect, it was surprising how her touch wiped the intellect void of all cares. A dream? For now, he wished only to experience.

Grasping, with reassuring squeezes, Christine had carefully and rather successfully, removed Erik's glove from his left hand, prying each finger from its snug-fitting cave. Suddenly, Cesar pulled up short and a flustered Erik sat bolt upright. Too late to realize what Christine had been doing, his hand jerked away, though he had already been divested of glove, leaving such in her possession! How irksome! He stiffened against her, his aggravation evident in the staccato breaths hitting her back.

"My glove," he expelled curtly.

"Your hand," she replied shortly, holding tight to that despicable appendaged leather, waiting. The idiosyncrasy had, as expected, come paired with a severe dose of obstinacy.

He could hear the smile. Was she so accustomed to his traits that she dared pull such a stunt? Was he so easily read? "It seems, my dear," he huffed, "we are at an impasse." Erik's chin strained to procure some form of comfort for his neck, unsuccessful as it was. *And*, he grumbled mentally, *perhaps you will prove more of an annoyance than an asset. For I detest. . . do not appreciate, being taken advantage of.*

"Erik," Christine sighed. Her voice was patient, allowing those four letters to roll off out into the ink of night. She had not turned nor did he wish it, she only moved her elbow outward from her side. "If you are uncomfortable, then I shall gladly return your glove."

Why does she do this? His mind brooded. *She has shied away in repulsion from my touch, why this sudden change?* Seeing the futility of resisting further, because he actually preferred the situation, he hesitantly threaded his left hand from the back, feeling his way.

"I will not break," she encouraged, "just as before."

The straps of the stirrups creaked under stress as Erik shifted, and his right hand clenched and relaxed on the reins several times before his tongue clicked, sending Cesar on his way.

His hand was exposed, skin luminously pale, thin in both structure and appearance, cold at first, but warming. Erik tensed when she slid her hand over his, and then he relaxed again. Interestingly enough, it was not long before the reins made a diagonal twist to rest across Cesar's withers, as the right glove with the slight-of-hand, not wishing to be excluded, was presented for *its* turn. Christine removed the covering and then it gestured for the mate. Once rewarded, the gloves were stowed, permitting Erik to complete the circle of a gentle embrace around Christine. A drop of moisture splashed along her neck, then another; she leaned back and Erik pulled, cinching her right up next to his chin. Was this how it felt to be accepted?

"N–never," he stuttered, "has anyone ever w–wanted. . ." his words were fragmented whispers in her ear as she kindly added a bit of pressure for reassurance and Erik absorbed every precious second of human contact.

Several hours had elapsed, permitting Erik time to review, on his terms, the events of that evening. He had discovered a flaw, an unsettling, quirky flaw in the character of Fate. What had she said? '… I find that I desire to learn *from* you, to be taught *by* you. . .' *Humph, I stare a gift horse in the mouth and insult the giver to his face. Worth? Upon what does my worth merit consideration?* His life always came with an agenda, an addendum, this too, was no different… this too, would pass away. Having been long within such close proximity to Christine brought the undeserving pinch, and a nervous stomach announced to Erik that at this stage of the journey, even Christine was having doubts regarding an intended goal; he felt the vibrations rise and abate then distanced himself, murmuring, "not far."

Unwilling to leave quiet to its own volition, Christine braved a question. "Would you tell me of our destination?"

"I suppose, yes, if nothing else," *I would prefer nothing else, I really do not mind the silence as long as I can be close. . .* "I guess it will engage the dragging of time," he prattled.

"Years ago, after I returned from my varied sojourns throughout sections of Europe and Asia, I was able to secure a great deal of property in a secluded area. I chose a site and prepared in earnest to begin building, but never commenced; the Opera House had procured my interest instead. I tendered for the foundations and was awarded the contract, and I actually found the situation suited me so well that I abandoned this outdoor project and took up residence where I could create, watching the birth and development of beauty emerge under my guidance. I reveled in the challenge and lost myself so completely and happily in the endeavor that it became a euphoric escape, and eventually my eccentric stage upon which to play out my will. It was not until, more recently," his voice emphasized, "that I had any inclination to erect this quaint little estate; finding it highly unusual that when the very boundaries I had built to protect against others, imposed too heavily, I would have to come back. . . here."

Erik gave the landscape a slow, panoramic sweep of his arm and, as if on cue, a looming shape rose out of the trees across from the base of a large hill. Their plodding advance toward this hidden niche had Erik aware of Christine's calm, it was the same comfort he experienced upon his returns. Squinting under the sliver of moonlight—for it was not much more—there were few specifics, other than ebon silhouettes upon which to rely, as sight gave way to other senses; there was a hint of moisture clinging to the air, and the soothing babble of water flowing nearby. Pulling up short, Erik dismounted, giving the two of them each an opportunity to breathe in deeply, separately. He then reached up and Christine's hands came to rest naturally upon his broad shoulders, for careful assistance to the ground. His head inclined, eyes lingering at the hand's chosen placement in turn, as though a piece of lint were waiting to be plucked from the immaculate surface. Quickly withdrawing the intrusion, she clasped both together in prayerful fashion before her. He listened, intently evaluating. Quiet had always been one of Erik's closest companions, but now it was he who dared to speak amid the stillness save the betrayal pulsing within his veins.

"Inside and up the stairs you will find a dressing room to your right. I should think it to provide. . . most of the essentials. I shall tend to Cesar," he directed.

Christine nodded, staying any hint of quitting his presence. "You will need to relinquish your hold, " she informed.

Erik dropped his hands and head in embarrassment, appalled by his own weakness to remain objective and aloof. "Forgive me."

"There is nothing to forgive, I am flattered," she gently expressed, touching the center of his chest before turning.

Sighing, Erik grabbed Cesar's reins. "All I ever dreamed of," he said, glancing back after Christine. Then, motioning to his friend, he leaned in and together they walked down the familiar gravel path to the stable.

CLIMBING THE STAIRS, Christine stepped meekly across the porch and pressed her hand against the smooth grain of an ominous set of double doors. Her hand slid down upon the handle and she entered unhindered, no lock to bar intrusion. There was a moment of adjustment, and though the pitch black within was altered little by the conditions without, a source of light would see to its defining role. On the right, and nearest the abutment of one neighboring wall, stood a library table, freely exhibiting its only wares of candles, arranged in varying lengths and widths upon a narrow platter. Striking a match, she lit the closest one to her; the flame flickered and sputtered to life, pushing back the darkness and, lighting a few more, the cavity of the room opened to gaping proportions, in much the same way as her mouth.

The main level, which seemed a vast drawing room upon first glance, was extraordinarily grand, while in possession of simple elegance. To her left, jutted a large, raised fireplace from the center of the wall. It had a smooth stone ledge for sitting about the heat and was central to the furniture, which edged an intricately woven Persian rug. Pillows, adorning the chaise, sofa and high backed chairs, spilled from their place of rest to the floor beneath. Then, turning a bit more, she noticed what had to be the most crucial fixture in the house, a concert piano, with accompanying musical scores strewn about in a haphazardly organized manner.

"If there is such a concept," she mused, "it resides here."

Brushing the yawing door completely closed, she moved to the panels at her right and slid them open. An "ah" escaped, "the dining area and just beyond, most likely a kitchen." Knowing there was still more to sate her vision she turned and began her ascent upstairs, leaving what she could, untouched. The staircase, broad as it was at the base, narrowed as it curved upward to a long, open landing spanning the width of the second level.

"Hmm, how strange," she said, steering toward the right, considering the mystery at each step. "Two doors, one at either end and nothing central." Christine shrugged the oddity in favor of boundaries, in which she decided to abide within the apposite limits and, lighting several wall sconces to chase back the expansive hollows even more, she moved in accordance with the directive given her. Again, the door's smoothness amazed her... *beauty*. The word forced pause for contemplation. "Perhaps Erik feels there to be compensation between the exquisite craftsmanship and outward appearances." Her brow drew low. "There is much we shall learn from one another, in this, your escape from an otherwise restrictive existence, Monsieur."

Christine was brought back to task as the next barrier folded in upon itself to reveal a magnificent dressing room. Cedar lined, mahogany wardrobes graced the walls from floor to ceiling. There were dresses, nightclothes, towels, soaps, and toiletries, all awaiting use. And the mirrors—not one, but three, placed in strategic spots—were meant as seen, to provide an adequate view from all sides, and lastly, tucked discreetly from sight, a bathing area.

Setting the candle down, a shiver ran the length of her spine. "It is as though he was expecting..." She shook her head.

He was clinging to what must be only a fraction of hope. To have prepared for, assuming in some possessive frame of mind that he could convince or hope to convince her to stay with him, and ultimately, to love him. He then freed her from that commitment because of her willingness, her compassion; he gave up what he so desperately wanted, for the happiness of another.

Christine crumpled inwardly, knowing that this man's heart was beyond bruised, Raoul's being the more resilient of the two, and yet he was casting a particle of faith out in hopeful anticipation, for the chance at a dream. "It shall be such, for us both."

ERIK PEERED BACK OVER his shoulder to see a faint glimmer move upward through the windows. *Good, she located the candles in the entry.* He looked at Cesar, wondering how often they had walked these trails, roamed the hills only to listen in silence, and scratched the horse behind a reliable ear.

"I cannot fathom what lies ahead, old friend. We have cultivated distrust, she and I, yet she is more receptive and venturous." Erik lit the lantern hanging above Cesar's stall and made the necessary preparations for his care, conversing in soothing tones. "You like her, do you not? Come, Cesar, honesty is best." Cesar wagged his head, stamping the ground in protest. "How could you feel to the contrary?" Erik demanded, giving the bridle a shake at the cheek piece. "Humph, it is just as well. I have most likely complained enough, but I have kissed her, her forehead," *that skin,* he thought dreamily, "and I touched and held her as any man, this very night! I cannot begin to describe. . . and she touched me as well, without reservation. You heard," he said proudly, leaning in to pick Cesar's hooves clean, "I flattered her!" Erik's mild elation cooled. "Though, if this is some fantasy, a hoax, or is some cruel deception, I warn! My mental stability may hang in the balance, let alone obliterate what keeps life flowing through my fading shell. What if she leaves, Cesar? There are so many unknowns."

His subconscious wound itself upon these points while he saw to Cesar's needs: fresh food, water, a good rub down and brushing of his sleek coat before being blanketed. The routine was calming, it allowed time to ponder and, as it had already been proven, sent the mix of thought around for digestion, a veritable feast for weeks to come; if indeed, their compatibility could withstand the test of the next few days or the hours of the initial twenty-four.

Cesar snorted, the rumination process had obviously snagged Erik, and his execution of brushing strokes over the same spot, far too long. "Forgive me," the apology came absently and Erik moved under the Percheron's massive neck to the other side. So much had occurred; all the preparations, each aspect, the months and in some cases, years, had all hinged on that one multi-dimensional variant of Christine. He grew weary from within and laid his head down across his arm, atop Cesar's back. "So long denied," he exhaled.

Erik had not realized the time. As a commodity, he usually had a surplus with no shortage or constraints, until now. When he looked back up he started, fumbling the brush to finally lose it successfully within the straw below.

"I am sorry, I seem to be rather proficient at startling you this evening," Christine confessed.

He stood transfixed at the visage standing in the stall entrance and had to admit, she excelled in the skill without any effort whatsoever.

Christine wore a deep blue gown, one with a wide set neckline and gathered cap sleeves lying lightly across her shoulders. The princess seams added length and form to her already slender shape under a silvery-laced robe, tied just beneath her bust, and her brown waves were pulled up into a loose twist, leaving several strands at liberty for affect.

Erik stared after her as she gracefully retrieved the brush in an offering for his acceptance. Moving back she explained, "When I realized you had yet to finish, I came to find you."

The trance broken, Erik replied, "You have been victorious, in many of your endeavors, realized or not."

She nodded and smiled then moved beyond the opening, near to where his cloak rested neatly over the gloves in his upturned hat. While finishing Cesar, Erik was very much aware of Christine's eyes and how they followed his every move. She seemed fascinated, as was he, and highly conscious, even to the point of—dare he mention the fullness welling in his chest—wanting to impress, to be thought well of. Therefore, he felt it somewhat of a necessity to conduct his mode with increased elegance, a testament to the lifeblood of music flowing within him. Though, if he had looked at himself twice, or even once for that matter, he may have reconsidered the show of poise.

Stepping out into the center aisle Erik closed the gate and pivoted next to Christine, his hand remaining upon the tangible. They observed Cesar, rightly content, but Erik's mind was far from oats and hay, and yet so close. He was more interested in a lock of auburn, lightly blowing across his dress shirt, and moved back a half pace to raise his palm in assisting the buoyancy as it twirled loosely, caressing his skin in its dance. *Guileless effects,* his heart whispered. *What am I to do now?*

"Erik?"

"Yes?" he responded mechanically, breathing in and dropping the miniature ballet to carry on without its stage.

"Would you escort me back up to the house?" she asked, gathering his things for him.

"I would take immense pleasure in doing so." Letting go the confined air, relieved that Christine had bridged the gap with her request, he grabbed the lantern and blew out the flame, plunging them into darkness. She waited expectantly in the thick unease until his guiding touch at her elbow, led them to light once more.

ENTERING THE HOUSE, Erik's attention drew upward to the waning fragments splayed against the walls from each candle, and he considered a similar phenomenon burning within his breast; just as he would exceed a milestone, the brevity of common interchange would rise up, lap at his unsuspecting wick of confidence, and nearly overwhelm any and all aspirations. And though he could not eliminate speech in its entirety, to feed solely on emotion, and knowing the option was not wholly viable, he let the optimistic wish fade.

"I shall relieve you of those," he said, referring awkwardly to the items in her possession. She handed them over without so much as a word. "Now, if you will excuse me, I too, am in need of some attention." Considering her informed, he bade a hasty retreat upstairs and to the left, ill concerned for any reactions forthcoming. Her eyes trailed him again. *Those eyes! Such scrutiny!* He was to his dressing chamber and then freely within.

Lighting a candle, he glanced down, not having heeded his unkempt look in detail, and cringed, recalling the display in the stable. How plain the smudges of dirt were to him now, the splashed wax, loose buttons and stitching, a cuff link gone, and seams having enjoyed better days. Seeing most to be of marginal significance in hindsight, the consideration dispensed occupation of mind. But, had *she* noticed? What was foremost in her thoughts? How clear was her remembrance of his cynical, tyrannizing oppression over her? *Hope, always hope, hmm. . . for me, there is only hope.*

Lingering was not a habit perpetuated within Erik's repertoire. Thus, his display of timely execution produced a presentably clean, well-dressed host, quietly standing before his descent; the sight below, giving rise to appreciation. The scene was set: Christine seated on the hearth enjoying the fruits of her labor, knees pulled up to her chest, eyes shut in contemplation, while the lighting grappled to feed a burgeoning appetite in its blaze to life. What had transpired during the interim to bring her back? Whatever the cause, he saw more clearly the self-assurance that shone from her, causing his to teeter precariously in reaction to it. *So self-reliant! It is well. . . a fire, and confidence to take charge of what affords one in a new environment. . . I am impressed, my dear, quite.*

Erik's dexterity of motion propelled him quietly down the stairs to the door. He dropped the tumblers into alignment, ensuring their safety, and flinched. *Safety?* His mind laughed at the lurid habit and at the attempt to prevent others from intruding. It was an odd gesture indeed, considering their seclusion, though it was somehow. . . symbolic. He had kept her locked up before, even restrained for her safety, to prevent self-harm when she found herself confronted with death or being taken to wife, by him. *I would have chosen death.* Erik rubbed the back of his neck and crossed the smooth hardwood to sit opposite her. Even before her lids opened, a cool indifference emerged between them, his glare, voraciously piercing. She shifted and looked at him, sitting there in his evenly honed clothing, the crisp lines of his trousers, folds in the lapels of his black and emerald dressing gown; she shifted once more, then lowered her legs, crossing them at the ankles to match Erik's propriety. He grinned. *Without a word, she conforms. This should be rich.*

The game wore thin after some time, watching and being watched, neither averting their gaze, and though he sensed the rising discomfort, in all truth, he did not know what to do next. This was her arena to face off in. Once he understood his role he would devise the necessary stratagem and join when ready.

"I suppose," she said firmly, while gathering herself to stand, "we could remain seated and stare each other down, though I would take exception with the fact that *my* point of interest," she emphasized in Erik's direction, "has yet to divulge any substantial knowledge of himself, thereby rendering this situation inequitable."

Was it? Erik had the distinct impression of inequity to be tilted in her favor. He squirmed inwardly and made to pull at the stricture about his neck, but discovering both tie and button to be derelict of post, his hand lacked purpose and dropped into his lap.

Cold embarrassment being the emotion upon which he was to play, he sat up as amusement crossed Christine's face, her brow lifted. *Oh, heaven forbid I give rise!* "Your observation is duly noted, Mademoiselle," *in more ways than I care for.* Christine had secured her cause.

"Seeing as it was I who returned, who betrayed and angered. . .

I will strive to explain," Christine's tone became solemn. She inhaled, resigned by the obvious burden of sharing, and began. "At that moment when I kissed you and our tears mingled, when you went to release Raoul and then gave the two of us leave to go. . ." she paused and Erik touched his forehead absently, "my mind seemed to be laden with a fog of misunderstanding. I had heard specific instructions to find a deceased body, to leave the ring and to bury with secrecy. It was a huge muddle of words. Part of me was relieved and yet I felt a great tragedy was consuming me, and before I knew my own mind or had conscious reign over faculties and scene, I was helped into the boat. My thoughts raced and swam in circles, but each direction sent me spiraling down. Afterwards, my first cognizant memory was of Raoul, commenting on how grateful he was to be taking me away from *that* nightmare. . . and of marrying quickly, and leaving to avoid his brother's objections. I found myself reeling and questioning these plans. Apparently, I looked almost ill because Raoul ceased to ramble and turned his focus to smoothing out the ride across the lake. It was not the rocking upon the water which caused the disquiet, but my soul in turmoil.

"As we neared the small wharf, I saw myself caught in the center of a life altering commitment. So many decisions had been made complete, and I had been omitted somewhere along in the process! I was assisted to stand, though I declined guidance. I think Raoul thought me to be disoriented when he said, 'I understand how traumatic these past months have been, tonight especially, but I wish to quickly put distance between us and the whole sordid experience.' I glared at him in frustration and asked what he would do if I refused his wishes. He went quiet. I know he was agitated at this point or too confused to say much, perhaps both," she bristled in recall. "He bellowed at me, 'What are you saying Christine, that you do not wish your freedom, to be rid of that monster's hold over you? You said yourself that you were most assured of his madness! How could you consider him an option after all his lies and deceptions?' I gained my full height and stood face to face with him and cried that that was exactly it! I desired my freedom most fully and was weary of being passed between two men as an asset or trivial amenity during some business transaction. I was not a possession!

"I struggled with the emotions Raoul stirred in me, I have since last year, trying to decipher all the conflicting thoughts, to be completely honest with myself. At the time, I was inarticulate and contradictory, both in manner and word, and it only served to impinge matters. Being shrugged off by Raoul, when I wished to discuss my feelings, only made confronting the situation more difficult, but on the whole, easier to bury, and easier to second guess everything. His accusation of my having some reliance on apparitions, in order to console myself in the death of my father, became viable. But it was not until Raoul was in the very belly of the Opera House that he finally believed. I told him, that when I thought of what I had done, of what *you* saw and felt, I was ashamed. He rounded on me and said, 'Ashamed? No, you should be wondering how it is possible to even look on him with the least degree of pity after all he has done!'"

Erik was sure she had seen the emotional impact churn in his eyes and mannerisms; the fury, the bitterness and pain, all were renewed from the past. *Sparing of feelings?* He scoffed. *She has spared nothing.* His hate for Raoul de Chagny deepened. How could he have trusted such a petulant imbecile with the happiness of Christine? Her pause snapped him back. Those eyes, searching and unsure, glossed over him before she averted her attention; it seemed, in preparation for further export. Was Hope to be their common ground? Absolution for naïveté *she* was granted, but for the other. . . his hands prickled.

"I told Raoul we deviated there because I felt something more for you, and he could be most assured it was not pity. I tried to deny it, cover it up with niceties, but I played right into the path of my own frailty, my own immaturity. And as hard as it was for him to accept, I explained that I cared for him—but it was unparalleled to what I felt for you. . . and that it would be unconscionable for me to continue in the plans set forth because he deserved someone who could love him completely, and I did not. I could see it in his eyes. He had risked his life and I had just thrown the conquest back in his face."

Truly? Doubt seized, his capacity to take in more quickly leveled, and anything said thereafter went unheard.

"Before our final ascent above, he understood that I would be spending time apart from you both; there would be no mad rush to return, but enough of a duration devoted to sufficiently search out my heart—truthfully, I was never in any danger from you, and could have spared us the pain by following my heart in the first place. We parted on good terms and were careful so as not to draw any undue attention, at least not in addition to what had already occurred that night. By then, things had quieted and no one saw us. Raoul promised me that he would not betray my trust, whatever I decided. When I think of the anguish my indecision has caused," she lightly croaked from the thickened emotion, "the destruction I saw in your flat, the loss... I feared for your life."

Here, her narrative was at an end, but Erik was still caught somewhere upon the fact that she held him in some regard, without pity, and that her feelings were unparalleled. The meaning of such words wrought a level of desire and excited wonder in his mind, sending a knot to rise up in his throat, all was a blur. She advanced in silence, knelt directly in front of him and touched his recently dampened hand. He flinched at the kindness, but was desperate for her. Wet streaks marked shimmering paths down the front of Erik's masque as Christine gently made contact with each side, to brush away the escaping emotion with the backs of her fingers. Erik breathed raggedly, pressing into her touch. "Oh, Christine."

Her hand fell away. "Please, forgive me?" she softly asked, head bowed.

Erik's hands rose, body trembling in uncertainty until his palms cupped her face. Drawing her chin upward, he slowly kissed the coursing stream of regret, his lips quivering, first one cheek, and then the other. The salty taste lingered, enhancing the moment he wished to savor. They parted, leaving Erik to search for a reaction as he unintentionally held his breath, eyes wandering over every detail, scrutinizing each feminine curve of her face. Christine covered one of his hands with hers.

Oh, foolish man that he was, how could he have missed it? He was no better than an ego packed in conceit for thinking this young woman to be capable of only loveliness and grace, whether her voice exalted or not, but it was all too clear why she felt as she did. The sudden exigency placed to these thoughts surprised him. He swallowed hard, and again brought her face close, committing to memory the indescribable warmth from feeling that downy skin. "I have longed for. . . hungered. . ." he whispered.

Christine traced the strong form of his chin to the well-defined jaw, caressing the limited access; his hands fled with the elicited gasp. Carefully she rose, and manners dictating that he do likewise, he held out assistance then stepped away.

Bending to rearrange space for them on the lounge among the pillows, she motioned for him to take a place, seating herself to his right.

Not exactly sure what to expect, he became rigidly statuesque, hands affixed to his knees. Of course, this pose pulled up on that musing brow of hers, forcing the variance in his behavior to surface; one moment he was reasonably self-assured then retreating and innocently brusque the next—with angry distaste and distance being the choice of binding mortar.

"If it is at all possible to sit any stiffer, I shall resort to using you for a coat rack. I do not bite," she teased airily.

"Your strain of humor is not amusing." His arms folded in agitation. "I was better off standing."

"Well, I should think with your capacity for learning, that you would be more open-minded."

Erik was suspicious about the whole exchange; the tender pardon turned whimsically comic, but comment or no, he remained stoic in posture. Each time they separated, he observed the brief irritation come and then go when initial contact was reestablished; he admired the persistent reassurance. *I must search for ways to maintain it for extended durations, but I am poorly versed in how to manage it. Thus far, it is she who has taken the lead, leaving me to. . . oh!* The voice of recollection kicked hard. *Yes, join when ready, and no better time to exercise that opportunity than the present!*

Christine filled her lap with a pillow, twisted sideways to her left and held out her hand as if waiting for an item to be handed her.

I have kissed her, lightly, he surmised, *her face, and now she wishes the same for her hand. Strange, these intimate little rituals. Fine, I can do that. I am open-minded. . . though I preferred her cheeks.* Erik's mind mumbled on as the tips of his fingers were brought under hers. Rotating the wrist over, he raised it toward his mouth, but felt a downward pull.

"Your gallant gesture is appreciated, though not what I had intended." Her goal seemed secure and he was not about to forego the contact, the recurring impediments of action blatant in his sight. With his hand compressed between her own, she began to gently massage the tension and divert his focus with praise. "Tell me, is it your craftsmanship that is beautifully evident in all I have seen?"

He nodded, responding well to the prompt, hypnotized by what was happening. It was marvelous. "Yes," he shot out to Christine's pause in rubbing. "I take great pride in shaping the wood and stone myself, molding it to the right contours, smoothing until the depth and grain are to my liking. It brings immense satisfaction to take raw materials and produce a tangible creation from the mental images. I trust no one else with that type of work."

"No one else, meaning. . . ?"

"Meaning," he echoed, "I arranged for the bulk of construction and did what remained, on my own. I am not a complete recluse, Christine, in fact, it was not until I returned to France that I became more so. By that time, I had grown weary of people."

Christine smiled lightly, having switched to his left hand mid conversation. He had relaxed noticeably quickly, extending his arm across the back of the chaise.

"Why the smile?" Erik wondered aloud.

"I am in awe."

"How so, Mademoiselle?"

"I am holding the hands of a master creator. . . and resident ghost."

"Hmm. . . now it is you who flatters," he murmured.

Christine worked in concentrated circular motions under Erik's admiring gaze while he fingered each stray curl along her shoulder. The silence between them was comfortable, not strained, as the fire crackled in the background. Intelligent woman, indeed, the longer she touched Erik, the more serene he was overall. Gradually, his sight became heavy and his head lolled against his arm. He had never encountered such a sweet feeling of peace, or slept midst. . . the touch of heaven.

Chapter Two

Morning came to delicately bathe the horizon with its golden fingers of warmth seeping into everything; it refreshed and renewed, shaking sleep from the earth.

Christine was first to stir from that hazy magic between wakefulness and dreams, where all is too often not what it appears. Taking great care to enact a credible amount of precaution by immobilizing her body, prior to mind reacquainting with bearings, lent the spread of fondness across her lips as she remembered the late hours of the night before.

Erik had slowly sunk to the cushion in her lap while she stroked each of his hands in turn, eventually running her fingers through his hair. And not having the heart to disturb him, she continued, gazing into the waning embers until she, too, succumbed to that peace, subconsciously wrapping her body around Erik in a protective manner. Christine detected a sudden flush at their newfound positions, and while not intrusive, may have been construed as a rather forward impropriety. He was curled next to her knees, his left hand hooked behind his neck, arm shielding his face, and her body was draped across his upper arm against the back of the lounge.

Extricating herself without waking Erik would have seemed the ultimate impossibility, knowing how aware he could be, and this being a complex issue of vicinity as well as contact, she was lucky it fell to the contrary; the skillfully handled maneuver left him blissfully intact.

This. . . she thought, kneeling down a few feet away to revel in the view, is a welcome change. The tables are turned, and now it is I who shall have the opportunity to observe him. I understand why he enjoys it so. It gives a person time to contemplate, to see what might not otherwise be present, and to find the real truth behind the masques we all wear. And, though his face is hidden, I find the contours of such a rigid exterior are softened under the power of sleep: he is handsome in his own way, and his lean physique, every muscle: tight and defined.

The daylight was an additional factor as well. It cast a whole new look, as though the sun had freed what the darkness below the Opera House held hostage, bringing his natural tones alive; his color, what little there was, seemed richer. Usually she saw Erik beneath artificial, manmade light: candles, lanterns, and fire, and those could hardly be considered sufficient amongst all the shadows. The façade of superiority he set out to command from, while seated pompously atop that throne of hell below the Opera, was gone, his standing reduced to equal.

Now, all shall become fair.

Christine stretched the resistance from her joints, stood, and gingerly ambled toward the door, unlocking it. She thought it odd, contradictory even, *a locked door, here?* His behaviors were most likely based upon some rationale she had yet to comprehend. Then, leaving the quandary behind her, and the door slightly ajar, she slipped outside to greet her new surroundings.

Ah! The fresh air is a blessed delight! Early as it was, she was eager to follow nature's lead and lowered herself quietly to the top step of the porch, trying secretly to blend in with her environment. All the trees, in their variegations of green, flitted in the soft breeze; small animals were up and busily chatting, whilst a few birds could be heard beckoning to the sun. Christine gazed out at the rising world to have her sight met with the source of limp moisture from the night before:

a streambed of gradient features, snaking in close proximity to that of the stable. *Of all the places I would consider a sanctuary, this would be the one befitting of someone wishing to shed the tempest of life.* Her shoulders lifted against a deep breath and her body settled, adhering her to that one spot for a good soaking in beauty.

FROM WITHIN, ERIK'S arm slid, startling him awake. Without an obstruction of some sort, there beget an endless distance for an incoherent mind to understand—not to mention the rudeness altogether. He rolled to his back, inhaling sharply at the pain fusing his right shoulder and neck together then exhaled perturbed, his hand reaching up to make a half-hearted attempt at a rub.

"Damned uncomfortable, this lounge. I should..." Suddenly, all was forgotten in a scramble to sit upright. Panic and anger collided as feelings of desertion flashed before him. "Where is she?" he fumed. "Get a hold of yourself... she would not... was I hallucinating?" his voice turned incredulous and uncertain. "Did I imagine? No!" By immediately refusing to accept this as a dream, he had lost every bit of mental acuity he owned and grabbed a pillow for a subconscious grasp on reality. Out of the corner of his eye a thin ribbon of light from the open door caught his attention, instantly ballooning his rage. "No!" he roared, sending the cushion flying back between the chairs and into the vase on the table.

Christine glanced over her shoulder at the rise of commotion exploding just as Erik gripped the door handle, the swift movement flinging the mahogany panel wide to collide against the wall with a sickening bang.

"Well!" she emphasized, promptly stripping him of all fury in the face of shock. "Someone woke up in a foul mood. I can see it will require time for us *both* to trust one another!"

The truth in those words stung. Erik went red with embarrassment, every capillary dilating under the heat of accusation, and all he could do was stand there agape, panting.

"Damn!" he murmured, turning. He hung his head in shame and retired to the base of the stairs. Not only had he cursed her unfairly for leaving him, but a tranquil moment had been shattered as well. After the assault of mixed signals surged through his system, he stood there trembling, and gradually leaned in for support against the baluster. Christine went to his side, her touch predictably causing him to shy away and withdraw from her. "When I woke. . . the door open. . . you gone. I. . ." his body shuddered, "assumed. . ."

Gently, she laid her hand to his shoulder then moved away to the broken pieces of porcelain strewn about the rug. Christine had just begun gathering the larger sections into her robe when Erik knelt with her, ash bucket in tow. They continued to pick up the small shards until reasonably certain they had found them all and he quickly disposed of the mess by way of the sliding doors. Hearing an expression of painful surprise when the back door closed, which was closely followed by muffled irritation and Erik swearing under his breath, she asked sincerely, "What is it?"

"Nothing. It is insignif—"

"Nothing does not cause your tongue to loose itself. . . here, let me see." Erik had every intention of opposing, but she had met him upon rounding from the dining room, leaving him little choice.

"Your hearing is quite sharp."

"Yes, unfortunate for me. And though you use a different language, it is still cursing."

"It seems Erik has much to apologize for and no darkness from which to reconcile, eh?" Her lips pursed thin, unimpressed. "At any rate, given the current score. . . chances are, you will probably give up—"

Erik winced. Christine's finger had touched his lips while her other hand maintained a grip on the injury wrapped in his handkerchief. "I am tolerant, to a point. Do not underestimate how often you can place blame or speak ill toward the one I care for and think I will permit it to continue." She had made contact.

Erik colored while watching her compress the white flag of truce close to her heart; his mouth twitched, spilling an application in the awkward moment. "I should like to take you riding this morning, before full light."

"You and I?" Christine clarified, half smiling at the discomfort in his voice. "I would like that."

"It is settled then, I shall make the necessary preparations while… you change." Erik backed up to give Christine some room to make her exit upstairs, reclaiming his wound in the process. She advanced up one step then leaned in, placing a brief peck on his right cheek. Her hand tagging closely behind emphasized the display of affection by pressing the masque in against his skin. This tender act left him breathless and completely taken. Soon, her door shut, bringing Erik back to the present. His hand wiped the length of his masqued face as he summed up the distress in the pit of his gut. *Great, nothing like a good jolt and a disgorgement of all composure to start the day off, Erik.*

It seemed but a few minutes and Erik was bounding up the stairs to knock upon Christine's dressing room door, which elicited a sound warning of, "Enter at your own risk," from the other side. He backed up cautiously, his retreat interrupted by the parting door. Their eyes silently roamed the other from head to foot, as they looked to be a duplicate, mirrored pair. Erik had provided riding trousers on a whim, should Christine desire proficiency in the equine arena. In his opinion, a woman in all her excessive femininity was strictly an object for public exhibition, and hindrance of little worth when it came to serious riding. Looking at her, he was well pleased to see she felt the same. The black trousers hugged her shape, every fine, detailed curve from her legs and backside to her slim waist. From there up, she was exquisite in a simple white blouse, and with her hair tied back, she was ready: short tailored jacket and gloves in hand. As her reflection, his shirt was the only difference; a billowy-sleeved linen, sporting masculine scallops along cuffs and center placket beneath his riding coat, which parted just below the base of his neck.

"You must think me dressed inappropriately." She blushed, making to don and button the jacket sooner, rather than later. "You would have said something otherwise."

"No, no, no. . ." he stammered, raising his hand to stop her. "I purposely. . . I mean, the fit is. . ." Erik's fist rose to his mouth to impede any further out-poring of wordy abandon and they both reddened. *I cannot even speak, how pathetic. And, my dear, you would not want to know my thoughts at the moment.* "Please, your steed awaits, and thus my stomach, for I am famished." Erik gestured, grateful that she was already in front of him to miss the roll of his eyes.

Cesar pawed the ground while anxiously waiting on the path headed away from the stable, a blanket and provisions tied down with a flank strap. She eyed the impending situation. "Um, no saddle?"

"You have never ridden without? I assumed because of your confidence last night that—" He shrugged and laced his fingers. "No matter. . . come, up you go," he encouraged, not about to let such an excuse hamper his plans or waste time. Once mounted, she looked non-plussed as to how she might remain there, having already overcorrected to one side. Erik resisted the urge to impose *do ut des*[1] for what he had been dealt last night and cleared his throat. "Grasp Cesar with the muscles of your inner thigh," he guided, pushing on her leg until he felt them engage. "Now, press your knees in a downward direction. . . that's it." Erik had not thought twice about propriety. His contact with her was wholly instructional, completely absorbing any and all thought. Then, grabbing a fist full of mane, he was up directly behind. "All right, let's get you settled in."

Erik quickly took Cesar through a few basic maneuvers to see if Christine would stick and adjusted her technique accordingly. "Do you feel how you are in conflict against the horse, how you bounce?" Christine replied with an affirmative bob of her head, saying "yes" in haste, when she realized it may not be distinguishable, and Erik pulled Cesar up to gently position her for success. He held her waist on either side and rotated her hips slightly forward. "Keep your weight centered, there... much better," he said in a gravelly whisper. "Now, feel his movement, Christine. Move with him, and with me."

THEY GALLOPED SOUTH across the carpeted fields with a clear sense of freedom expanding before them until all three became as one fluid motion on the wind. Doubling back, Erik headed east, up into the wooded hills, slowing Cesar when they merged once more with the trail. Christine had a sly gleam of wonder flash through her mind about how receptive Erik might be this morning, considering his left hand had yet to leave her unsecured since their start. *It has something to do with barriers, his gloves for one... the touch is marked as different in his mind, I am sure of it, but a little experiment should prove invaluable.* She leaned into his chest and was pulled tight. Yes, he was distracted, cruel woman that she was, the light sighs being proof alone, so she began without warning. His glove, being midst the removal process for a repeat performance, deterred his introspection and Erik tensed, signaling Cesar to stop.

"You have a bad habit of spontaneous activity, Mademoiselle," he addressed her coolly.

"Well, if I were to forewarn then it would not be labeled as such." She peered briefly over her shoulder, eyeing the recovery of his balled fist; as swift as the blink of an eye his behavior had changed, leaving him irrational and surly with arms folded in resolute fashion. Christine had to bite her lip to keep from smiling at his childish pout. He had had his moment interrupted before he was ready and she could tell he did not approve of the infringement. Christine's brow raised in understanding when they began moving again. Their hands were separate and a divergent aura emerged between them, one of diffidence, which signaled to her that he would be setting the pace, at least for now. The experiment had been conclusive; there was a distinct difference between gloves on and gloves off, as well as contrast in instructing someone innocently and holding them around the waist. She knew he desired touch, yearned for it, but the how of going about it, and the appropriateness when offered, eluded him.

Placing the incident behind her, literally, Christine smirked at the relevancy and decided to relish the experience as a whole. It made a world of difference, especially the part of not dwelling on what could not be controlled, which took the lead in her ability to appreciate her surroundings. She reflected upon the thought of variance between light and dark, thinking that even light came in fluctuating degrees; the newness of a morning sun would perhaps, be all the diversity needed. Its prelude was nearing completion and soon an appearance would debut, marking their first *day* together. She grinned during this mental exercise, all the while twirling a piece of Cesar's mane to busy herself, when she heard an overpowering growl come from Erik's stomach. It was so empowered that it would have set the ground rocking if they had not already been in motion.

"Cesar," the horse's ears pricked back, "I suggest haste, a storm is brewing and from the intensity, I fear it shall be a most insatiable one to quell."

"Pardon me," came the sheepish voice behind her, "but I did warn of my hunger, did I not?"

Christine grinned and nearly burst out laughing when it grumbled again, but she knew Erik was already uncomfortable, due to the shifting after the previous ungentlemanly rebellion, and stifled her impulse thusly.

THE TIMING, NEVER *better,* his mind began, *first your mouth, then your thoughts, and now this most recent uncomfort. . .* When *had* he eaten last? *We are here, good thing, there's no telling which feature might be unleashed next.*

Cesar came to a stand still, allowing his master to dismount, and

Christine slid off of her own accord right beside him. He gave a mere bow of the head as if to say, "As you wish." And, leaving the horse to fend for himself among the luscious spring vegetation, the two hiked along the edge of a cliff until they came to a small opening in the brush. Leading the way, Erik helped her to a spot below, just a few feet down. It was a peculiar outcropping of rocks, completely hidden from view and well protected from the heat of the afternoon sun by the grove of trees above.

Christine's mouth fell slightly open as she established her footing. "Oh Erik, what a spectacular vista." Her eyes panned the eastern countryside for miles. The ribbons of blue that wound in and around the rolling green hills were peppered with wooded glens, ashen mounds, and the occasional farm or outskirts of a town; it was flat out astonishing.

"During the night it becomes more impressive with pin points of stars glittering in the background." Erik spread the thick blanket across the ground, the edges fluttering outward to await its morning buffet. Christine was enthralled and walked farther out for a better look, but immediately met with resistance from Erik's grasp on her arm. "I would not wish you to lose your balance and tumble. I prefer you stay close," he gently suggested, with an open gesture to sit.

Neither had eaten for some time, he specifically, which was evident as they ate their fill in silence, eyeing the other in turn. Christine finished first.

"Thank you for sharing, it is absolutely gorgeous."

Yes, his mind agreed with a wry smirk. *You being the one highlight, that one-degree of intensity missing.* "Beauty is by perspective," he offered. "One could stay all day or night, perhaps in combination, but the stone would soon render the opulence in nature intolerable with its unforgiving harshness and cold."

Christine looked down, her fingers drumming in frustration. Was she inept at a speedy redirect? And had he, determined as he was, tossed up the insufferable and demeaning analogy to convince her of his detrimental influence while trying to foreshadow what was to come, assuming the challenge to be too great? A test? Oh, he was indeed, a work of art.

"That is why there is sun," she proposed, looking to be quickly inspired along a suitable line of reasoning. "It warms the surface of everything it touches until it has penetrated, fulfilling even the stones' limited potential. The stones take over, expending their reserve to continue the effort of the sun and then wait to be touched again, once spent. The capacity to retain heat expands as the beauty around increases. And sometimes, all that is necessary is but a particle of desire for that beauty to take root and flourish."

He was in awe of her counter explanation. His comment had been hard and lightly pessimistic and she took it, returning it to him better than it had been received. Their eyes met for a moment, staring, until Erik was unable to tolerate her gaze; he looked away out into the distance. He wanted so badly to believe, to accept, but all those years of torment, the scars, and the conditioned hate, every component of his past weighed against. . . her.

She was quiet, too quiet upon moving to Erik's side. His stomach lurched as her form, having been slightly obscured by his masque, appeared. Their upper legs touched, and then that all too familiar movement toward his face, too many motions, too close; those years of being coiled like a spring, his reflexes poised to strike at a moment's notice suddenly let fly, and his menacing grip snared her wrist spot on.

"Erik! You're hurting me!" Her words, like her action, threatened his well-being and he released her and propelled himself away, placing a barricade of space between them.

"I did not mean to. . . I thought—"

"I know what you thought. As soon as I saw your hand come up, I knew what I had done. Forgive me," she expressed genuinely.

Erik whirled on her in aggravation. "Why do you so readily accept blame, when it is glaringly obvious it is I. . ." he pointed vehemently, "who should confess responsibility? I cannot even control myself when I know, here in my heart, that your intensions were not meant the way my mind comprehends them." He turned his back, throwing his hands up in frustration. "Why? Why do I do this when I have a chance? All I do is succeed in pushing you away," he cried. "I am pushing my dream away!"

Without warning Christine seized him from behind and held on. Erik fought, not physically, but he writhed in her emotional immersion, and struggled against the overwhelming constriction in his chest. "Then I will embrace you until you no longer resist."

His body shook, legs weakened by the blatant assault of warmth and kindness, and he wept uncontrollably. Shocking as it was for his system to accept her constrictive touch, he took all she could give. When at last the tremors subsided, he rotated. "Don't let go, Christine, please, do not let go." He was dazed, she had stayed true to her word, her arms encircled about his chest. That one unselfish act provided so much stability that she hugged him tighter once they were away from the edge. Soon, he had his arms around her and she eased up in determination.

An overwhelming urge to touch her had Erik raising his hands to stroke Christine's delicate skin with the backs of his fingers. They slid easily, caressing everything upon her face; her smallish nose, the natural rosy color up her cheekbones, the contour of her wide jaw and her sensuously soft lips. Oh, those lips! His thumbs carefully flitted across them, her breath lightly moist, and as he pressed his lips to her forehead, they lingered. His shoulders lifted, intensifying that pleasure of sweet touch and condensed splendor of awareness. Their eyes were secondary to fulfill understanding, his quiet breathing, uneven, as he rubbed a small portion of his jaw to hers. There was another kiss to her temple, her jaw, and then he placed her lips to his forehead—a token gesture, for he could not feel them. He held her face, his fingers barely entwined in her hair while she leniently bathed his lower face, each blessed kiss a soothing balm to his parched senses. Then, ever so gently, Christine placed her hand to Erik's heart and closed her lips over his. An amazing burst of color flooded his body; she kissed him!

Not trusting these feelings without first looking, he stared into Christine's warmed face, and blinked twice, sending one tear trickling effortlessly as it was he who now sought to draw her close, his arms unyielding for a long, long time.

The early morning yellows gave way to blues; the pair gradually separating at the same rate as the ascending sun on its unfailing path. There was nothing more worthy of time, at that moment, than how they proceeded. Unfortunately, nature often takes the driver's seat and helps the flow, leaving little control, but this is where the aptitude for one to compensate is greatly honed.

"I. . ." Erik began, his stomach finishing with a loud, unsatisfied rumble. His hand clamped onto the site, rubbing in an effort to squelch the rude gurgle of juices.

"Still hungry?"

"Not particularly," he replied, embarrassed.

"I was not referring to your physical status," she smiled wryly.

Erik reflected a mixture of concerned surprise; to think she could be so forward, to have a flirtatious vein, struck him. Knowing her thoughts, seeing that cheek flush with guilt, made the lapse almost worth the prick to her sense of better judgment.

"Forgive me," was her gentle petition, head lowered. "I have gone and made the situation uncomfortable. I should not—" Christine had opened the door and he took full advantage of the invitation, pressing his mouth to hers mid-sentence.

"I will starve no more," he muttered, his heart pounding erratically. The beating was so extreme that he likened it to a regime of taxing exercise for the sake of one's stamina. The sound was loud enough to be heard shamelessly, at least by his ears. *How deafening and wondrous all at the same time; she wanted my kiss!* Pulling back, Erik could have sworn he felt an undeniable upward slope tugging at his mouth, a spark igniting in those orbs of the deepest blue. Was this true joy? She grabbed on to his waist and snugged into him. At first the tension blared, then dissipated. Her daring had broken through.

"Erik?"

"Yes?"

"What significance does this place have for you?"

No! Erik's eyes squeezed tight as he fingered small pieces of Christine's hair. Talking, what frustration. Perhaps this was to be his penance, a way to release the past in exchange for having this beautiful angel with him. After all, she had stated her ignorance of him, knowing only what he chose to impart or what she had herself observed.

"I come to this spot when I am. . . most lonely," he confessed, feeling her grip the back of his coat. "I learned to listen when I was young, mostly to stay alive, but in part, as a way to console myself. . . the plaintive cry of night, its mourning winds, and the success of those who survive. They are all too numerous to recount. I learned to hear music in everything that existed around me; it helped bring peace to my soul, to know that there were other sounds, other than those of humanity, to which my heart could connect.

"For the longest time—*fifteen of those eighteen years, to be exact*—I remained focused on the Opera House construction and the creation of a dwelling far below in the cellars, away from the eyes of man; a place unknown to the world, where I could allow the mischievous-artistic side of my nature to run rampantly unchecked." He felt another squeeze and responded in kind. "When I needed to feel harmony, as unrest hindered my flow of ideas, or if frustration bothered me to no end, I returned. Between this place and my Persian conscience, for so he is, as the current state of affairs stand, I became quite the upstanding fellow."

Suddenly, Erik's heart grew heavy. Not knowing exactly what to say further, he took Christine by the hands and gestured for her to sit back down. If she were to make an informed decision about her true feelings for him, then he must be honest and forthright, just as she had been.

"I think clearer when I pace. . . there are fewer interruptions and distractions," he explained, looking directly at her. She nodded her understanding and he rejoined, "I come to forget, as well." This subsequent task, one that enslaved him through memory, posed most difficult indeed. He took small, contemplative steps around the edge of the blanket and repeated this until his comments mentally took shape—abominable as they were, he was scarcely guaranteed of what was to exit. He had never wanted, or had never been required, to explain himself to someone, never felt accountable, but something prodded, something compelled him, spurred him on, despite the lie of silence pleading to remain closed.

Then his subconscious took a stab and toyed maliciously with his emotions. . . *A few idyllic moments before the ambush, you know they will not erase nor temper what you have done. Nice strategy, Erik, securing your first and last kisses. . . how efficient you are!*

Without warning Erik stopped and stared at Christine, and wished he had something in his hands to alleviate the fraying nerves; his fingers, rolled into a fist at his back and one at its leisure, for gesturing, would have to suffice. "Erik has. . . *no*, I," he strained then clarified. "I have a history with that Persian gentleman, the one you helped tend to the night he found himself in my torture chamber. He is known by the title Daroga of Mazanderan, a rank in his country's law enforcement agency, which is similar to our chief of police. He and I were present during the political upheaval in the Middle East. He carried out the legal desires of the Shah while I came to be employed for a number of other reasons, some of which plied my skills for immense inspiration while others were heinous, monstrous practices to satisfy the morbid wishes of those I served." His eyes darted from hers as he shamefully spelled it out for her. "I was a political assassin, killing for gain and the pleasure of others and occasionally, for personal reasons of my own."

The relation sounded monstrous to his own ears! How utterly detached! Erik could feel the recent contents of his stomach roil and imagined the same of hers; that light in her earthen brown eyes had gone dull. No beating could have prepared his heart, no exposure suffered, compared to the loss of her opinion, her seedling care. *Monster!* How loath he was to trudge vicariously through these experiences. He suddenly hated what he was, what he had been, and hated every crime justified under the guise of legal hierarchy! His soul groaned; the face suited the man all too well.

Moving on, he tried to reduce the enormity. "Years passed and my duties began to grow tiresome, but I persisted until I could no longer tolerate the atmosphere. There had been attempts on my life, as it is an unfortunate fact that one does not simply fall out of that ruthless profession." He shrugged. "I owe my life to the daroga, in more ways than I care to express.

"I disappeared for a time, traveled to Asia Minor and Constantinople, where I made myself indispensable within the service of another and had to later flee because I again knew too much. Then, there is this *little matter of the heart* and you." Recounting the events most recently pertinent in their lives, he sighed, clasping both hands behind his back. With his penetrating words, arrived Christine's tears of comprehension for what he had dealt with his whole life, and how she had, in turn, compounded and eased the chains of hell anchoring him to this world. He stopped and looked at her, her head devoutly bent. "Though I have kept my oath to the Persian, my hands having remained without stain since returning, I am partially responsible for the death of Joseph Buquet. He found his way into the same chamber that the Persian and Chagny were in. . . I did not find him until later. . ." his tone saddened. "And just so you are aware, because you will eventually hear, the Comte de Chagny[2] was found in the lake the night all came to a head. The banks surrounding the lake are treacherous in that void of darkness, but it was not I who caused his death."

Having finished, his twofold efficiency repeated, Erik hung his head, pained to have heaped such hate upon her narrow shoulders, but it would spare them worse heartache if his past proved to be too much for Christine to handle. It was all there. Done. And, as he had feared, it may have crushed the sweet woman before him. The jacket she wore was stained in tears about the collar and moisture dotted the blanket in front of her. Erik stared at his hands and wondered if she would ever permit them to touch her again.

Taking a deep breath, Christine rose slowly. Neither made eye contact and successfully averted direct attention of any kind, and Erik, having already resigned himself to the transparency of the situation, started when Christine spoke.

"Do I have your word. . . that what you have told me is true?"

"Yes."

"That you did not," she coughed, wiping new tears from her cheeks. "Raoul's brother. . ."

"No, I did not." Erik's answers were solemn and concise.

"If it is all right with you, I would like to return." Christine knelt beside what was left of their meal and helped prepare to leave.

Erik gathered the blanket and mumbled quietly to himself, "No, it is not all right, but I will not force you to stay against your will."

"Thank you," she whispered, to that small voice of hope.

THE JOURNEY BACK was uneventfully awkward. Erik refused to make any contact whatsoever, except in gallant assistance, and Christine would not ride, which left them both in reflective thought on foot, and the provisions to a free and unencumbered passage back to the estate. Common sense was reading Christine the list, in succession of importance, as to why she should be running and not casually walking. Behind her on the path was a man who had, at one point in time, committed unconscionable murders and managed to still attract such occurrences, whether he was to blame or not. But then, her heart had a different agenda. There was more to him, complexities attached that raged on.

All that had taken place before the fifteen, no... she calculated, eyes blurring, *eighteen years! Oh, why?* Why, indeed. Why did he bother being honest in the first place? Why would the Persian risk personal detriment, endure the loss of imperial favor, be banished from his own country and come all this way to France, if he did not think there was some measure of underlying good? What did she feel? He inspired beauty; he constructed, composed, sang, and who knew to what extent other talents were possessed. Animals responded as though they found kinship, a kindred spirit with him. That was evident, as she cast a quick glance at the two, head to head behind her. *He is easily accepted because there is no cruel dominion. If I stay—I start from square one again. He has already retreated from me... and if I decide to move on? Raoul is not an option, I don't feel that way for him and yet, I do for Erik.* Tears welled and she quickly dabbed at the corners of her eyes. *Do I let you, God, worry about his past while I center on his present and future? Can I begrudge him a change in life? He has paid all these years with a life consumed in hate. What sense is there in exacting revenge by leaving, especially when I know it is forgiveness that he seeks?*

UPON THEIR RETURN to the estate, Christine offered to clean up, which was met with Erik's flat refusal of wanting to take care of it himself. The ultimate goal was to have enough time for thought, was it not? He figured, as had she, that a tree seemed to be the most prolific place to employ that task and the decision was made. But, before retiring to the house, Erik walked down to momentarily join Christine at streamside.

Agitated, he stood with his hands clamped together behind his back, putting the last few hours through its paces. His jaw hurt, holding it unconsciously taut the whole way back had been a gross err, one easily avoided, and one he was sure he would pay for later. Right now, Survival was demanding he put forth his bravest effort and all he could muster was hope. A *taste of heaven. . . it is more than I had yesterday.*

"We shall leave for Paris when you are ready, but. . ." his confidence faltered briefly, "if you could find it in your heart, I would prefer. . . you stay." He turned abruptly, glued to his spot for an instant, and whispered, "I want you to stay." Then he strode hastily toward the house, up the porch steps, and through the doors.

Hours dragged throughout the late morning and afternoon, the minutes stifling in their quantity. What was he to do if she left? Absence of force, yes, it was decided. She deserved the freedom and had a right to choose. His patience thinned. Several inside doors were heard to shut harder than normal—not an uncommon indication of his unrestrained emotions in waiting. Angst trailed Erik from one place to the next. He could not distillate on any document in his study; moreover, reading material was out of the question, period, as he could not manage to sit long enough. He felt an unexplained omnipresence of woe and wondered if these were the feelings of those who met their demise under the watchful eye of the Shah-in-Shah, in Persia. A smattering of this for the conscience was plenty, and apropos under the circumstances. Music aided, but only served to rifle the thoughts of malcontent fermenting in his mind; thusly, whatever was dumped onto the ivory medium became a mass of discord. He glanced outside again, fully expecting to see Christine's still form next to the tree she had befriended, and received a shock instead; she was coming toward the house! He had fretted, wished he had never had this day, but gave thanks that he did, then Erik lifted his hands and they dropped into a lifeless pile in his lap, the last resounding notes vibrating into naught as she entered.

The words came, thrusting deeply, burying themselves to the hilt in his chest. "I. . . am ready," she said. That was all, hushed and to the point.

He walked in leaden shoes from around the piano, each pensive step bringing him closer and separating him farther, until he stood in front of her. She touched his arm gently and he stared, but did not shy away; he wanted every moment afforded him to be near, to be as close as possible.

"I am ready. . ." Her repetition was unwarranted. Why torture him? Why bloody his heart more? "To stay," she added.

The phrase did not register initially, but the meaning soon pierced, his tears coursing openly. He heard a voice airily trill the syllables of her name. It was his! Felt the cold of her hands warm within his enfolding care, and delighted when her smile broadened. Each hand was kissed, held dear to his heart and kissed again. He dared not embrace her, as it was too presumptuous a liberty. He stayed firm, *no force, patience and caution shall beget reward enough.* He had no right and yet, his arms ached.

"With the passing of time, I was certain you would leave, you had to know, I had to tell you. . . everything!" Erik choked out.

One of Christine's fingers rose to hush him, so he employed his free hand to begin wiping his own tears dripping from beneath his masque. "I felt your sincerity, your trust. You gave me the darkest secrets that could, and should have, divided us; you gave them to me and believed. My heart belongs. . . here, with yours, Erik." She touched his chin and laid her palm to his chest. "I stay because of what I feel for you."

Erik was slow to respond, stunned by what he was hearing. She continued in the same path, her feelings were steady! While this digested, Erik reached for the moist dew descending her cheek. She inclined toward him. "Hold me," she mouthed. He nodded, and taking her by the waist with one hand, he guided her until they tightened in upon the other in a mild embrace.

"Teach me... Christine, teach me how to be loved," he pleaded. "Believe in me."

The moment was complete then, finished, as though one season of life were ending and the next, beginning anew. He had opened up and she listened, hearing his sincere desire for change.

"I do not wish to let go," Erik mumbled.

"That may pose a problem of repeat embraces if you choose not to relinquish your hold after each one."

"Yes," he said, reluctantly drawing away. "I see your point. I should think missed opportunities to be a waste, if presented and not accepted graciously." A light touch of pink seemed to infuse directly from where Erik had taken Christine in a courteous gesture, from the exact spot of his lips against the back of her hand. He noticed her fidget and the height of blush rise, *heat exhaustion,* he smirked, *hmm... do unto others?* Then he rotated with a grand sweep of his arm, this movement launching a change in topic.

"Permit me to show you the rest of the house before evening sets in?"

"Of course!" Her voice pounced at the relief, rewarding her earlier decision to keep that *womanly curiosity* in check while at the same time minimizing the effect he was having over her.

He rather liked it, especially the contact, enslaving his delicate prize of a single hand all the way to the rear of the great room. Being about certain prospects of loss for the better part of a day had made quite an impression.

Pushing on the double doors, Erik opened up his private study. To the left was a full wall of bookshelves and backdrop for a sizeable desk, and on the right, two low, overstuffed chairs stood on opposite sides of the fireplace, and two sets of French doors, at the other end of the room, provided access to the adjacent portico from both the study and guest room next door.

"Looks as though you have a good deal of paper on hand," Christine commented, noticing the documents lining one side of the desk.

"These? Financial affairs. I can assure you, they are of little interest. *Some may require a reverse of finality. All in time. . . patience.* I secured a comfortable salary while employed about in other countries, compensation due me for the lasting scars. Penury was not an acceptable status I would stoop to, so, I invested in sound opportunities, leaving myself without the fundamental concerns of most people; I am well-enough off." She nodded, satisfied with this short response.

On the other side of the stairway stretched the dining area and kitchen. "Do you possess culinary skills as well?" she asked, interested in taking just a peek.

"Some, a foundation is all. And you?"

"An elusive venue for me, I'm afraid. I would be ashamed to admit past anything basic, though I look forward to expanding my proficiency, to learn."

"It is but edible art. Here, this way," he directed. Going down to the basement level, Erik prefaced the look around. "I was not quite sure what to do with this whole area, so I decided that one large studio would be most appropriate for the space."

Lighting a candle gave the room a rather eerie glow, as the shadows from the flame skittered across canvas and wall. Erik noticed Christine focusing on the blueprints lining one side, and moved to address her curiosity. "Since I had plenty of room, I spread out. Design access aided any necessary changes while building progressed. I have not had reason to remove them."

"I am astounded," she said reverently. "The whole milieu speaks of creativity, as the expended candles would attest."

"Hmm. . . if you would like," he detoured, "we could go upstairs.

There is something I was most pleased to incorporate." His boyish pride gleamed, increasing when she allowed him to escort her to the upper level. *What pleasure.* While setting foot on the landing, Erik released her arm. "This is my favorite room," he smirked at the altered current of her brow. Was it consternation or curiosity gone awry?

"Favorite room?" Christine asked, hands pressed together.

"Looks are deceiving, my dear, watch. I was able to conceal one of my pressure-released doors, usually hard enough to do when it is of standard width, but even more daunting to construct one nearly five feet wide." While speaking he ran his hands over the paneling, depressing in a specific area. "I am sure you found the two doors, on either end of the hallway, to be very odd, no?"

She affirmed and encouraged, "Go on, please."

"Our dressing rooms connect to this. . ." A large doorway receded between the walls and he finished, "the master suite."

Completely enthralled by what met her eyes, Christine gasped. The flat, for it could be referred to as such, based on dimension alone, had an outward facing bed, one directed away from the hall and central to the décor, indeed, a grand presence. The rich mahogany headboard was enough to keep the eyes spellbound for hours with its intricate carvings of the majestic night sky, the stars accompanied in detailing the glorious heavens by cherubs and angels. The angels were of such detail that they could almost be plucked by their delicate wings of gossamer and laid peacefully across the palm of one's hand. Chests, from different parts of the world, were placed in balance to the chairs opposite them, on the other side of the room surrounding the stone fireplace, and tapestries hung from the walls in their vivid, unique designs and colors. Christine touched one, finding it to be as soft as silken air while another, rough and unforgiving.

Erik could see she appreciated the fine workmanship; the fascination and honest countenance expressed as much.

"Oh, Erik," she breathed.

Rounding the end of the bed, she was met again with carvings. The footboard was adorned with spirals of music running the full width, but there was something else, almost secreted away in the lower corner. Upon closer inspection, the discovery of a less significant, faceless angel with bent wings caused her sight to immediately intersect with his. His gaze dropped away from hers, the meaning understood all too well by either.

Thankful for her sensitivity to his feelings and pleased that forbearance prevented her from dwelling on the exchange, the moment passed. Another set of paned glass doors stood wide. Erik leaned into the frame, permitting Christine a direct line out onto the balcony, which spanned the length of the upper floor, forming the covered entrance below. The view was splendid, one of the sun already engaged in its slow descent, its amber hues streaking the sky as the last bit of light filtered through the clouds.

Bringing her hands together, Christine rested her elbows along the railing. "Just. . . there are no words to describe it."

"Yes," he agreed incoherently, "indeed." Erik was not looking out over the landscape as was she, but standing several strides behind, gazing unfailingly at her.

She turned her head and, realizing his focus, blushed furiously. "Perhaps, I should go change."

"No. . ." he spoke languidly then straightened with a jolt. "I beg your pardon!" His hand combed through his hair, dismayed at how intensely he had been staring at her.

"Come," she cooed, holding out her hand, "then we shall complement each other in coloring."

Not to be told twice, Erik took up what he quickly deemed as *his* place and was at her side. She linked her arm through his and laid her head against his shoulder, both content.

Chapter Three

As the last call of eventide swept its calm behind the shade of dusk, Erik stood looking out upon his land, pondering on the events of the day, listening to Christine hum in her dressing room.

She is extremely patient, compassionate and kind. How often has my name crossed her lips? And not my nefarious counterparts, but my name... mine! The mere mention of Erik invokes none of those connotations associated with any of the other labels I am known by. What a blessing, a clean slate awaiting an author to commence their prose afresh. She has chosen to stay, makes witty remarks to relieve the tension I create and has taught so much in so little time. Who knew that my preparations would be used, though I wonder what she thinks. That I assumed? No, not after I sent her away. She has indeed compounded my life; even my thoughts are full of unconventional mishaps. Hers, in contrast, produce clever results, he smiled, *the gloves. She is no simpering girl, for that I have done her ill in my superficial regard. I never gave credit to the potential of her mind. I, of all people, should have known better! She is an asset of great worth to me and it is I who am the annoyance, the gawky annoyance; I cannot keep my eyes from her, my mind runs around in pieces, which becomes unmistakably glaring each time my mouth opens, and I love every bit of physical connection with her.* He rubbed his lower face where she had let her mouth linger. *That is it. . . I love her! I have professed this, but will not do so again until given leave by her, realizing there is more to this 'matter of the heart' than meets the eye, or any other sense.* Sighing lightly, Erik pivoted and headed straight away to clean up and prepare for the evening meal.

And whilst engaged in said preparatory duties, it is from this exact point where his mind continued. "What could be taking so long?" *Women,* his mind poked, *unpredictable. . . the whole of them.* "Yes, but intriguing nonetheless," he responded.

The meal was simple in every sense of the word, bringing the necessity of provisions to arrange his priorities for the following day. He had been to the estate recently, though hardly long enough, his life having necessitated little intervention to sustain him with no other desire. *I wished nothing more than to place distance between the whole sordid experience and myself.* Those words sounded vaguely fresh. *Chagny! Damn! The narrative last night,* he chilled. Not only did Christine place the men in her life as being of the same mindset, but he was also utilizing the verbiage of that. . . that BOY!

His head snapped to the side at the sigh of inadequacy, redirecting his attention to a most welcome distraction, away from the dull throb at the base of his skull—*Pain; she is always extremely inconvenient*—an oncoming bother since the relaxing moments on the balcony. Erik walked toward her with arms outstretched, gently motioning for her to circle.

"How do you do it?" she asked, finishing her rotation.

"Do what?"

"This!" She gestured to the dress. "The correct size, perfect fit, color, everything. How?"

The dress was a deep, plum-red linen, flounces and lace done up in a cinch beneath the bustle, a sweetheart neckline accented her alabaster skin and enhanced her figure in all the appropriate places.

"I don't know," he lied, for he certainly did not wish to grant her knowledge of just how often she preoccupied his thoughts. Had he been obsessed? Perhaps. "I simply choose what would, in my opinion, enhance your natural characteristics." He took her hand and bent to kiss it, stopping short of his destination. There, on her forearm, were traces of discoloration, apparent below the sheer attempt at a cover up. He turned her arm over, rubbing it, only to discover that the bruising continued around the full diameter of her wrist. He checked the left. There too, were the spiraling marks, twined in a familiar pattern. Regret was evident in his eyes, and she immediately tried to make light of it.

"It is all right. They will heal. You were only trying to protect—"

"No!" he interjected, "it is not right at all." His countenance was already deteriorating. "No one should ever cause such marks on a woman, least of all... on a woman he loves." Erik wanted very much to undo the bell that had been rung, along with its deafening repercussions. "And you are too swift to forgive," he said curtly, "too kind for one as undeserving as I." Erik tenderly caressed the underside of each arm, bathing each with his tears, hoping that in some way he was easing the pain he had inflicted. And she allowed him. He was not denied the guilt he felt nor the process the conscience required for it to feel cleansed. There was one final kiss and he returned to the kitchen, placing the mistake aside.

Their evening progressed in a pleasant manner. Dinner was exceptional, and the conversation, enthralling, as it encompassed the appeal of the adjoining kitchen. Especially desirable were the options created for a sense of togetherness, including those formal, business or casual circumstances, where topics could be discussed and enjoyed by all—whether in the kitchen or enjoying the fruits thereof. Additional topics were joined in, such as art, literature, music, and the most fascinating one of all, that of people. It appeared they both had a fetish for watching people, wondering what might be on someone's mind or where they were going, and upon occasion, would place a person in a "what if" situation, which proved most comical, based on the individual's personality traits, those known or otherwise conjured. Talking afforded them the ideal opportunity to scratch the surface of the other's interests, to see the commonalities and differences they could appreciate. While listening, they understood about exclusive passions, gained insight when one became animated upon a subject or respectful, if a point of view were to the contrary. One discovery or reaffirmation—which proved as no surprise—was Erik's affinity as an instructor; his sharing of intelligence already evident in music, had now been manifest through an exhaustion of subject matter, for it would be a shame to retain partiality in the pursuit of knowledge unless one could enlighten and enrich the life of another.

Erik caught Christine's eye and folding his napkin, laid it across his plate. "Would you care to sing?"

"I believe I would," she replied. "It seems ages since last we. . ." her voice trailed as she searched her memory.

"If one cannot remember, then it has been far too long," Erik countered, leading her toward the piano. "Shall we revisit something, a work from Gounod, perhaps?"

With a smile of consent, Erik drifted to a place only he could access, that he might produce the perfect accompaniment for an angel. . . his angel.

EVENTUALLY, EVENING MELTED into the black of night and a fire lit the room. The pupil, having been excused, was curled up reading while Erik composed from a deluge of effortless thought, and his gaze shifted to Christine. *He is connected again,* she reflected.

He was. To a work he had begun months ago, and he would continue to indulge the alleged tendency, preferring not to quit until the notes rested in the appropriate score. But every so often, silence commanded the room, causing Christine to look up in Erik's direction to observe the ongoing repetitive actions; he would first squeeze his eyes tight, rub the back of his neck, sigh, and then try to refocus on his music.

Something is not quite right. She squinted suspiciously at the behavior. Standing, she cautiously closed in, each movement deliberate and visible under his wary eye. She placed her hands on his back and began rubbing, his reflexes, being a firm testament to his religious distrust, went taut until satisfied of her intent. The tension Christine felt was immense; muscles cinched and twisted under her very palms from the knots rippled about his neck, down the upper part of his spine and across both shoulders.

"Erik, tell me how you feel."

He sighed again and she figured it was from the frustration of being interrupted. "Better," he said, patting her hand. "I have not experienced this before... it is similar to your endeavors of last night."

"And, your head?"

"Throbbing."

"As I suspected," she murmured, moving in front of him. This was, in itself, no mean task, considering the confining space in which she had to crowd her skirts.

"Christine, I have had headaches, it is nothing new. Pain and I are not strange bedfellows, you know; sleeping it off when I am finished is usually sufficient. Though, you are proving to be a most bothersome obstacle to that end."

"Yes, and your reply is unconvincing. I will remain here until you have sense enough to rest when your body is screaming for a reprieve."

"Women," he said derisively, his mind cheering heartily in unison.

She could see a stubborn... no, it was worse than that, a belligerent side to his personality. "What is that inference to imply?"

A look of determination coiled within Erik as he stood up, nearly upending the bench to lean over Christine, and hearing his papers shift and crunch from behind her, he spoke in a rather terse fashion.

"It implies—" he began to say, his arms grappling from all sides to rescue the sheets that would soon be of no use, except to replace the bellows of an accordion, "that I will not be compelled to quit when I—damn, another one—am perfectly able to continue. I have, in my own way, crossed paths with plenty of chits at the Opera to know of the domineer—" Erik staved off that spill. "Now, if you would please move, I wish to create music!"

Christine's finger jabbed him in the chest to make a point. "Well, Monsieur," she challenged, "you may have to find another, less taxing way to make music, because *this* chit refuses to budge. I can be every bit as bull-headed, and shall oppose at your earliest invitation." Then she kissed him before anything else could spew from his mouth.

Disarmed, Erik sat down hard, slapping the pages in a stack to the floor. He glanced at her then down to the scattered composition, ending with a touch to his mouth. "You make a persuasive argument, Mademoiselle, most persuasive indeed." His thumb and index stroked his chin. "We should go upstairs and listen to the sounds in nature, the balcony awaits. . . come."

Finally! Christine thought, as she stood behind Erik in the soft breeze, massaging his shoulders. *Domineering, indeed!*

"Your hands are cool, a blessed application against my neck."

"I am delighted."

"The places you knead on my back, to loosen and disperse," he grunted, "I never knew they could harbor such stress. I daresay there is a level of pain attached, but it is positive."

"Hmm. . . you push too hard, someone stops you from abusing yourself further, and it is decided good. Is this gratitude?" She did not shrink in her affront and waited for a reply. *I shall not say more. I have seen evidence of that fortnight he talked of, how time passed unmarked, except for the prolific expanse of paper and diminished wax, but it must come with physical and mental detriment. . . such a price.*

Erik kissed her palm and caressed it to his lips. "I appreciate—"

"Never mind, you felt warm just now."

"Yes, whenever you—"

"I am completely serious Erik, when you kissed my hand, your mouth and throat were exceptionally warm." She set her lips to what portion of forehead she could, then gestured. "Let's get you inside."

"I will be all right. I am quite adept at taking care of myself, and have been for some time now. I do not require one of those, *bonne d'enfants*."

"Fine time to allow your humor to surface in this confused state. Come," she encouraged, ignoring the shot while getting him to his feet.

Erik stood and all the blood rushed to his head in one painful explosion, folding him in half until he could regain balance. With all the stress released, and his emotions merging after being in such chaos for months on end—not to mention the nutritional famine and anxiety—his body had begun to erupt in excruciating glory.

"No arguing, inside," she directed. "If you have some sort of medicine, it may be wise to tell me where you keep it, and far more beneficial to the few herbs I know of."

Erik pointed. "My dressing room, top drawer in the armoire, ugh. . ." He pulled at his collar and sleeves to unfasten them as Christine helped him to the bed. "Really Christine, I can go downstairs."

"I think not," she insisted weakly, as need to debate the issue ceased to exist. Erik had already succumbed to his body's rise in temperature and was out cold.

"Now it is my turn," her hands planting jointly at both hips. "Men!"

First off, she saw to his comfort; his shoes and stockings were easy enough, but his trousers posed a discretionary problem. So, off into his dressing room she went, boldly at the onset, but increasingly meek when greeted by the foreboding cavern, and she with only a timid candle in hand to slice through the black. The act was necessary, not meant to be intrusive, but Christine's eyes still darted around the room. Everything was in order, *right down to the most implicit detail,* she noted reverently. *I suppose being rigidly acquainted would give rise to anything out of the ordinary.* She shuddered. Not wanting to stay longer than was needful, she located his dressing gown, and what might possibly be a variety of natural analgesics, but she was hesitant and put the idea of use aside; an illness was no time to experiment. Upon leaving, she saw something that disturbed her and a piercing thought of that faceless angel tore at her heart, her hand administering only a gentle touch in acknowledgment. There, laying face down on a shelf in the armoire was a small hand mirror. *You provide mirrors for the beauty of others, but use only what is requisite for yourself.* She moaned in a moment of reflection, and closed the notion away.

By the time Christine figured out how to maintain Erik's privacy, without embarrassment to either of them, and had him comfortably situated, she knew his fever had increased. His flesh was hot to the touch. Rushing, she gathered clean cloths, a basin of water and made a quick change of clothing herself, before returning to his side to begin sponging.

His trembling body beckoned to be covered, shivering uncontrollably while his temperature rose. Once Erik's body had reached its culminating limit, sweat broke out to diffuse the heat, and Christine worked in conjunction, to assist in dissipating the fire by dabbing at his exposed skin; this self-same cycle viciously renewed itself throughout the next thirty-six hours.

Christine rarely left Erik. When the fever did subside in intensity, his eyes would open, searching, and she would be there. His feeble attempts at communication were seldom more than one syllable and were regularly lost among her endeavors to keep fluid entering his body. Most often, she would rely on a moistened cloth to squeeze lifegiving droplets across his dried lips, while his lightly dressed form lay under the sheets within the raging grip of Hell. Though, when his coherence profited him, a few swallows of water or tea made from the Borage flower[3] aided greatly.

At one point, Christine dozed off during a spike in the next spell of the fever's unrelenting vice. She was thankful that her weary body found a moment of reprieve, but started awake at the sound of a voice calling her from the misty recesses of her mind. It was Erik. Her response was a mixture of disbelief and alarm when she looked over at him. The pillow covering was stained, smeared with blood oozing from beneath his masque, his breathing shallow and uneven. Christine's mind raced back to that morning on the ridge, not less than two days ago. He had speared an assumption, and now this! Again, he whispered in delirium as she moistened his skin against the burning torment, theirs; one amidst the throes of helpless suffering, and the other, consumed by a struggle of knowledge, hidden knowledge of what he expressly forbid, and the decision she was about to make.

Grave misery called once more and she heeded the summons, removing the masque. An insipid inhalation followed, made by both on the tail of that one relieving gesture. Between the heat, and the existing condition of his face, the tender, thin semblance of skin had been chaffed raw. *His face.* She looked away, remembering his anger. Would he be so again? Her gaze returned firm, to avail the impulse of coming to terms with his appearance. She must move past the surface. Why did it breed repulsion? She had seen photographs of war, artistic renditions, and the wounds sustained. *Erik's disfigurement is no different, but the lasting impact. . .* she stifled the force of a sob. *Inflicted while in Persia? She had heard tell of brutal punishments, loss of limbs for stealing, tongue removal to ensure silence. . . or was it further back?* Her hand reached out, hesitated one last time, and then touched his face. Carefully, she cleansed the sores, permitting the air to heal them while again soothing the unquenchable flames.

The hours ticked by, dropping Christine inch by inch into a well of time, regardless of the life that seemed to dwindle. Finally, not knowing what else to do, she leaned in and cradled his head against her breast so he could hear and feel the beating of her heart, placed her hand to his chest and *his* heart, and sang. In between songs she would hum softly while encouraging Erik to ingest whatever liquid he could. With the patience of a saint, her hand cupped his chin, drawing his mouth upward after each spoonful of water, and massaged his throat until he swallowed. *Baptism by fire. Oh, Erik. It seems we are to experience much these first few days, and there is nothing like an illness to familiarize one's self with the needs of another. I serve willingly, grateful that I can give you tender care, something not partaken of or bestowed on, I am sure.* A gentle smile stole across her lips at the warming thoughts of her affections held in reserve, and she whispered, "There will be time. . ." *as I am quite confident in my sentiments, and in my love. . . for you.*

She did not remember much after that, except being awakened later that night by a hand coming to rest on her cheek; she only recalled resting her head upon the edge of the bed for a moment. Erik's fever had given way, his breathing had become deep once more, and for the first time in more than two days, Christine grinned wide, allowing thanks to float heavenward and relief to cover her in a dreamless sleep.

A trace of sun peeked over the horizon as a new day suffused the land. And as Christine's body gradually began to shed its stupor and stiffness of form, she sat forward from the all too uncomfortable chair, her cushioned post near the bed, to check on Erik. "Good, still breathing steady and only lightly warm to the touch." Being careful not to disturb him, she stood, shed the weighted confines of a blanket, and spun a half circle to do a visual inventory in preparation for the day, and to discover whatever else should be met head on.

Christine remained vigilant, busily determined to have order within, taking only short breaks to check on small duties or Cesar. Erik's dressing gown and clean trousers lay at the foot of the bed, his masque, clean and resting on the nightstand, fresh pillow linens. . . yes, everything was ready.

Erik slept soundly the whole day, with a welcome difference from those previously experienced; he was calmly moving and changing positions. Each time she left or returned, she made a point of either touching or kissing him in strategic spots: on a cheek, forehead, hand, or temple. There was nothing like lavishing him with as much attention as possible before he realized and became reserved again; though, it seemed as much sport as anything else. She could see the tranquil response and near delight the connection educed, but he purported an unrelenting slumber, which aroused her suspicions greatly.

When evening approached, a depleted sun spread its colorful fan against the end of the earth before an appreciative audience of one; it was Christine who sat out on the balcony, watching the rays fold up to dip behind the hills. *I wish Erik could see this one tonight*, she exhaled softly. Her eyes closed to allow listening an opportunity to replace her other senses. The birds quieted and the night's music began to fill the air with subtle, restless stirrings—emanating from both inside and out.

ERIK WAS AWAKE, coherent for the most part, and intent on one purpose requiring all of his strength and concentration, what little there was. He could see her outside and desired to be near; he needed her. Focusing, he sat up, grabbed his trousers and hastily tugged them on. The action, once done, left him realizing indolent movements and frugality of energy to be wise, and that walking out onto the balcony or tending to personal needs would be a far greater chore, engaging his utmost perseverance. Grasping the end of the bed, he stretched and stood unsteadily, his muscles balking use right and left from their preferred state of atrophy, until all succumbed to the arduous task of hobbling from one piece of furniture to the next. Finally, arriving at the door by feeble transport, he leaned his waning shape into the frame and called tenderly to her.

The evening's orchestra had become soothing. She listened, reaching mentally to identify the individual sounds until there came one, which entered to encompass her replete with its silky tone. "Christine."

Her head turned to see Erik clasping the door. Looking as though he might collapse at any moment, she moved quickly to embrace his thin frame.

"Your touch," he whispered shakily, leaning against her to avoid falling.

"Come, you're still weak," she stated, helping him back to the bed.

After propping him up, she was gone, scurrying downstairs on a mission to bring him something fresh to drink.

Taking in a deep breath to clear his head, Erik tried to think, but found it most painful. It was like reconstructing remnants of glass, bit by bit, after being shattered. "I cannot remember much," he said. "I only know how I feel and can deduce only from what I see." He blinked solidly. "I woke up to find myself lightly clothed, but covered well enough... and my masque..." he reached over and immediately resumed the barrier for comfort, "was on the nightstand, dressing gown and trousers at the foot of the bed."

Erik's rambling had ended before Christine reappeared with additional tea to help in the remedial process. She sat gently next to him and smiled, noticing that he had replaced his masque. "How are you feeling?" her shyness of voice rasped.

"Self-conscious." Erik grimaced, face deepening a shade or two into the coloring of his ears and throat.

"I shall put your mind at ease by assuring you that I maintained your privacy at all times and kept you modestly covered. But *that* was not my meaning."

Laying her hand on his chest, she asked again as he slowly lifted his eyes to hers. "In here, how do you feel?"

"As though I've been drugged," he began humbly, "severely

beaten, and burned from the inside out. My soul, deep within, feels like it has been nearly purged of life itself. And. . . I hurt. . . everywhere." A moment of quiet passed between them before Erik wondered aloud. "How long have I—"

"Three days," she answered, her expression pained. "I could only rely on my limited knowledge of what is commonly used, to reduce the fever, what I have seen done. . . the other herbs. . . and the medicines. . ."

"I know, I shall teach you. They contain wondrous healing properties that are as yet untapped in our country." His finger brushed at the hint of a tear. "Why?"

"Your masque. . . I removed your masque." Her eyes drifted in shame for betraying him. "You called out in pain, your face was bleeding from the heat and. . . forgive—"

This time it was Erik's finger that quieted the unnecessary plea as he led her hand to be addressed, palm side to his lips. "I am not yet comfortable without the protection my masque affords, but I feel no malice, only gratitude that you could bear to look upon me, when I know you could not do so before."

Christine kissed Erik's tired eyes; the pallor of his exposed skin looked ashen when compared to their darkened circles. He leaned in, to absorb the affection while taking her hands in his.

"I've missed your touch."

"Considering the frequency exchanged," he whispered, "I must be doing something right."

She blushed lightly and their foreheads met softly.

Erik became solemn. "I heard you, Christine, and I heard. . . your heart."

Chapter Four

The afternoon blaze from the summer sun met with a shield of green overhead as Erik lay gazing out at a small swarm of insects, hovering about the water's perimeter. They seemed to have difficulty deciding on how best to proceed, but they clung to their mass of safety. "And I, alone," he mumbled.

How peaceful he was, his mind, his body, his soul. Christine would come soon, her approach audible. To feign sleep, to lure her unsuspecting figure close was possible. Unfortunately, his mind had other plans. More tired than he realized, and still recovering, his charade quickly became reality and plunged him into blissful revelry.

"Ah," came the soft remark, "looks like someone needed more rest than they would admit to; we shall eat later." Putting the covered tray aside, she knelt next to him to watch. He was on his back, hands folded behind his head, his breathing light and rhythmic. *Prodigious learning ability, I daresay. I desire to know so much about you, my gentleman of mystery. You are calmer, less showy, and more genuine, though your past is guarded and emotions still so veiled, but I shall remain ever patient... a hard trait to maintain at times!* She sighed. *We shall see how things unfold.*

A loving smile formed on her lips, then widened. His shirt was open, exposing a bit of definition. Touching his chest she began to swirl the hair beneath the tips of her fingers and a look of uncertainty crossed Erik's face. *What sort of intrusion is going through that brain of yours? Does it never allow you complete rest?* She stopped her ministrations to let him sink back below the surface.

"Oh, so unfair," he groused. "You cannot stop... please? It feels... too good." Erik peered at her through narrowed slits as she started again.

"Are you hungry?"

He lay there pondering, assessing the query. "I could take it or leave it."

"Well," Christine said sternly, "taking it would certainly be the wiser of the two choices." Surprising herself at how direct the words were presented, she hastened in earnest at an explanation. "It's just, it would assist... Well, look at you! You need to regain what you lost during your illness, plus... whatever you were doing in the past," she tugged on the waist of his trousers, "you cannot continue, obviously. 'Living on music for days at a time,' I believe is what you said, and that, Monsieur, is beyond unhealthy."

They stared, watching the other as a clear understanding passed between them that there had been more than a passing glance. He flushed outright!

"You would have me overweight?" he quipped.

"Of course not. You know there is a difference. Just looking at your face I can tell it has yet to fill out." She was examining the outline of his masque when she saw his eyes moisten and instantly regretted every word. "Forgive me, I was far too pointed with my comments."

Swallowing, he whispered, "No," and lifted his hand up. "No one has ever worried about me in such a way. I have grown accustomed to people recoiling in fear because of what they see or do not see in my face, that there has been little cause for care of the whole. Your thoughtfulness for my well-being, in addition to the fact that you are interested in how I look physically, is appreciated. Though, it will take some getting used to."

Christine brought him up to a sitting position. "I would prefer to look after a well nourished male, not one who is neglected, at least if I have a say in the matter."

"You may have as much 'say' as you deem appropriate."

Erik was hungrier than either had expected, surprising them both, finishing all of his and what was left of her meal. Rolling over on his stomach, he sighed, and expressed how excellent he felt; he was full and satisfied as the workings of a back rub lulled him gently back under the curtain of repose.

"Erik, may I ask you something?"

"Hmm, certainly."

"You have mentioned, several times in fact, of your return to France. Would this mean, you are originally from here?"

"Yes, I was born in a small town, not far outside Rouen, but would prefer not to devote any time in the present to its remembrance," he said, dismissing more by closing his eyes.

"Then sleep, you deserve the rest, no need to concern yourself," she said, her tone softly leading to a distant hum. *I consider myself lucky on an increasing basis. I have discovered hopes and pain, knowing I will eventually learn more. When I hear a passing comment it helps me comprehend, and this most recent makes me aware that even from a young age, his memories are not fond ones, so treading into his childhood may be long in coming. The gentleness and strength that cohabitate, move forward to bind us together each hour we share.*

And, at present, his kisses, I cannot put words to the desire they already invoke from me, and I know he feels the same.

HOW LONG HAS it been? Erik wondered, rising to one elbow while rubbing his face just under one side of his masque; a quick, upward glance at the position of the sun gave him an approximation on time. *I am usually unable to sleep so soundly.*

Christine had cleared up and was lying inversely on her side, watching him unseen. Erik was lightly stunned by her persistence when he lay back down. "You have been studying. Repeat acts can become tiresome, can they not?"

"Sorry for the start, sleepyhead," she greeted. "Now, to your comment; I should think that having an accomplished woman to converse with would be highly stimulating, and second, the answer is a most resounding no. This performance has yet to repeat, no matter how often I attend."

Erik grinned slightly at her wit and rolled over to stare into the most alluring brown eyes; they were so compassionate, so soft, and there was something else, something he could not quite put a finger to.

"Feeling well?" she asked.

"Yes, quite well, thank you."

"Good, then tell me, how is your temperature, I have been waiting to enquire."

"My temperature?" Erik was curious as to the meaning.

"Yes, my insatiable feminine interest would like to know if you feel the least bit chilled and are in need of some heat to bring you up to normal. Mind you, we would not wish to go the opposite direction and overheat you."

Erik's comprehension sharpened quickly. "Ah! I am experiencing a slight chill in this vicinity." He pointed to his mouth. "The air passing through continually causes me to shiver."

"Well, we shall see if we can remedy the problem," she said, leaning over his face upside-down and kneeling on all fours. Amusement passed over Erik's face when she provided a peck on his lips.

Interesting twist. Most amiable, kissing her from this perspective... definitely has its possibilities.

"How is the temperature at this stage of recovery?" she queried.

"Seems to maintain well then drop again when you start talking. You are extremely frustrating." He was enjoying this game, and wishing it to continue he reached up behind his head, lifted her by the waist, turned her around and placed her across his upper body. A delighted squeal spilled forth in the form of his name. "Mademoiselle, I require better, no... more consistent temperature regulation services." He brought her hand to his mouth, kissing slowly, each one of her dainty, porcelain fingers in succession. *Only she could taste so sweet.* Rising up to sit, Erik's eyes never wandered from hers. Having given individual recognition, with her hand curled over his, it was time to address them as a whole and he brushed his lips to each knuckle, the availability of breathable air becoming at once suspended without complaint from either of them.

This type of situation had a habit of recurring, the more comfortable he became with his boundaries. Dropping her hand to his left shoulder, he was now free to caress the milky sheen before him. Her fingers explored the outline of his mouth; the malformation drawing across a portion held her gaze momentarily before her lashes slid together, an unexpected tremor snapping them open. Erik's cheek twitched, knowing it was he who induced such a response, and she relaxed once more under his spell. His hands were skilled, eliciting unhindered senses, to mold, stretch, and coax into pure delight. His lips diminished in weight as they danced from place to place along her cheeks, asking her to move with them. Upon nearing her mouth, she joined his, raising the tempo to an even pace. Christine's lips parted and a sliver of moisture heightened the conduction, bringing everything to a stand still.

Erik was instantly skeptical, but receptive to something new. Her fingers pushed up through his thick hair and drew him to her, eyes closed, breath magnetically taunting until their lips came together.

So many sensations erupted at once that he was quite unsure how best to proceed. The intimacy was intoxicating; her lips, her mouth as a whole, its texture, shape, taste. . . every particle.

He broke away, chest heaving, and felt a ripple of indescribable pleasure surge through him. A low, airy pitched "hmm" was all he could manage while sitting there, staring at her. Mutually, they wasted no time in immersion once more as Christine's arms closed around Erik's neck in possession. Reluctantly, it was he who put distance between them, and kissing her lightly on the cheek he moved away to stand with his shoulder pressed relentlessly to the trunk of a massive tree, eyes unwilling to meet hers. Erik chastised himself mentally, the self-irritation due in part to a loss of control, which was clearly exhibited by the distress during his struggle to regain composure.

"These feelings that flood my mind and body, I. . . am not fully prepared to experience what may be unleashed if I allow them to run undirected. To partake in. . ." he cleared his throat, "I shall not take advantage of the situation, our emotions, and especially you." He fought desperately to relax his voice as he continued. "And. . . though I am not intrusive in nature, I would hope for other moments, to learn."

A gentle stroke to his back brought Erik to face Christine. There was such kind interest that he felt greater ease. He was being totally honest. The gravity of concern about wanting to remain chaste, at this benign level of their affection, was standard, an unwavering must, which secured one to the other even more.

"I look forward to multiple opportunities," she said timidly, "to become familiar with meeting the needs and expectations of the other, but always with the utmost respect."

There was a nod of agreement, and taking it to mean that an end had come to their conversation, she took his hand until he was ready to go on with their day.

Christine gives me purpose. Coming with provisions from Amiens today, she sent me to lie in the shade and I did so in total submission, ardently obedient to her slightest command—strange, these sentiments, and after only a few weeks. I have hated for so long, pursued knowledge, power, and possessions, anything to span the void that could never be filled, where joy ought to have been, where she. . . is. Where I shunned, I now greet eagerly, I accept her touch, and her sweet kisses, and she mine. I still harbor a strong sense of doubt, especially about myself, but I have begun to feel a deeper passion, which overshadows the negative. I have never allowed myself to think that I was worthy of having joy.

Chapter Five

By summer's end a routine had emerged alongside a level of comfort. Walks during the evening hours, to watch the sun go down from different vantage points, brought opportune moments to discuss the events of each day; adventures in the kitchen were among those favored—the disasters as well as successes (baking bread was just such an enterprise, one which recurred and that Erik was kind enough never to tease about, but soon it was Christine whose comments rounded upon the initial loaves). Erik, having openly professed a limited repertoire in the kitchen, allowed her full lead and discretion, as it was she who was determined to hit upon more than mediocrity in regard to the casting of golden dough. One endeavor yielded a wondrous beauty, to which she and Erik instantly wished to indulge. The rising steam from the finely textured slices excited them to partake, its looks, anything but deceiving, and scent, enticing. Alas, Erik grinned at Christine's frustration and asked at what point she had been interrupted. She thought, then raised her eyes, and hand to mouth. She had forgotten the salt! Both laughed heartily, saving the loaf to feed the birds when next in Amiens.

Continuing on. . . there was singing, Erik's conferring over musical works with her, whether his or that of an established composer, riding, shopping and people watching in Amiens or talks and reading by candlelight while curled up amongst the pillows. Their relationship flourished in the present, whereupon an occasional moment would touch the past to become as an exposed nerve, cold and sensitive, shuddering and resistant to any effects of penetration. Christine knew his odious nature—his occasional temper flares were quite colorfully displayed—but she hoped he would begin to trust enough to allow her to go beyond the surface, to strengthen their foundation. What more could two burgeoning souls wish?

This was the subject Christine sought to ponder as she walked upstream to her favorite place for deciphering solutions. Weeks ago, right after one of Erik's belligerent outbursts, she had found this spot most suitable, resolving the distance, sufficient. She could still hear his music wafting through the air, emotions all too clear, but it was adequate space for thought and cooling off.

Wading in up to her ankles, she climbed out onto the large flat stone protruding away from the rocky bank into the lazy flow, grateful for some time to herself. She always enjoyed the way the sun filtered through the protective screen above, to dance upon the ripples in the water and penetrate her very existence. For now, the world stopped so she could think on the complexities she was learning to treasure about Erik, and of the fortitude used to shore up her patience. They had both refrained from telling each other their deepest feelings, recognizing the bond of friendship taking root. He told her once that she would have no better friend than he, but she wished for things to be more than they were and feared that he was too content or that he waited for some other reason.

Christine let the thoughts mellow in the breeze while she turned her attention toward her fascination with the stream. *It is truly a marvel; water in any form. Its undeniably strong force, the way it meanders in and around the obstacles in its path, inevitably unhindered, patient too, until there is a solution.* A butterfly gracefully flitted by, alighting on the upper most tip of a blossom without disturbance. She watched, discovering this creature to be very particular about which flowers

Beyond the Masque

it chose. The bees, on the other hand, were indiscriminate and visited all that were available. *That is an interesting correlation. How many characteristics are possessed by humanity, which are but a mirrored instinct of God's creatures? Some take arbitrarily from anyone while others are graciously specific. I am amazed at the delicate balance we all flirt with. Words, thoughts, and actions, all governed—in some form—by unconscious principle and all set upon pretext of upbringing.*

She had been surrounded with gentle structure all her life, but as she learned about Erik, she was actually dumbfounded at what a lack of compassion and love had done to the soul of another human being. For nearly four months they had adjusted to their differences, but one concept eluded her, that of aloneness. She found Erik reveled in self-dependency, the timeless hours he spent unfathomable, as something deep within compelled a determination for perfection, a drive to complete and to accept nothing inferior. She, dissimilarly, considered moments of solitude a place to go to, to visit and appreciate, a status that had never been forced, and could accept if something was beyond her scope, if her best was put forward. Even now she wondered if her presence was a hindrance or bother to such a state as his, though, for the most part, his actions portrayed kindness.

Christine lay down to rest her head in the crook of her arm while dipping her hand in the cool stream. Pulling petals and leaves from a nearby plant, she spread them over the water to watch them float about, confused on the surface, and her concerns dissipated as she admired a petite flower peeking up from a small rocky fissure. *Look at you, so tiny, yet vivid in your coat of blue. The odds are against you in this world, you know. What makes you think you will survive? Perhaps the odds are what incite your heart to succeed.* "Erik." His name escaped her lips and she sighed heavily. *What makes you who you are?*

GLANCING UP FROM his piles of musical scores, Erik listened to the quiet of the house; he could sense the distance between him and

Christine. Looking around and finding his music in methodical disarray, he decided that a balance must be established, personally, as well as collectively. He felt a sense of contentment, more so now than at any other time in his life, but was unsure of Christine's true feelings. *I am accustomed to being alone, though I have rapidly learned to find unrest. My whole life I have been dependent on silence to bring solace to my weary soul, and now, I can only feel peace with her at my side. There is also a strange frustration of late,* his eyebrow cocked; *it seems that my focus is attached to my preferred distraction. Perhaps she has felt this and tries to help by staying out of reach and sight, giving me time to work. Unfortunate, I have my intolerance to blame for the imposition of solitude that I place upon her. So it is together that we must claim ignorance in our regard toward the other, for neither discloses honestly what we so centrally hold dear. Such confusion.*

He shifted, smiling at the dust particles he had disrupted from their place of hiding. They hung in mid-air, and drifted through a shaft of light coming through the corner window seat until buried from view again amongst his papers. Rising from the bench, he strode out to the porch to have a look around, and spied a misty visage not far upstream. An idea, spawned by this fair sight, quickly turned him on his heels, and he dashed to his studio to retrieve a sheet of paper, art board and chalks. Fully equipped, he silently proceeded to locate an unobtrusive place, one that would permit a good sightline from which to sketch Christine.

Erik gained an early appreciation for artistic detail while in his youth, astounding those who were as much as four or five times his age, with the intricacies and skill of someone who had studied for decades. His gifts of genius materialized on paper as effortlessly and precisely as a bird in flight; the lines and shading blended, evolved and changed until a point in time had become immortal. Awestruck, he serenely observed, drawing the beauty that held his heart, while his mind took to wandering over the previous weeks. *If I were to use one word to describe this moment, it would be "inspiring." I know so much about her and she in turn, knows only what I have chosen to share, I am the limiting factor. She has not pried, held me under contemptuous inquisition, or made any requests related to my masque. I suppose, in some way, the masque continues to guard against the monster that glares back at me from my haunted past. She knows, she has seen, but I have not permitted a subsequent removal to happen since my illness because I wished for her to become familiar with the man, behind the masque. I can feel my blood boil even now, the hatred festering in those open, unhealed wounds. I am pained as well, to think of what she beheld. Perhaps it is time for her to confront the man as a whole, to see if the seed of happiness continues on the winds of indecision or whether it will anchor itself within the depths of my love.*

As the rendered depiction neared completion, Erik heard Christine sigh, his name escaping her lips.

"What could be so grievous as to evoke such burden at the mention of my name?"

"Erik! Oh, you. . . how long have you been there?" she cried out, shaken from her inattention.

"Long enough to thoroughly admire." He grinned, eyes twinkling, as they remained affixed to the portrait.

With her arms out for balance, she slid out onto the smooth stones and walked haltingly through the icy water back to the bank. "May I see?" she asked in interest. Erik held out his hand in gesture of welcome, inviting her to sit beside him. Christine entwined her arms around his and rested her head to his shoulder.

The final touches produced a sensuous surface, shading as he was with the tip of his fourth finger. Although the portrait was in tones of blacks and greys, one could almost see the sky blue of her dress enhanced by the fickle shadows, swaying to and fro across her back and the deliciously smooth neckline encircling her shoulders. The hues of light, drawn through her hair, reflected from off the sparkle at the water's edge, intensifying the beauty against a natural backdrop of summer color.

"You have captured more than what is evident at first glance." She pointed to the drop of her garment over one shoulder. "How *does* one man possess so many talents?"

"Perhaps it is to compensate for other aspects of my life that I lack, I am not sure why or how, the ability is innate. And as for this, my dear, not all must be visible. That which is left to the imagination is far more alluring to the mind's eye than anything overtly exposed." Putting down his supplies, he took up Christine's left hand and kissed her palm affectionately, then placed it to his chest. "I hope I have captured far more." He melted into her touch, as he wished for embracing penetration straight to his heart and with it, her warmth, never wanting to release that rose soft skin.

A light blush shone.

"Christine, I have yet to understand the reasoning behind why you stay, to put up with my selfishness, with the unknown. Sometimes I think it is out of pity that you demonstrate such kindness and tolerance, but I feel in the depth of my soul that that is not true. I am learning to trust, slowly, and should like to become more trusting, more open." Apprehension gave pause as prelude to the next invitation he was about to extend. "What is it that you wish to know of me?" Calm resignation filled his eyes and overflowed down his cheeks in preparation, head lowered. "You may ask. . . anything."

She was hesitant, "You are sure?" The question came as if she had only waited upon opportunity.

"I am." He held on even tighter.

"Then, I should like to know about your masque."

Erik inhaled stridently. The one thing that brought the most pain in his life *was* his masque and all it covered. It was the one burden that guided comment, thought, action, and emotion. . . everything stemmed from that one heavily rooted aspect. *Naturally, she wasted no time with trifling preface and went straight for the jugular!* Well, the monstrosities he committed were exposed, why not the history attached? A wave of nausea hit, his mind spun, and his past gripped his vitals. But the image was so appallingly real. Pieces set to floating, spinning about him, each summoned as witness to his life: mirrors, water, glass, horrified stares, whips, laughter, music, and death. Each fragment meshed with the next—there were millions—until he was ultimately entombed. *My masque!* It burst. *Christine!* He clasped her hand solidly and the dizziness subsided. He would not be letting go of her any time soon so she leaned over to his bent knees and settled in.

"I have always worn a masque," Erik began solemnly. "I have worn it, or something contrived, since the day I was born." He arrested momentarily at an airy "oh" from her.

"My very existence spurned terrifying excitement in those who knew of me and I have known no other relief. My mother found the idea of contact with me distasteful... I repulsed her, thereby initiating the creation of the mitigating insensitivity. I grew up having never known touch or the gentle kiss of affection, for she would always run away and beseech me, for God's sake, to wear the masque. I felt that if I displeased her so, I must also be displeasing in God's sight as well. She was completely and utterly detached, only providing the necessities to survive those beginning months and years, as she drained from me every drop of life she had given. As a result of this indifference, I developed a self-preserving connection with silence... alone. Alone became my companion, and together we spent hours with Curiosity as our instructor.

"My progress quickened during the time I had to myself. Sleep was not easy to come by, so I utilized this time to my advantage. Both my physical and mental developments were enhanced, striding far outside the confines of what a normal, intellectual environment could inspire, with music as the catalyst. Being young, the imposing limits that were forced upon me were accepted; I was content with the varying explanations, as well as those I had placed upon myself, and whereas no one seemed to give notice, unless I posed a problem, I was left up to my own volition. I quickly learned to cope with disappointment, to rationalize shortcomings, for it was my inexperience with the world that dealt me numerous blows in the face of reality. It showed me that safety came only by being hidden and later, that people would take advantage of another's misfortune, unless it was unknowingly taken first.

"The masque was a similar issue. I wore it obediently, but acquired a strong dislike for the sores and heat that were caused, not unlike those witnessed during my illness. Leaving my room without the masque was forbidden, as it was only up in my room where the masque could be removed. My face was granted a stay of reprieve, if you will, while I slept or became otherwise engaged, and I often preferred refuge in my sanctuary to escape the painful chaffing. I guess I never really questioned why until age clashed with comprehension.

"I recall once wondering what my mother looked like beneath her masque; young as I was, I thought we all had one. Disappointment is a harsh instructor, for it does not take long for a precocious child to figure out that certain restrictions only pertain to them. I would postulate—and I say this because I have no recollection of what happened just prior to this revelation—that I threw a grand fit of displeasure when I realized it was I. . . I who was different! I had never seen a mirror before, but I discovered one in my father's room, a place forbidden me. . . hah! In my state of rebelliousness I went in, just to spite him, and was soon face to face with something no child should ever have to confront. . . my exposed flesh. I was horrified! I could not fathom what I was seeing; all I could do, all I wanted to do was lash out. I pounded, screaming in fear until the reflection before me disintegrated. I bled profusely, but continued my tirade, trying to beat the image from my mind; I was unsuccessful. When I calmed down, I was entreated to wear my masque, told that it would make the face go away and hide the horrid picture from my eyes. . . I believed, I hoped, but it did not bury the terror from my mind. Nightmares filled my dreams and darkness loomed heavy over my innocence; only a candle was given to console and disperse my fears. Alone and I did not seek out Curiosity for quite some time. I hated Curiosity for tempting me that day, for deceiving me.

"Over the years I have been displayed, humiliated, loathed, hated, and hunted. I gradually realized that, even though I wore a masque, I would never escape the monster beneath. There would always be those who were curious and those who despised because of what they could or would never understand.

"I later developed the skills to create masques, to keep myself obscure, eventually improving until I could fashion them to give the appearance of someone with normal features. I shall continue to experiment as I discover new properties and materials, hoping that I may find success for all aspects in one design and that it will look aesthetically appealing. They have provided me with an eccentric air to hide behind and structure to that which has none. My masque has protected me from the fear in others' eyes; it has always been, Christine. . . until now."

Erik had caressed her hand throughout the whole bitter recounting, had slid emotionally by paling degrees, hitting bottom with a jarring thud. Darkness, he wished for darkness. Chancing a wary look, he could see her face was wet, but that was all before the rush to close his eyes. Raising her hand from his chest to his mouth, he kissed her palm and wrist, then gently placed it to his right cheek, and together they removed the masque and hairpiece. The barriers fell to the ground as he sat, laid open, a fresh wound rent to air. He no longer held her hand, only his breath, and soon felt a small stir next to him.

Christine rose to her knees and leaned in cautiously to stroke the tawny strands of hair away from his face. Her hands explored the terrain, from the barren scars to the fullness of joy coursing in streams beneath her touch. Erik felt the shy curtain of trepidation gradually draw open to expose confidence along this unsure journey. And when her fingers made an end to their wandering, her lips began. The sweetness of contact long denied came as rain, to nourish. She covered each portion, soothing the scorched flesh with her salve of compassion and love. Erik slowly felt for Christine's waist; he held tight, and struggled for breath. Then, pressing tenderly, his face nestled into the comfort of her breast and his chest heaved. "Hold me," he softly pleaded.

Words of sorrowful disbelief attached themselves to the conjured image of a callous woman and an indifferent father; Erik wanted to forget. He had shouldered this since birth and could, in Christine's embrace, feel shielded from the memory, safe. Tears came easily.

For some, the capacity to love unconditionally is given and for others, it is too much for them to bear. One cannot condemn, but only think that the world would not have abused the spirit of this gentle man if they had known the desire of his heart—to be loved for himself.

"I am sorry," she offered, gently kissing his forehead.

"Oh, my dearest Christine, do not think on it, even for a moment. You have given me more than I would have ever thought possible."

Christine released her grasp and tipped his chin up. Waiting for his reddened eyes to greet hers, she smiled. "When a person loves someone, as much as I love you, they are willing to share the burdens of the other."

He seemed genuinely perplexed by the statement, blinking back his emotion.

"Erik, I—"

"Oh, blessed words!" he exclaimed, following her lead to stand. Christine moved right in front of him, her hands bracing against his chest for balance. He watched her eyes following the path traced by each of her hands ascending along the sides of his neck until woven at the base of his skull. Christine's sight rose as Erik's head bent to receive her forehead against his left cheek in a caressing rub.

"I love you... Christine, you are my salvation," he intoned lightly, his voice gradually darkening under the smoldering desire in the depths of his soul. "I shall never be convinced of it being otherwise." Then, without another word, their love gained mutual ground; they embraced, lips moving in an empowered seal of affection. They remained on the bank that afternoon; arm in arm amidst the leafy bower, impassioned by the strength of discovery... in their love.

Chapter Six

Dearest Angel,
 I shall be down stream—there most of the day—gathering dead wood and felling trees to cure for replenishing our firewood. Look for Cesar; I'll be nearby.
  Your love, Erik

"My love... yes," she agreed. It was interesting, the change which occurred in Erik over a few words and the course of a week. He walked taller, was light hearted, and found peculiar ways to surprise Christine. They came by note, folded ingeniously into clever spots and pockets, a dressing room washbasin filled with flowers, and a key tied with ribbon—an odd one, in a way. She had the hardest time trying to figure out what it could possibly open and Erik allowed her the better part of a day to think on it before she understood that it represented *the key to his heart*. Remorse had been felt keenly by both; her folly, mistaking the meaning to be of literal content, seeing him perturbed that it had taken her so long, and his, to fancy himself just, in his show of irritation when it was he who thrust presumption. And then today, this note, found lodged between the panels into the dining area was obvious to a fault. Deep down, they held appreciation for the attempts of the other, in addition to the kisses and reciprocation rarely experienced by him.

Christine read the note once more, tucked it away and set out prepared with ample fare and drink, slung about her shoulders within a haversack.

The sun had yet to reach its peak, as she hiked through the trees near the stream; a smile softly graced her appearance, lifting her frame entirely, an effect from country living, no doubt. She was quite robust, skin lightly hued, and the pace here was detached from the stressful confusion associated with the business of performing. Vanity was perhaps another aspect of unimportance, or was at least weighted less in the scheme of all things natural; the rise of color after a brisk walk and the brightness of eye were all the brilliant enhancements deemed necessary. Clear, quick thinking—though not always evident—increased, to match the masculine wit and heightened awareness in the importance of environmental components; the ability to learn from listening, to read people more skillfully, their tone, mannerisms, and words. Trips to Amiens provided plenty of targets for random practice under Erik's tutelage, in addition to those presently residing at the estate, but a question arose in Christine's mind of whether Erik would one day rue the door opened to that inducement. A grin broke out. Time together, devoid of others' influence, was of such great worth. They were a prime example that the power encompassed by the positive suggestion of words could accomplish spectacular feats: patience cultivated trust.

The jangle of harness chains alerted her to her destination. "Well," she surmised in a glance around. "I suppose the definition of 'nearby' will present itself in due time. He probably knows I am here and will swoop down as if on the wings of an owl, when least expected." A patch of summer grass lent a comfortable setting next to the weathered face of a rock. It was the perfect place to display the bounty from a fully ripened sack, atop Cesar's blanket. Grabbing two apples, she stuffed one in the pocket of her apron and carried the other to Cesar, who accepted the treat and pats of affection greedily. "You are a handsome horse in your suit of white, as much as your master is in contrast." He nudged her sideways and snorted. "And impatient!" Cesar's ears pricked and Christine grinned. "He is behind me, no?" she mumbled to the horse's rather persistent mouth.

A pair of hands descended upon the situation, pushing Cesar's muzzle away to encircle Christine's waist from the back. "Such manners, you rogue! Pilfering a lady's pocket. Surely, only *I* may be so bold." Erik plucked the juicy sphere from Christine's apron and took a meager bite. "You shall be required to bow down before the fair maid. . . come, all the way," Erik ordered.

Cesar tucked his foreleg and lowered his head in submission to receive his reward. Christine laughed at the horse's antics as Erik's lips prefaced his words with a peck to her temple. "Your perception, my dear. . . well done, taking your cues from Cesar's ears."

"With such a valuable *key* in my possession, sir. I take the responsibility of your heart to be quite serious. It is in my best interest," she said, falling in with Erik's British accent as best she could.

Erik laughed. "An Englishman would be right in taking offense to our imitation." He sobered instantly. Her hand had reached up behind her to caress his face, but met instead with a cold, familiar obstruction and sighing, the hand quickly retreated in its wake.

"What?" Erik exclaimed. "I have on my masque I suddenly become unworthy of your touch? This is the first time you have reacted—"

"You're keeping score?" Her voice raised in surprise, body twisting out of his grasp. "Or, is this some sort of valuation, where as soon as there is some unfavorable, uncontested response, the subject is disqualified, then has to work twice as hard to resume a respectable level in your mind? What of trust?" she demanded.

Caught! Erik backed up from the scorn being served him and shied away in guilt. He *had* been testing her, and had succumbed to his mind nodding permission.

"I'm sorry, Erik. I did not mean to lash out. I was expecting to feel one thing and touched another in disappointment. The ease and comfort in which you function without your masque led me to believe that it would become a natural transition to be free of it altogether."

"I consider myself enlightened," he admitted, his chest rising, "and must ask your forgiveness as well. It was unintentional to anger you and unfair of me to plot your reactions. There is always a method to my way of thinking." Erik saw her brows peak. "Almost always. Since my masque has been a protection throughout my life, a conditioned life, I calculate risk because a masque is a part of *who* I am, Christine. It will never completely go away. It creates peace of mind and is a barrier against the elements." He looked wistfully back in her direction. "And, you are correct, I enjoy the freedom afforded me, especially your touch, in all its forms. I have no qualms if you wish to remove it for those purposes. . . I do trust you."

Sauntering toward Erik, Christine bit her lip while closing the distance then assisted him in shedding his gloves.

"Do not ravage your ability to share affection," he said, sliding his finger vertically across each full lip. "Uh, I recall a certain, reassuring comment about not biting, eh?"

"Ah, 'nless rowvowkt or tented." With the tip of his finger ensnared the words were horribly garbled.

Surprise registered quickly. "Provoked or tempted? There was no disclaimer!" he protested. "Or is this *your* way of telling me that the rules adapt to fit the moment?"

His question was answered with a nonchalant shrug, and a relinquishing of the digit as she drifted into his arms for a deliberate kiss. The masque tumbled onto the ground, all resistance to the petal soft veil of her hands gone. They caressed his uneven flesh, reaching farther to curve around his neck. Impassioned, he sighed lightly when feeling her press into his chest, then she pitched off balance in his arms and giggled, breaking contact.

"Get away from her!" Erik grumbled, swatting Cesar's pestering nose from Christine's backside. *Damn horse!* "Have you no discipline, thinking only of your stomach and nothing else?"

Christine picked up Erik's masque on her way over to their small oasis, grinning from ear to ear at the comments she heard Erik griping about through clenched teeth.

"Spoiler, ruining a perfectly splendid situation. I ought to stick your nose in that oat bag she brought." He followed a few paces behind, cuffing Cesar under the chin with his gloves.

"He would not be the first male with a one track mind." Christine caught Erik with a peck on his cheek and he dropped to the ground in front of the rock, running his hand over his face.

"No, I suppose not," he conceded, minimally abashed at this turn of subject.

"Erik, your honest emotion is something I cherish. Being included in your thoughts, and a partner to your discoveries, makes me grateful I am witness."

"I would have it no other way."

"Though, it cannot be easy. . . I mean, the dynamics of our situation. Yet you seem content at any given point, and a gentleman always."

Content? Oh, yes, more than he could express! But the dynamics, those. . . there was a jolt to conscience. *Dearest Christine!* What manner of impropriety he had committed! *Foolish wretch!* He had treated their situation as a mere condensing of the Opera House. They lived under one roof there—logistics aside, for levels traversed—separate apartments, visiting, sharing meals and music. . . none of this had registered as *wrong* to him then. His eyes shut briefly.

"Christine, I hope you will forgive the conditions," he began slowly, trying to regain hold over the discomposure. "I relish the incremental progression in our relationship. There is no reason to push for more when I am satisfied at present. I value, as you say, your witness in discovery and enjoy learning with you. However, a part of me feels guilt because I do not wish change, nor do I wish to share you, though. . . I know I must. Selfishness would only land me right back in circumstances similar to those I imposed upon you before."

He took the food-laden plate in appreciation and their hands touched in passing. Her skin made his limbs weaken. Was he a liar? Not totally. He was not satisfied, desired joy and wished to be longer in her presence during times apart, so much so that his very being cried in jubilant recognition when reunited; this he had suppressed, to respect in order to sustain her good opinion. Patience had done right by him.

"I have not minded, really. I like the limited distractions, but I must confess to the odd feelings I had when I came to a place where my very presence seemed. . . expected."

Erik squirmed, waiting for a clear mouth to reply. "Yes. . . well, my plans were instigated after I overheard conversations between you and. . ." he refused to verbally recognize Chagny. "I felt threatened, and for me, that was sufficient to justify eavesdropping and anything else I wished to set in motion. In a way, I have always been double-minded. I think it is how I maintained a level of sanity in my life, how I distinguished right and wrong, but then I had to deal with the instability as a by-product. Being madly in love also does something to one's rationale."

Christine bowed her head. "Your state of mind when I first found you."

"Yes. . . not one of my better moments," he admitted. "I was determined to hide you away, then realized, that for you, there had to be more. Keeping you below in darkness would not have been an acceptable option, hence, the motivation for actually finishing the estate."

"But, your motivation dissolved. . . what would have become of all this had I not returned?"

"When you took your leave of me with. . . I came here to place my affairs in order. It was quiet, removed, and then I returned to a short interview with the Persian, though it was largely one-sided and highly accusatory on his part. I talked of that tragic night, of the astonishing events, finally imparting to him of my plans and those intended for you. I would have left everything in his possession. Those documents you noticed on my desk. . ." he inferred. She gave a nod to the pause. "He deserved no less for placing his faith on the line in my behalf. He is the only one who knows I am still alive; he thinks I am alone. . . I have posted several letters from Amiens." Erik assuaged the possible thoughts brewing with those last words and an errant wave.

"I see. So, you have not been back at all, not even during the night?"

"No."

"I thought you might have, while I slept."

She is aware of more than she lets on. "What leads you to conclude that?"

"I tend to retire for the evening before you and no matter how early I rise, you are already up, busily engaged. My suspicions were lightly confirmed last week when you mentioned that sleep rarely came easily as a child."

"But I do sleep," he offered in defense, "just not for long stretches."

"Or regularly," she added. "Care to elaborate on what does occupy your time?"

Erik set his plate aside, brushing his hands off, and gathered Christine next to him. "I read, draw, conduct experiments, prove or disprove theories, compose, sometimes ride Cesar, and—"

"Draw up a chair to sit and watch me?" Christine broke in,

stunning Erik. "I know when I am under your gaze, Monsieur."

"Does this bother you?" he asked innocuously.

She shook her head. "I feel safe with you near, but I can tell it is not reciprocated comfortably, at least not at present. The longer we talk, the harder it becomes for you to look me in the eye."

Erik's heart beat inconsistently, his eyes, a wall of regret. Suddenly, sitting in her presence was like being left to swelter beneath the desert sun without reprieve. "You look on me, sustained. . . how can you bear—"

"You would prefer me to make contact with what, the ground? I think not. When one is addressed by another, he or she must be allowed the courtesy and attention of focus." Christine searched his features, raising her fingers to trace his marred face. He closed his eyes too soon. "No!" she demanded curtly. "I want you to watch me. I want you to see that I desire to see you. I will not shun the man I love." Her hands held steady, and he observed her study her captive. "There is actually a good deal of emotion expressed, and is far more attentive than the earth upon which you sit."

Erik's face brightened, his countenance elevating several hues as a bit of contempt was erased. The woman, to whom he pledged an unfaltering love, could gaze at him, speak of her love as well, and find no repulsion! For a moment he did not know whether to laugh or cry. His hands came up to lightly rub Christine's arms, slowly drawing them up. She enfolded his neck in the crook of her elbow and waited for their foreheads to touch. "You are the world to me, Christine Daaé. . ." And he pressed his mouth to hers, whispering between a series of weightless kisses, of his love, his undeniable passion and unending devotion.

His breath warmed her neck, leaving a sigh echoing in his ears. "It used to be your voice that caused me to soar, and now with your sensitive touch and kiss I am aloft in unthinkable pleasure."

Erik's chest inflated confidently at her soft, emboldened praise.

If his smile were as broad, no one was aware but he.

"I love you," they professed in unison, withdrawing in mild laughter.

A glint caught Erik's interest and he glanced down at Christine's lap where a passel of juicy red grapes lay; he cleared his throat. "Ahem, and how long were you intending to hold out on me?" His finger pointed at the patiently waiting treat.

"Hold out? You tell me which you would prefer, a kiss or fruit?"

"Both, what sort of question is this, that you divide my wishes?" he blurted, attempting to pluck a few, meeting with no success as Christine covered them and drew up her knees.

"That was—" his phrase came up short when a grape made its debut between her teeth, a wink calling him closer to partake. He grinned.

"Making me work for that which I desire?" Christine nodded. "Ah." Spreading his arms wide Erik bowed gracefully and received the grape with double the reward. The system was good for the first few, but Erik wanted them quicker, resulting in Christine hand feeding him.

She slowed on the delivery of one, her face thoughtful, and asked, "Erik, can you smell?" The question came from out of the blue.

He eyed her keenly and grasped her hand after the most recent delivery, hoping to lessen any betrayal of mind with action. "By day's end you shall not be this close," he murmured, pulling her nose to nose-ish in dance hold, "until I have met with a tub of warm soapy water."

She scowled, tongue clicking because she knew he understood her meaning.

"All right. Yes, I can. I may not be packaged as well as some," he jested, touching her nose, "but all my senses are extremely acute—another gift or curse depending." He rotated her extended arm and his lips passed over her wrist. "Come," he suggested and rose quickly.

"I shall help you wrap everything for your return."

If she had not known before, she certainly could see this brusque turn. She had struck a nerve, uncomfortable as it was, but graciously and quietly followed his lead. Oddly, no more was said. They walked to the back of the flatbed wagon; the water set down and the blanket tossed up beside it, he turned away. The coarse grain of the sideboard swelled from the moist tension of his grip, felt thicker. Did she care? Erik knew she did, but he remained sensitive. The masque, and the face, promoted—it was a mathematical result, a summation of pain no matter how he looked at it—shame, he was ashamed. His grip clamped down. It was not like her to protract and stave off wonder; her query would come, but how would he answer? This was quite a disquieting exercise for the emotions. He should stand up to it, should he not? *Blast this face, getting in the way.*

"Was my question. . . was it upsetting to you?"

She was direct, as usual. He made several kicks at the dirt before he embraced her from behind, ending their time as it had begun, with his mouth at her ear. "No," he replied softly. "I am experiencing a bit of discomfiture, it will pass."

Christine reached up, tenderly feeling her way to his cheek. "I ask because I care, Erik. It is not idle curiosity."

His breath became rapid, his chest rising and falling, and his embrace tightened. "I know, Christine. . . I know." His lips visited just below her ear and she leaned into his shoulder. He gasped her name and groaned slightly.

"I should go," she said, squeezing his hands in her rotation.

"Yes," he agreed, shaking his head to the contrary. "One more?" He winked.

Christine's hands rested on his chest, their eyes trained on the other as Erik's fingers combed through her hair, smoothing the strands from her face before they nestled within its comfort.

With their goal realized, they parted. "Go," he rasped, "I shall see you tonight." And he sent her off with a brief seal to their last kiss.

Waiting until she was out of range, he rounded hastily, breathed deeply, and clasped his laced fingers to the back of his neck before an open, triumphal gesture in mid-air. "I cannot believe how I feel! I love her!"

Chapter Seven

Patience, few week's time. Safe return. A.G. Her mind reviewed the dictated line once again; it was simple. Done. *Yet another of his wishes fulfilled, one of many, for O.G.* Weariness etched her face as she sighed.

"Madame?"

"Yes, Monsieur?" she replied, somewhat distracted, her memories groping for a firm hold upon the bustle of present.

"If you would confirm for the evening paper."

"Oh, but of course." She looked over the message approvingly. It was not obvious, but satisfactory for the eyes that would eventually read it. Shaking herself back to the moment, she responded, "Yes, it is correct. Thank you."

The gentleman nodded, his bored eyes peering at her over the drooping glasses perched at the end of his nose. "For one week," he reminded.

Pivoting on the ball of her foot, Madame Adèle Giry made a concerted attempt to pass through the crowded lobby of the newspaper, but to no avail. Her stride was interrupted at every juncture and her mind let loose what a lady would never verbalize. She rolled those striking, ink dark eyes in silent exasperation, as a very flustered page, bumping and apologizing in a stream of guffaws, trampled the side of her foot. "Monday!" she grumbled.

"Beg p–pardon," he stammered at the unforgiving stare and rolled off to the next unsuspecting victim.

"Too many people, unorganized, unruly. . . at least I can control my piece of the chaos existing in the Opera House," she said in a dignified huff. Relieved upon extricating herself from the rush of morning deadlines, a frigid wind knocked her head-on when she opened the door, giving her cause to bemoan the next perturbation of the day: "Fall." *I should have been more attentive to the weather, but the note has. . . it has consumed my every thought. Seeing his deliberate script again has me bordering on obsession—not something I would readily admit out loud—with all those questions put to rest months ago.* "All right," she said, encouraging herself, "out I go."

Head bent in determination against the crisp biting air, she wrapped the thinning shawl around her shoulders and hurried home. Not toward the Opera House, as one would naturally assume, but numerous streets in the opposite direction. This set Mme Giry off on another mental tangent, a detour of equal proportions to the other, one related to the construction and refurbishing of the Paris Opera House.

She softened, *I must remember to give Monsieur Mercier credit, he has done well.* A smile crossed her lips and she felt her face warm at the thought of him.

Monsieur Edouard Mercier was, on the whole, easy to look at, a solidly framed gentleman in his early fifties, the dark hair and thin, well-groomed mustache belying a man of his age. He did not, however, rely on features alone to set him apart as dignified, but his straightforward personality instead; to this end he was able to command attention and acquire the respect mandated in his position, that of sole manager. Most people, upon meeting Mercier for the first time, were very impressed with his fairness, kind demeanor, and serious upstanding business scruples. The Paris Opera had been under

Mercier's management for six weeks and already the improvements were clear; from this confidence, an undeniable calm had at last permeated the theatrical milieu, despite the accident.

It was but a fortnight ago when an unforeseen flare-up, in a basement subsection of the more than ten miles of gas pipe, set part of the auditorium ablaze, before the firemen could bring it under control. Fortunately—or not, perspective dictating—the damage occurred when the gas-man, M. Mauclair, took himself off on a brief summer hiatus and left all responsibilities to one of his capable assistants. It was just an unpredictable fluke, but one that the new owner handled rather well. While the fire set the newspapers alight with fashionable gossip, with some even going so far as to pin blame on their old nemesis, the Opera Ghost, Mercier rose to the occasion and had plans drawn up, using the incident as a precursor to the electric light. This was one area in which Mercier prided himself, his forethought. The refurbishing had unearthed a series of well-twined plans, each progressive of the next, which were soon to commence beyond initial preparations.

Monsieur Mercier was completely resolute and a man of vision, patient, and had waited for years to strike financially. Until recently, the position of business manager had provided him an opportune vantage from which to observe the workings of the Opera. He could see the stress had taken its toll on both men, Messieurs Debienne and Poligny, upon their announcements to retire, and then came the mismanagement between MM. Moncharmin and Richard. Mercier surmised that his moment would occur soon enough, for he knew neither of the latter pair trusted the other. There were decisions given without thought, hastily attributed to a whim or what would resolve the matter posthaste, and they were frequently too absorbed with the *in-house farce* of the infamous Opera Ghost. To this, Mercier was heard to directly state, 'It has perplexed me as to how the two ever came into partnership together; their long-term considerations were devoid of planning and almost non-existent.'

Going back, Mme Giry remembered her initial impressions of Mercier, while being questioned on a prior matter of a certain "disappearing twenty thousand francs" and Box 5 in the auditorium. At the time, when she had been continually probed by an excited pair of managers, MM. Moncharmin and Richard, she had the awful experience of seeing what unsurety could do to the stability of men's minds; it was not a desirable sight. Both MM. Mercier and Remy were among those privy to being entrusted with the hush-hush of the behind-the-scenes goings-on and were always somewhere close by when the Opera Ghost became the main course of discussion or point of heated adjectives.

There was one side note, unknown to Mme Giry: Mercier was also of like mind with the newspapers when it came to choice of perpetrator. He was not, however, convinced in any way that everything was laid to rest. For this purpose, but not reason alone, Mercier kept in regular touch with Mme Giry. Being the shrewd man that he was, he saw she was wise beyond her years when dealing with those in his employ, which secured her future value; Mercier preferred to utilize any and all resources to avoid repeat mistakes, if certain issues were to rear their ugly head again. Mercier was one of many who considered Mme Giry a specific, self-disciplined woman, a woman whose input and advice one would do well to heed.

"The imbalance!" Mme Giry murmured forcefully, shivering at the mix of memory. The only solid fact acquired by the commissary of police was of the unaccountable death of Philippe Comte de Chagny, and even then there was no evidence, neither physically apparent nor otherwise known to prove it to be more than an accident—a situation unpublicized out of respect for the family. The other mysteries, regarding Raoul Vicomte de Chagny and Mlle Christine Daaé, were clueless wisps in the notebook of the detective. And the Opera Ghost? Her response was based on the truth, as she knew it. The Persian had informed her of his encounter with a gratefully happy, but heartbroken Erik; there were no doubts regarding his future. "I know nothing Monsieur," she had told the commissary. "I can only assume, mayhap piece conjecture, but I can tell you what I do know. He no longer lives." She had believed, and Mercier believed her.

"So, whether by his own hand or by some other means, our ghost has been excised," Mercier reiterated, his emerald eyes portraying just a hint of skepticism. Mme Giry saw the suspicion vanish just as quickly as it had come. Then, unfettered by the past, he was free to conduct business more worthy of his attentions, the refurbishing and perhaps, her.

Yes, her. Somehow the former thoughts, in conjunction with the latter, had kept her warm the whole distance home. The situation caused Mme Giry's walk to seem half the distance with all she had floating around in her intellect; the noise, men unfamiliar with the genre of theatre—eyeing the girls of her *corps de ballet*—equipment lying about everywhere; the past, the present, the whole tedium had become so distracting that a flat in the tenth arrondissement[4] became a welcome commute. For someone who prided herself on being in control in all facets of her life, she felt disjointed, but mostly irritated at herself for allowing the conundrum to dominate and beat her down.

Mme Giry entered the modest courtyard serving their flat (she and her daughter, Meg), and latched the gate behind her; she would enter through the back door and ascend quietly.

"Think, just go in and employ your methodical side to work," she ordered. Giving her faculties a thorough shake upon arrival helped to sift out the questions plaguing her, allowing placement of events. "First," she spoke verbally, using the sound of her own voice for reasoning, "there was the announcement of his death. I marked such a time with peaceful relief or, as I feel now, ignorance. Then came a hand delivered note last week from that unspeaking foreigner, who greeted me with silence and a congenial bow, younger than the other, perhaps a servant, and... oh, how could one ever forget the oil-black depths of Persian eyes? He knew, servants always know." She had unsealed the small waxen 'E' fixing the paper into thirds and read...

Dear Madame,
  From my hand to yours... yes, alive. I wish to speak with you.
    The favor of a reply, for a moment of your time.
      Erik

That was all it said. But why come back, why contact her? This note churned up memories, unwanted, just as the sediment of query around the events of the previous spring began settling.

"Such a belligerent man—*a phantom, rightly*—confusing others with arrogant justification. How grateful I am that I could answer honestly. At that point, he no longer lived, but dissolved into the darkness of his own soul." She gazed out the window at the leaves drifting through the streets, tiny boats on a windy sea with no control over their destination. Her breath fogged the glass. "Well..." her soft comment began; *you live on, my dear Opera Ghost. I should have known you would never just vanish. No, you are too clever...* "but I am sure you will tell me soon enough."

"Who will, Maman?"

"Oh, Meg, I did not hear you come in." She turned and went to welcome her daughter. "It is nothing, nothing to worry about."

"I see the concern in your eyes, Maman. We have shared much since the disappearances and upheaval in the Opera House," she stated, tossing her coat to the back of a chair. "I have put together my own opinions based on my experiences and the old gossip that filters through the back corridors in the theatre. Besides, I believe there to be some validity in the contrived stories. Those of us that have been retained since that time will probably keep and pass on the tradition of touching the horseshoe before we set foot on the first step of the stage." Meg paused and stared at her mother's tired complexion. "I am no longer the naïve girl I once was."

"You are right. I need to be truthful," she said, leading Meg to the sofa. "We may soon have an unexpected visitor."

"Maman, how can one be unexpected if you know of their coming?"

Mme Giry sighed. "Meg, please. I do not know his frame of mind, or the basis for which he includes us, but I would like to offer a listening ear. And he is unexpected because. . ."

"The only *he* that has ever been referred to with such anonymity is the Opera Ghost. But I thought—"

"So did I." Mme Giry glanced to the floor. "You do not seem afraid, after all you know."

Meg smirked. "If anything, my curiosity heightens. Somehow my insatiable desire for wanting to know leads me into trouble." Her eyes doubled in size at the thought. "Just think of the things we can ask. . . face-to-face!"

"Meg! I will not have you turn his time here into a self-serving interrogation for the rumor columns." Seeing the calm, rational side of her daughter resurface, she went on. "He is a private man, choosing only to share what and with whom his parameters say are trustworthy."

"Then I shall be a model listener. . . in confidence."

A nod and light caress to Meg's cheek brought an understanding smile to thicken the ties of their bond.

Chapter Eight

The hands on the clock stood nearly at attention as Erik finished the last of his preparations. It was to be a night of business endeavors, a succinct time schedule, documents and basic provisions, his company. Except for an occasional late ride, he had become used to Christine going along and this, this felt unnatural. Mounting the top stair on padded feet, Erik paused to listen, relishing the soft, rhythmic breathing from within the master bedchamber. *I hate to wake her when she just recently retired, but I know I would be hard-pressed to receive forgiveness, especially after our discussion.*

These days, the door remained open for him to spend more time in front of *that* fireplace, reading or stealing glances when he became restless. He walked around to the foot of the bed, a light exhale—which was nothing more than a flicker upon a candle flame—exiting his lips. He lingered, eyes wandering, caressing every inch of her celestial outline, he glanced at the obscured little angel. *Perhaps there shall be a face for you after all.*

Erik sat next to Christine's form on the bed, his weight causing her to rouse. "Shh. . ." he motioned. "I am ready. I should return before sunrise."

"Be safe. Paris is filled with all manner of characters."

"Fortunate for me that I may see to business unnoticed." He smiled, gliding a finger over the pout beginning to swell.

"I will miss having you close."

His grin became comical and his eyes danced. "As close as one room under another?"

"Hmm. . . and how much time do you spend inhabiting the guest room verses that chair over there?" She waved toward the cushioned evidence with a yawn, a book resting where he was last seated.

Christine smiled lazily at Erik's interception and gentle indulgence upon her wrist.

"Guilty—" The word was punctuated by the first stroke of midnight, impatience signaling an unbidden reminder of departure. "Sleep well, my sweet Christine." One final kiss, placed discreetly to her shoulder, and he was gone.

NOT LONG THEN, *a few weeks at most. It is well.* Erik sighed in relief, his eyes passing over the line once more. *I was somewhat apathetic as to receiving an answer, but this is a good juncture from which to have Christine emerge. Madame Giry has never disappointed, she is a very meticulous woman who gives attention to every detail. Perhaps this is what endears her to me, apart from the attached anonymity. . . so much like myself.* Erik flinched at the vaunted comment. "Cocky, most egregiously cocky," he said to Cesar, stuffing the paper under his arm. *Dreadful, this attitude that begins to wreak havoc on my personality. Riding through the perimeter of the city I could feel an instant change, and like a chameleon, the transformation nears complete in the vicinity of this hell. My thoughts spiral downward to the depths of an impoverished soul as a beacon summons me from within these cold, unfeeling walls. All the years of torment, self-hate and pity that filled my veins, giving me an artificial sense of existence, lies here.*

Erik laid a gloved hand against the brutal, unmoving stone of the

Opera House and spoke in earnest, an incantation uttered in guttural calm to ward off the force that claimed ownership. "No more will you bind me as prisoner within your bowels, doomed to an endless digestion in misery. Never again will I be bound into darkness, never." His breath hung in clouds, each inhalation piercing his heart with an icy evil, taunting, luring him back under the numb blanket of the cellars below. "No! I know the warmth of touch, experience and savor each caress of love. I will not be deceived, you were not the panacea touted to rid me of the spoils of mankind!" Erik's hand dropped, severing contact, immediately wiping the mist of doubt with an infusion of welcome reprieve. He leaned into Cesar and thoughts of Christine surged quickly through his limbs, to strengthen him, as he replayed her angelic face after his kiss spirited that soft, malleable skin before leaving, just hours ago. Closing his eyes, Erik tried to hold that memory, to keep it vivid. . . alive. *Several hours until any hint of daybreak appears,* then his thoughts leapt to another, *there should be ample time to visit her. . .* He fostered the thought because, as Erik reasoned, the end justified the means. He would allot time.

Erik had been engaged in her presence more frequently for the past month. For some ungodly reason, presently unknown to him, he felt connected to her while his plan took shape and so far, he had managed a veil of secrecy. No mention of specific activities provided the ultimate cover necessary for rides on Cesar, which eliminated the need to be conciliatory or play false. He had been exceptionally careful, only staying for limited durations, so as not to arouse suspicion. Months ago he found her, abused to the point of death, her spirit completely non-existent; it was empathy which made way for her to have a piece of his heart. He saw the way her beautiful eyes fixed on his, and though troubled at first, she came to trust and finally allowed him to heal her. The world had turned its back; recipients of this pain, they were both ungrateful partakers and allies for the other. Not long after their initial meeting, it became his turn. Christine betrayed and impaled Erik's heart with disbelief in that profession of love for Raoul de Chagny, the denial forcing him to her understanding side. By then, a fondness had developed, something he had yet to understand; it was their bond, it was... different. Erik's intent was to help, assist, and to console, but after having his hopes clatter to the ground, to be trodden once again under the foot of misfortune, he took refuge from the disappointment.

She has been so understanding, no judgment or condemnation, and she listens, responds to my every touch, to the qualities of my voice, not unlike Christine. I cannot turn my back on her now, abandon what we have meant to one another, but the visits must end. That sheen of ebony hair... Bowing his head in resignation he climbed Cesar, then, as if to convince himself by speaking aloud he said, "Tonight, tonight I will finally take you and be done with it. Yes, tonight... my sweet Desmoné."

CHRISTINE'S LIDS THINNED annoyingly, parting just as her arm lowered, and a beam of sunlight, sinister and sharp, accosted her. "Ugh... I should have stayed in bed, at least I would not have to deal with the intrusive shock up there before I am ready to wake!" she snipped mockingly. Rolling away from the bright, uninvited guest, she went to bury her face under an absentmindedly tossed pillow and was met with a more pleasurable display. "Oh, Erik. What a gorgeous vision," she gasped.

From a water glass on the chair side table, where she assumed the placement intentional, was quite a phenomenon indeed. The water bent the sun's rays in just the right way to project a varied spectrum of color to transverse the room. As Erik explained it, theories often lead one discovery to a surfeit of queries, and his most recent fascination with light fit the mold perfectly, boosted their childlike wonder together, and caused her jaw to drop.

She stood up, smiling at the thought and was quickly buffeted with disappointment when expectation failed to produce any sign of

Erik's arrival home. A pang of concern swept across her normally smooth face, leaving furrowed lines to mark the level of severity and his words 'I should return before sunrise' reverberating in her ears.

"It is just barely light. . . *sort of*. . . he will be here," she muttered to herself unconvincingly.

But time marched on relentlessly, waiting for no one, least of all Erik.

Poised with hands on hips, Christine took stock of her accomplishments, though she looked set upon the act of disciplining an errant child; the routine duties were done with ease, in a timely fashion, the house orderly save the usual scores—of course—and, her increase in stamina with which to endure these fair tasks, her source of pride. Remembering how the challenge of exhaustion taxed and vexed her, despite Erik's equal part, she was well-pleased with her body and the way it had continually adjusted. It was of little consequence that she had been active, busily involved in rehearsals or dance routines, for here, nothing compared to the physical demands of living far from the city, and with no maids, it was up to her. *I do have to give Erik recognition, he is mindful of even the smallest detail and has never expected that I go anything alone or that certain duties be labeled according to gender.*

When she and Erik spoke of his traveling to Paris, the mere thought felt foreign; a distant memory, one that had been carefully carved away from her life, left her childhood wanderings as close as the back door, to pick up where she had left off. She strayed to the window seat with these recollections and stared blankly out into the past, rubbing her arms against a sudden chill. *Is this how you felt when you went to Paris, Papa? As the days blended together, you were not the same man you once were when we traipsed the roads of our native soil from village to village. It was not until we went to the Bretagne[5] shores that you recovered some of your vitality and spirit. Was your heart constrained to seek simple freedoms and joy through sharing your music? Is that why I feel the way I do about this place, the feelings of comfort confirming the decision I made to stay? Unfortunately, the overall comfort I feel is not enough to keep my mind occupied from the nagging fact that it is now late morning and Erik has still not returned. I just hope he is safe.*

Her inner thoughts undulating between bother and concern had her leaving the visit of the preceding decade for a chance to secure some finishing touches on a project in the present. She went to retrieve a sheet of parchment from its hiding place, centered within the leaves of a book. For the past several weeks she had been working on a gift for Erik, having completed it the night before. Searching for the right words, to fit the pattern she had established, became an enjoyable passion, even a demand on her intellect, to fly in the face of insecurity. Had she succumbed to her first inclination, and not tried for fear her work of poetry would pale in comparison to the numerous talents belonging to Erik, the worse condemnation would have been enduring her conscience and the disappointment for not having made the attempt. This was her private battle, waged behind her own wall of intimidation, not one egged on by any competition. She knew the very thought was ridiculous because Erik always encouraged.

She looked over her scripted verse, gave it a few quick rolls to encase the scent and presence of rose petals with a kiss, then fastened all by ribbon. Next, was entering Erik's dressing room. Nothing was ever out of place; she was counting on this to prompt notice of her poem on the dressing table, amongst his personal toiletries. The room itself commanded an unearthly reverence, like accessing the chamber of a king who had servants to attend to his every need or desire. The act of entrance opened specific images from the stories she envisioned while listening at Erik's side: the palaces or tents of royalty, the veils, the robes, and the traditions of Persia. Turning, she reached her hand out to caress his clothing and released the aroma of spiced musk. He stood before her momentarily, in the midst of that scented divination, wrapping his magnificent arms around her shoulders. . . The vision diminished and receded into a corner as the clock chimed on the half hour; it was now eleven-thirty.

Frustration sparked the momentum carrying her downstairs only to climax on the way outside. "I need to move around, take a walk, do something," she said, jamming her hands into her pockets. Pacing the width of the porch did nothing but escalate her anxiety and she quickly ended, staring out to the northeast. "What if. . . he's hurt? I have no way of knowing where he is. I would have to walk to Amiens! How long should I wait? Ugh!" she spurted. The clock made its complete half-day's revolution known and was fast becoming the enemy. "I have to get away from that ticking reminder!" So, with her duties crossed off, she ventured out toward the ridge.

Christine had scarcely been gone twenty minutes when a flurry of dust billowed in the distance.

"I have been absent far longer than promised, blast! How am I to ever explain this away?" Erik pushed the limits at breakneck speed; thick froth dripped from Cesar's mouth, spattering across his opaque chest, lungs heaving as sweat seeped from the creases of skin and saturated coat under the saddle. Indeed, the consequences of obedience to his master's wish to hasten home. Pulling up short in front of the house, Erik dismounted and called Christine's name, the letters distilling in rapid vent. Not here!

Heeding the immediate needs of his horse, he apologized. "I beg your forgiveness to the point of exhaustion and promise a handsome reward for your service." Erik dumped the tack from off Cesar right where he stood and sent him to roam the paddock with a pat on the rump. "Plenty of water, sweet grass, shade, and rest for you my friend. . . the reward, later." He paused in dramatic thought and swore to himself, nervous about what Christine would say.

"How could I have calculated my time so poorly? Everything required so much more than I had planned." His mind raced on, urgent to come up with something to smooth this contravention while putting away the saddle and bridle, but to his chagrin, nothing came.

An unmistakable whinny out in the paddock brought Christine running back home to greet Erik at the foot of the steps. He turned at his name, his arms spread wide as she lunged into his embrace.

"I'm so glad you are home safe." Her exuberance broke upon him breathlessly.

Yes, safe in your arms, he thought. He kissed her cheek and held close, cradling the back of her head. He started to tear at being missed, and then it evaporated under the heated guilt elicited from her comment.

"I have been worried sick, missing you this morning, thinking what might have happened."

Kissing her forehead he distanced himself while replying, "I had to overcome a slight obstacle—"

"Obstacle? What obstacle? You're not hurt?"

Holding up one finger to stifle the barrage of questions he was unprepared to answer, and wishing he had the wherewithal to appreciate, he made a roundabout request. "I am not injured. . . yet. . . but if I might, I should like to explain later, after I clean up and eat. . . we shall go for a ride and I will satisfy your curiosity, yes?"

Christine's mouth parted, but she had no time to object or accept his suggestion before he dashed up the porch stairs and into the house. He could not have disappeared quicker had he stepped through a trapdoor.

A sigh of relief exited Erik's lips and one of exasperation in tandem from Christine. He had been kept out of harm's way, and yet she could not help but notice the avoidance when their eyes met. "Something is definitely askew," she spoke to no one specifically; conversing with herself suited the moment. "But I am unsure how to broach the subject. Being straightforward should meet with some measure of success, though. . ." The longer Christine mulled over the situation the more irritated she became. "He just left me standing here. . . that weasel!" she glowered. Not prone to cursing, Christine resisted the blatant urge, but let the door seek its resting place securely within the frame upon entering the house. "He arrives home, says he had to 'overcome an obstacle' and then evades questions. Men!" Then, her disgust mellowed. If she confronted Erik while possessed in such a display of ill temperament, it would do nothing to open him up and would have the converse reaction of shutting her out just as quickly. "I shall wait," she said calmly, slipping through to the kitchen. "I shall wait to see what the greased vermin comes up with in defense of himself. Keeping the knives out of reach would probably be in his best interest as well, until this matter is resolved."

Upstairs, Erik moved briskly around his dressing room to ready himself, and ducked with a shrill intake of air at the sound of the front door slamming. How often had the fine wood been on the receiving end of *his* anger? He shuddered to think, his skin prickling in one mass of goose flesh. He rounded at the sense of something amiss, locating the discomfort with a perusing glance; a delicate scroll purposely laid on his dressing table. He finished tending to his attire then seated himself to read in his usual chair by the fireplace.

The smooth texture of the parchment smelled of roses as he passed the cylinder to his upper lip. *Christine.* Upon release, the coil sprung open and showered his lap with petals, blessing his hands with softness. Fingering several, he read. . .

> *To my beloved Erik—*
>
> *Through the guise of darkness, as an angel you came*
>   *My soul aloft to heights unknowing, exquisite, sublime*
> *Teacher, Master, Lover. . . in dreams beheld, imagined*
>   *In slumber, my heart touched, resigned*
> *This angel bound, shunned, forever alone*
>   *Chained to night, a shadow lost and forlorn.*
> *A hope indifferent, illusive, reflective in thought,*
>   *Truth hidden, a masque, his face would adorn.*
>
> *Talented genius, mirrored beauty within,*

> Shared gifts of worth, yet no one to learn.
> A life blessed, though not for himself,
>   Beautiful spirit, humbly tangible man.
>
> Love graced a heart, entered, piercing replete,
>   Infused, enfolded, immersed in full sight.
> Gentle, kind, trusting... emotively deep,
>   Belongs now embraced, forever held tight.
>
> Cherished, remembered, love openly shown,
>   Redemption, forgiveness, gracious mercy impart.
> You are accepted, adored and set free,
>   My sweetest angel, my Erik, my heart.
>
>   All my love,
>   Your Christine

Dampened lashes gave liberty to a silent trickling down his cheek, which blended harmoniously with the elegantly chosen words—at least to him they were. His breath, tattered remnant that it was, became fluid once again at the firm handling of cabinetry. Thinking of the repercussions attached to the noise below rooted him to the chair, as it would be far more tolerant of his presence than she. He scanned Christine's poetry for a second time and smiled. "This is what had her so occupied of late." Closing his eyes he soaked in the last two lines. *Her poignancy and ability to comprehend my emotion is humbling. As a man corrupted for too many years, driven by hate and want of power, of control... I suddenly find the need diminished and unimportant. What I want in its place ... is her love, for it is of far greater worth. To live without... I could not!* "We shall soon see whether she truly accepts." He sighed at the rise of doubt come to gnaw at his defenses; concluding that, where she was involved, his reserves were sparse.

Leaving the poem available to be enjoyed again, he silently stepped downstairs, feeling the tension increase with his intrusion. He peered around the dining room entry like a wayward imp dreading a possible reprimand, assessed his options then turned with his back to the wall. The options were plain; take care of the famine complaint and/or look Christine in the eye. The "and" was out of the question, so by default, it was his stomach that won out. He waited for the timing to present itself aright and made his move.

Christine had just finished setting up a plate with an array of food and had her back turned to the imminent crime: smoked ham, camembert and brie cheeses, and a crusty bread, all pending consumption, when an act of stealth grabbed a variety of the offerings and disappeared. The only thing left in the demise was a swift kiss and thank you.

A towel smacked the counter. "Twice have I been left wide mouthed and without retort against your near wordless pranks. Master of evasion, eh? Momentary evasion, but you will have to explain eventually," she announced, indignation permeating the cool tone as her voice lowered. "Needless to say, the way in which you are manipulating this hidden agenda has begun to work against your cause."

He was doing a fine job of frustrating her. "Dodged the questions and *the eyes*," Erik remarked under his breath, "but I know I will not hold out much longer." He devoured his prize on the way out to the stable, then headed for Cesar, clean blanket draped across his shoulder.

Sensing an undesirable outcome, Cesar made a hasty retreat to the far side of the paddock, a fresh shearing of grass all but lost against the shake of his head. *Everyone is non-confrontational today.* "Come now, old friend, do not make this harder on me than it already is. I appeal to your good nature," he pleaded, laughing at the sway in Cesar's determination after Erik gave the horse a hearty scratch about the withers. "I am lucky you accept me again with such a simple gesture; I can guarantee it will not be so with Christine."

Erik led Cesar, without bridle, up to the house where Christine awaited their approach, arms crossed, anticipating the next feat of legerdemain he would deploy. What Erik was not prepared for was the expression accompanying her stance; it begged honesty from him.

"Are you prepared to ride with me?" His confidence all but melted in the shy enquiry.

"That all depends on you. So far, you have done well to walk the outward rim of your conspicuous ruin, though your greatest ally is ready to shove you into consumption because you have given nothing of worth to souse the raging doubt."

"I am aware," he replied to her fiery metaphor, mounting Cesar.

"Will there be resolution of the situation or more unanswered issues?"

"Resolution..." Erik nervously whispered, "one way or another." He was sure she heard the fear by her puzzled expression. Seeing her hesitate in thought, he pushed the advantage concern would allow, aware that she may be wondering if he had compromised their trust. "Sooner would be preferable to later. I would have you join me as you are, we shall not be negotiating a huge distance."

"All right," she relented, and grasping his forearm, he pulled her upright from a step atop his flexed boot. Once Christine was seated to the side, he gently nudged Cesar's flanks.

The unease between them was dreadful, it was as awkward as riding together the first time, but there were no gloves to break the ice. He felt her nab both his wrists then pull them around her. *No talking, please,* he wished. *I cannot bear more.* Touching his hand, she began to tenderly knead each joint and eventually found a soft spot to focus on between his thumb and index finger. It felt wonderful to have his anxiety erased.

Erik had, during those uncertain moments before the ministrations centered, focused almost exclusively on his frailty of spirit. Always first! She astounded him with her generosity. When a misunderstanding occurred, she sought to apologize, tolerated, never sharpened her tongue against his deficiencies; he recognized this. Learn from him? What could he possibly teach her that she did not strive to nurture in him. She must be in jest, of course, unless... he was schooling her by *his* actions, indeed! He scoffed quietly. *For one who did not want to converse, I have done a fine job of carrying on alone.* All he desired was to arrive at the designated area he had located when felling trees, it was a place without any prior connections; then, he would let the cards fall where they may.

Veering off the path to the east, Erik coaxed Cesar on until the dense undergrowth became a barrier of unease. The combination of riders and horse were not a successful mix, thereby casting a somewhat foreboding presence upon the discomfort. Erik remembered the backstage crowds after a performance, how the bodies would press and oft times limit breathing. As a bystander, he watched it—interesting that the memory was doing nothing to alleviate the existing condition. Halting abruptly in a wide spot for dismount, Erik's arms surrounded Christine once they were on solid ground.

"I shall begin here, by apologizing for my distance and rude behavior today, though I must confess my fondness for our current proximity." Christine stepped up in height and his eyes shut, feeling her fingers brush across his forehead in an attempt to tame the course, unruly hair. All burdensome concerns were thrust into the deepest recess he could find when she tipped his face down and kissed the void beckoning her lips. "Shall we?" he asked, head snapping back, his shoulders heavy with the intrusive worries once more. Christine released her grasp and they continued.

The earth around them had a pungent, moist odor, consistent with the natural decomposition of the previous years' leaves and debris. Erik followed Christine's glance above, noticing how unsuccessful it was for any light to penetrate the interwoven canopy overhead. The knot in his stomach rose to his throat, its ends not about to leave any portion excluded from the turmoil. Erik stopped and turned in front of her.

"It grows thick. Would you mind closing your eyes?" His finger lifted quickly to prevent any bursts of womanly curiosity. Seeing as vocalization was out of the question, a guarded smile, coupled with compliance sufficed. Erik's arms engulfed her petite frame to carry her onward, quickening the pace to their nearing destination. Considering the day's progress, he looked askance as to how foolish she would see herself, or him, for the next request.

"As I set you down, keep your eyes closed until I direct you otherwise, all right?"

"Odd that you seek my trust," she quipped.

There it was. "Humor me, please?"

"If it is what you wish."

So calm, and completely at his mercy in this strange circumstance was she. He darted away noiselessly, was detained, and then returned, seeing no more nervousness from her than a twitching leg; not a wave disturbed her countenance. Such trust. Her hands taken up, Erik gently kissed them, and while moving slightly to his left, instructed, "You may open your eyes."

Silence dominated until she found some semblance of voice. "Oh. . . Erik," she breathed. Obviously overwhelmed by the sight, she said no more, but stood stock still in admiration. Christine's reaction was as he had hoped, and a relieved smile radiated from ear to ear.

They were at the edge of a small, partially shaded clearing, the sunlight drifting in and out upon the lea of grass and purple heather before her. Erik wished she would say something, anything, as he moved her in a benevolent manner toward the visage, his eyes transfixed to her face. In the center of the clearing, scattered in droves, were thousands of variegated rose petals, producing the effect of netted butterflies threatening flight from their carpeted meadow, the slightest movement causing them to flutter and twirl at will. Standing in the midst of this floral cloud was a most exquisite, onyx colored horse. Its mane and tail were stunning; the crest was intricately braided and twined with rosebuds in their finest detail, as long, white ribbons trailed in the subtle breeze.

As they approached, one could see a solitary red rose at the base of the animal's mane. Erik reached to untie the delicate messenger from its place of rest and offered the gift to Christine. He watched in anticipation, her fingers carefully trained on the extraction of a gleaming diamond, held secure to its thornless stem by a black ribbon. There was a broad, expectant smile to meet hers as he softly suggested she read the inscription. Turning the ring over, she mouthed the words "Erik's Angel." When their eyes met again, he cradled both her hands within his and gracefully descended to one knee.

Silence suffocated the laws of nature for a moment and Erik took a deep breath. "I have struggled with our commitment, on how best to proceed, that is. . ." *Good articulation! Half dozen languages at my disposal and I trip over my native tongue, that should reassure her.* "I mean, the option of choice seemed to encompass every sentiment I possessed, therefore, I deemed it would provide me with knowledge of yours as well. Christine. . . I. . ." He swallowed and his mouth went dry. Dry? How could this be happening? Near to panic with numb disbelief, he almost stood to search for the lost phrase and wished to heaven he might rescind his position. He detected a kind squeeze and glanced up into her face; that smile amended everything.

"Yes?"

Now! Ask her! "Mademoiselle Christine Daaé, I would be honored, feel blessed, if you would accept my hand in marriage and consent to be my companion, now and forever. To be. . . my wife."

Poised to spill, tears brimmed their eyes as Christine guided Erik to come to full height with a touch under his chin. She rested one hand on his chest and dabbed at her eyes with the other. The diamond was placed gingerly into the palm of his right hand and his fingers coaxed to enclose the treasure. Sweat menaced his brow and his chest tightened. Then, in sweet repose Christine responded. "I belong here, in your heart, Erik. This is where I want to remain. . . always." She paused for emphasis. "Yes, I accept."

That one phrase caused a tremendous explosion of joy to ensue. Erik snared Christine at the waist and lifted, spinning her until dizziness loomed, their laughter wafting through the air on the tail of the ever-present wind.

"You asked me!" she stated in amazement when Erik set her down. "You did not assume, you asked!"

"I learned my lesson," he explained, eyeing her meekly. "I almost missed having dreams and hopes realized because I assumed you would be happier in the arms of someone else. You deserved to be courted and asked properly."

"I see. . . and this has been the focus of your endeavors?" came her wistful taunt.

"Yes, Mademoiselle. And though my tactics will require smoothing, a gentleman does no less. Now, per chance, would you happen to have another ring on your person?"

Reaching into the pocket of her skirt, she extracted a dainty, white handkerchief to gently pull from its interior a circlet of gold, and placed it into his palm with the other.

"I thought on what might have befallen this symbol of my love, but it quickly departed with the other current affairs occupying my time, until the morning I left the flowers in your wash basin. In doing so, I knocked the ewer askew. . ." he mused at those preserving contortions, "and while preventing its ruin, promptly brushed my sleeve across your things; they all went to the floor, spilling the ring into view. It startled me at first, that you—"

"Had not lost it. . . again?"

"No, had kept it," he replied, fingering the smooth surface around the end of his index. Erik lifted her left hand and kissed it plainly.

"This one reminds me of a time when I had to demand a choice, coerce and threaten an answer by force... and to beg. At the time, I was willing to do whatever was required to have you as my own, to sing my music, and feed my delusion." Looking down, he briefly admired the insignificant piece of metal, then placed it in his pocket to suppress the stinging image before continuing. "Quite a colored past associated with its simple beauty." His sigh of cool indifference ended the recall.

He raised the diamond up to catch the sparkling light reflected from inside the prism and went on. "This ring is clear and brilliant, not tainted; it is void of all darkness. It reflects the spectacular light you have brought into my life, a new start by your desire to share your love, and your life with me." Erik gently slid the ring onto her slender finger, sealing this token with a kiss. "Every day you add another facet to my comprehension of what love means. I have never experienced such consecutive felicity, and I desire to deepen the dimensions between us.

"I once observed the love of a woman for her husband, her devotion so complete that she would have followed him to the ends of the earth and beneath, to her death, if she could not be with him in life... there are tales depicting such. I decided then, that if I could not have *that* type of unconditional passion from a woman, I would not have any woman at all. I shut those emotions off and locked them within my demented soul, never permitting them to emerge. These months together," his voice rasped out unexpectedly. "Christine, you have assisted me in releasing all I have suppressed. Feeling floods through my veins to resurrect a forgotten part of life I once denied and forbid myself." His lips curved, as she tenderly brushed a kiss to the heel of his hand holding her face. "You give me affection, kisses and touch. You do not deny me your love based on the corrosive stains that I can never erase, and it has not deterred, nor limited the sweetness with which you patiently teach. The openness and nonjudgmental capacity you possess leave me in awe and asking why, though I am learning to accept.

"Then, there is your playful, feisty streak." He poked at her nose in humor. "It endears me to your mischievous side and the diverse qualities of your personality." Christine's eyes creased at the corners as she took hold of his hands, entwining their fingers.

"You accept me physically, now that I have regained some weight," he modestly commented, releasing her to pat his firm abdomen. "I am made to feel that my appearance is aesthetically pleasing to you, and I no longer find it alarming to be seen without my masque because I know I will not see shock. . . and you never hesitate. . ." Deep emotion welled unexpectedly and sprung forth. "Y–you never hesitate to touch. . . my face," he choked, "I am loved. . . for myself."

Needing oxygen in his suddenly deprived lungs, he inhaled tensely before pursuing his next line of thought. "Forgive my gush of words. I have so much to be grateful for because of your decision, and. . . I hope I will never cause you to regret your choice, but I do ask that you allow me mistakes and help me to learn. . . at least before I am condemned."

Christine listened, had given Erik an uninterrupted opportunity to share, their eyes glistening; his battered heart had begun to heal. Erik firmly embraced the woman who had just promised him her love and the distance between them fused. His hands found their way to her innocent face, lifting it and wiping her tears. Their lips, secured to the other, deepened the voice of their hearts, flaring as mouths moved in tune. Erik drew back and dropped to his knees amidst the petals, speech deserting him at length, feeling heaven secretly infuse his soul, and with a reverent bow, Christine kissed his forehead.

Chapter Nine

*E*rik sighed contentedly while surveying their situation; he had had enough sentimentality and desired amusement. Surmising he had a low center of gravity, beneficial to the sudden, infectious impulse that assaulted *his* mischievousness, he made a direct attack on Christine and wrestled her to the ground.

"Erik! You!" Ecstatic squeals pierced the scene as the two rolled to a stop, blossoms bathing their hair and clothes. "You, Monsieur, are incorrigible!" she exclaimed, positioning herself for a counter-assault.

"Yes, I am encourage-able, am I not?" he proudly announced. "Is the spontaneity adequate?" Meeting with success, Erik was unwilling to forego the advantage and lunged in her direction, but she was prepared, moving quickly enough to leave him with only an armful of flowers.

"Ha–ha! Missed me Monsieur—" Christine sat up, severely distressed, and looking to have been accosted, every ounce of joviality drained from their play.

"Christine?"

"I am at a loss," she said perturbed, "that I have not thought of this until now."

Erik sensed the short-lived elation crash, thinking perhaps, some circumstance they had yet to discuss had come knocking and was now at her mind's threshold. "The suspense, Christine, please!" His hand gestured openly, as he sat back on his heels.

"What name will you share with me once we become husband and wife?"

"For a moment," he coughed, "I thought something to be seriously amiss. My last name, legally attained for business purposes, is Gautier."

"Close to Charles Garnier, is it not?" she observed.

"Yes, and you have been reading."

"I have. History is an absorbing pastime."

He nodded and freely volunteered the required addendum. "I revered the man, Christine, and felt to align myself with him in some way because of his sincerity, his kindness toward me, and because he treated me as an equal. In the past, I managed to retain titles, labels, and other self-fulfilling terms, most of which provided me with a peculiar power over people, an aura. Look at the title of Opera Ghost. It is the very essence," Christine watched how his fingertips drew together, "that consumes and lifts the individual to unimaginable heights... so, for a time, I never used anything more than Erik, and have, since I was young, rejected any connection with my own relations... too much hatred."

"Monsieur Gautier, the complexity of your background is intriguing and disconcerting in equal portions," she said, tossing petals to distract him. She sprang and thumped him square in the chest with her shoulder, knocking him flat, and with it, any latent air.

"I guess," he wheezed, "I deserved, hmm."

Christine maintained a dominant position perched across his upper body, she had him pinned, arms extended helplessly above his head.

"I do believe... I am captive and shall submit to—" Her insistent lips obliged his ultimate surrender. "Do not torment me, my dear.

When one assumes control one must be ever vigilant and wary against any who seek to overthrow." With one twist, the tables were irrevocably altered. "See? Though I am conditioned to take the upper hand, I may be retrained."

Erik's actions had put him in a most tantalizing position, directly above Christine's chest in his embrace. His lake blue eyes glanced down as her fingers caught his chin, raising the errant movement to a more respectable level. "I am only admiring," he protested, centering one kiss and nestling his head to listen to her heart and its rhythmic comfort. Her fingers stroked his hair and his body tingled at the supplementary attentions radiating gently into his left ear.

"Christine, please do not become too. . ."

"Oh, not I!" she confessed. "I shall never accept the blame for my current lack of agility."

He cocked his head and came face to face with the horse. They laughed. "Hmm, she has a flawless temperament, one that will be good for Cesar," he stated, chiding the interruption before returning to his place of preference.

Christine started rubbing the wonderfully downy soft muzzle that was offered for a caress. "She is absolutely stunning. Thank you, Erik. Actually the whole day will be one to remember," she declared, tugging at his ear. "Though it seems I am at a loss again."

"How so? Certainly, it cannot be for *lack* of words."

"Erik. . ."

"Forgive me, but your talking has become mildly irksome. Perhaps I shall make reparations of my own so I can relax." He maneuvered himself back into their previous arrangement. "Now, you may talk as much as you wish. You were saying?"

Leaning back against his bent knee, Christine took his hand into her lap and found that soft spot once again. "Recently, it would seem that the names of those who have mysteriously joined my life are rather important. So, that said, does this fair equine have one or do we become creative?"

"Already done, her name is Desmoné or Dezi, if you prefer, it means desire. I had been craving compassion at the time I discovered her, but found that she required it more than I, though, we will need to come up with something Arabian when we register her." Erik glanced at Christine's posture and the way she settled in. "I feel I have commanded most of our dialogue today, are you sure you wish to listen?"

"I think you are making up for shirking earlier explanations. You know I enjoy listening to your voice, when have I not?" she asked, laying his wrist on her shoulder to roll up his sleeve.

He relented with a smile. "Yes, well. . . having had numerous occasions to ride close to our nation's thoroughbred capital in Chantilly, and figuring this trip to be as any other, I gave greater birth to the area one particular night last winter, to take in some of the spectacular animals housed by other breeding farms. The open, moonglazed fields provided ease of sight, sufficient to see all that I desired, which started me thinking. My imagination flooded with ideas of what it would be like to own such marvels, to dream a bit. Then I turned north, directing my travels toward the estate, but was prevailed upon by what I at first thought to be Cesar's uneven breathing. I stopped and listened further to discover it was the sound of wasted desperation. In locating the origin, I dismounted and proceeded slowly and unthreatening toward a dark, dull mass, huddled with its muzzle to the ground. She was far outside any boundaries or claimed acreage, hidden away within a glen of trees. Her legs were folded beneath, she moved little as I held out my hand, but there was no gesture to meet or familiarize. Usually an apathetic attitude is a sign of a dispirited, broken soul," Erik explained. "I assumed it to be due to one of two conditions, either injury or abuse. I cautiously traced her form, thinking there to be something wholly unsound and could find nothing on my initial examination save the glaring crime I suspected.

The skin hung hideously between concave ribs, indicating a substantial duration without nourishment, in addition to several open wounds interspersed along her body."

Erik looked up as Desmoné exhaled and nuzzled one side of his face then she went back to grazing. His arm lay resting across Christine's lap while she stroked a patch of lightened hair, her eyes rimmed pink. *Dear woman, touched by the pain of a creature.* He sought after her soft eyes, they were but a fraction of that pause behind in seeking his, and he went on.

"As difficult as it was to get her feet up under her again, she did, astonishing even me after seeing her in daylight the next morning, that she was able to support her own weight. The wounds looked to be varying combinations of whip bites and the teeth marks of other horses. I assessed her needs and looked for a glaring flaw, but the only defect I found was poor alignment of her left foreleg; someone's opinion of imperfection and inexcusable justification for abuse. I was saddened by the cruelty that rendered her unwilling to graze or fend for herself.

"So, I treated her wounds, fed her, and gradually relocated her to the estate, which is why there are two, fully equipped stalls in the stable. When I attempted to groom her the first few times, her muscles knotted, eyes widened, and nostrils flared in fear of being handled, but slow as it came, at least I knew her spirit would emerge with a desire to fight. Singing seemed to soothe this condition, and once she regained strength and her physical health improved, I secured a place for her to be boarded. By then, we had an interesting bond, I believe we connected and understood one another's pain. I took refuge in her training and rehabilitation when frustration overwhelmed my better judgment, and in turn, she listened and responded to my touch. When my presence was required in other matters of life, such as it was, a young man by the name of Taylor Rossi looked after her at his place of employment and researched her background. She has excellent Arabian bloodlines and should make a fine broodmare."

"Were you able to discern the status of an owner?" Christine asked, concerned.

Erik could not help but react to the inference. "I made arrangements based on mutual understanding," he growled indifferently in defense of himself. "I did not steal her, whatever you may think. I set up reasonable funding for her care, including an allowance for Rossi to search out her past; he was to become my mediator as well, should the need arise. There was never any admittance of loss or claim to the abuse, despite our efforts, but we had our suspicions and checked records, finally locating her lines.

His voice calmed. "The owner, as Rossi related the incident, was abominably irrational, refused to compensate me for the time, care and expense, none of which I desired but for the determination of the man's intent, which later became evident. My offer of payment was declined, and her papers relinquished forthwith. He had already cut his losses and wished to have any connection to said maltreatment, dissolved. This worked to our advantage until the morrow, when the previous owner must have had a change of heart—and an empty pocket—thinking as I had already planned. A steward from his estate confronted Taylor to establish conversion with intent to defraud." Erik scratched his chin absently. "I am not quite sure how they would have succeeded. Taylor had witnesses to the transaction. . ."

"You said he was irrational."

"Yes, though it seems whenever *I* try to use correct legal channels there is always an impediment of some nature, no matter how trivial. And," Erik intoned, "I rectified the situation with Cesar at the same time."

"I was not accusing you."

"I realize that. My only wish is to make amends," he clarified. "I desire my wife to speak without reservation of character when she utters my name, at least where possible."

Christine moved to stand and Erik joined her as they shook the remnants from their jaunt among the flowers. Turning, she spoke to Desmoné, "Well, sweet Desire, I appreciate your compassion and consistent listening ear while I was thwarting this gentleman's love." She encircled Erik's waist. "However, I would now prefer you leave his heart to me."

"It is yours."

Hugging her tight to his chest, he could not imagine being any happier or expressing verbally the depth of passion he held for this woman.

Chapter Ten

The sun had nearly gone down as Erik plucked Christine from off Cesar, her slow descent in his arms alighting her upon the front steps. She leaned forward, directing a sensual smile his way, the meaning all too transparent.

"Spending the day with you, Monsieur Gautier, has proved most pleasant."

"*Whom* do you address?" he asked wistfully, having immediately noticed the level at which Christine stood and, coming closer, their breath, as it swept about with passion, had the distinction of name all but forgotten.

"You. I should. . . dinner."

Her answer shook the inviting trance in time for him to collect her hand from attaching eyes and mind to the backward reference over her shoulder. "Wait, I should like it if you were to defer for a moment." Erik's sentimentality had returned and he wished for her to remain eye to eye with him. "I must seek your forgiveness for the irritation caused earlier. It is difficult for me to conceal secrets when I have to be near the person for whom I am planning. Accounting for my actions is. . . new. I only wished for this day to be unlike any other."

"You were successful, in more ways than one. The petals. . . where—"

One kiss secured silence. "If innocent wonder is inspired by beauty, why not let it be and accept that it is, to preserve the moment?" Erik raised Christine's left hand to admire his ring upon her finger, kissed it and laid the palm to his face. "Thank you for accepting my proposal, and for the beautiful poetry. I love you and believe fully the depth of your words."

Her hand lowered, thumb lightly brushing along his jaw, eyes glittering. "Would you, Monsieur, think affection appropriate at this time?"

Erik's breathing went short and airy. "Yes, he would welcome a most ardent display." Waves of delight broke over him as he, without thought, encouraged. *Lovely Christine!* He inclined his head, tenderly advanced then drew away, teasing. Again, he neared, and she heard a seductive, beckoning echo in her ear, "Kiss me. . . deeply."

A brief exchange shared, Christine patted his chest as they moved away in silence, both reluctant to meet the other's gaze, their furtive behavior indicative of the now evolving connection.

Christine went straight to the kitchen while Erik turned and headed toward the stable. His step lighter, he took to work in haste, soothing the horses with his luring hum and soft comments. "What do you think, eh?" he queried his two steeds. "She said, yes!" Then, with a bit of reflection in his voice, "This should greatly change up the dynamics. . ."

Back at the house, practice and interest had long stirred confidence in the culinary arts. Each aspect came with great satisfaction, but especially that of presentation, the blending of colors, textures, and complementary characteristics for balance. Accomplishing the meal, she set it aside for later—as the task of stable chores were now double—she smoothed a few of the pleats on her dress and several rose petals tumbled into view. There was a quick smile, a sigh, and then all were gathered into her pocket before she, and a handful of raspberries, went to escort Erik on his return.

Her approach stretched out in the greys of evening to the satisfying glow emanating from the stable. Entering quietly, she could see Erik had just finished Cesar.

"Erik." His name, though barely audible on her lips, was heard; he glanced up, brow aslant. "May I be of assistance, or would you prefer I stay out of the way?"

He motioned for her to join him as he moved across the aisle to begin on Dezi, Christine's step proceeding to intersect directly with the path of his determined stride. "If you prevent or prolong this, your worth shall be deemed questionable."

Shocked at his coolness, as was he, but undeterred, she placed a berry into her mouth. He watched steadfast when it disappeared, riveted, as she closed in on him. Their lips parted, allowing passage of the ripe, moist fruit to the back of his tongue, bursting its flavor in the process. His hands came dangerously close to entrenching themselves in her hair, but managed instead to give an affectionate touch to her chin before moving past her into the stall. He wanted space, jealous of her and her ease at which she had regained control.

She has yet to comprehend how her mere presence rouses me to distraction now, my feelings are a torturous avowal of this and serve as a constant reminder. How can I be rendered into such a weakened state when I have maintained the utmost control? It must be her acceptance of me that has caused. . . and because I am unfamiliar with these marvelous struggles I have lost all gentleness in my embarrassment. Erik colored at this fault while working opposite to Christine, which by no means went unnoticed by her, causing her countenance to be equally affected by her own unrestrained looks in his direction. Was she too? There, the flash of eyes. He glanced at her to reaffirm. No, not even a hint of glazed rose adorned that flesh. *I must be a grave disappointment to her. . . far too bold. . . the silence.*

The grooming process and unbraiding of the ribbon and roses from Dezi's mane became all-consuming as they continued, wordless. Soon, the brush dropped into the straw and a hand appeared stealthily to the left of Christine, on the horse's shoulder, the other, reaching slowly for the halter. Each motion was extremely subtle and hardly detectable, except for the sudden nearness behind her. Her eyes shot to the void where Erik had been, then spying his hands to either side of her, she became keenly alert. Rotating bit by bit she faced him, her hands grasping at the back of her dress, an indication of shy nerves. His azure orbs burned through her as he mouthed the word *silence*, his finger placed to his lips for emphasis. His warm breath caressed her ear, the sensuality forcing her eyes closed, his fingers trailing languidly from her neck to descend the lightly hued skin of her arms until their hands laced. Erik gazed at her in earnest, memorizing, heartbeat increasing as he whispered his lips luxuriously along her neckline. *She smells so sweet. Never have I imagined a woman to allow me these blessed freedoms.*

Christine trembled at his touch, so tender, sensuous. Such enticement! *What is this spell, this merciless spell, which lures me eagerly beneath her power? Is she aware, does she know? Our resolve must bear all, but the will, it signals a mandate for fortification.* Relinquishing his grip, Erik placed her hand intentionally to his right cheek and rested his head within the safe inviting curve of her neck. His upper body heaved once as he kissed Christine's warm skin, her breath was ecstasy in motion floating across his ear. Wrapping her in his muscular vice, Erik pulled close, never wishing to be parted and knowing beyond doubt that distance would be a most prudent action. He could not believe the difficulty with which he was faced, how his limits ebbed and flowed against the dam of restraint.

"Erik. . ." she said, tenderly pushing away.

His firm but gentle grasp was upon her shoulders, he had placed her at arm's length. The fierce longing consumed every thought. How was such an ongoing battle to be handled? He stared at her, saying nothing and everything until notwithstanding their unease, he kindly intimated, "I have gradually allowed myself, over the course of our relationship, to experience the varied ranges of affection you so generously bestow. I thrive on your encouragement and at present, desire more, whereas I had been content only days ago, *hours ago.* What I now experience washes over and through me, leaving nothing unaffected. The intensity, I am ashamed to say, may tempt me past what I am able to cope with." All was quiet, leaving a vast precipice of tension spilling awkwardly between them. Her hands pressed against his chest, fingers clumsily tinkering with the unfastened buttons on his shirt. He felt her touch, that skin. "We should, perhaps, take leave of one another for a few days," he suggested.

An incredulous look came over her that seemed possessed of mild apprehension. "You mean, that you wish for us to separate until *you* are capable of dealing with this situation."

Oblivious to the emphasis applied toward him, he nodded. "I think it best."

Her hands dropped. "*You* think it best?" she clarified indignantly. "And what if your companion disagrees? What if she feels support and conversation to be of wider benefit?"

Erik cocked his head at the rise of inflection. He was, he felt, justified in making such a request and it to be perfectly reasonable, not at all aligned within this discourse veering for disaster. "I am sure that if my companion understood," his voice patronizing, "that *she* would appreciate—"

"Appreciate what, that your caprice on separation should be looked upon as gallantry to preserve us both?" Her voice cracked as she shed his grip. "Giving space and establishing boundaries have worked thus far... we have always discussed our concerns, together!"

The resentment heightened his complexion, he being lightly appalled that she would overlook the difficulty, which had him just moments prior, totally confounded. He sincerely observed his position to be one of duress and his opinion, to be of moral worth.

"Then it is obvious that you are ignorant of your effect on me; your lack of consideration toward my regard for you, for us, is not appreciated." Erik shifted in irritation, arms laid to Dezi's back, fingers twined white at the knuckles. "The immaturity," he continued, "which you so willfully demonstrate in recogniz—"

"'Immaturity?' How thorough you are!" she crisply mocked. "You barricade with insults then protect yourself from such a time of joy with isolation. And. . . what makes you think you have an exclusive hold on maturity in this instance, Monsieur, your age?"

"No! I would. . ."

"Or, as you say, it is my naïveté or youth which predisposes me to ignorance of feeling, specifically *yours?*" Christine rounded from her sideways stance, turning a rheumy glare to his stiff, unbending frame. "How dare you!" she cried. "How dare you assume you are affected singly. . . how arrogant to think that you are the only one to experience impassioned moments. And how selfish, after all we have discovered together, that you would want to be alone." Christine's hands clenched, the anger finally giving way to despair and additional tears, as she backed toward the already opened stall door. Erik's pronounced astonishment, purposely subdued for fear his exasperation would prevail over his better judgment, whilst she was but a few feet away, procured his disinclination to rebut. The understanding complete, she gathered her skirts with one hand and made a quick exit from the stable, leaving him with his own thoughts and to his desire of self.

Erik's countenance paled, his shoulders beaten, his mind rehearsing the surprise he was sure had registered across his features at the accusations garnishing each of his brash claims. "Brilliant," he murmured sarcastically. "How else could I possibly inflict more disgust than to engage her scorn?" Frustrated, he channeled his fist into the wood of Dezi's stall, lightly cracking the planks, incurring a satisfactory amount of splinters and torn skin from the roughened finish, and quickly turning a wary Dezi broadside, should she be next in line for his wrath. She snorted, eyes wild.

Christine heard the unmistakable termination of some inanimate object under Erik's hand. "Yes, gloriously mature," her whisper intoned disdainfully, while the sound imposed once again. "Twice! Oh, now I am quite satisfied. With such gracious proof bestowed, how could I be otherwise?"

After a time, Erik's footfalls made known his presence on the path. Christine's darkened silhouette did likewise, huddled against the base of a largely rooted tree, her form discernable after a mere glance toward her placement near the stream. Such was the detour realized with lantern in tow as several advancing paces closed the distance in caution; Erik was there.

"May I. . . join you?"

"Do as you please, it is your land,"—*Ours*, his mind corrected—"but be forewarned, if you sit in my company, you may no longer declare yourself in a state of solitude."

"I'll take my chances," Erik whispered, grateful that she would at least speak to him, though it came impertinently accented. He quickly chose to sit on the other side of the gnarled anchor before she had the opportunity to reconsider. The ground was unbearably hard and he wondered how Christine could possibly have endured. He hedged a peek. *Ah*, she sat upon her heels, arms clamped about her knees; hence, his answer. Erik's disturbance of thought would not permit him leisure and he fidgeted until he could not tolerate the engulfing quiet—a shuddering oddity.

Then, standing abruptly, he stepped in front of her, offering his hand. "Please?"

He was glad that she did not have the meanness of heart to further her enjoyment by way of his suffering, though, she may have been disposed to such when first seated. She accepted and he, seeing little inclination of pursuit, held her hand within his own and addressed her kindly. "After a lifetime devoid of human touch, pleasure, and love, I cannot in good conscience return to that sort of deprivation. I do not wish to be. . . alone." Emotion burned, constricting his throat with remorse as he reviewed the spectrum in which their civility had roamed since his departure the previous night. "I have reflected on our separation earlier this day, the deficiency in communication; the behavior it brings about is contemptuous. I should like kindness instead, to mirror itself in your face and prefer success from our togetherness."

Tipping her chin upward to the exceedingly diffident bow of her head, Erik met her eyes and her confession. "Forgive me," she offered. "I fear the pent up emotions of midday led to my vile spray of temper. It was—"

There was a direct end to her acceptance of any guilt with a long kiss. "Stop," he ordered, when his lips became free. "Please, stop. You have burdened yourself unfairly since our initial arrival here. You allot me far too much in the realm of justification. I have no right. Your reproof of me stands, well deserved. My condescension regarding our relationship was abhorrent, and the way I addressed you in my state of discomfort, gave way to nothing but honest derision. It is I who must seek for reparation." Taking her by the waist he pulled close, pressing his forehead to hers. "I hope you will indulge me because I must digress in order to obtain some level of forgiveness." He waited briefly and felt the slight pressure of consent.

"I could not have predicted such a turn of character in myself, willing to admit fault, calming rationale in lieu of rage, and none would exist if it had not been for your gentleness and patience. While I thought on this, I also realized that singleness of mind has proven itself to have nearly replaced the diverting thoughts of split sanity; it plagues me little. You must concede on these matters, at least."

"I do."

"Good. Your sweet nature has made a lasting impression on me as a whole, I wish it never to be erased, but to work internally as an improvement." She chuckled at the contradiction his choice of words offered, in accordance with her current actions. "Though *my* personality may be of consequence in reverse," he added. "Next, you said that you were clearly aware of my frame of mind."

"Yes, keenly aware," she emphasized.

"As I perceived you indifferent, your desires where I was concerned were... ?"

"Never to leave your embrace, vulnerable, and wishing to experience everything under your touch."

Her frankness surprised him immensely. "You mean. . ." he stammered, feeling a flush of self-consciousness.

"Of course," she exclaimed softly. "How else does one feel toward the person to whom they will share their life? The sensations are wondrous, naturally flowing passions meant to bind us together. . . and mine are most generously entrusted to the gentleman standing before me; our commitment has not wavered, but expanded."

"Indeed, I shall endeavor to be most attentive to, and protective of, this responsibility."

"As will I."

"Now, Mademoiselle, I have been too long in misery and would like absolution, if you deem my suffering adequate."

No objection was made as the two embraced heartily on the outskirts of light, bidding their trespasses adieu among the comforting, tranquil strokes to the other's back. Neither had any immediate plans to dismiss their subject of interest and so they stayed, unfailing. It is to be known as well, that their high opinion, one for another, reigned absolute in the caring hands of the other, and an agreement upon a short engagement, decided wise. Consoled in these resolutions, Erik ventured to expound on an issue that had yet to be faced, that of age. Until Christine revealed it during her moment of heat, he had not put thought to the matter, but perhaps she had.

"Christine. . . I cannot help but think. . . there to be. . ." he began, the inelegance of tongue and lip powerless to produce fluidity without a repeated accounting of strokes along her arms, distracting his phrases. "The difference in age, are you bothered?"

She looked up from where her cheek had rested against his chest. "No, not in the least." Her answer was simple. "Why do you ask?"

"Our quarrel. I was given the impression, if you found ease in bringing my age to light while upset, of the possibility existing."

"No, that was only a statement of fact. Your youthful looks—"

Surprised, he laughed outright and quickly apologized, but the temptation to comment prevented her from furthering her cause. "Only here do I find hope for the expression of love being blind."

"Will you stop?"

"Yes, yes," he assured with a sarcastic tone.

Christine ignored him. "Are you able to see through my eyes?"

"No." Erik regretted his insensitivity and wished to clamp shut the uncouth propensity of his mouth to reduce probability of recurrence.

"Do you perceive or believe as I do?"

"I am learning."

"Then, there is no excuse for the self-deprecation. Now, back on point. I consider your agility of form, sharp mind, and overall appearance as evidence. No one could repute your age as being but a handful of years older than myself. Though, you would not have mentioned the situation unless it afflicts you."

"Some."

"Well, then I shall strive to eliminate those doubts which captivate and sabotage your confidence in my love for you. I am quite sure that I could not feel what I do for any other man; no one else could make me happier." She smiled. "No one would dare try, for the fearsome attachment and violence of heart that joins our souls.

Nothing, not even the span of time would ever be so bold as to keep us apart."

Not being able to control himself longer, Erik bent to gather Christine and walked with her cradled in his arms out into the stream. She laughed at his solution to a possible repeat of flaring ardor. "I shall remain until I have respectfully sated the desires which flood my body or until I can no longer withstand the numbing chill, hoping that the former proves attainable." Feeling balance resume, he engaged Christine at once in sweetly deepened adoration amidst the liquid confines. But, unbeknownst to Erik, he had, upon picking her up, entangled his right hand in her hair, and while not normally a focus of being caught up, would soon prove problematic, an obvious flinch removing him rather hastily back to dry ground for relief.

"Forgive my urgency. . . when I set you down," he grimaced and gave a short inhale, "please, do not move."

Christine followed his instructions, smiling patiently while he carefully unthreaded several strands of hair from around the ragged skin. When he had been successful, he glanced at Christine, seeing the hint of a grin playing in her eyes.

"If I did not know you better and had I more light, I could swear that you were about to tease me for my actions, and if this *is* indeed the case, I would advise against wounding me further with your womanly pride."

"Perhaps you do not know me as well as you might like to think." A sigh of dismay audibly exited. "So to this, a longer courtship would be in order, Monsieur Gautier. Sad indeed, for I was in fact, prepared to offer my heart-felt sympathy. . ." She left the comment unfinished as he chimed in with gratitude for her concern, and then she concluded, "yes, sympathy. . ." she sighed again, "for the unfortunate object on the receiving end."

Erik's mouth drooped a bit and she teased him on that as well, saying that it was most unbecoming, to consciously leave an exit for something to spill forth, seeing as the event had a habit of resurfacing when least expected. All said and done, Christine took hold of his hand, gingerly attending to *its* status, the pride she had so recently poked at, and the lantern, then led him inside to have a closer look at his injury.

Extraction of the embedded wood required the better part of two hours. Erik sat immobile at the preparation table in the kitchen, watching her take great care, wincing upon occasion when she had to probe deeply, but never recoiling. He ate, they talked, and as the balance of the time moved in silence, Erik observed that, despite whatever their relationship was to weather, he could be persuaded to enjoy all encounters, considering himself blessed beyond comprehension with such a privilege. This was the station from whence he began meditation on all future possibilities between them.

She must have seen the corner of his mouth bend upward, his eyes, though focused rigorously on her hands, seemingly enchanted by other entertainments, leaving his cheek to fold gently about his implanted fist.

"Care to include me in your thoughts?" she suggested, casting him a furtive glance.

"That, my dear, you may always be quite assured of," he murmured, his grin increasing in breadth. "The *content* surrounding your inclusion, however, shall be withheld. . . as I do not wish for reproachable damage." Repositioning his elbow against the table's solidity, he watched for a reaction to his knee coming alongside hers.

"I should think that with all the trouble you have incurred today, you would desire to keep your distance," she said, circumspection giving pause to her tone. "But you are a man, a gentleman, yes, though a momentary scamp nonetheless." Erik's leg collapsed beneath the chair in guilt. "I shall now be obliged to forget your lapse since you have regained your senses willingly."

"Your scamp is indebted, Mademoiselle." He smiled at the wink she imparted, and toward the bandaged wound when it received a timid address to the exposed fingers. Grabbing his chin, Christine led his mouth to hers for a light caress as well.

"For purposes of recovery," she explained.

"You may apply to either effected area on a daily basis, as often as you wish," Erik replied honestly.

"All right, off with you." Her waving hands fluttering in agitation, like those shooing an unwanted fly. "You. . . are in my way, now go." Erik left at her request, but noticed the sudden glow up her cheekbones and sighed happily to himself at the soft, flustered comment and the way she cradled the heat of her face in her hands. "I do not wish to be responsible for any other altercations tonight."

Chapter Eleven

A few evenings later, satisfied with the completion of certain events being recorded well enough in her journal, and the addition of petals pressed, Christine made her way from the bedchamber to look for Erik. The seasons were at the height of their ever-present rotation, each having brought characteristics that combine color in its splendorous entirety. Fall was no different, taking hold with vengeful jealousy; daytime temperatures still warmed, as the brilliant hints of orange, ocher, and red tinged leaves splashed over nature's canvas in response to the unpredictable, fluctuating nights. This was just such a night, more tepid than the last and not at all guaranteed to be likewise tomorrow.

Erik's habit, of disappearing and reappearing when least expected, had become less of an annoyance, but continued to elicit occasional frustration. *Where is he? I would like to change the dressing on his hand before the hour becomes late. What a hindrance to have to search, and I fear my attempts are futile unless he wishes to be discovered. . . part of his unpredictable charm.* She whimsically wrapped a spiraled curl around her finger as she continued her exploration about the premises until a soft, mystical tone slowed her pace to a stop; she listened, placing the distance of the sound at its closest, toward the front of the house. Opening the door exposed her to a welcome pleasure, one that had been overlooked for a time but not forgotten, the celestial melody of violin strings, producing in ecstasy what could only be achieved beneath the caress of Erik's hands.

Christine inhaled, desiring to breathe his very essence through music, noting how effortlessly it gratified. Quizzical brow that it was, a degree of perplexed curiosity rendered height impossible, spying the muted glow of a candle under one of the larger ginkgo trees. "What a majestic sight," *though perhaps my remark should be, otherworldly.* Indeed, the fan shaped leaves followed in a subdued state of delight, as though the vibrato provided an undulating breeze to which they moved. Standing at the bottom of the porch, she beheld the star lit sky above then tread languidly en route to the flame, hands resting behind her back. *Erik has said the ginkgos, of which there are several right here, possess an interesting variance to the other trees in fall. Some specific change occurs to signal a moment when all their golden wards are to take a final bow. It happens rather quickly, some actually shudder and drop their leaves in an hour or two, but will never release singly over the course of weeks. I shall be glad for the opportunity, if I am fortunate enough to be in attendance.*

Christine could still hear the faintness of a note drawing into silence, the sound, likened to one hand passing just out of reach of another save a momentary brush of skin upon the ending cadence.

"Erik?"

"Look up," replied a voice in her ear.

Oh, and ventriloquy too, frustrated her, but not always. "Ah, and how shall I ascend to your realm?" she laughed. "I have no means by which to aspire to such a task, Monsieur, and my attire, as you see, can hardly be effectual to any specific goal of—"

Stifling her, his arm was immediately offered for her acceptance. "I expect that you would trust me." His response captivated her, as did the grasp upon her forearm; he accomplished such, to lock them together and pulled her up next to himself. "Do not look down, focus on what is before you," Erik advised.

Proceeding to assist her along to each subsequent branch, one hand would encase hers, securing a hold in place, while the other encircled her waist to lift until they reached the upper most spires of his leafy retreat. Erik made sure Christine was well seated in the crook of a wide bough, prior to a repeat indulgence in his musical reverie.

Her eyes closed to the comforting elegance swirling around her; the technique so powerfully exquisite. Gratitude for the deep of night, and the inability to judge elevation, soothed what bit of tension existed, permitting a reasonable level of relaxation. *Climbing down. . . that may be something else,* she mused.

As the partita concluded, Christine paid Erik a compliment. "Bach himself could never have played so beautifully."

"You honor me." He gave a slight bow in her direction from a few branches over.

"Such a creative place to be lost in music. . . why?"

"I enjoy the sense of lofty distance I can procure between myself and others."

An "oh" was supplied, or rather decidedly set as bait, to the seemingly including remark. It was hard enough for her to see his darkened features, let alone grasp intent by inflection with so little an exchange.

"Present company affianced. . . excluded," he rambled on, "from the generalities, of course."

"Indeed," began the string of words her mind was accumulating, followed by more quiet. He seemed relieved! Was this guilt? Pinched scruples? Fleeting bits of conscience? *Interesting, I should think his Persian friend to be out of employment one day soon.* "Your point produces a dramatic effect."

"Yes, infinite possibilities." He looked up. "Detaching from the unpleasantries of humanity helped me to bear up, to center and hone. . . when at the Opera House I sought out the highest pinnacle atop the statue of Apollo, and this tree," he patted the nearest limb, "is the closest to attaining what I will no longer experience there. Mind you, as I do not wish my mention of this to be misconstrued, I miss only the familiarity of that endless domain, and as I see it, that too will be short-lived."

Ah, the commanding air. . . "What of your ability, what of the inducement to play?" she delved.

Erik dropped the instrument from his shoulder, grew somewhat pensive then repositioned the violin. He plucked and adjusted to align its sound, finishing with a test to each of the four strings, their performance gauged by quality under the bow. Sighing at length, after much fidgeting, he spoke. "In order to capture the emotion necessary to perform in any artistic genre, one must have experienced it from within. If it is not here," his hand went to his heart, "then it cannot be portrayed sincerely, it is empty. An example of this would be your voice. The talent has always been, but the depth of spirit had yet to resurface. . ."

Christine appreciated him avoiding the mention of her father's death; still, it was an uncomfortable quiet between them, then he went on.

"Intense passions of the darkest kind have given fuel to the creativity in my life, but that has changed. . . so much has changed." He let go a soft exhale. "You are the one who inspires and gives rise to my expressions in every form."

Suddenly aware of his cessation in speech, she glanced up to find his head cocked in observation, eyes transfixed. She looked away in embarrassment, unable to bear the severe stare of wordless sentiment into which he engaged, and realizing this, he dropped his gaze in haste, returning his attentions to a less affected object. Erik stored his violin and refastened the cords holding the case safely between a few smaller branches, climbed through the tree's separating arms, and positioned himself directly in front of Christine, perched to one side as if sitting on a park bench.

Taking her hand, he began to caress the patient fingers. "If you would permit me... I should like to apologize."

"Whatever for?" she exclaimed, giving his request the brush.

"For throwing the other day into such a tail spin. I was highly successful in evoking all things negative from you. It... it should have been a time of elation."

"Your compunction regarding the situation is shared and all forgiven, unless... Do you do this to receive additional affections from me?" Her amusement turned his body rigid to the allegation.

"I do not say this in jest, Christine," Erik's direct tone piqued. "Are you aware of how often I have ever admitted to wrong doing in my life? Pride and justification were tools used *against* humanity. I could commit no wrong in the face of the injustice shown me... until your example... I am all amazement at the relief I am afforded." He shook his head, disbelieving. "I *seek* forgiveness, wish to atone and desire to repair so much. Your opinion of me is motivation to prove myself worthy of your love."

Erik felt a tug and leaned in closer, slid closer, his forearm coming to rest against the trunk above her. "Then I shall find it in my heart to bestow as often as I am petitioned."

"You are so good for me," he said, touching his lips to her temple, "have provided stability... say it shall always be."

"Always..."

"I thank you. Let us descend," he suggested, as abruptly as his kiss addressed her hand. "I have in mind to solicit your undivided attentions elsewhere when we are down."

Once they were again on firm ground, Erik cradled Christine in his arms before sitting her next to the candle at the base of the tree, then promptly taking up residence, he laid his head in her lap in anticipation of her hands upon his face. Their cue taken up, the whispering ministrations of her fingers began; alternately, one hand would play with a strand of his hair while the other tickled his skin.

"So sensuously soft. . . hmm. . ." was his contented murmur.

"My mother used to caress my face, lulling me to sleep while she told stories or sang. I never remembered her stopping because she maintained contact until I had drifted off." Erik caught one of her fingers with his lips, kissed it and sent it off again. "You seem to enjoy it as much now, as I did then."

"By far and yes, if allowed, I prefer this position in which to indulge. I melt inwardly to nothing, but the tingling sensation exists in filling my mind, it is a pleasure I celebrate at every opportunity."

Seeing that she had managed a captive audience, Christine made good use and asked how soon Erik would consent to marriage, considering their prior discussion of making the engagement brief. "I could definitely be convinced of tomorrow being quite as amiable a time as any other." An absently wicked smile raised the corner of his mouth and he rolled over, taking Christine by the waist to pull her between his upper body and arm. "You may choose the place where we are to exchange our vows, but I have a specific wish for our first night. . . together." A blush infused his sincerity.

"And. . . is your 'wish' to remain undisclosed?" she asked, combing his errant hair back from his eyes.

"Not at all, though my wish may increase anticipation, due in part to distance, but I would desire to come home, to come here. There is no other meaningful place. We have learned to trust, have developed a solid friendship, and the foundation of our relationship as a whole, began here. I desire our love to be brought home, as well."

Erik's arms wrapped around her shoulders supporting her lightly from the ground, and hers caught the back of his neck by clasping her wrist. All was quiet, except for a low, menacing growl emanating from deep within his throat; aptly drawing her nigh he pressed his mouth to hers.

Interrupting their felicity, the unexpected din of crackling and rubbing leaves stiffened Erik's back. He listened, and when the sound gradually rose in volume, his silence paralleled to alarm Christine. He swore cautiously under his breath, "the inconvenience" and "talking" were all she could make out before he pushed up to stand. She supposed it was his way to lessen the severity, knowing as he did of her distaste for the abominable pollution of mouth, and her mention of intelligence finding more suitable language, that worked on him.

"Stay where you are," he ordered mysteriously. Christine watched him lick his fingers, quickly snuff the candle's flame and toss it headlong into the stream, then scale the tree to retrieve his violin from the upper limbs. Returning in haste to where he had been, he laid back down, inclining his head to one side for a thorough look above, and grinned.

"You may pick up where we last—"

"But I. . ."

"Patience, you shall in good time," he purred soothingly, reassuring her while nearing the juncture of her neck and ear. Christine giggled, a leaf had settled lightly atop Erik's head, then over her eye. She tried in vain to whisk them away and Erik just chuckled at the futile effort, for others replaced them one after the other in their last, soft, continuous ovation to the earth. "Enjoy them, my love, they will soon cover us."

Laughter rang out, permeating the air with joy as their forms were tenaciously swallowed beneath an insulating quilt, in harmony with one droll comment. "Darkness has fallen," he said, nestling against her. Soon, the only hint of life became an occasional rustle, whisper or guttural moan of content.

Chapter Twelve

Time became a fast, headstrong enemy as the end of another week drew to a close and plans for Paris, though at once settled upon for the upcoming days, approached undaunted; a visit to the Giry's was in order and again, to one most deserving, the majestic Daroga of Mazanderan. Wedding details were as yet undecided, leaving an earnest pursuit of explanations to dictate the duration of postponement until resolved: duty before blissful design.

Thoughts weighed heavy, more so on Christine than Erik; there was the unease of timely execution for the aforementioned plans and blatant disregard exhibited all these months for her punctilious upbringing, but however unintentionally meant, it filled her with dread of the deepest sort because she would be facing those to whom she owed much. She took heart at what little consolation was profited her, recalling when she went again to stay with Madame Valerius, provisionally of course, between her dealings with both the men in her life. Her plans, thoughts, and feelings were left in confidence with Mme Valerius, Christine being reassured that when all had been set aright, a detailed communication of the outcome would be enjoyed. That said, Mme Valerius beamed and imparted to Christine of *her* intentions, which up until that moment had been but a faint wish.

With her husband deceased, and Christine to take leave to follow her heart, she would, after so long an absence, be returning to her old home of Gothenburg, Sweden, while she retained enough strength to that end. Madame confessed she had pined for friends and family when alone and that it would be best. And so, the generous considerations, ones strictly adhered to these months past, would now discover relief in word being conveyed and received, especially in regard to Madame's health.

These thoughts, coupled with inexplicable bouts of emotion, occupied a great deal of Christine's energy, setting forth a strange pattern of display. As it would happen, Erik often came upon her tearful figure, huddled in a chair or other small confining space. When he tried entreating her to work through to the cause, it would elicit such anguish from her, and frustration from him, that Erik found it best to remove himself from her sight. This behavior confused him immensely, but was not completely incomprehensible. In some aspects, she was as he used to be, sans the tears, in experiencing a level of emotional madness: the irrational comments, finding fault with petty issues previously overlooked, rounds of tears shed, and the desire of solitude. He attributed some to the stress of their return, to the more familiar society and social circle of Paris, but the other thoughts plaguing him were increasingly difficult to handle.

Descending the stairs with Christine's poem in hand, Erik realized that the tables were turned, that he would be the one from whom patience was now required, only the approach was less certain. He shook his head and ran a hand over his face, then leaned within the corner window to sit. He felt empathy regarding her dilemma, for all she had ever struggled with in relation to him, but there was something far deeper than either of them suspected. Even her conduct began to wreak havoc on his self-worth. She no longer found happiness beside him, but contentment when she pondered away.

My chest is pained with misgivings at the thought of her reconsidering, regretting the choices made. Each time I bring this to mind my heart skips for she is seared into my very being, he clenched a fist; *surely this hypothetical banter will do me no good and be my final undoing!*

He glanced in the direction of her stone then at the sky, its greying depths importuning his mood. Not able to contain himself longer he stood, and leaving the poem in his stead, went to seek conversation. He was following their conviction, their commitment; it was time to talk, to resolve the matter.

The scuffle of sole to ground, the clack of a rock against others as it found a new residence, had Christine looking over her shoulder to see Erik, tossing bits and pieces of a small branch into the waving grass before him, on his way to her. Entering the water without heed to boots or clothing, he was met with a kind gesture of welcome, Christine's smile.

"Would you join me?"

Erik acknowledged the invitation, saying nothing until seated next to her, right shoulders pressed together. "We have neglected our promise, Christine." He watched her straighten, shoulders squaring to withstand a possible reproof. None came.

"I find 'we' to be too kind," she admitted. His saddened eyes roved her face, the concern at his silence, enough to bring her head low. "Forgive me. I have not behaved well at all. . . on the verge of atrocious may be a better description still. Leaving you with assumptions as I pitch ridiculous fits, pout; crying unmercifully. . . continuing on without any real answers, partial thoughts, and those are a befuddled mess as well," she confessed, leaning into him more solidly. "I know I am anxious about returning, but excited just the same. Still, the fact that no one knows I have been here with you all this time has given me little cause for concern. I would have wished for nothing different, and I can deal well enough with the remarks of impudence that I shall be accused of. It is just, I do not understand the why."

"You sit for hours in thorough occupation of mind, and yet, nothing."

"Yes, I know. I have been assessing, giving rise to some sort of inventory regarding the decisions made in my life thus far. I was hoping to find the source while deliberating upon the outcomes, had I chosen otherwise."

Erik's self-doubt flashed and he braced himself for rejection, an emotion too often experienced during his young, impressionable years. "I. . . I am. . ." he repeated warily. "I am unsure of my wish to hear."

Christine wrapped her arms about his. "You may not, but it is for you to decide," she stated openly to his hesitance. "I have deliberated on, or have at least come as near as one can, to predicting what our lives would be like, had we kept strictly to our original paths."

His muscles grew taut, but more than a sharp inhale he would not let pass. Erik had control.

"I can fearfully presume what you had resigned yourself to, your comments alluded finality. As for me, I was brought back to sweet memories of a time spent in youthful joy, all too innocent of the political and familial responsibilities to be borne at length. When I was in Raoul's company more often, I became swept up in the possibility of the dream. He dazzled me with things, places, and the people we met, but after accepting his proposal. . . I don't know, something knotted from within, and I refused to acknowledge my acceptance outwardly. I know I was afraid of hurting you, and in my inexperience with such attentions lavished on me, I found myself caught in a hopeless triangle. I had two men vying for my love, one seemed the safe choice, reasonable and prestigious. . . Tell me," she queried, her voice gaining a rhetorical air, "who among women would not desire to be on the arm of a Chagny? While the other was mystical and fiercely passionate, something of which I wished to know, but denied myself out of embarrassment."

Embarrassment? Surely not! He thought of her as reserved; she was all openness and guarded passion, the sepal-clad bud now in bloom. In effect, he was astonished by the rigorous assessment, felt intrigue moment to moment, in which his contempt diminished and where he could declare his esteem for Christine all at the same time.

"When I think of the quixotic environment into which I was blindly acceptant..." She shuddered. "It makes me almost ill to see how extensive my gullibility had become. Unaccustomed as I was to the flittering and fraternizing Raoul exposed me to, I tried to blend with the other women of sophistication and I suppose, became as false as they. The gossiping, backbiting, and change of subject matter under their scrutinizing eye was, as I too often observed, all dependent upon connection, and who was in their party as a whole or within possible earshot. I can only imagine the conversations when one was not in their presence. So, to this insight arrived an understanding that I would have become a prize to be shown about town, flaunted even, and I felt unfit for the match or challenge. I grew up in humble surroundings, and was later given a taste of the more delicate side of upper society by the Valeriuses. Trust amidst aristocracy does not come easily and is indeed, an anomaly. I feel one would be truly hard-pressed to find someone to retain in such a reliable confidence."

Christine sighed, moving slightly to catch Erik's gaze, gently touching his face. "The regular company Philippe kept, to which he opposed so vehemently because his younger brother desired it on a more permanent basis, was deplorable, an example of hypocrisy and selfish pride at work. I would never have survived the dreary façade with Raoul, and feel it no real fault of his, to have an honest pride; even now, he would have valued outward appearances as a means to flatter himself. Those who claim superiority, due to their breeding and rank, would do well to find themselves some sort of masque to sport. They are certainly two-faced enough to be the ones wearing them, not you. All the same, it should be interesting to hear of Raoul one day."

Erik stared, as he was yet unwilling to interrupt or add to the conversation, and was hauntingly entranced by these conclusions her perspective granted him on the high society of France; his doubts had diminished quite readily to a different level of awareness.

"You must know that you are and shall be my confidant," she

assured, smiling, "when I know what it is I wish to confide. I know that I value honesty, simplicity, and trust, and would not have decided any differently than I already have, however complex the journey." To this, Erik raised an eyebrow. "But it is not one sided, as you have recently discovered. I possess as many or more frustrating attributes. We have experienced so much emotional intensity, some regretfully so. Forgive me for complicating things, for all the tears. . ." She hastily looked away, attentive to the threatening rise.

Coughing unexpectedly, Erik broached the preceding trail unfinished. "Do you feel me incapable of dealing with as much convolution as I cause?" he asked solemnly.

"No. . ." she said shyly.

"Am I less of a man in your eyes for the resurfacing sensitivity I demonstrate?"

"No, you are more. . . my words were not meant in this light." Her lips quivered. "I am deeply in love with you, your tears warm and endear my convictions. You are so much more, so much. . . I adore you, grateful you deem me worthy to be your companion."

Erik's hand rested over hers, stopping them from twisting the fabric of her dress to ruin, his other, softly guided her cheek to a reasonable elevation so she could see his tears, spilling unhindered. Her representation was quite an extensive first, for such an intimately, intense sincerity had yet to be uttered past general admissions of affection to this point; it touched him.

His eyes said it all, beckoned unceasingly, breath unsteady as he sought tangible valuation of her words. Wasting no time, her arms were unerring in their goal to encompass his neck, as he gently pulled her tight against his chest. "I am passionately unashamed in my love for you, Christine. And if you will permit, I shall avow my sentiments."

The moment he spoke, her hands were at once lost and tangled in his mussed shock, forcing the very air from his lungs. *Too good, blast it, it feels too good!* He was well on his way, he knew he was, she in his arms, he partaking greedily of her tender kisses and that hand, venturing slightly, running the length of her side and back.

"Stop me, or I shall be in dire straights by the. . . oh, Christine, I. . . must not. . ." his words burst in a jumble as he moved from her embrace into the numbing confines of the stream. "You are a most wicked temptation," he moaned, wagging his finger at her. "Beautifully wicked and sumptuously. . ." His lips found her uncovered shoulder irresistible, he apologized—*what torment, where is my control?* He must distance himself completely, further out into the current. The stable was first in recall and this, a close second, as hands splashed face with a bit of propriety. Turning for a quick look at her, he saw a flash of what he thought was enjoyment, a bite to her lower lip, a reddened face. Obviously, her sympathy would not be forthcoming for the repercussions now felt, and he plunged into the water, restoring those brilliantly sensible limits.

"I must admit. . . the water is quite refreshing, reminds me of the lake under the Opera House," he said as he waded, glancing up at the ominous clouds continuing to darken. "We should head back inside, there is sure to be a deluge by the looks of them." His head motioned in an upward gesture.

"I am not afraid of getting wet, and you are already sufficiently soaked," she observed, giving a startled blink from a raindrop spattering on her cheek.

"Good to see that we think alike. Come to me my sweet angel, I was not yet finished," he confessed, grinning impishly. Sweeping Christine from the rock, Erik rounded and headed for deeper water. "No one else could possibly make me feel this way, my love, I am ardently impassioned."

The few spots on their clothing and skin, from an occasional drip, more noted by her than him, soon gave rise to a constant drizzle amidst their joy, the moisture providing voluntary ease at which his tongue and lips could glide along her jaw. He dropped her legs slowly into the water, shock abusing all nerves until past feeling. The back of his hand brushed the damp curls from her shoulder and became entwined at the nape of her neck to affectionately draw her in, her hands on his waist. Their kiss intensified, and the rain drenched them, petitioning the need for a more centralized placement in the chill. Erik moved against Christine, pushing her back gently, but misstepped, throwing the two of them off-balance. She screamed in response to Erik's contorting spin, which made possible just enough space so he would not injure her with his weight, and they toppled into the cold flow.

Christine regained her footing first, grabbing at Erik's shirt, both sputtering and coughing between fits of infectious laughter, neither successfully keeping their legs beneath them.

"I sincerely apologize," he confessed, falling once more after he tripped in the shallows.

"You planned that!" she accused.

"Honestly, I wish I had." Erik eyed her from where he sat on the stone to take in their predicament. "You know," he panted, slicking back his hair, "you are quite wet."

"Yes, and to which award are you applying, most observant?" she choked, sending a shower of water back in his direction.

"You are also quite seductively gorgeous in drenched garments." His brows elevated.

She looked at herself then at him and crossed her arms to hide the penetrating coldness. Light mortification spurned the incentive for her to navigate a retreat, but the load of skirts proved cumbersome and difficult to manage while trying to maintain modesty. "I do not appreciate your expression," she grunted, "at all! Serves me right, blast my thoughts." The last words were but an absent murmur.

Seeing that Christine's lips were fast becoming a purple-blue, Erik collected her and headed for the porch, the rain itself, warm in comparison.

"You are taking great delight in every bit of this situation."

"Yes, every bit," he replied breathless, setting her down. "Remember, my dear, I am intoxicated, influenced beyond reason, honest always, and unable to hide behind false pretense." Then he thoughtfully stated, "You shall require warmth."

"And y–your recommendation?"

"My embrace."

"Come n–now," she stammered, her teeth chattering from inside her trembling chin. "You expect me to p–perpetuate the crime?"

"Yes, you and your thoughts. Come here," he demanded. She obeyed, tucking herself to his chest and his solid mass of radiating heat for close on ten minutes. "Better?"

"Much, but... I must have your back to me, please, this millstone of clothing should be left off out here."

Sighing, Erik swung reluctantly to his right. "Christine?"

"I know what you are thinking and the answer shall be a most resounding, no!" she chided, running her finger little by little down his back.

"Even with my eyes closed?"

Christine nuzzled lightly. "You know as well as I, we would be pained for our momentary lack of control when we are close enough to sharing liberally. We have... ugh... taunted and stretched the limits plenty; moreover, what sort of gift is completely enjoyed if handled or peeked at prior to its appointed unveiling, hmm?"

"Sweet voice of reason, I heartily concede. Go in haste, my dear," he responded, his back chilling to the click of the latch.

That evening came off rather amicably pleasant, despite the direction of Erik's earlier conduct, and as he claimed to be unpardonably untoward, it had all been examined agreeably, with blame allotted to the pair in equal shares: Christine's being the lesser and his, rightly regaining their gentleman-like flare. Christine relaxed out on the balcony, the braiding of hair making an overall industry of dexterousness favorable for thought, or spell. Erik stared intently upon his subject, observing every action, the way she combed through those long dark tresses with her fingers, deftly separating and weaving them enslaved. Their expressions being foremost in the advantage now, when remembering what had been alluded to, resurfaced all too soon.

I daresay a change to have commandeered my assurance of 'not being intrusive in nature' to be altered irrevocably—and we, providing extenuating disservice to the other. I shall never be the same now that I am loved, for there are certain liberties a heart may claim: the most critical being the declaration of abiding fidelity. I have done nothing but show devotion to that end in my search for reassurance of her affection. Though, her emotions have invoked grave consternation in my present quest to understand the workings of a woman's nature, complex creatures that we all are.

He secretly wished to be under the power of her hands, but he vowed—strictly promised, to distantly admire and be respectful. This was, however, secreted intelligence for himself alone, established to aid in valiance through the course of the next week, as they would be wed on the Friday upcoming, indeed, just six days from then.

Such innocent beauty would be lost on someone more than fifteen years my junior, his chest swelled; *maturity. . . is quite advantageous, but relationships and concepts of the heart have without doubt, placed me in a most enigmatic dilemma. Nothing is static!*

Her hair complete, his eyes continued to devour, breath catching anew, each time the breeze would accentuate a sweetened curve obscured by her dressing gown. Almost a third of an hour passed with Erik standing so enraptured. Suddenly self-conscious, he looked down to the violin under his arm and smiled. The gentle pianissimo, invoked from the master's touch, caused a shy glance to be cast toward the balcony doors, the music brightening the countenance of its premeditated goal. He glided to her with his offering, an endowment for her pleasure. When the effect ceased, she held out her hand.

"Thank you. Nothing could have lifted my spirits more." She

breathed deeply. "I adore the cleansing qualities of the rain, how it penetrates the mind and body."

Erik nodded in agreement. There was the lingering, earthy scent and sovereign serenade of crickets, but he wished nothing more than to hold the hand bound within his and caress lips to prize.

"I am a pathetic heathen," he stated abruptly, "unable to keep an oath, even to myself. I cannot. . ."

Christine focused on him. "What sort of oath?"

"To protect our commitment, I promised not to. . ."

"What, you would refuse to touch me? I believe that to be a little extreme. The most civil of courtships, when exposed to public, address the other reservedly. Besides," she whispered, "I would not get on well at all, Monsieur. It is nonsense to be contact poor for nearly a full week; such a premise might force irreparable distraction."

"My abstinence, if I am to understand correctly, does not meet with approbation then."

"Not in the least." Her grin returned from him a lightened heart.

"I fear you may think less of me because I was barely able to last a handful of trifling hours," Erik responded dolefully. "It seems my romantic inclinations have rendered me without discipline all day, and I scarce can predict what may be thrown in our path, but should like, in any event, to propose a diversion prior to our arrival in Paris."

Quiet.

Taking her wordlessness to mean there were no objections to what he had said, he went on. "I feel impressed," he sighed, grasping her hand ever tighter, "that we should travel to Perros."

Tears welled, and a hand flew to cover the startling appearance of emotion. Erik released her other hand and that too, retracted, seizing hold about her waist. He vacillated then reached for her shoulder, softly touching it. Christine rotated in a blur to welcome his embrace, taking refuge in the solace offered and pressed close.

He had no idea she would react in such a manner. A few gladsome drops he might dash from her cheeks were expected, but she held on as if his being near had everything to do with living. If he moved, she clung and was nigh on shadowing his very breath. *Hold her, it is all she needs,* urged Compassion.

Crying for nearly half an hour Erik sought to calm Christine with his voice. He was persistent though gentle, knowing the default of emotion earnestly wished for drought. And at length, while slowly gaining control, she was able to brave the task of speaking and drew back slightly, appalled by the storm's havoc wreaked upon her intended.

"What you must think. . . he has been gone for so many years, but I cry as though it were a recently fresh occurrence."

"Only your tenderness of heart is considered, as I have seen this in your regard for me. I know you miss your father, and I would never desire to replace the feelings or make light. I only wish I had made the connection sooner. Your demeanor changed the night we climbed above in the branches of the tree; it was the violin music."

"Yes," Christine agreed.

"I am sure, despite the lack of understanding I have of such religious concepts, that he is aware of our happiness, though I should like to have had the opportunity to ask for your hand, to seek his blessing."

"Would you?" she breathed raggedly.

"Yes," he chuckled, "though your supplication in my behalf may have been required in earnest."

"I know the discomfort you will be subjecting yourself to, and this you would do to accommodate me?" Christine asked incredulously.

Erik lovingly kissed her forehead. "I shall do anything and everything in my power to ensure your happiness, nothing is too great a price to have you at my side, as *my* companion." A new round of moisture dampened her cheeks. "Christine, please, tell me what I may do to end these tears that pain me to see shed."

"We are. . . so much alike, yet different, Erik. Neither of us has any real family to speak of, only a few choice people who have impacted our lives."

They both stopped to contemplate this, her youthful features aged by the insufferable anguish, alongside the swollen, red eyes, gave Erik all the excuse needed to console her in the realization he had lived with his whole life. "Then, we shall be alone as one, and therefore, together, my sweetest Christine."

Chapter Thirteen

In the interim of darkest night and predawn, rain revisited—a most unrelenting guest—until morn brought steam rising from the ground to greet Erik and Christine's early departure within the disseminating clouds, encircling all that remained unmoved. Amiens waited reverently, hushed to the eminent tumult of citizens that would take to the streets on their quest for spiritual nourishment.

Erik sighed again, his agitation increasing with the very distance to the outskirts of the city readily diminishing. Who could mistake the violent exhalations he had willfully sounded out?

Pulling Dezi up short, Christine confronted the issue. "If it is to be this painful, then I shall not tread on your good intentions, however well meant they may have been last night. It will be of no worth to inflict the anxiety I see building and will certainly lead to an unpleasant journey."

Shifting atop Cesar, Erik came about with his head cocked to the right. He looked at Christine then dropped his gaze as he drew alongside her. "Forgive me, it has been years since I have ridden a train in the presence of so many. I dread the stares and whisperings annexed to my past, but it is time I set aside my general distaste for people and start believing them to be *fairly* tolerable. I shall resign myself to this fact, as I owe much to you and to the Persian. It is only right that I take my place among those in society and begin attending to my own affairs, personally."

"Erik," she said, concern threading her query. "Are you quite sure?"

"I shall conquer this, master all, indeed I shall, for it is my desire to be most worthy of you. You are all that matters." With that, he leaned over, his hands set to either end of the saddle on which Christine was perched, and kissed her exceedingly well. She smiled at his bravado, but was unconvinced by his admission, this declaration of his. He could read it in her countenance plainly; *another challenge to get over*, he knew, guessing it would be the entailing actions that determined the merit of his word.

Their horses boarded, minor personal effects attended to, a letter posted to Sweden, and tickets purchased for the morning train, they traversed the quiet streets to one of the grandest sights in all of France, la cathedral Notre-Dame d'Amiens.

"We have come often to Amiens, and I find it shameful that we have yet to enjoy a few of its historical diversions. Would you indulge my passion during these early hours?"

"It would be my pleasure, please." Her expression gratified the desire Erik had for sharing knowledge, and so he tucked Christine's hand securely within the bend of his right arm.

Confronting the ominous side to the west, they were immediately transported to the late thirteenth century, all the intricacies presently attesting to this elaborate feat at the time it was conceived. Erik stretched forth his hand and with reverence, touched the aged stone. "There is always an existence beneath. Anyone who labors on such a masterpiece leaves part of their soul to breathe life into their creation. It is unavoidable." He sensed pressure to his forearm and knew of her comprehension regarding the connection he had with those creations bearing *his* genius; he responded to her kindness. "Indeed, there have been many, but only a select few have ever been purposely seeded and nurtured in love, Christine." A gentle pat came in return as he proceeded.

"This cathedral is the token centerpiece of Amiens, suited naturally for this by its height, of course. It is the tallest cathedral in the whole of France, and one that is fully complete. From here, the infrastructure radiates outward, similar to the spokes within a carriage wheel, a rather interesting concept upon which to found a city really. Here, as we move along the west façade, you will see a rose window... there," he pointed up, "and directly beneath, the kings gallery and three portals. Each of the sculptures shown is deeply etched, a labor-intensive affair, not merely a superficial representation. And, despite the complex details so skillfully rendered, as most cathedrals require more than a century to construct, this came to fulfillment between 1220 and 1270, with restoration occurring as recently as twenty years ago.

"This is Gothic style at its best, Christine. It evolved from the Romanesque at the turn of the twelfth century. The rooflines have undergone a vast transformation since that time, from near-level to these high vaulted peaks. But in order to attain the desired effect of height, maintain the integrity of the structure and gain unblocked access internally, the supports were built on the outside of the walls. See these piers?" He gestured toward the tall arched columns surrounding the north—their present position—and south façades at even intervals. "They are known as flying buttresses or simply flyers. A temporary wooden frame, referred to as centering, is erected to maintain the shape of each arch until the mortar is solid and thoroughly dry. Then, once the system is in place, to manage the downward thrust from the rising pitch, with the counter thrust from the buttresses, the thin walls become as a creative canvas for the artisans of stained glass."

They looked up, interfacing enlightenment with sight, and Erik's exuberance rose. "The concept is fascinating, is it not?" he asked, quite impervious to deflation or aware of more than a few quiet murmurs and affirming nods from Christine. "Having the supports outside the building itself allotted for an increase of light internally, and more warmth of spirit."

Rounding the south façade, they beheld actual passageways constructed through each pier, a visually pleasing addition of ornamentation to the otherwise stoic blocks. Erik led Christine through the narrow sections, glancing back upon occasion to the besetting curiosity reflected in her features. At times, she was uncertain, untrusting of all the purported strength among the exhibiting piers, and stooped warily.

"You are concerned?" he asked, stopping.

"Although you have explained the massive restoration, the fact that it has been here for decades, difficulties incurred and resolved, the excessive height, and the changes made in conjunction with the lessons learned here, to other cathedrals in France. . . perhaps I am consumed with awe, or not," she shrugged, "but I find the structure somewhat intimidating."

He pulled her close into his protective embrace. "It is but a conglomeration of materials, nothing to fear, except for what we attach to it symbolically." A bewitching air lifted his left cheek, noticeable, if only by a hint along his hairline. "Our dear O.G. was, in comparison, just as untouchable and intimidating until you anchored him, destroying the sails of that implacable façade *he* so cleverly developed."

She looked quizzically to his masqued face and rubbed the underside of his chin with her index. "Am I to understand that an accusation has been *thrust* in my direction and I, with no means to retaliate, must defend myself?"

"It is your touch, your loving touch to which I allude." His eyes rolled back beneath their lids. "What is it that you lace across the surface of your skin prior to caressing mine?" His question was asked in breathless astonishment without want of answer. Pressing her hand to his lips, Erik's eyes found hers. "You are infectious, utterly and indisputably infectious and I, sorely tempted by passion."

"Then I shall not compound the issue," she whispered softly, blushing while resuming her grasp upon his arm.

"Yes, thank you. Come, we have a previous engagement, one in which I must brook the wanton attentions from the bees of humanity."

"I am glad to see your manner in jest," she laughed.

"My dear Christine, I must have some outlet for my innermost feelings, repression will only make for an unhappy man and unfulfilled promise. The question now, is whether you will sanction this harassment to be unleashed upon your hearing alone."

"Yes, Monsieur Gautier, I shall accept your humor, delightedly."

IT WOULD SEEM reality comes to those who place themselves within the path of another; no one is exempt from the journey, and thus it is, when thrown together as the confined burden of the railways. Steam billowed from the engine during a brief respite on the smoothly forged rails; passengers mixed and repelled, those arrived and departing within the station and upon the platform, being conducted as they were, in a frenzied dance by the experienced hands of time.

Erik retrieved their belongings, rejoining Christine in a less occupied area; the diminished exchange of comings and goings stemmed and they eventually boarded, choosing to situate among a facing set of double seats toward the rear of the car. Once their bulky outerwear was removed, and he had his hat, cane, and personals stowed within reach, Erik placed Christine near the window for her protection, away from the aisle. Taking up residence himself, he plied the art of observation, meeting the disparaging stares with little success.

"The incessant glares burn through my masque, Christine. The fleeting glances and roving eyes. . ." Erik kissed her hand during the frustrated mumble.

"We have no obligation to anyone, only to be content ourselves; that much is manageable."

"Perhaps, but nothing would give me more pleasure than to oblige their curiosities."

"You do not mean that," she said, careful not to betray her tone by volume.

"I most certainly do!" came his sufficiently hushed reply. "I am just belligerent enough that I may feel justly inclined to do so, no matter the consequences." His agitation had mounted during those few minutes' exchange to an alarming degree.

"Look at me, Erik." Her quiet demand forced him to dwell on her and the removal of her left glove, looking after the actions with interest. Anyone who was rude enough to trespass now would be in for a surprise as she placed her jeweled hand to his masque, directing his left cheek to touch hers. Erik calmed.

"I can be as mischievous as any, employing their minds to wonder what could have possibly been said to the man by his intended wife. And if nothing else, they will at least know you are loved and of great worth." Her comments were closely followed by a discreet kiss, one heard, more than felt.

Sweet pride enlarged and heightened the esteem in which he regarded Christine. She could have simply refuted the depth of her attachment to him by depicting mortification, sitting across, rather than beside him, or reproached his ridiculous behavior, but instead, he received compassion. Of significant relevance, and of worthy notice, as the train lurched forward, was how much the eyes receded into the background of importance, enabling him to then settle gratefully into a diffident tranquility of his own.

"If you care to read. . ." Christine offered him one of Tolstoy's works.

"Thank you, but I may wish to try a bit of our favorite pastime of people watching. Seeing as I am to be without choice in the matter of visual privacy for the better part of a day, I should like to return the favor." She nodded, glad that his lightheartedness had returned.

Leaning back, Erik crossed his legs, folded his hands loosely into his lap, and began with a glance to the right, across the aisle. From where they sat, there was a rather tall, unobtrusive gentleman in a grey suit. He had thinning hair, a twisted moustache, and pointed features all fixed into his newspaper, ignoring life around him. *Would that I could be as indifferent, making productive use of my time or at the very least, the example marked. Perhaps I am too trusting of his exterior, and it is he to whom I should place my guard and not those more conspicuous.*

Further up the car was a group of men, six in all, dressed in fine business attire: long trousers, colored tail and designed waistcoats, each encompassing the whiteness of shirt and ascots strangled up about their necks, imbibing freely in a rather raucous display of youthful impropriety. It was from them that most of the condemning looks were bestowed. Erik shook his head in distaste of the flaunting peacocks, considering it a most unwelcome siege to the lulling atmosphere, and huffed. Others became an unchallenging framework of boredom, being decidedly labeled as tedious and limiting, *so unlike the menu available from the passersby on the streets of Amiens,* thought Erik, but it was of little consequence in this inert scene and must be made sufferable.

Having taken stock of the conditions surrounding him, possible exits, humans to be dealt with, and all manner of scenarios run, Erik was at last satisfied. He did locate, however, amidst the general gloominess, one desirable, weathered bloom among the chaff. An elderly woman, frail, but not weak in spirit, as denoted by the way she represented herself. *Not unlike Madame Giry.* If there were a duplicate of her, this would be his expectation in later years. She was valiant in her daring. If their eyes met, she would hold his gaze until a smile caused him to shift under her kind demeanor, and then she would again be attentive to her needlework.

Discomfiture having cast Erik into a fit of melancholy, he re-situated, feeling Christine's hand entwine about his. "I should like to agree, idle wandering of eyes does rattle the nerves after a time." She referred casually to the group of young men.

"I appreciate your empathy and intuition, which is unashamedly accurate. I needed the connection," he said.

"I know you have not slept well for days, perhaps you might try relaxing?"

The emphatic suggestion, joined to the book in his hand, encouraged the deep repose in which he longed to engage, and in time, his sight succumbed to the rhythmic movements of the train, and thereafter, success in achieving several hours of needed rest.

"I beg pardon, Ma'am." The British accent was courteous but exceptionally high strung and intrusive, causing Erik to start awake. Christine held on to him, knowing he had been caught off guard, but his abrupt rise to confront the impertinence of this direct address to Christine rendered her grip ineffective, in much the same way as Erik's ennobling display left shrinking the resolve before *him*.

"Forgive me, sir." The young, blond haired man gulped pityingly. "I certainly did not intend. . ."

"Well, you most effectively did," Erik quipped, hands resting eagerly atop his walking stick. He could easily strike, and would do so if the behavior, however ill-presented, provoked in the slightest. Christine's eyes widened in silent alarm, seeing Erik's fingers poised about the spring mechanism of the cane, which would release the imbedded sword unfailingly.

"Perhaps, Monsieur. . ." she suggested with a nervous smile, "you would like to begin anew?"

"Yes, please." Then, looking to the impatience looming in wait, he addressed Erik. "Monsieur, if I may?" Erik bowed his head as the young man continued hastily under burgeoning suspicion. "Madame. . ." he addressed in assumption, having corrected the honorifics used. "My associates and I concur, after a somewhat lengthy deliberation, that you are indeed a most uncanny likeness of a soprano we have had the privilege of hearing at one time or another, though we *hope* you are she, a Mademoiselle Daaé?"

Christine blushed lightly, but responded in a reserved manner. "You flatter me, Monsieur, I thank you, but your deliberations have been in vain. I must apologize for unconsciously occupying so much of your time."

The young man bowed. "Forgive me for troubling you." And, taking his leave of them he returned to his clutch of fops, set at naught from the dissatisfaction of misfortune.

Seated in astonishment, Erik asked, "You denied your identity, why?"

"I desire only your attentions, and enduring a possible uproar in their haste to expose who I am, knowing they would be only too glad to congratulate themselves, is not. You, on the other hand," she whispered, "were prepared to flay him open on the spot for the dissolution of our privacy."

"His manner was too gay and excessively immodest for my taste."

"You are entitled to your opinion, but think, upon what is your foundation based? I would suppose some form of jealousy to be suspect for your haughty disposition."

Erik glared at her, thoroughly disgusted. "Jealousy? Jealous of whom?"

"Not of whom, but of what. The situation is foreign, is it not? How often have you dealt with other men, in my presence, outside an environment not in your control?"

He opened his mouth then closed it promptly. Christine could see him mulling the premise from every angle. He crossed and uncrossed his legs and arms, rubbed his neck and finally rested his chin across the thumbs of his clasped hands, elbows to seat arms. "I am all admiration for your eloquent insight. There are. . ." he struggled without confidence in the subject. "I suppose, the feelings of superiority I bestow upon some men, are due in part because they take ease in what I am just now experiencing at my age." The color elevated along his neck. "And I meet it head on, the only way I know how, of this I am guilty."

"You mistake the reason for drawing your attention; it was not to induce guilt nor incite pain, but merely to demonstrate the passionate flare in your character."

A huge grin spread his contours, turning his head in a sideways glance. Yes, he would survive this yet, and in reasonably good humor. "Flare, eh, not flaw?" The enlightenment hung as bait to the unsuspecting.

"To that trap, my witty love, I shall not reply." Her voice taunted mercilessly. "Let it be your lone transposition sparing me the agony of future rebuke."

Their travels nearly complete, Erik could feel his nerves prickle. Despising the unproductive use of his time, he mentioned thusly in quiet to Christine and she agreed, amending the fact with a suggestion of it having been a creative hiatus. Amazed, Erik spoke to his pessimistic nature and then to her rage for eager depiction of the positive, again resuming the discussion to the contrary, and finally concluding it beneficial to not always be one way or the other, but a healthy blend.

The balance of their confining sentence drew swiftly to a close, ending this last conversation with an in-depth recall of their personality traits; during which, Erik perceived the heat of prying eyes. The older woman had taken an interest in, and more fervently now than at any other period along their journey, his dealings with Christine. It fascinated his mind and normally obdurate senses, baffled them actually, and stranger still, his composure was in no way affected but by curiosity. Whatever thought and fixation she may have caused, it was soon forgotten in the crowd clamoring to ready themselves for the long anticipated exit. He and Christine patiently waited then gathered to leave in a more leisurely fashion.

"Excuse me," the elderly woman said, her cautious hand in motion toward Erik's arm.

"Madame?" came the reply. Their eyes met upon his rounding to meet the gentleness, her touch light and unthreatening.

"I hope you would permit an old woman the indulgence of a moment." Her smile brought a radiant sincerity from each of the creases lining her well-worn face. Christine turned graciously to attend the request from Erik's left, to see him tenderly encase the frail age beneath his.

"Please," he encouraged, "we are in no hurry."

The woman nodded, applying to their mercy. "First off, I shall beg your forgiveness; as you are well aware, Monsieur, the two of you became a point of observation to me early on. I tread upon your privacy unconsciously."

Erik grinned. "Do not trouble yourself further, there was no harm—" he tried to reassure against her rapid interruption.

"I do not wish to argue, it was impolite, and would prefer to offer, if I may, my reflections as a way to make amends. My heart warmed at the tender regard shown by each of you for the welfare and comfort of the other. You are a handsome couple, exemplary in the honest portrayal of your love." The woman held out her hand to Christine, looking at them each in turn. "There are, Monsieur, those who are singular in their ability to see beyond, to care deeply, when the world is replete in cruelty. You are truly blessed. Honor her, cherish her with a vibrancy of passion from the soul, but above all else, protect the love that you share." And with that, the woman gave Erik's arm an affectionate squeeze, released Christine's hand, and was gone. They were stunned and moved alike.

"I should like to become a woman as lovely as she, her austere beauty of heart. . ." Christine murmured in admiration.

Erik cleared his throat and returned a faint "yes," stepping back to help Christine shrug on her coat, eyes distant to the mechanics of politeness. From his experience, she would achieve such a state, and had already done so by working her powers on him, he was positive.

Christine pursed her lips as a kind "ahem," nudged the lapse, startling Erik into speech. "Yes, 'beauty of heart,'" he copied, replaying those well-chosen words: 'singular in their ability. . . to care deeply,' and 'vibrancy of passion.' The impact of these courtesies, and the overall consideration, had rarely made his acquaintance; that another person validated possible feelings of resentment, was compelled to apologize, and had sentiments specifically approving his bond, their precious bond. . . there were no words.

Chapter Fourteen

"Does this meet with your satisfaction, Monsieur?" the slight man questioned from the doorway, his eyes pushing the boundaries of decorum to one side and then the other. The young concierge stood waiting, all manner of thoughts loosely flitting after this mysterious man in the masque; the young woman, the silence and prestige the gentleman was able to secure with his presence, all had engaged the young hands in a battle of nerves behind his back. "I shall provide options and secure travel arrangements to Paris when you are ready, Monsieur."

"Quite satisfactory, that will be all for now, thank you." Erik gestured dismissively with a short flip of the wrist while removing his cloak and gloves. The concierge bowed, taking his leave.

Luxurious as the rooms were, adjoining and facing toward the coast of Perros-Guirec, Christine preferred the breeze outside on the balcony to the stuffy exchange of airs within. Erik joined her and aided in the removal of her walking coat.

"What is it," her tone shocked him, enough to prevent him from doing anything more than allow her coat to fall across one arm, "that coerces people to behave in such a pretentious manner and conform so conditionally under the eye of public scrutiny?" Her sweetness resumed quickly. "Why can we not all be sincere?"

Erik cocked his head, grateful she was not starting a topic in so disagreeable a way as he thought. "Am I being included or specifically referred to?"

"Both, I imagine." She averted her eyes while rounding. "Your character alters when trapped behind that masque. The grounds for some I understand, others confound," she explained, concern creasing her forehead.

His finger rose to massage the blemish from her flawless skin. "Yes, can you blame me? This masque grants me freedom of movement and multiple benefits when I deal with people in general. If I do not posture my expectations in an undeniably, resolute fashion, commanding respect, then I am seen as someone to take advantage of, and I will never permit that again. Ever!" His gravity of determination held fast. "I shall not apologize for the eccentricities that guard my privacy, however impolitic they may seem, for they will shield yours as well." Signaling the need for a moment, he stole inside, draped her coat over top of his and made accommodating his embrace. "Tell me, are these habits so unsavory?"

"No... no, you are constant with me, undeviating. The influence comes from external sources, of that I am confident, in a rather abstract fashion."

Christine watched him while listening to the prevailing vocal distraction. "Hopefully, your patience will assist me in regulating... the unsteady, hmm... fluctuation..."

The late afternoon sun brought the reddish undertones of her hair to brilliancy, suddenly demanding his full and undivided attention. His hands recalled their domain a familiar comfort, as they toyed with the loose waves at her temples. The world blurred without care, his finger teasing forth a length until the dark ply lay fully extended, buoyed across her chest by a light breeze, its texture, a downy feather, drawn wistfully to the skin. Inclining his head, Erik reached to one side, feeling for the pins securing the detailed coiffure, extracting each, which produced small cascades trickling down her back. The removal complete, he combed his fingers through, immersed his hands and pressed his lips to her forehead, employing a smooth decline to bury his face at last against the sweetness of her neck.

She smelled of dew-flecked roses at the end of a summer's eve rain. His breath quickened, his mind wandering sensuously, like the scent that caressed her soft skin after bathing. Christine's lashes set low on her cheeks, his touch drenching all senses, those hypnotic coils entwining her under the spell of his chanting whispers. "You are my refuge, Christine."

Strength subtly found a firm grasp upon her limp extremities after an unexpected tremor caused surrender to both composure and color. The satisfaction derived from such a response was complimentary to a man's affections, *his* most explicitly, which gave encouragement and excited anticipation. Tender phrases and trading of names floated between them, his gestures respectful. Soon, the taunting could go on no longer with her lips so close. His demise sealed, Christine's hand gently lifted the masque from his face. The warmth on his naked, translucent flesh was natural to behold, and the anguish of exposure drained with her light, brushing kisses. He could not keep quiet.

"During moments such as these, I forget. I imagine what it is like to be whole, that I am whole," his voice strained. "You make me feel as any other man."

Clearly vexed, Christine could not prevent the gravity of his simple comments from suspending her gaze at the uneven, improperly developed features meeting her eyes. In the past, her normal tendency had been an increase in compassion and optimistic praise, but this time, Patience staid entry into the campaign. Erik was continually fraught with doubt, always wading through the inescapable cruelties for a chance to feel worthy of common decency; then, when given his deepest desire, to be loved and considered—and not only by Christine, as the fortuitous interview with the old woman could attest—he slipped back under the accursed disbelief to be swallowed whole. His lids had descended at the gentle, weightless stroking, the velvety contact, and he, in a state of oblivion, saw nothing cross in her countenance as several nurturing passes eclipsed the need for speech; her actions meant more and the irritation dissolved.

Without warning, his palms pressed unfailing at her shoulders, fingers curling about the fabric of her blouse, massaging their hold to draw her near. His steps receded blindly, luring her to yield while yet in his grasp, all the while removing their presence from the balcony. "May I request," he began, his voice breaking the intensity of the moment, "your company for a walk along the shore, as I am in desperate want of a diversion."

She grinned approvingly, gave him his masque directly with a pat to his cheek and chest then prepared to depart.

Several levels of stairs lent their guidance, abutting on the lowest, to the winding path above a menagerie of pink granite formations; an architect's dream unfolded in the rough, just waiting for the right hands to coax some foreordained image from its inclusion. Erik, struck by the possibilities of what could indeed be extracted if given the opportunity, had excited the old memories of construction: Mazanderan, Constantinople, Paris, and the estate. He supposed it was not all reprehensible, architecturally speaking; some were rather warm and inviting, sections he would soon be sharing with Christine—those lower sections—those in the Opera cellars, which remained unknown to all but him these many years. *Yes, mine to ours.* These thoughts were dispensed with, upon an unrestrained inkling in Christine's designs, in reference to Erik. And, taking him quite by surprise in an expression of what may have seemed to some as an act of frivolity, she insisted it a necessity and he, feeling inclined to try something new, agreed.

"Sand... hmm?" he commented dryly.

"Have you never?"

Erik shook his head while removing his shoes and stockings, which were closely followed by the rolling up of both trouser legs. "No, never... at least not like this. I mean, I have certainly walked where there is no shortage, but barefoot and wet..."

They strolled hand in hand, unconcerned with time or destination, permitting Erik's mind to drift far from the present... *'Never' is forever a recurring negative leading me to experience happiness at the hands of Christine. We are days from being united and I am playing games of "what if." What if she had not entered my chamber of her own free will, to claim my heart, would I have sought no life at all? The blackest depths of my mental hell should have provided me plenty to explore in death, gladly adopting an insignificant exposure to compassion as sufficient. Ignorance is truly an idyllic drug, dulling all senses to remove pain of the unknown. Not knowing, that would have certainly kept me safe, blind from the worst experience of all: to have had a deep and abiding love, and then naught. The longer I reside near her, the bolder my conviction is of being entirely unalterable on the subject... that I cannot live without her.*

I look forward to what my Persian friend will have to say. He may consider my disposition quite changed for the better, my motives enigmatic, or improper and untrustworthy. I can only hope for approval. Tolerating my abhorrent personality and actions... after my treatment of him he should be considered a saint, if Allah accepts them.

Erik raised their clasped hands to lovingly grace Christine's with a kiss. Smiling shyly, her eyes chanced a quick look, to catch his eye perhaps, but instead, proved him otherwise employed.

Air caught in an embarrassed gasp of air, interrupting his thoughts as Erik realized he had stepped right into Christine. "Forgive me!" he exclaimed, moving to one side.

An evil smirk laced her expression. "There is nothing to apologize for. I intentionally placed myself in your path, Monsieur. I would prefer to engage all of your faculties."

"That garish an impasse, eh?" Tossing their things into an errant pile up the beach, and snapping her around, he pressed their hands to her lower back. "It might shock you to know just how often you weave your web through the very fibers of my being. I smile, laugh, play. . ." He looked down as the tide gently brushed over each foot. "If I stand in any one place for too long, I feel sand oozing between my toes and the foundation erode beneath my feet."

Christine moved to occupy the same space of sand by covering his feet with hers.

"You," he breathed sharply, "are impeccably close."

"I determined this to be the most rewarding stance for nomadic attentions."

"You did."

"I did, Monsieur Gautier."

"I see." Erik's cheek twitched unconsciously.

Her hands were slowly released to slide along the lapels of his waistcoat, where she pulled lightly on the end of his ascot, displacing it entirely for a remedy to bind up her flowing tresses. A languid sigh of anticipation marked the affection he most desired, as her arms continued their journey to curve around the back of his neck. His eyes dipped closed.

"I have been deprived most of the day, of my own doing, of course, but now," he asked deservedly, "would you consent to kiss me?"

The warm sweetness of her breath teased his mouth open, her lips barely there and then gone as she abruptly bypassed the intended destination to attack the weak spot below his ear.

"You!" Erik's eyes flashed wide and shut tight in an instant. "Oh, Christine, you are not fair in choice of location!"

"Am I not? There were no specifications. Besides," she sulked, "your masque is in the way."

He smiled somberly. "*That* is easily remedied,"

Looking to the few people dotting the vicinity, he felt secure enough to remove the unwanted barrier, allowing it to slip from his grasp. The cool air blended with their fond regard, his tears pouring undenied as they openly shared.

Unprepared for such a response, Christine tried to query, but was rotated to stand in front, permitting him partial anonymity. Then, touching his lips to her left ear he enlightened, "You liberate my emotions, desire *all* of me, the innocent requests seal my heart to yours. I stand here to be seen, but care only for you." His tears streamed down her neck as he shadowed her hand upon his cheek, pressing his moist face within the delicate protection. "I," he breathed slowly, "do not know if you will ever comprehend the depth of my love."

Erik shuddered, his arms and chest molding against her. He pulled tighter as if drawing sustenance to his unique existence; it was a solid mass of strength, asserting power to terminate life itself or caress the fragility of a butterfly. Once the quiet sobs tapered to stillness, and composure was attained, his hold eased.

"I need to talk, please," he said, leading her away from the encroaching tide.

The air was tepid, blowing indistinctly from the south, waves almost nonexistent in the calm lapping of water up against the white sandy beaches. Hues of purple and orange streaked the forefront of the evening's pastels as the blue faded to white, just above the horizon in drawing the day's performance to a close. Sitting together on the conforming sand, he was all strange contemplation void of sound. Severity had commissioned his conscience to set himself apart from pleasure and to think on why they had come; his thoughts presumably organized, he at once positioned himself most advantageously to be the recipient of Christine's enduring care.

"Your father," he commenced thoughtfully, reclining in her lap, "was he fond of Perros?"

Taken aback by the caprice, she glanced away, attempting

mentally to place its meaning in the awkward pause. Erik's hand rose to guide her sight to his.

"Yes," she said. "The sea reminded him of the old country, of the Scandinavian shores. He spent much of his time playing the violin along these beaches, dreaming, listening, remembering, rehearsing the legends. . ."

"And, what of the Angel of Music, what did he tell you?"

"That all great musicians and artists, at some point in their life, receive at least one visit. Sometimes it happens when the child is but an infant, and for some, not until age and effort twine."

"Christine, you know it was I who tended to your desires this winter past. I should like your forgiveness, if you can bear it, for the mockery I made of such a sacred remembrance."

His request startled her, eliciting an intake of breath, but oddly enough, no emotion. She sat stunned for several minutes. "How peculiar that I am not awash in sentiment. Your honest interest and desire bring a sweetened peace to my heart, a feeling I have not often experienced when in reflection. Perhaps it is a blessing, a way to venerate our union." Blinking, Christine dropped her distant stare to his. "I never considered the event anything other than a tribute, but I appreciate your solicitude, thank you." Erik gave a quick nod as Christine frowned. "Though, I am not sure I understand your interest."

"I should think several reasons plausible and seek, where it is most promising, to clear past folly prior to our marriage, wishing too, that we might limit our contact. I hope you will not be offended. I have no music nor occupation to channel these pent up, undulating emotions and thoughts that blindside me. Even now, I cringe at my conspiring insinuation of adjoining rooms—such juvenile entertainment, that my room had gained a respectful position in reference to the one in which you have lain all these months, yes, quite juvenile, I must admit. And I confess, willingly too, that I cannot always remain as celibate in thought as I do in action." He heard her breathing spasm and saw, upon an upward glance in the dimming sun, the shade of her coloring change. "I have said too much and at the same time, not enough." Erik could not contain longer the passions burdening his mind, and stammered on. "I will apologize up front, but you must know how I manage, how vulnerable I am. You should know of my natural concerns in regard to the more private, intimate matters of our relationship. We have been quite open, thus far, and I should feel secure in confiding such things to my wife, should I not?"

Christine smiled timidly. "Erik, I can assure you that I am prepared to listen and proceed in accordance with the course we deem fit. I shall take no displeasure and wish to confer no feelings of guilt."

Kissing her hand he encouraged its welcome journeys about his face and neck. "This," referring to her current endeavors, "I can tolerate well, the motion subdues the want to test the parameters we have justly set. At present, I do not trust my judgment during such moments out on the balcony and must keep myself busily employed. There will be much to engage our time once we arrive in Paris, to be sure, but it is the simple joy of being idle that becomes dangerous."

"Your feelings are quite valid and I respect you for vigilance in adjusting for the unexpected. Indeed, I have nothing but admiration."

The sun, as it was nearly three hours below the horizon, had departed, leaving Erik and Christine to finish their conversation under cloak of night. Neither minded, and before it was too late, they shook and brushed vigorously the sand from their belongings and returned to their rooms; cordiality parted them at their outer doors with a soft, albeit short, show of affection, which had both glowing in the discovery a renewed verve brings with honorable intentions.

IT WAS A RATHER tedious night of unease. Why could he not relax? He should have slept soundly for the walk; the canvassing of topics, the contentment from their choice of mild sentiment, was all very satisfying. Agitation and nerves forced him to his feet to make ready for the day, despite Dawn having neglected any hint that Darkness renounce its hold on the morn. The affable passage would be soon, he felt it, and checked the small clock upon the mantle. *Five.* Erik heard nothing to affirm Christine had awakened. He sighed, his mood declining with hasty steps out to the balcony. No comfort was found and all he succeeded in accomplishing was an exciting of his circulation while pacing about in the chill. Turning from the scene outside, he reentered the room and had his sight drawn immediately to an envelope resting just his side of the adjoining door. Snatching it up he greedily devoured the contents, paled, cursed his lack of conviction and denial of instinct then speedily gathered coat, cane, and hat for a rendezvous at sunrise. The contents of the note read as follows. . .

Dearest Erik,

I am gone to set plaguing memories behind me. The churchyard and my father's grave are excellent just prior to sunrise, a time to mentally refresh. I will be fine, as I have been in the past. I would enjoy your company atop the moor overlooking the sea.

Until daybreak,
Christine

Walking to the sound of her own footfalls in the hush of the early morning, she felt invigorated, as the damp, moist air purged the veil of rest from her lungs. The moon shone low and inconsistent from the pewter-laced clouds it hung beneath, having found a full night's quest mounted in vain for its equal, that it might commune before returning ever-faithful the next.

Christine meditated now, the same as when she had closed her eyes to retire, freely able to rehearse some of the questions and subsequent discussions from those hours before. *It appeared that Erik* was making a concerted effort to know my father as I knew him; perhaps he sought perspective on filial connection or as an example for some future reference. I should have asked; he seemed intrigued by the experiences, and I could not oppose his wish as I felt no anxiety from his interest. In any case, I dearly appreciate his noble effort.

Slipping unseen through the gate into the churchyard, she paused, reluctant to press forward beyond the shrouded remains of the past. She could make no accounting for the strange feeling of being unwanted, but it was not until an ominous shiver spilled the length of her back that she dispelled with fortitude, the gloom affixing her to that entry. Reverently, she moved through the rows of tombstones, aimlessly diverted by the differences people seem to impose upon those departed, the affluence and simplicity, side by side the uncaring souls they lay to rest.

"Oh," she inhaled softly, when she happened into a freshly mounded site, a doused lantern and shovel not yet collected. Prayer was offered, the sign of the cross made and her pilgrimage continued in relief, grateful that the unexpected was nothing more.

Having pulled her cloak in closer to guard against the morbid bite, her warm exhales mixed with regularity in the chill, forming a ghostly fog to linger in the air. Polished surfaces, varying inscriptions etched, stories shared; her mind wandered over the notion of so many gone and those yet to arrive, and of ancestral experiences to be repeated and generationally enhanced. Turning at the foot of her father's grave, Christine knelt in prayer, not sorrowfully, but in joy and thankfulness of heart to share.

Finishing all she had come to do, she gained her feet in anticipation of her beloved's coming and glanced to one side. *The roses.* They were there, clinging to their stony trellises, adorning several and eclipsing some almost entirely. Most of the blooms had arched, sighed fully open, and were singed brown by the light frost save one; a bud, hidden between several others, it had been protected as a protégé of hope for the spring to come. Her finger traced the perfectly formed, tightly closed petals, waiting for the sun's rays to encourage a burst of crimson. *Ours is a similar circumstance. Each petal cleaves to the next in trust, the crucial key to unlock the secrets unknown beneath each whisper thin layer. All it would take to crush the refined precision is one malevolent hand mista—*

The vice clamped across her mouth, suffocating her thoughts, replacing her solace with burning terror as the grating voice dripped menacingly through her mind.

"Well now, looky wha' we 'ave 'ere. Young women, such as yo'self, ought t' know better than t' be out alone."

Wild panic widened Christine's eyes as she fought back the urge to cry. *The feelings, the premonition. . . I should have waited. . .* her inner strength chastised in retreat. Frightened tears escaped their restraint, making way for conditions to swell and heave against the floodgates then erupt.

"Oh, poor, sweet li'l bird, yo're scared. There, there, I wouldn't do yo' harm, such a pretty thing. . . come!" he snarled.

She could smell a putrid mixture of whiskey and vomit radiating from the right side of her head. It was excruciating in pungency, enough to make her insides churn. She silently pled as the man's body moved forward, her only option, compliance, and however minimally established it was, was done in order to keep whatever hope of distance she had, maintained. Tender skin flared from the abrasive assault, her arm wrenched painfully up the center of her back as she was forced toward the little Breton church. He pushed the doors open, entered and haphazardly shoved at them with his heel to conceal the crime from the light of the world. What desecration to be had within the walls of a sanctuary! The pressure against her arm compelled quicker movement as she was constrained to kneel in submission before an altar.

"There'll be no screamin', Mademoiselle," he hissed into her ear. "Am I understood?" She nodded. "That's a good girl."

His tone patronized, making insignificant the delicacy. Oh, how that phrase spurned and roused her ire! People had always referred to her as 'a good girl,' remembered the 'good little girl.' It was Erik who treated her as a lady, a woman esteemed, and now to be violated? *Erik, forgive me.*

The man uncovered her mouth slowly, apprehensive that she might still cry out. There came nothing and he relaxed, but the very moment the man released her arm, Christine pushed back, knocking him off balance. It was enough for momentary freedom.

Angered by his own stupidity, having underestimated this to be an easy catch, he reached out unerringly, grabbing both her legs. She fell hard to her forearms, again at the mercy of this squalid demon. His hands were at once upon her; grasping her by the hair, he yanked.

"Feisty, eh? All th' better," he grunted. "And jus' so I'll 'ave no more trouble..." She saw the glint of a blade flash in front of her face, his weight imposing as his dark form loomed hideously above her. "Wi' such a prize fo' me patience, a bit o' insurance will keep yo' quiet." He sneered, the knife coming closer, it pressed up under her chin, causing her body to become rigid.

"Please, do not..." she pleaded, unable to bear the sight.

"Ay, an' a proper one, eh? Do not?" he scoffed. "Oh, now beggin' jus' ain't very 'tractive. Of all th' se'imental gifts placed about these 'ere gravestones, *yo'* are me bonus. Yeh see, wi' people leav'in all manner o' precious trinkets fo' their dear'st departed loved ones," he bragged, pulling at her clothing, "and as guardian o' these 'ere grounds... well, I jus' takes care o' things at no charge to 'em." He was exactly above her.

She gasped, lightly wailing as the searing pain burned the full length of her jaw, the tip of the blade, unerring.

"Yes, how fo'unate." His hot breath wilted her to a mass of numb flesh, his hands groped, his face twisting in glee as he began to force himself upon her sweetness, but then all froze, suspended; an abrupt halt to all premeditated action came with a hard, purposeful gulp and quick intake of air. What despicable dragging and stretch of the imagination could one endure? He moved not, his eyes dilated in a stroke of panic and screwed up tight as a cold blade of steel found its calculated resting place. Now it was he who would quickly empathize with his prey.

"You, sir. . . " the words were coated in mesmerizing venom, "would do well to take your hands from that which does not belong to you. Defiling what *I* have gone through great pains to keep clean will ensure a most untimely demise."

The man was at a loss as to how he might proceed in such a position. Erik's sword had penetrated his clothing and was positioned well to his crotch; one wrong move and vital parts would be irrevocably separated from their God-given placement. The knife slid from the man's now shaking fingers as he gingerly backed up in canine surrender, emancipating Christine from the disgrace and horror inflicted.

"Your *brief* fortune is indeed great, that I should choose not to defile holy ground with your blood or expose tenderness to the dreadful shock and brutality I am most certainly able to commit. You should run, and run hard, before my capricious mind is persuaded otherwise, for death will seem sweet in comparison."

Haste had never engaged such a tenacious pupil, as fear and the excruciating, almost incapacitating bite of the sword upon removal, sent evil to flight.

Upon the dull thud of the chapel doors, Erik carefully deposited the sword at the altar's steps where Christine had withdrawn. She shook uncontrollably beneath the torn cloak, unresponsive to activity, blind and unaware, far away from his presence and comfort. He gently reached to her and she cowered, avoiding him. Numb from the ordeal, but in tune with her most primal feelings, she knew Erik's intensity had yet to recede; it was that lust to kill preventing contact. She wished to hide and was desperate to be clean, even her subconscious denied relief. It was her fault. Home, yes, home was safe; she wanted home and. . . where was Erik?

Already standing, Erik paced the floor in an agitated fashion, fist pressed to his mouth in comprehension, and then he returned to kneel before Christine. Tears burst, silently washing away the stains of filth and grime from her cheeks. She gazed into his eyes then suddenly turned from him, bent in shame. "Forgive me," she said humbly, reaching out to him.

Without delay he took her up in his arms and rose, walked hastily to the back of the church, set her down on a pew and knelt again at her feet. "Hush," his voice soothed, ignoring the recent petition. "Tell me, please tell me. Did he hurt you? I arrived before. . ."

Without word, she tipped her head up and back toward the left, exposing the gash along her jaw line, shutting her eyes to the breath that had seized in Erik's chest. His ungloved hand inspected it at length. "And?" he enquired, fury garnishing his clipped tone.

She shook her head. "I. . . he. . ." The shameful scene engulfed her physically and she bolted for the door, her success at relieving the contents of her stomach inconspicuously being realized upon immediate exit from the church. Erik held her steady, pulled back her hair as she wretched, and held her exhausted form when her body had nothing left to expel but tears. No more was asked, no more was spoken, as Erik secured his few belongings before carrying Christine back to the inn, cradled against his chest.

"MONSIEUR! WHAT HAS happened?" The concierge met their bedraggled appearance in alarm as Erik exploded through the doors.

"Summon a physician quickly!" Erik's guttural demand elicited urgent attention as his figure stormed, panting through the foyer and up the stairs.

Within a matter of minutes a flurry of people converged: several maids, the concierge himself, and soon after, a Breton commissary and finally, a physician; most were lightly astonished by the masqued gentleman, but paid little heed as the young woman was attended to and her needs genially met.

After a time, the physician pronounced Christine to be suffering from light shock, had cleansed the wound, and upon a thorough examination, found her to be free from violation save a bit of soreness and bruising. This, to the relief of Erik, was pinnacle to the situation, for now he could concentrate on other more pressing necessities. Christine was assisted, as much as she preferred, with her personal toilette while Erik changed their itinerary, requesting that Mademoiselle's clothing be removed from sight and disposed of discreetly. The concierge made himself out to be a most affable benefit, useful in multiple venues, but especially in his locating a clothier to attend to the specific desires of his patron, alleviating a wealth of anxiety in the process. Once the aforementioned details commenced, Erik turned to the patiently waiting commissary, a first, in meeting the world head-on. Having never had the occasion to rely on others to dispense a pronounced verdict determined in his mind, this would indeed, be a most difficult feat. An accurate account of all that took place was given, then Erik let go the responsibility and debt of possible repercussions, hard as it was. Pride expanded his chest, Christine would be proud.

Late morning saw a surprising resolution with a speedy apprehension of the man in question, which provided Erik with a satisfactory conclusion to his nearly implacable opinion of legal systems in general. Just as Erik had predicted would come about naturally in the course of the day, the perpetrator had sought help for a most embarrassingly incurred injury, one that would have proved risky if not treated properly; and lastly, the knife was recovered in evidence of said crime.

Straightening his tailcoat, Erik took leave of his room and met with the maid recently exiting Christine's. "How is she?" he enquired.

"Very solemn, but well, Monsieur."

"And the clothing and flowers?"

The woman could not help smiling at the attentiveness and set his mind to rest in a hurry. "All has been replaced to Monsieur's specifications, the bouquet and clothing were graciously received. Do not trouble yourself, we have made every accommodation."

"I thank you, Madame," he replied with a bow.

The woman curtsied and went away privily, leaving Erik to walk the hall and pace the confines of his hotel room. How he wished to be within the passageway to Christine's dressing room at the Opera, to hear and know. But here, he was ostracized *again*, destined to be the stranger, the outsider in their love because of the cruel ignorance of another. Leaning against the hard paneled barrier his hands balled in resentment. He hated, cursed in righteous indignation then waited for some meager scrap of acknowledgment. Feeling he may as well become mad, he shoved the doors wide to the balcony and went to lean at the rail. *There is absolutely nothing to be done; I know I shall become insane if I remain longer without intelligence. Her thoughts, countenance, spirit. . . I shall have to refrain from any assumption and stress fortitude in awaiting inducement to know how we are to bear this misfortune, for the repercussions may be heavy. Why now? Why, when I have yet to experience, would another presume it a right to steal from me? How am I to manage without her touch. . . damnable, selfish man. . . ugh! The both of us! I am no better than he, for I think more to myself than to her. Oh, Christine!*

A timid knock startled the wallowing, he pivoted, drawing to full height, and placed his right hand to the small of his back in a majestic display of nobility; the latch clicked open. Erik dared not move, terrified of frightening the trusted advance, he permitted his gaze to be put forth in regularity, leaving breathless the awe in which he stood.

Christine entered cautiously and he yielded implicitly with a deep bow, and she, responding in kind did likewise. They were riveted in all aspects for neither moved nor barely breathed, it was as if meeting for the first time and anticipating the hope of an introduction from an acquaintance of both.

"Erik, I can no—"

"Christine, you must allow—"

Their layering of speech brought a blush and an awkward smile to each. How especially evident to Erik it was that her composure was altered, exquisitely reserved, and to Christine, that his could not be any more formally dignified.

"For two people who seldom find themselves at a loss for subject or in requisite of prompt to keep a conversation lively, we neither of us in fact, seem inclined to forge the mode of communication in comfort." His direct observation helped to set ease, but the difficulties brooked would not be as trifling to overcome, so he began with attentions to her basic well-being. "You are improved?"

"Yes, very much. Your mental acuity and consideration to details, some of which I would have to admit to overlooking, were and are, greatly appreciated. Nothing," she expressed sincerely, "has been lost on me or gone unnoticed."

Relief overspread his countenance, for she understood all his efforts. He made sure that a woman should meet her needs for emotional sensitivity, of which there came to be several, the least of these, to alleviate the mortification of hovering men; the meaning of purity, as it related to the deep blue color of the skirt and short tailored jacket, with the white, pleated blouse laid prettily underneath; and in reference to the flowers, a variegated spray with a single, white rose in the center.

"Will you not come inside? I do feel rather strange conversing with your statuesque frame outdoors, primed as if for some bird to perch on your shoulder."

Rattled from his engrossing gratuity, he slipped back into the room, soundless and nervously distant.

"I have much to say," she stated hastily, guilt motivating her to jump right to the point. "And much to apologize for."

"Nothing could be further from the truth," came his unrestrained comment.

"Please, just listen."

"All right, all right." His hand went up then gestured for her to continue.

"Because of my headstrong independence I placed many cherished aspects of our future at precarious risk and I feel it a most grievous err in judgment. There are sequences, too numerous to play out, any one of which may have resulted in a tragic ending. I could have spared us the agony. I could not even bring myself to confide my pain and suffering when you were so willing to accept whatever I would impart. It is hard to bear the assumptions, but more so then. I regret so much."

Erik paced, too distraught at the very idea that she was now mitigating the role that that filthy swine had played—words failed him, but not her.

"I have led a sheltered existence to deliberate evil, which taints or smothers good, and despite the crime, I am glad for the perspective gained, if only by a small measure... all the brutality endured by you and I shrink at a mere repulsing taste."

"Christine!" he blurted. "You are being irrational, what that man did, and I am thankful he was wholly unsuccessful, is not your fault! There is no possible way you could have foreseen what took place. Nor, for that matter, would I wish my experiences in life to be 'tasted' by you in any amount."

Stunned by the passionate rise to defend, but remiss at the unsavory decry pronounced, Christine weakened. Doubt, confusion, and reticence all shown, she went quiet. Erik believed it resolve, to maintain some level of control on herself.

"Independence is a fine quality," he said, rubbing his jaw in forced calm. "I did not mean to belittle the valid feelings brought about from this morning, I am pained for a strategy and depend entirely upon you. Please inform me of how I should best proceed, what you would have me do."

"Please," she asked softly, her view of him blurring. "I need to know how you feel, toward me."

"I love you, Christine." This declaration was bestowed in earnest while stepping in her direction. "My sentiments are unchanged, unconditional, and unwavering."

Suddenly the tumult of her heart spilled freely, bewildered in the extreme as she reflected on the contradiction of his words and behavior. "Then, why such indifference of familiarity?"

"Oh, my dear, I was afraid you would shy away from touch and wished not to burden you with the imposition of choice nor of discomfort. I guess my desire to see things in a prudential light overshadowed common sense in the matter and drove me to excessive insensitivity the other way. Although, I ought not to have presumed more for this is nothing related to practicality but due in part to a mode of self-preservation; I would rather have deprived myself of your touch than have you shrink from me." He shied from her vision. "Perhaps, I could not have done right whatever I chose to do."

Christine's complexion sparkled at the timidity displayed. "Women amidst emotion certainly take an unfair advantage."

"They do. May I?" he asked, motioning for her hand. "I shall make a comprehensive endeavor at research, which may or may not consume the balance of my life."

Christine blushed as his lips pressed firmly to her palm. "Erik," she said, "if you would not mind, I should be glad to bid farewell to the Bretagne coast for more favorable conditions."

"You are sure?"

"I am. Our time here is spent and in every way, complete."

Chapter Fifteen

Almost as quickly as a carriage could be sent for the couple set out, and by midday had reserved themselves into a compartment on an evening train bound for Paris. In comparison to the previous day's situation this was, as determined by Erik, so far above amiable that he vowed never to accept travel accommodations of anything less, whether or not plans were known in advance.

Their northeasterly journey proceeded from one province to the next as they talked amidst many types of illumination and without social constraint. From the unrefined coast through the relatively sparse stretch of inland, night's view faded to naught as a smudge of coal, to overtly descend and prevent the mind's eye from any undue stimulus. It was a scheme ill refuted as Erik made frequent returns to the window, though he could do no more than see his reflection in the glass. He would stare, and then walk the compartment with the brevity of a caged animal, while Christine brought forward the most prominent subject of that morning. Apart from his past, the horrific sight—to behold the loathsome rape of innocence at any level, especially when it threatened such a precious gift, their gift—was exceeding injurious, because the particulars prefacing his arrival within the church had been out of his control, and now, all he could do was listen to the escalating narrative. Erik, in turn, sat across from her, bridging the awkward chasm with her hands in his, stroking them nervously before sharing the pent up, angry frustrations and shock mentally linked to the picture now emblazoning itself. In most aspects, the incident was too overbearing for more discussion, which left him incensed.

"Will you not take a seat here?" She motioned next to her when he stood to wear upon the floor for the umpteenth time. "We have ventured from our own insecurities in order to address many considerations of the other; the impact seems less, I think, and the concerns are narrowed, except you still resist being close."

Erik quit the excessive pacing and spread the tails of his coat in such an agitated fashion that he looked to be genuinely put out by the suggestion.

"It bothers you still, that I flinched when you offered to console me."

Rubbing the light stubble along his chin he looked at her, guilt stamped across his countenance. "Yes," he whispered. "At the moment, a lifetime of conditioning cannot be helped."

"And it bothers you that he. . ."

"Yes! Yes, and I am ashamed for thinking it, for being so selfish as to burden you, but it hurts Christine, it hurts to feel betrayal again. Though unsuccessful, he. . . It pains me to know that the person I value most, cherish beyond life itself, was touched and exposed to such abhorrence of actions, actions that should be sacred and tender." As elbows dropped to each knee, his hand deliberately rose, ripping the masque away to bury his face tearfully into his palms. "Forgive me."

This revelation at once drew forth a long, forlorn sigh from her and she pondered whether it would be well to leave the topic. Talking only succeeded in unearthing more than they were able to put to rest, but to her astonishment, and certainly before she had a moment to recollect the path she was tending, he was as near as he had ever been with her hand draped about his; it was pressed tightly to his lips.

He quietly expressed his love then released her hand to run his finger along the delicate flesh of her cheeks as she leaned into the palm cupping her face. She needed his acceptance.

"I cannot wound you further, I cannot," he professed.

"Hold me, please?" To this entreaty Erik put his arm gently around her shoulders and hugged her.

Memory served Christine a feeble dose of amnesia when she woke some hours later to find herself similarly positioned in Erik's embrace, the exact moment fatigue claimed ownership, unclear. Neither had budged a particle, for the exhaustion had procured their reserves and was yet in effect. She moved little whilst she studied the tenderness of his hand, resting protectively over hers, and endeavored to make a closer inspection.

Erik had long, captivating fingers, sleek lines filled with enormous strength, the veins bulging under his tanned skin. This coloring had been absent for more than a decade with his compulsion to remain below, in the Opera House cellars; with only moon and candles to hue his flesh it was but a slight wonder he evinced more than a waxy coating back then. The rough exterior belied the deftness of touch underneath, and as she turned his hand over in hers, there was seen a melding of both experience and opposition; the calluses showed the skill of a craftsman, but the smoothness of finger tip, so often preserved by the gloves he wore, safeguarded the sensitivity of his strongest, most dominate sense, that of touch.

The act of upending Erik's hand caused a large intake of air, a constrained moment rousing him to awareness and then, once realizing, he pulled Christine snug, kissed her temple sensuously and whispered, "I look forward to waking with you in my arms."

They looked deeply into the other's eyes, the moment igniting an instant of passion to drive away all foreboding thoughts and phrases last mentioned. His steadfast gaze roamed the view before him in its entirety and lowered, centering on her mouth.

She smiled, disarming him completely. "Air is not in short supply, leastwise that I am aware, and though your avoidance of waste is admirable, it is unwise. Breathe, Erik."

"Thank you, no," was his reply as he kissed her full on, both hands tenderly cradling her head on either side. At this point, he donned blinders in a demonstrative show of affection, his heart soaring in her reception and approbation. This meant the world to Christine as well, that his feelings were as he related. His lips slid to her chin then ghosted along the wound beginning to heal, caressing in their desire to erase even the physical memory that existed.

Gingerly, her hands defied the fervor venting undirected and suspended the ardor by pushing against his chest. Erik gave a modest bow of his head, a wry grin lifting in the same intensity as the flush up her cheekbones.

"See?" He gestured to dawn's first light making known their surroundings, and stole an additional kiss when Christine glanced. "A new day and the outskirts of Paris."

"How daring," she stated.

"In every way, for I shall not have many opportunities afforded me."

"Not likely. I believe you will create opportunity at every turn. Come now, I wish the return of your hand, I was not finished."

"Finished?" Erik's brow creased. "How is it that you may finish and not I?"

Christine raised hers in surprise. "And how is it, Monsieur, that you, in all seriousness, could ask such a question?" A conclusion favored by both was indeed the granting of his hand to her as they sat content the short distance into the Gare de Montparnasse station.

Chapter Sixteen

Erik handed Christine down from the brougham amid the autumn leaves swirling the streets. The diverse groups gathering and disbursing her attention were caught by the transformation of what was once a pliable green, into dry, fragile crumbs beneath the city's livelihood of commotion; an interminable dust blowing from the wings of winter's prelude. A touch to her arm channeled the subconsciousness of thought to the present, at Erik's side.

"Monsieur, Madame, enjoy your stay," came the exhortation from the young gentleman, bowing almost prostrate upon excusing himself from the room. Christine nearly laughed.

Erik nodded absently as he watched Christine head straight for the double doors emptying onto the balcony. One grand sweep pushed them to capacity, opening their welcome to the City of Light. She breathed deeply, embracing herself against the differences. The smells, sights, sounds, and feelings were dissimilar to what she remembered, now that she had reference to compare them with. Her father knew, he could differentiate between the city and country styles of living; this is what drove him into solitude. It was the abundance, the synthetic replication in society that all was well through gaiety and false pretense, which assaulted his very being, knowing suffocation of the soul was bound to occur. Christine understood because she felt the unrest and longed to return home.

Erik moved directly behind to blanket her with his embrace. "Are you chilled?"

"From the inside." She peered right. "I have lived a fair portion of my life here, but the past six months have made a stranger of me and I am ill at ease. The only thing which gives any measure of comfort is the Seine River."

"If this is your only means of comfort then I shall sink into despair." He felt her tighten in upon his grasp. "Perhaps I have committed a disservice by keeping you too far removed."

His hold loosened, allowing Christine to circle and meet his gaze. "Need I remind you of my love?" She searched for acknowledgment and received nothing but blank disbelief. "I can assure you that I have no intention of relinquishing my choice. If I had any inclinations of deserting you I would have executed them in haste on the first day, but I did not, and the incentives which bind me to you are now of greater strength, they cannot be severed."

"This is how you feel?"

"It is, yes. So, why burden yourself with such destructive skepticism?"

"Because... whenever I have hoped for, or sought after the desires of my heart, it ends in disappointment. Yesterday, doubts began anew. If the felicity of the past months ceased here and now, I would savor in my mind and heart all that I have learned, everything I have experienced with you, and I would be grateful." His voice trailed to a reluctant mumble. "You have not denied me, apart from that which we intentionally prohibit, and rightly so," a tear of confession brimmed, "... I fear the chains of reality clamping down on my brief fortune."

Christine considered his claims prior to commenting. "You may recall a certain young woman who had vocal possibilities, superficial at first, with a quality ascribed by some to be the mimicry of some garroted creature?"

"Humph," he snorted, his memory serving him all too well. "I believe I know this woman to whom you refer. And it is your opinion that she would forgive so readily the verbal debauchery?" The diva Carlotta and her stream of insults against Christine blared.

"I suppose, to have such a perfect recollection would be persecution enough, but only for she who remembers and that, in and of itself, is a waste, a petty triviality upon which to dwell. It would be more prudent to exemplify the change in humility, to express gratitude by showing what marvelous works may be accomplished with guidance and belief to infuse one's confidence. The influence of one can do much, just think what will occur when the effort is redoubled between two."

"This," his tone roughened by emotion, "is one of many reasons for my love of you. You speak truthfully. There is nothing we cannot endure or make successful if we have the best interest of our relationship at heart, thank you." With his fervor recommitted to their love, he grasped her longingly by the shoulders, palms touching and lifting her arms to rest around his neck; he held her madly to his chest, not wishing for the moment when they would depart to commence preparations.

Erik and Christine stayed only long enough to freshen, then set out on foot to call upon the Girys. Despite the early hour, as it was considered by some standards, they knew they would not find Madame unprepared. Each walked in quiet thought and expectation; to be comfortable was quite impossible, wondering what may or may not proceed over the course of the next three days, but they had resolved to bear all, come what may.

The knock came at precisely nine, a firm, demanding petition exacting immediate notice.

"Maman! Do you suppose?" Meg jumped to supposition.

"Meg, please! You have leapt upon every knock this week!" Mme Giry quickly stifled the excitement. "Now, compose yourself."

"I will. There is nothing to fret about," Meg said, gripping the rail. "I can assure you."

Mme Giry descended the stairs from their living quarters and opened the door to a gentleman, to whom she had never been formally introduced, but to one she was well acquainted through mysterious correspondence, and one fixed account given her by the Persian; there was no denying who he was. Standing at full height, just above six feet, and dressed in dark tails, an emerald and copper waistcoat, and a luminously white shirt and ascot, he made a formidable appearance. The masque and cloak, the gloves, his attire, and air as a whole, embodied the very essence of whom she pictured in her imagination, if she were ever granted a chance meeting.

He bowed. "Madame Giry, it is a pleasure to meet, at last."

"Yes, indeed, Monsieur, that it is. Please, you are welcome." She gestured inward, moving back to allow unhindered passage.

"If I may, I have brought someone with me who claims familiarity as well and is desirous to be reacquainted."

"By all means, Monsieur—" She wavered internally before this stranger, hesitating at the lack of surname, and now there was to be another? No notice was taken and no outward countenance was lost.

He stepped back and held out his hand, which was soon joined by a slim set of feminine fingers wrapping over the top of his. "I should like to introduce, my fiancée." He smiled broadly as he led her inside, entering afterward afore the astonishment. "Really, Madame," he whispered in passing, "it is as though you have had some spiritual enlightenment bestowed to your features."

"Christine! Christine! Oh, Maman what a wondrous surprise! Come, Come!" she beckoned from the double doors of the upstairs drawing room.

Mme Giry had yet to display emotion or comment, and relied

solely upon Meg's zealous personality to bridge the awkwardness of thought preventing her from being more civil. About the time Mme Giry entered the room, she had managed to become quite hospitable and was soon echoing her daughter's invitation to sit. Erik kept his guard up; the repetitive glare he elicited from Mme Giry was unmistakable and accusatory in nature, hardly the damper he would have wished for Christine's return. His intuition summoned a wary mandate that he resume the stance of an outsider, to beware a provoked sting from the female gender, however unsolicited.

Christine and Meg were already thoroughly entrenched in greetings and girlish ovations that accompany such a long absence, but quickly quieted when a lull declared them to be the only participants in their party of four. Erik had removed himself to the window, cloak over arm, occupying the initial moments by looking out over the garden, but charming as it was, it would not curtail the sullen atmosphere foreshadowing the conversation to come.

Meg had just seated herself on the sofa as Christine walked to Erik's side. "I see your discomfort, what can I do?" she inquired softly.

"You have already eased," he responded, shaking his head. He tenderly kissed her hand. Then, taking her coat, he draped both over the back of the chair where Christine felt inclined to sit, near Meg, but across from Mme Giry, which left him to wander lightly with an arm adhered securely behind his back.

"Oh, Christine, you are so lovely," Meg openly complimented. "You seem at peace since we were last together."

Christine flushed. "Very much, in fact, more so than ever before. I am glad that it is evident." Erik was but a stride from where Christine was seated and reached for her shoulder at the mention of her happiness; she covered his hand affectionately.

"Yes, I would have to agree that your distraction is greatly, reduced." A sly grin pierced Mme Giry's grim features, carrying its couched meaning to her intended target. Erik's brow shot up, signifying reception. "And I guess, since we presumed one to be dead and the other to have gone off to some distant place with another, never to grace us with even minuscule knowledge of her well-being again, that the next obvious query to pose should be relating to your whereabouts these past months, if you care to include us in such matters."

"Swift and to the point, are we not, Madame?" Erik asked in cool civility.

"Always."

"I," Christine ventured quickly into the conversation, "should like to apologize for my lack of consideration. At the time, I felt the decision best, not involving more people than was necessary. My guardian, Madame Valerius, was well aware of the situation and advised me to forego correspondence, even to her, so I might focus on addressing the issues confronting me; she saw what I had yet to discover. I knew I would be causing concern, but I had to commence with who I was, before reaching out to others; the very foundation of my happiness depended upon it."

Meg listened intently to Christine, but found herself unable to prevent the darting glances from recurring in upward abundance to the gentleman situated neatly behind the woman, who so clearly captivated *his* attention.

"Mademoiselle Giry?" His voice startled Meg in such a violent fashion that every ounce of composure drained from her; she colored afresh, flagging her deplorable manners. "You will forgive my interruption." His excuse was directed toward Christine with a gentle brush to her cheek. "I do believe we are proceeding under a rather false, if not untoward presumption and omission, which should be rectified sooner than later."

"I beg your pardon," Meg said, "I did not mean to stare."

"Unfortunate fact, intentional or not," he stated in nonchalance. "Comes with the eccentric display; an embodiment or reminder to us all of what we choose to keep hidden." He shrugged, gesturing to his masque. "I am curious, does the personification satisfy the rumors I hear told?"

"Yes. . . uh, well, no. . ." His sincerity and direct front unnerved Meg's answers. "Forgive my blundering and childish curiosities. It is just. . . well, I have postulated from the stories, and from what Mother has conveyed, and you are more, in every sense of the word, than I expected. I could not imagine such a refined human being, flesh or no, Monsieur."

"I thank you." His dignified bow made her blush deeper; he seemed pleased.

Christine looked directly at Meg and mouthed a heartfelt thank you. Her friend could not have conferred a more meaningful compliment upon their first meeting than she then had.

"And since you have the floor, Monsieur, you might as well—"

"Not one for depth or breadth of conversation, I see," he broke in curtly. "I too, if you must know, felt the necessity seclusion offers; however, mine is quite a different matter. Death is rather final, a burden upon those it touches, but it can often be the means of relief and rebirth. Would you not say, Madame, that a direct relation of truth is a most gratifying release?"

"I can, Monsieur."

"Then it could be said, of the deceased, that his passing was in the best interest of those intimately or remotely connected with the Opera House, could it not?"

"Yes, Monsieur, it could." Mme Giry watched his peculiar stance, eyeing the calm while at the same time listening to the sound of accountability slip from the shoulders of one so cunning.

"Then, I believe the matter to be closed. The man who you see standing before you, is Erik Gautier." Another graceful bow put an end to this explanation, but exacerbated Mme Giry's frustration, her eyes flecked with heat, the gall! Erik caught the economy of her glare.

He had involved her and her daughter, alluded to his own death as though it were that of another, when it was perfectly obvious that he, as *said deceased,* was standing in a lively manner in their presence; a most certainly presumptuous and highly contemptuous display, not to mention morally wrong, he knew. Mme Giry knew. He twisted life to his benefit by deception if possible, *had* done so, but what of Christine? She knew of the reticence they must maintain. *Trust her, she loves you.*

"We shall leave well enough alone, when this last item is laid to rest." Mme Giry rose and drifted in purposeful fashion, everyone's gaze following in apprehension as she made her way to a small writing desk. Erik leaned on the mantle to his left, agitation building in distaste for the impertinent treatment Mme Giry purposely disbursed. He could see well, the deliberate gait and poise closing in for that sting, pausing—yes, the pause—to await some sort of reaction, like she knew the letter given over into Christine's possession would thus educe. She was not long in standing, for an intake of air came immediately, hitting a vulnerable spot between Erik and Christine at the sight of the addressor, Monsieur Raoul Comte de Chagny. Erik shifted, backing up a step as Christine sat motionless, eyes fixed unseeing in the present.

"The letter arrived not a full week ago." Mme Giry's voice became factual. "Monsieur Chagny enclosed it within another, posted from the Americas, where he mentioned briefly his commission aboard a ship sailing from Brest."

Christine's hands trembled and she turned, looking for Erik, who, upon immediately sensing her distress replaced his hand to her shoulder. "I should like to read it aloud, if I may."

"Are you sure?" Erik asked.

"I am."

Unsure of what to expect, the seal was unfastened to place before her eyes several pages of script, which were unfolded with a touch of reserve and awe, the unknown written in an unsteady, nervous hand, and dated 18 July 1878.

Dearest Christine,

If this letter should ever grace your delicate hands I shall be forever grateful to place an end to that which remains sore between us. I have found myself, upon many occasions, prepared to write, but felt constrained by lack of will and desire to express wholly what resides in my heart. Apart from our history, which I shall address momentarily, I had news of my brother's death after my arrival here in America; this has also been a contributor to the reluctance of lending pen to paper as a mysterious business indeed, but I return now to the former.

Parting from you on that painful night, with your words ringing in my ears, 'how unconscionable it would be for you to continue in the aforementioned plans when your sentiments lay elsewhere,' I believe is what was conveyed, has haunted my very existence for weeks. I pondered long and hard. Needless to say, I was under the prescribed drugs of Shock and Denial, which were wondrous for subsistence at that time. I was numb and past feeling, but as the encasement around my senses began to dwindle and wear, I was finally able to accept the turn of events as they applied; more than a few perspectives were made apparent, and came off as a great deal more reliable than my own.

A blow to the male ego is always hard to swallow at first, and I think I can easily pronounce this defect upon all of my sex; to be given leave to take you from one who I considered entirely devoid of sanity, only to have you quit my designs as well; complete mortification to say the least, and how utterly humbling; to think I had triumphed in your behalf, only to succeed in securing your preliminary felicity to the unhappy ending of mine.

I willingly admit to the fantasy of being the gallant hero, to being the one who would save you from your inexplicable connection to the past, from the intangible, and inevitably from yourself to the freedom you were unable to attain... this was the crux of my motivation. A childhood relationship stood behind me as foundation, but it was a hollow wish. The enjoyment, which I felt during the reprieve of winter, though it was surrounded with vexing confusion at every corner, gave me hope and lightness of heart, but it was short lived... sweet, but short.

At this point, there has been no knowledge come to light of the implied decisions regarding your future and I can only hope for your finding the peace you desired. I do maintain, however, that prior to my confessions here, I know there is a part of you that loved, or loves me in some context, whatever that may be, of this I am sure.

A continual evaluation of our time spent together has declared itself invaluable, and much to my dismay, has also produced a vast truth behind the pretense. It is hindsight, coupled with experience and patience that is too oft the mode in which understanding becomes brightest. I am ashamed to say that deficiency in the latter has only been made clearer with time. For a while, we partook of the affluence high society had to offer, in all its diversions, and I ignored the person to whom I should have been most attentive. I had expected that those whose circles we frequented would, in time, permit the differences noticed. For this deficiency in recognition, I apologize. The discontent was there, and it, like so many other signs I am guilty of not seeing, plagues me unceasingly, but I know now that no matter what I would have attempted to do, the fact is... I would never have had your devotion, this I comprehend.

Again, what a fool a lovesick heart can play one for; blind deception of mind and soul. If I have learned anything, Christine, of which I will apply most generously to subsequent relationships, it is of the necessity of trust between two people who claim an attachment and mutual fondness.

My sincere admiration for all you have bestowed on this wretch of a youth, I will be forever indebted. And now a sigh, as I draw this scene to a close, it is right. I know I would never have had you to cherish fully, but when you look back at our moments together, my wish is that it may bring a smile, that is all.

I would only amend my address with one desire, that you have attained the happiness for which you so dearly longed.

Raoul Chagny

Not one set of feminine eyes remained dry for the compassion and regard so tenderly expressed by M. Chagny. Erik was quite astonished, completely taken aback at the change; there was no more hatred, no superiority, no good versus evil, only maturity and generosity of soul. Christine stood and rounded the arm on the chair, being mindful of the company in which they were, she laid her hands to Erik's arm in a modest display of affection, but the deeper feelings were professed unmistakably by the brown sparkle she affixed to him.

"You can see," Mme Giry spoke quietly, but with far less sensitivity, "that with as much communication as Monsieur Chagny imparted in his instructions to us, we knew him to be safe, and could then guess that Christine was not in his good company."

"No, I was not, but amidst far better." Christine bristled at the scorning tone. "And, I shall not insult your intelligence by reiterating what is obvious."

"Well said, my dear," came a whisper to her ear.

Not one for being argumentative, Meg could not tolerate the ebb and flow of tension in such prolific quantities and stood, to tactfully decry as much. "Well, now that we are clear on the subject of where we all were and are, I should like to steal Christine away, for I am dying to know the particulars, her desires, and what must be done. If you would allow me, Monsieur Gautier, to occupy her for the time being?"

Christine smiled at the refreshing attitude of Meg's insistent exuberance, but waited to hear Erik's response. "Would you mind?"

"Not at all. I shall take my leave shortly to attend to other matters, go." Erik touched her chin upon her extrication by the whirlwind of a friend, and what a dear friend, to rescue her from such tiring disapprobation.

The door closed and the once playful aura, lighting the blues and greens of the room, dimmed in the engulfing vacancy. All distractions removed, the two circled predatorily, one to the sofa from seeing the young women out into the hall, and the second, to the window, as a place of reference to begin a regimen of pacing. The latter was not at all content to prolong in games where he was untried. He had watched the posturing of language, the behavior and overt looks, and decided to draw her into the ring of discourse, first. "Time is a cultivator of wisdom in a great many ways, is it not? Both young women have improved much these past months."

"Yes," Madame agreed. "Christine. . . she has a calming effect, one which I am sure has been of benefit to you."

Erik could feel the accusations ready to fly and despised the courting. "All right, let's have it out. I know you do not approve, but before you even venture a response, I will have you understand that we are not here to seek approbation!"

"That is well with me, for I would not oblige the petition. How could you have taken her, why her, Monsieur?" she demanded.

He scoffed. "Of all that is wondrous about this relationship, *that* is the core beauty of it, Madame! I did not take her. You heard the description of Christine's parting from Chagny himself. I gave them leave to go and she returned days later, to me. It was *her* decision!" His voice heightened in emphasis, but not overly so, much to Mme Giry's amazement. "What is it that plasters incredulity across your harsh exterior?"

"I, in spite of your brash diffidence, am impressed. You hold your temper, as well as your tongue, to an extent, despite what has been told me by the Persian gentleman."

Erik shot her a petulant glare. "Do not push me too far."

"Agreed, Monsieur." Madame nodded while weighing the importance of the other issues upon her mind, and then speared him. "You have considered her youth—"

"Please, spare me the questions about age. There are numerous gentlemen who enter the prime of their life before marrying, and they wed easily enough without an inquisition. You know," he smirked, "I could never have imagined the circumstances to which I am indebted, to the relationship I am involved. Do you honestly think time would have afforded me a woman better than she? In society, I daresay that the weight of my wealth would have turned up some mindless tripe, but would they have availed themselves to the love I desire? Shallow greed cannot look upon my face, only compassion, trust, and sincerity of love, and that, my dear madame, is exactly what Christine and I have carefully developed!"

She shrank from the truth with downcast eyes.

"Am I not entitled as a human being, to some measure of joy or happiness; to love and to be loved? You would deny me that much, condemn me?" Erik was suddenly near, his arms stretched across the back of the sofa. "Look at me!" he ordered. "Why is it not possible for her to love someone like me? Why?"

At first, the poignancy of his questions roused Mme Giry to a sense of decency, she could not refute anything he put to her for consideration, but all at once she colored in defiance, finding herself unable to withstand the very fundamentals of compunction deficient in his character; she retaliated verbally. "Because, you are capable of abhorrent actions... have committed crimes unspeakable. Did you think me blind, that I would not notice the mark along her jaw?" Her condescending tones tore him apart and plunged just conviction through his heart.

"How dare you insinuate," he seethed softly. "You know nothing of what my life has been. You comprehend but a particle in comparison to the depth of knowledge possessed by her and should not presume to cast judgment upon another when you lack every detail." He grabbed his belongings and turned his back menacingly, leaving his final words hanging in the din of quiet. "This conversation is over!"

Christine and Meg had been privy to the vocal inflections emanating throughout the hall as they were both just come from Meg's room moments before. The drawing room door opened and closed in haste, with Erik exiting between. He glanced toward Christine in earnest then moved silently down the stairs without a word.

Patting Meg's hand, Christine hurried off in concern for the scene held aloft in such contempt of feeling. "Erik," she gently called as he reached the front entry, giving him reason to pause, and sufficient time for her to gain on him. "Come," was all the encouragement required for him to trail behind in her grasp while rounding the post at the foot of the stairs, being led willingly toward the garden entrance.

"You came to me." He sounded surprised.

Beyond the Masque

"I did. Would you care to tell me?"

"Later, perhaps." There was no mistaking his anger as he pressed his lips to her hand, his teeth were clenched, and the irregular breathing, it burned inside, consuming his consciousness. She knew because he barely had temperance of mind to realize how close Christine was standing.

"Your grievance is with Adèle, not me, though I can envision the proceedings. The accusations will arrest in time, and all doubts shall be laid to resolve with truth. Oh, Erik, how weary you must be," she whispered as her fingers caressed his throat. "Always defending in the face of confrontation. No one need know our heart's desire, it is for us."

Erik shivered under her touch. "I cannot believe the influx of serenity you give. No one must ever take you from me, no one! My desire deepens! Hold me, close." The grip with which he induced Christine to return his ardent embrace left them both flushed, and grateful to the gardener for having much to accomplish that morning. As the man unloaded an armful to the patch of ground needing to be tended, he inadvertently dropped a spade to clang upon the courtyard bricks; a shadow at midday could not have disappeared any faster, after gracing his intended's forehead with a peck, than he.

With his spirits reinstated, Christine would endeavor to meet the next headstrong personality with as much civility as possible, though she would enjoy consoling the other, for it was certainly a more affable engagement.

Christine came upon the Girys when she reentered the drawing room, sitting in a flustered state of togetherness upon the sofa. She looked at both, worry knitting her brow so recently addressed in affection.

"If you would permit me?" Christine began, holding aloft her hand, finger extended to arrest Mme Giry's impulse. "I must preface my brief remarks as they may be construed as impertinent. I have no wish to insult or compound what has taken place, but I must express my thoughts." That said, she folded her hands and continued. "I will not speak to the subjects discussed or why the need was felt to affront the character of the gentleman I am to marry, but that is for you to resolve with him, Adèle. I will mention, however, that what was once a trifling ploy turned obsession, has since grown into a relationship built on trust and honesty, and neither of us will allow deviation from our present course of choice." At the end of that dictation she smiled. "And now, if you can tolerate me longer, I should be glad for your assistance."

"Oh, Maman, can we not set aside these dreary opinions and indulge in happier plans, like the wedding?"

Mme Giry nodded. "Christine, I shall ask pardon of Monsieur Gautier, for your sake. It was wrong of me to behave in such a way that offended and brought unwelcome feelings when the opposite was meant. My trepidation on the matter heightened upon learning of your involvement, and the implications…" She sighed. "All right. I believe we have a wedding to prepare for, do we not?"

Chapter Seventeen

Late morning procured an illustrious view from the glass panes of a second story window, one blessed in the picturesque colors of the Tuileries gardens in the mix of fall, and another, brought forth from the more verdant recall of a time earlier that spring. The dark, tired eyes softened beneath the resurrected memory as a smile eased the heaviness so long in wait for relief.

"He will come, and soon. I stand where I did when last he poured out his innermost gratitude for the slightest taste of compassion bestowed, when I then believed his confessions. What is to come of him? What has occurred. . . death, in a manner of speaking, to be sure, but since then? Only he can answer this," were his thoughts, given leave by reason.

A knock startled the Persian, and the fibrous inmates of the book, those held open at chest level, turned restlessly from where he had been reading. He closed its pages and folded the thin wire frames upon the cover.

"Master, a gentleman, an Erik Gautier to see you. May I show him in?"

"Please, and some tea if you would, Darius."

"Of course, Monsieur." The manservant rounded crisply, closing off the study.

The door soon reopened and there, to his astonishment, stood a different likeness than he had expected would grace his home, different than the one who had left his presence all those months before, broken, weakened, and weary of life. This gentleman had lightly hued skin, not chalky and deathly pale, but represented in contrast a confident elegance, he was full of purpose and seemed to be, quite stable.

"May I, Monsieur?" The manservant availed Erik of his services, his hand extended.

"Thank you, no. I shall retain them here, if I may. I have much to do and shall not be too long invading your master's time, I should think."

"And why not?" the Persian asked, answering his man's quandary with a quiet, "I shall see to him," and made the exit simple to execute, for privacy's sake. "See, you owe me *some* time at least, enough so I might enquire after the affairs of the deceased in a more thorough manner." The Persian grinned lightly and held out his hand to which so hearty a reception was borne, he hardly knew what to make of it. "You look. . ."

"Alive and more than well?" Erik supplied.

"Indeed! Please, come sit near the fire and tell me as to the origin of your apparent turn of events and rise in countenance. All of which are most contrary to who you were a half year earlier."

Erik sighed, *just how much to divulge is the concern.* "Finality has a way of never taking hold when I am the recipient, I suppose. It is an aspect I have wished for, exacted in behalf of others and now desire to forego, personally." He pronounced a seasoned glare at the Persian. "Must you?"

"Forgive me, Erik, but the rationale, I am. . ." He rubbed the lower portion of his face.

"Obviously speechless. Does it suit, the rationale?"

"Remarkably well, and the leveled civility, the transformation is unbelievable, and the cause?"

"Unbelievable as well, immersion to the fullest extent beneath the uncommonly positive influence of a woman." Erik rose animatedly from the chair opposite the Persian, his heart having leapt from the joy sharing brings, and came to rest an arm against the mantle before staring into the flames. "It is true, Daroga. I courted her, she accepted my hand, and we are here to wed this Friday." He turned sharply to see the reaction his news excited.

"A woman... yes, I scarce can explain the impact of a female upon our gender." The Persian's tone cooled mildly amid the tumult of mind, to reconcile with whom Erik could be referring. Calmly, his hands folded as elbows lifted to the arms of the chair. "Do I know this woman?"

The conversation with Madame Giry played out before Erik's closed eyes; everything flew across the backdrop, all of it, his eyes warily parting into slits. "I am unsure whether you claim an acquaintance with her or not. You will excuse me, I should go, thank you for permitting me to trespass on your time."

The Persian stood quickly to barricade Erik's departure. "Erik, please stay."

"Forgive the abruptness, but I am unwilling to be the recipient of more decision related contempt. I have had plenty to fuel my determined independence and wish to avoid any additional well-meaning adversaries, thank you."

"It is she, is it not, Mademoiselle Daaé? You would only behave in such a way if it were true." Inches separated the two, the Persian planting body afore a clean pass to the door.

"Would I? Would you not have the same thoughts if it were anyone else?"

The Persian grasped Erik by the shoulder and was rounded upon, sword unerring in its placement to the base of his throat.

"Erik, be reasonable!"

"This is reasonable for a man such as *I* am, is it not? You have plagued me for years, Daroga, gnawed at my resolve of character, telling me that I was responsible to you for my conduct. And now, I find happiness beyond my dreams, in one small corner of this miserable, hypocritical world, to meet with nothing more than disagreeable, unceasing queries! Do you think insanity a satisfactory option, that I should be exiled to the confines of my own genius because of this face?" Suddenly Erik's natural features were staring directly at the Persian. "Take a good look, Daroga!"

In all the years he had known the Persian, Erik had never offered to expose so spontaneously what lay beneath his masque, nor was he given to freely exhibiting himself. It was all the Persian could do to master the recalcitrant wish to turn head or avert eyes; every dark inch of his face was canvassed, waiting. "Am I not a man with feelings or does my present state deem me unworthy? Perhaps it is only logical that something without semblance of form should be thought devoid of emotion? Why does the world, why do you, feel the need to deny me this?"

The sword changed point of destination with such slight of hand that it was nearly a minute until recognized; the double-edged blade lay grasped by Erik, palm down, and tip to breast. "Go ahead, Daroga!" he exclaimed wantonly, "Take my sword, pierce my heart. I bleed as any other man, but perhaps hate has made me unfeeling, impervious and numb to pain. Shall we see if I am able to feel... *this?*" And he pulled slowly, purposely, livid resolve forcing the blade to enter silently, cleanly separating the callous exterior to spill forth life's fluid, the cloth thirsty to indulge. The Persian's expression deteriorated openly into alarm while anger ignited the other's fortitude in a clash of wills.

"Erik! For pity's sake, don't—"

"Don't what? Inflict myself with what I *should* feel? There are laws conversely established in this world, but for the most part, I seem to have only experienced one side!"

Mere seconds elapsed, and Erik's eyes shone luminescent green, the flecks of gold submitting to the fury of blue while the blade penetrated still, his hand shaking as it suffered similarly in restraint. Steady resistance brought a swift conclusion, and the Persian was able to remove the sword from accomplishing any more needless damage.

"Quite an accursed demonstration to bring about a point, damn irritating!" the Persian chided, pulling Erik over to the chair he had last occupied. "Come, I will listen." Once seated, Erik was given a handkerchief to wrap his hand while clean cloths were requested to attend the other wound. "I suspect your emotions are in a continual state of upheaval while undergoing some form of mutual cohabitation. Your customary traits have become subdued, but are available when the need arises... foolish passion, being the most recent to surface. You are an extremist, my friend," he said, having retrieved scattered belongings, handing over Erik's masque for him to resume.

Nodding, Erik glanced up from where he had been nursing his chest. "I am, but not around her, never with her," he sighed. "I have come so far, lived so complete." The look of surprise placed Erik in mental reverse to clarify. "Please," he huffed, "you could elevate that prepossession and give me a little credit. I may be monstrous in many ways, but to intentionally take advantage of a young woman... that is where I have always been morally sound; I am a gentleman, you may be well assured, Daroga. I will do whatever is required of me to have this relationship succeed, but despair when I observe the same patterns beginning to recur."

"This is where you are too eager to condemn, obligating me carte blanche by auguring my response with the majority. Circumspect I am, no doubt, but I do not pass judgment through emotion as a woman does," the Persian said in his defense.

"Forgive me," Erik readily atoned, then cocked a brow at the gaiety behind the rough-cut eyes. "What now?"

"I may take a liking to this civility and delightsome wit, it becomes you. Quite an improvement over the insufferable hauteur of the past." He lifted the decanter and poured two glasses of wine, holding one out to Erik. A hand rose, staying the Persian's genial offer. "No wine either?" He eyed Erik disapprovingly. "You are a Frenchman, a connoisseur, have been since—"

"A connoisseur gone dry; the tea will be fine." The Persian set both glasses aside untouched, transparent interest petitioning him to be seated, for there was more to be told. "I abstained from the moment Christine left. My emotions had run the gauntlet by then, and I desired more than anything to relive her kiss, the one I related to you." A nod. "Yes, well, the thought of losing all I'd experienced to a rummaging fog, did not seem fit. You know me, a servile host to any ghastly deed; I protested to spite my nature! Best," Erik's mind lit up, for there was more than one to list! "*One* of the best decisions I ever made. Had Christine returned to find me in such a blind state of *ivresse*. . . I scared her then, the destruction, my discomposure. . . She would certainly have forsaken an inebriated wretch. Heaven bless her."

"Heaven? Gone religious too!" The Persian slapped his knee.

"Let us not go that far!" Erik postured his reserves, hoping to minimize the breach in his callous past. Little did the Persian know how often he thanked God, and while not presently engaged toward a bend in pious living, he respected, and would not deny from whence his fortune came, knowing the key to this reformation was Christine. How his chest swelled to share with another.

"Well, I should like to know better the woman who can employ such magic to the benefit of many."

"She loves with a fiery conviction and is never afraid of me." Erik glimpsed the brief disquiet. "I saw the repulsion in your eyes. You forget how well I know the emotions of those who look upon me;

nevertheless, you kept your composure and for that, I thank you. Now, imagine gazing into what you have witnessed, on a daily basis. She sees beyond, Daroga, deeper than I am able to comprehend, and loves."

After the wounds were tended, a light meal and a round of chess became the course of the engaging hours surrounding noon, during which time a succinct dissertation of events provided the enlightenment necessary for a thorough understanding of prior occurrences, which now led to their current goal in review. The Persian conveyed news pertaining to their business dealings, with Erik listening only halfheartedly, paying more heed to where he might land his knight to block the progress of the Persian's queen. Though, when a turn in topic cast a dour mood about the game, he was all interest and curiosity for the sharing of an unfortunate situation. The daroga had secured an accounting from a rather ideal source, and felt bound to inform Erik of the demise of a common friend. It seemed that the examining magistrate, M. Faure, had closed the case of le Opera Ghost, to the vexation of several. The scoundrel was never discovered, if there had indeed, ever been one, and speculation circulated yet again, concerning a body found within the sewers, horribly decayed and unclaimed, which leant credulity to vague possibilities and aided in arresting what little doubt resided in M. Faure's shallow mind.

Their eyes met and a sorrowful comment made, regarding the mishaps of encore performances, then the subject was abandoned.

Chapter Eighteen

Christine sat reading among the bed covers early that evening, pausing every now and again to jot down another point needing to be remembered. *How will this all come about? The more I think, the more I find requires doing, and no doubt I will run out of time and ink before ever accomplishing my plans. Oh, thank Heaven for Meg!*

She glanced at the small stack of notes upon the writing table, sealed and cleverly wrapped with explicit notation, to be particularly stationed for use two evenings from then. This is how she found herself focused, when a shy, apprehensive rap addressed the door. The knock was delivered as though it were fearful of waking the occupant, and likewise concerned if it did not, but either way, intrusive upon the subject of her endeavors.

"One moment, please," she replied, grabbing a shawl to wrap modestly about herself.

"Pardon the intrusion, Madame," the young girl said, rising from a curtsy, "but the orders were to hand it over directly. Good evening." The envelope was held out and instinctively taken.

"Yes, thank you," she answered absently while shutting the door. Christine leaned right where she was and pulled out a card with the words, *I love you*, scrawled across it. "I deem you to be a most hopeless romantic," came her soft observation.

"As hopeless as they come."

The voice took her completely by surprise, as one startled "oh" would attest, its companions following closely behind with the shawl and card drifting from her grasp to the floor. She blushed violently and made to recover her things, but the loosely drawn nightgown slipped from one shoulder, causing even more distress.

"Forgive me! This was not my intent!" Erik quickly knelt to retrieve the dropped items and gently draped the shawl, collaring it about her neck while at the same time lightly caressing the sleekness of her throat. "I had not expected. . . you were already retired? The message was to. . ." he stumbled amidst the phrase, so thought it better to quit altogether, take a seat, and quiz along a different line. "Tell me, your day, you were able to achieve a great deal?"

"Yes, and you?" she returned his civility with a tender squeeze to his arm, as she moved to cozy up against the bedpost.

"It began painful enough, but has since, dulled." Then it was off to the races, and she so ill-prepared, could not curtail the deluge of information. "I have made arrangements with my tailor and a couturier, choosing materials that I hope will be pleasing. Your compliments in my taste gave me confidence to do as I saw fit in this area, though I shall be leaving the choice of wedding attire to your discretion. Once finished, the clothing shall be sent directly to Amiens. The chapel, I. . . when you mentioned how overwhelming the cathedral in Amiens was, I felt the Madeleine to be too ordinary, and so the church, well, it is not really utilized as a church as it once was, but is now an historical monument. They were most appreciative of the donation and more than willing to perform a small ceremony in the upper chapel, at two o'clock, that is to say if the time is agreeable to you. Oh, and the license, timing was sufficient to draw up the document, and you would not guess! The Persian, knowing that I would not come back so soon after alerting him, went below.

This I would not have allowed in the past, he certainly tried often enough, making his existence unbearable to me, but he was successful, and I am not aggravated in the least. He went to sort through the calamity left in my destructive wake, obviously leaving the ultimate decision to me of what I wish to keep or remove. Such kindness. . . I—"

There were several opportunities to attempt participation during the rapid fire, but none made it farther than a slight inhale and oral gape, such was his lively frame of mind until a carefully tossed introduction of verse came at him through the air.

"Your reflexes do you justice, as I suspected they would."

"Am I that imprudent in conversation that it causes you to retaliate?"

Christine smiled, disarming him even more within his present state. "Erik, for all the conversations we have ever had the pleasure to engage the other, a newspaper could not put upon its reader to absorb as much, and. . . Listen to me, now I am as unnerved as you sound."

He stared momentarily, still clasping the book as he stood to walk about. "There is this feeling, perhaps it is nerves, but it is the second episode today." He stopped to glance beseechingly. "But it only happens when I am near you." Erik's concern glistened at his temples as he advanced toward her. "You seem so tranquil and yet, I feel coincidently similar to the disrepair of my home on the lake. Taking this into account you, I. . . your smile." He scratched his head. "If I slow for a minute I swirl in this emotion; please, if you would, help me to understand?"

"You may have to come close enough to be touched, hence the necessity of glove removal. Come. . . here, near me." Erik hesitated at her request. "Yes, on the bed, as you can see there are no other items of furniture that will situate us both. I shall begin with your left."

"My left? Oh, of course."

"I think a good amount of anxiety shall be allayed, you know you are not alone."

"No?" His expression opened as he tossed cloak to chair and sat obediently.

"No. Between Adèle's treatment, the letter, and our parting in the courtyard this morning, I was left so flustered that I walked the downstairs hall a good quarter of an hour, and I prepared for bed early so I could think. I find reading aids the resurfacing of what is important because it employs the mind differently."

Erik watched her fingers, adoring so completely the relaxing spell cast over him by her genteel application of pressure. "I. . ." he coughed then looked up in cold realization. "You too?"

"That embrace. . ." Her cheekbones heightened in recall. "Yes, I too. You do not comprehend the effect you have."

"I should like to say it goes both ways." He beamed.

"It is well that fortune played out in your favor then, escaping as unscathed as you did from the clutches of we females. And though your perspective may be contrariwise, there is a reason for the comment. It seems you and I are not singular in our secrecy."

"Interesting." Erik was glad to hear that he might part with some of the blame.

"Madame has some connection to the *new* management, a Monsieur Edouard Mercier. She sees him often, though Meg said she would deny this outright if ever confronted; and to this, we add a young gentleman for Meg, British Baronet Richard Castelot-Barbezac. So, my dear Erik, change is the only constant; besides the beautiful sky that joins above us all, how can we not possibly have some affliction of nerves?"

"True."

"Furthermore, the time is fine, and I trust you implicitly in regard to a couture."

Christine took hold of Erik's right hand, when he, having been preoccupied with the simple affections received, lost all vigilance in concealing the evidence from the morning's outburst. He pulled away in such scorching fashion that Christine's shock stunned them both.

"I suppose alarm will do me no good, unless I am steered otherwise!"

"I fear this is another, perhaps more viable reason for my agitation. You are correct, there is no need for worry." He grunted. "I forgot while busy and shall be forced to pay the price. Would you?" Between the two of them they were able to extract his hand, leaving his fingers and thumb quite sore.

Erik saw Christine's compassion surface as she gently examined it. "Was it tended to properly?"

"Yes, the daroga. . . hmm. . . it is a minor inconvenience."

"Whose?" Her soft tone pained him. "This is from *your* sword, is it not?"

Erik nodded then saw her eyes moisten as they drifted to his chest. His followed. Her hand moved a portion of his ascot to the side then drew back when the speck of red swelled beneath contact. How often had he changed the dressing? Not as he ought. And clothing? Erik withdrew from those brows, set heavy in concentration as she let go his hand and touched his face. Did he truly comprehend trust? If he did, then why the disguising downplay and evasion? He could only imagine what was going through her mind. Oh, what had he done?

He would not have prevented her, even if he could, and her imploring wish for permission came, her fingers ready, poised at the top of the waistcoat buttons until his consent bowed in resignation. The buttons caved one by one, spreading their folds to the crimson betrayal, awaiting sentence to be discharged. She removed the ornamental stud, untied his neck cloth and pressed on until the final layer was exposed; the droop of her countenance, the pale wilt of lashes and wash of emotion combined to deepen the injury. '*Extrem-*

ist!' the Persian had rightly called him, to which he added, *rash fool!*

"Who?" she required of him.

Erik had hardly formed the words "self-inflicted" when she gasped and uttered a strangled "why?" to break his heart. An eternity fled in those humiliating moments, with her hand pressed tight to his suffocating heart, his thoughts gushed in bitter rebuke to fill the quiet.

Slowly, she composed herself, sniffed, dabbed at her cheeks, and ordered him to lie back without so much as a word. He wished for condemnation in any form but silence. But silence it was; it was not like her to make a scene. A shake of her head rendered him speechless then she gently spoke, "Your life is not yours to take, only to be given for another. Please, don't ever choose to leave me," she implored.

"I promise," his penitent reply.

Eventually, all was related to a level of satisfaction. Erik declared idiocy in the matter, labeled the action as a sheer lapse of rationale, and accepted an especially pertinent bit of candor after Christine had mumbled something about "this proving to be an unfailing example of his ability to bleed as well as the next man." Although, however well *bled* he could be, Christine accused his wound of being just as stubborn to begin healing as Erik was to diminish in passion and therefore, a shortage of surprises were to be highly unlikely. The edges of the cut itself were too cleanly severed and had refused to knit easily, the continual seeping denoted such, and throughout the day's business there had been no notice taken to reduce activity, which set the course of repetitive separations and soiling of dressing and garments. The only way, as Erik saw it, was to have Christine apply pressure while he remained stationary.

With him reclined upon a pillow in her lap, their degree of comfort returned and they smiled often at one another throughout the next few hours as they read aloud, leaving time to converse about their day in full. Erik rehearsed, at a more leisurely clip this time around, the finer details of the couture ordered; texture, color, and fabrics all described, he noted next that an early arrival at the church would provide ample opportunity for a tour, in addition to those hours required for female bonding through preparation. Christine grinned at the idea.

Erik was later pronounced rested and serene in all aspects. He kissed her hand, thanked her, donned his cloak, and excused himself out into the night. She watched him go as the darkness welcomed his form, swallowing him away under its protection, right hand and all—the one that always seemed to take the brunt of punishment, from the gash of a vase and the unforgiving wall in a stable, to the latest; an unfailing pattern, why? He paused and looked back toward the light, his light.

If one could have encountered Erik's meandering trail back through the streets of Paris to the Opera House, the delight effused across his countenance would have told of his happiness. He walked but a few feet shy of the embankment along the river, his step borne in majestic silence, remembering the enduring heavens and the love he shared with someone who was just as faith provoking as the natural laws were in motion. Erik stopped and breathed deeply, feeling for the first time what he supposed was evidence of a light heart; it was a glorious sensation.

Chapter Nineteen

Darkness nearly proved impenetrable in the dead of night, rekindling those overpowering emotions; the clamp of a hand stifling her into submission and the unrelenting wind against the waning efforts of fall, pressed violently together. A sudden gust added to the pallor of shifting greys cast through the glass doors to the balcony, but none quite so bothersome until the slamming of a distant door woke Christine. She was conscious and very much aware of what lay ahead with that fearsome prospect of sleeplessness. Her eyes lowered, centering upon the glow of a candle, unlit by her, dancing its solitary sway to ease the disturbance of mind; it tempered the various noises upon her ear and set light to a few articles. She quickly retrieved the flame to her bedside table and climbed beneath the safe warmth of cover, her face awash with intrigue, hands eager to unseal the strange messenger for relief of content. The letter referenced a companion, whose divine softness and scent rested at her bosom, she read. . .

> *My love,*
> *This guardian of the night, while not a substitute for the arms aching to envelop your treasured form, will pierce your darkest fear as it did for me so long ago. It was the only hope*

I had until your gentleness upon my soul. The rose, a symbol of such, that we are susceptible to the other's influence, forever bound.

Know that I am near.

She sighed. One petal, loosely adrift from the tightly cleaved bud, had successfully detached itself from the rest, making it easier to study its singular qualities. Its wavy edges were hued crimson, as though blessed by the touch of a painter's brush, infused to a flawless depth within the purity of white, each instilling acceptance and temperance. Christine nestled into the bedding, assured now that she could weather the tedium of hours yet to come before light, but it was not long before weariness overtook her unremembered.

The next sound to rouse her was the rasping of draperies crossing the rod above the balcony doors.

"Well, if Maman could see you now, sleeping half the morning away! Perhaps someone is becoming lax, or keeping late hours, hmm?" Meg's impish grin, coupled with the implanted fists at her hips, made her stance almost laughable. But try as she might, her dark hair and complexion could not muster the countenance to look put upon.

"And hello to you, too! How is one to get any sleep?" Christine asked, pulling the sheets over-top her head. "Between the annoyance of bad dreams, and visitors calling at odd times, is it any wonder that my eyelids and body are leaden? Oh, heavens. What time is it?"

"Rehearsals would have started an hour ago," she said, yanking the sheets from Christine's grasp. "When you did not answer the door I went in search of a key and found what I was looking for."

"As you see," Christine groaned.

"Yes, but you were expecting *me* by nine. Who were the others?"

She smirked. "Erik. His sleeping habits are. . ." she reflected for no more than an instant, "are not even that, and hopefully subject to change. He was here on two, perhaps three separate occasions." She glanced to the table, seeing the letter and rose tucked inside her book for confirmation. "Yes, at least three."

"You're not sure?"

"No. Well, not exactly. I was only conscience for the first. And," she pointed at Meg's dancing glare. "Do not even ask, he just can... the doors, all of them were locked, were they not?"

"Fine, then I shan't quiz. But really, does it not bother you, just a bit? Having his eyes on you when least anticipated. I should think it queer to be *watched,* very queer, and every part abnormal."

"Really, Meg. You are making him sound as though he had some sinister motives when it is quite the opposite. His interest is always thoughtful and never intrusive. Here, read this." Meg blushed a hint then sat squarely on the bed in Christine's stead. "I do not mind, it came with the rose and candle last night, there is nothing intimately personal, only caring, promise."

"Oh! I nearly forgot, the woman who opened your door... this is probably from him as well." Meg removed a note from her pocket and waved it in the air.

Christine verified with a quick look. "It is. Erik would have me become better acquainted with his Persian friend, so we shall make allowance in our plans." Turning around, she left the invitation on the bed to continue her nimble preparations.

"Christine? Are you sure this is from him?" Meg called after her, comparing both notes now in her possession. "I mean, I would not dream of offending either of you, but..."

"But what, the penmanship?"

Meg nodded. "Yes, this one is steady, but the other, though legible—that much I credit him, is just not what I would have expected."

"His script, I will have to admit, is atrocious. When you think of the marvels that cascade so elegantly from such intelligence and talent, and then to be favored with an example of *this* skill, the likes of which you could put to the level of a child, makes one wonder, does it not? Moreover, he is somewhat sensitive about it, has realized his neglect of late, so much so that he began practicing."

A fast end was made to criticizing what would, at length, remedy itself and instead, a shift in focus toward more pressing details employed the two vivacious minds. When women have a notion to accomplish a great many things, they can set forth in a zealous blur, which most often bewilders men; their effortless gliding about with the alacrity of hummingbirds, setting motion to a world of complacency.

Christine's prospects, among all she endeavored, had left little if any room for censure or disappointment; she would not have either, only success. To this positive accompaniment, she and Meg applied diligence and good nature to employ kindly services from those proprietors whose talents were required. Not to say that all went smoothly, enabling them to secure the first visited for their bidding, but through perseverance and happenstance each task met with a rather genial outcome. A young jeweler, trying to establish himself at the completion of an apprenticeship, agreed wholeheartedly to the specifications requested; another, eventual triumph, came with reference to an older, retired gentleman, an expert luthier, who accepted the charge; though somewhat reluctant at first, he caved generously after such a unique circumstance and touching story were related. How could he not help, seeing as the young women gave his wife much praise for a hearty dose of encouragement in behalf of love?

Fortune smiled indeed, above as well as below, for the occupation most popularly engaged in became any pursuit that would further preparations and hasten time, but worse was one effect than another. For Christine, fatigue received some measure of repose as an interval was spanned each night, while Erik had the contrasting dilemma, being perpetually hounded by insomnia, to which Christine was cause as well as cure by diversion. Thrice he had ventured to ensure her safety the night before; to partake of her calm, to confirm his presence in reality, and to ensure that being below again had not thrust him into the past.

Afternoon brought Erik from a sojourn to Amiens, and as he entered the interminable disquiet of his sanctum, he was resigned to prescribe a treatment contrary to that of his earlier procrastination, and began immediately addressing the waste. He had intentionally put off the onerous chore, not desiring to look upon the decimation he had created while in such despair. In a matter of moments, what had required years to collect was laid to rest in a soon to be empty cavern. This would serve as a brutal, just reminder, however sorrowful the loss, and would point to the importance of people and relationships, not things, as a way one could account for *self* in the world. Truly, if he were to look at each item, it would be the means by which a memory could be recalled, but when all was said and done, worth came with the aforementioned and knowledge acquired, which, when at once secured, none could take away. These thoughts stayed with him above several hourly rotations as he plodded through the organized chaos until a few musical scores and drawings did more to distract.

"Master of silence you will never be, Daroga, try as you might. Good day to you." Erik greeted the stillness, not having faced his guest. No movement. He was amiable, no burning anger or cynicism. Did the man honestly think himself sneaky? "Daroga," he encouraged sympathetically.

"I am hazarding a guess that any queries into how you knew, would be futile." The Persian mused at the civility proffered him and pushed open the door.

"They would be, yes. Just know that I can. Christine has learned to accept and so must you." There was a pause, which Erik soon realized to be related to the interest of his guest. "Oh, and pardon the disarray, but the situation shall remedy itself in good time. I fear it looks worse than when you were here."

"Implacable arrogance... tolerable, but just." The Persian grinned broadly.

"Arrogance?" Erik repeated. "Acute senses and instinct cannot be erased, nor should they be, if beneficial. And what, pray tell, are you amused by?" He whirled about. "Your smile is audible from here!"

As the regal step neared, he expounded, "All my previous attempts to enter your home were overtures aloft in colorful threats, but now, even when surrounded by *this*, you are cordial."

"Surprising, is it not? I have learned not to waste my energy in foolish spite; what is done, is done. I cannot change it, only affect differences elsewhere. And, regarding my home, it is of little consequence since very few have ever located its whereabouts. As I see it, sealing the place off will be best."

"What credit to you—"

"Ah, not to me, Daroga," Erik quickly interrupted, "to Christine. Her loving influence tames and smoothes the rough edges, but one may incur scrapes if they approach from the wrong angle."

"Indeed, I look forward to reacquainting myself with her, as our previous encounter was borne under less favorable light." He shuddered in recollection. "Our roles were nothing but a farce on your stage; your Christine, a quaint, genteel sort of nun in her devoirs, and I . . ." then deciding a reference to only himself a wise move, he purposely omitted Raoul de Chagny, wishing discord to remain untouched. "I was a half-drugged, unconscious afterthought, and you, a pious mockery in your condescension to we mortals."

The art fell to the desk. Erik did not appreciate the tone, nor replay of the night they were all found below, and it was clearly seen in posture—if not in face—as he took on an inclined look of disbelief during the snippet, but any snide retorts were kept in check. "Just how far would you see me irked, hmm? . . . maddened in my lawless domain? You can be rest assured that I still possess those capabilities to which you refer and speak of so contemptuously."

"I regret the pain caused, but so it was and is; honesty is often unpleasant."

Erik glanced at his watch, preoccupied. "As well as a host who has not prepared for his guests. Here you must forgive me; I shall clear a place." The Persian seemed pleased with the changeling; his face lifted at the rush to tidy the room, then looked down by way of recovering his features to neutral, sorely mistaken in Erik's purpose of heart. "Christine will come soon enough. Be seated, please. Tea is here," he led with a hand sweep to the table, and seeing that all was right, bowed. "You will excuse me."

IT WAS NOT AN extraordinary evening, only mild, as most weary Parisians shuffled off from the center of town to their quiet homes; a full day in its entirety under a cloud-streaked sky. Christine was not unlike any other, partnered in a similar vanishing act, her radiance settled with a commitment to ground; the distance shortened and the contrast became less obvious between the rotations above and the enduring crypt of sameness.

What a strange sensation, this returning below; the Persian in *his* flat, and Christine, she was there, occupying each portion of thought, his significant reason for life. She had been an *obsession* in every sense, her word 'possession' aptly sharp, leapt upon the other to devour it whole. He sneered at the former thoughts, the words *'implacable arrogance'* echoed, and his shoes scuffed against the stone, *how blaring!* His wants then had mainstreamed his every action. And now? He was learning to be less, he was certain of it! *Imagine, thinking to keep someone! That was arrogant.* He was appalled, repulsed, and thought on what her reaction might be, what her memories were. Considering her frequent journeys below, those conducted through fear, they were not an indomitable terror, but compelled by the madness of love, his, a terrifying irony of imprisonment and escape. What it meant to be free quickly became foreshadowed among these separate peculiarities, scattering the past among the living. He pressed on, his chest aching inside and out as he moved toward the underground passages of the Rue Scribe, and Christine.

Erik smiled at the wonder that surrounded the impending reunion, of sorts, an odd one, where not all would be invited—nearly, but not all. Cognizant of her whereabouts from the indulgence in thought, Erik had not expected the delight from which he now feasted quite genially. She knew of his proximity to her, he was sure, could sense the energy, knew she felt his gaze, and wished that he would dispense with these games of cat and mouse. He preferred the upper hand of observing, and adored the anticipation of the clandestine art of seduction.

"Erik?"

A gentle pair of hands encompassed her.

"Do not turn." His voice stayed her impulse of foot. She trembled at his warm breath upon her neck and ear, and fell back lightly to his shoulder to be engulfed by comfort. "You have come," he said. "Oh, the passion, Christine. You cannot possibly know what I hold in reserve for times such as these. These two days, our limited moments, have been a torturous separation, like partial living, waiting for an atrophied appendage to join the whole in functional union once again. I can hardly bear this stifling behemoth, traversing the stony corridors or crossing the barren waters when you are not within its walls somewhere; they have become as desolate catacombs, lamenting the departure of their very soul. I desire you for my own, to make me complete." His lips rested upon her cheek.

"If you insist on filling my heart by intimating such emotion, I may be required to oblige."

"Required?" Erik's tone turned grave, and he stepped back from her. "I shall not force." Christine circled to face him in light exasperation. His eyes rolled. Damnable language, his construing of literal context habitually arose at the most inopportune times! She retreated, but his arms surrounded her once again, though the passion was gone. "And, are you well this evening?"

Looking at him cautiously she answered that she was, "quite well."

Silence commanded for some minutes, both on the verge of drawing away, when Christine gently rose up on her toes and brushed Erik's chin with the back of her fingers. His sudden, civil indifference puzzled her.

"Do you," he began, "in all sincerity, wish to be my wife?"

Understanding lit her eyes. "Most sincerely, Erik." Patient creature that she was, she clasped his face tenderly on either side and directed him into submission until his cheek touched her shoulder, cradling his head dearly to her. "I love you."

"I will see to your happiness, you have my word," he whispered. The intensity of grasp belied the softness of tone, and his arms collapsed about her.

They made their way to the house on the lake, finding one content Persian sitting near a small table sipping tea and perusing a stack of artwork. He had been pondering rather loudly, lamenting the very idea of "never visiting this hideaway again, after finally gaining welcome," and was entertaining the "probability of there being other places secretly set aside, as it would be unlike Erik to play *all* his cards face up."

"Talking to yourself, Daroga?" Tea sloshed from the Persian's cup. "Beg pardon, but one must be careful with whom to engage in conversation," Erik teased, watching the comical display of unnerved man, papers, and saucer trying to locate a favorable position prior to gaining his feet. Christine was led within the makeshift drawing room upon Erik's arm. "Daroga. Mademoiselle Christine Daaé."

The dark-skinned gentleman was duly impressed; *this* was not the same young woman who had been easily swayed in mind; the same timid, leggy reed she was not, but a healthy copse, generously potent of spirit and highly esteemed. Yes, he could see, and would ascertain the operations of time that flagged them both.

Taking her hand in his, the Persian bowed courteously to Erik's proud introduction. "It is my pleasure," he responded readily, "to formally meet the woman to whom I may credit with taming such an insidious wretch, by laying claim on his heart."

Christine heard Erik's light "humph" at the insult, and softly laughed. "It is my wish, Monsieur, that you would not flatter me so, for if one does not truly desire change then it is a hopeless conversion, is it not?"

"Beautiful, and witty too! Hmm, a fortunate match indeed."

A genuine squeeze from her bade the Persian chuckle, and no sooner had they withdrawn contact than Erik retrieved her cloak and gloves.

"The tea could be freshened, I shall return shortly." And she hastened away, becoming attentive without uttering another word, leaving the two men, one to sit in comfort and the other to pace. Her presence was quickly restored to the gathering, her tenacious affability breaking forth upon rejoining the incongruous angle she had created. "At last, Monsieur, we are able to greet each other on more amiable terms, that we may judge clearly of the other's character," she began, as she passed him his cup, her frankness in manner speaking immediate confidence.

"At last, Mademoiselle? Has someone been giving narratives of my background, to which I may now be obliged to either uphold or defend? Please remember, that there are always two sides to every tale, and this a most arduous saga."

Erik received his tea at the mantle, wary and quiet. He was watching and listening with great interest, the exchange linking the best parts of his world together; they were as political allies, representatives forming the stern and bow of his life.

Christine seated herself on the sofa, opposite the Persian. "You need not worry. Erik has only given me illustration under the best of light. I believe it is your friendship to him where I must be indebted to you."

"What? Come now, I would have expected Erik, of all people, to paint me in a supercilious fashion. I have dogged him tirelessly to no end, held him to rigid expectations, blamed him, and all he can do is color me illustrious, eh?" the Persian concluded with doubting amusement.

"I know the past you share, and I am of the opinion that if one were to have an unfaltering memory it would place many of us in peril."

"Well said, Mademoiselle. Now it is my turn to inform, but I may be as enlightened as you, for our source is the same, so I shall venture down another path. Do you have relations who delight in your news?"

"Only a guardian." Erik heard her, and was suddenly glad he would not be required to wade through more scrutiny; his chest ached as it was. "Madame Valerius, she is not well and is presently in Sweden. We hope to visit her when the time is right, and expect to share our happiness," she confirmed.

"Yes, quite." The Persian grinned unmercifully at Erik, but unable to catch the down-turned eye, he was again moved in speech to gain it. "Then, I am compelled to look beyond the artifice, beneath that hardened exterior because you intimate that therein lies something of worth. I had held out hope all these years, though was never rewarded."

Christine followed suit. "Indeed, Monsieur, as I am sure you are aware, the ever-present existence of merit was buried by debris and clutter of pride in disparagement for the world, but all that is being swept about and will find repose in modest conventions." In turn, both cast furtive glances bent on the subject at hand. Christine winked at the Persian; their banter was finally rousing the indignation of their host. "I should be remiss, however, if in my haste I neglect to mention the endearing stubbornness."

"By all means!" encouraged the Persian.

"Do you mind? I am present, am I not?" Erik interposed. "At first your comments were tactful, but I find they are now indecorous and insupportable. You speak too personal." Erik's plumage was quite ruffled.

"How so? Can you deny that neither of us has claim to knowing you in such a way?" the Persian asked.

"No, but you carry on as though I am not able to account for myself," he responded hotly.

The Persian stood and looked at Erik straight on; both were of similar height and build, and well adapted in respect to the other. "Able, yes, but disposed to?" he twisted and bit down on the last word.

Finish! Erik demanded silently. He felt eerily cool headed and straightened for the challenge, the Persian checking him mid-thought.

"Before you become too unsettled, hear me out. Let us not forget how often you spoke as though you were *not* willing to do so." Erik looked as a chastened youth, dubious to what outcome may be arrived at. "This should be nourishment for a starved mind, Erik, feast on. Just when were you thinking of atoning for the blame you placed on your *other* self?" There was a visible twitch. "Ah, third person is now distasteful and impolitic, hmm? You should try being the listener, for it is immensely frustrating to hear all manner of comment thrown about, with the responsible party present, while at the same time artfully dodging any hint of accountability, and, if you detest being the center of discussion, participate in the conversation and defend who you are! Time shall be proof of expiation or it will be the undoing, the execution. I, for one, appreciate what I see, what I hear, and am pleased." The Persian rested his hand atop Erik's shoulder, and giving it a hearty grasp, admonished him sincerely. "When one has discovered the right companion, when reciprocation is in abundance and the heart is full, it is reward enough. Look at her, Erik!" He chuckled at the color suddenly flooding the countenance of both then whispered, "I much prefer giving rise to this sort of fire than another. You had better treat her well, Monsieur Gautier, and love her passionately."

Erik stared at Christine, humbled by the charge issued.

The Persian offered his hand to Erik, and to his surprise, it was accepted. "Good evening to you, Mademoiselle Christine. Erik. I shall see myself out, now that I am able, and would enjoy future visits to become more acquainted." He bowed and quit their presence in elegant calm, leaving them several moments in awe of his behavior. Was it audacity or just friendly pretension?

Christine glanced laterally, her vision staying to study at length the emotion apparent in Erik. He removed his masque slowly, deliberately tossed it into an empty chair, and leaned with his back to the mantle, arms crossed and chin seeded into his palm. He had yet to fix his sight on anything but the void in which he was now focused. *Feel, feel something.* He was numb at the mental banquet his friend had given him for perusal, though it was not until the mild rain of tears that motivation to breach the pregnant silence became provisionary for *her* approach. The movement startled him; he had forgotten he was not alone and reached for her, burying his head to her shoulder, taking succor in her embrace. "He is pleased with me, Christine, sincerely pleased."

"Very much so. I know that I am."

Erik gathered her, entwined his arms round about her and held tight, speaking softly, "I have thirsted from a man whose opinion I have quietly valued and revered. I drink his praise, and am quenched at long last." He sighed. "His upbraiding I could have done without; it came poignantly, but true."

"Followed swiftly by a showing forth of greater love," she murmured. "Your friendship, it is perhaps deeper than either of you is willing to admit to the other?" A nod from him finished the observation.

"Look at me, Christine." Her eyes met his, bright and piquant. Queer, this request for another to look on him, and how bold, no masque, and yet she eyed him sensuously. Passionate? Dear heavens, yes! She pulled from him his best. Six months in review had proved the man of thirty-nine, a stranger to that of forty; he who stood in the arms of such a lovely woman and partook in her intelligence, a man who now heeded improvements; for this man he had fond regard, and all because someone cared. "Hmm?"

"I said, dear wanderer, that the chambers are much improved."

"A little here and there."

"Your nightly occupation?"

"No, you are my diversion," he put out seriously.

"Ah, regular *rites* of visitation based on, what? Tell me, how is it to be tolerated, these forays, this restless vagrancy?"

What a tease, sweet lady! "Sad, there is nothing much to be done that will do me any good save marrying me." He shrugged as Christine began to gradually withdraw from his arms during the change in topic, but he eagerly snatched her closer. "You are not to retreat from me, for I cannot give you up just yet. Perhaps a taste would satisfy, if you will not concede." He was again regaining his playfulness.

"Tastes only whet the appetite."

"They would keep me nearer to being anchored. Yes, I should think it a positive thing to be secured." His tone importuned hope. "Marry me!"

"I shall, on Friday at two." She winked.

"More waiting, blast!" Erik slid the curl he was twisting from his finger. "A few suggestions could be entertained in accordance with stringency, could they not?"

"I know I shall regret any agreement, benign as the request may seem."

"No faith in me, imp that you are!"

"Oh, I have faith aplenty, and trust that you will use it to your irrefutable advantage, such as you have over me, for I know not what stratagem is forming in that scheming mind of yours."

"You wound me," he said, clasping hands to breast.

"It is fortunate for the world you are not an actor,' she goaded. "I remain unconvinced. Your suggestions?"

"Critic! Fine, I wish to know of your success in locating a wedding dress, what it looks like actually, so I may engage the imagination."

Her brow arched then settled when Erik's lips broadened. "Well, it is white, long sleeved, high necked, and has a flowing train."

Erik's eyes narrowed. "Do not play coy with me; it better not have all of your beautiful skin covered. It would be a burning shame to barricade me completely; you know how I thrive on contact."

"I do. The dress is in good taste, but you shall not weasel from me any of the details. You know enough, as much as any bridegroom should."

"Should!" he scoffed. "Well, since I am now wholly unsuccessful on two fronts, I may desire to take liberties. Would you accompany—?"

"I have heard those words before," she broke in, "and look where I am now."

Erik's hands had circled around to repose easily, folded upon the small of Christine's back. "I believe, my dear, that you must share equally in the arena opened by your gentle penchant for me, hmm? Come, not another word, no more debate."

He disengaged himself and sought their cloaks then escorted her quietly above, hailing the nearest cab. But it was not until the driver was given direction that Christine had any meager hint of where Erik desired her to go; they were destined for the Bois de Boulogne.[6]

The day had wasted, leaving the raven sky to boast its orbed beauty, a dangling ornament of the heavens surrounded by opalescent gems, unassuming against their infinite, opaque curtain. Walking for some time in protracted harmony, Erik and Christine strayed through the leafy-veined pathways amidst the shorn grass and colorful trees in their evening gloves: oaks, chestnuts, locusts, cedars, and beeches lined dense woodland galleries to form seasoned gardens, scented and quickly yielding their sacrifice, unnoticed till dawn.

A clean surge of air rushed over the open lanes, fiercely waving its patrons cloaks, and roaring past the fingered branches above, then it eased. Christine was braced against Erik one minute and the next, led in hurried fashion to a grove near the lake; and it was here, behind the trunk of a broad resident, that the two sought refuge from the change in weather.

"We should—"

"Too late," he chuckled, "it already begins."

Christine heard the jovial intonations, for it was indeed a light misting drizzle which veiled the park on the heels of their retreat, together held at the mercy of an outpouring from clouds laden past their prime.

"We should stay fairly dry, but there is no guarantee the duration will be short. Would this," he paused in emphasis, "be an acceptable suggestion?" He had picked up in conversation at almost the exact point in which he had left, as though seconds, not hours, had elapsed between. His arms gestured wide.

"I suppose it is more than a suggestion if it is realized, Monsieur?" she stated in a soft voice, her cheek pressed to his. "Your arms are paradise to me."

"Then come," his expression bid deeply. "Idyllic peace awaits."

Moving confidently into the shelter proffered her she was gathered close for warmth, and kept safely to his breast as the sky met relief of burden. A keen interval elapsed in which the sharing of solitude was akin to communion with one's self in nature. Soon, an austere revival, purified and marked by the deep inhalation expanding the breadth of Erik's lungs, awakened his gregariousness.

"Christine, if I may ask, what do you think on? Neither of us has uttered more than has been needful. Minimalists that we now are, I discover my latent curiosity in want." There came a short sigh from her. "Sounds mysteriously significant."

"Erik." He chuckled at how his teasing promoted that vocal inflection. Her fingers directed their caress to the coarse stippling along his throat and he calmed. "You may laugh, but I have been in earnest. I endeavored to be in the present, as it is. The very moment I felt you near tonight, I shed the past, though it was heaped about me. Nothing mattered but you, though I did relish the sardonic wit of the Persian. He is priceless—"

"Is he now?" Erik mocked, his arrogance vexed. "I refuse to allot more than a centime for his blackened hide." He quickly atoned, then asked rather sulkily, "If. . . if he is priceless, under what light do you consider me?"

"You come at great expense, Monsieur," she said, having tugged mercilessly at his jealous pride. "*Precious* expense, Monsieur. Not a day sets where I am unable to account gratefully for our valuable union, one in which a lifetime of industrious devotion will be required to further its depths. My desire is to place worth, to make known in as precise a way as possible, why you are most dear, most beloved."

Erik's heart was full, so full that he risked spilling forth if he made instant comment, so he postponed and lightly displayed the contents thereof with a sweet kiss. "You were saying, when I interrupted."

She allowed him to guide her head against his shoulder before continuing. "My mind strives for tranquility, as such is in limited supply right now, every minute consumed by what is complete, what has yet to be attended to, where to go, what to do, and remembering. Tonight focused solely on events of the moment, no past, no future: sounds, sights, scents, and delightful sentiments, all of which have enriched the flavor of your company by ten-fold. I have listened to my soul's content, and pondered on the sagacious conversation, how it engaged and touched. Then melancholy pricked while traversing the impenetrable dark. I discovered I no longer dreaded any second of unsurety; your stealth became a detectable, audible energy of reassurance. I enjoyed as a child would, the novelty of clapping hooves against the streets while being borne rhythmically between two points; brusque protector, as your air demanded, seated at my side. Our forms, once divested from the convenience of transport, ere long became gypsy-like. I devoured the pulse of your wrist as my hands clasped tightly to yours, skin-to-skin, feeling the resonance with which I am most familiar."

At this point in the narrative, Christine stirred briefly, repositioning her arms to draw both in closer, and Erik pulled his cloak about them. He appreciated the trees, screening them from the city, could hear the majestic wind summoning all to bowing reverence, and kissed the crown of her head.

"I've felt as near to home as ever I could. The beating of your heart, its steady resolve welcomes, beckons my soul to yours. I shall never leave. This is my promise, my word, my pledge; I love you as no other."

Regularity of a peculiar conflict had troubled Erik throughout the evening flow in a manifestation of verbal actuation, his ability to loosen his tongue coming more languidly than his prompt show of affection. It was thereby displayed in a sweetened caress along her soft skin, and shone as fire, kindled full within the horizon of his glowing eyes, but all came unseen behind the ocean swell and poured lavishly as a wealth of ardor onto her lips, sealing them unfailingly for life.

Words were wholly unnecessary.

How he wished to stay until dawn, holding her, listening to nothing but her breath as it cast a moist fog across his shoulder. There was little else to avail him pleasure, except being with her, but it was not worth taxing either to an extreme. It vexed, frustrated him to no end, when he desired nearness and she was elsewhere or he became detained. How he despised Separateness and called Distance wicked!

Our return from the park gardens reminded us both of home. She looks to it as I, the time was a treasured, resplendent pause, for we will again bustle about, haunt, and wait for another day to expire. No sooner were we trotted off than the tranquility arrested with a suggestion I proposed—and she had the audacity to refute me, dear angel—that we marry first thing today. Obviously flustered by the reduction of time, she said 'it will not do' and pouted, chiding me for taking enjoyment from her plans. In truth, I have arrangements as well and must be resigned, blast! But no matter, I will check on her soon, and shall await her coming to take breakfast with me. Then, I shall delight in bringing her here, to this lower chamber, to this place I have concealed from all other influences. It is here, in this inner sanctum, where I can and will share more of who I am with Christine, within an environment created, rife in the glorious beauties of knowledge.

AS THE BANE OF an overbearing dream—one ill-wished for—obliged its presence, a birth of agony squeezed forth in droplets along Christine's hairline; dampening the thick mass, they receded almost as swiftly, one after another until each successive bead trailed its predecessor into the pillow.

She was standing behind a curtain, staid in manner, content in position within the muffled depth, for she could not see, nor hear, beyond the suffocating constraint, then the barrier was drawn away from before her. It fell, a pall; rent in twain, as clouds parted for the bluely, moonlit sky, to shroud two coffins among a congregation at rest. Regret bemoaned the passing in a sullen wind, which churned the mantle of repose and whisked the coverings from their eerie, silk-lined abodes. On having her sight renewed, she turned to her left, finding her father at peace, the lid shutting in final recognition. At her right was an empty shell, it confused, cast doubt and completely unnerved, but the lid shut tight as well. Lifting her eyes to a remote hill, she could see a shaded form, one known best to her, and set out to accomplish the distance in earnest. Her pace was rapid, but the void between increased with every footfall. In frantic haste she sought the vision without lessening the perilous gap. Stopping, her arms thrust outward, he responded. Joy ensued, though his endeavor became equally as fruitless. Numbing cold gripped their hope of reunion as terror closed over her mouth. No scream could she emit, no call of warning came. All ability was dissolved by panic in her struggle to usurp the bands that held her freedom. Lungs burned, jaw seared, and the pressure, immense. . .

"Christine!" Erik's tone was passionate as he held her wrists, staving off the wild frenetic swings. "Stop, it's all right, I am here. It is only a dream. Hush, Christine. . . shh, shh."

Her consciousness jolted and gave rise to the present, leaving her panting and wide-eyed while regaining her bearings. Once subdued, her face contorted and her body convulsed in grief. Erik leaned near and she flung her arms around his neck.

"I couldn't find peace, my safety. . . gone." She clung in desperation, wetting his shirt collar. "You and I were as distant as words uttered in vain across the wind." She halted, shaking involuntarily. "He touched me. . . restrained me. . ."

Erik attempted to embrace and protect as much of her as he possibly could. "I am the only one here, it is I who touches you. We are not apart," his whispers came reassuring to her ear. "I should never have left you to bear this out alone. A candle is not enough when my arms were the only solace fit to quell the storm raging upon your subconscious." He bore her up and drifted not one whit from her side, nor permitted release from his grasp until the dispelling of fright was complete. It was she who drew away first, patting his chest softly where his wound lay beneath.

"I am no better than a silly child afraid of thunder," she said in irritation.

"I beg to differ. *Our* experience, my love, was more than just a superficial disturbance."

While nodding, she gazed at him for a substantially long duration. Christine watched Erik's cheek flush under scrutiny, and then she smiled herself. The awkwardness had since dawned on them, and seizing the furtive opportunity to disengage her stare, he had taken to examining her jaw line.

"We have an innocuous habit of wending our way into the path of the other, no?" She looked askance upon Erik's unmasqued face.

"We do. Although I enjoy the tastes and dream of feasting heartily."

"Confiding those thoughts will only. . ." She turned suddenly, noting he had ceased his gentle caress only to catch the descent of his lips, which required her to put the effort aside before they ensnared their goal. "Erik, please, there are too many temptations here."

He stood sharply, inarticulate at first, then conciliatory in countenance. "Soon then?"

"Yes."

"And you are steady enough?"

"I am."

"When you are come to me, you will permit me a decent welcome?"

"Most certainly."

Satisfied, he departed subdued in spirit, though not in heart. She could see the smoldering flame of passion gleaming in his eyes and the exclamation of acceptance in stature; there was no brooding, no feeling of deprecation, only love and respect.

Chapter Twenty

As Christine rose later that morning, she thought of what the day would bring, and then what it might be like upon the next. While readying herself, she looked at her reflection in the mirror and applied an evaluative eye upon her features, similar to what she had given Erik's just a few hours before. Nothing of significance could be detected; it was she, the same autumn brown hair and fair hued complexion; all were unchanged, but somehow altered. An enigmatic look controlled each aspect while her mind pondered on. It was not the reddened streak that made any difference in appearance, nothing quite so easy. Perhaps she was searching for something that could only be seen through emotion. Was it being the giver of unconditional love or that she was so well loved herself? Maturity? Hope? The sharing of life? She sighed; the time of day was early, but would not keep for such poignancy or harassing of mind, and she finished arranging the last of her curls. Closing the door behind her, she instructed the maid on where her possessions were to be taken then hastened to meet Erik.

It was a joyous bidding of dawn, as Christine half walked, half ran through the streets of a slumbering Paris. Her destiny neared, not unlike the veiled wraith of the dream experienced, for it was here that she succeeded in bringing *him* to her grasp with each step tread; the ground did not gape, nor would it recede beneath the expectancy, it was sure.

Erik met her on the shore as she fell gladly into his waiting arms, and then he pronounced the day superb when her promise was at once fulfilled; a shuddering breath, his only reply.

"Good morning."

"That it is. Does the sun lift its head?" he asked briskly.

"Not entirely."

"Then we shall enjoy the morn in leisure, come." He took Christine's hand and moved her in front of him. There was a mysterious air lingering about the implication of leisure, and her curiosity heightened even more as they passed through Erik's flat to the rear of his personal chamber. Often, this recurrence of full circles situated itself in linking them together, and now was no different. The door pivoted, just as it had six months before, but this time, a glow flooded from the passageway, beckoning gaily to its visitors. Erik stopped at the familiar bend and performed in reverse, the removal of cloak, hat, gloves and masque, and then added Christine's belongings as well.

Without warning, Erik resumed his memorable grasp upon her forearms, and understanding without error what had been meant, she did likewise; her movements retraced precisely until he held her nestled to his breast.

"You remember specifics quite well," she commented.

"Humph, double-edged," he murmured. "How could I forget the very place which fastened me indissolubly to you? I trembled that night, scared out of my wits at the foreign deity thrust near, and was utterly lost. I did not know how to act. I disbelieved, doubted. . . I still do."

Placing her hands to either side of his face, he was gently drawn to her. Lips brushed, and then she pressed hers to each of his piercing eyes, then to the concern etched upon his brow. "Am I not real? Does this feel as spirited emptiness against your skin? Do you encircle your arms about a vacant hope?"

"You are real enough, but promise me that you will not cease to remind my fleeting credulity until it becomes stable."

"I will often, though I cannot vouch for even temperament."

"What!" he exclaimed. "Is patience now to become as conditional as biting? Please, spare me these exercises in caprice! I shall be a case of pitiful infliction, not knowing whether I am coming or going."

Taking both her hands in his, and kissing them exuberantly, he grinned rather wide, much as a young child unable to contain a confidence long kept. They went lower, negotiating an additional level, down into the deafening quiet where no one ever goes, and where no one would ever hear, down below the fifth cellar toward the Communists' dungeon. Walls of stone went before them, surrounded them from all sides, the very foundation above loomed and stretched out into every Parisian crevasse and void unknown to man; deep and foreboding, a dark, impervious to light, but where the starburst from each torch illuminated. Erik hesitated, turning beneath a flame.

"I have never brought anyone, wholly conscience, this far below," he confessed. "No one knows. It is a place safe from the influences of the world, concealed. . . and now I share it with you. Perhaps it will become a special sanctuary for us. I am unsure about its use, knowing in time we will define how best to appropriately incorporate it, if at all. You shall help me decide."

His speech was unclear and protracted, enigmatical at best. Christine was perplexed, but she knew revelation would follow swiftly, for if there was one thing Erik relished, it was the suspense preceding disclosure of some piece of lofty genius, and she, perched on the edge of that emergence, waited.

The stone wall submitted to his touch and a second barrier, hinged inwardly as any heavyset door might, opened by a mere twist of the handle. They went in, crossing the raised threshold into a place of awe and inspiration, a museum-like chamber, one in which the most inquisitive of intellects would have been satisfactorily invigorated. A general blending of antiquities suffused the room in simple fashion, and the floor coverings were no exception, being limited to thick woven area carpets, with little or no design. Within direct sight were bookshelves, abundantly lined by volumes in their antiquated dress jackets and all manner of peculiar, scientific workings; near to these, a chair, ottoman, and small lamp topped table, sat as cozy accoutrements. Upon absolute entry, the room took form altogether—one would have thought themselves in a strange representation of a theatre—the shape was curved, larger at both ends, and narrow at the center, its right wall covered in a wide, velvety sapphire curtain, and to the left, its mirrored opposite on a smaller scale, a portière, complete with tapered, straight-backed chairs as matching sentries.

Christine felt the splendid virtues of good works as she passed through. Glancing sideways, she beheld an eager Erik, skirting the edge to keep out of her way. She almost laughed, but maintained her composure well enough. He behaved anxiously, conditioned to the least bit of praise from her, to which she had given none on this relegated hideaway of his. She continued to the other end and took in the pianoforte, couch, and a marble-capped table strewn with music, paper, and calligraphy supplies.

"Someone has been practicing," she said, picking up a sample.

"I have," he stated proudly. "What do you think?"

"Your hand improves quickly."

"Christine..." Erik compressed his lips testily. "I entreat you, tell me what you think."

Smiling, she turned. "I think, Monsieur, that you have far too many secrets."

"And *you* are a tyrannical tease!" he growled, seizing a fistful of hair at the nape of his neck.

Striding toward him she grabbed his waist and ran her eyes thoroughly over his facial features. "It is a haven. One I shall gladly share with you."

He seemed pleased. "Good, there is more," he whispered, throwing his arm round her shoulders for control, while pulling on the tasseled cording before her. The curtain rose thus, parting and drawing upward in overlapping swags to reveal an alcove. It too, was unpretentiously furnished, a bedstead in rich mahogany, with dressing table and wardrobe. Before she could gasp out the tiniest of accolades, he circled and led her through the opposite set of curtains in a whirlwind of motion, letting the cloth fall behind. Christine's eyes widened and focused under another dim torchlight: it was a vaulted cavern, unimposing, but a most fascinating void. Here, not more than a few yards away, was a natural spring enclosed by smooth Parian marble;[7] the effervescence swirled, rising unopposed until it overflowed the lower boundary, returning to its earthly depths in rivulets, one edge heaving a bounty ready for reaping.

"You are hungry, I hope? Your table awaits, Madame Gautier," he said, the title rolling out in a fiery accent as he stirred from her side.

Christine barely snagged his cuff before he was out of reach, drawing his attentions abruptly from those intended. Joy lifted her mouth and played at the corner of each eye as she took hold of his wrist; a stride brought him back to her.

"Christine." Her name broke free from his lips, feathered and impassioned. "I had always imagined you would find. . . what I lived contentedly with—*and damn contented at that*—unappealing and oppressive. You came back only slightly willingly after I freed you during our first encounter, and the other times were anxiously compelled. I was no fool despite my fantastical behavior, but you were at least kind. So, that said, I was unsure on this trial and feared you might wish to never partake in the world that hid me, that I would wither your delicate spirit if I held too tightly." He smoothed a few short hairs from her face. "When you. . . last night, when you said you would not leave, that you would stay. Will you accept this, as ours?"

"Many perspectives have been transposed, Erik. Yes, wherever you are, there will I be." Then, gently kissing him, she answered "ours" atop his parted lips.

CHRISTINE GRINNED AS those thoughts of her morning vividly played out while standing in front of the full length glass; she had since been with Meg.

The fruit juice dripping uncontrollably amidst echoing laughter in the *Whispering Spring*, to which she had fondly christened the chamber. Peaches had not worked quite so well as raspberries, but the experience became priceless. Erik's attempts at containing the rich fruit in his mouth created a sticky mess, making for the most amicable of affections.

"Christine! Good heavens!" Meg waved her hand in front of Christine's face to summon her to the present. "I have been calling for you to show me the dress. Our afternoon is full; such nerve, to stand here day dreaming, though whatever the male distraction, it was more than likely a delicious vision."

Christine flushed. "Why would you say such a thing?"

"Because your distant gleam made me wickedly jealous, and you have been giddy, almost recklessly giddy. Richard is not scheduled to arrive until tomorrow morning and I will already be with you. I miss his animated conversation and attentions."

"I apologize on the first account, but you claim I am reckless," she gasped, "that I can never be."

"Silly, don't think twice. You are only carefree; a woman in love, and my Richard has been gone a month from me, a whole month away from this continent, and in England no less! He was to visit a few of the coastal provinces then finish with his return here."

"Meg?" Christine seized her arm pointedly. "You have told me much about your dearest Richard, and though I look forward to meeting him, you must promise me something."

"Anything."

"If your relationship with him or any other should become quite serious, you must swear to me that you will never make reference to Erik in any way but the present tense, since we have returned. From this time on, his past, his connections, the stories, it is essential for his well being that it remain buried. I know it is asking a great deal, but this one confidence may never be shared."

Meg stared intently, then took a short breath. "I give you my word."

Christine's hold slid to Meg's hand, grateful for dependence upon a friend, for the somber mind, less will-o-the-wisp traits, and retention of zest for secreted schemes. They had evolved. "He has lived for so long without goodness, and still he doubts. I just want him to go on without hesitation, to experience what I give him unconditionally." The cloud, which had attached itself so quickly to her countenance, gave way to a show of relief. "Thank you."

"Mademoiselles?" An inquisitive knock on the doorframe forced them to look. "You are satisfied? It is to your liking?"

"Oh, Madame Bailleul, I could not have wished for better, it fits perfectly. Do you think Monsieur Gautier will approve?"

"The alterations were minimal, and if he does not approve, my dear, he is a fool," replied the sweet couturier.

"That he is most definitely not!" Christine laughed. *Most decidedly not!*

Chapter Twenty-One

A note lay upon the bed; Erik had made the discovery shortly after Christine took leave of him, without escort. He thought it strange, the request to make her departure alone, that he remain. Her nervousness sent the previous intoxication of pleasure to bind in mass and swell in his stomach. He was expressly put out, she, not to be accompanied, and he not to be graced by her presence every valuable moment was very disconcerting in every aspect. Erik forced himself to remember the comforting peace her narrative afforded. *Trust her! She will not leave.* The note was testament to this inner voice. He listened, glad to dispel the negative havoc. *Another of her simple acts of kindness. I appreciate finding traces of love to indicate that I am in her thoughts, though perhaps not as much as she occupies mine. But this is cryptic, bothersome and resolute, yet my integrity constrains me from mastering its desires.* Erik creased the fold open. He had fingered the writing most of the day, kept it tucked close at hand where he could soothe the distance and read it often. *'Not to be unfastened until designated time,'* and its counterpart, with the directive on the accompanying card. *'Your presence is requested at an intimate rendezvous. Please wear appropriate evening attire. Further intelligence is detailed within the enclosed message. You may commence at precisely eight-thirty tonight.'*

"How frustrating!" he exclaimed aloud. "I am held hostage, me, of all people. One who has resorted to extortion and unscrupulous behavior, bound to a mere fragment of prose whose mystic contents await."

He had prepared early, righted the chamber, and paced about incessantly in his sleek, pantheresque habit, even his pocket watch, if it had any sense of touch whatsoever, would have been handled raw with his continual checking—but then again, one would need to pity the stone under foot as well.

"She tries my fortitude! She knew full well that my thunderous impatience would drive me to distraction. This game, the challenge. . ." and he lapsed into thought while biding time, seating his figure squarely into the chair cushion. *I've not ever been employed in such a manner, an interesting quandary, but she does this purposely, to test me, perhaps, or because. . . she truly loves me.* He ran his fingers over the writing. *She cares, and we shall wed tomorrow.*

The words had venerable poignancy, as did the time, for it was now eight-thirty, and not a moment was wasted in stripping the paper of its seal.

> *A place of consternation posed*
> *Assumed a prank in jest,*
> *Ensuing patience worn too thin*
> *A shadow's view deemed best.*

Erik's mind sifted through the meaning. *Of course!* He left at once from the lower cellars, closing everything tightly in his wake, stealing his way—as only he could—through each level and ensuing passages to the adjacent stages, its theatre, and inevitably. . . to Box 5. Engaging his facile stealth, he slipped out to behold a dimly lit house, taking a moment to inspect the progress, and he, having heard of the impasse regarding the counterbalance beneath the stage and imperial side entrance, was beyond resisting a gander. All was on hold until a suitable course could be agreed upon, but as theatre performances were not the sole reason for the Opera's original conception, the societal events filled in rather nicely, without undue pressure placed on the renovation schedule. "Humph, Parisian contractors." Erik shook his head, while his quick stride had him entering Box 5. "Now where?"

He searched; running his hands over every inch of the red velvet ledges draped about the grand tier, under the chairs. . . nothing. Finger tapped chin as his eyes scanned; he turned slowly, at last glancing toward a small shelf from where he stood opposite—it was a second note, clearly visible.

Well done, Monsieur! And on we go:

> *Beauty engulfs by silken form*
> *Deity's song, vocal discipline replete,*
> *Her name, upon an angel's lips*
> *To guide earth's soul to heavens keep.*

On he went, back through from whence he came to the Communists' road, which led behind the last hallway of dressing rooms, a glance, the silent trip of a spring, and the mirror pivoted inward into Christine's old room, which was a most depressing sight. A dismal grey-green, seeping from a gas light outside the door, rendered the walls, floors, and all its furnishings, dull and lifeless. No living warmth but two roses, their stems crossed atop the next verse, lying on the bed.

"Singleness of beauty," he mused, "white for innocence and red, impassioned love."

Please include nature's celebration of verve in your journey:

> *Rocking hearts from shores apart*
> *A vessel beckoned glides,*

Silent sky of blackened glass
Bids music ere long abide.

Tucking the floral companions safely within his cloak, he headed below again. *Now I am the bearer of gifts, quite perplexing.* The boat was moored obediently, as was he, his broad shoulders hunched in contemplative thought, stroking his chin. *The most logical places would be the bow or stern, seeing as how either is used interchangeably.* Kneeling, he examined the ends and found nothing, then slid his hand around the rim, finally locating a compact bundling of paper tacked under the upper frame. "Not obvious, well done," he murmured.

From heaven above to ground below
Purification reigns supreme,
Sacred swan, cithara blessed
Height attained beyond one's dream.

Erik sat down unsteadily at the edge of the dock and cried unashamed in broken gratitude, astonished at the words chosen. He had traipsed through this enclosed kingdom, from the farthest vault encased and would now ascend to be with his angel, heart strong and soul light, no condemning limits, no enmity-forged chains. *She gives joy, love, and laughter in measures I have never partaken; I do not want, as she provides, and nothing is beyond her scope. Her forbearance carries innocence to cleanse, virtue to raise merit, and strength to an indomitable will. This is to whom I shall cleave; she is my life.*

Leaning against the post, he composed himself and rose. His steps began slowly enough, he thought, as he pressed those bits of script into the confines of his waistcoat, but hastened midst the sobering cadence of quiet; uninhibited he soared to roof level without grievance of discovery, a whisper among spirits. Up among the cupolas and statues, above a city bursting with night life—which, were it not for the rustling of carriage wheels on the streets below, would have seemed in a state of absolute hush—an inky sky shone clear of all but a pale moon fixed still. Poised on a bench, mere steps afore the parapet, her back away from him, Christine sat with her eyes closed, head primed to listen; a single candle flickered from its glass display, resting in unison on a black, wrought iron table next to a fluted vase.

He approached solemnly, treading unseen, his steps languid and fluidly black, poured on toward the mesmerizing apparition, his sight riveting all emotion to her light blue form under the vibrating fringe of her white shawl. Erik could not deny the eagerness he felt, but he wished to observe, to indulge in the beauty of wonder and allow Christine to direct this sequencing of events. He interrupted his motion forward, waiting for her to make the first move. Her head rotated over her left shoulder as though detecting he was near, then she smiled softly and made way to stand, looking straight at him. Breathing became an abstraction, a muffled effort when her hand beckoned. Common interchange was needless; the roses were placed, gloves and cloak removed, seats taken, and their left sides near, gazes intent.

"Tonight, we are on the cusp of fusing our hearts and bonding our souls, the last night we are to be apart. I desired a special evening, wanted you to experience something different, something only for you. You have blessed me with your voice, opened your heart, shared burdens, and trusted. Tomorrow we shall begin life again at each other's side, as husband and wife."

Erik took hold of Christine's hand within his own and pressed it ardently to his lips. "My dearest, you have provided me with far more than is comprehensible. Do you realize what joy I derive from doing *for* someone instead of *to* someone? Real happiness floods my veins; there is purpose, good and clean. And... I delight in our love!" He exclaimed with such sincere conviction that he had to pause and look away; minutes passed before he could resume. "It has been a pleasure to be the center of your attention this evening."

"You found the amusement to your liking?"

"Christine, it was refreshing, and provided a unique, endearing twist, but it was more than just an enjoyable diversion of thoughtfulness. The last segment of verse," his heart suddenly filled again to spill down his cheeks. "It bore down with such weight," he said, ending with a shake of his head.

"Mythology's Apollo?" She smoothed a lock of his hair.

"Yes, though I do not believe in mythological beings, I am aware of the more common gods."

"When the idea came to me, I sought ways of including symbolism within what I wrote, considered the resolute fixtures adorning the Opera and read accordingly about several gods. I focused on Apollo specifically, only to discover that many of his traits and circumstances correspond with yours."

"Well, some at any rate." He kissed her soft hands. "I am not an Apollo in looks, but have been more fortunate in love than he. He thinks of swans as sacred, is the god of music, the arts, and light—mind that that segment came only with you." Erik shifted and steadily looked at her. "The reference to the purification rituals he performed, done in behalf of those guilty of lurid crimes, reminded me... we have not mentioned my offenses for some time. I should like to hear your feelings in regard to them."

"Why?" she demanded. "Why must it be dredged up? I thought this would express our understanding, Erik, that we might put it to rest."

"It does," he said apologetically. He had clearly made her cross. "But I need to hear you, to know once more where I stand. My conscience will not allow me to marry you if you have any reservations, any at all."

Upon her hearing the last, she exhaled in terse recollection. "What we have discussed has grown faint, and fades from my memory at least. I could never condemn or act against you because *I* know who you are. I know who you would have been all those years ago.

I willingly accept, choose to accept; the man I love is here, not in the past."

His drawn out sigh preceded the gentle touch of his thumb caressing her temple, and his palm cupped her cheek. Guiding her close, their lips pressed sensitively and often. "Please, I wish to feel your delicate care. . . take off my masque."

Christine obeyed, liberating his tears with tenderness. "Erik? There is more," she said calmly.

"More?"

"If I may, I should like to proceed."

"Proceed? All I desire is before me."

She smiled, "I pray you accept what I wish you to have. There are many memories, some life long, but all of them sweet," she explained.

This puzzled him; he needed nothing, wanted nothing, what more could she possibly impart to him?

"Close your eyes, for me." He glanced at her dubious display of behavior then followed her entreaty. Once amenable, she produced from beneath the bench a leather case, richly aged and graced with a white ribbon. "You may look."

Saying nothing, Erik's gaze rested on the *cadeau*[8] taken into his lap. The violin case told of travels, though not extensive, and was used, but not overly so.

"It was one which belonged to my father," she offered.

Unhurried, he retrieved the instrument from its soft bed and skimmed the burnished surface in adoration, his touch resting as though it were fragilely spun glass. Christine must have caught a glimpse of his renewed emotion in the candlelight; she smiled satisfactorily. This night was filled with sentiments, tokens of love and tenderness and the very essence of memory.

"Very few people," he said tentatively, "have ever given me

anything which did not have some tie of obligation knotted and strung from it. I am unaccustomed to this sort of reciprocity."

"An older gentleman, a retired luthier, restored it for me. He said it was a Cannone Guarnerius." Erik's eyes lit up. "I knew the name would have more meaning for you."

"But, I was under the impression your father had. . ."

"And how many do you have?"

"Two. . . three."

"I kept the other, less often used violin instead of selling it when my father passed. Would you play?" her voice urged.

Erik kissed her forehead, tucked the instrument under his arm, and ascended to the pinnacle of Apollo's statue, the only place that seemed altogether appropriate at the moment to place bow to string. He perched himself with solid demure, securing the violin with raven wings, and there, commenced brilliant music. *The Resurrection of Lazarus* came to mind as the notes soared to unfatigueable heights, only to glide back under the master's command. The tones that emanated from the agile splendor pierced air, arresting the heart, and by force, made a resounding connection upward until Christine's vision clouded. When the last, full vibration drew to a close, she gently addressed her emotion and brushed the drops aside.

"Thank you. That was beautiful," she extolled reverently while he made his descent.

He replaced the violin within its leather cradle, and bowing, offered his hand to Christine, they embraced.

"I am blessed," he said tenderly. "My love is yours."

Looking out over the city they observed the world before them and kissed, lips touching in acclaimed fervor, moving in affection, ending their evening thusly complete.

Chapter Twenty-Two

Morning came early as Christine lay soaking under the warm covers, basking in sweet thoughts. So content was she that she dared not move a muscle nor open her eyes for fear all would dissolve. *Last night, it was totally uncharacteristic of him, every moment, every touch, and every single kiss!* She grinned impishly while the evening replayed, her skin tingling even now.

A knock rattled the dream's intensity and chased it away to play on—back stage—whilst new scenes began. Meg peered in at her friend from around the doorframe, then burst in brightly upon seeing she was awake.

"So? What did he think? How did he react?" she asked, bounding onto the bed.

Christine sat up with her nose raised in a matter-of-fact way and said nothing.

"Oh! You promised! Ugh! How can you not tell? Christine you are simply awful." Meg went on, pouting miserably, chiding left and right for being denied the details and finished in a grand huff by folding her arms and collapsing backwards onto the bed. "A big tease, that's what you are. I hope Erik knows about this side of your temperament."

"He calls me the same thing, so yes, he is aware of the danger he is entering into. Besides, he is an even bigger tease, when he sets his mind to it." Christine watched Meg fume for a moment. "All right, sit up. . . I'll tell."

Meg righted herself to listen.

"First off, it was fortune that put me where I needed to be. Erik's invitation to breakfast fit perfectly; I just had to extricate myself from beneath that scrutinizing eye of his, to set up the initial note and the one requiring the tuck and tack along the rim of his boat; the rest were situated later. I knew he would figure them out, little doubt there, but for his reactions, I was very ill-prepared." She envisioned him in the candlelight, his tears, private. Meg had to reach for her arm so that she might continue. Christine smiled. "He came to me, dressed in black. If it were not for his white shirt I should never have seen him, though I felt his presence. You cannot believe how nervous I suddenly was, weakness and strength tugging in various degrees—*and I shall be a wreck by two this afternoon.* The violin sincerely touched him. He caressed the strings as if petitioning Father for my love. . . then he walked me here. He was so out of character, Meg, laughable even, but so passionate. Each time we came upon a shadowed niche or side street, he would pull me into his embrace and lavish me with affection."

"How roguish! Such impropriety! My Richard would be appalled, the English gentleman that he is, and then he would proceed to do the same."

They had a hearty laugh, which required several minutes to recover from. "And the courtyard garden. . ." Christine subjoined with a gasp. "That became as a jungle for his flagrant ardor. He refused to release me, threatened to carry me off as he had done before; there was the textured lure of his voice, the smoldering touch, and the depth of intrigue. He said, 'love's fire ignites and shall burn until quenched on the morrow,' then he vanished."

"Disappeared? He left you? Ah, romance," breathed Meg.

Christine fell among the lofty down and wondered aloud. "What do you suppose he is thinking and feeling at this very moment?"

"Oh, please!" Meg cried in mock disgust and tossed a pillow at her. Christine was about to return the favor when Mme Giry entered.

"Come you two, we have a wedding today or have you forgotten?"

Inhaling audibly Christine exclaimed, "Whose wedding? Today? Odd, I do not recall seeing an invitation, are you quite positive?"

She smiled at both young ladies giggling amongst the bed covers. "Yes, I quite assure you, but if this is not the case then I shall send *this* away with your regrets."

"What? Send what away?" the two young women pled excitedly.

Mme Giry held up the tiniest of ring-sized boxes tied with a white satin ribbon.

"Well, it was odd, having a man show up on our steps early this morning, to give me his ward under the strictest of stipulations. First, that you remain ignorant of it, and second, that the gift be delivered into your hands at precisely eight-thirty, and is it not that time now?"

"Oh, heavens, Christine! Maman!" decried Meg.

Eight-thirty, she mused at the time. "Was the man mature?" Christine asked, making the distance short to the door.

"What does it matter?" Meg chimed.

"It matters to me. Remember, Erik is not above playful antics."

"The gentleman was indeed mature, but dark," Mme Giry replied.

Christine graciously retrieved the little treasure, had turned, and was now with Meg, ready to open it. "That, Madame, could be applied to either of the two we know."

"It was not Monsieur Gautier, if that is your meaning."

Satisfied, the present shed its bow and lid to produce a small, carefully folded note about the inner case.

If you are as yet undecided on specific accessories, would you do me the honor of wearing this star, which came into my possession during evening last?

All my love

    Meg blinked, her breath catching lightly when Christine draped a diamond pendant across her hand. They stared at each other, then at the necklace and back, mouths hanging agape. It sparkled, as did Christine's eyes. Meg had already sought out a corner of the bedding and was busy whisking the tears from her cheeks. Mme Giry stepped toward them and quickly withdrew the unnoticed intrusion; their behavior had puzzled even her indifference, but all would come to light as most things did, one way or another. Understanding seemed to pass simultaneously between the two of them and the room's boisterous smile died away to an inarticulate din. Could this be? These young women, who once set the Opera at naught with their stories and fettering gossip, held silent? The type of ladies they were becoming, each in the other's confidence—trusting deeply, and girls at heart—who could enlist spontaneous bouts of ridicule with their chasing around, friends always, to finally claim a sisterly bond in the face of decision and evolving futures. Smiling, Madame's judicious discretion bid her leave.

    Meg heard the door close. "It makes me shiver sometimes with the coincidental, uncanny occurrences. How could he know?"

"There is no possible way, Meg. He could not."

"Then how would you explain it?"

"I... cannot."

Awake most of the night, Erik lay central to the shamble of bedclothes, estranged from sleep; the unrest, mid the even greater tempestuous surge of emotions reigning through his reality, had again rolled him over to bury his face in Christine's scent, lingering on the sleeve of his shirt. He felt such happiness, cast sanity to the wind and triumphed! He serenaded her and behaved as a love starved youth, stealing as much affection as he dared. . . *all those kisses in the garden.* . . How he should be cursed for nearly robbing her senseless prior to his timely desertion. *Beautiful woman!* Cursed? Certainly he was, by an uncharacteristic plague. He had checked, everything was in order, he was sure of it, the tedium of legalities, yes, his mind was freed from all but her, and it was this plague, *her* image, which so sweetly played upon his exhausted mind. Unable to snap up more than a few hours, he breathed her scent once more and rummaged for a pillow in the upheaval.

Several hours later, an intense pounding assaulted the door, shaking its fiber all the way to the hinges. "Daroga!" Erik's voice thundered impatiently, as a second round of pummeling ensued. *Damn!* The door suddenly relinquished its phlegmatic hold in defense, producing an enduringly calm demeanor, at ease within the storm's eye.

"Will you desist? You will be demolishing everything in your path today if you do not take hold of yourself!" the Persian softly chastised. "And," he went on while admitting the flurried groom, "*you*, are late!"

"Very good, Monsieur." The sarcasm darkened, "No brass ring as yet. . . and you don't think I realize?" His chaffing query directed fault solely upon himself.

"Information unwanted, I see." He gestured up.

"I. . . overslept." Erik tugged airily on one of his cuffs, setting the length aright.

"You?" the Persian clarified. "Will wonders never cease?"

Erik's glare reduced the Persian from a vibrant awe, to an abject grin. "I have slept fitfully all week and never as restful as in those hours most recently spent. I was thinking, *of her*. . . and the next. . ." *I am nothing but a clot of nerves.*

The Persian led the way into his study, Erik hot on his heels. "Not to worry, I allowed for this."

"You. . . allowed?" The already present glare gravitated to a perishing scowl and remained, being the only substantial witness to life infusing his veins. Erik's stance resembled that of a statue, rigid and unbending. "You deceived me? Lied to me? There are matters which still must be resolved for this day to come off smooth, are there not? You said certain items must be done the day of, and now?" Erik moved briskly to the window and managed to regain civility in as many seconds, which were slight on either side of this swinging pendulum. "Daroga, I do not wish to upend a day that should be filled with joy. Christine has taught me that I am above the temper which seeks to canker and control me in moments of impetuosity, forgive me."

"Done. I have been involved in many unions, personal and general, and I know you. If I had intimated three days ago of there being a remote possibility of something going awry, you having a lapse in recall about things relegated to your care alone; would you have believed me or reassured me of the *impossibility*?"

"The latter," Erik agreed.

"Then, I must allege you to be as those who are despised by you in this world." He peered tentatively from a lean in Erik's direction.

Erik was listening, reluctant to admit or deny, neither appealed to his judgment save interest in how *he* was like humanity. What the deuce was the man trying to prove? Feeling wrenched over a barrel, he watched without reaction.

"There are certain tendencies innate to men, and it is because I desired this to be a most memorable day that I risked a bit of your indignation in categorizing you with others in predictability. And for as many faculties as you would lay viable claim to, the mind usually disengages quite involuntarily, as though defenestrated." He shrugged, looking again to Erik, and was rewarded when cautious appreciation looked back. "Everything is in order." Now, if you are ready we can proceed to the chapel. That is, if you have *all* items on your person and have forgotten nothing."

The man was insufferable! "How much of this patronizing treatment am I to endure?" he asked in a self-righteous fashion while reaching into his waistcoat. "I. . ." Erik fumbled verbally, "I seem. . ." Cocking one brow, he cleared his throat. "I should meet you there perhaps?"

"You will do no such thing," he said, flashing a triumphant smirk. "We shall retrieve whatever it is and be on our way, I am here for support."

"More like torment. I can see you are taking great pleasure at my expense."

"Really, Erik?" the Persian chided lightly, laughter playing in his eyes. "Pleasure, 'at your expense?' There is nothing wrong with having a slight upper hand, as I am sure you will concur. But if you must know, I do enjoy every precious moment that you writhe. It is all well and good that you experience a bit of what you so generously dole out." He rested his hand on Erik's shoulder. "It is time to relax and permit the day to unfold."

Erik studied the fine gentleman standing next to him, and then gazed out from the latticed window to the nearby gardens. "We have been through much, you and I, even unto death." They regarded each other in turn as he continued. "I am proven wrong again. I once assumed I could exist without dependency upon another person, but discord causes me to become pliant. As much as I desired solitude and professed contentment in such a state, I always denied what I could never admit until now. . . my gratitude for the friendship you have extended," Erik uttered respectfully. "I appreciate you seeing beyond the hatred."

The Persian's eyes misted and a tear slowly descended the golden hued cheek. It was indeed a day of happiness, a day of gratification for years sacrificed in hope, and a day of dreams realized. He bowed his head, and in a muted whisper said, "I am amazed, Erik."

"I am as well, she has been *this* influential. I love her."

Their hands clasped securely, haste soon replacing delay, and they departed.

In another section of Paris, just west of Notre Dame on the Ile de la Cite, lay Sainte-Chapelle, a glorious historical site, upon which the greyness of sun-lit stone stood unyielding against the marbled blue. The sight of brightness and clarity welcomed, as a guest faithfully expected—though unheeded—assured that if officious behavior were to threaten, to change from balmy to foul, the invitation advanced in good faith would certainly be despised.

Erik worried needlessly, his folly smothered with acclaim for Christine filled the carriage, despite the Persian's confirmation of women being found just as absentminded. He would not hear of such a thing. Women were about fastidiousness, they were orderly creatures, especially these, but upon the step's thud and drop for their exit, it became evident that the feminine half of the event was at a similar level of turmoil.

"What did I tell you?" The Persian jabbed Erik in the side, turning him in time to see Mlle Giry dash inside.

The gentlemen entered quietly and were immediately greeted by a spry elderly sister—a sprite, if ever there were—petite in stature, experienced in face, but serene in demeanor. "Messieurs, welcome." She dropped proper recognition to their bows.

"Madame. The young lady, Mademoiselle Daaé, she is well, she has arrived?" Erik enquired.

"Yes, Monsieur. She and her companions are in preparation."

"She does not want for anything, she had a tour?"

The woman's smiling eyes glided to the Persian and back to Erik, her creases deepening. "The young lady is settled, was provided a tour, and is getting on splendidly, Monsieur. Soon, when the time nears,

I shall go to Mademoiselle, and then she will come to be placed safely in your care." Her felicific contagion did wonders. Erik nodded.

"Come, Erik. I should like a tour. It will level my nerves." The Persian steered the bridegroom to a preparation area of his own and sat him down to relax. "I have secured your orders. Darius stands ready, your violin is here. . . now, my tour, if you please."

Seeming to be without choice in the matter, Erik would go about the motions of guide, transparent in effort, he knew, but it was for the best and would prevent dwelling, wondering where each of Christine's feet trod, her precise path, what she touched, thought. "We shall begin upstairs, Daroga, in the upper chapel where the ceremony will occur." It was a start, his mouth moved at any rate.

A winding staircase was climbed, the very one which would convey her presence before him in few hours' time. He held onto the railing; could not subdue the thoughts no matter his persistence. *Her hand.* Did she hear all the bits of historical import or was there no helping those organs to shut out that kind, exuberant voice of the elderly woman? Erik observed the visitors dwindle, knowing one o'clock would see the room clear.

The chapel's length traversed, the Persian nudged Erik for more background. "King Louis. . ."

"Hmm, King Louis IX was affixed here in his royal hierarchy, remembered among these sacred family relics. The cathedral was a representation of religion and nobility, a place of worship and high profile as their connection to French power succeeded."

"How unfortunate for the damage," the Persian remarked. "As I understand, it was a great loss."

"One sustained during the French Revolution," Erik completed. "None were left untainted, the furniture and choir wall disappeared, but in preservation, Sainte-Chapelle was set aside as a National Monument in 1862, and completely restored to its grandeur by 1868."

"Choir wall, whatever for?"

"I build the things, not dismantle them. People do strange things in declaration of war."

"Architect's insight? Go on."

Erik grimaced. "Stories, more than one thousand of them, are depicted in detail within the stained-glass windows held tightly between those slender columns, which give the ceiling an airy suspension; they are read from top to bottom and left to right, as verse in scripture."

"Ah yes, you *are* becoming religious."

"Common knowledge!" Erik ground back, playing quick to recall his tongue. He did not wish to be lumped in falsely with some pious sect of their race. "Let. . ." Erik let the phrase ease out to nothing. His friend had him pegged. One more word depicting those finely sculpted impressions of the twelve apostles marking each bay, or nigh on peaceful communion, and he would be pronouncing *himself* wed.

More of the same awaited their descent to the lower chapel. *There is no escaping it.* Erik bemoaned the incredible fact that it was religion by quantity, continuing the tour with a dismissal of the Virgin Mary to expound on station, and how palace staff and commoners alike felt the sting of royalty. Humanity dealt him wrong just as birth segregated those in reduced circumstances.

"There will always be those who wish their status to be known in excess and overbearing dominance."

"It is true, Daroga. But you will notice the heavens above," Erik said. His heart lurched. All he could think of was Christine's eyes. "The resplendent stars overflowing their limits upon the ceiling, down to those whose memories lie beneath the floors, those who were once servants within these walls." He hesitated, thinking seriously. "I believe we should end here. No one could have kinder support, but my mind is at odds with yours, and more than anything, I wish to entertain mine. I shall be with you shortly."

"As you wish." The Persian fell silent and quit the hallowed chapel.

Erik felt relief and strangely sacrilegious—having laid foot over the top of someone dead was not among those sensations listed for a wedding day. He checked his watch, *an hour*, and pocketed it again in his waistcoat. Alone and somber, he looked to the stars overhead, touched the wall, and then crossed his arms to his chest. Pivoting around he leaned into one of the gabled columns and gazed up, re-creating the beauty of Christine's smile, her sparkling eyes, how her hand could reign up its defiant charge with a hairpin, and brush against her delicate face, and his, with no more than a whisper. A dear father absent—she would miss the safe transfer of affection from a father's security. So, too, in acknowledgment for reception of this sacred gift, this angel, to cherish for whatever duration God would grant, he humbly bowed. It was time.

Chapter Twenty-Three

Erik's commanding apparel portrayed such meticulous care; he was at his best in black, a full dress tailcoat, with its rounded lapels and trousers trimmed in satin, a pique front shirt and wing tip collar, freshly done up by a three button waistcoat, white tie, and ornamented with white gold pocket watch and cuff links.

"Monsieur?" The manservant gave one last whisk at each shoulder, catching Erik just as he turned for the door.

"Darius?"

"The mirror, Monsieur."

Mirror. Erik rounded and froze at the image seen. He may have asked whose, for the blank recognition that pelted the figure. It was he, no stranger, his figure. . . white masque and all. He stared for a moment. What would *she* see?

The Persian knocked and pushed open the door. "Erik?" Erik caught both sets of eyes reflected in the glass.

"Thank you, Darius. I am ready," he breathed out, then straightened his back and looked away.

The violin from the previous evening lay in reserve, waiting beneath Erik's arm for Reverend Manois' signal to commence. The nod came and Madame Adèle Giry entered on the arm of a young, fair-haired man, and the melodic strains of Wieniawski's *Legende* lifted heavenward as bow applied to string. Mademoiselle Meg Giry drew forth and moments thereafter, Christine. A deep sense of longing sighed and awakened, permeating each meaningfully to the core; from sentiment to soul, the very music bore admirably as catalyst in its migration straight to some impassioned well embodied since birth. His eyes refused intrusion until the final vibration died full away and a hand was brought firm to his shoulder, the instrument melting from existence.

Several strides apart, that first sight of Christine left Erik in quite a state, in search of his racing heart while managing to put forth adequate will upon body and mind to stretch out his hand, and slowly move her forward to join him. Her touch was his undoing and strength alike—from here he would accept no rescue—her beauty pleased, radiated. The natural hue of each cheek deepened as she took her place at his side, and giving her single rose to Meg, her skirts cascaded to the floor about her feet. He watched, heaved deeply then made himself guardian and possessor of her grasp, and where the shallow bands of her neckline set wide to the graceful slope of her neck, there lay his diamond at rest.

No gloves separated them, only time and ceremony.

A light throat clearing and the minister began. "We have come here today, to witness the union of two hearts before God, to observe separate lives, become one. You have expressed your desire to exchange personal vows along-side tradition, and so I shall dispense with mandatory custom post haste by asking if there be any known impediment as to why these two may not be lawfully joined, if such an one exists, it must needs be confessed."

Erik listened, held his breath and moved not a measurable distance during that life-altering pause; he felt humbled, called to his knees by past actions, knowing pronounced judgments could well interfere and strike down all that was good, but it could not, not today, not at Christine's side.

A calm nod and blink of confirmation from the clerk along the back aisle gave a welcomed release, and soon progression carried on.

"If you would face one another. Monsieur, the time is now yours, when you are ready."

There was a spark, which seemed to ignite his gaze, and then his eyes were hopelessly upon her, his searing vindication, his right to avow and sincerely commit. "Christine... I humbly take your hands in mine, to pledge unwavering devotion, to respect, honor and cherish, that which we bring together. You are first in my life, and I shall strive to set my will at naught, learning continually of the permanence in change. I wish for all that is possible as our bond strengthens. I need you beside me, as you are my freedom from solitude. I desire now to become your husband, to be worthy always of your love."

His vision sharpened as though he could hear through sight; her smile warmed and she hesitated for only an instant. "Erik... I give you all that I am, that we may become more together. I promise unconditional love, support, and highest regard as our paths merge this day. We will be henceforth inseparable, never to be alone again; companions, sharing all that life encompasses from deepest sorrow to incomprehensible joy. I desire above all else, to be your wife, to place in your hands my love and trust, to believe as you once believed, from this day forth."

A sweet silence ensued, a breath and the question asked, "Do you, Erik Gautier, knowing this woman's love for you and returning it complete, promise to realize her strengths, to learn from them, and recognize her weaknesses, helping her to overcome them, take Christine Daaé, to be your wife, legally bound?"

"I do, yes."

"And, do you, Christine Daaé, knowing this man's love for you and returning it complete, promise to realize his strengths, to learn from them, and recognize his weaknesses, helping him to overcome them, take Erik Gautier, to be your husband, legally bound?"

"Yes, I do."

"You may exchange rings, if you wish," encouraged the minister.

Erik retrieved the small, white gold circlet from his waistcoat pocket. He looked at its simple beauty and commenced. "I give you, Christine, this ring, as a symbol of my commitment to you, to us. May you wear it with love and joy." He slid it effortlessly down her forth finger to always remain close to her heart. She then replaced the diamond given her, as she turned back to him from Meg, producing a ring of her own.

However subtle the surprise, she was amused by his unnerving and winked. "I give you, Erik, this ring, as a symbol of my commitment to you, to us. May you wear it with love and joy." Her palms surrounded the token with warmth and gentleness.

"Erik and Christine?" Reverend Manois smiled. "The two of you bring unique aspects to this marriage. Remember to confide the deepest parts of who you are, be of comfort and refuge to the other, and as your foundation begins with trust, so shall your love endure in forgiveness. Cherish your differences, rejoice in the variance you discover, then use the bond, which secures your love, to solidify and reaffirm this commitment professed today." Then, looking at them in turn, the minister pronounced them husband and wife, in the name of the Father, the Son, and the Holy Ghost. "You may seal your vows, Monsieur."

Erik's heart pounded, deafening his ears and causing him to tremble ever so slightly as he placed his hands to the sides of Christine's face, tenderly raising her chin.

"Christine."

Unaware of just how long he remained staring, a faint reminder at his elbow assisted. "And you are waiting for. . . ?" the baritone behind him needled.

"I only have the opportunity to kiss my wife for the first time once," he whispered.

Christine placed her hand atop his and mouthed, "I love you," and immediately the warmth of his lips pressed sure, was multiplied twice and shared against the softness of her forehead. Smiles grew broad all around as the reverend encouraged the new couple to present themselves officially, and then Christine immediately became Meg's prize to hug and fawn over. Erik was quickly resigned to the fact that he would have no control until he could extricate his bride to the carriage outside, and therefore permitted the Girys their moment while he in turn, focused on the Persian, who was keeping him locked within a grip so unimaginably strong that Erik dared not be dismissive.

"I should like to be the first to congratulate you and. . ." he referenced to Meg's confiscation, "I shall contain my rush there."

"I have no words, my friend. If. . ."

The Persian pulled Erik into a brief embrace. "No ifs, she is yours to love Erik, hold her close, treat her well." They released and Erik's form was given a light shove and told, in no uncertain terms, to go attend Christine.

The conversation, upon closer approach, was a flurry of laughs and interestingly enough, a jaw dropping coincidence. Meg's flaxen Baronet, Richard, was none other than the foppish peacock they had encountered on the train to Perros. He was handsome at any rate, of average height, slim build, had slicked wavy hair, a narrow, energetic brow and steel blue orbs, which absorbed information from all sources, and found life a comical rage to rejoice in. The whole story was rather promptly reenacted from start to stop, as portrayed by Richard's fertile animation for the benefit of the Girys, and at the end, left Erik in little doubt as to the necessity of an apology. Contrition was dismissed, for it became of more importance to Richard that he had been right, than to absolve any admission. He actually thought it made for a better, more intriguing bit of fancy to entertain the mind and said so, though upon that thought, and as part of his character—making habit of capricious junctures—he was off again along some other avenue, with immediate company suspensefully in tow.

Erik gave an ardent tug, from an arm hooked about Christine's middle, toward the stairway. He was in a mood for pleasing no one but her, and by indulging the one, he hoped to reciprocally satiate the other; selfish as it was, he wished to leave civility, deal with others minimally, and have finished the church scene, but most specifically, the charismatic thief.

"You are a *tactress* if ever there were," Erik confided out of earshot. "I am afraid I may have tarnished the moment had we tarried much longer. At second meeting, and under different attachments, the pleasantries require some steadiness of tongue and massive doses of a taciturn disposition to abide in the same proximity without searching for the most convenient exit. Perhaps, a trapdoor?"

"Erik, he is not that bad."

"Well, he is not *jolly good*, either! The flaunting is absurd."

These last words were but a sarcastic mumble as the Persian checked the door of their carriage. "Madame, it is an honor," he said, taking her hand. "You are beauty, rare amidst all forms. Erik worships you for gracing his life, as do I."

Christine touched the Eastern bronzed cheek and kissed him tenderly. "I love him and you flatter me, thank you."

Erik eyed the enamoured complexion, took hold of his bride and handed her up. "Yes, sweet, is it not? Now, as much as I enjoy your company, it is time for you to make yourself scarce."

The Persian grinned. "Your eloquence in tact is deficient still." He received a friendly pat to his face and shoulder for the observation.

THE CARRIAGE CONVEYED the new couple along the outskirts of the city, to the Buttes Chaumont, a beautifully romantic park, noted for its panoramic vistas at dramatic cliff top heights, which look back over the whole of Paris. Her arm drawn within his, they walked in comfortable silence beneath the blending foliage of rustic oranges, golds, and plum fringed reds, all eager participants in their hush to disclose nothing of the planned seclusion, until a final escort through parting hedgerow proffered visual relief from a tremendous waterfall—meant as a scenic dinner companion.

The meal complete, and the most basic of their needs met, Christine excused herself to stroll near the edge of the gently lapping water, under Erik's watchful eye. He had done more of this activity than any other since their carriage door closed in behind them, and for some reason, conversation was inexplicably last in importance or last to be skillfully summoned. In every minute way, a subtle record of how Christine looked, moved, touched him, and how she gently conducted herself, inspired beyond what he was even capable of expressing. To place one source of dependence where true felicity became naturally tangible, she was his hope.

"You know, the first time we met on civil ground, you studied me, unsure of my motives." She looked briefly over her shoulder. "I have been well scrutinized today and am curious as to your confidence in me and whether I please you."

Two warm arms embraced her from behind at the conclusion of her query, and his familiar tones resonated passionately for her to hear and feel. "I trust and confide in you alone. You could do nothing else but please, this I have experienced in every way thus far. I rejoice that the description of this dress was a mere tease, the neckline is delicate, has but two-thirds of a sleeve and does not prevent me," he sighed, "from being close."

The softest part of his lips prefaced at her ear and recalling a tender moment, he bade her lean into his shoulder and pressed his mouth once again to her waiting neck. His hand countered hers as he held it firmly laced within his hair and it was she who gasped at his attentions. "Beautifully sweet," he commented lightly, determined to express gently his innermost desires. A tear suddenly reached his awareness, adding savor to her skin, and he rotated her to look directly into his eyes, fiery as they were. "Does the intensity frighten you? Tell me of your thoughts, confide in me, please," he pressed in concern, trying to read her countenance. "I do not, that is, I can be incrementally more sensitive. You know I can."

More tears took leave of their boundaries, repeating the inclination to compound Erik's blundering all the more, leaving his voice aquiver and hand to comb aimlessly through his hair. Too much, he pushed too soon! What is the course, to do or to say now? He had the evening planned and to derail so... painful doubt and confusion cast upon his heart. *Talk, ask her to forgive you, discover her thoughts!*

"Forgive me, I have offended you." He backed up. Absolutely contradictory, he wished to proceed with their relationship, but was scared of rejection.

"Erik, there is no offense."

"Then, what?" The agitation shone brilliant, he was fretting.

"I belong to you."

"And this saddens you," a pause drew out, "I see."

"No, you do not see... far from it." And she repeated softly. "I belong, to you." She had rearranged the emphasis. "No frenzied, worded caution need beset what is natural in the course of time. I am filled with joy to be yours."

"This is not fear or sorrow that I wipe from your face, but happiness?"

"Of that, you may be certain."

His penetrating gaze came alive once more and he bent toward her to kiss upon their embrace, tight and sure as he clasped her to his breast, shuddering under the enchantment of touch. Being perfectly suited in their understanding, they found themselves convinced for the present, of the favorable outcome silence would bring, and made no effort to disturb providence for a time.

"Oh, you must know how you affect me," he said, his emotions taking voice. "I could not comprehend what it would be to marry without love, such a desolate institution; to encircle with my arms emptiness and to press my lips against the dust of indifference, but that I shall never be required to experience as I have the privilege of your compassionate affections to fill my arms and my life with what I deem valuable." He sighed wistfully. "Now, if you would be gracious enough to set my mind at ease about something."

Christine smiled. "We are getting on wonderfully if I need only mitigate one other issue." He offered her his handkerchief and she pressed it to each eye.

"I know of more lurking about awaiting your assurance, but I shall narrow the range drastically." And he held up his left hand to a simple, enlightened tilt of the head.

"Ah, you did not expect one?" she asked while brushing her lips across the token. Shaking his head to the contrary he swallowed and had drawn a blank the moment Christine attempted to place his open hand to her heart. It was that supple skin beneath his touch which had him pulling from her those flamboyantly singed nerves. Coaxing his hand ever so gently, she steadied it beneath her own, inviting the liberty.

"You are my husband."

"But I have never. . ."

"I suppose there may be many firsts shared by day's end, and if you are not adverse to this slightly more intimate position, I should like it to remain."

He acquiesced as she began. " When I was a little girl, Mother would sit at my side and tell me stories of heaven while I watched out the window from my bed. I would envision such glorious kingdoms and create such wonders as only a young mind could. There was one tale I remember vividly, for it developed a special meaning to me later on. She related that the vast array of stars in the sky represented all the people who had ever come and gone from this earth—I decided there were many, too numerous to count, and likened them to the sands washed by the sea. What became granted for viewing were their shining smiles, radiating hope back to those of us here. Each giving faith, winking until dawn could impart strength anew.

"She had a necklace; a small, solitary diamond, one my father had given her after their first year of marriage. Having only afforded a set of thin, steel bands to exchange, he felt to do more, and was impressed to bestow a pendant, rather than a more lavish ring, to be worn closer to her heart. Each evening, as I was tucked under the covers, she would lean over me to kiss my forehead, and the diamond would twinkle, suspended by its chain above my eyes." Christine's own eyes dulled solemnly. "To my knowledge, she never removed the necklace, and it remained until my father placed it in my care. After she passed, I would lay awake for hours, gazing up into the night sky, wondering which of all the tiny luminaries was hers, and when my father took me out into the country with him, that is when I felt the closest to them both, nestled between their love."

Strong feelings emerged fresh, sentiments from which most are never fully able to subdue when fond and poignant remembrances stir the boundaries, and she dashed away several of her own tears, looking to him. "The diamond seated in your band, is hers."

Her mother's, his emotions struck, a bead of dew at the base of Erik's masque was gently caught before opportunity allowed it to fall. He thoroughly enjoyed being tended to.

"Your thoughtfulness touches me," she subjoined, "in many ways."

His? What had he done more than she?

"We have spent much of our time as connected as possible to the outdoors; the parks, the Giry's courtyard, our whispering spring. . . but I am partial to our home, which awaits our arrival because it confers a level of nearness to all *I* value and hold dear. I share this memory with you as we begin to treasure up our own. Mine shall begin with the necklace you have given me as a cherished continuation."

Erik could hardly suppress the emotions welling. He looked at the ring Christine held violently to her breast, then to her eyes and bowed his head as he now seized her to himself. "It is too much, Christine. The kindness, yours. . ." he said, trembling. "My masque, if you would remove it."

The unique features patiently accepted all Christine had to offer, and as lips moved together he claimed her, his hands caressing along her back, feeling naturally the meaning of bliss.

ON RETREAT FOR the afternoon, the autumn colors migrated skyward to gain benefit from the horizon's farewell ovation, cast long in shadow by eventide; as two, whose fastened cares most critically hinged upon the companion now bound to, pulled into the Amiens station.

It is happening again, she thought. "It" had become a recurring phenomenon, a queer theme, and the almost unsettling deprivation to one's comfort was now unusually predictable to Christine, but part of the choreography fitted to Erik as these were the staging elements observed: carriages awaiting their presence at every leg of their journey, the concisely timed walks, a leisurely meal, the train, and as they disembarked, *their* horses, readily harnessed or tethered to a new carriage, depending on responsibility. Even Erik's violin, and their personal belongings, appeared to be lounging content and well cared for on the plush seat cushions for their return home. Erik took pride in the bewildering unease—that shiver of having one's whereabouts foreseen—her safety was assured, and everything was unfolding to the miraculous will of a performing genius who wished nothing more than to astonish, but somehow it was on the verge of affixing a permanent wrinkle to her brow. His kiss seemed to soothe.

Range of conversation, on and off the train, had them speaking of hopes and dreams, goals and ambitions, then as these last few horse drawn miles passed, they were each seen to turn quietly introspective. His thoughts, what there were, celebrated. He was married, of all things, attached to someone and gladly responsible! She belonged to him, and he to her, joined in heart for all their tomorrows. He glanced over to his diversion—she had her head pressed into his shoulder—and studied her in the glow of the lantern, the strands of white flowered ribbon adorning the crown of the veil, his lips found the hazel wisps highlighting her forehead soft.

Lately, in a round about fashion, the subject of family resurfaced. Drawing her out on the sands of Perros could not have produced memories more fondly related. She spoke easily of the Valeriuses, her father, their lives. They were stories, hers, pleasant to hear and unconsciously presented in happiness, happiness he had tried to grasp, yet an elusive concept of fantasy for him. Did he wish for them to become more than two, did she? He imagined the two of them content, they had been marvelously so, but she was young. Perhaps she would desire, demand more of him than he was able to give. And had he, in the most remote confines of his heart, cauterized the desire for children?

During their discussion, talk had alluded to individual desires, more self-centered perceptions, and had made limited inclusion of others or none at all. Time together had seen Erik evolve from his selfish singularity to encompass the needs of another; a reconciliatory apex had yet to be reached, but he would discover a steadiness in character, yes, indeed he would. *Leave off with it, heavens! The problems of the world need not be solved the first night!* He made no mention nor detected any inkling in her of such things, and purposely excluded what might tug at her womanhood.

Erik felt Christine squeeze his arm from their conveniently positioned entanglement, he smiled to himself, his grin becoming evident as the snorting and bobbing heads anxiously displayed their sense of familiarity with the environment.

Erik patted Christine's hand and queried, "To what do I owe this attention?"

"No reason."

"This day, this week, has been beyond my expectations, but that is an assumption of its own, really." He traced the porcelain fingers clasped with his. "I've done well, have I not? Perhaps too well. . . being tranquillized by your touch and the movement of the train for an embarrassing length, I would not make a very attentive husband at first glance."

He was searching for praise and she baited his ego unmercifully. "Your sleeping habits are deplorably erratic, though I shall give leeway for exhaustion. Mind you, expiation is requisite for neglect on your behalf; there will be no excuses or exoneration, and you being gentleman-like is always apropos, whether one is courting or married."

"By your account I shall never be reconciled and should consider my sentence acceptable, or one day I shall wake to find all vanished, and then where will I be?"

The leather reins licked the palm of his hand, making a languid escape during the exchange, a wry smile signifying the only hint of mischievous play afoot. His enjoyment of sparring with Christine, matching wits and sagacity, never diminished; her charm increased and his delight in intelligent banter now expanded to include bits of spontaneity from him.

"Vanished? Oh, Monsieur, I could never forsake my investment, but if it is permissible, I should like to remain for a time, to see if interest accrues. You must understand, too, that I have not had cause to strike out on my own in business before and hear it can be a risky, speculative venture. However, I have not delved blind nor do I jump without the net of counsel as I am sure that that nice, ebon-skinned gentleman will be more than happy to take notice of my welfare, if errant developments should arise."

"You wound me! I speak to the care and attention of the companion I love and she becomes as a mercenary, extorting from me all I cherish. Such incentive! I should have known, I should have guarded myself, but I shall know how to act."

"And how is that?" she asked, reaching up to rub her fingers along the top of his collar.

"I shall take things into my own hands." And he gathered her into his embrace.

"They are unemployed at present?" That furrowed brow appeared with a vengeance under the lantern's glow.

"Cesar knows the way, he needs no guide for this last mile, but. . . I do," he whispered. Erik's eyes closed as her lips gave stir to the embers smoldering within, allowing their devoted hearts to engage the dance begun so many months ago. "Share with me, Christine. Entrust your love to me as I give of myself. . . love me."

Holding Christine tight, Erik contemplated his next advance, but was moved to sigh at the steady decline of the carriage to a premature stop, interrupting the interlude with a pawing of the ground. "You could not have managed just a bit closer, Cesar? I gave you your head for a mile and you came up at least an eighth shy." Cesar's snort brought irritation. "Damn horse! Rebel that you are!"

"It's all right." Christine chuckled while weaseling out of his grasp.

"No, it is not!" he fumed and pouted. "Now I have to find the reins, it's dark. . . *I am not holding you.* She deserves to be delivered to the front door," he murmured to Cesar. Bending to retrieve one rein, he tied it securely then circled the carriage to find the other. Dezi's lead was long enough that she came up alongside for a quick pat from Christine and the carriage suddenly lurched forward, too quickly for Erik to gain a foothold.

"An equine conspiracy, is that possible?" Christine called back.

"Yes!" Erik bristled. "You ornery. . ."

The rest of what Erik said faded and would have been stifled by her light laughter had her options included stasis, but they did not, and she was kindly removed right to the front porch to await the wrath of one frustrated master.

She grabbed at his sleeve. "Don't stop me, Christine."

"Erik, why punish him for adding humor? We are home." Her hand cupped his cheek, turning him to face her. "Would you at least look at me? Being so inflexible only causes—"

"No lecture, I beg you." Agitation made him impatient as he rested his forearms to the rails and held up a hand to quell her good intentions. "I have plans, wanted things to be a certain way and will not tolerate the impudent nature thwarting. . . my. . ." Erik listened to the last words exiting his mouth and glanced furtively to Christine, then to the star dangling sweetly at eye level, his gaze bent downward, suddenly realizing how ridiculously petty he must sound. "He *is* intelligent," came the comment, after several minutes of silence hung between them.

"Yes, *he* is," she quietly replied. Erik wondered if she were referring to him or Cesar, and smirked.

When next he looked, Christine was temptingly close. His finger lifted to touch the diamond and moved slowly until it gently stroked the curve of her face, coaxing her nearer; his lips caressed hers, brushed against her left cheek, summoning her into his arms.

"You must not stir from whence I place you. Do I have your promise?" he asked, setting her on the first step. "If I cannot have said horse conduct himself as I wish, I may have this, mightn't I?"

She kissed him soundly and answered, "I would rather be at your side."

"I would also prefer it, but not tonight."

"Then I shall be patient."

Nothing is better incentive for motivating hands than guarantee of a reward, which sent Erik on, post haste; the horses were led to the stable, a lantern lit, and the reverberating jangle of a harness clattering against the wall was signal to the zest in which he was earnestly employed. *Quite a sight associated with the noise emanating unheeded from beyond these doors.* He chuckled mentally. *Not much of a phantom either, I would be classified as its troublesome opposite, a poltergeist, no less.* Then he mused on Christine's wandering attentions, wanting to be busy, not wishing accommodation, and was reminded of the seemingly unaccounted for glimmer from within the house. He grinned, he knew her leg would be nervously twitching beneath her gown, his moment of reckoning for last night.

Having finished, Erik shut up the stable and gave the grounds a brief scan, and seeing little change during their weeklong absence, he stared up to admire the constancy there, fortunate that it was in just such a position that he found Christine, entranced and entrancing. She startled easily at his approaching form, then as if on cue, settled her eye warily to survey with what intent this black plumed, white-breasted bird came bearing away on the night air. But the answer was left for curiosity to unravel. He unloaded the carriage, blew out its lantern, and walked past her to stow things just inside, then returned to the foot of the stairs before her.

"Welcome home, my dear."

"Our home."

He took hold of her hands, kissed them and placed one to either shoulder, as his found their way to circle tightly and pull her securely to him. "You once kissed your fiancé from this vantage, would you do your husband the same honor?"

Smiling, Christine pressed her mouth inviting to his, soon deepening the affection until breathing was more requisite than determined. His auditing gaze fixed on her and again he sought as she consented, an airy groan of satisfaction prefaced a burst of energy before Christine was whisked, cradled in his arms, up the stairs and across the threshold. Neither remembered much of the stairway, except to have presence of mind to douse the lights in each wall sconce, but it was the illumination from their room, the lucent echo of specifically located candles, that intrigued.

Erik set Christine before a stand-alone washbasin without their room, symbolic in every way; a pitcher of refreshing water lay just beneath the pedestal, with soap and towel nested in the bowl. Draping the towel over the rail, he poured the cleansing water, pushed back his sleeves and invited Christine's hands to join his. Skin-to-skin their palms mirrored and fingers merged, washing gently the touch of the other. Once dried, Erik led her to traverse those few steps midst the wonder, and the panel slid into position. Almost instantaneously he watched her countenance cloud over a shade, then brighten in an eclipse of mood. He knew the look, the fits of frustration he gave her when something astounded and surpassed understanding, and he took great joy in refusing her wishes to know *how*, by simply telling her that it was for her to accept. She dealt with his benign secrets well. The great irritation provided all the self-discipline necessary to place the kibosh on enquiry. He saw the mouth compressed in defiance and knew she was not about to allow him any additional pleasure of gloating at her expense.

Grasping a rose from the spray of crimson against the rich blue and emerald bedding, he made an offering while quietly leading her to a chest at the foot of their bed. *Theirs. . . how joyous it is to say.* It was of the same deep purity as the other fine mahogany wood used, but near black in color and handsomely polished to defy its own dimension. The key, an ornate, medium-gauge silver, rested within the labyrinth for anyone taking a fancy to things unseen, to unlock the mysteries.

Christine looked at Erik, who bowed and stood back, permitting her complete accessibility. She knelt, twisted the key and displaced the lid, pushing up until it was secured open. Dipping her hand in, an abundance of white gently met her touch and materialized as nightclothes: a gown and pair of loose fitting trousers, and a set of dressing gowns, all of which were examined in turn and arranged across the lid. Erik observed the careful attention allotted to each and then most expectantly, when she retrieved a letter nestled in the bottom corner. Here, she regained her feet with his assistance.

As Christine released the message, Erik came and settled in behind her to read the following over her shoulder.

> *Tonight, my sweet Christine, is a time when we shall exchange a gift greatly esteemed between husband and wife, one that may only ever be given away as a precious first, once in a lifetime. This gift of purity is for us alone, is shared by us alone, that which I give, I give freely to you. I am yours at long last.*
>
> *Erik*

She trembled within his protective vice, he sensed trepidation and held her, speaking softly to her heart. "I would never do anything to offend, to harm. . . I shall be tender and sensitive."

Reaching up she began to slowly feel for and remove the hairpins securing her veil to the crown of her head, though her attempt at retrieval was interrupted by his greater delight in assisting. The pendant was set aside, leaving his finger to trace the center of her back. She was absolutely gorgeous. Erik heaved a contemplative sigh, one prefacing the eventual manipulation of each beautiful, opaque pearl button. "How many of *these* lay foremost to my ultimate destination?"

Turning to face Erik, Christine shyly replied, "fifty-eight." Her impulsive shift caught him unprepared to confront her eyes and a brief glint of embarrassment shone through his valiant exterior, assuring them both of an equal experience. A generous smile from her calmed the restlessness just before her mouth merged with his in a sweet kiss. "I trust you."

Erik's mind erupted with those permeating words, every fiber. . . she trusted, and she loved. . . she wanted him! This became evident as Christine now slid the tailcoat from his broad shoulders, entwined her arms about his neck and drew him, weakened, into repeating more ardently what she encouraged. Her hand brushed his masque, an innocent enough occurrence. How often had she touched or removed it? How often did he wish it? And now, all at once, an icy thought cinched its threaded cord. These minutiae that wait to malign good with the infirm, to infest and torment right with seeds of impossibility, choked efficiently, and from the depths of his weary soul elicited a moan to shake even the most hearty of men. Grabbing Christine gently, he pushed her away, stormed out onto the balcony, slammed his fists down on the railing, and bellowed in agonizing fury, "No! You cannot, you must not!"

Erik glanced back at her. Christine stared, arrested in panic by his words, her hand rising in an attempt to ward off an unseen, mind reeling blow.

What had happened? *Breathe!* He could not. What was this sensation welling in his chest? One moment they were engaged in affection and the next, a polar explosion of anger. Was this to be the precedence set? Would they encounter these engulfing crossroads rarely or had they embarked on a journey more complex than either of them fathomed? *What have I done?* He saw her, heard her light, hesitant footfalls and withdrew, weeping in humiliation.

"Erik, tell me what I. . ."

"Nothing!" he spat as a rabid dog. "You did nothing, can do. . . nothing."

"You're scaring me!"

He groaned at the phrase and shouted, "I. . . I have been a fool, have ignored, denied—I am so proficient at self-denial. I actually made it to the altar, and arrived at the threshold that I might have had as others, but when I tread to the very edge, it showed instead a precipice, unforgiving and sure. I thought I could have more than a taste and see my thoughts are as yet, stained and mistaken." His speech calmed to a calculated articulation, Christine neared, dared to make contact with him, but he jumped back, calling out in desperation.

"No! Please, don't touch me!" He recoiled, fearing some reprehensible demon or that retribution would smite him for considering himself deserved, partaking as normal men. Breathing returned erratic, and he looked away in shame for the pain felt and inflicted unjustly.

Christine defied him, tearfully and openly an indomitable strength imprisoned one of his hands. "Erik, you cannot always perceive unbiased!" she cried out.

"You do not understand. Please, Christine, release me for I am at a breaking point. I cannot fight this if you continue in such a way."

"I do not wish you to fight, only hold me. . . you must."

Looking from her face to the hand firmly gripped and the closing distance in sequence, he made one last entreaty, a shake of the head, a tug of resistance, but it was futile. Fists crossed at her waist, relaxing acceptant as they melted gently against the other, filling the other's arms. She stroked the back of his head and he situated into the comfort of her neck; it felt right, as the hot rain of tears streamed.

"Tell me," she urged, but he made no effort for minutes on end, pending the curtailing of deluge. "I am here."

"I cannot risk," he inhaled raggedly, "perpetuating. . . this." And he raised his head, pointing to the masque. "How could I knowingly condemn a child to this fate, to the burden I have carried all these years? How Christine? How in good conscience could I do that?" His voice cracked and a new round of tears flooded down his face.

In case she had wandered upon that query of children, of blissful increase, he had just presented her with his tragic answer. What a topic for such a night, to tear hope in different quantities from the hearts of both!

Seeing Christine's eyes swim, Erik wondered how he would repair the passion rent by selfishness. "How am I to bear the sorrow imposed, for the discharge of *your tears* come entailed to my remarks on the abhorrence of conception. Perhaps it will be this truth which drives you from my grasp."

"Erik, I love you, wholly. There are no inhibitions or limits to my sentiments, but as there are now two of us to consider, the feelings of one are infinitely significant to both. And, if I love you, how could I not love our child? How could you not love our child any less than you love yourself?" These words came lightening fast and suddenly gave insight as to where the difficulty lay rooted, leastwise on her side. A true reflection of where Erik's heart might be swayed from seemed to revitalize Christine's prospects.

Love himself? He did not comprehend the concept of self-love. Love for another, a creature, traits, characteristics, talents, art in all its varieties, and perhaps that another loves him, yes, but he had nothing to offer upon that plane to himself, as a human being. Conditioned throughout life to hate *who* he was, he went outside himself for value, for worth.

Confusion and suspicion garnered Erik's thoughts while he mulled over the idea upon being led inside to Christine's dressing room. Once seated on the vanity bench with her back to one of the mirrors, she motioned for Erik to be seated, facing himself, and he visibly tensed. Right now, any feelings about mirrors were nothing short of volatile—his image, this scheme, hang them!

"I hardly think a lesson to be necessary, Christine. I am completely apprised and current on the appearance of my face. I am not amused," he bit out derisively, his eyes darting from her to his reflection and back.

Ignoring this logical response, she asked, "Who do you suppose I fell in love with?"

Erik gestured belligerently to the small portion of flesh exposed below his masque, glowering intensely. Christine overlooked his behavior, childish as it was, and stood slowly, pressing her palms to each of his shoulders.

"You have made decisions and assumptions regarding issues that concern us equally. Neither of us truly knows if your condition is hereditary; the impetuosity... cursing ourselves to never experience the possible blessings our future may hold, that would be far worse."

Parting his lips, as if something were about to pass unchecked, he closed them and sighed at the distraction of having his tie unfastened. Then tactfully, and with compassion, Christine motioned to remove his masque and hairpiece. He took no steps to oppose, but his countenance took a drastic turn; his defiance clouded, his spirit became mournfully quenched, and upon meeting the dreaded physiognomy, he chose instead to bow his head, and kept eyes bent to the wood flooring as though he preferred to slither beneath the grain.

"I do not expose to shame you, but to show truth." Her gentle caresses lulled him into welcome submission, the kisses soothed, and his eyes fluttered closed, breath leaden. He felt whole, floated contentedly. Each touch, the way she methodically ran her fingers over his scalp and through the collar length strands. Curling up against her breast or within her lap was all he could think of. How she controlled, manipulated him. He was lost.

"Erik," she whispered.

No, he did not wish to be summoned from her lily soft spiriting, it elicited such sweet feelings.

"Erik, look at me."

With her request came more than just a requirement to listen. She rubbed his chin and throat, rotating his face so an eventual gaze rested on her, and then she kissed him, deeply. As they separated, he caught a glimpse of what it looked like in the glass, for her to lavish affection on his hideous deformity; he recoiled in shock and involuntarily distanced himself by putting his face aside.

"No more. It would be punishment to continue," he sneered in disgust.

"For whom? You explain to me the change that occurred. You and I are no different now than we were five minutes ago."

Erik was distressed about the reasoning. She was right, and yet the sight of what he enjoyed, violently repulsed. "What I see... how can that ever be sensual or attractive?"

"That," she said, pointing to his likeness, "is the illusion. You speak of what you see as though it is a separate and distinct entity apart from yourself, and the masque does nothing but perpetuate the deception. All these years you have successfully created this perspective for your mind to adhere to, and now I am asking that you comprehend the differences appropriated to what you see *and* feel. You have learned to love the capabilities, attributes, gifts, and talents you possess, mistaking these to be the extent. You have yet to love the man who possesses them, and if you never confront yourself, you will always maintain the façade," she explained, speaking while kneeling in front of him, aligned and set between both the abstraction of self—his alter ego, which was what his mind had utilized for third person reference—and the physical, visual reality which formed the concept that he was, indeed, one with the embodiment she beheld and touched.

Christine began addressing the buttons on his waistcoat and shirt, enabling her to successfully evaluate his injury, and finding it pursed shut and healing well, her hands lingered across his chest.

"Remember how it required time for you to realize that when I looked at you—especially your eyes—it was you personally and not just me gawking at your face?"

"I do, yes."

"Now you must see *this* man, Erik, the man I married." She took his face in her hands. "This is the face I brush with kisses and caress gently. This is the face I love. I love the man behind the face, the soul beneath the man, and the heart, which beats in harmony with mine. Beauty, my dear Erik, is more than just here." Christine caressed his cheeks and tenderly encompassed each feature mentioned. " Beauty is here, in your mind; here, in your heart, and wends its way from your hands. Give in to your heart, Erik. See through my eyes. Let me love you," she entreated. But it was her final, beseeching words, which seized all senses and sealed their fate. "Love me."

She was so close. He inhaled her scent, devoured the feeling of her skin against his, her curves, his strength of vigorous prime; her lips pressed to his forehead, kisses rained upon his eyes, it was beauty in its entirety, hers. Life thundered for Erik, renewed belief, kindled passion, and he only hesitated briefly to admire the woman in his arms. Silence reigned in the pounding dissertation between their hearts as Erik gathered Christine for his own, and under the muted blush of night's shadow, ardor flowed unhindered; gentle, tender caresses opened up the gates of heaven to a deftly maneuvered dance beneath the splendor of nature's sweet rhythm. (Despite those pearl buttons.)

Chapter Twenty-Four

The buoyant flames had long since diminished to a frail, red orange in the fireplace. An errant foot, too far removed against the bedclothes, retreated and came searching for warmth and drew up to find the perimeter at its source, only a marginal improvement. Christine stretched out hoping to tap some portion of core heat but discovered that which she desired was not to be had, and had not been available for quite awhile, the coolness of sheets testifying by vacant decry. She stroked the place where his head had lain. Could she really expect one so saddled with unrest to change, to harness his habits in ready expectation for alignment with hers? Consideration and compromise, in regard to accepting some things as they were, must be prudently and sensitively handled. Of course, there would be many adjustments; to say all was paradise and felicity would be a gross err when fairly judging life with another.

Sitting up, she could see Erik had not wandered far, just out onto the balcony with a small candle for company. She made no concealment of motion, the knob rotation was sufficient to profess he was no longer singular in his wakefulness.

"Erik, are you well?"

"I suspect that I am." He welcomed her to his embrace. "Forgive me, it was not my intent to disturb you. I could not sleep and wished to remain nearby."

"You have been up for some time."

"I have, I. . ." Erik paused and looked directly into her eyes. "Sleeping near someone is a different sensation."

"Is it?" she returned.

"It is. I was unsure. . ." he hesitated awkwardly. "Promise not to laugh?"

"Have I ever?"

"No." He paused. "I feel ridiculous at my age pondering on concepts which perhaps should be second nature. Most people never think twice, I am sure."

"About?"

"Is there etiquette which governs how one chooses one side of the bed or the other? How much is to be shared or relinquished, and what is appropriate. . ." he stopped abruptly after feeling a light spasm at his side. "You promised, Christine! *Damn!* I knew I should have just kept it to myself and figured it out on my own."

"You should not have." She loved when he became embarrassed and sullen. "And I am not laughing, just thoroughly delighted and highly pleased to discuss something so sweet."

"Optimistic rhetoric, you are proficient at that. Sweet? Humph, I was not trying to be sweet, merely sincere in seeking your advice. You may go back to bed at any time and leave me to my thoughts."

She had injured his pride, a bit deeper than she meant, and must make to alleviate the brooding taking hold with a vengeance, which became worse the longer she remained. Erik let his grip loosen and drop, an unmistakable hint. And, had it not been she who was just moments ago, reminding herself of how any number of topics might become sensitive? Christine shook her faculties for the impudent abandon.

"I do not wish to part, especially to sleep alone when I have been the cause of upset. I treated your concern lightly and trampled on your feelings. I am sorry." She sighed then began to offer up what knowledge she had for his query; she toyed with the wax, making the candle her focus of communication. "I am not aware of any etiquette, leastwise related to societal norms, and would feel it quite oppressive to be governed in such a way. And knowing your struggles with compliancy—the how and the why—I should think you unwilling to submit to the world imposing its beliefs in any form, if it did not suit. Keeping this in mind, I might imagine courtesy our guide and that we conduct our private affairs, as such. If you are accustomed to one side or the other, I am easy because I can do either, and as to the sharing of space, I do not feel compelled to require an amount, but should like to occupy whatever is closest to you, knowing that there will be times when more distance is preferred, and if that becomes the case you most certainly will be awake and busying yourself, with projects and the like, because I shall not think on it for one moment that we could possibly. . . be one next to the other and not desire. . . to ever really consider. . . never wanting. . . or limiting certain aspects. . ."

"Or could ever remain irritated for a duration, which would protract yourself from my side or touch for any length of time due to an intermission of a lengthy run-on discourse. Your speech is at an end, come to me."

Erik's touch along a shoulder had caused inarticulate surrender. "I much prefer here," she acquiesced.

"Yes," he breathed seductively. "Yes, close and in my arms. I wish to do right by you, Christine. No details overlooked, no deficiencies that would cause—"

"Me to laugh at you or think less of you for lack of common knowledge?"

"Exactly."

"Sweet man that you are. I think we, as husband and wife, are left to figure a great many things out for ourselves. Discovery is an adventure, and there is much I do not know. Remember, I am here to learn with you."

He kissed her hand and sent it to roam and explore the uneven contours of his facial characteristics. Her fingertips traced the translucent flesh; the blended greys of midnight and mottled skin tones all melding as one under her care.

"Erik, are you content?" she asked, watching him move his head in synchronized fashion with her tender ministrations. He pressed her palm steadily to his cheek, and a moist sensation trickled through their tightly clasped hands.

"Immensely so, Christine." His voice faltered. "Truth hurts, you know as I do, but it can lead to healing. You say I must see past the delusion my masque has caused me to become prey to, see through your eyes. So, in light of this, I ask because I wish you to be honest with me, however painful. And, I shall warn, I am not a fool. I know the reality of my appearance. Whether I learn to *perceive* alternately or not, my face is still a harsh reality and physically irreversible."

"Oh, Erik."

"You must. Being the incredulous and self-conscious wretch that I am, you must not spare me, once and for all. I am married, have a beautiful young woman who loves me, who stares into my eyes and gazes undeterred, and I cannot let it alone. Our intimacy was so beautiful, I was made to feel utterly complete, but I must know *what* you think of, or who, when you touch or look at me." She sighed, obviously perturbed. "I know... I am awful for asking this of you when you are so generous, it cannot it helped."

Gloom descended upon him in a most desperate way and Christine could see that he would not be put off or consoled with the usual generalities, he required specifics. Troubled in heart from her earlier mistake and grieved by the prolonged impasse to joy, which she had the means to relieve, she smiled genuinely while he seemed to brace for the worst. "This has occupied your mind all evening?"

"Among other subjects, since facing myself earlier today," he finished ruefully.

"And you wish for me to tell you straight out?"

"I do."

"Then I will not conceal a particle, though you know I lied to spare your feelings when I first knew you."

"My profile at the time was such that I could hardly have expected more."

Christine fidgeted, stopping as Erik steadied her. "I was weak minded and I am unashamed to say so. Standing before you six months ago humbled me. I realized the pain I caused and was devastated... I had truly hurt the person I had begun to care for. If you would have revealed yourself then, illness aside, I could not honestly say whether I was strong enough in character. You were wise in allowing our relationship to flourish and solidify because when you finally decided to share with me, I had come to love the man beyond the masque. My commitment to you was that *that* fear no longer existed. I was afraid of the emotion, the hate I did not understand. Never had you given me reason to be afraid *of* you. But *for* you, was a different matter." Erik nodded at various stages in agreement during the brief recount.

"Thereafter, I became intrigued, sought keenly that my motivation should stem from the appropriate source of love and not idleness. I proceeded to ask myself what I actually saw, took every advantage availed me to study your face and have since, found a pleasing image which has given me joy to bestow. I do not see another man, I could not, and could never designate a face as a label, your masque dominates that illusion, but I reserve our lifetime for any work of art to evolve. My preference by far, is as you are with me, no masque, no pretense, only natural. Erik, your face is a reminder to me of all the rugged beauties that God has ever created."

Allowing the comment to be thought on, she stroked a spot on his chin and he gently lowered their hands to his chest, intent on listening, curious as to the analogy.

"Somehow, you seem to look on your birth as a cruel mockery. What else could account for such genius being conferred upon someone, if it was not in compensation for a rift in his physiognomy, hmm? Nonetheless, I believe that God has never, nor is He capable of, purposely creating anything other than beauty. The perception of *ugly* is found only within the hearts of mankind. I am grateful for the earth in all its variety, from the grandeur of the loftiest mountains to the tranquil scenery meandering about the hillocks below, the colors and contours; all that could be agreeably distinguished and appreciated. This, my dearest Erik, is what I see, who I see."

This comparison had never been considered and astonishment registered involuntarily, causing his spirits to soar. Christine was taken up, gathered securely to him and promptly shown affection. Oh, how her heart cried out to his, rejoiced and trembled in awe at the benevolent, virtuous companion who would always stand at her side.

VERY EARLY THE next morning, at the first prospect of light, Erik woke to a dull ache in his right arm and grinned, Christine lay huddled against his outline over top the numb appendage. Not an entirely disagreeable situation, but likely the one making it necessary to move sooner than desired. Extrication was successful in surrendering the blood to its proper location and left Christine undisturbed. His arm tingled as he donned his dressing gown and made to freshen, the sensation pulsed to the tips of his fingers and he yawned, stretching every inch of his frame from both ends to the middle in satisfaction. Upon returning, he took one glance around the room and colored. Every item bespoke novels from the spent candles, the roses collected and placed in a vase, to the note, chest, and clothing. He reread the message inscribed, *I could not have brought any gift more worthy to be given or received, nothing compares.*

Erik stooped to retrieve some of their garments and finding Christine's corset among the articles he laid across the chest, he evaluated it. *The things women do for fashion, to support and slim their figures. . . must be damned uncomfortable. How does one breathe? Or sing? Whoever comes up with these maniacal contraptions, and to encase the soft body of a woman no less, should be tortured and strung up in his or her own invention. Lasso or corset, toss one of each into my mirrored chamber and either would produce comparable results, to be sure.*

He shook his head while collecting other belongings, set them on one of the lounges and entered Christine's dressing room. He blushed slightly as the recollection of what she had done crossed his mind. *Philosopher. . . I bow to the skillful seductress that you are.* Picking up the cuff links, he replaced the bench to the vanity, exited and returned with a low-backed armchair, thus seating himself in direct confrontation with his nemesis. *I have been fascinated to the point of obsession,* his mind raced to list out the experiments with positioning, curves, and angles, and his thoughts wore on; *it is merely a piece of glass bearing an alloy on the reverse, nothing more, but how it absorbs and transfers, reflects as much as possible from the smooth, exacting surface to surpass such potential, despite the limitations, is enchanting. I have broken plenty in disgust, created feats of wonder in other countries, and yet I can barely tolerate its use for my tedious, daily rituals.* He buried his face in his palms, and then slowly raising his chin to rub the gruff stubble, he raked through the sparse natural waves about the rear and left side of his head. "Not much to obscure one's sight," he poked in quiet sarcasm. "The rugged beauties of God's creation in all its glory." *It is how she saw him.*

Leaning back and lacing his fingers together pensively, index's pausing against his mouth, he challenged God and everyone else. *How do I begin to see as she does? I want to believe all she said; it tickles the ears and placates a wisp of desire before the enduring slap. However, I shall accede some measure of beneficent intervention or Christine would never have come back, least of all to marry my sorry excuse of a carcass. All right, convince me, change my perspective, purge the engraved horror, erase the brand of monster, and while you are at it, a bit of enlightenment as to what my purpose is would be appreciated.*

Having sent his arrogant plea heavenward on the wings of asperity, he reclined, arms folded and stared, patiently waiting for some condescension.

Again Christine awoke without his arms, creature of habit and twice in not less than a quarter of a day. She stretched and rolled to that familiar void then commenced the same routine of dressing gown, a brief interaction with the scene and flush of a ruddy complexion then smiled as her legs carried her toward the sound of a husky exhale.

Peering cautiously around the door frame to see Erik fixed in front of the mirror, his image in the process of a strict schooling, her shadow receded from intrusion and was sharply bade a hasty return.

"My arms are empty and you retreat?"

"Not on that account, only that you seemed occupied."

"Will you join me?" he asked kindly. Walking past him, she avoided his grasp and flailing limbs. "You imp!"

"No, just practical," she chided, taking a moment for herself.

Absence was not long and she was at once behind him. Bending low to the right she pressed her cheek to his. "So, tell me of the view this morning."

His smile broadened. "Much improved. My face value increases with each contact."

"Then we shall nourish its worth often." Her lips kissed Erik's uneven skin while crossing her palms down his chest, causing his lungs to heave. His arms shot out, pulling her into the chair and his custody, her legs drawn up, with toes tucked down the side of the cushion.

"Your skin is so silky." His fingers wandered aimlessly over Christine's face; each large, lash covered eye, her petite nose, sumptuous mouth, and the curve of her neck. "Christine?" Her lids opened fluidly, eyes prepared to read in earnest any sentiment he would inscribe. "You know, other people will not see my face as you do. To them, to anyone outside the few who are closest to us, I shall forever be a terrible prospect to lay eyes upon." He laid a quiet gesture to her parting lips and pointed behind her. Her presence obstructed his ability to see himself full on, but there was enough to reference toward. "It is a fact, one I accept. And, if we are blessed with a child, I do not wish to be a source of shame, in any aspect."

"Erik, there are many who have made your acquaintance and not once has your masque been remarked on—that is not to say it is no less unique, courtesy of value dictates privacy there, but you did not marry humanity, you married me. You are my husband and may claim peace of mind knowing that I accept and love." Her hand slid to his heart. "You are most sincere, a gentle man, who will know how to discuss this topic with our children at a time appropriate to the situation, and they will understand and love as I do." She hesitated at the emotion beginning to well, and then pressed on. "I desire children, with you."

Lowering his head, their tears mingled, and as their cheeks drew together a humbled, heartfelt prayer filtered upward. What more could one possibly say after receiving such an answer to impertinence; and, to be delivered by this intermediary, appropriated to keep fully engaged his embrace, would be the means by which to achieve the perspective wished for until confidence was attained individually. Doubt eased from deep within his soul, realizing each experience brought him nearer to having affirmed that he, indeed, belonged to her.

"Christine, thank you for thoroughly loving me, nothing wavering."

"There would be no other suitable option, it is all or nothing. I have proven my affections cannot be divided."

He grinned.

"Now," she said, straightening.

"Seems serious."

"No, not really. Although, waking to discover your mind troubled at regular intervals during the night has me concerned."

"I don't know how to inhibit my thoughts, Christine, but if it is any consolation, I appreciate your willingness to search me out and listen, in addition to any other ways you inspire me by joyfully punctuating our union."

Christine flushed. "You certainly know how to—"

"Do I?"

"You always have, you know."

Chapter Twenty-Five

Christine sat curled up within the dependable comfort of the plum-colored armchair, it lent support as she placed pen to paper; a pause lifted, suspending thought, sending her mind to wander amid the sweeping tendrils of the golden blaze. Warmed thoroughly, her exposed toes dangled over the front of the cushion while she enjoyed the varying degrees of quiet each night introduced: the way the fire licked the wood about its crevices, the northern wind outside, and the drawing of pen across the finely textured journal, its black ink scoring permanence into the fibers. These sounds, despite the fact that they were categorized as making such, actually became welcomed companions when one was solitary and content beyond silence.

The first full week of their return had worn through to the next. In all, five weeks had passed clear, and only the initial few days of blissful reverie could be looked upon as specific to enjoying the wonders of blending love and play into the facets of marriage; then a ride to Amiens brought news from Sweden. It was not unexpected or sudden, but devastating, to be thrust so low upon the sunset of life when on the dawn of one's own.

Madame Valerius embarked, knowing the extent of her condition, never regretting anything more than the separation between she and

Christine, and now that their connection had been reestablished, hope held out that they would be reunited ere long. Erik set forth from that moment to arrange for their departure, and as timing would have it, their couture arrived, making travel all the smoother.

"No, no sorrow, it was for the best, my dears," she said to them. "My days were filled, I could not have wished for more. And now that you are come, my needs are met." These were Mamma Valerius' words, so calm, and how strange her reaction to Erik. "So, this is your Angel of Music?" she said directly, with a gentle pat to his hand. He was shocked, unsure in her seeming recognition of him, and all Christine could offer was a shrug. When they could confer upon the matter later, she had no more of an explanation to offer him than Mamma's belief in her father's story, the product of their lessons together, and what had transpired at the time of their parting (between the two women).

It was a tender week, as Christine recalled, one that touched Erik most profoundly. The housekeeper and personal attendant confided one evening, as Madame dozed contentedly near the fire, that it was the strong determination making up for the frailty of health which they observed. Madame Valerius had held out, knowing they would come. The move had been advantageous in the beginning, she rallied some, visited extended family and friends, and it bolstered her spirits to be near, but was eventually short lived. When she became home bound, people called regularly, and did so up until and while Erik and Christine were there. Never a day was left to expire without her knowing someone cared; a message was left at the very least, if she were unable to bear someone's presence. Christine and Erik were grateful she could live out her desire in comfort, in ease, and at home.

Madame's final hours were spent among her very own angels, who played and sang at her wish. She passed peacefully.

The two remained for an additional week, touring the Scandinavian shores, then returned to their home and country, and here Christine sat, as she had every evening since, alone. Change had occurred. From threshold to threshold Erik was not the same man as when they had left. The carefree, newly married gentleman, the one who sought regularly for his wife's affections, who turned restless when he could not detect her presence at any given moment, was surprisingly, gone, leaving melancholy to reign in its stead.

Erik was altogether absent, had yielded to the urgency of rapidly materializing ideas, and finally, taking to reclusive behavior, busily tended to the surge of inspiration, despite the kindness shown or temperament leveled. He put off regular nourishment and tenderly extinguished the carefully served amounts of persuasion as well, much to Christine's disapprobation. Oh! How the frustration swelled, subsided and resolved within her mind.

In an honest attempt at gaining insight, she mounted the studio stairs after one, two-day trial estrangement and found herself shunned by an agitated, "please, do not come any further." As much as she would have liked to imagine herself ignored, technically she was not; her queries received a vague, but kind response; invitations were politely declined until a later time; random comments were given a reserved acknowledgment, and the food trays were at least picked over. She could not chasten or berate, for it was feared a longer sentence would come as a result and she did not wish to be restrictive or to become selfish and demanding; that sort of companion would stifle even her into seclusion, and she chilled. No, her desires included the conditions previously enjoyed. The question now was how to achieve it.

Those thoughts had worked on her until before long, she happened on a bit of insight. When she looked at the situation square in the face, Erik was expressing himself, was emotionally charged in ways foreign to her. Noticing the folly, her hand suddenly raised to the emotion up her cheeks; she was jealous, perhaps even envious! Being the center of attention for such long periods of time had had an interesting side effect! "Oh, how simply awful," she had gasped. "Dependent in too many avenues, I cannot expect Erik to. . ." Her enlightened expression arched. They were at fault in different ways: he still avoided contact and was mercilessly secretive, but she was as responsible for her own happiness as she was for theirs together.

Therefore, the powers of realization befell her justly and she ceased to fret about what would, in time, work out. But from her perspective, as the present pushed the limits of all things reasonable (being ten days complete), there could be nothing wrong in hastening the situation with a dose of enticement. Her eyes flashed, closing the chronicle before her to commence the luring of one entrenched mole.

ERIK STARED AT the configuration and smiled. Separated from home when the deluge of thought came was overpowering; the people, the creative stimuli, the questions—especially those—had muted his outward expression in lieu of the dominant inner process. He sighed. The tumultuous wealth was at last waning, but he knew the marathon had taken its toll, for the sense of accomplishment came bittersweet.

He smoothed the disheveled hair and gripped his neck in deliberate rumination to fumble between thoughts, his smile soon fading under the weight of guilt. *How do I manage these predicaments? I am inattentive, unfair, and wholly indifferent to her needs. I frustrated her short term, I know I did, then she left me to self-indulge, gave me sufficient rope and I successfully hung myself. I've. . .* An unexpected aroma permeated the studio, filling his lungs. *Usually her cooking is unable to reach. . . those notes at the top step. My actions mirror those of. . . my weeks of brooding. . .*

Erik's brow contracted heavily, the piecemeal of thoughts shamed him as he tossed the lead to the center of the drafting table and doused all light sources, placing his own shadow amongst the silvery-greys of each dwindling memory. Squinting, with head inclined, he walked toward the stairs under an unexpected glow and found the door ajar. *Odd, a single candle perched at flight's end and a small card beneath the waxen press that says. . . Come.* It was the only word contained thereon, no clues as before. In a moment, he was scanning the darkness for a successor, locating the next in progression from the foot of the grand stairway, up. *Kisses, Massage, Caress, Love.* These four lured further, sounding most advantageous and very positive. Cresting the last step, he slowly peered around the doorframe into the bedchamber, not knowing what to expect in this game of sequence; *Nourish body, mind, and soul* (center of the bed), *Cleanse and dress* (atop his obsidian dressing gown and trousers in the armchair).

A distinct click from the dressing chamber door sent preparations into motion below. There was a hearty repast set up in front of an easily lit fire and candles, staged prior on, which left Christine time enough to take her place against the railing. A drawer slid open then closed, and she tensed when an elegantly attired figure stood silently before her.

Erik's damp, wavy mane hung to one side until one graceful movement rectified the situation, raking every strand smooth. His chest rose at each terse inhalation then fell languidly, though no other muscle budged in observation of her delicate approach. His eyes devoured every natural curve accentuated by the sleek, blue gown, and his legs weakened. They were now not more than a few inches shy of touching, a thundering storm ready to let loose upon a starless sky. Her head inclined to the side, planted a soft kiss beneath his right lobe then drew away. "Welcome home," she whispered.

Erik's eyes drifted closed, savoring every feeling that kiss ignited, the light voice near his cheek uprooted his body, compelling him to heed her will to come. Her hand took his and caressed it as she led him downstairs, seating him comfortably before his meal.

He looked almost unwilling to accept. "I have deserted us and you spoil me. I cannot possibly—"

"You can and must, my fair camel. Forgetting to forage, or ignoring provisions when they are supplied, does not increase my confidence in your abilities to take care of yourself."

"I ate." His defenses shrank sadly. "More than in the past."

"Our perspectives vary greatly there, and I should think my patience to be tried enough, Erik. Please eat."

Concession came and with it, pleasure in conversing. He ate well, filled his stomach and warmed her heart, placing the more in-depth enquiry until after supper.

"Christine, thank you. Supper, your company, pulling me from my obsessive behavior. . . your efforts are greatly appreciated."

"I had begun to worry."

"I did not fade much," he teased, and pulled her from balance into his arms.

She righted herself. "I realize your requirements for sleep are less, and when ideas come they need freedom, but you always sought me out, would blame me for infecting your common sense by derailing all focus and concentration; I loved what I did to you."

He loved what she was doing to him that very moment, how she pressed close.

"When we came back from Sweden I no longer held your attention, swayed your mind or your eye. I thought our connection a novelty worn thin and found myself dreadfully jealous of all that was in your thoughts or beneath your hands."

Here, Erik could not decide whether he was out of humor with himself for being slack in thought or not. His jaw stiffened, that soulful breath given in self-recrimination had immediately affixed reproach, and she became shy and unsure.

"I had been central to so much, to so many, for too long. So, with my selfishness admitted, I left you in peace and found things to keep myself engaged, but I missed you."

"You are always first, though I chose a dismal way of portrayal. There was so much for my intellect to digest in connection with our trip, I just. . ." He groaned at the oversight. "Forgive me?"

"I am here to listen."

"Where to begin, the words to use? My own mortality," came the startling rush, "has weighed heavy, a force imposed and hence the course taken. I am afraid—" Erik stopped cold at the graven fright marked on Christine's countenance.

"Oh, no, no, no. No, my dearest, no." He pressed her hand and face with kisses, unable to dispel the moisture blurring her vision. "*Thoughts* of mortality, *thoughts* and contemplation have brought about the deep moods I have experienced." He shook his head. "This will not do! I must preface my narrative, account further back." Quickly gaining his feet, he removed the tray, clearing the area to accommodate pacing and movement before he went on.

"Christine... the tenderness I observed while in Sweden evoked curious views, most in stark contrast to what I had always related to death. My perception was harsh and unfeeling, a fate I felt to reap myself one day, but as I watched the differences there, Madame Valerius had nothing but kindness to express, to everyone, regardless of station. Her servants esteemed, revered her even. Friends and relations cared that she had someone with her at all times. She accepted me as an individual, I had worth, and she appreciated our gifts of music. I could see respect gained by gentle courtesies, and I wished then, that when my time comes to exit this life, others might remember me with fondness, be glad to have known me, care if I am alone. I also wondered *why* I was here; what purpose had I for being on this earth? If you had not returned, Christine, I would have gone from this world a scoundrel, as someone forsaken, to be pitied for an existence lived in wasted abhorrence. I would have died alone and without love."

He could go no further at present and coming to her, knelt by her side. Christine made no comment as Erik laid his head in her lap to be stroked, his arms wrapped about her waist. A comfortable silence was applied to the next few minutes, and then he again took up his relation.

"What purpose do *I* have? Ambiguity weaves such a tangled mass, how am I to know? In many arenas I squandered my talents for and upon those who were self-vested. It was never to uplift others, always mercenary, and always selfish. But for you, I shared. What use are gifts if not to bless the lives of others? What use are they if horded and hidden away? We set a soul free on the wings of music, Christine. I assisted in the happiness of another, I went outside myself and found acceptance again, with you!"

"Perhaps, for any of us, purpose is to exact a difference, even if it is within one's own life." She paused briefly. "You are *my* difference, you inspire me."

"I should think that statement to be conversely understood. In my mind there is no doubt as to who made me who I am, who exacted their influence upon this abject soul."

"Made you, Erik? I could no more make you do something than I could stop time; no one can force another to change. No amount of encouragement, coercion, bribery, or any number of strategies could manipulate, especially you. Your will is too strong, discipline too firm to alter unless you desire it to be so. I am sorry, the credit belongs to you."

His head lifted, chin stretching with a shake. "You know perfectly well the affect you have over me. What about upstairs?"

"I have no claim on you. Your resistance for ten days is proof." Her response was kind, not injurious.

"My ability to work a task from cradle to grave has interfered with so much. I did not intend for it to be. . . ten days? Old habits. . ." he sighed absently. "I do desire differently, of this I am most sincere." His head tilted up in childlike wonder at Christine's smile as he pulled her into his arms in front of the fire. "I desire happiness for you, but I seem to bring tears and frustration more often."

"You bring much more than you realize; oft times it is the tears which help us to see clearer, and the aggravation that engages consideration for the other."

He looked into her face, amazed at how the flame's charming trance across her eyes melted her to him, each surprising the other by the rejuvenation drawn from shared affection. Upon separating, Erik labeled himself foolish for his dismissive ignorance. A kiss had qualities such that he should never want to disregard again. How could he be treating this newly acquired blessing so readily trivial when in the reciprocal process for nary a year? Repetition was the order, and then came a settling in to ask what she had done with her days.

"All right, my love, since I am no longer *away*, I wish to hear how you occupied your time." Erik had expected menial, womanly types of pleasures, but for her mannerisms giving prelude to response, the ordinary attracted interest. She dropped her gaze and fixed upon a myriad of objects in the room, other than him.

"You may be slightly indignant toward my independence, but however the headstrong display appears, I took precautions..."

Erik's finger helped her to focus. "Christine, protraction only serves to detour the listener down paths of needless concern."

"Yes, well, I maintained a healthy regimen of exercise for both horses, alternating them each time I rode into Amiens—"

"Each time?" Erik interrupted, sounding out his mild astonishment, though he was determined to listen.

"Yesterday, we had a letter from Adèle requesting your consideration in regard to the renovations at the Opera; there are architectural and structural issues, and some meeting that shall be conducted in two week's time. Meg and Richard are engaged... I enquired into the purchase of Arabians from Haras du Pin, Normandy, and contacted Rossi for his advice; he is employed at a training center in Chantilly. So you see, a certain pursuit has made frequency a necessity."

"Being independent and self-reliant are amiable qualities, some I can honestly admit to favoring in your character when coming here, my dear. Reckless, you may have been, due only to my negligence. I am grateful you are safe."

"You are not upset then?"

"To what would it signify? No, in actuality I am in awe, that you would take such risks! To think, a woman, my wife, on a quest to fulfill one of my passions. I could not have conjured such details, but," he warned, "promise me a swift kick to gain my attention prior to setting out on any other bold excursions?"

"Done, if I am allowed near enough for application."

Pleased, he held her close and laughed. "The letter can wait, commending your culinary applications cannot; my skills pale in comparison." She smiled at his compliment. "Is this, I may as well seek answer, the 'nourishment' I was assured of when following your bait?"

"Implications! I suppose I must be careful how I phrase things, for you tend to read far deeper when plain facts are meant as they are." She grimaced.

"Do not play ignorant with me, Madame! You know very well the extent alluded to."

"Do I? You should think about meddling fancies and insinuation because absurd, empty threats will do nothing to hasten what may unfold naturally."

His narrowed eyelids insured a voracious attack upon the neck, which produced in turn, an urgent response of escape, sending pillows sailing as Christine clamored for freedom. Laughter ensued then escalated the moment a pillow was sent in his direction to nail him in the back of the head, his stunned expression quickly becoming the source of her convulsive glee. As was commonly known, Erik would never tolerate being bested during anything remotely competitive, and so she grabbed what pillows availed her general vicinity and dashed behind the sofa in preparation for the onslaught of a possible battle. Erik marked her position, picked up an unclaimed portion of ammunition and strategized while speaking.

"I have never been accosted by pieces of décor until now, although the furnishings flung in the heat of my anger would not have been so forgiving." He watched for an opportunity; none presented.

"You would do well to become accustomed to the flight of these lofty birds," she forewarned, "as I am ruthless in the midst of a fight. Beware, Monsieur!"

"Ah, the truth flushed out!" He grinned while removing the tray farther from the line of fire. Another plump fowl rained in his direction; it was intercepted and added to his growing collection. "You know, I do not intend to create an adversary of my wife by participating in such an immature war," he stated flatly.

Christine stood immediately from behind the armchair, mouth open to protest, and was thumped directly by two of the insolent cushions returned in jest.

"I quite deserved that, falling for a ploy of neutrality. I shan't commit that *faux pas*[9] again," she admitted.

Erik snickered at the rising disgust and the pillow she held in reserved security, then he countered her direction by way of the supper tray to gain a portion of bread from his unfinished provisions, his means of retaliation spent.

Rounding the lounge, Erik coughed several times, holding up a finger for Christine to permit him time to clear his throat; he backed up to the hearth, pounding on his chest and sat down, coughing repeatedly without relief. Christine was at his side, water in hand, which he gratefully rescued from her grasp before wrestling her to the floor.

"Touché, my dear." She was no match for his powerful mass and caved instantly.

"Unfair, playing on my sympathies."

"All stratagem is fair when pitting two forces. Where is your callous exterior now?" he asked, maneuvering them comfortably into the nest of pillows.

"Gone, to resume when least expected."

The joy Erik derived from such deliverance of play, to a revisiting of more serious sentiments, found him grateful he would not have to endure a prolonged inducement and was content almost at once with the sensation of Christine near to his heart while he caressed her shoulder. He stared, the hypnotic dance performed by the flames consoled and his ease shown in his softened contours and warmth of attachment.

It was not above a half hour, and unsurprising, that the two, satisfied in their connection, made no effort in voice, indeed, all remained calm but for Erik's breathing which became more frequently short and shallow. Comparing the deep, penetrating blaze to that of Christine's touch, and the way it caressed the disfigured wood, he shivered against her and pressed close, his hand shaking as it rested upon her neck. He felt the pangs of the inequitable relationship he had with Christine, how much she gave tallied at a distressing rate against the quantity replenished. Why was *he* the recipient? Unable to control himself longer, he placed the heels of his hands to his eyes, and wept privately.

Turning her gaze, Christine found him, eyes reddened, looking blindly toward the ceiling. "Erik?" She touched his chest in solace. "Tell me."

He motioned to the fire and choked out, "Look what you do for me!"

Christine twisted to scrutinize the meaning he had interpreted, and not drawing the intended conclusion, he reached for her hand. She understood without delay, her lips moving whispered affection across each sunken, taut portion of his face where his cheek had nestled against her palm. Emotion forced more tears as she tenderly wiped and stroked.

"Christine, the pressure," he moaned.

"Give me your dressing gown and roll over." Obediently he complied then seized, hand pressed in alarm to his chest.

This phenomenon, which occurred as a result of inhibited ebullition, was first experienced on the ridge amidst Christine's immersion in touch, though it was not readily apparent; her embrace had suffused the stress, disguising much of the attack. Another episode sprung easily upon the conclusion of Erik's narrative and masque removal. The suppression of violent emotion, which promoted such eligible conditions, subjected Christine to a grievous display, panicked her, and added to the anxiety of the situation. Once handled, they devised a course for relaxation, alleviating any future postponement of address—deciding exclusion of restrictive clothing to his upper body optimally wise.

Christine situated a pillow, kneeling with Erik prone before her, his hands clasped tenderly to her thighs. "Let it go."

"Damn, this one hurts!"

"Because you're tensing, relax," she softly directed.

Within minutes the immobilizing constraint loosened under her timely ministrations, leaving him in a state of quiescence, as she continued to rub every muscle along his torso. "How would you like to feel like this every night?"

"Void of the introduction, I'd prefer it, but would accomplish little. As it is, I cannot move, your hands render me as weak as this contemptible malady, though the treatment is heavenly."

Christine seemed pleased. They spoke infrequently, a word here or there, and with nothing of weighted import cast abroad, they both became lost in thought.

Again she tends to my needs, accommodates me, caresses me and is drained. I cannot deny this established wont as wishing it to cease any more than I can stop my own life-blood flowing from each beat of my heart. Yet my conscience scorches mind and soul because I cast words to the wind.

A warm, moist sensation upon his shoulder startled Erik from his shortcomings to a quick reminder. Memory recalled for him Christine's gentle face, pained over the sight of his back. Situated as she was now, she had fought the urge to gasp at the indelible, finger-wide scars latticed across his skin, the fine, silken strands stretched taut and smooth, but she could not contain the ache, and he wondered if she had taken to remembering. At the time, her tears tore at something within him that he could not explain. It actually hurt more to see her cry for him than it was to be mindlessly abused; one he could detach from, the other, he could not.

Erik felt her cry over him and his hands clenched, the softness of her gown gathering within each fist until he could contain himself no more. Pushing away from her, he sat up. "Enough." The tone came coolly. "It is enough."

Averting her head to one side, her auburn hair drew against the shocked chill and hid her distress, a shield to the all too familiar preservation by denial, by separation. He made to brush the hair from her face, but she interceded, rejecting his attempt.

"Do not turn from me, please."

"Reciprocity works on many levels," she said evenly, "does it not?" And she carefully withdrew to stand. Erik grasped her wrist lightly. "Please, do not cause me to pull away, Erik. . . let go."

He released her and watched her retreat with the supper tray to the kitchen, perplexed at the grave, sullen tones by which she addressed him. Scratching his head, Erik tossed a few pillows to their rightful sections, then stood and leaned heavily upon the mantle, waiting for Christine to reappear. Would he ever comprehend women, least of all, the woman to whom he was now irrevocably attached to? *Perhaps, I must learn to be forever flexible.* Erik had sought to spare her and found he was at a surprising loss.

The time was not so interminable as to cause agitation, and the dining room doors were heard to slide shut. He rounded, arms crossed, and she adhered to the panel.

How scared she looked. Erik sensed her fear, the palpable aroma of confidence wiped clean, saw her move, heard each breath while she struggled for composure and each tear contact the floor with a dull thud from her penitently bowed head. Were their prospects for repairing this dilemma dwindling so far beyond reach that she feared what to say?

"Christine?" The mention of her name affected a sharp inhalation. "I don't understand."

She forestalled speech, crossing to the corner windows. "No, you do not, and I am having difficulty coping, managing the doubt," she said timidly, her response barely audible. "Do you regret you are my husband? Sorry I know? Do I cause you so much discomfort when I look past what others cannot, that it causes you to feel unappealing in my sight?" Her hands parted the lace curtains, permitting her to gaze out into the night. "Are you trying to convince me not to love you, thinking that if I must repeat my convictions, see your countenance and your scars often enough, I will inevitably question myself and discover something intolerable?"

Erik was close, his commanding energy near. He knew she would not turn, understanding her only assurance to a position of determination was to avoid his eyes; she had had occasion to tell him as much. His fingers raked through the ends of her hair and played with the curls as a voiceless whisper filled her mind. "The answer to all your questions, is no."

Relief came to both, though neither saw nor wavered, and realizing their conversation was yet in its infancy, he braced as the next barrage of queries flowed.

"Then why do you rely on such caprice, opening yourself up to criticism for the inconsistencies?"

"Because. . . I find embarrassment in my faults, physically as well as characteristically, when compared with yours."

"Stop it, Erik! Just stop it!" Christine cried out wearily. And circling abruptly, she glared at him, fists balled. "You cannot compare yourself to anyone! I have faults, Erik, many unbecoming traits, or do you selectively dismiss them? Perhaps we should freshen the course. I have been disloyal, deceptive, impatient, curious, stubborn, moody, irritable. . . have betrayed you, and I am highly emotional! I feel you're testing me again. Are you? Are you really willing to see the results of how far you can push? Do you want to know how your scars affect me? Do you? They cause me to ache for a time I was not there for you, for the stupidity and ignorance shown you, but your appearance does nothing to change my feelings, except to widen the understanding between us. My love is unconditional, I've told you this, and I feel my actions do nothing to the contrary." She breathed hastily and went on, despite the dejected complexion sinking from the sting of her words. "It is your distrust that hurts and aggravates. I am always at arm's length; you permit me just close enough, then thrust me off in a fit of incredulity. Why won't you let me support you, Erik? Why can't you just let me. . . just let me, love you?" Christine's voice trailed to a silent plea.

Her wrath had heaped plenty upon Erik. She hugged her arms as he turned from her and sat, stunned at the piano, weighted by an unforgiving gravity of heart too heavy to lift on his own. She stretched forth her hand only to be met with the cold shock of despair she inflicted.

"Don't touch me." The negation hissed as he snapped out.

She froze and retracted the gesture.

"This is not a game, Christine. I do not bait your emotions to observe, like I once did. Our relationship is too important for me to engage such a plot. Most lessons are internalized quickly. I do sincerely regret being the cause of this anger and agree, you are not tirelessly patient for I shall require more than you have given—*much more*—but your compassion endures. Of this I ask forgiveness because I have indeed, taken advantage." Erik looked to the side, seeking cautiously for the touch he had again, cast away. Christine stood blankly in a haze of sorrow, her back to him, perfectly still. "Our love," he ventured, "has a strong, embedded foundation—*I feel it*—there is no guise involved. You have been honest and completely up-front, and though I seem to struggle. . . no, I struggle," he corrected. "I struggle, with sharing all that I am, and with accepting, but I give only *to* you."

He shook his head at the last segment, misconstrued as it could be and most likely was, it had not been imparted well. An almost obliging pause ensued, which had Erik half hoping for and Christine nearly turning from, her place of resolve. But an exertion of will curtailed the inquisitive nature of the latter and left the former with naught but continuance.

"I long prided my ability to dominate those who were less than I, and now loathe that I cannot seem to conquer the impulse to shy away. How am I to explain?" He frowned darkly. "Deep inside, I have an ongoing conflict, a daily war I wage where the past occasionally prevails, but it is less so. It is a war, where nearly forty years of life are pitted against one with you, the odds are stacked and not favorable, but you triumph a good deal of the time." There followed an anxious silence before he took up again. "During these blinding circumstances, I sought and tend to seek the old comforts, difficult as they are to repress, instead of what you so graciously offer because I am scared as hell, especially now, that you *will* decide it is enough, and that you *will* stop loving me and leave. In truth, I can see I have done this to myself. And, how? How can I love you despite all you mention, and overlook? Because I see change, though I do not permit the same *of* you for me. I thought I had allowed you to love me completely and obviously I have not, I have not. . . allowed. . ."

The repetition was a sharp acknowledgment of arrogance not yet considered, of subconscious control. Erik sighed and was quickly deterred into a state of self-enforced withdrawal, unaware that Christine moved toward him. Her touch came lightly to his shoulder, and his joined hesitantly, securing as much surface contact as possible, neither meeting the gaze of the other.

"Love me, please," he entreated.

"I will. . ." her voice came hoarse and slow, "fight your war with you, by your side. I shall never forsake. I *do* love you."

"Oh, Christine," Erik breathed, as her other hand encircled his neck; her lips lovingly come to bid his despondency flee. Grasping at her arm, he coaxed her to sit and pressed his forehead to hers, brushing the tears from her cheeks and she from his. "The art of marriage, how I shall endeavor to learn, to be taught."

"To enjoy all and to love."

"To love and to be loved." He embraced her with an emerging lightness of heart, "Would you care to see what has so thoroughly engaged my mind?"

She grinned sweetly. "I would indeed."

"Come then," Erik encouraged.

Detouring temporarily to secure a means of light, the flame did right by them, cutting through the darkened studio to his drafting table. Being layered in an orderly fashion with blueprints, the diagrams were fixed by small sandbags, and smartly so, as the diversion of entry brought on a vivacious animation of activity—the likes of which blurred and ruffled anything he passed—to be kept secure while gathering up all he wished to share. He kissed her and began telling of the plans he had drawn up for expanding upon and improving what they already had at their estate. Here he poured, nearly gushed in exuberance to finally make the intelligence, which he had at one time barricaded her from, known. The excitement was infectious and had her asking questions, urging him with interest then, while pointing to a specific feature, he stopped mid-sentence and stared at Christine. He was sure she had not realized his thoughts to be so divergent, however, when his mysterious side took hold it was a time to pay heed, so she returned his attention firm. Stepping from opposite her, he moved until he nuzzled in against her from behind.

"You were saying?" she urged.

He held tight, lowering his hands to rest about her lower abdomen. "I am at your mercy, your discretion. There, above the kitchen. . ." his voice directed.

"Here?"

"Yes. That is the nursery." The very declaration obliged a gasp, and Erik embraced closer. "Along the upper corridor I have designed several bedchambers, and my study shall be reconfigured, remodeled if necessary, for the purpose of teaching our children."

"Neither of us seem to have been far from the other's thoughts," she sniffed.

"Never! When you are near to me as you are, my mind brings such clarity of recent experiences, so fresh. After Sweden, I resolved we should not be solitary, whether by our own volition or," he kissed her neck, "God's. We can begin in the spring, but first, your thoughts. I wish for your input."

Fingering the papers, smoothing the delicate sheets Erik had so carefully introduced, as becoming quite integral to their lives together, she sighed and rotated around to face him and laid her tear stained and glowing cheek to Erik's chest, constrained by emotion and unable to express anything to be readily understood. Once in control she drew back. "I have been mistaken, misjudged. . . thinking that you delved, solely to express for yourself, whatever the inspiration. This confounds even the most remote ideal." Her tone rose. "Spring, hmm?" He saw the suspicious nature twitching at the corners of her mouth. "And to what do you owe your *second sight*, to scheme in such a way?"

"To one. . ." he mused at the insinuation of foreknowledge, "experience, but to the other I, as was stated, am at the mercy of other laws, be what they may. I desire, as do you, to share. I love you, and from our love there should come children."

"Children, more than one?"

"We shall see how the whole of it unfolds as I am not opposed to the idea, now. I. . ."

Suffocation of speech beneath her lips, and the wickedness of satin, brought them too near for verbal sentiments, each assuming a responsibility created by governing the sweetness at once benefitted by the other.

Chapter Twenty-Six

It was nearly a fortnight passed, and the relentless pace across the office flooring, to which M. Edouard Mercier employed himself, secured no pity from his onlooker. He refused any guarantee and would therefore deal with the worry creasing his brow. Mme Giry watched, lightly amused by the comely performance, but she was tactful, not altogether devoid of common courtesy when direct in her cheeriness.

"Less than a fortnight since hearing from this gentleman, Adèle, and no prior introduction. What am I to do, the meeting is tomorrow! Blast!" He halted, confronting the irresolute twitch of her lips. *Was that. . . no,* he doubted. But he could have sworn they had harbored the shape of an upturned smirk just moments ago. "You think my plight humorous, do you?"

"Of course not, but you decline—"

"Decline? To what, join your confidence of a man I have yet to make an acquaintance, when I am to recommend him? Yes!"

"Edouard, you shall not meet with disappointment, I can assure you. Monsieur Gautier knows the Opera House, more thoroughly than you could have wished. He is a blessing dropped in our lap, one who shall bring ingenuity and experience. He is concise, adept, highly skilled, and well educated. His character, perhaps, hints to a self-serving pride, but none that would interfere with the seriousness for which he is retained. I know what he is capable of, trust him to keep to his word, and if he inferred his attendance tomorrow, then he will not fail you."

Disbelief flitted across the forested depths as he took her hand, breathing a deep sigh of resignation. An unexpected heat rose to pinken Mme Giry's face, forcing a girlishness to take hold, a state one could not easily shake while standing in his absorbing trance. She came to herself soon after, and placing her hands to his shoulders, straightened all manner of peaceable accessory, whether needed or not, retiring thereafter from his close proximity to regain total composure and firmness of will. M. Mercier, as he was fast becoming a connoisseur of this woman's traits, preferred her paradoxical changes to that of youthful predictability. They were well-suited, strong to a fault, both stoic and persevering in nature—but only slightly less so in the presence of the other—guarded, daunting in ways that would dare to attach their proud hearts, as if by chance they might lower the tendency to send compatible intimation.

"All has progressed well, albeit those specified sections," she spoke, picking up directly as though nothing had passed. "You are at your best when convincing others to support your cause. Telling the investors they shall have the advantage of an original contractor will, I am sure, persuade. And as a gauge of such, look how well your conversations have been taken to print while overcoming scandalous rumors. As for me, I await the information necessary to establish a full rehearsal schedule and shall provide ballet performances aplenty within the interim. The auditorium is usable toward that end, even if completion must be postponed."

"I may satisfy the queries of the communal gossips, Adèle, but I have yet to sate my own theories. I know with what I deal; I still feel the Opera jinxed for any who assume control. I, of all people knew, thinking I could tame, and it curses me thusly. . . oddities cropping up. What goads me is that it is *his* spirit haunting postmortem, an insolent mockery, one who seems to win despite the realm in which he exists."

Mme Giry listened, said nothing and remained quiet on the topic. If he only knew the experience from which *his*, *Erik's*, perspective was drawn, he would not conclude in such a way, but Mercier would never know, nor would anyone, not from her.

HAVING ARRIVED DURING the previous intervening hours between dusk and dawn, Erik and Christine were comfortably situated below, preparing, unbeknownst to any until a message lay in wait upon a certain desk early the next morning. It was addressed to one Monsieur Mercier, resolving all concerns, and reserving the right to Mme Giry for the expression of a short, well-founded speech of, "Well, it was as suspected," when the contents came to her intelligence.

Erik made his rounds, surveyed the existing conundrums, and finding all as he had when last there, spoke his mind in much the same fashion, "It is as I expected," and returned to the lower cellars.

"This meeting should prove interesting," Erik rehearsed, whilst tying up an ascot about his neck. "Mercier is oblivious from whom he seeks assistance, though... of the managerial glut over the years, he shall be a worthy opponent to keep an eye on, and dear Adèle, she conceals everything, even our connection. Can you imagine their faces upon our first acquaintance?"

"I can. Is there a direction in which you are steering them, or not?" she asked.

"At present, my decision is to relate nothing. If they know anything at all, in terms of the profession itself, they may speculate as to a misfortune with bitumen, and I shall leave it at that, as gentlemen usually avoid such personal affronts."

"Since I am not a gentleman, would you explain?"

"It fits rather well, my gentlewoman. You see, the foundations of the Opera House are sealed, along with inner and outer walls of brick and concrete, but are made impervious to water by the bitumen, which is a petroleum-based product requiring high temperatures in order for it to be utilized, hence. . ." He gestured to his face. "One tragedy."

"Erik."

"I hope their reaction to be likewise," he remarked, taking notice of the involuntary tremble run through her as a wanton chill. "It would be an unpleasant image for the mind to dwell upon all the particulars," he said, sitting before Christine. "Would you?"

She smiled gently as his humbled dignity submitted to her practiced hands, permitting her to position his hairpiece. He had shown her the meticulous process that ensured the illusion for others and in turn, she took it upon herself to employ a level of sincerity for learning well; she would do no less. Smoothing the raven hair, she tilted his head back and gazed tenderly into his warm, familiar contours before he resumed his masque.

"Thank you," she said, placing a set of tranquil fingers at his temple. "Thank you for allowing me to love you."

Erik wrapped her tightly in his arms, and kissing her breast lightly, pressed his ear to her heart. "A fortnight with you, riding, time with you, examining Arabians for future breeding, extending an offer to Rossi to join our estate next year as stable master, more time with you. I am a different man," he rambled.

"Yes, and lingering too long will make you a *late* man, you are already repeating yourself."

"Not often enough. Will you be here when I return?"

"Unfortunately no, a bit of time and space is apropos, I should think. I shall be with Meg."

"Her wedding details, I suppose. Take care then."

"And you."

Erik slid back the chair and bending low, took his leave by kiss.

A quarter hour placed him patiently waiting, reclined in an overstuffed leather chair, taking in the sight surrounding him. Mercier had quite the touch, his furnishings were basic, *no use trying to impress oneself when alone immersed in business most of the day*; the deep black walnut set off against burgundy drapes, the private desk, table, chairs, bookcases, all required, nothing gaudy. The corner of Erik's mouth moved, a tic pulling it in recall to each ruse imposed upon the managers from within this very room. "Poligny," he airily clucked. *Such an easily excitable puppet in my theatre. . . on my stage, humph. . . my theatre, indeed. I certainly poured enough of myself into its tidy confines of an empire: hidden chambers, trapdoors, slight-of-hand, extortion, and possible murder. Hell, I could be locked up for years but for lack of proof. . . should be in another country, and yet for all my genius, where am I? Smack in the middle of it all with a pack of ignorant wolves at my bidding.* Sighing heavily, and feeling like a sacrificial lamb to slaughter, in one sense or another, he quickly shut off any sentiment and placed his confidence forward knowing it would sustain, for above all else, he held all the cards; he could impart his wisdom or not.

Voices roused Erik to vacate the chair and rise as several men entered the room in succession to discover his early admittance—made privy by Mme Giry—and as this intimation was already understood, Mercier led off with the introductions of Messieurs Gabion, Sharbonneaux, and Martine. Shaking hands, the gentlemen each made an effort to avoid staring at the impeccably dressed individual until they were obliged out of necessity to attend his face with the whole, in a civil manner. *Miserable failure, discounting what is obvious. The masque is a difficult element to ignore,* he thought honestly. *Well, at the very least they averted their sight.*

Then, before a table amply endowed in seating, Erik gave one comprehensive glance and threw himself under the scrutiny of the aforementioned. He became comfortable and unaware of himself in supplying a lengthy intercourse of expertise, and he quite enjoyed watching the skepticism fade in light of his command over the subject. Hands, initially interrupting the gravitational momentum of the long dour faces, soon slipped to support the countenances in their fancied interest. Queries came simply, and the responses convinced and appeased.

Nearly an hour passed and only once had there been cause for vexed annoyance on Erik's part—but more so to his credit—as M. Sharbonneaux, who was unwilling to allow presupposition, veered along a more personal avenue, to dispute and test what he had been hearing. A thickened pause released a visibly tacit expression of hauteur from the former, the cock of a galling brow from the latter, and induced suspense upon those remaining. M. Sharbonneaux monitored the relevant effect this deviating challenge could pose. Erik's eyes burned hot, but were no more than embers after taking a moment for composure. He apologized, explained directly the presumptions under which he had been functioning and briefly provided the gentlemen with his qualifications. Erik expressed regret for the undue stress a detained schedule puts on all involved and mentioned M. Mercier, for his endurance was worthy of applause. He also assured them he would do his best to successfully coincide the finishing work with the other renovations concluding by years end, thus avoiding any comparison with the previously prolonged governmental intermission.[10] This snip of candor brought laughter and respect from all sides, whereupon, receiving a gracious nod from the *instigating germ*, Sharbonneaux, Erik pressed on. The meeting had become a rightful interview, and as it migrated from office to auditorium, all envisioned the project aright; what with mistakes exposed, cuts in quality discussed and points exacted for the improvements, approvals were made alongside a trusting relationship, which had turned to bring about a successful negotiation. Inside, Erik grinned broadly, swelling his chest to capacity. To be blindly out maneuvered or outwitted by sheer anger was not control, what he had accomplished, was.

Christine's day had shortened, landing her and Meg back in the Giry's flat at one-thirty to partake of a fascinating tale that had transpired that morning. It was obvious to the initial listener that M. Mercier was impressed by Mme Giry's mysterious acquaintance and thought nothing extraordinary in his conduct, but to the subsequent narrator and listeners, it bespoke novels. Christine could not put off her departure, and left.

Arriving below, humming could be heard in the upper chambers and as she rounded the doorway she observed a busily contented man, tinkering with the replacements to his organ. He sensed her—he always could down there—but relished the pleasure of anticipating her touch, which would not be long in coming, or so he thought. When some minutes of vacancy piqued, and his curiosity was well tormented, he rotated from the console too chafed to wait out the half-day's separation and went in search. The lower vault doors were open, and upon entering, two lithe arms seized from behind.

"My angelic tease," he grumbled wistfully. "Why did you not come to me?"

"You seemed too calm to disturb, and because you knew I would."

"Ah, spontaneity, your indomitable incentive."

"Someone must keep your senses alert, mind sharp, and abilities flexible."

"Self-appointed to keep me from becoming stale and musty, eh?" he asked over his shoulder. "How am I to ever appreciate you enough?"

Her arms loosened and he turned to face her. "What's this?"

"Happiness for you." Her eyes were moist.

Light dawned. "Adèle, how much did she divulge?"

"Her focus was specific to what she alone understood. I heard only enough to bring me back in haste to hear of the account from your own lips. I thought it better than second or third hand." His cheek rested to hers. "I was aware of the possible outcomes, knew of your mindset then, and felt a difference at my coming now. The air within these cellars has a charge all its own, a passionate energy and today, this afternoon, a reverence envelops it."

A full disclosure was immediately bestowed from husband to wife, one she could not have been more overjoyed to partake in, especially his rendition; to hear of the covert winking, brow signals and furtive, disbelieving glances, were at first to her, amusing, to realize that grown men would stoop to such nonsense. But the impact of such tactics was apparently ingenious because it had begun to erode Erik's mental stability. Defeat was not an option and the struggle for composure, a blessing, for it sharpened his purpose and honed his reason for desiring to sway them to ally.

There is a warm peace felt when necessity intervenes on behalf of pride; this was the difference Christine sensed.

Chapter Twenty-Seven

A month of relentless days melted from one to the next and a routine emerged, however short term. Erik's occupation of time was spent managing several crews during the week while it became Christine's responsibility to keep him mindful of social affairs for balance, which were anxiously monitored dinner engagements twice weekly with the Girys—one never knew if M. Mercier would show unannounced. There were walks, visits with the Persian, as well as the inclusion of holiday and wedding preparations, just to please Meg, for a man's input became part and parcel to her; and once, being lightly cowed, Christine gave in and accompanied Meg to a rehearsal at the Opera, to which they later received a severe chastisement for carelessness from Mme Giry and were told straight out, though nobody recognized her, that it would require but one wagging tongue amongst the rumor mill, and speculation, to ruin opportunity. Of course, Erik was told and Christine had to endure his disappointed sighs, though he was more understanding; their roles, such as they were, were in reverse, which bridged meaningful insight to empathy.

Christine longed for weekends in the country, coveted them, and would not allow talk related to the tedious building to creep in until the eve of a new week came.

"You make no advance for a return, are you unwell?" he enquired.

"No. I lack motivation. I do not care much for the way we have to orchestrate our lives around those who *might* recognize some connection. There has been sufficient turnover in the past six months alone that it is highly unlikely, except for Edouard."

"But this is not the only reason."

Christine shook her head and sat upon the edge of their bed, arms looped about the post. "I am tired of late. Trying to keep up with you is quite a task. Besides, I can do more here, the horses, walks. . ."

"And you would be more content with the pace, yes, I understand." His words said one thing, but he could not help the disappointment flooding his tone or face. "I shall be away for three days at most, there will only be the finishing out and details of a walk through to complete the contract."

She suddenly looked exhausted to him, the wan distance in her eyes telling more than her voice. "You have enjoyed the physical aspect of this 'purpose' I believe."

He sat with her, taking her by the hands. "I have. But it means nothing if I neglect you. How have I been?" he asked. His thumbs nervously rubbed the soft warmth of her skin then he pressed them against his mouth. "Be honest."

Christine kissed his forehead. "It has not been easy to share," she admitted. "I wish to do everything with you, keep you near to me as you are now. But this I have gladly replaced with the comments Meg and Adèle bring me from those working closely with you." She tucked back a wave. "You are described as hard, unyielding in your expectations, but fair. If a task is claimed as impossible, you are kind and direct to instruct until comprehension takes hold. Adèle has heard curiosities and wonder regarding the masque, some supposition, and you were correct, she said that members of your crew have mentioned the bitumen."

Erik seemed pleased, and she talked on, stroking his gruff, two-day growth affectionately. "The remarks, none are derogatory, they are factual and show respect."

Feeling the looming presence of a conjunctive rejoinder, he silently braced as she rose and moved toward the balcony doors. Dispassionate melancholy reflected her inner mood as her gaze rested on a hint of receding sun twinkling along the edge of some crusted snow.

"But. . ." he pushed.

"I am proud of my husband. Joyous for the purpose engaged in, but. . ." She traced the moisture beaded along the glass pane and her intensity doubled as if the very thought of parting gave pain. "You must not go. I do not wish you away, nor can I bear separation as yet." And then all was silence and quiet entreaty. "Our desire is to keep you here longer, your presence tonight is imperative, to us."

Erik stared; his eyes firmly adhered to her form, then they narrowed as a keenness of hope sought for that sharpened, intuitive ray; they in turn dilated, heightened in concern at the incremental rise and drop in pitch. He was baffled and confused, but this too, shed in seconds. There was an intake of air heard, the treading of bare feet, and what was yearned for most, touch. He stepped up from behind, sliding his hands in a gentle caress to encase her lower abdomen.

"Tell me," he whispered.

Her hands moved to encompass his in wordless reply and Erik shivered as emotion tenderly gripped his heart. The confirmation welcomed him, brought them together, whereupon they could reestablish enlightenment upon a plateau within the commonality of love. Christine stood quite still, saying naught. With only a hair's breadth of movement visible to discern life, Erik basked in a period of reverie, and then one graceful rotation in adagio drew him comfortably into a sanctuary shared by one more.

Erik went down on one knee, laying his cheek to her flat stomach, as she stroked the base of his neck. "My mind goes blank, nothing shall exist tonight beyond us. I am bound. I cannot, I must not leave, for our souls shall imprint yet again, reaffirm and renew with purpose." This precious avowal of commitment burned as he sang through touch. Her ears warmed to each intonation, the beauty flourishing between them. . . a child.

Morning came, had drifted in lightly under a veil of white repose and with it, such leisure that one should not so willingly give up. Christine sat up carefully against the pillows as a bleary eyed Erik stirred; only to resettle again with a limb contentedly draped across her lap in confining affection. She leaned to one side above him, gently circling the tips of her fingers in a feathered motion over the skin of his shoulder and arm, to watch the icicles precariously hang from the roof, their lengthening process begun in reverse beneath the sun's unrest. Several weakened, could bear the tenacious adherence no longer and came to an end, crashing in a heap of glistening fragments. A look of uncertainty furrowed the manly brow awhile in response to the brash, unspecified noise, as though the subconscious were trying to decide the worth of venturing too close to the surface of awake.

"If you persist," he half grumbled into the bedding, "I shall be required to put down roots, and thus lies the difficulty in which I struggle. The longer I stay, the harder it will be for me to take my leave."

"Would you require incentive of some sort?"

Erik's body vibrated in laughter as he rolled out, gaining his feet. "For what, to remain or to go away?"

"I suppose, from the looks of our situation, it would be to stay, but I shall sacrifice so that the Opera may have her precious stage. Go, do what you must and then return."

Erik grimaced at the convincing tone of indifference and the waving flick of her hand. The mere mention of leaving brought a foreboding chill and he could not help but resume his most recent circumstance, which would prolong the agony of this repeated see-sawing affair, much to Christine's dismay.

"First," he remarked, taking her into his arms. "I am not a fly you can whisk with your tail, and second, to know you are safe, to know you are secure and well. . . I sense I ought to be here and not gone from your side." A dull tremor suddenly affected his voice, and Christine's grateful tone made light, hoping to reduce his concern.

"I will be fine, Papa. You shall be home the day after tomorrow to find all is well."

"Christine. . ."

No amount of verbal convincing could be done, but her gentle ways bolstered his faith that what she had said, should indeed be the relied upon course.

Erik was now into the better part of day two, arduous in both capacities as might be experienced mentally and physically, and though he was immersed, he could not hasten progress, people's tendencies, or time. The last, in its infinite, colloquial whir, was vying as commander of wills, never one to be commandeered, only obeyed. Above the main level, and by way of the administration hall, Erik stood within one of several temporary offices let for those employed in the renovation process, his attention bent toward checking over the Opera plans, thoughts naturally bearing eyes and heart elsewhere. . .

CONFLICT OF CHOICE had roared and pulled at every fiber from the moment he could no longer see Christine standing alongside the estate. She waved until movement became futile, then switched to a raise of the hand. He would circle around on Cesar every so often to take in the sight of his beloved bidding him well, but it did nothing to quell the raging disquiet in the pit of his stomach. While aboard the train, he realized the incident to be their primary separation since marriage, his mind dwelling on the odious discord generated from the day of their engagement. *How unsettling.* The distance removed all options from their agency; there lacked a level of control, of choice, and he determined at once that this was not to become an enduring friendship but an infrequent acquaintance—Absence was to be tolerated only when necessary.

With mind industriously split, but without Christine to settle, and the true Parisian façade drawn, Erik was free to attend directly to details upon arrival. He became almost instantly distracted, had an aloof, but civil air, and gave the distinct impression that his presence could be more effectively engaged otherwise; that he would prefer it to be so, overt. The one bit of intimacy holding his heart aloft was the knowledge of life that he had helped to create, and he grinned lightly.

Enduring until later that first evening, Erik had found himself in the Persian's company, partially absolved from the afflicting preoccupation, but not totally, which may have permitted the topic a seat at the chess game Erik seemed to be wholly disengaged from.

"Care to have out with whatever is troubling your mind?" the Persian asked offhand.

"What makes you think. . ." Erik began his response absently enough, when the Persian captured his bishop and ended his sentence.

"*That* is what makes me think. Tell me, when have you ever granted me the privilege of capturing both your bishops?"

Erik sighed and leaned back to contemplate the line of conversation that would best suit. Nothing did, and so without preface, he shot up out of his chair and spilled the intelligence ineptly before the quiet auditor. "Christine, she is. . ." A flush heightened along Erik's neck and brought an immediate grin to the Persian's face. "Daroga, she carries my child!"

The Persian sunk back into his chair and breathed out nearly complete before uttering an astonished "well."

Beyond the Masque

"Yes." Erik fixed his eyes to the fire.

"Then, I should enquire why you are here."

"Because she is not, she wished to stay at home, in the country."

"And your heart is there." He grinned, his winsome semantics having gone unnoticed.

"It is. I was torn between responsibilities; she encouraged me to be done, though I felt I should not have left."

"Then my question stands. Why are you here? The contract is finished, is it not?"

"The day after tomorrow is the final inspection."

"Push Mercier, he'll understand."

"Daroga, I have kept a low profile, and despite the pain and soreness of tongue, have been cooperative. Mercier knows nothing of my marriage to Christine, that I have any relations or a wife. Christine and I thought it best not to arouse suspicion."

"Which is wise, but there is nothing wrong with the intimating of family concerns, is there?"

"No," Erik replied simply, taken aback by the unimagined ease of such an answer. He was quite appalled by the revelation, but as all incommodious thoughts must be given their time to soak, he left them for the very place from which he desired to be released, the present. . .

"MONSIEUR GAUTIER?" A gentle, but firm hand grasped Erik's shoulder, startling the self-absorption, much to his consternation.

"Hmm? Oh, forgive me, my—"

"Mind is elsewhere?" Mercier finished.

Yes, it was, and how careless of him to be wandering, to be come upon and found in such a fashion. It did nothing for his pride, but for some reason—peculiar really—it mattered little in the scheme of things, as they were. He was at once attentive.

"I received your message when I came in but was detained with other matters and unable to make concessions until recently, though I sympathize completely with the presentiments explained. You have exceeded all expectations and have made good on your word. I am witness to your wish for nothing more than to attend to that which rends your loyalty. What would you say to having done with our final inspection, now?"

Not wanting to seem too eager to satiate the deign proffered him, but feeling his distress begin to dissipate nonetheless because of it, Erik bowed in reserved acceptance and joined Mercier, thus hastening the termination of that decidedly despised company of Separation—relative of one he wished to know rarely.

Dismounting in the twilight of eve, Erik dropped Cesar's tack in the gravel at the base of the front porch, and leaving the horse to his own devises quickly entered the house calling out for Christine, the summons meeting with little but an unused void. Erik climbed the stairs to find the door to their chamber closed, as well as the entrance to his dressing and bath area, all secured from the inside. Turning, he found hers to be open and strode directly through to see Christine curled up asleep in the chair before an ashen fire. He knelt and let his sight roam about her slight figure; her face was pallid, matching the ghostly echo he now agitated from its lazy state into a renewed blaze; dark circles shadowed her normally flawless skin, which felt warm to the gentle touch of his lips. His fingertips slid softly around to the underside of her wrist. . . *faint, but regular*. . . he breathed in relief, then he carefully draped a light afghan over her to aid until the flame's heat took hold.

Erik's eyes adjusted as he perused the room for evidence to satisfy an accounting of the past thirty-six hours. He found the remnants of tea swirled in a coin-sized pool, the bed was left unmade, a basin and wash rags. . . It was not much to give rise to more than the sudden onset of an illness, the memory of which needled his conscience to send him off pacing as if trying to avoid the sharp reminder of her unfailing form at *his* side. His frustration eventually placed his step in front of the window, adjacent to the open door of Christine's dressing room.

"I should have been here, sent word at the very least. I promised to set her needs above my own—" The muttering chastisement came to an abrupt end as he rounded to face what had been obscured from view upon his initial pass through. There, hanging just barely visible was one of Christine's chemises, clean, but horribly stained. Erik spun unerringly and leaned against the doorframe in an unforgiving manner, head limp, lungs refusing exchange of air and soul weary. "When?" he demanded, dragging himself to look once more at what she had to deal with alone. "When will I be able to accurately interpret and follow the disquiet which preys on me physically?"

The sound of a fist colliding with an intended wall was all too familiar, albeit unnerving, as Christine struggled to make sense and gain a clear perspective. "Erik?" Her voice rasped out in a timorous whisper.

"Yes," he replied, shaking off the despondency. "Yes, I'm here."

Those words were a sweet mixture of sanguine comfort and hope reunited. His silky tone infused both a rush of energy and desire to be near, but for her, was brief and sadly expended in untangling her extremities. By the time she stood, her legs gave way in rebellion, buckling in a conjoined dance with the spinning of her head. She had no cause to worry, for Erik, in his desire to close the imposed distance, gathered her to himself, embracing her solidly before sitting with her nestled into his chest.

"Hold me tight," she murmured at length.

Erik clung desperately to the beautiful young woman who lay in his arms. Minutes passed unheeded, tears fell, and he dared at last to speak. "Forgive me, Christine, my sweet Christine, for not being here when you needed me most."

Pushing herself upright to face him, Christine removed the forgotten masque and looked upon the sensitive spirit penitently staring back at her. "You are home now, a blessing come. I prayed you would finish, that the work would not linger."

Erik watched her face contort mildly and her eyes close to block the light wave of pain. "When did it begin?" he asked, setting one hand atop hers, the other massaging her lower back.

"Last night," she choked. "I. . . too hasty."

"Christine, it was not yet meant to be."

She nodded. Erik pulled her close and held her for hours as they shared their sorrow far into the night, but the outpouring of tears rained despite what the mind comprehended, and hurt for what the heart understood.

Chapter Twenty-Eight

"For posterity's sake," was what Christine had used to ply him into trying his hand at journaling. His excuse—or reason, as he called it for not doing so—was that he felt impressed his legacy should be encased upon the staves of a musical score; there was little need for leaving the other. While composing on a regular basis he expressed so infinitely and clearly the emotions yearning to overflow their boundaries when poised at the keys or strings of an instrument. Language was entirely different, an author of poetry possibly, that was at least artistic. *Utilitarian, prosaic, prose... blast, I am not a writer!* Erik smirked. Christine had noticed the inconsistency of his penmanship, sometimes his hand looked so elegantly smooth, steady and effortless, then there was the right, for it was the ability of the right in which he endeavored to improve. Needless to say, Christine was not amused with the feigning lack of aptitude; hence, her persistent request to put down experiences, manually.

Erik removed himself to the window of his study in the hope of inspiration from the elements drifting peaceably in a congregation of white. It was no use, such a torturous waste of his talents! All he could think of was applying ink to paper, and snow only emphasized this in volume. Sitting once more, he reflected... *inspiration, betrayal, love, joy, love, sorrow, and love.* The word had a continuous well of meaning, thus, his thoughts congealed about their most recent events.

After Christine's miscarriage there came a few days of attentiveness, almost to the point of absurd, as though she felt to make it up to me or to us by over compensating. (What I told her, about the timing, I feel was more to convince myself of there being another opportunity.) We have since discussed the officious behavior and see balance, and are stronger upon reaching the other side of this experience. She amazes me, the wisdom possessed and the fierce devotion lavished me. . . I shall never want from another.

I have remained here, at home. I avoid separation and have left the Persian with our investments to manage. I figured since I was not occupying such a large portion of his life, something might as well. There is also a small matter of remuneration to procure before the month of January is completely expired, and perhaps, as a favor, I shall use what is due me and become a viable patron of the Opera. Mercier complained of Box 5 being unsold and the seemingly unending tales associated with its participatory grandeur of the past, but what do I care of superstitious rumor? After all, one should rectify mistakes if the occasion presents itself, should they not? It is a most befitting paradox in my mind, and why should I not keep the best seat in the house? "Why not, indeed," he spoke up. Having finished with his quarterly contribution, Erik blotted the ink, shut the book, and went in search of other activities to employ his time. This kind of diversion was ill suited to a restive mind, especially on a day when occupying himself out-of-doors was unthinkable.

Opening the study doors brought the sweet scents of home, such splendid tokens providing ample feast to lungs and soul. What he decreed as *the labor of love* now filled the great room in combination with the cozy fire, and sent his stride headed straight for its source, patting his stomach. Excellent! He was in time, Christine had a towel slung across her shoulder, his signal to relieve her of its burden and commence dish drying. She handed off the first, the hireling paid in advance with a kiss.

"Bread?"

Her brow arched sharply.

"All right, so there is no prize for stating the obvious," he countered to the non-verbal display.

"Writing?"

"Task complete." He feigned notice of the silver pattern to escape meeting her eyes, for an essay it was not.

Drying her hands on the backside of her apron, she looked at him then gestured for the towel and being duly returned, it came with his hands wrapped at either end to ensnare her.

"You have something to ask?"

Erik studied her smug expression. "I do, and how is it that you perceive this?"

"Whenever you have something on your mind you attend to it in a round about fashion, usually by way of trivialities. Perhaps I am likely to find the topic distasteful or that my will shall be uneasy to dissuade; the symptoms profess as much."

"Am I that simple to figure out?"

"Certainly not, but I have been well taught and work in earnest to dissolve all inhibitions."

"Specifically mine."

"A worthy goal, considering. . ." Her thought failed as his long fingers stroked rhythmically at the base of her neck. "You are hunting for an affirmative concession."

"You know I do not seduce to get my way, that is beneath me." His wry grin broadened at the choice of wording.

"Beware your humor, Monsieur! Now, are you going to ask, or not?"

His humor, right, she was sucking the play right out of this situation. "Yes. I was extended a personal invitation to join in the festivities of the Opera's reopening. Mercier is hosting a Masquerade Ball in one week's time. I was wondering, since the rich accommodations meet the criteria, if you would allow me the honor of escorting you."

"There are memories." Christine gave him the once over. "And you would be comfortable?"

"We shall replace the old, with *ours*. I should like to show you that I know how to be social. My previous attempt was pompous and haughty; behavior mirroring that of an imperial demigod, or so the Persian would have categorized me. I paraded around like those peacocks Richard keeps company with and whose characters I hold in hypocritical contempt. I made quite a daunting spectacle of myself while you spent those first hours after midnight, guarding Chagny— you gave more credit to my power over you than I actually had." *The boy's* name popped out without notice.

"Erik, your reach went farther than I was willing to admit." She scowled, wishing to keep from revisiting stagnant subjects. "This is old news and I much prefer the new. So, yes, I would enjoy having a proper escort without the dodgy male attachments; it will become me quite well."

He measured the distance from his mouth to hers in leisurely, amorous breaths, her lips spirited his, forcing his eyes to close out distractions under their dreamy shutters. They were so evenly smooth, full, and wet. Her tongue made its journey across the threshold to the depths of his moist well and then her teeth clamped gently upon his lower lip, snapping his heart and collapsing his lungs.

Christine's eyes flew wide, she quickly drew back and swung away from Erik, muttering an errant "oh, you!" to save her prize from incineration.

"The loaf is more important than I, typical," he said, clasping at his heart and swooning in mock despair, all the while backing up to watch the response just stirred, the towel being tossed aside in haste. "How unfortunate for the mind of a woman to be put upon with multiple tasks. Should have let it burn, I would have helped to make more, seeing as I have nothing much to amuse myself with."

"Than to persecute! You had better run fast, Erik Gautier!"

(And he did, but not quite so fast as to impede capture!)

THE FORETHOUGHT AFFLICTED by only a few days in prior succession to the gala event was of short duration and went virtually unnoticed as the designated night prevailed at week's end; the appointed time being sufficiently welcomed.

The vibrancy of color in attendance alone flooded the corridors with a richness to shame their natural counterparts in depth and breadth, flaunting hues so vivid that the statues attained the greater benefit from an immoveable vantage upon the scene in the grand foyer. Guests arriving to fill the Opera came in all manner of anonymity, waking in unison the unused echoes from the farthest recesses imaginable; people in every corner were devouring its quiet with the din of gaiety, laughing, talking, and reacquainting themselves with the business of others.

Erik found most conversations tediously based in trifling, gap filling nonsense and figured, that had his hearing been any less acute for the occasion, he may not have minded, but if he just smiled and nodded absently, no one would be the wiser. He certainly had had enough of Richard; a few hours in the same vicinity as that raucous laughter, due in part to his lack of moderation and want of a situation in which to drop propriety, left no doubt in Erik's mind as to a difference in taste for entertainment, but seeing that many others were enjoying themselves by the same mode, he concluded that Richard was at his best in these environs.

The more pleasant encounter of M. Gabion occurred quite by happenstance as one came upon the other. It was in avoiding a jovial group, headed for another round of champagne, their thirsty glasses handled carelessly in testament, that both dove for the outlet a conversation balcony offered. They shook hands, reaffirming acquaintance, and found that they had much in common in regard to preferring more intimate engagements and introductions. They laughed, for neither requisite seemed required by Mercier, if one was unfortunate enough to be detained by him, and M. Gabion had, but Erik had not. Soon, the exchange turned to investments, which always made for a profitable topic when in good company, though the discussion, by no fault of either participant, was brief. Mercier had spotted the familiar attire of M. Gabion and delighted in the discovery of connection. M. Gabion apologized generously with a vigorous cough, and Erik gave a dismissive gesture along with his comment of "stationary targets" then quickly canvassed the room for an excuse to use at *his* earliest convenience. Mercier would not be put off, much to Erik's misfortune.

"What has your attention diverted so that it keeps your jaw clenched with little reprieve?" Christine asked, at the conclusion of the set they were dancing. He kissed the back of her hand and deftly maneuvered her among the crush of partiers; some being on the verge of forgetting themselves and a few, who had surpassed this barrier, were in the midst of behavior that would ordinarily find reproach if in their right mind, but most were under suitable conduct for the hour of midnight.

In an unoccupied room several floors up, one adjoining a deserted sector of the gallery, they gained the privacy Erik deemed necessary, as he handed Christine inside and closed the double doors. Passing her, he stepped quietly before a window and began, his speech low and guarded.

"Recently, each time I have shown myself openly within these walls, I feel eyes riveted to my form, boring a hole into the back of my skull. Nowhere else is it felt but here. And strange as this may sound, I do not recognize the sensation unless *I* am noticed outright."

"And you feel it now?" Her eyes followed the solid black outline pacing in bursts through the shafts of moonlight.

"No. . . it is sporadic, perhaps I have fallen prey to my own paranoia, but I think not, at least not yet."

"What about during construction or. . ." she shivered, recommencing her thought in concern, "when we are below?" Her eyes stared blankly, a hollow emptiness taking up residence behind their normal warmth.

Erik went to her side, to embrace and reassure, her image, his opposite in silver. "Below is secure, but the infrequent premonition scratched at my subconscious throughout the whole of last month. It began tonight while you were with Meg."

"Where were you?"

"With Mercier. His unabashed pride, however cordial, wedged me distastefully within his grip for acknowledgment all around to his immediate acquaintances." He exhaled deeply and went on. "You are first in my life, Christine, and I worry that my past will trap me only to entangle you. . . it must not happen."

Their eyes met. He knew she understood, that he deserved— and it would be her right—to have her say something poignant if she chose. But when being dealt a measure of sobriety such as this, with consequences unknown to them both, he was grateful she would not.

Gentle conveyance of his appreciation, for her accompaniment to the event, was expressed as was hers in return, for spirits raised in the lighthearted atmosphere; and then a decision was made that there could be no more benefit in rejoining the glut of indulgence, so they danced together beneath the resonance stirring their own designs, peaceful and serene; knowing that the quiet misgivings could be abandoned in the moment—abandoned, though not forgotten.

Chapter Twenty-Nine

A much-needed spring snow encapsulated the worn husks at the end of each stem in little, frozen spheres of ice. What was once a fragile cluster of misty-blue buds now waited to burst forth from winter's last hurrah; at that precise moment warmth would cause the frosty weather to retreat. Christine pulled the downy thick barrier around her shoulders, trying to keep the early morning chill at bay for just a bit longer. The late snow would be a memory in a day or two and she would forget the variant conditions, naturally. Erik seemed impervious to the cold, acclimatizing on a whim when there was something to be accomplished, which was most of the time. He had been up for hours in preparation for his contractor's arrival. Not one to be without some project in progress, they would commence building the new stables, not quite one quarter mile beyond the existing structure; the construction on the house, by the end of May. She smiled at how innovative Erik was, always revisiting the ingenuity of his mind to access some uncharted lobe.

The creations he can busy away the hours with to contrive some marvel in order to fill a need, astonish me. The writing desk, located at present near the piano, was made so I might compose in the same area as he, if I wish, and I do. His studio has been, and still is, a mass of designs for an improved masque, one that is lighter in weight and flexible. I liked the prototype very much; its coloring matched his skin tone so well it startled me. "A good indication," *he said, and we discovered the sharing of affection to be less cumbersome as well, though I find, and I am positive he will agree, that to be without the masque whenever possible is our ideal.* "I wonder," *she sounded out,* "what he would do if the masterpiece of a lifetime were ever supposed complete?" *Heaven help us that he never finds such an one, that God pushes forward to enhance and inspire the minds foreordained to bring about good works!*

I rejoice that Erik has his focus shifting to a grander scale, carrying him outdoors and away from the shelter downstairs. Learning gives him motivation to live, that purpose desired; this venture should present some new twists. Our relationship has been first and foremost, but the future, as I see it, will bring increased opportunity to rub shoulders with more people and expand his ability to cooperate through association.

At length, she had come to the end of her allotted time and sighed. Knowledge that the initial bite of morning air would come and go as she began moving did nothing to motivate, notwithstanding the generous fire Erik had left for her.

A FEW HOURS LATER, two figures, hands outstretched, greeted the other under a thinning, steel-grey sky.

"Monsieur Gautier, good to see you!" crowed M. Minot.

Lightly astonished by the term, Erik hesitated. "Good to be seen, I guess. I trust business is well?"

"How could it not? I have put into practice many of the techniques learned at your side and await the opportunity once again!" M. Minot's smile split his face most amiably, almost too sanguine and certainly befitting of a pleased grizzly that is either exceptionally full or aware of a profitable catch soon to come his way.

In any event, Erik's mind quickly accessed what it could, and though the information was sketchy and not at all in-depth, he recalled the man's good nature as the reason for taking up with him again. "Come, we shall discuss preliminaries over a late breakfast," he said, suddenly alight with anticipation. "There is someone I wish you to meet." To this, Erik gave a slight squeeze before releasing the gentleman's hand and trudging the distance to the house, prepared to openly reacquaint himself once more.

Monsieur Chanler Minot had worked with Erik during those formidable, brooding days—just for that, one should bow respectfully to M. Minot, consider him a saint and ask for a disclosure of where the well of patience was located into which he had dipped regularly. He was a tall gentleman, a finger's width above Erik. His stature broad and muscular, one aptly matched to his profession, as were his features; they consisted of a wide base, the jaw and cheekbones set squarely beneath a pair of round, emerald eyes and a short nap of curly brown hair. He was a hard working, self-made man, trustworthy to a fault, one self-taught in the finer points of his business from the ground up with a foundation of common sense, attention to detail, and the humility for being teachable. Having had an occasion to be spared when he was but a foolish youth, M. Minot, it is noted, lost his left ear to a piece of machinery on a dare—a fortunate and inexpensive price for such a lesson.

The door opened and a shrill gust blew through the inviting warmth of the kitchen, raising the hair on Christine's arms.

"My dear, this is Monsieur Chanler Minot, my right hand and soon to be common fixture about the premises for the better part of this year. Monsieur, my wife Madame Gautier, Christine." How pleased he felt in this first-ever introduction. She fairly beamed.

While M. Minot bent to grace the back of her hand with a light kiss, Christine shot Erik a look of astonishment, for she seemed quite taken with his bold advance and quickly made use of her limbs to return the courtesy. M. Minot's grin deepened, and having a will of his own, set out to survey the place in a most unrestrained fashion.

"What?" Christine heard the near voiceless word confound only her ears, as Erik kissed her temple and surrounded her at the counter.

"Later, it can wait," she said, and pushed him away to attend to his guest.

"Perhaps I cannot." Erik sighed dejectedly in the process of shedding his thick coat and meandered through the dining room to where M. Minot stood at the foot of the stairs, arms folded and sight roaming.

"I hope you will forgive the trespass. I felt somewhat justified, seeing the project finished after all those disjointed months of wondering."

Erik grimaced.

"Ah, I see your comprehension is intact. Well, at least I did not want for pay, only dependability."

"You know I preferred my privacy, Monsieur. I still do," Erik informed, revisiting the intrusion. "And there are but few times I tolerate such insolent comments from—"

"From whom, your subordinates? Oh, please! And call me Chanler." His invitation was so cheery that Erik almost choked. "I can only imagine there to be some lenience in your character for me or I should have found myself out on my ear long ago." There was a subdued shrug. "So to speak."

Erik chuckled and proceeded to show Chanler around. He owed him, and truly did not regret the forthright initiative; Erik was actually glad of it. There was something he felt from this man, from being in Chanler's presence, that he was possibly—in some odd way—sincerely liked for himself, and a level of comfort arose hitherto on entering the study for the intended purpose of the morning.

"She has been a blessing, no?" Chanler tossed the unexpected forward, as he headed for what was presumed to be the blueprints.

"Blunt as ever."

"Discretion, valor. . . only in mixed company, Erik. Life is far too short for evasion and prevarication."

At the mention of his name in such an affable, frank tone, he shed all pretense to answer, "In so many ways."

"Good! Then you shan't be jumping down my throat or—"

"Whose throat?" Christine asked, interrupting upon her entrance through the open doors. "From what I have heard thus far, I would characterize you two as formidable opponents for either, in equal amounts. Neither cares much for incongruitous circumstances, both are strong willed and have such pertinacity that I suspect you strive to outdo yourselves in order to encourage the other to success. Yes," she stated agreeably, while setting their meal upon the desk, "I shall look forward to the diversion!" Christine winked at Erik and made herself scarce at the conclusion of her comments by hastily quitting the room. The men glared after her then pointedly at the other, each standing on opposite sides of the newly erected drafting table. They grinned simultaneously and glanced over the plans spread about.

"I like her fire already!" Chanler laughed. "I like her quite well, yes, quite well indeed!"

With their discussion complete, Erik saw to establishing a start date, a retainer and remuneration for the project upon completion, and then with a handshake, Chanler was away until the following week. Erik stood perplexed, trailing Chanler's receding frame from the doorway while mulling over Christine's elusive "it can wait" phrase. He soon located her up in their room, sitting in front of the fire.

"You know," she said when he entered, "this addition has already excited my anticipation for all the prospects it will employ. I rather like envisioning and entertaining all the good that will inevitably come from the thoughts flourishing about, and what better time than the spring to be acquisitioning such a considerable amount of business."

She had a way of dishing up optimism in streams, and when the tongue could not find its end he knew something was up; it was charming really. Her outbreak of speech and the way she furtively sought for his attention, the little gestures she did with her hands, but it was always those unearthly eyes, which succeeded in catching him.

"What?" Christine's rush had found cessation.

"Is it later, or shall I occupy myself elsewhere?"

"Why? No more Monsieur Minot to banter with?" she teased.

He did not reply at first, but ambled up to the mantelpiece and lent his arm against it, the light taunt going virtually unnoticed in the face of deep gratitude. "I appreciate the impression you left him with, Christine. He seems to have developed a fond opinion of you."

Standing, she encircled him from behind. "I like him as well, his character is unpretentious and genuine." Her expression became suddenly quiet. "See? Our world is already expanding in a most benevolent manner with blessings from the addition of a friend. Now, Monsieur, if you would indulge me by rotating with your eyes closed."

"Whatever for?"

"*What* is quite the theme for today," she quipped, gently positioning herself in his blind embrace with her back to him. She placed his palms to her stomach and whispered, "Remember?"

Erik knew. His hands caressed and found a hint of swelling, his lips, the curve of her neck and his voice, her ear. "You are several weeks further than before?"

"I am. I wished to spare you disappointment, in case I was mistaken."

"But, Christine—"

She turned sharply and placed her mouth to his then slowly drew back to look at the worry beginning to effuse his softened eyes. "We cannot have certain joys without first submitting our hearts to faith. I have you, Erik, and with hope, we trust again."

Chapter Thirty

Glorious spring! The seasonal enigma of an unfailing rebirth—being professed by people and landscape alike in verdant hints—seemed accomplished with fresh air and open windows. Such a connection is often easier to reestablish along with the cycle of nature whispering her cheer. . . which is exactly where Mademoiselle Giry began her letter, and rightly so, if the scribe were to make mention of all the glories before expressing the fancies of one's mind and heart between friends.

> ... Oh, Christine, I can hardly contain myself with all there is to do. I laugh and cry, wishing you were closer that we may rely and confide upon the other. How we ever accomplished so much for you and Erik in less than one week I shall never know, but Maman says it was Erik's undeniable will to which we are to attribute our success. I know better! And the mind, it roams to such vast places. I took a walk along the Seine River, something I have not done for years, and I remembered learning about the miracle of life.
>
> When I was very young, perhaps six, I recall looking at

the dead trees and brown sticks lining the banks; it was the simplicity of wondering where all the green had gone that had Maman showing me the difference between what was dead and what slept. An explanation ensued about everything being stored deep within a safe place until the season warmed enough for them to loose their reserves. I feel like those plants now, Christine, and all I want to do is burst! All those memories of innocence, how wondrous they are; as a child we are so in tune, we want to know, learn, experience, and then as an adult it all changes to responsibility; we are no longer innocent, and fondly digress. I am there.

Richard has had a profound effect on me. You know his tendency to speak in rapid succession? I have recently been accused of such. Imagine! But I rationalize that I must keep up if I wish to converse at all with him. Actually, I am afraid of being left verbally sprawled to find he has talked circles around me only to return for another go. Listen to me... thus his dizzying British influence.

Now, to more pleasurable things! Maman wishes me to take some leisure, and since I miss you something horribly, I should like to take you up on that offer you made, and visit. You must decide on a time that is best, for I shall adhere most willingly.

Your most devoted, Meg

Christine perused Meg's letter for a second time, ruminating from over a bowl of strawberries atop her front porch vantage. Seeing her, Erik carefully tread down the stairs to the open front door, a distance not half so quiet as he would have liked, her already keen senses attune to the bothersome creak on the bottom step. Melting in behind her, having already been officiously announced, his hands slipped to the smallish protrusion of her abdomen and his mouth over the berry held upright in her hand.

"I see... hmm... Chanler has arrived early, per discussion, and brought correspondence, too."

She murmured in the affirmative reaching back to hold his face close to hers. He waited with a grin until the unfamiliar surface had snapped her around. "Ah, so this is where you have been, finishing up modifications."

"It is."

"I assumed you to be monitoring the relocation of those huge rocks found during the initial excavation so we might use them for the gardens." Her attentions were beginning to transfer from the wistful greetings of the letter to more pertinent matters.

"I made arrangements and secured the equipment last week. I shall check with Chanler in good time, his men know what to do. You are my point of interest at the moment. Now, if you would look at me full on and tell me your opinion."

"I think," she said, examining the masque with a critical eye and after a brief pause added, "as remarkable as this one is in structuring your facial contours, it may be an acquired taste for me, though extremely pleasing in the ways we have tested. I'm sorry, I'm afraid that my opinion is not so very reliable... my judgment stands too biased."

"An acquired taste, eh? I suppose this to be true with or without." He gave her a peck for the comment. "No matter, the improvements are as they are. It is lighter, more flexible and was a good deal easier to mold. I thank you for your assistance, rendered in each stage of development. I am glad of your approbation."

"I like it, Erik, possibly as much as your humor in relation to its necessity in our life."

"Good!" he exclaimed. "Then we shall be on to more important issues. What does Meg have to say in all those pages? And what of Chanler? I wish to know his frame of mind upon making an appearance by dawn. He is not so early a bird as he would like to think. And then, we shall address those," he ended, referencing the fruit with a nod.

Christine sighed fondly and glanced at the hand gently rubbing her belly. "Meg wishes to come for a visit, though I know she cannot bear to be separated from Richard, any more than I can from you, but we shall see how she copes. Next is Chanler, he was all merriment and smiles. I fear he saves most of his gruff behavior in a special cache labeled for you, or so he has told me was the case before." She laughed. "I believe he has found you changed and suspects the levels of tolerance might not ever be reached, for the affable sieve at the base of this course prevents it."

"Affable sieve?" Erik returned speculatively.

"I like Chanler," she went on brightly. "As a matter-of-fact, I like him on an ever-increasing basis. He is well balanced, fair, respectable, and most thoughtful. And listen to this, he *informed* me that his wife would be coming out to the site, as she often does when time allows, and that she would be much obliged, if I find no objection, to call on me."

Erik had seen felicity skirt her countenance more than once midst the narrative on being the recipient of guests, for it was an agreeable amount of joy he took himself as to the excitement it procured. Christine was proud to welcome others to their home, and had no second thoughts, reservations or apprehensions whatsoever.

Suddenly, a clamor of voices yelling out panicked directives breached the hum of machinery. Tones rose and fell, and then mayhem rapidly ensued midst a rider bolting in the direction of Amiens.

"Christine, meet me at the back door."

Forsaking his calm, Erik quickly stood and ran, rounding the corner of the house toward the confusion, meeting the foreman already en route to him. Several men were lifting another from the foundation pit. *Who* was his only interest, seeing the disengaged chain hanging in a disproportionate manner, he knew it could not be good.

"Monsieur..." Erik's stomach knotted upon hearing a brief sketch of the incident. *Chanler? It's Chanler?*

While lifting one rock over top the other, one of the chains loosened, causing the bulk of the load to shift and swing. It was lowered, and the restraints reset and tightened, but being an unwieldy shape, it shifted once again. When it was lowered yet a second time, Chanler went in to assist just as the chain gave way; he was pinned between the masses, the damage done before they were able to gain control long enough to get Chanler out from under its weight. Minot's men compressed shirts and anything they could readily grab to the bloodied extremity.

Erik knelt over Chanler. "I'm here," he assured, finding a weakened pulse just as Chanler looked up. He spoke Erik's name and immediately passed out. Instructions were given in haste while Chanler's body was quickly conveyed indoors, preceded by Erik. Christine had been waiting with the door open, and as Erik stepped through, he requested she retrieve his medical instruments from the studio then proceeded with dexterity of knowledge to ascertain Chanler's condition. *Left arm crushed past the elbow, broken ribs, but nothing that indicates his lungs to be punctured. If I apply a tourniquet, here...* Erik worked on him with forethought, no procedure undertaken that would be irreparable, only those to preserve life. The physician arrived, was ushered in by the messenger and fell into sync comfortably at Erik's side.

MIDMORNING SHONE HOT, and with it, one Madame Minot, to alight before the gates of the unanticipated. She could not deny the obvious buzz of activity: idle forms rising to greet, pain creased faces, wordlessness, all communicated an event of severity. The situation demanded collection of self and nimble reflex of thought.

The woman breathed in deeply. "Tell me," she said. Being an attending nurse herself, and despite what she might hear, she wished to know all the particulars. The foreman, ambivalent as he was—relating in more detail than was customary or comfortable, to someone female—gave a full account to Mme Minot's satisfaction. Christine continued assisting about in other capacities, and in time, she relinquished most duties to be out of the way and remain as a close companion to Chanler's wife. What a welcome!

Madame Cerise Minot was a sturdy, well-thought woman, poised and deliberate, except that being the recipient of long awaited news from the outside, instead of the compassionate giver, ready to disburse from her possession the right amount of necessary intelligence, was driving her to frustration. Christine provided support and light enquiry to divert focus, though she could never fully dissuade the severity of mind for long and was left to her own thoughts and observations at odd intervals. *Such an iron-willed female! I am amazed at how civil and specific she is in her ability to exact knowledge. Surely, I would not have the slightest idea of what to ask, except for one's health in general. Her countenance is so vivid, and the color of her lips each time they compress does not leave one to wonder long after the Christian name of cherry; it is a most befitting description, and the eyes, they are most strikingly cognizant!*

Anxious to have "finished" and "successfully done" be in joint harmony, the physician wearily opened the doors to impart all to those of similar sentiments without the room.

"He does well Madame Minot, and far better due to the skill of the man attending him when I arrived. The tourniquet permitted me the necessary time to supplant cauterization with ligature, which, as you know, is not often an option in cases such as these when the tissue is heavily damaged. However, enough muscle and soft tissue along the exterior surface remained that we could do a flap-amputation. The ribs," at this point he left off in open gesture, "they are on their own. He is a fortunate man."

Erik shall explain later, Christine thought, for the uncommon terms confused her. All she needed to know was that Chanler did well and the physician was pleased. She caught Erik's attention and he smiled. She could see the exhaustion as he walked alongside several of Minot's men, accompanying them but a few steps as they carefully transferred the patient from dining area to guest room at the back of the house. A firm hand deterred Erik in its grasp for a wholly unexpected interview as gratitude was expressed upon several aspects. Mme Minot begged leave to tend to her husband, but the physician, not having released Erik's hand, talked on in praise about the procedure. Erik was not accustomed to such accolades and nodded in mute humility, excusing himself from the grip so he might assist those to right the soiled area.

The workmen were sent away for a few days with a relief only positive news could induce. Christine, too, sighed in perfect contentment as though the whole had been a beautiful orchestration of charity. The Minots felt their imposition great, yet were obliged to stay after much effort was exercised on their behalf to explain the benefits, none of which could be more advantageous than convalescing without care or burden of the mundane. Thereafter, reasons mounted for everyone involved: medical advice and holistic remedies were discussed on both fronts, conversations came alive upon further acquaintance, equally advancing between couples, and the men could consult regularly on the construction without delay. But most prized of all was the condition of self-worth; the trait had increased in large degrees, causing the Gautiers to retire each night with glad hearts from the services shared in turn.

Less than a fortnight elapsed and an exchange of guests proceeded. Meg Giry came, replacing the Minots and with it, the meaning of *busy* took on a whole new look, that of a dark-haired whirlwind, as if Meg's visit could be labeled anything to the contrary.

How monotonous the house moved in comparison to its lively visitor; shrill torrents of phrase, near daily jaunts to Amiens to absorb yet another feature of the rich textile industry, and the continuous wonderment of marriage importuned gaiety at each blink. And then she was gone home.

Listening to the birds one evening, not many days since quiet had returned among the lengthening shadows, Christine grinned. Erik claimed he was glad their guest enjoyed her stay, but she knew him to be even happier that he could walk the halls and rooms without feeling blown helter-skelter. *What will the flurry of children do to him?* How she treasured these peaceful times when he could not spare one moment more from her, the steadiness limiting time designated to each aspect in their life.

She heard the door close to the study, boots drop in succession and a deep sigh, all while standing in the balcony doorway, and then came silence. It was but once that he mentioned his awe of seeing the profile of a woman with child, that she placed herself where he could have the experience whenever possible: how profound it was for him to be in love all over again. A trace of movement at the threshold told her he had paused to admire. She looked sideways, her eyes finding his, the gleam therein rendering him weak at the knees, and saw him visibly swallow.

"I do not understand the control you have over every faculty I possess, my mouth becomes inexplicably dry, my heart throbs. Tell me," his intonation thready, "how it is that you stir every sensation now as you did the first time we kissed?"

There was a playful tenderness in the way she said naught, the way she freed him from the heated environment of his masque to the healing breeze, such undeniable meaning confirmed and elicited comfort. "The designs of love," were her breathless sentiments.

Christine gracefully consumed every portion of his face in brushing caresses, smooth and vulnerable, nothing was left untouched but his mouth, satisfied on the eventuality that her lips would remain in the specified vicinity. As they did, she grasped his hand, almost in earnest, and placed it to her stomach; all motion ceased save one.

Tears streamed and Erik pressed again, his countenance dramatically subdued before Christine's watchful eye. "Our child," he said kneeling, his cheek tucked up against her. "Our child moves. So vehement was I that my condition not be flagrantly imposed, to miss such joy because of selfishness, because I coupled fear and hatred to produce an incomprehensible burden. I am humbled by your conviction and the beauties so elegantly entailed in procreation, to risk giving life for us. . . I love you in so many ways, Christine."

This newest experience bred sweet rituals into their daily routine, where there had been one to share affection with, two became purposeful; what was once a slight stroke became kisses, comments, and inclusion.

Chapter Thirty-One

It was a week of unmitigated temperature; the last in June and just down right hot! Fortunately, not a more pleasant situation could be had for employment than one near water or to feel the rise in spirit when the presence of someone often thought of returns.

Chanler sat in a wretched frame of mind in an attempt to cope with some of the agitation, which had, since his arrival that morning, found liberation at strange and uncivil moments in relation to an unforeseen inadequacy. He stared bewildered out into the moving water at stream's edge, the motion soothing.

"Would you mind me joining you, Chanler?"

"Ah, Erik, not at all." A sense of premeditated quiet passed between them as Erik took his place, determined to leave the precise instigation of subject up to him, knowing in light of the behavior mentioned, a few minutes constraint would be all that was necessary before Chanler spoke.

"I like this place and the tranquility it offers a troubled soul," he said heavily. "I imagine," he continued on without want of response, "it is the same for you."

Erik's hand rested on Chanler's shoulder then fell quietly away in another easy vacancy. How right he was.

"Where do I go from here, Erik? Are such simple acts, those that have become a complicated challenge, to be done by others simply because they have the use of two working appendages and because they are able to complete the task quicker? All I see is paperwork, a confining office, and overbearing, fussy well-meaning people. . ." He shook his head and pointed. "I can't even tie my own damn boots, Cerise does it."

The despondency surprised Erik. He thought the inconvenience might slow Chanler for a short time, hamper the usual intuitive nature amid boundaries, then figured his tenacity would engage and do him credit as he found innovative methods to accomplish his goals. "First, you heal. . ." Erik offered, "the rest will take care of itself with time and patience."

Chanler glanced at Erik. He looked lightly insulted then picked up, talking along his own agenda as before. "I feel a siege rain upon me with all there is to deal with; the explanations and stares. . . When I lost my ear, I managed the harassment somehow. . . hats, longer hair. . . fact is, I am not as young and resilient to what I hear and see happening around me. I am disheartened that time and advances in so many avenues do not alter the latent tendencies of people in general, and it is to my disadvantage that the defiance of spirit lacks behind an inflexible heart. There is such limited mercy in the eyes of strangers, their blatant pity. I can even see it in the faces and eyes of my own men, feel it follow me, taste it even, and I hate it!"

Erik listened, empathizing all too well. "Cruelty toward others is perpetuated by humanity, Chanler. It is where the ugliness of character festers in cancerous ignorance, growing until it discovers an undeserving form to latch on to and consume. I am sorry."

Chanler's complexion whitened, he heard Erik's glazed explanation spoken in resigned calm, no bitterness ready to sting as it had in the past. "Forgive my insensitivity, my disregard for—"

An understanding hand flew up to end the worrisome thoughts. "You have every right to feel as you do. I am just grateful you felt you could commiserate with me equally, though it was done unconsciously. I know what it is like. I know of the putrid, undignified treatment dealt, and of the treasured relief of consideration. This is what you have shown me by never making reference to my masque, my eccentric demands or flares of indignation that were perpetuated by forces unknown to you. Around you, I feel as anyone else."

"I suppose we make a fine team, you and I. We are doubly blessed by the blindness of love, eh? Your Christine is full of a determined strength and my Cerise is a realist to a fault. We must always move forward, even if we wind up being knocked flat on our backsides." He snickered at Erik's expression. "I guess a bit of humility wrapped about the male ego is not such an awful trait to incur, now is it?"

"No indeed." Erik's thoughts betrayed his voice and he dared not speak more upon that sweet truth.

Then turning serious, Chanler gripped Erik's arm. "I have little recollection of the experience as a whole, so in the process of being made aware of all that took place, it has only recently struck me as to the extent I am indebted to you and your insatiable desire for knowledge. My arm heals without worry of infection and, all accounts considered, is appealing. Perhaps," came the arched expression, "this conversation was meant to evolve as it has, in benefit for adjusting the perspective of one so etched in his ways. Well, for whatever reason, what is most important is that I am alive, and for this I sincerely thank you."

This was a strange twist, having someone owe him! And, while he did not feel entitled to the right thus bestowed, it felt hauntingly good nonetheless. Giving a mere nod and a friendly pat, he rose, excusing himself to head off toward the house.

NOT FEELING QUITE up to the charge of disengaging herself from bed that morning, Christine lay for a longer than normal period, trying to relax away the persistent ache in her lower back; the prescription having remedied a similar complaint several weeks earlier. If she continued on, she would be giving Erik more cause for concern than she was sure she already had. Hiding emotional issues was an utterly futile endeavor, especially in her condition, as she tended to wear outwardly much of what she felt. It was a deplorable plague, and with Chanler on site again, she was at once troubled and unsure of whether or not to be thankful for those unfailing senses.

She stretched to another position and prepared to roll out from beneath the soft linens. Her body rebelled slightly, but not so much that she could not make do if her advancements were gingerly executed. Walking into the dressing room passed on the sigh of hesitance as she glanced back at the bedding, just to check—a frailty of human nature as dread entwined hope and faith—all was clean. Then, within as many seconds, her shift in focus caused relief to retract in the face of what lack of sleep could create. She was a ghastly sight, standing limp against the wall, her pallor a terse, unwelcome reminder.

Grabbing for the nearest seat, her vision burst into strings of light across the backdrop of her lids, forcing her to sit hard to combat the dizziness engulfing her balance, and then the symptoms ceased, leaving her extremities to involuntarily shake. She breathed slowly, steadily attuned as her body, taut with expectancy, went lax.

"You're all right. . . breathe," she told herself.

Christine sat for some time in calm evaluation, her head resting in her hands. Sniffing, she stood. Dreadful mistake. The back of her hand pressed to her mouth as she leaned over the basin feeling quite suddenly, very ill. "Oh, please, not again. It can't," she pled. Tears mounded and the turmoil inside whirled; it hit, her hand clamping down as the pain cinched unforgiving, her only thought for Erik. The pain abated and Christine reached for the door, desperate at all cost to cast herself into the path of another, when a second, brutally unyielding contraction cut her in half. Bracing squarely against the corridor wall she called for Erik and threw a hasty glance over her predicament, knowing in retrospect that whatever happened, she had no regrets.

Two strong arms gently lifted Christine, collected her flaccid body, and a thunderous voice called out, "No, not again!" as a weaker cry of despair petitioned from the heart.

Chanler entered through the front door in a blurred rush to see Erik, cradling Christine at the top of the stairs. "I need. . ." Erik's request never made it audibly past a rasp, but there was no mistaking the urgency. No other words were exchanged; time had been issued an ultimate request as Erik turned to head for their room.

ERIK REMEMBERED THE scene in fractured segments, his actions coming automatically until he finally stood without the room: linens, towels, anything absorbent to staunch the hemorrhaging; Cerise taking control with an authoritative air, a place to wash, sliding past a lanky gentleman, who seemed perplexed at the absence of a door. Erik looked dumbfounded by the situation, his hands nervously raking through his hair in an alternate fashion.

"Erik?" Chanler spoke evenly, gaining his attention.

Rounding toward the voice, Erik stared blankly at an armless man at the foot of the staircase. He rubbed his face and neck, his thoughts dazed in an emotionally induced stupor, and then pointed. "What the deuce just happened?"

Chanler was gnawing the inside of his cheek, hoping that he would not be witness to any outbursts of anger and cautiously answered, "Umm, ousted by disregard would be my guess, it is their way."

'Their way,' his mind tripped. Again, Erik ran his hand through his hair and turned back to the murmurs coming from the room, unsure of what to do. His bottom lip quivered as he gazed from where he had picked her up, the tears welled forth at the scarlet streaked flooring.

"Come with me, Erik." Chanler issued the order gently.

Tensing unintentionally under the warmth of a firm arm, Erik jerked away, searching in agitation to equate reason for the unnecessary navigation. "No. I cannot." He shuddered. "No trace. There must not be any reminders."

Chanler understood. "Then I shall help."

The rate in turns about the great room increased, and Erik's path shortened as did the fuse of Chanler's nerves under the quiet, vexing strain, for neither had said word one since the previous exchange on the landing above.

"Erik, talk to me."

This verbal intrusion startled him, like hitting a wall unprepared. "Chanler, if you don't mind, I wish to be alone with my thoughts. Pointless verbiage is of no interest to me."

"Well," he began, looking Erik square in the eye, "I would prefer not being alone with mine."

Erik smirked at the wit and the smug manner in which Chanler folded his one arm across his chest. "All I have are questions, unanswered ones at best."

"Shoot," Chanler encouraged. He donned his most serious pose of chin situated between thumb and index, which in reality was an almost ridiculous looking stance, causing Erik's brow to raise.

Shoot? Come now... Lassos are much better, in fact, they are as silent as the wings of an owl, no chamber rotation or hammer click. Erik chilled at the errantly induced thought and sighed. Pain had a way of jostling old retaliatory habits. "All right, what of this doctor? Tell me what you know of his background." His eyes darted upstairs in reference and then back.

"Cerise would not be working at his side if she did not agree with his ethics, procedures, and the perspectives employed. I know he spent time in Edinburgh, personally substantiating techniques prior to adopting them into his own practice in Amiens. Dr. Dubois has also been most accommodating in furthering Cerise's education and does not wish to place constraints on her ability. Then, there is Cerise, who at one time discovered herself within the very circumstances your wife currently experiences. We have been there, Erik, and are grateful for our son. Complications left her unable to bear more and consequently, in her desire to support a purpose, she has devoted her life to the profession of obstetrics." Chanler grinned lightly and added an abstracted, "The condensed version."

"I suppose I shall trust as I can," replied Erik.

"You would do well, I am proof of that, but there is too much emotional attachment to remain objective when the subject of your affection is beneath your own hand." Chanler's gaze moved upward, signaling a possible communication of news. Erik was at Mme Minot's side at once.

"She is resting comfortably and is in no danger at present. Dr. Dubois will speak with you."

"Thank you, Cerise." Erik entered wary, his approach circumspect in passing.

"Come," the physician invited, "she sleeps peacefully enough that we may converse openly without disturbing her."

Dr. Dubois was drying his hands and arms as Erik looked at him and then to Christine in her dreamy, motionless state. He ran a finger along her cheek, causing her to stir lightly.

"Monsieur?" Erik circled to meet the physician head on, their eyes locking, the former and latter gazing in gratitude, gracious curiosity, and respect. "Madame Minot will stay at your discretion." Another pause of emptiness asked the next question and Erik fixed upon Christine's face.

"I regret we were unable to spare—"

"I understand," Erik said sharply, cutting him off, then his tone softened. "Can you determine if this will reoccur?"

There was a deep breath taken. "The body, it is a marvel in and of itself that fascinates me, how life develops and ends without explanation; her case is one such marvel. I discovered her womb to be shaped differently, which is a perfectly plausible inference; meaning, it is likely that as the muscle stretched, a weakened section tore, causing enough trauma to disrupt growth and progression. She may continue to miscarry or not, but she is young and strong; give yourselves time to heal."

Erik scoffed at the phrase, his own words turned on him.

Hearing the disbelieving huff, the physician felt prompted to kindly explain. "If she stays quiet and does not become too emotionally distraught, she should be much improved by this time next week. Madame Minot shall visit and report to me on how well she mends, in all facets. Monsieur, there is no reason to think that she cannot carry to term," Dr. Dubois reassured. "I shall take my leave, *au revoir.*"

"Yes, thank you." Erik whispered.

He pulled up a chair, gently placed Christine's hand in his own and became engrossed in their finer particulates, every other private or worldly care instantly devoured by the delicacy of her situation. Looking down on her, the dissimilarity of age seized his heart and buried its iron fist deep. He seemed old and careworn and she, so small and childlike, such an insignificant wisp pitted against the gale force of importance that her hands took on a rather copious obligation as the instruments of love. Upon this renewed quest, Erik's thoughts widened to explore the worth of hands, weighing the journey commenced at birth to the adventure a lifetime provides; each detailed taper, a slender, feminine match of perfection against his blend of calloused grace. *Hands are the body's one attribute most salient in versatility. They are replete with a measure of ability granted from all our senses; hands give sight, feel sound and texture; they bridge communication through language, they teach, learn, and are the means by which the mind and soul orchestrate the emotions. To be the recipient of Christine's... Her long determined value of me has aided my imagination in coming to terms with what I might have been, had I...* His lips pressed timidly against the sweetness of skin. "I would have been so different," he muttered.

Erik observed the flattened surface of the bed, her lone form beneath the linens, and his eyes misted over. *Our child,* he lamented. *You foolish...* He stopped. To what would name-calling signify? It would do nothing more than confirm his idiocy and he did not require proclamation for that. Oh, what quantity of misery could one endure? Conscience had stirred plenty, no mistake. He knew he should not have attempted more; music was enough at one time, then one kiss, which bloomed into the love of a woman and the hope of a child. If he continued to want, what would be the consequences? She was spared, a warning to tame his selfish fancy for normalcy. If he lost her, he could not bear life. He berated so completely, was cornered so authoritatively by the guilt that its affect finally paralyzed any desire until diminutive pressure countered his hold, causing him to glance up. Christine peered at him from under her lashes, between barely cracked lids. He knelt close, brushed a stray hair from her forehead and replaced it with a kiss. She smiled weakly and had an unexpected presence of mind rush in that Erik could not curb. It was too much for her, too much, and she gave way to pain in the most acute sense.

No one came the next day, Chanler made certain of that, nor did anyone come the day after, and so it was, leisure was imposed and affixed until further notice; the dividing distraction of self, between wife and work, was in every instance an absurd notion among all that had transpired.

Feeling a tad untoward in his unaffected indulgence of bitterness, but not enough to end perpetuation of its fueling, Erik surveyed the graveyard of abandon from his vantage on the balcony, and easily admitted that the quiet to which he had once been imprisoned, was now an anomaly midst the calculations, sheer quirks of misfortune, and life. It reminded him that music and the simplicity of joy within this befuddled mixture of business, had hung the notes of inspiration out to dry. He strained to organize and segregate all that tumbled about randomly in his head, but numb, done in as he was, he could only envision her.

Christine is up, infrequently, and I have wished to give her every support by consecrating my time and devotion toward her, though Madame Minot has made it undeniably clear that I am but a nuisance when she comes to call, a mire to be avoided at all cost. She and Christine spend large quantities of time in each other's company and I am beginning to suffer the results of jealous wonder, indeed, a jealous heart beats inside the chest of this wretch for no one to hear. "Confounded woman, here at odd hours to agitate my peaceful vigil," he grumbled, wishing in vain that he would have placed those words, and more, to Cerise's ear. But he dismissed the inkling. *Making unannounced entrances so I have to clamor for personal effects to avoid a confrontation, though, looking back, it would have been most gratifying to see the response my face would evoke from such a person. But I could not, and yet there is something profound sent in my direction. I am impressed that that sort of mentality would only be a shameless mistake, much as Medusa looking in a mirror.* His mind turned to other thoughts, which left him wondering how his conversation with Christine would progress when he was finally able to verbalize the friction building on his side. So far, she only spoke with Mme Minot; she had an outlet, a place to channel her emotions, but he was excluded and his concerns were ever increasing. Resting his face in his palms, Erik sighed, his lungs convulsing gently.

A shy, timorous hand glided forward in search of the crook made by Erik's elbow; he peered from between his fingers to see a pair of fierce, tired brown eyes staring up at him. Looking the other direction, he began to wipe the moisture from the base of his masque, much to Christine's consternation.

"You have never hidden your tears before."

"I am ashamed of their source."

"Regardless. . ." she said, removing his masque while leading his sight to join hers. "I have not *seen* much of you."

"No, I suppose it a difficult task when a great deal of your waking hours are spent conversing with Cerise and my cue is rarely taken up." He lifted his head away after the sharpness of language pierced, and Christine's touch fell absent.

"I see."

"I beg to differ," he carried on, retaliatory. "When you miscarried the first time, you were dependent only upon me. But *this* experience has introduced a whole new set of modifiers. I have been superseded. I am informed, never asked, scolded and chased from where I ought to be, for my own good, and treated verbally as if I were the inferior sex, like it is my fault that all of a woman's misfortunes are a direct result from knowing man. And, if Adèle Giry ever had a twin in this world, it is she; both have an intrinsic way of wheedling under my skin that I am unable to fight. I know their requests," his voice suddenly reflective, "are not unreasonable and have our best interest at their core, that Cerise has an impeccable bedside manner is irrefutable, but *we* have not shared past the super. . . fi. . . cial. Christine?" Erik rounded slowly, expecting to find her close by, but she had seated herself to listen, finding the pressure easier to manage.

"Damn!" His expletive gleaned a mournful look and he dropped to his knees in front of her. He could see from her countenance that he had done a fine job of meting out guilt.

"I had not realized. . ."

"Please, don't." He stopped her from saying more; despite its resounding familiarity to a biting retort, he needed to vent. "Intellectually, the benefit is understandable, there is something to be said for female companionship, there is a need satiated by the nurturing trait that the male gender cannot ever come close to; I know at least I do not, nor can I duplicate the perspective. . . I am extremely selfish right now. I want and come up with a massive deficit, as my choice of expression is especially pathetic. Forgive me." Erik's gaze remained bent on the hem of her dressing gown; he folded and released it, his emotions swirling anew. "I scorn people in general and feel an immense disdain for the neglect dealt me. Every bit of wretched sediment from my past has been dredged up, the anger and injustice, the hatred. I fought, but have succumbed, I just cannot suppress the resentment." He abruptly tore away his hairpiece and flung it to reside with the masque on another chair, his visual distaste pelting the two inanimate objects as a rain of colorful produce upon an inept thespian. "And, I detest having to wear those in my own bedchamber."

Christine captured Erik's returning attention, procuring his hands alongside her in the chair, and drew him into her lap by ruffling his hair and stroking his scalp. He melted instantly, contracting his arms around her.

"Your feelings are valid. I'm sorry, I know you hurt."

"I do, Christine."

"As do I. . . still. My discussions with Cerise are, and have been, very one sided, a monologue of her medical history really. I did ask her to share and will take the blame for perpetuating the retelling of experience, since many concepts are gauged in a vastly different light than when she conceived her son. She was able to explain the physician's diagnosis and dispel a few false assumptions in such a way that I am more comfortable. But we did not canvass the emotive lot; that remains for us, in our territory. I hope this helps, to know of our parity there."

He nodded and turned the other cheek, saying nothing while he struggled desperately to curtail the force tearing through him.

"I might add," she said in disbelief, "that despite what you have alluded, your feelings have been held successfully in check, I saw nothing that would have led me to believe otherwise."

"Because," he cried, sitting up with his hand clutched to his breast, "I could not bring myself to contribute to your sorrow while it was so fresh. It is in here, inside where my heart has been decimated by the loss of life, I have ripped it to shreds over the undeserving taunts chastening me. To think that it is I, of all people, who hazard such an attempt at creation when I lend no merit to the right, and when I meet with grief and suffering, the likes of which I have never borne, I realize that *I* caused these feelings in the souls of others, those whose lives met an end at my. . ." He inhaled painfully. "They were mourned." Christine lifted his chin, her eyes swimming at these thoughts that had formed and given rise to so sobering a madness. Then, Erik's voice slipped to a hollow whisper. "And to risk losing you, I cannot. . ."

Chapter Thirty-Two

Even now those words 'and to risk losing you, I cannot' brought heartache to Christine, as much, she supposed, as reality had pricked Erik's conscience, but one was always in forefront to the other and somewhat overbearing in nature, notwithstanding the remonstrance for either's legitimacy. Their initial discourse had them operating under the presumption of latent passions, and further examination had only excited a tumult of emotion. The incident was so raw and fresh back then no one could be blamed for metering the amount of feeling exposed at one time, however negative or positive.

More than a month passed in overt civility, each unwilling to yield in their point of view; to one, which was his, that no risk be brooked in temptation of bereavement: life was to be preserved at all cost. And the other, which was hers, that life should be a blessing to live and share, not to be hidden from, in addition to the countless uncertainties—for these were too many to warrant a final decision of "never" when it was such an opportunity to rejoice in being a parent. With both perceptions starched and inflexible, they became propriety laden in excess. When choosing to revisit the topic, the consideration given began as one would test hot water for comfort, the angle different each try, thinking that if postured correctly, one would be able to coerce the other to accede, but all they accomplished was to serve frustration because neither were motivated by a similar spirit in the matter.

What conflict we rouse! Were Christine's ending thoughts, rendering her unable to claim success in fluidity of writing save those feelings she wished not to permanently record—having written and burnt *their* mischievousness to ash—she laid her journal and letter aside. *I cannot function with this sort of impasse between us. He works himself to exhaustion, behaving like he must prove something, and the crossover of personal concerns into professional has been caught and redirected by Chanler, several times, which is evidence enough that our situation must find even ground. But right now, I desire to be somewhere other than here, and a horse may be just the ticket to a bit of quiet from this outsourced pounding.*

Taking satisfaction in her choice of escape, she sighed in relief, pulled the blanket from Dezi's back, and headed up to sit upon the ridge. The action itself was beneficial, just sitting with one's own thoughts gave her an appreciation for an opportunity to ponder, which had been so recently ignored and difficult to do, especially when the days came filled with construction and the evenings were left in suffocating avoidance. Yes, it was here she remembered the balance of their relationship, but the notice taken could do nothing unless embraced by two, and she wept.

After a time, when Christine could no longer constrain her thoughts, they spilled quietly forth, hand in hand with the tears. "Why, God, do you punish him through me? He thinks it is because of him that we have lost twice, that he is unworthy and that he has drug me to his level. Erik has suffered a life of disappointment, has he not? Doesn't the fact that he improves, learns, and feels remorse merit any more joy? I love him!" she declared. "His significance in my life is everything. Why can he not have sufficient happiness to negate the memories of his past?"

"Because happiness does not exist in the quantity required for such mercy."

The cynicism in his tone of voice caught her off guard on all fronts, as did a small stone tossed high above her; she started, luckily staying put while several more stones went sailing out over the cliff in irritation. Wonderful! Unbeknownst to Christine, she had nailed his feelings superbly, an accusation she must now prepare to face. She turned warily, afraid of what would meet her gaze and was correct in her caution, for the sight elicited a justified gasp.

"Adds color to God's gnarled upheaval, does it not?" he said with a sarcastic air of indifference. He was standing there, leaning against the rock with his ankles crossed, contemplating the toss of another stone being rubbed in-between his thumb and index. Christine made to join him as Erik dodged to avert the oncoming charge. "I am here under duress and would prefer you to—"

"But Erik, your face. . . the bruises and—"

"There's nothing to be done now, though Chanler said with my attitude you would most likely need an excuse to pity me. I thank you *so much* for supporting his conjecture."

"Chanler did that to you?"

"He did. Caused me to break my own rules, too. I let fly a most colorful round of expletives, in several languages I might add. I'm angry beyond what I dare express, aggravated with every aspect of my life because I have allowed my egotistical nature to forego what I promised you. I don't want to risk your health or what we have together. And, you cannot deny that I have an obvious right to be furious at God and everything good that has happened in my life because, the proverbial *rug* has been yanked yet again. My illogical fortune remains aloft only so long then plummets in response to the ugly plight of gravity."

"Well, finally!"

Erik's chest rose sharply in response. "Finally? And what is that to mean?"

"Two things! First, that Chanler had had enough, and second, that we are in a position to talk," *his least preferred option.*

He backed away and turned upon that premise, placing his hands to the harsh surface. She touched his arm.

"Don't!"

"Why? Because you wish for this state of affairs to continue between us?"

"No! It just feels good to spew, to be livid! I have to do something, remember? I no longer hurl objects. Words?" He shrugged, clenching his fists, his jaw flexed. "The control of those are under advisement and inapplicable at the moment."

"Look at me!" she challenged.

He spun, and came within inches of her, towered over her, panting. "Don't do that!"

"What?" She knew exactly. Her scent was foremost to assault his senses. She could see his jaw set hard, the veins throbbing willfully to maintain the feverish resolve, and then their eyes locked.

"I. . ." he spurted without follow up. The finely detailed skin and the way small crinkles formed at the corners of her eyes caused momentary rapture, then her voice dissolved him to present.

"Erik, hold me."

"Christine. . . no, please, my insides are hopelessly tangled."

"You are unreasonably obstinate."

"So I have been similarly accused by Chanler, though your delivery is more to my liking, being exceedingly more humane than his."

Erik flinched, the motion of Christine pressing her cheek upon his chest and the fresh memory of face and fist colliding entwined. They stumbled awkwardly against the rough exterior behind them and he rolled instinctively to one side to prevent her skin from making contact and wound up holding her tightly, and she, him. The moment was right.

"Christine, don't let go."

"I have no intention of doing so."

"Curse my resistance," he rasped. "How I wished to settle this sooner, still, every effort to talk reaffirmed *your* position. I had long since sealed my already tattered heart from any common sense, knowing full well the destitution it might create. Each time we dared open this chapter I would slam the bloodied binding, trapping the fragile pages, then toss it headlong into a darkened well. Seeking that book in preservation of what was within it became infinitely harder and I cared not, for your feelings or my own, it hurt far too much." A long pause registered with his sigh. "I felt life, Christine. It still hurts. And it has required someone with a stronger character than I to haul my reluctance to its knees, to extract the apathy I had permitted to so carelessly spread. I was wrong."

"Erik, it is not that simple; I wish that it were. Our double sided circumstance is not about right and wrong, it is about finding an answer that will suit the needs of both, comfortably and without—"

"Resentment," Erik ended.

"Yes. I cannot have you despise and be embittered toward me."

"Christine. . ."

"You know it is true."

He took hold of her shoulders and pushed away, gaining distance to better perceive her feelings. "I know no such thing. I have only desired for an element which lay in conflict with yours, as one cannot be achieved without possible detriment to the other; I wish to place all else secondary to us, to be reconciled. To this, wrong *must* be included. I heard what you said, listened unannounced at the peak of my belligerence and intruded on your privacy. It was imprudent of me. I'm sorry."

She smiled tenderly as he clasped her to his breast in earnest, and wondered where he would find peace in the knotted unease.

"I am a man of opposites and passions midst logic, my very nature would speak to inconsistency if it were not for you, but I know not the course in which to lead us, for either way... Christine, I *love* you."

His tenderness was shown in the skepticism clearly professed and as she repositioned herself to entrench more securely in his arms, she whispered, "Oh, how I do love you."

AN ACCEPTABLE QUANTITY of time passed, enough that Chanler asserted the taking up of advice to have occurred and be intelligently heeded, at least he hoped this to be the case.

What a tragic necessity, but I could not tolerate the argumentative self-centeredness and brooding any longer. Perhaps my crew and I shall be enquiring after another situation tomorrow. Chanler shut his eyes against the chill as he dipped his throbbing hand repeatedly in the icy current. Between Cerise and Christine, their dropping of comments, and what he beheld on his own, he empathized, to a point. Weeks went by before he was able to come to terms after he and Cerise stumbled along that similar, jagged path of elation coupled with disappointment and fear. *It is when your personal issues cross the line and interfere elsewhere. He was extremely irrational! Someone had to shake his world up, and who better than I? I would have done no less had he been my son.*

The cold at the base of his neck felt good, though insufficient to relieve the image etched upon his mind. He had not expected to explode as he had done, only continue their already heated discussion away from his men. Regrettably, Erik would have none of it. Chanler's goal was to send the men off early so Erik might use the quiet to make amends, but ignoring his wanton attitude as catalyst, he blatantly refused. The workers were sent off during the first break from his presence they had, despite Erik's orders, dispersing quickly to leave Chanler waiting at the site within full view. It was the silence that brought Erik fuming from the back door of his study. Chanler could not help but grin at the predictability, seeing exactly what was coming at him: sleeves loosed, no waistcoat from earlier, and the determined stride holding the posture of superiority. The dam had risen to a level of malcontent, which could not be contained longer, and it burst, gushing debris in all directions.

"How dare you take it upon yourself to usurp my authority! Of late, you and I contend at every juncture on this project; our current circumstances being in model form, find you meddling where you have no right!" Erik exclaimed, his fury parading in all its grandeur.

"I have every right, Erik. When the safety of my men is threatened, then I have an obligation to remove them." His speech was neutral in affect and completely irksome as he calmly sighed, seated upon a stack of framing lumber.

"What threat? This site is beyond safe and you know it! The only problems I have now are delays." Erik stared menacingly and turned away in disgust.

"Really? You would not convince me with such shortsightedness. And at this moment, *you* are the contemptuous hazard I speak to."

The observation came as an unwanted insult and Erik rounded sharply, meeting with the fist of one infuriated Chanler. He hit solid, the connection sure, one which knocked Erik to the ground, among other items. Erik was shocked, mortified and enraged, immediately resorting to an offense of hatred upon Chanler—the fact that Erik's masque had been totally dislodged went unnoticed by Chanler in the surge of emotion and acrid words.

"You have some nerve, referring to your wife as a delay!" Chanler drug Erik to his feet. "You've created deplorable working conditions, worse than before, and I've had about enough of your childish outbursts and paltry attempts at soothing conscience. Now..." he stated, pushing Erik back slightly to pick up the masque. "You take your sorry excuse for a carcass, find your wife and don't return until you make things right with her. Bless her heart to have pity on you now because I sure as hell don't. Get out of my sight!" With that tongue-lashing he shoved the masque to Erik's chest and propelled him in the direction of the stables.

Preoccupying himself with incidentals had become all-consuming since then. He tried to justify the actions, the attitude... Heavens! That face, or lack thereof, plagued his mind, contracting his brows in pain. The scene replayed; he could hear the anger, how it merged with the shame of discovery, for it was not attached to the blow received, but to the privacy uncontrollably torn away. He saw the black privation imprisoned by those hateful words—not Erik's face—and remorse swamped Chanler's heart, filling it with understanding: the contradictive behaviors, caprice of thought, his character, it made sense, not excusing the folly, and explained so much. "Christine," he breathed. "What a lovely woman to care for and love him."

His deliberation was deterred by a light snort and he stood, coming away from the stream, eyes and ears keenly riveted to the couple walking hand in hand with obedient steeds following close behind.

Christine felt Erik tense when he saw Chanler, his fingers repositioned about hers and she squeezed. "He cares, Erik," she reassured, and taking the reigns she veered in the direction of the stables, leaving him to reconcile with Chanler as well.

They approached, regarding the other, Chanler purposely refraining from an overtly direct gaze.

"Chanler."

"Erik."

Erik's sight cast furtively about. "Seeing as how our altercation has left memory in tact, we are off to an affable start, are we not?" he quipped.

"We are," Chanler agreed, looking after Christine. "Your wife, she is remarkable."

"Thank you, yes. The gift of her presence in my life..." he stopped mid-sentence and cleared his throat, looking right at Chanler. "It seems however, that I am susceptible to a lapse in gratitude. I needed my head straightened out. I thank you upon this count, too. Never having had a father or brother to learn from, and only fleeting male role models that I considered worthy of my respect, I have had no one to keep me in check."

Chanler understood, but the guilt beckoned resolution. "Erik, I. . . about your masque. I wish to extend my most sincere apology."

Erik grinned, or so it looked to be. "I am fortunate that this one is a bit more forgiving, the others would have succumbed to breakage and more damage, though I shall revert to their use until the swelling subsides." There was an uncomfortable silence. "Apology accepted and, if I may be so bold, I should like to petition for your forgiveness as well."

"Done!" was Chanler's hasty response, and holding out his hand, to which Erik grasped in appreciation, all was settled.

"Hell of a face, is it not?" Erik mused when their hands parted.

Chanler glared steadily, as if digesting the remark, then he lunged forward to firmly embrace Erik, compassion staining the man's face most heartily. "This is for all the times missed between father and son, I'm sorry."

Erik trembled, amazement engulfing him. Rarely had tenderness or affection been included in his life from a masculine direction. It was foreign, but not wasted on a poverty-stricken soul such as his; he returned the embrace.

The lesson experienced left all to wonder why blessings seemed to flow on the heels of resolved discord and why they occurred in less than obvious ways. Why, indeed.

Chapter Thirty-Three

In the days following, there began to be a perceptible difference in which Erik and Chanler viewed each other—a rather curious variant really, noticed among those at work on the site. Respect and high regard were in realms unequaled as Chanler fostered the fervor, genius, and passion, as Erik reshaped his moral insight and ethical fortitude based on the example shown him. All in all, it was a thriving camaraderie. Truth be told, embarrassment doled Erik a fair portion of gratitude with his display; luckily, one masque, garnishing the standard aplomb, and it was business as usual. Had the unlikely salvo not been secured, his bout and miserable loss would have met with easy interpretation.

Erik relaxed upon one of the rear benches within the Madeleine, making notes on these and other past thoughts, when he was struck by the stateliness this church came to manifest. He had once professed having designs to be wed here because he wished to be as everyone else, to do as others in matrimony in order to achieve the pomp and circumstance. *Heavens.* His throat narrowed. Looking back, it was not only in matrimony but littered throughout his whole contrived existence as well, an integral part of who he was as a person. The very fundamentals he wished to hold himself aloof from were those he yearned most to have. *How fitting too, that the revelation be had inside these religious confines.* In his estimation this was progress, it must be. He could see change, felt altered for the better. *And our wedding? I would not have had it any different. The intimacy and historical, peaceable quality befit us. This grandiose display,* he glanced about to confirm, *is too imperious, but it all becomes Richard's relations most satisfactorily.*

He breathed in deep. *Eleven months ago. . . used well, not fettered away alone, actually longer if I include the courtship, although this past week has been a protracted, unending circle of hours in solitude. The crew can hardly be a substitute. And, here I sit, having not yet seen my wife.*

Erik's eyes closed to savor the delicate past when a hand closed carefully over his shoulder. He smiled.

"What is this, keeping notation? Jots of intrigue and holder of conscience? And look at that, since when are you right-handed?"

"Ah, my friend, will your infernal list of questions never cease?" Erik's eyes danced in greeting, as he gained footing to properly address his partner. "Yes, truth be known. . . I must account in some way. Christine cannot read my mind, although she comes close, nor would I wish to impose points I seek to ponder more fully. And no, I am not right-handed, I only practice as a diversion."

"Naturally, enough said."

"And how are the haunts about the Opera, quiet?"

"Uncommonly so, everyone and everything in religious order."

Religion again, Erik's face warmed. "And Mercier?"

"Genteel, definitely genteel and polite in his condescension to a lowly intermediary, who has his interests locked into that of justice."

"Lowly?" Erik returned. "You, of all people, should be overjoyed you no longer need be compelled to shadow my behavior, anything would pale in comparison." Erik's mock arrogance caused the Persian to lighten. "Besides, it is not an option to have that section of my life reopened for your sole enjoyment. I am quite content."

"It is well that the outlet for your genius is such, and how pleasant for you that she has summoned the virtue I had always hoped for. Oh, and I appreciate you making good on your word to seal up certain disagreeable entrances."

"Not at all. I cannot have uninvited guests showing up unexpectedly then go missing, it would be extremely impolitic."

The Persian grinned derisively at Erik's response and at the joy he derived from tormenting him with his warped semantics. "Come by later, we shall talk then."

"I must decline, for I have not seen Christine these last eight days. I shall catch up with you when I am next in town. Forgive me."

They parted with a bow as the chapel began to be a bit more frenzied, not wishing to have their contact misconstrued, they gave an air to their meeting, making it seem more of a formality. The Persian was always evaluating factors at risk, but then, was he not guilty of the same? Erik rubbed his chin in consideration and walked down the aisle to his left; a disturbance of calm rushed behind him and then away, reappearing again from the support column just up ahead. The mysterious imp, dressed in deep green, placed a finger to her lips and smiled. He immediately fell into step and followed the alluring suggestion into a nearby anteroom in a less occupied section. Waiting for him to enter, the beauty quickly closed the door and became a barricade to Erik's only means of escape. Awestruck, Erik backed up and bumped into a desk.

"I was sent as a spy to commandeer visual information, but my mission has gone horribly awry. You see, I have set my sights on another, more worthy target for my attentions." Christine's dulcet tone lightened.

Erik listened, enthralled by this detour of sorts, and watched her glide to him. Her hands gently crept to his lapels, his heart beating wildly upon seeing those moistened lips; they reflected the afternoon sun then met their rendezvous, tenderly touching his.

"I've missed. . ." were the only words uttered. The exchange of passion left her colorfully flushed, necessitating that she withstand his ardor by arm's length.

"I must return. . . hmm, and make my report," she expressed, bodice heaving.

"You gorgeous vixen."

Her smile spread slowly and evenly. "I sought to inform my husband, lest he forget that I love him."

"And I feel, according to protocol during times such as these, that," he swallowed dryly, "that clarification is mandatory."

"Hold that thought," she said. "I do bring interesting news as well. Edouard Mercier shall be attending today, though I have yet to see him. The two of us have crossed paths twice, today will make three."

"He knows that you are married then, just not to whom?"

She nodded. "Questions burn his tongue. I have not been in his presence long enough for him to catechize, and I know he would do so if he had been given the opportunity. He carries himself with deference, however there is something ostentatious about his manner when in the company of those familiar."

"He matches every other in society. All right, enough with the business, back to more enjoyable reiteration."

His hands cradled her face, thumbs tracing along her jaw and throat, awaiting some reply, when Christine's elbows collapsed with a sigh. "I am a mutinous romantic in want of fulfilling my own designs, but shall now meet with disapprobation and wrath upon my return. Oh! Wretch that I am. Who shall ever trust—?"

Erik chuckled at her dramatics, hushing her with his fingers. "I shall always trust you. That you hold me first, above all else, means much my fair maiden. Kiss me and be off, tempt me no more."

Thereafter, Christine became as those around her, purposely destined and task oriented under the constraint of time. She looked in place, not unlike any number of busy people, and hastily threading her way back to the bride's dressing chamber was to be expected. Richard's sisters waited at the door with a smattering of queries for the determined Christine.

"Where were you?" asked Victoria.

"Yes, fess up!" demanded Suzanne. "We send you out for a quick look-see and you disappear. It was quite discourteous of you, you know."

The first remnants of music broke through the air in time to dash the young ladies' polite façade, and they pounced greedily for more information.

"Yes, do tell us what you found!"

"Yes, yes! Oh, and did you see our uncle and his wife, you know, the one we told of, the one with an outlandishly gaudy hat?" Suzanne cringed at the mental picture.

"Let the woman in and me out! Good gracious you two, behaving with the manners of someone not yet out, and silly to boot! Heaven help your father and me that neither of you become shameless flirts done up in silk and satin; dreadful mess it makes of a man's true affections."

Both young ladies rolled their eyes at the lecture, being careful not to demonstrate the rude orbit until their mother quit the room to take up her place of prominence. Their mother gone, they clamored to pull Christine from the hall.

"Well," she dawdled, "I do recall a remarkably posh nesting ground somewhere near the front." The girls laughed at her description of the feathered excess. "But, I must confess to experiencing a minor deterrent, you see, I could not leave him pining and me lamenting that I had not taken care. One kiss was insufficient, and so it was that I befell his enticement." She feigned a meek swoon and clutched her heart, laying wrist to brow.

"Really, Christine! I am about to walk down the aisle and my matron of honor is out cavorting with her husband."

Christine grinned. "Turnabout is fair, is it not? I did, however, see another lively chap. He was standing with his father and brother off in one of the side vestibules, his blond hair—"

"Point made, you may stop. I do not wish to know," Meg said.

"Meg, enjoy the moment for what it is. It will not last and shall be done sooner than you think."

"Christine is right, my dear." Mme Giry peeked at her daughter's reflection in the mirror.

"It's no use, just look at me! I've chaffed my hands raw. With so many people to make an impression on, and all those thoughts of not being good enough because I am not as *they* are, oh, Maman!" she panicked, shaking out her hands.

"Steeped in tradition means too lazy for change. Listen, we have been through this and have resolved to quit the subject more often than is healthy. The most important person out there is Richard. You love him, my dear, and I have seen the care and fuss he makes over you, focus on that."

"Yes, and if something goes oddly askew, I shall be ready to intercede that you may have a tale to remember, but Richard may beat me to it."

Meg nodded at Christine's sobering good nature, then looked to her mother.

"Meg, you are beautiful, we have prepared all these months for this to be your day. He is a good man, now go, enjoy a new life with Richard."

A few kisses transpired, with some well-placed dabs to save face, the same moment ending in an abrupt merge with the interests of Meg's sisters-in-law, both reengaged with the imprudence of gawking from a gap in the door.

"Oh! Look at him," commented Victoria.

Playing along, Christine asked, "And, just what does *he* look like to make you become so giddy in voice?"

"Madame Christine, it was but a glimpse as he passed through the foyer."

"And what a glimpse it was too!" added Suzanne.

"He has the darkest raven hair, walks with a majestic air, and wears a masque! How mysterious is that? Appearing like he's a character from one of those novels you read, Suz, the ones Mama grumps about."

Meg elbowed Christine and they both burst with laughter.

"What?" plied the girls in unison.

"That gentleman, to whom your tone so audaciously covets, is Christine's husband," Meg chided.

They gasped and said not one word more; they dared not.

Christine sighed inwardly. Yes, it was her response exactly!

"The wedding came and went," or at least this is how much Erik would have penned if given responsibility of the announcement. It was enough, in his good opinion, as the only virtuous particular to pay mind to was the woman standing to the bride's left. Richard would have an alternate bias, to be sure, but since he was nowhere near to dissuade him otherwise, Erik's thoughts were free to continue along their current path. His heart swelled and the words "thank you" crossed his lips. *Thank you for choosing me to love.*

Chapter Thirty-Four

The boat slid quietly across the night-colored water of the lake, each oar propelling effortlessly to shore beneath the light of a small lantern fixed to the bow, its challenge to the darkness. Christine watched the glassy calm distort into ripples, then lift to caress the stone in its continual undulation, their singular movement giving life to the tenebrous depths. Sighing, she gazed absently in thought, *What a wondrous day, today. . . the 27th of September 1879, one year ago.*

She knew Erik's eyes were upon her; observing everything, they had been irretrievably adhered in just such a manner since the middle of Act II, when Don José pledges his love to Carmen during the *Flower Song*. Pulling her trailing fingers from the water she reclined into a set of newly situated cushions, took a deep breath, closed her eyes, and rested an arm up above her head. She lay there, still and motionless then suddenly spoke, "You have barely uttered a word all evening."

"A word." Erik smirked at the piercing eyes now wide and staring, the phrase returned with a touch of sarcasm.

"I see, you wish to carry on. But I believe your reply, coupled with a vacant 'hmm,' 'yes,' a few grunts and an 'ah,' do not a conversation make."

"Then obviously, my dear, you have missed numerous visual messages, for my eyes have been composing in earnest." He drew in the oars and went down on one knee, bringing her hand to his lips. Christine felt the heat spread up her cheeks; she watched, mesmerized by his gallant habits, those perfectly captivating, gentlemanly tendencies, his touch causing her eyes to float uninhibited past their evening shade.

It was only a kiss, though one awakened by the savor she applied, he had taught her well; to take the most simple of feelings and expound on the virtues contained therein. He told her, "If one understood the deepest foundation of emotion, they would be more guarded as to the random individuals chosen to share such a gift." Nothing within this sphere was ever frivolously expressed or received by him, and in beneficent consequence, Christine learned to experience the fierce intensity of touch—he actually thrived on the contact and reciprocation. What one, brief kiss of affection could do for the senses, if not taken for granted, and knowing the near impossibility she faced of never being able to resist the mode of his declaration and kind consideration. . . Oh, how could a man have so endured, have had such fortitude? This was the beauty behind their bond.

Releasing her hand, it drifted lightly by her side and was all at once replaced with radiating warmth, an arc of desire from the lips brushing against her forehead and temples, to finally rest at her ear.

"Who is devoid of word now?" he whispered perilously. Without warning, a jolt crumpled Erik's partially bent arms, landing him in a convenient approximation to his wife. "Forgive me, are you all right?"

"I should think I could not find myself in a better situation, being most fortunate that you are a trim man." She tapped his chin. "We have arrived."

Erik stared longingly and his lips closed over hers, his scent to her, passionate and fresh. "We have yet to arrive, as I have not even begun to suitably thank my wife, so, *that* was for breakfast in the spring. And this," he pressed his mouth deeper to her acceptance, "is for the late afternoon walk and feast beneath the trees in the park." Erik removed a few strands of hair caught on his cuff, and going on said, "I would be remiss if I were to forget to convey my gratitude for your tender care and belief in me, for not leaving, and, for loving me enough to consent to be my sweet companion." His face descended once more to claim her as his own.

In like fashion, Christine re-situated to her side, which facilitated a more advantageous position to afford more completely the full expansion of her lungs; she then continued the gratuitous theme. "I enjoyed Bizet's *Carmen* tonight; sitting with you in the infamous Box 5 was a pleasure. We were on the same side of the curtain without any type of combatant or vested interest as to how all should proceed. I preferred it most gratefully." She wrinkled her nose and unfastened his tie. "I am curious to learn whether *this* was the subject so intricately consuming your partiality."

"It was. I desired your voice, tried in vain to block out and replace what I was hearing on stage and was finally successful by reminiscing back through to our most significant moments together."

"Do you have favorites?"

"Yes." He smiled as his finger lovingly caressed her mouth. "There are two which dominate. When you asked me to explain the origins of my masque and the moment you agreed to spend your life with me." Her dubious glare puzzled him. "What? You do not believe me?"

"I would have assumed the first to be one of the least pleasurable. I know it caused a level of discomfiture and embarrassment to reveal so much of yourself, in more ways than one."

"Exactly the reason I hold it in such esteem. I was blessed with an acceptance I had only ever dreamed of, which came through the challenge of releasing the burden I had shouldered alone."

"Dreams are wonderful things."

"They are."

"Then, my dear man, the matter of knowing to which time you refer when you say I agreed to, 'spend my life with you,' is enigmatical, for I feel there to be more than one."

"I mean to imply all, for each confirmation of your devotion to us signifies a commitment I desperately cling to. I love you, Christine, and in every way you have introduced a most kind-hearted felicity into our relationship; it is choice beyond measure."

Gazing at him, lying beside her under the soft glow of the lantern, she encouraged the finger's ongoing sojourn across her skin as his eyes drifted in tandem.

"Erik, my love... come," her request piqued in the mellifluous suspension of word upon his ears and she bid him rise. "The night is young."

ONE QUARTER-HOUR and then nearly two elapsed awaiting a summons; such frustration! How much more was he to tolerate? Erik tucked his watch back into his waistcoat pocket and shrugged away from where he had been leaning, rotating around from heaven's angel humming pleasantly from below. As distance set between himself and the familiar stone, he headed back up toward the organ chamber. Christine had entreated a sufficient length of time for mysterious preparations of some sort and left him to the leisurely act of pacing about. The gentle melody had since ceased; he paused to make out her footfalls, but nothing came.

Reentering the organ chamber bore witness to an inceptive canvas of endless possibilities, blank and sterile, and so different from its former years. Not that his flat was warm and inviting, but the flourish of heirlooms and piecemeal of rich, Mideastern ambiance was no more, and with its purpose removed, it would remain barren. He smoothed the varicolored drapery to carefully cover the sides of his organ and gave it a final tucking in for a long season of rest, a first. Erik recalled the fortnights of brutally naked emotion pouring in torrents over the keys, bearing in wont the burning flow of hell from his veins. *Don Juan* had yet to triumph, it was incomplete, a life's work on edge, poised to mock and weighted by love. There it would remain while celebrating joy. He had intended it done, to be quite done, but while there was a glint of hope, he somehow could not bring himself to make it a completed work. Christine's departure, if wholly realized, would have sealed its fate in a timely ending, but it did not.

Erik reflected solemnly to find his conscience bothered by this and by the fact that more than three quarters of an hour had gone missing without retrieval. He fidgeted, and feeling thusly warranted, he snubbed the past in favor of the present.

Christine had been humming pieces from the evening's opera, all the while surveying the well-positioned candles; each tendril of smoke writhed hypnotically and mirrored an echoed resonance across the chamber walls that maintained continuity of warmth. Erik's library, being the incongruous exception by absorbing more than its fair share, quickly found itself with her gaze fixed in an attempt to shove a few books securely into their designated slots. But as they were not to be thrust further, she was resigned to the variation in size and shape of each and left them as they were, apart from one. Her attention was drawn to a wispy trail of dust, clue enough that it had been drug from off the lower shelf at the far right, perhaps recently used. She inclined her head and carefully extracted the worn text from between its neighbors. The pages were gently skewed, their soft leather cover, thin. Intrigue—heightened by Christine's nature in general—turned the book over in silence, her hands, going the length of the binding, passed it close to inhale its antique scent, and Erik's.

Splitting the parchment wide permitted the contents to breathe once again, the air infusing vital urges to entice the reader. *Ah, just one look, and then another,* abide longer with its temptations; it knew. Evil: it could span decades and reap rewards still. There were pages of science, sections of mechanical devices and still others. She squinted, her eyes unbelieving, and fingers momentarily rendered inept. The tainted subject matter was difficult to wade through, in addition to the tears and implacable lure drawing her unmercifully through the glut of blood and masterful intellect. Christine's eyes closed against the images, and a sob shook her frame, right as the book's heinous material became suffocated with a flick of Erik's wrist.

"I fear my carelessness has given your vague inclinations detail that is far more graphic than you ever imagined. Forgive me?" he asked, his voice thick with regret. "Your innocence, I am unsuccessful in guarding, but I shall not deny your right to be knowledgeable of my crimes. The level is discretionary and is what I promised."

Tender pressure to her bare shoulder could not bring her around to face his pain-stricken countenance, her head too heavy to be torn away from the safety in which her hands gave.

"You knew who I was, Christine. I have no secrets and have sought to keep nothing hidden from you." Was she listening? Of all the books there, how did she ever manage? One glance at the shelf revealed its tale. Yes, the story of his life. Bliss turned sour, excellent timing as always.

A soft, "I know," came at length in the long silence.

"Then why do you refuse to look at me?" he asked strained. "Why do you keep your gaze bent away?" *Don't push,* his rationale flagged. *You know to see is a far cry from how the brain illustrates the unknown.* He knew, yet his heart pressed for justice. "You think I do not feel shame enough without more condemnation from my own wife... she who would believe in me?" Again, the silence crept on. "Christine!" The intensity startled her. "I am not that man!"

The moist dark of the cavern welcomed him as he left their chamber in little more than a blur, throwing his cloak at random to some chair, his hat, gloves and tailcoat arriving in a heap thereafter. *She knew!* The velvet churned after his stormy entry then calmed to nothing. He stared blankly, at a loss for what to do, and a choking cough shook him, rocking him hard enough to warrant he clasp his arms about himself for stability. How he longed for them to be hers, to explain what she had seen. His mistake was instigating separation. Up snaked his hand to rub at the base of his neck. *Tired*, he was so tired.

Christine stepped slowly through the curtain. He looked down at the outline cast from the shaft of light, faceless and without detail, unknown, just as he had always been; there was the illuminating white of his shirt, he was at water's edge, his back to her.

"Erik," she said, "I'm sorry. I should not have pried. In doing so, I have wronged your belief and trust in me, slighted you when I promised I never would. If I had left well enough alone, we would not be feeling grief and injury, would not have strayed so far... especially since our day has been so enjoyable. You were right, what I saw and read was shocking in its portrayal and left me unable to respond for a time. I should not have shunned, no matter the level of knowledge availed me or color added to the sheltered life I've led."

The last comment was in want of taste and produced a sigh of despondency from Erik.

She winced. "I am deficient in tact as well."

"Please, come to me." Erik held his hand out in invitation.

She readily accepted, was received in a grateful embrace and there they stayed, undisturbed. Erik did not fault her; he could not. How was she to be led except by wonder and trust, and no guide? He hurt rightly, conscience and heart alike. When they could at last manage a tolerable amount of composure, she offered a few meaningful words of affection.

"I love you, Erik. I always will."

He kissed her head. "Our evening has taken a direction that neither wished. Perhaps it would be best if I were to explain the book."

"If you like, but may I say something beforehand?"

"Please."

"I should like you to know that I appreciate your conviction of character. You are not the man that book depicts, nor is it who you are now. You are my husband, caring, sensitive, and honorable. One who has given temperance to anger, which shows strength of will, who yearns to bring peace where nostalgia has rent aim by detour." Her hold of decency revisited, she silenced her tongue.

Loosening his grasp, Erik gestured toward the spring and once seated, he took both her hands in his and began the narrative. "Historically, I desired to remember specific portions of original, uplifting endeavors, but the book soon incurred all manner of baleful accounts. As I strived for the unique qualities my superiors had come to expect from me, the book helped to insure the novelty from wearing thin. Sadly, it was my prideful arrogance as always, in wont of reliving control, to see the power of my will reign supreme and unchallenged. Its pages include some of the abhorrent assassinations, and serve as a just reminder of how lethal I had become. There are also a plethora of ideas obligated therein; everything from scientific interests to the mechanics of automaton and curio oddities, to architectural designs, trapdoors and tricks. Most important, is the latter. I have drawn the whole of my passages, a blueprint of the Opera's cellars, the entrances and so forth. When I seal one off in favor of another, I refer to this to make sure it is duly noted, that it will be an advantageous change. It is for this purpose that I had removed it from the shelf and none other." A defeated look sunk his posture, his thoughts clearly communicated. "The information is so extensive that there would be no need for trial or representation by those legally bound. It is an irrefutable warrant for death in Tehran."

"Why keep such a book?" she asked.

"Why, indeed." Her hand was given a light pat. "Assiduous feeding of superiority, arrogance and stupidity would be my first pass; I do not understand it myself."

Christine nodded. "In my decision to read on, notwithstanding the pain inflicted so unnecessarily, I gained a greater comprehension of why specific concepts are, perhaps, more moving and poignant in their application."

"Sentiments reserved for those pages are marked in vastly different degrees, but my past shall always be one fact I cannot ever be divorced from." Erik stroked her cheek while she absorbed all he had shared. He wondered if his honesty would cause her perspective to alter or her to love him less. He need not have worried, for Christine would not be so easily chased away. Sliding close, she grasped the ends of his tie and drew him in, filling his need for air, much to the joy of his lungs.

Sweeping her up into his arms he sauntered to the piano and enquired, "Do I have your permission to torch the bridge between what was and what is, for tonight?"

"You do." Her mouth covered his briefly. Then, holding up one finger, he put her down gently, moved quickly to set the doors, and returned.

Erik's hands rose to her face. "Oh, my dearest Christine, as well as you understand me, I think you shall never fully realize what your companionship and our union means, despite the challenges."

"I will listen, if you wish to share."

His chest broadened under the encouragement. His mind light, he rounded to sit before the keys; minor adjustments were made and fingers poised then with one defeated breath he dropped them into his lap. "I cannot."

"Cannot?" Her questioning rise let him know of her interest.

"Without proper inspiration, I am hopelessly lost."

"I would gladly heed any reasonable petition."

Perfect. Tilting his head to one side he eyed her keenly and touched his mouth most sensuously. "Right here, long and deep."

Settling next to him, Christine loosed the top button of his shirt and traced along the outline of his masque, the anticipation causing his eyes to roll back and lids to close languidly beneath her caresses; her touch slid easily between the weightless material and his uneven contours, to remove that which he surrendered freely. She pressed her lips softly to each eye, trailed them across his forehead and alternately to each temple. Their proximity, and Christine's reassuring gestures, roused his withered, shock beaten heart to a pleasant cheerfulness, which was now fast recovering with a descent upon his lips, into the sweet void of his mouth. Erik broke their impassioned moment to study her face in the throes of awe. He tenderly stroked her chin, then without word he patted his shoulder and she took her place behind him.

Gently, and with the delicacy of a breeze upon the skin, he began a composition Christine had never heard. Smooth and effortlessly the notes entwined through mind and senses, to embellish their spirits with the treasure of his musical forte. The melody sang of contentment, of tranquility in thought, and the harmony spoke in terms of ensconced souls, the rich passion blending from depths unknown to heights of the unimagined.

Upon completion of that glorious piece, neither could transcend the spell until the resolving dissidents rested among the hushed silence once again. Erik was first to move, and brought her to sit opposite him for a more ideal view. One small, opalesque drop fell quietly to the center of her cheek, where it was met by a kiss.

"I wrote it for you. It is entitled *When Angels Kiss*." Another drop rolled to the tip of his thumb before he could brush it away. "I have this as well," he said, producing a scroll tied about with a white ribbon. "I would prefer to recline in your lap, if you would permit me."

Before moving she pronounced a well-earned kiss, then he carried her to the desired comfort midst the bed, where she set free the sentiments upon the paper. Christine gazed in astonishment, the hand, which had so exquisitely penned the contents, was of Erik's doing; there was no mistake.

He smiled openly. "My left hand merits all the credit, for the right remains apprenticed." To this stripe of wit was brought the charming ministrations he sought, and for her, a gift of time.

> My cherished Christine,
>
> I must be a hopeless romantic (you may laugh because I know that I am). Anything remotely related to us has significance deeply embedded within the innermost recesses of who I am becoming, and as this is not an endeavor to be lightly taken, I do not use past tense because I shall, and must always, claim myself to be a work in progress.
>
> You have awakened choice freedoms, the concepts of patience and forgiveness, and have given me the gift of love, in all its forms. Knowing this, I undertook to express in earnest as much as I could, by use of music and by placing our story in verse.

Beyond the Masque

Ages gone, these years progressed
Within a vault confined
Musical connection, an oath
Truth measured, beat resigned.
Buried far, deep release it came
Intense, affecting power
Raw passion flowed, creation sought
Design in worth did sour.
Imprisoned thusly with each bar,
Between each metal stave
Professing love, though desire grand
Remained upon the page.

Your dream, my hope relied upon
Deception, mastered task
Inquisitive, pressured slight of hand
You pried Beyond the Masque.

In time, the game reversed its course
Frustrated love, to choice
When truth found out, an angel fell
Such rapture held in voice.
A gift, a kiss, collapsed demand
Set freedom leave to go
'If only,' were the words unsaid
A love forsook to depths unknown.
In stunned confusion, silence burned
Determination set in motion
Location shift, beneath black night
To heal, to learn, mind open.
A trust began, mistakes forgiven
Light changed the dark at last,
Erasing grief with gentleness
You touched, Beyond the Masque.

Deprived of simple kindness,
Starved to death, was just a man
Nourished at all junctions crossed
Endured, a guiding hand.
Ingrained were threads so bitter
Imposed by guilt, unceased
Escape, the only answer found,

Curse imprisoned alone, for peace.
To transcend a surface marred since birth
Exiled, cloak forced by humanity
Through devotion, patience, love unfeigned
You've taught, the heart can see.

Accepted whole, my confidant
You understand, and know, yet love
You own my soul, conviction strong
Complete, steadfast above.
An imprint of your life is set
Against mine, forever cast
Your heart beats full, in time with mine
Beyond the Masque.

I love you beyond words...
Erik

Feeling blessed in such a joyous manner, Erik benefitted by having his ear most affectionately attended to. Soon the location of her hand shifted to his chest and he assumed the verse to be thusly perused and glanced up. Her eyes glistened and his beamed; then clasping her hand, he pressed a kiss to its palm and laid it tenderly to his ravaged cheek.

"A hopeless romantic, every woman should be so fortunate, except, I shall not share for want in society, no, this is a rare find indeed, and one I shall forever cherish. Thank you." Her tender hold emphasized.

"Rare..." he sighed. "I believe it is you who are rare and that I am unique. Aïe! Blast!"

"This is not a competition in semantics. Come, up with you." She extricated herself from under his head, gaining amusement from the disappointment corrugating his brow as a most unwilling party to the idea.

"A poke. . . no kiss. Such an unfair exchange," he pouted.

"Hasty conjecture is most ill-advised," she warned, moving a chair into position near the footboard, paralleling the bed. She motioned for Erik to take a seat and then stood directly in front of him. After his waistcoat and cuff links were removed, there began a circular application of fingertips to each temple and, while continuing on in an upward arc, down to the base of his skull, he conformed beneath the soothing care. Christine finished off with a kiss to his cheek then disappeared from sight. His eyes chased to the farthest confines of their peripheral ability, unable to discern the purpose of her intent. He certainly did not wish to spoil the intensity, but could not resist the urge to enquire into the silence.

"Why the mystery?"

"Often," her voice projected from a distant section of the room, "words are an unnecessary hindrance and distraction to cover insecurities."

My own medicine mete out in return? His forehead rose, bewildered by her form returning with a steaming basin of water and towels draped limply from an apron girt about her waist. Kneeling before her husband, Christine tended lovingly to a Mideastern custom: with trouser legs rolled up and dress shoes and stockings eased from his feet, each were in turn washed, massaged, and dried several times over. The warmth absorbed up his limbs to allay the fatigue from the day's activities, a welcome gift. Had he not been familiar with this type of cleansing ritual, the act of which Christine took upon herself to sincerely express, would have seemed to be more of a subservient role, to be accomplished by a hireling and not a service into which his wife should condescend, but his knowledge paved way to understanding as this was instead, an exceptional display of love. Christine's adept handling of each foot had him so relaxed that it could not be helped, and he dozed during the splendorous moments.

"Erik? Open up," she cooed softly into his ear, then laughed. "Not your mouth, your eyes. Come, I need you back up on the bed."

"Am I never to be left in peace?" he groaned.

"Moving one meter is but a mere sacrifice. Now, I shall leave you in peace, if it is what you wish."

Erik rolled into the pillows and smiled. "I shall refrain from further complaint."

"Wise choice," she responded, reaching over him to retrieve a slender document portfolio from beneath the bedcovers. He mistook the gesture and was faced with a mandatory relinquishing of what he thought to be an honest conclusion, considering. Christine asked for patience and Erik smirked, propping himself up to read, her position by his feet being curiously marked, prior to focusing on the papers before him.

Erik's interest quickly honed when he saw Christine take a small vial of oil from her apron. With several drops dispensed into her palm, the spicy scent permeated the air and gave rise to immediate recall of the pleasantries from the east. Though, he preferred to attach the tenderness of her massaging caresses, positive that this was truly a wondrous experience, for which many untold virtues could be affixed. When all could be deemed serene, he visited the opened case and the sheets therein.

Erik, my love,

Since the day we became engaged I have made a concerted effort to compile a record of gratitude, a conscientious remembrance of moments noticed which depict a trait, action, or reason for me to be grateful for who you are and why I cherish our love. I wished for you to know how many possible ways

there were to be appreciated, it is endless. . .
Your Christine

"What is all this?" he demanded straightaway, glancing up. The coquettish grin he spied was interpreted as her suggestion to go at it solo, of course. He snorted in frustration and gave the extensive list a quick leafing through, which slowed for random picks until he finally reordered the lot to indulge from the start. Page after page, both sides covered, the dates. . . *daily*. The whole of it caused inspiring intrigue for Erik, the tenacious collection of thoughts, the tranquil moments and consideration; so much about himself that he never considered loveable or of worth to anyone, lay in comment; in effect, captured in essence by her. Especially noted were the portions associated within that time frame of siege upon their loss—Erik found tongue-in-cheek observations connected with certain dates off to one side—*at least she was gracious enough to find something optimistic to say.* Erik heaved a sigh of content then reached for the quiet blessing, industriously employed at his feet.

"Erik, I have oil all over my hands," she chided.

He directed her palms to his shirt, and the buttons, no longer needed to maintain their attire's appearance, melted into repose. "Wipe them here, my beloved," he breathed, pleasuring in the release of each hazel rivulet flowing unchecked over her satin nightgown, he cupped her face gently. "You have given me more than I knew I could desire, thank you for providing my life with meaning." She seemed sincerely happy. "A record to keep my doubts from wandering, am I right?"

"I wish you to stay close."

"I will. Now, if you would help me to understand how best to please you, so I may keep the reserves of your love full, *I* should be forever grateful."

Gazing at him unwavering, she sunk within the circle of his warm embrace to nestle against the comfort of his heart and after a short time, expressed her sentiments. "Stay romantic; sing to me and love me with every fiber of who you are and will become. Caress my heart with your music and vibrancy of life, my mind with intelligence, and my ears with the breath of passion, but most important, touch my eyes with the beauty that unites our souls."

The kiss he had long been waiting for came at the exact point Christine finished; entranced by her words and taking mental notation for later reference, he was completely unprepared when those lips came crashing into his senses. Thoughts disintegrated in seconds as remnants within her scorching fire; he hesitated, gasped and was given no hope of escape; not that either preferred or found it a compatible option.

Chapter Thirty-Five

What a joyous occasion! It was the eve of a new year, a time for all the world to celebrate, the young and older alike, (the term *old* is disallowed by perspective, for if one considers their inner self, they might but discover that being a child at heart is the only requisite to add the sparkle of wonder). Indeed, a time to ponder over challenges as well as the reprieves, closing doors on the past to turn and burst wide a window for the hope of opportunities presenting change. Parisians are no different than most; in fact, being such improves the outcome of gaiety nearly ten-fold. Even if one is removed from the city, the festive ardor accompanies the individual in spirit when the chill of the season becomes shed upon entry into each home.

Having an unusually harsh winter for the year's inception had many stranded in their travels between family and friends since Joyeux Noel, especially this eve. Moonlight glinted off the ocean of white subduing the countryside; muffling distractions beneath its icy sheet, it amplified the sharp qualities of sound as the wind blew unrelenting waves of flakes to twirl about the land in its desolate sleep. At first glance, what at once seemed bleak and uninhabited had only to happen upon the warmth of a brief gathering, happily extended, with prospects of weather looking to clear over the next few days.

The newly constructed guest wing of the Gautier estate was completely furnished and in full use at the invitation of their host and hostess. There were the Barbezacs, Adèle Giry and Edouard Mercier, the Minots—those presently known and their son and his wife, Nicolas and Valery—and the Persian. This evening, as with those previous, found the gentlemen engaged in various forms of amusing occupation from chess and billiards to conversation, but the room was somehow in want of females, who were assembled in the kitchen.

Erik had taken a solitary moment to deliberate on the joy he experienced in decorating with Christine, the traditions begun, and on the group collected—their intricacies of character had several improving upon better acquaintance, and all while in the company of those who need not be impressed. He turned slightly at the approach of the Persian, nodding in acknowledgment.

"It seems," the Persian began dryly, as he drew up to join Erik by the corner window, "that my endeavors to make acquaintance with your abodes manage to procure some form of natural element, which must be endured."

Erik smirked at the inference. "As I recall, Daroga, being an uninvited guest does bring its consequences; you deserved your near drowning. At least you are warm, and not overly so, and welcome, as you shall remain."

"I appreciate the inclusion."

They grinned and Erik made enquiry after several different subjects altogether. "How is our newest diversion with the railroad and your arrangement with Mercier coming off?"

"The rails are unmatched by anything past. By the time I return, there should be word to send, and Mercier?" He sniffed and brought up a rolled fist to subdue the wash of mock tedium. "In a word, dreadfully boring," he whispered to Erik's faint chuckle.

"That would be two."

"Alas, even the word requires dressing. But, it puts my mind at ease to compare you then and now, the lighthearted banter, participation and interaction... just think of all the lives you are influencing."

"Please, don't."

"I apologize." The Persian firmly rescinded his conclusions and went quiet, though his eyes leapt from the otherwise poised reserve.

"And Mercier himself?"

"Well, I can certainly tolerate him to a higher extent while out from under the Opera. He is amiable, to be sure, and definitely finds being the center of attention to his liking, but he is more reserved in this atmosphere, though well enough favored."

"I find we are of similar mind. He took my marriage to Christine in stride."

"Is there any reason why he should not have?" he asked, staring.

"Daroga, he is suspicious by nature and is the last connection we have to, he-who-is-eternally-silenced." The hair on Erik's neck bristled. "You know I do not enjoy the sensation of that glare; it is the same one I felt while inside the theatre."

"Ah, you have pinpointed a specific location for my efforts then?" he asked, pausing at the irony of his next comment. "Perhaps it is the spirit of our ghost in a state of unrest."

"Your humor eludes and unnerves me."

"I am sorry to hear that," the Persian teased. "Actually, there remains a steady demonstration of normal activities, the usual superstition, the touching of the horseshoe and such, nothing out of the ordinary or interesting to report. That alone is enough to haunt—"

"You really ought to find another occupation to sink your teeth into, as the taunting of your current ruse has become tiresome," Erik countered.

"Oh, quit, both of you!" Christine intervened on that note and grabbed Erik by the waist. "You sound like two young boys with nothing better to do on a snowy day than to pick a fight! Now, come join us, we are pulling everyone together."

The women had moved into the room, bringing with them their lively sense of the holidays, in addition to an assortment of sweets and tea, of which Meg, Cerise, and her daughter-in-law, Valery, were setting out.

Without warning, the whir of conversation came to a halt with an unbelievably loud crash, followed by a vile chain of expletives spewing forth to a draught of irritation. "... No! I can't believe it! Blast and damn! Bloody hell man—"

"Richard!" Erik's voice thundered. "Such abuse of women and guests in my home will not be tolerated! You. . ." he caught himself before he was reduced to the bitterness of something he would be unable to recant and ended with a less toxic form of reproach. "I ought to cut your tongue loose from your throat!"

Meg's countenance flashed a full palette of color, comparable to the variegated language of her husband. With all eyes riveted to the "what next" of the scene surrounding Richard, no one dared move. Mercier was gingerly retrieving a few pawns from the floor in front of the hearth, his composure entirely disjointed, he being the clumsy oaf responsible for the ruckus. Mercier had inadvertently caught the toe of his shoe on the small table where Richard and Chanler were going rounds at a game of chess, upending the board and its contents, as well as Richard's recent turn of fortune, while on his way to seize upon some after dinner refreshment.

Mme Giry and Chanler locked eyes, obviously having the same, in chorus sensation, they looked in opposite directions; first, to uphold their approbation of the management shown toward the impropriety, for it was an abominable *faux pas*, and second, to avoid wounding the already feeling Richard, who sat mortified, as any spoiled child captive to its folly amidst mayhem.

"Forgive me, Erik. . . Sir, I," he blundered and flushed. "I meant no disrespect, though my language betrays me to the contrary, I was absorbed."

Not more than a second was allowed to elapse and laughter suddenly roared from Chanler, followed by Mme Giry's gleeful burst, which lightened the thick cloud of tension looming to dampen what was left of a wonderful stay. Chanler glanced at Erik, shrugged and leaned over toward a dejected Richard, slapping the young man on the arm.

"Couldn't help it boy, your face," he breathed raggedly, "was classic!"

Mercier breathed easier. Seeing the attention was channeled accordingly, he rose, letting the gathered pieces in his possession spill quietly back onto the board, then, with his composure thus reclaimed, he set a course away from the scene.

Displeased, Erik shook his head, patted the Persian on the shoulder and traipsed behind Christine, his need to be close, increasing. "May I help?"

"Certainly." She finished pouring and handed over a cup of tea. "You take this, kiss me and go relax. You have worked hard in more ways than one. Thank you," she whispered, "for everything."

Her eyes spoke sympathetically to his tired ones; only she comprehended to what length he endured this many people around him, his one salvation being able to close off their end of the house from the main section, for privacy. It was he, he felt and she agreed, who had made the greatest sacrifice, conceding to the idea of having a home filled with guests so soon after completion. 'After all,' she had quoted his own words, 'is it not one of the greater reasons for the expansion to the estate, after personal requirements?' And now, with the weather turned foul as it had, she truly had the maximum benefit, albeit at the price of his fluctuating discomfort.

Erik circulated about the room; there was no denying the commanding energy infused from the graceful ease and civility of his presence, despite his more reclusive tendencies. So much ability in a public arena, yet to put up with the shortcomings and undisciplined actions of others had rarely been met without comment. Christine lauded his display of fortitude and dignity in the face of all he may be feeling. At present, he smiled at the insecure glances from Richard, for he seemed to be the only one who felt on the cusp for some type of residual condemnation, and guilty for appearing to be so.

The evening calmed and with it came conversation as mainstay, a background of music from Mme Valery, with momentary interludes of applause being the only factor rousing the smaller groups—the former opponents now heavily engaged in a rematch—to commonality.

Making a point of delving into the young man's interests, Erik stood with M. Nicolas Minot near the foot of the stairs, remarking on the abilities of the younger Minot's father and upon his wife's talent, though not in that order. Being a younger version of his father, the dark hair wagging as Nicolas Minot claimed ignorance in all mediums related to the arts, although, however inept in knowledge, he quickly made up for in appreciation, and mentioned it quite often to the blushing gratitude of those amply blessed. His real preference lay in science and research, with an affinity for the betterment of people in general. Erik was impressed with the man and would have probed more into the particulars had his eye and focus not been pried away by the odd, clandestine actions and *tête-à-tête*[11] of Mercier and Mme Giry.

"Are you positive you wish the subject broached here, Edouard?" Mme Giry asked quietly.

"Yes. This week alone has been a pertinent reminder. Seeing her at your Meg's wedding put it into my mind, then to be practically given a private audience, and repeatedly too, I am in no doubt as to what I should like her to consider. It makes me ill to think a gift like that is being unutilized and underappreciated, hidden, if you will. I find I have enjoyed listening to her more than any other diva."

"I agree," Richard said, overhearing. "Ha! Check!" he stated to Chanler.

"Keep your voice down." Mme Giry glared at them.

"I have the upper hand for a moment and you want me to be quiet. I applaud your wish to impose humility, but you know me, Mother Giry."

"Evaded successfully," Chanler replied, referring to the game.

"Blast, Chanler. But I think you are correct in your observations, Edouard."

"Good, at least I have the approbation of *someone*. . . and," Mercier mumbled excitedly, suddenly including those who would support and not put him off. "Gautier has the audacity to keep her to himself this far from Paris. He plays beautifully, but he is an architect, not an opera connoisseur and perhaps has no idea!"

Erik could not help but see the obvious; Richard's glances his way, Mme Giry's disagreeableness and Mercier's animation, and so excused himself from his present company.

"No idea?" Mme Giry snapped. He was, perhaps, the only man in years who had had superb taste and understood what the quality should be. "In your exuberance you may have spoken a bit too loudly, both of you, and now we shall have the privilege of knowing first hand."

Chanler played his last move. "Checkmate," he announced, and vacated the area; passing Erik in the interim, he went to enlist the aid of his wife for fixing up the hunger growling away, much to Richard's disgust, and those who were left became awkwardly silent as their host joined them.

"Edouard." The men exchanged nods. "I thought there might be something amiss, I caught mention of my name."

Richard sighed when Mercier fumbled over his own words, which was anything aside from normal, but Mme Giry stepped up with encouragement in the form of a question to fashionably advocate.

"Perhaps you would like an opportunity to seed your idea?"

"Idea?" Erik's tone heightened.

"Yes, I. . . I am sure your wife has told you something of her success on stage, ephemeral though it was, and since you most likely have not had the privilege to attend those performances. . ." Mercier's confidence had all but resurfaced. "Humph, what am I saying? Of course, it was implausible because she was involved with that, that Vicomte, you and she were not yet acquainted." Mme Giry looked at Erik and saw perfect control with a hint of amusement in his eyes, and as Mercier waved a hand, their sight crossed and returned to the speaker. "That is neither here nor there, what is critical is whether it would be agreeable to you."

"Agreeable, to me?" *Oh, that the other managers would have been so complaisant.* Erik savored the consideration. "I am aware of her past, and fortunate that I hear her talent often. My misfortune, as you are quite right to point out, was that I did not have the pleasure of enjoying Christine's accomplishments from the theatre, as I would have liked."

"So, you approve?"

"We shall discuss the matter if it is a desire of hers, but you must pose the question to her, personally," Erik explained.

"I shall do just that." Mercier grinned at Erik and stood abruptly, causing Erik clarity as to how the table came to its earlier upheaval and Richard, to scramble to keep the chess board from a repeat dive. Mme Giry gasped, light shame coloring her cheeks at the presumption and brash action, yet all seemed to be accepted in stride by Erik.

With a few clanging taps to his empty teacup, Mercier called everyone to attention. "Ahem, if I may?" The room quieted. "As I have been given leave by our gracious host, I should like to make a formal proposition. Now, I am sure we must all concur that the melodious voice of our hostess has been a treat and blessing on the senses, must we not?" A bit of applause and murmured accolades were expressed by all, taking Christine by surprise in her modesty. "Shh, good, good. Then you shall be my allies when I make the request of Madame Christine to favor us once again from the stage of the Paris Opera."

Richard gave a hearty "Brava," and the Persian's falcon eye dared a hasty glance in Erik's direction, as if to ask whether or not there was coercion to be confessed. He received a negation for his distrust that only he could hear. Meg flew to Christine's side in excitement and told her without hesitation that she should take up the offer.

"Well?" Chanler prodded.

"Oh, for heaven's sake, leave the woman alone!" Cerise warned. "Let the thought digest!"

Piercing the confusion with ease was Erik's calm tone in her mind, giving her the security she sought. "We shall decide later."

That was all she needed. "Monsieur Mercier."

"Call me Edouard," he insisted.

"Edouard. If you will permit me, I should like some time to think on your proposal. I have not performed in nearly two years—"

"That is all I ask." He nodded genially.

The delight in which the balance of the evening was captured came through the relation of all things opera. Mercier led out, having found fresh ears to bend. Those whose employment revolved around the entertainment portrayed descriptions and general life, but the most enthralling portions were the thematic narratives of mysterious intrigue shared singly and jointly, much of which was unknowingly leveled toward Erik.

Erik watched the fire, as it became a soothing narcotic paired with Christine's touch to lull his senses, and while thus encamped at the end of the sofa, he listened to the subsequent dialogue. The perspectives were exceptional, some fairly laughable, knowing he should have flinched more often save the aspect that could not be denied: *He* was the mortar holding that unique edifice together on both a figurative and literal basis, and would most assuredly remain an integral legend for years to come.

When the chimes sounded, they all rose to make an end to the familiarity of the retiring year and to welcome the new. Erik put forth a concerted effort, restraining any hint that his mind and body had preempted interest to already bid them depart, until he and Christine had seen the last of their guests off to bed with a sincere "good night." Having done his duty, he turned and took the stairs in haste, leaving Christine to discover the determined man draped face down across the width of their bed, exhausted.

"Tired?"

"Most thoroughly."

"Quite a busy fellow during your days as a bachelor," she commented, while closing their door.

Erik rolled over with his finger to his lips. "Walls have ears, my dear. Please, no more talk, all I want is to nestle in my wife's arms and sleep. Come," he said, patting the covers. She sighed, crawled up next to him, and sat cross-legged.

"Uh oh," he mumbled.

She peered down at him. "Your meaning, Monsieur?"

"It means you are unsettled." His hand touched her back and began rubbing to ease the tension. "Edouard's proposal, perhaps?"

"Not really. I was hoping for your undivided attention."

"I'm listening."

Christine stared at him without interference of word, which stirred his concern and any wish to slip unhindered into peaceful oblivion. His eyes soon fixed on her and her behavior caused him to rise up on his elbow.

"I am listening, tell me," came the silky tone she was unable to dismiss.

"I should have said something before now but put it off with all the preparations. In a way, I'm glad of it because Edouard's prevailing expectations, in comparison with the simplicity we have cultivated, has me even more resolute. I do not have any wish to be in front of an audience, at least for now; I don't want to sing opera on stage."

Erik took her hand and kissed it. "If you feel this strongly about it, there is no need for us to discuss the issue further."

"You're not upset?"

"No, I am not upset."

"Disappointed?"

He shrugged. "I love you and am enchanted with your voice—among other things—but if there are to be only one set of ears to hear you, they must be mine, of that I am firm." His eyes narrowed at the mix of emotion he read in her countenance. "Is there more?"

"Yes." She smiled softly. "There was one particularly noteworthy item I wished to share tonight. However, after the discomfort I felt from the officious exuberance, I thought to keep it to myself and share it with you in private. May I?"

"Please."

Christine reached into one of her dress pockets and produced a small, white box tied up with a burgundy ribbon, and placed the gift into his stewardship. Interest made an attempt at discerning the contents, but only succeeded in securing an upright posture; Curiosity had the advantage of giving the enigmatic cube a few shakes, to no avail; it was too light and made nary a sound. Finally, Logic took hold and loosed the bow from its reign atop the unknown treasure then dislodged the lid. Erik's gaze was transfixed, as if a portal to some future wonder had opened. His shoulders heaved once and a lone tear escaped from the corner of his eye.

"Christine? You. . ." he could not complete the sentence until she rescued him from doubt with her gentleness. The masque came off and their foreheads touched. "You are sure, quite sure?" He looked inside the box again.

"I am."

"And you will take great care, allowing me to pamper and spoil you, no arguments?"

"No arguments, from either of us," she whispered tenderly.

"They're so tiny." His voice was low and husky as he extracted the newborn sized, white satin shoes from their nest of wine. "Such a keeper of secrets are you, I never suspected, what with the completion of the construction, the furnishings, and decorating. . . your energy. . ." Erik caressed her cheek, amazed. Gathering her, he laid his hand to a measurable bulge and sighed.

For a third time, Erik threw his hope to the wind and prayed from somewhere deep within his heart, that the promise of a fragile new life would soar.

Chapter Thirty-Six

And soar it did! In a magnificent flight through the cadence of a fresh spring it flew, as this prospect replaced the tragedy of the last with a rhythmic flow of green; nature's symphonic reintroduction to the world.

Being completely convinced and immensely disappointed that she would never have enough snippets of rest together in one night—or day—to compose sleep, Christine stretched from her place on the lounge, pillows wedged in strategic locations for as much comfort as was humanly possible, and unattainable at this late stage of her confinement. Already the weeks had multiplied to that of the second in mid-May; the sun ever faithful on its climb this day, chased any remote chance of slumber under the covers, of which she had none to prolong those fleeting moments.

"Ugh! So unfair, absolutely unfair of you!" Her arm tumbled across her face in defense against the light. "Becoming active the instant I am not; it is a conspiracy! No sooner does your father adapt to a more reliable pattern of wakefulness than you take up his shed, nocturnal habits." She moaned and nearly leapt upright to rub her left side.

"Madame?"

"Yes, Liana?" Christine rotated while donning her dressing gown and faced the eager expression awaiting an order from beneath its honeyed net of curls. The young girl of seventeen stood in the doorway leading from the breakfast-parlor.

"Forgive me. I heard your voice. Monsieur said I was to attend you upon waking."

"Monsieur is too explicit." Christine softened at the shy retreat. "I am glad for the company and extra set of hands these past weeks as my time nears. And, if for no other reason, it gives the eagle and hawk a break from their vigils."

Liana stifled a giggle and blushed.

"Go ahead, Liana, do not be afraid to laugh at something which is perfectly deserving. The descriptions fit them both, do they not?"

"They do, Madame. The red in Madame Minot's hair is—" she stopped, her wide grin suddenly turned upside down. "Do you have pain?"

Christine knew she was only acting as instructed, but all too often the questions and concern hovering about every minute movement were exceeding the limits of cumbersome. "I am fine, if sore and cranky are on par for the resulting antics of *this one*."

"I am excited for you." Liana's smile returned. "It will be soon, I am sure, perhaps sooner than we think, no?"

This was news to Christine and her forehead wrinkled in dubious response. "Predictions! Ah, the supernatural, hmm?"

"No, Madame. I have worked with Madame Minot for nearly a year, and though I am by no means as experienced as she, I do observe. She said that all women are easily agitated, tend to ache more, and have a feeling of urgency as the process comes to an end."

"I guess," Christine gave a swift sigh in preparation to mount the first step, "I fill each of those to overflowing." They both laughed at Christine's honesty. "Well, I think *we* shall make ready for the day and take a stroll out to watch the eagle work with the horses this morning. Thank you, Liana."

"Madame." Liana gave a light curtsy. "Enjoy."

HALF PAST EIGHT found Christine stepping out onto the narrow garden walk behind the house. She roamed about the new inmates of the estate and gained measurable pleasure from the hedges, lawn, and flowers midst their experienced surroundings. What with the early rains, all had taken well to ground and were now showing signs of establishment. Touching the large stone nearest her, her brow lowered in brief objection to some thought then rose calmly. There was a kind pat before she turned to admire their home. Construction had changed a good deal of the layout; the kitchen expanded to accommodate the increased need, and a formal dining hall was added beyond what had been and what now became the breakfast-parlor, for less formal or daily use; the guest wing, in conjunction with the original section, formed the angular shape of a hook, which housed a more formal drawing room, servants quarters, and bedchambers aplenty.

Drawing up her skirts to cross the dewy grass, Christine intersected the path down to the stables. Erik could see from his position astride one of his new mares that his day was about to brighten, as a rich glow emerged in the near distance. Dismounting, he leaned into the railing and drifted, enrapt by the memories of the past four months, in contrast with the current view. She was more beautiful to him than ever, and sighing, he changed his plans and went to address the head of his stables.

Handing the reigns to Rossi, Erik asked if he would mind putting the bay through her paces without him. Rossi grinned, having already seen the oncoming distraction; he grasped the implications and moved to continue where Erik had left off.

Erik gave a gentle pat to the mare's rump and strode toward Christine, who was now waiting patiently on the far side of the arena.

"Don't tell me I missed the session; you know how I love to watch you ride."

"No," he answered, shaking his head while scaling the fence, landing with a deft jump next to her. "Change of plans."

"Oh." Her lip swelled in disappointment.

"Good morning," he greeted warmly as he reached out to embrace her, and to rub the swollen belly pressed close, "to you both. How did you sleep?" The question brought an immediate reaction of a tear trailing the skin of her cheek. "You detest my persistence." No response. "And you are a little depressed, too, I think."

Christine shook her head then hesitated, nodding once. "I feel like a specimen being critiqued under glass, there is an enquiry about everything. I cannot sleep nor control my emotions, and I feel selfish with no one to dote on but myself."

Erik closed his eyes to block out the flash of recall from his past. "I understand. . ." was all he needed to say for a full round of tears to gush.

"And I say things without thinking, I'm sorry. I'm a wreck, Erik, and so unprepared."

"Are you scared?" he enquired timidly, and then grimaced at the ease in which doubt performed. Good, his old nemesis here at last to have a go at the circumstance too far developed. He braced against the unwanted answer and fear, the same anxiety of finding that familiar childhood nightmare residing in the face of his own unborn child. He was certain she had seen, she always did. Christine guided his hand and thoughts to the movement of the unsettled spirit between them then kissed him tenderly.

"No, not for that, never for that, Erik."

He was grateful she knew of his concerns. "Then, today is for us. We need to be together without the cares of others interfering. Where would you like to lose yourself?"

Christine's features creased, heavy in consideration of her options.

Observing the fine determination, Erik pressed his thumb along each line in an attempt to eliminate the hardened indecision and lighten the mood, but it was only when she came upon a conclusion that her face softened.

"I should favor losing myself miles away from here in a secluded location, in your arms, having arrived by secreted means with enough nourishment for a day of leisure."

Erik held her, and as his fingers twined into her hair his words caressed her ear. "Talking of everything and nothing. . ."

The day promised to be unseasonably warm, for a cloudless sky could not provide respite to a sun-lavished earth stretched among the forested lots of shade. It was for just such a reason that Erik and Christine meandered along the stream under the leafy bower, listening to birds singing about in their lofty canopy to the lazy pace of the travelers on horseback. Time was not the dictator of limits now, but distance, and when such criteria met with the desired surroundings, all ceased to exist beyond.

Erik slipped quickly from Cesar to bear Christine gently to the ground, the genuine directive to "go sit" given while he set the stage for their engagement of privacy. There was a dreadful look of uselessness that paled her complexion; one short lived when pitted against the remembrance of pampering. The vow, too, had been most willingly and faithfully kept, whereupon she expressed he took a bit too much pleasure bestowing in abundance. Erik laughed, turned her in the opposite direction, and gave her rear a tender slap to send her away. This gesture would not do either. Instead of eliciting the kindness in which it had been delivered, it brought a fistful of grief; a woman throwing her hands up in exclamation, storming off through the trees, mumbling something about how she was only fit for attention mete out through a slap to the hindquarters. Erik took exception to the comment, conceding in part that spending long hours with horses may have influenced the action, but the action itself was not derogatory, merely a playful show of affection. He suggested, by way of observation, that the cause of offense might well be a sassy attitude in need of an adjustment, then he discarded the discourse with a shrug and snapped flat the blanket draped in his hands.

An angry hornet could not have returned more speedily, barring the awkwardness of stomach and terrain; Christine slowed to a stop within inches of him, his eyes shut and body recoiled in anticipation of her. Erik had seen the irritation, was assured of a tongue-lashing and prepared for such, though it never came.

"Forgive me." Her submissive tone lost not one moment in rousing him from the conditioned reaction. "You expected me as though I were a headache descending upon you. I apologize for my insufferable behavior, it must be awful to live with."

"I was far worse."

"That is no excuse for me."

"Christine, I love you despite your emotional flares, though I am disposed upon occasion to bear the brunt of them. You can be sure that I'll not desert you in your present state, as it is known to be temporary."

She smirked at the quip and her hand brushed along the turned up sleeve to his well-forged upper arm, then to the surface of his masque. "May I?"

"There is no need to ask, Christine, I trust you."

"Just because we are familiar with each other, does not mean I cease to extend politeness, I obviously need the practice," she explained, lifting the shield from his already-perspiring features. "I love this face, Erik."

The remark was so casual and simple, yet it struck him in so profound a way as to constrict his throat.

"What?"

"You. . . are sincere. When I asked if you were scared, your reply was honest. You really do love me." Erik expressed this as new revelation, and dabbed at his face and eyes. Christine spirited affection until his lips could no longer stand the deprivation; a tiny thrust being the only deterrent, he detoured to kiss the site requiring instant consideration. "Seems that someone would prefer additional space, hmm? One more and I shall let Maman go, promise."

Christine adored the inclusion Erik purposely afforded their child; she sighed and drew away, rubbing *his* stomach. Guiding Cesar from the trees she turned a seductive glance back over her shoulder. "We chosen equines shall be nearby until our master wishes otherwise."

Erik smiled.

Shadows marked the passage of time as the two fugitives whiled away their hours in the pursuit of existing; short walks and discoveries in nature became prolific, the admiration of iridescent wings on an insect, a fawn tucked motionless in thick grass, skipping rocks, mud sculptures, and the entwining of some dainty, pearl white and yellow flowers into a chain. They cherished every sweet morsel of *now* occupying their minds and hearts, eager to satisfy and overflow.

"What are your thoughts of, this very moment?" Erik asked.

Finding her position increasingly uncomfortable, Christine took the opportunity to move into the invitation of Erik's shoulder and a lower back rub, proffering him an opportunity to restate his enquiry. "I mean, dismissing the present, physical consistencies, what are your thoughts?"

They had since taken to skyward sights. "That clouds are more than they appear to be. . . and yours?"

"That my life is more glorious than ever," he chuckled. "Neither subject could be any less contextually complex." The current rate at which Erik methodically laid his hands coaxed her into relaxing far more than she had anticipated. He sensed she had no intention of succumbing to the temptation her body yearned for; she resisted, but it was the tranquil lure of his voice that did her in.

"You are. . . so. . . not playing fair. . . singing. . ."

"Fair does not apply, rest."

No more to be heard or said, Christine curled up beside him with her legs cradling the baby, fast asleep, while Erik sang to her heart. Then he lay there content to listen in the quiet as only he could, venturing a goodly distance in mind to deliberate on the word, "if."

My world hinges, circles infinitely around the implications of such an insignificant letter combination. Irony is stacked, interlocking its fortification within the links welded to prevent what my hands embrace. Humanity dictates that someone without conscience should never experience beyond Fate's prescribed boundaries and that goodness would be a waste, yet, I finally feel to have been given an opportunity specific to me. The challenges have stretched my comprehension to extremes, my faith—what there is—has been tested repeatedly, and a light burns inside, a light I am sure I was born with. He cast his eyes upward. *I shall be proven by the stewardship entrusted to me. She is my treasure; they both are.*

Erik traced lightly over a hardened spot near Christine's ribs, marveling, then giving it a tender massage he watched how it slid under his touch to protrude farther down, his kind persistence following the small bulge until it disappeared altogether. This had become his most cherished aspect of Christine's confinement: to feel with her. He knew she tired of his stroking and pressing, her comments of having "frayed nerves" and an acute case of "attentivitis" were telltale signs of the fascination he had with the developmental process, his connection, and the fact that this child was theirs. Erik knew Christine to be correct; he would love no matter the outcome, and his capacity to do so had indeed reached out to encompass another.

Even breaths had floated across his chest for a substantial duration, denoting some form of relief, though it was never enough to chase sleep in order that one might catch up. Christine's body flinched and a groan stirred her peaceful solace, her hand rising to push just below her ribs. Again, groaning from pain, irritation or a combination of the two, Erik could not tell; in retrospect it was but the precursor to a set of arms shooting out above her head.

"Aïe!" The harsh peal ejaculated twice more.

When the spasm subsided she lay extended over the top of Erik, her back arched in vain to escape the knobby shard jabbing unmercifully.

Erik chuckled. "If someone happened by at this very moment, they would mistake us for an established collection of mortally wounded bodies."

"That is so morbid!" Christine said, slapping his arm in distaste. "Though," she grunted at the exertion to stand, "my insides feel ravaged in this ongoing battle."

Laughing because she continued to hold her arms aloft, Erik immediately closed in behind her. "Lock your elbows about my neck."

"How will this help?"

"I'm not quite sure, it just seemed a natural place for them to be," he confessed. "Besides, you have yet to kiss me."

"Oh, please! An affectionate mercenary! I have been awake all of five minutes and preoccupied for the whole of it."

Extrication was unsuccessful, a useless effort, now that Erik had embraced her. "Christine." His voice blended into the sweetness of skin at her ear.

"Yes."

"Do you know exactly how much I love you?"

"I was not aware we could measure emotions in precise amounts." Her statement was tinged with play then she turned and noticed the weight of expression, changing her mood level in return. "This much?" He received a kiss to his right cheek.

"More," he sighed, and there came a kiss to his left. Shaking his head, Erik gently embraced and soundly quantified a portion for her.

They lingered in relation to the dissipating heat and decent of the sun, finding at length their leisure to have been given an ample dose of attention and justifiably administered, they made to reverse their journey. Cesar's gait mimicked the easy sway of an evening breeze kicked up through the branches and meadow grass. No one moved bent on haste, least of all the fine steed as he came to an unsolicited halt. Unpredictable as ever! Was there no end to the cheeky antics of this animal?

"You know, for the stubborn streak that runs as deep as you are broad, I would think it to my advantage if I were to purchase an ass!" Erik ranted while positioning to dismount, but a small hand, clasped tightly to his wrist, detoured his intent.

"I think you. . ." there was a tangible pause as Christine drew in a sharp gasp of air. "Ugh! You ought to give him some credit, he stopped moments before. . ."

Her face wrinkled under the burden of such sudden, intense pain, and she was so unprepared that the shortness of breath and surprise seized upon any ability to relax, making this ambush tensely unbearable. The birthing process had indeed become an imminent eventuality, leaving Erik as dumbstruck as Cesar was intuitive, words failing him.

When Christine's grip lessened, which seemed to be key in function for horse and master, Erik found voice. "Steady, Cesar, as you were." His hands encircled the distended womb, taut as it was; it then gradually softened beneath his touch. "Breathe deeply." Feeling her lungs expand, he released a breath of his own.

"I would suppose an early debut, Papa."

"Yes, it would appear that way. We shall await the next few to see if they are at regular intervals, then—"

Christine grabbed at his wrist again.

"Another? So soon?"

"No, no," she replied apologetically to the wave of unease sent through him. "I had the most disagreeable thoughts. If Cerise happens to be at the estate when we arrive, she will be displeased about the horseback riding for one, blame the onset of labor on the excursion and possibly you, and you know how she is about her profession; she will not want you to *clutter the natural flow*, as she calls it."

Erik clicked his tongue, moving Cesar on his way. "What are your desires, Christine?"

She pulled one of his arms around her and the baby. "For you to be with me every step of the way."

"Then it is settled; nothing shall keep me from your side. I would have insisted despite Cerise's mandates. If she causes trouble for me, I shall make it my responsibility to take matters into my own, capable hands."

"Sounds unfeeling and obstinate."

"If the glove fits."

"Erik."

"Perhaps we shall say nothing, remain covert. You know I am a non-conformist, my dear." He moved her hair to nestle his lips against her neck. Cesar stopped and Erik kissed Christine's cheek while she held onto him in her anticipation.

As expected, they came home to an irate Cerise pacing in and around the garden, and rode directly to the side entrance—formerly the front—bypassing an immediate confrontation altogether until Erik had Christine safely atop the porch.

"Look." His chin and finger referenced Cerise. "I could swear that every time I am in the vicinity, her hair ignites and becomes a deeper shade. I'll hold her down while you pitch a bucket of water at her; the steam generated should be plenty to heat a whole tub of water."

"All right, enough debasing," she laughed, flashing him that undaunted smile.

"Or possibly, devise some Mideastern form. . ."

Christine laid a finger to squelch the unethical flow of thought. "You cannot torture the poor woman simply for being concerned."

"I assure you, it would not be simple," the sardonic tone tagged phrase and eye. "Adding Adèle to the mix. . ." His brow shot up. "Ha! I could have done with them both, and resume a peaceable life!"

"Erik, for pity sake, would you quit?"

"Pity? Fine, I shall. . ." he paused as Cerise was coming into range of their conversation, "go play with my horses and be in shortly." Then he heard Cerise grumble something inaudible as he descended the porch stairs to remount Cesar.

"Forgive me, I was unable to make that out."

Cerise glared at him. "I said, how could you? And on horseback too! At first I thought I was mistaken, but then I remembered—"

"Excuse me." Erik interrupted calmly. "It would be best if you were to end right there, Madame. Suppose for a moment that you see things from my perspective, hmm? I took my wife out for the day, as a diversion from the boredom and unending scrutiny. I have her best interest at heart, as I do claim some level of intelligence from being an ignorant member of the opposite sex. I am not a brash youth without direction, and I would never do anything to endanger Christine nor the welfare of my unborn child. Though, the latter may be in effect, experiencing that mode of transport bringing him or her into this world. You should give me *some* credit, Cerise."

Erik bowed curtly, winked at Christine and rode off, leaving the formerly disgruntled and recently chastened Cerise, quietly pondering.

A LONG, WEARISOME night begat the customary event of dawn; though little heed was pronounced, it came faithfully as precursor to that which consumed all else about the Gautier estate.

"When I tell you, give me all you've got, Christine. . . good. . . yes. . . all right, push!" Dr. Dubois ordered.

Leaning back hard into Erik's chest she squeezed his hands, forcing the blood to recede from his thumbs.

"Wonderful!" the doctor exclaimed.

If looks could rend a man in two. . . *Fatality of nuance*, Erik thought. . . he would have done incalculable damage with the glare Christine imposed. Dr. Dubois was without clue in the matter and unaware that torture was increasingly probable. His lips twitched. The change of heart would have been a charming taunt had the circumstances come less strained. But no, he was exhausted and she, sweet dear! He could only imagine how Christine felt to see the cheerful energy, a freshened physician, arrived at their door prior to sunup. Her progression decided the man instantly that remaining was in the best interest of his patients.

"Push!"

She sneered. "Push? I'll give you push!" But she was too tired to expend more strength or breath necessary than empty threats as Erik let her temporarily recline before the next pain.

"Again, push!"

Up she went with Erik bracing against her efforts.

"Marvelous!"

"For whom?" she finally shouted at the decline of her torment. Everyone smiled silently. Christine looked to Erik, eyes pleading. "I don't want to do this anymore."

The pressure wound tightly for another bout and he whispered against her damp forehead, "I'm here, we shall see this to the end, together. Push. . ."

Within moments a robust wail pierced the room and all was forgotten. "Madame," the doctor addressed her first, most deservedly, "Monsieur, you have a son."

Erik thought his heart would burst with such news and it was delivered in such a way that all seemed a normal everyday occurrence. He glanced at the physician and Cerise. What had he expected? Shock, disbelief, horror and pity all came to mind, but no response from either matched those debilitating reactions. Cerise whisked the screeching rebel away to be cared for.

"Wait! Are we not allowed to see him?" Erik entreated after her.

"This," she began in a firm, albeit quiet voice, "is where I draw the line. I will not permit the presentation of child to mother to occur until properly attended!" Erik's eyes focused on the deft navigation and her tone softened. "If you would care to assist me, you are welcome."

The substance of the moment was intrigue and trepidation while he sat, unmoving in a stupor of silence, and however exhausted Christine was, it was she who gave the gentle pat to rouse and engage his mind. He studied her features; weary and serene, hair drenched, skin glistening, but it was her smile, that radiant smile which encouraged the most. She winked.

"If you do not move yourself quick," Cerise cautioned, "I shall..." Startled by the stealth in which Erik materialized at her side, the threat was abandoned in favor of instructing the eager pupil now attentively watching; all animosity dissolved between them as each of her instructions were executed to the letter. Erik maintained a close watch over both mother and child, and when Christine was at last settled, comfortable, and all things medical dispensed with, he laid their slumbering bundle within the embrace most dear to him. A dense reprieve was soon awarded the new mother and she drifted off, eyes barely parted, hearing subtly attuned to her heart's calming rhythm. Voices overlapped and forms hovered about her stillness in thought. *He has a child, a son; another long-awaited miracle who will love him.*

The clock chimes announced the evening hours to Erik's hunched form. Odd... that so many rotations had gone unrecognized before then. He'd seen to the departure of both physician and nurse, extended his gratitude to them in unison with their congratulations, his confidence secure on behalf of his wife; that her condition was as any other young woman post-childbirth: healthy, with the prospect of being quickly recovered if allowed to indulge upon self and her infant son. There were no complications to be anticipated in consideration of the past, their son being similarly diagnosed, with the adjunct comment of having a set of lungs to rival those of any long-winded politician. Erik took great relief in knowing the risk to be low, lightly amused at the remark, then turned his focus to the faint cooing and fascination holding his attention since. He shifted his body forward to the edge of his chair.

"Christine, my darling. Christine?" Her smile told him she heard the warm, familiar texture and welcomed the call, along with the smacking noises of a ravenous appetite in the arms of his father. "Christine, he is not to be pacified much longer by someone who cannot satisfy his hunger."

Her eyes fluttered open and she gingerly propped herself up among the pillows to receive her son and husband. "Hello, my dearest gift, fresh from heaven."

Erik carefully seated himself at Christine's generous invitation, to observe the natural course of bonding, something devoid in his life, he was most assured.

Christine handled the infant expertly, held him close, conversing in low, coaxing tones. How he wondered upon the nature of his wife. To her it seemed natural: to love what had, hours before, caused horrendous pain. His son's foot hung limply from the blanket; he could not resist the softness and ran his finger along its center, up under the base of the perfectly configured toes, which curled.

"What are your thoughts of, this very moment?" Christine asked, having seen the wonder and awe narrowing Erik's eyes for a short time.

He smiled at his own words. "I am thinking of how different my life would have been had I a loving mother." He glanced up and stared sincerely into Christine's eyes. "And how grateful I am now, to know that our son will be raised with the love I cherish, the love I am no longer deprived of."

"Oh, Erik," she sighed. There were no outward displays of emotion, only the sorrowful healing of regret underscoring the lack of involvement. "Here, lay him stomach down, his head in the crook of your arm, there, rub his back."

Within minutes, the desired response emanated in a sound expulsion of air, and Erik laughed. "Of the traits there are for one to master, I do not recall belching as a skill *I* endeavored to polish, but he seems to have a knack."

Christine adjusted her position, motioning for Erik to join her on the bed. "Now, tell me your feelings."

Laying their son between them, Erik sat cross-legged and began to unswathe the babe. "My emotions are exhausted. I ached for your suffering while I watched you writhe, laboring to bring forth life while secretly dreading the moment Dr. Dubois and Cerise would gasp in horror. It never happened and I had to rummage for some sort of composure in haste before I was preempted. . ." he stopped briefly to look at Christine then went on. "Cerise apologized to me and said I had every right to speak to her as I did yesterday."

"Erik, she has a good heart and respect for you."

"I guess."

"Go on."

Erik considered his time earlier with the babe. "I am overjoyed to have created life with you. He is perfect. . . ten fingers, ten toes, velvety soft skin and dark wisps of hair, and a beautiful face. His face. . ." Erik spoke reverently, and raking his hand through his own hair, he removed his masque. "Perhaps I would have looked like. . . how am I to know which features he shares with me?" Hearing himself and seeing Christine's mouth bend upward, he held his finger aloft. "Don't answer that."

"I shall leave you to figure it out in good time then."

A light convulsion breached the scene; Erik's chest rose and fell in rapid succession and the back of his hand stifled a sob. The overwhelming feeling eventually forced him to succumb and his emotion sprang, sprinkling the infant unhindered. "He's beautiful," Erik whispered, gazing into Christine's moistening eyes. "Hold me?" he asked.

Opening her arms to him, Erik quickly gathered their tiny boy and sought that sweet embrace, encircling one another, and kissing her forehead, she heard him repeat distantly, "thank you, Christine, thank you."

THEY SAY THE most cherished of blessings come in the simplest forms: a kiss, the touch of a hand, kind words; none of which can be purchased, but given only from our souls and hearts to that of another. It seems our littlest angel, Chèver Matieu Gautier (born May 12, 1880) possessed a wealth of these tender reminders for sharing, and does so on a daily basis with his father.

The name, Chèver, came about in a most curious way. Having been shut up in our room for several days, already bored past what was reasonable, Erik thought a change of scenery would do me good, but said nothing more until the next day. I heard the baby crying for his morning feeding and wondered why Erik had yet to seek me out, when he appeared at the door to petition, at the bidding of his son, for my presence downstairs that very instant. Collecting me in his arms he brought me to the corner windows and nestled me among the soft cushions and pillows there arranged, tucked a light blanket about me and retrieved Chèver from Liana's hold. While feeding, Erik reclined opposite in the other window, there physically, but seeming mentally removed as he watched us from his slightly obscured position behind a lace panel. The peaceful view and bright spring flowers displayed on the desk where he had placed tea, my journal, and a few books, gave me pause in gratitude for his thoughtfulness. He breathed lightly and enquired if I had considered a name for our son and if not, he should like to impart his thoughts on the weighty honor. I confessed the subject to be untouched, which pleased him all the more. He mentioned how a name should reflect particularly who a person is, as it would remain with them their whole life, explaining his desire for a specific meaning, to draw a correlation between my name and an enduring word. He said, "our son is a constant reminder of you in my life and his name should reflect it as such," so there it is: C̲hristine + For̲e̲v̲e̲r̲. My tears were his confirmation.

Erik is quite industrious too! The time I spent downstairs gave him uninterrupted occasions necessary to do a bit of carving, this I later discovered on my own; the angel at the foot of our bed was bequeathed a gentle face, I know it belongs to Chèver—Erik's model, for what might have been. Perhaps we shall talk about it one day when he is ready, but in our relationship thus far, it is an unspoken understanding between us.

And, needless to say, he has been in perpetual motion, exposing Chèver to music, instrumental as well as vocal, and to the written word, reading out loud and through sweet discourse on innumerable topics. "There is no better opportunity than the present," he said, and I believe him. According to the way Erik explains his childhood learning, we should have a precocious miniature following closely in his father's shadow. I only hope that that portion of me contained therein will allow for him to experience being a child.

Oh! An old acquaintance visited unexpectedly: Jealousy! I had to admit being in its grips at the end of a fortnight. Erik, leaving me only the hours to feed as my time to interact with our son, dominated most of his waking hours, but this situation was not at all acceptable, however enthralling he found our newest novelty. We discussed the imbalance, at which time I warmly explained that I was more than a wet nurse, and amusing as it is now, even that description stretched the amount of contact between us, for he attended to all else so I might rest.

I write of my selfishness that gratitude may expiate the reconciliation I wish to perceive Erik's actions through; I am truly fortunate and cannot repeat the realization often enough.

Chapter Thirty-Seven

Erik had only been gone three days from his wife and ten-week-old son, and yet the deprivation of their presence had him tangibly quaking as they neared home, his senses heightening in the knowledge that he would soon embrace them both. Rossi eyed his employer keenly, watched him clench each fist then extend the fingers to release the tension, and though he was a private individual, one of purpose, Rossi was privileged to observe the solid devotion this man possessed for his family: M. Gautier never wavered, was steadfast, and was dependably kind and fair. No one could have a better situation in which to work than he; unlike the drama played out amongst the relations of other families, one could not be assured of complete autonomy, hence the state of his previous employment. Here, there was trust and nary a cross word uttered, stern perhaps, but never uncaring, and with the purchase of another stallion, there would come additional hands for him to train as stable master, under the prospering *Gautier Winds*.

"Taylor, you have something to say?" He had clearly shaken Rossi.

"If I may."

"Certainly." Erik glanced at the lanky, densely muscled young man and smiled. The melancholy behind the wide set, dark grey eyes, wore a constant look of determination etched across its brow.

"Taking an extra day to ride, instead of arriving by train and carriage to look over the newest prospect for stud, had me wondering at first."

"About what, my sanity?" Erik queried, as Rossi chuckled at the willing self-implication.

"Well, n–no, the tactics," he confessed. "I guess I judged this to be somewhat dramatic, based on prior transactions."

"There is always more than one way to address a situation. With this gentleman, steeped in superstition, religious beliefs and tradition as he is, I knew it would be more to our benefit if we did not arrive as though conducting business, and so we followed what is customary for a desert Bedouin, especially where the horses were concerned. We came with two of our mares so he could see the quality and be assured that our concern was of maintaining Arabian purity."

He applied the information and his eyes widened. "Impressive, Monsieur."

"It is research and experience, nothing more."

Rossi's smooth complexion furrowed beneath his short mop of flat brown hair; his lips drawn straight in skepticism to the forthright response, he was recalled to the anxious behavior and ventured a remark. "After surveying our surroundings, Monsieur, I should think these prized mounts find the countryside somewhat tedious, no?"

Erik smirked. Rossi was always looking to challenge. "Shall we give them their heads?"

"Ready when you are, Monsieur."

Lacing his fingers through Arzu's mane, Erik pulled up short, the horses sensing competition; ears alert and nostrils flaring, their well-suited forms coiled for action. One nod from each rider and they were off at Rossi's "go!" Seconds separated them as Erik held back, releasing the power to its fullest potential with a belated, "Now! Drink the wind, my sweet, and out-run Neziah!"

The horses skimmed the surface of the ground without effort, the natural movement of their flowing reach evident at each collection and extension made, their sure-footed confidence compelling the resilient legs toward their final destination of home. Miles sped by in a blur with Erik and Rossi upon the supple contractions of muscle bearing all through this test of endurance, the training exhibited in compact elegance.

Arriving on winged hooves, Rossi was left scratching his head. "How do you manage? I mean, no matter which one you ride they always perform at greater their capacity."

"It is possible she felt a sense of urgency and was obliging, is it not? I did wish it most emphatically."

"No," Rossi disagreed shyly and dismounted. "Too simple. There is more to it; they pour out heart and soul to please."

Erik grinned as only he could, his eyes reveling in some deep secret that led Rossi to believe there *was* more; the mere presence of the man brought a desire from the core of one's natural existence, to do more, to become more beneath the tools of touch and voice. He even found *himself* mesmerized by the innate, authoritative control.

"If you would?" Erik requested amiably, handing the reins of Arzu to Rossi. He acquiesced in quiet, observing Erik turn to leave. The questions, which came to mind during all hours when alone, seemed to vanish in importance like breath to air, in wondering how a man, such as Erik, could stride through a stable in refined harmony.

Leaping up the stairs, to bound uncaring through the side doors, had been the plan, right up until Erik laid his hand to the latch itself, but somehow that very contact drained all exuberance, replacing his zest with a docile silence and click of the door. The grandiose announcement diminished into a straightforward entrance, the door closing without prodding on his part, to a most unexpected welcome in both directions. Christine had less than a syllable executed, when she at once discovered herself embraced and mouth occupied; the shock subsiding altogether as recognition took up the position relinquished by the former.

They parted, Erik's lips twitching at the corner. "I missed you."

"So I gathered, and I you." She flushed.

"The Minots and Liana?"

"Knowing you would be home, they left, which gives us the whole of an evening."

Taking both her hands, Erik raised them to brush each with a kiss, then stared into her eyes and the delicate details of her face. "When I took my leave, my heart became laden; I wandered blind in a desert among the shifting sands of remorse, through the mundane I trod, unable to retrace my steps at the end of each day, and compelled to move forward from where I stood until it was finally time to return." He touched the diamond resting upon her chest and fingered the small gem. "You are my guiding star."

Sincerely touched, Christine glanced to Erik's hand. "And what of Chèver?" she wondered aloud, troubled by the fact he had yet to mention his son.

Drawing her face upward, he brought his lips to her forehead with such certainty. "Do you recall the first time I kissed you?"

"On my forehead?"

"Yes," he replied, softly encircling her at the waist. "I suppose you were never aware of the difficulty that posed for me, how painfully inhibited I felt at that moment. Then you reciprocated the gesture. I thought I would die from the sheer ecstasy of your flesh innocently connecting with mine, the sweetness of that long awaited touch, and I would have. I would have passed from this life, satisfied." He drew in deeply and slowly exhaled. "Chèver is every bit as important to me, but you chose me, Christine. I would not have him if it were not for you. You shall always take precedence, you are my first reason for living and first in my life."

She leaned into his affection, cherishing his strength.

The evening meal done, Erik lay in a perfectly agreeable situation with his son peacefully asleep across his chest. Just then, even though he felt as such, he knew he was obviously not the only man who had ever taken pride at the sight of their slumbering child. Having given an account of his travels he remained, doing nothing but contentedly soaking in the languid sensation, caring little for change. In some ways a pang of frustration was often the accompanying emotion, when less time weighted in greater increments than more; and though the enriching quality inevitably made up for the quantity, he was fast learning to savor a vast array of treasures, including sleep.

"How is it that he can sleep so soundly in the oddest places, and in the strangest positions, without waking?" Erik juggled the barrage of thoughts and soothed Chèver's small, squirming frame back into stillness. Lifting up the flaccid arm with two fingers, he dropped it carefully back to his side, amazed once more by the level of relaxation attained.

Christine turned from her writing to look at her men splayed in comfort on the bed. "Someone with your abilities should be able to deduce that," she offered vaguely.

"Indulge me. I bartered for the better part of the day yesterday and prefer my mind to remain in a state of *off* for the night, please?"

She scowled at his lame entreaty. "What is this you are developing?"

Erik smiled triumphant. "A lazy streak. I thought I might engage the characteristic for valuation purposes." The gleam in his eye did nothing to further his cause.

"Well, for the record, it is very unbecoming."

"Such intolerance will never do and shall come back to haunt at a later, inopportune moment." His acerbic tone agitated her into closing her journal, the cover meeting its contents with an unnecessary slap. "Your behavior is very unbecoming as well."

Christine knew he was teasing and went to join him. "If you

desired me at your side all you had to do was ask."

"I know."

"Here, place your arms above your head," she instructed. Erik was wary to assent. "Tell me what your feelings are when in this position."

"I feel vulnerable, submissive."

"Correct, but do you feel that way with me?"

His expression arched. "Depends." *My sides are usually attacked mercilessly.*

"Erik."

"All right. No, because I trust you," he replied, intrigued.

"And whose voice captivates?"

"Mine."

"Chèver has no reason not to trust us; it is experience that teaches distrust. I have seen the way he looks at you, with and without your masque. He knows goodness, which is how you have bonded with him. He shall judge love based on tender interactions, security, and acceptance. At this point, I think the masque causes him to be unsure and a little confused because your emotions are somewhat skewed." Erik's brow knit. "He sees as I do, Papa. He is not contaminated with the world's opinion of fear; you do not represent that in any form. I know you have noticed."

Stunned by her observation he was suddenly filled with unanswered concerns, and addressing her gaze head on, he sought counsel. "Your perspective on the matter?"

"Do what is comfortable, do the same with Chèver, as with me. There is no need to alter the course and over time we can adjust accordingly. You have my support, however you choose to manage."

He cupped his hand behind Christine's neck and gently dislodged his son from the rhythmic throne. "Maman's turn," he told him, as Chèver scrunched his body and face disdainfully. "Oh, Christine," he whispered. "What did I do to merit such love?"

"You did not contend my choice when I followed my heart, the second time," she replied.

Erik righted himself, drawing her face to him, filling her thoughts with his voice. "Love me forever."

Chapter Thirty-Eight

Summer's long hours began to recede and with it, innocent youth of color to that of seasoned experience. Nature receives but a fraction of time to mature and to stretch the instincts when humanity has the abundant advantage in repetition, gleaning what may be pertinent at that moment, and to bypass all else until the mind is ready to comprehend a deeper meaning the next time around.

Erik filled his lungs slowly. It was too early for some, and not late enough for others, as he lay in bed thinking on the innate abilities of one so young, listening to the persistence generated in blatant disregard, or so it was considered as such for one venerable party. Christine stirred in his arms.

"I am astonished at the accuracy one has when predicting the wakefulness of a small soul, just by being immersed in other worthy activities. No matter how often I reassure Chèver that his presence is not required, he seems to have an opinion to the contrary." Erik received a shove, pushing him away from the center of the bed.

"Yes. . ." Christine mumbled, "and you adore every minute. In fact, I might assume, at the ripe old age of five months, that he has begun exhibiting his father's dominant trait of wishing to spend every spare moment fully engaged in learning, therefore, he sleeps only when absolutely necessary." She slid out from under the sheets to rescue Chèver from the pangs of hunger before Erik had any thought to prolong her stay in his scramble.

The cool flooring felt exceptional on such warm nights, appreciation of both time and contrast, priceless, with the extra set of hands that always accompanied her. Erik was completely involved, desirous to know of things missed, giving and experiencing in multiples of two, to comprehend and reinforce.

Christine paused at the railing, pulling the bulk of her hair to one side in a loose braid, which gave Erik a clean shot at her neck as he passed on his way to the nursery. Turning, she gracefully descended the stairs to sit in the welcoming respite of the temperatures below. Erik soon appeared with a bundle of wide-eyed curiosity snuggled into his arms and placed Chèver into his mother's protection, then settled in next to Christine on the sofa.

The tranquility of moonlight penetrated through all availing means, driving visibility up to full as the shadowed visage of daylight displayed a ghostly equinox across the room; a few choice rays lit the threesome, reverencing their forms. Nuzzling Christine's cheek, Erik vied for the attentions of her free hand and successfully gained a silent caress when she pressed his face near. Chèver stopped feeding to watch the brief kindness, which instantly brought his parents' gaze to his. He smiled and giggled lightly, and soon stared transfixed, studying the aspects of both while reflecting from one to the other. Reaching, Chèver's chubby hand patted his mother's chin then stretched toward his father, the little fingers coaxing the air as they entreated contact. Erik lowered his head to meet the request with a kiss to the palm; Chèver smiled momentarily, his countenance lifting to wonder in exploration of his father's face. Erik closed his eyes to the tender, imitating softness of that unpretentious touch and drew away; Chèver gave a content sigh and resumed feeding.

Exhaling slowly, Erik's eyes pinched tightly to savor the pure gesture, where he remained unmoved until a kiss from Christine roused him. "A sweet, sweet moment," he whispered.

Half an hour elapsed quickly, but did little to convince Chèver that it was too early to start the day, much to his mother's disapprobation on the issue. Erik had quit the room minutes before to dress and ready himself and descended to confiscate the rebel not long afterward. "I shall take him into the study with me. Come Chèver."

Christine passed him over, guilt tingeing her conscience for the good nature of her husband. With an occasional exception, Erik's habits had mellowed; he was less adamant in regard to keeping a full schedule. He surmised the trend linked to exertion, variance in activity, sunlight, and emotional expansion, summing it all up as having plenty to make his life complete, often to overflowing.

She kept an eye on them until they disappeared behind the study doors and acknowledged quietly, "sessions with Papa, man-to-man."

Erik lit the lantern at one corner of his desk, glided around to his chair and reclined with feet propped up, setting Chèver in his lap. He was sure, from Christine's reluctant offering, that she felt it an imposition to have time to herself, especially after bringing the matter of obsession to his attention.

"She deserves moments to write, ponder, sleep, and take care of herself. What Maman has yet to understand, Chèver, is what she gives me when the two of us are together. You see, my father never had anything to do with me, never saw me, but I will not hide from you, I cannot." He was who he was. "Ah. . . the glories of being male! . . . To ignore and disown for the sake of convenience or embarrassment! But, I do marvel at the ability of the female sex, all species inclusive, at the pain endured to bear life. The gift of procreation should never be taken lightly, as it is by far the greatest gift of self, to come so close to death in providing life. . ." He sighed sorrowfully. "You are such a delight that I can hardly fathom the loathing caused by my birth. I often contemplate on the advances that will surely come in the field of medicine. . . what if your grand-mère had a way to foresee my condition, would she have thought it more humane. . ." Another sentence incomplete, Erik pulled Chèver to his chest for a hug. "Sadly, we know the answer to that query, do we not? Now, what do you say to more optimistic ventures? That stallion being shipped to us from the Crabbet stud farm in England is quite impressive. He has a proud head, elegant crest arch and high tail carriage, a stunning creature. Then, we await the official certification which shall make our stables a prosperous contender for breeding. . . I am sure we passed."

Erik noticed the shrouded barrier preventing light above a foggy grey and shook his head in disappointment. "Underground, deep underground, the seasons and temperature were all rather consistent, and a completely unnecessary triviality to bother oneself about." Upon occasion, the fact that he had become subject to the suffocating changes in weather became irksome and he noted there would be no training unless the clouds broke. Dullness of routine chores and paperwork, he did not much care for; music, he could revisit.

"But the people," his fist rested against his chin in thought, "were quite diverse. They still are, even those with whom I invest in the elite upper class. They are so full of superficial qualities, especially when money and status become the ticket into their ring. . . if one had the intelligence to manipulate everything to an advantage—in addition to enjoying the political games—a gentleman could rise to unimaginable heights; whereas, I can tolerate only a limited exposure to that negligible palaver. I suppose, there may be a few who deserve respect, and who carry on a meaningful exchange, but the rest. . . I truly comprehend Maman's experiences. Sometimes I wonder what they would do if forced to listen to their own drivel."

Chèver sneezed, balling up in response to the convulsion.

"Exactly! A worthy ending to the petty dialogue." Chèver giggled, receiving a kiss under his chin for such a spontaneous reaction. Erik gained his full height and strode directly to the outer door at the sound of an ominous clap of thunder, which had at last removed all conjecture from the day's course of rain.

"So active, and the attention you give. . . those eyes, they are crystal blue like mine," Erik observed. "You seem to solemnly consider

Beyond the Masque

my words and the music I play; perhaps your development will come rapidly, as did mine, to devour your surroundings. I am prepared little one, for whatever comes. There is much to learn, and much to impart."

RAINDROPS SPATTERED AGAINST the windows, sparingly at first then at regular intervals, eventually creating rivulets for the passage of cleansing beads to follow.

Christine rolled over, extending her writing hand to shake the stiffness from the bent wrist and looked out at the ceiling of yellow-grey, a dreadful combination of color, yet needful, nonetheless. She had been recounting a few memories while attempting to wrest a decision one way or the other on the topic of performing.

Strange how foreign the feeling of performing is to me, and how my perception of what or whom has been altered in level of importance. Erik and I took a hiatus when Chèver was born, but we have since resumed practicing. And though I have discovered sentimental connections to some music, an affinity that becomes so strong I wish not to be estranged to begin anew, I feel drawn to the challenge. I should think late winter on to spring would suit, as Chèver will be nearly a year in age. I am swayed by guilt over what I should do with the gift Erik has cultivated. Not surprisingly, it is the same guilt that rouses such an intense need for expression, and one that is contrary to the innate nurturing which is vividly impressed upon my soul. I know Erik shall encourage gently and it is I who fights with excuses. Oh, why can I not rejoice in the fact that the profession importunes me to honor Erik's genius by sharing what he clearly inspires? I wish to be led, have another make the choice, but then, then I would be where I was before, and that would not signify intelligence at all.

Christine slammed the nettled unrest between the pages of thought and lay there on the rug, content to do nothing.

"Ah... look, Chèver, it is Maman. She moved just enough so we might distinguish her beauty from that of the Persian carpet upon which she lies."

Erik drew in next to her, flying Chèver amidst loud, echoing chortles from behind the presently gnawed-on fists, to gracefully land atop Christine's stomach. She pulled her knees up to support Chèver and had her ears addressed in a most sensual fashion.

"I love you, Mademoiselle Daaé." His tone affected her with such an intense blush; there was something unsaid wound through those five words making his gaze burn.

"Do you not tire of me?" she quizzed.

"I no more tire of you than you do of me." His voice returned her challenge.

Christine's head fell lightly to the side, her silky lips having made their way under his chin to rub against the smooth, freshly shaved throat.

"Our answer…" she began, "is what you feel at this moment." Speechless, Erik could only nod as his lips found hers. "We are in no danger, at present."

"No danger exists. . . at all," he added.

Erik tipped blissfully over to his back that he might watch Christine hoist Chèver above her head in play. Their reactions to one another were so natural. Christine would bring him close, kiss his neck then lift him up again. Delight beamed from the soft face, his nose wrinkling as Christine's mouth began opening for a repeat attack to his sweet neck. Suddenly, and concurrently, his little legs kicked out in spasmodic mutiny with a hic from Chèver's rounded belly, which expelled a sizeable volume of spit-up, precisely filling Christine's mouth and bathing her face in the curdled liquid. She burst upright, coughing and gagging, spewing forth herself in an effort to breathe. Stunned, Erik quickly grabbed Chèver and tossed her a cloth, observing the frantic gestures of disgust and disbelief until Christine was able to place a resounding whine to the experience.

A rumbling snort churned in Erik's throat just before he exploded into uncontrollable laughter.

"Well, I'm happy to. . ." she sputtered briefly, wiping her face and evacuating her mouth again. "I'm happy to have provided you with your dose of amusement for the day!" she pouted, feeling about as rank as she smelled, but noticed that Erik had yet to cease laughing. He was hugging Chèver to his chest in near convulsions, wheezing and rolling on the floor as tears streamed freely down both cheeks. She had to admit, if one were to take in the whole scene, it would come off rather hilarious, but the most blessed moment received was the opportunity to see her husband lose all composure in pure enjoyment.

Chapter Thirty-Nine

The shrill wind brought February soon enough, as well as Christine to the knee of perfection, so to speak. She had made the decision to begin seriously training once again, and with Erik's support and approbation they focused in earnest. But today, for some unknown reason, there seemed to be an acute frustration brewing; it hung menacingly above their session, dampening even the most remote sense of enthusiasm. His irritation rapped pensively against the instrument before him, his eyes flit from the score to Christine and back in turn. She stood there; hands perched at the rim of the piano, torso aligned properly. What directive would she receive next? Smiling at the severity of temper only inflamed him and one knew not to tempt too far.

"Once more, Christine," he exhaled passionately. "Begin at measure forty-two, and this time, control your breath and carry through to the end of the phrase!" His instruction came sharp, a trace more pointed than the intent, causing him to wince mentally and glance apprehensively to the music and then to Christine; there was something amiss, something that had been left unaddressed, not. . . *damn*. The word swept across his thoughts. "How do you expect," he questioned, "to attain suspension when you are strangling your airway?" Rising, Erik took hold of Christine and attempted to position her body for ideal sound flow by pressing her abdomen in and up, though, much to his dismay, he discovered she had been appropriately situated.

"I am close, but have yet to fully regain my shape. I gave you a son, remember?"

He patted her gently. Erik's voice rose in justification then dropped to concede as he cautiously resumed the bench. "Yes, well... yes."

Christine's eyes darted to their corners and then back straight ahead, her focus steadfast. "Measure forty-two, I am ready to proceed when you are."

The phrase held a level of sarcasm he could not understand. This was important, was it not? This is what *she* desired, she wished to sing, and here he was, willing to set aside a specific time to rehearse, then why? Why was the task to be mete out as a tedious waste? He glanced at her and she winked.

"Pa?" The light tap at his leg, accompanied by the small voice, drew him from the confusion and detached all concentration, agitating him to anger.

"Liana!" Erik called, "Liana!"

Christine jumped as the doors slid open. "Erik, hand Chèver to me."

In his haste he had forgotten to take up his masque and was now forced to stand with his back to the room, disengaged from the music entirely. Christine sent their son off to be entertained and closed the doors for privacy. She settled herself in Erik's place and watched the tense rooting of his figure while he stared outside, arms folded.

"I sense discord, a feckless disregard for a valued passion. Not to mention the lack of discipline, which seems to be plot ripe and precisely calculated to incur wrath." He allowed the theme to die in his stern recount.

"Glad to see you at least recognize the symptoms of the infection."

Her tone was delivered with such impudence that Erik turned on his heels, incredulous in every respect. "I should think a reasonable amount of time and distance from here adequate for cure."

Such a comment! If she aimed to confound beyond words, she had succeeded. Erik reeled, his legs weakened, and he reached for the window seat to buoy the unsteadiness. Raking through his hair slowly, his shoulders sank; he felt baited, like his emotions had been strung along, and now he was the hapless, cold-blooded vertebrae who had accepted the tantalizing lure, unaware of the hook bent on stripping him completely of oxygen.

Exhaling at the response her words evoked, Christine quickly stepped to him. "Why must you torture yourself with doubt and pessimism? I meant distance from *here* most specifically, not from *you*." His chest heaved, and grasping her, he laid his head cradled to her breast. "You have been severe of late, and far too serious for too long."

"My behavior has been quite wretched, if I understand you correctly."

"Unsavory, indeed, but not yet contemptible. I felt to test you, to see if you might accept some good-natured ridicule to help revive your senses, alas. . . you failed miserably, requiring urgent intervention," she whispered secretly.

"Blast." It was his own doing and fairly dealt.

"Think, Erik. Think of all the changes experienced in your life these three plus years. You have a wife, a son, an ever-expanding circle of friends and amiable acquaintances, many of whom find themselves gainfully employed here at the estate; and the Arabian stables, which have and shall prove quite profitable in many aspects, in addition to all you had prior."

"I see. My ears are burdened just listening," he admitted. "Your highlights have me disbursed as a wave across a cliff, returning to the swell below without hope of reaching a restful shore. And because of these changes and diversions, I have accrued their inescapable responsibilities, of which I had none but myself in the past." There was a brief moment of quiet and then he concluded. "The singing, it has since become one of these diversions, so much so that my actions profess it to be more of an imposed drudgery?"

"It has, yes."

"And, I failed your test, how thick." He stopped, disgusted with himself.

"You are not thick," she immediately professed, "nor thick headed."

He pulled back to look at her long and hard, and then asked, "Where would you like to go?"

"Beyond my own back door, and somewhere, *non françiase*."

He smiled. "I believe in all that stretches the capacity of an individual, seeing for the first time, the benefits a trial separation might bring to my mind. I shall refocus on the most critical element, our love."

"And you will forgive the test?"

"Absolutely not!" he proclaimed indignantly. "You think to mollify with your feminine wiles, and I daresay it has worked—occasionally—in the past, clever woman that you are," he breathed, taunting her with a disciplinary finger as she chimed in.

"I had an experienced instructor."

He sneered. "Well, yes. . . but you owe me time, and you owe it to your public to be well-rehearsed. Remember the patrons, the ones who strut about the grand foyer?" Erik made a swirling motion with his hand, ending with a stiff reference to the piano. "Posture appropriate to the desire of said instructor, if you please."

Blinking hastily at the haze erected by that ghostly voice and those mannerisms of the past, Christine backed up and took her place where Erik could monitor the instrument so beloved, a revelation parted; master and protégé, timidity in the face of ability, an angel awakened and the silent, trance-like state of obedience. No longer was she as she had once been—change had procured a steeped hold within her, a mind of her own and the will to guide destiny where she wished.

"Prior to commencing, I believe clarification to be in order." Erik's tolerance contracted and Christine hurried, surprised at the gravity so suddenly possessing his countenance. "Monsieur must understand that I 'owe' no one anything save he who truly appreciates. I sing for him alone." She swallowed to suppress the rising emotion, took one deep cleansing breath and reclaimed her composure. "Measure forty-two."

His hands plunged into the ivory, her voice climbed steadily, languidly vaulting at the peak of each phrase, and from one musical platform to the next she carried the sound to its end. Erik listened to her soar, watched her perpetually as his accompaniment became a linear expression to the delight he inspired beneath. Their tones died within seconds of the pedal's release, but a tear sustained its vantage until Erik brought Christine to sit beside him.

"Why?" he asked softly. "Why do you choose to perform, if it is only for me?"

"Because I wish my angel to share, to triumph with me. Each time I tread upon that stage, you reside in each note, echoing, filling the hearts and souls of those who could hear, if only they would listen. I sing for the man most important to me now because he has waited long enough for a spirit to ascend with his, for an escort of music home."

Their cheeks touched.

"Forgive my audacity? I treated you like the child I once thought you to be, when it is I who retreats into youthful comfort in your arms. I often live two lives simultaneously, trying to capture some small portion of affection missed when young while enjoying all manner of love as a man, husband and father, though here I shall not scruple to admit. . ." he gently took her hand in his, "I may never make up ground."

He felt the brush of Christine's lips repeatedly; their intrinsic motions fluid, and he inclined his head to partake of her sweet caresses.

An unexpected bang reverberated around the room, prefacing a wealth of glee and followed closely by a breathless Liana. "Mam'n! Pa!" exclaimed a little voice, pushing the door aside to locate his absent parents.

"I beg your pardon Madame, Mon—" She seemed perplexed. "He eluded my attempts before I could stop him."

Christine met the rushing imp, directing the attention away from the piano and Erik. "There is nothing to trouble yourself about, Liana, we were nearly finished."

"We, Madame?" Liana queried, seeing no one else.

"Monsieur Gautier just stepped from the room. I'll be in shortly to review next week's schedule."

"Yes, Madame Christine."

She squeezed Liana's shoulder lightly and winked before latching the door against prying fingers and turning, she instructed, "Chèver, go find Papa."

How Erik had managed to relocate in such a stealthy quiet dumbfounded her, though from the way her son was now positioned on all fours upon the floor, no one could possibly rebuff this game as having been played often. Chèver peered low and under, a puzzled look wrinkled his nose momentarily and he sat upright, contemplating his options. Pushing to stand, he stole carefully toward the piano bench, nothing. Next, he rounded to pass the large fronds on the fern and headed for the lounge, peeking slowly around its side.

"Pa!"

"Smart boy, come here you!"

Chèver squealed in delight as Erik threw him into the air, sandy blond hair sticking straight out, gravity returning him to the safety of his father's arms.

"Maman, come see what Chèver can do!" Erik cried excitedly.

She met them as Erik slid in front of the keyboard with Chèver on his lap. "Papa's turn," he directed, prior to a well-executed page of an aria. Once concluded he said, "Now, Chèver's turn."

Two tiny hands jutted out to the keys and Christine prepared likewise, eyes diminished and brows raised, to have her ears assaulted by uncontrolled pounding, but in lieu of the assumption, came a precise pattern repeated as taught. Erik's face glowed while he viewed each successive key depress, and then with finality, innocence went atop deftness to play a stacked duet.

Christine clapped in a glorious ovation, making the young cheeks rosy with pride. Erik kissed his son for a job well done and sent him off to pull out a few toys; husband joined wife, embracing her from behind.

"His development is astonishing, sharp, thoughtful, and he has the appropriate amount of his mother's patience," commented Erik.

"I am happy to have contributed proportionately," she said cleverly. Reaching back, Christine pressed his cheek to hers, and together they watched Chèver consider the workings of a top. The spiral handle disappeared into a diamond-shaped cavity which, if set correctly on its point, produced a spinning motion. Chèver slowly pushed the handle in evaluative repetition, then he gave it one forced shove downward and it twirled. Glancing up, his eyes met with the smiling approbation he must have sought after, for he retrieved the top and repeated the trick.

"Just like his father... a little magic, a bit of praise, and he scuttles back hoping to enthrall his audience again."

Erik chuckled at the comparison drawn and pondered on the traits that would emerge over time. He pulled Christine securely to his chest, wondering aloud at the charming attributes, and what fascinating creatures of learning children were, to which she dubiously rejoined in polite jest, making mention of this as coming from he, who-had-adamantly-objected-to-such.

Clearing his throat he stated, "I changed my mind. I am now under the opinion that children are a blessing to the relationship between husband and wife, a natural expression of love shared."

What more could be said to contend with Erik's simple observation, which led to an agreement of allowing all to unfold in due time.

LATER THAT NIGHT as Christine sat in evaluation of the morning hours, map before her, her fingers running the length of the European coastline, she thought on Erik's ease in professing himself to be under a different opinion. *Change*, both had come a great distance since their first days in the company of the other: change flowed constant. Their life was rich, challenging, and despite the gruff belligerence of habit, it was a relief to know one was not locked into a certain set of tracks, nor was one forced to bend mind and spirit if the course ahead was rutted unfavorably. The question now was why she felt the need to tempt Fate, even consider merging with the unknown stresses. Pride? To prove they could do more together? Strength of will would see them test their ability to circulate amongst the past—as they had succeeded thus far in a more exacting fashion—but here they would be aligning resemblances, placing her to sing once more upon the stage.

This opportunity did not come as an indefinite marker, but was deemed wise to accept, to acquire closure. Justification was a phenomenal ally to subdue the unrest, and the knot in her stomach loosened some.

Chapter Forty

The room carried a disparaging air—once adorned with life and critically purported to house only those highly sought after leading ladies—scantily furnished as it was, a bare frame of its former years; its commendation only recently bestowed in the past week by the return of Mademoiselle Daaé. Christine stared into the faceless item affixed before her. Its mimicry precise, the gilt-edged mirror had been left unchanged, but gone were the vanity table, sofa, bed, and bureau. All the articles previously lavished were allocated to those more permanently situated, leaving her with a writing desk, chair, and settee, which is exactly where she sat. Having been attended to by the dresser, the maid brought a few things to amend her toiletries, straightened and fidgeted about—what little there was to trifle with—and quit the room.

Alone and waiting for the timed warnings, her thoughts found voice. "I am here and yet miles away in Italy. . . *Venice, Rome, Sicily. . .* from one end to the other we roamed." She sighed, heart heavy. "I can blame no one but myself as I fight the inner turmoil and rending of allegiance to sing publicly. It was my decision." Her brows met with intense fury as her fist pounded the bench, the knot in her stomach growing tighter. "Ugh! Those infernal notes and cards!"

Agitated by varying means and inconsistency, someone had found a way to fluster her with their unsettling adulation, and she did not take kindly to the intrusion.

"If I were not a lady, I am quite sure I would not hesitate to cover the walls most vividly!" In conjunction with that threat, the mirror swung open to reveal a debonair figure come at last to her rescue. Erik's black cloak melted in elegance across the chair and Christine flung herself instantly into his arms.

"Ah, yes. A bit of red and orange would do wonders to wake the dull pallor from the cheeks of this room."

She gaped, pushing him away. "You were listening?"

"Gaping is also unladylike," he chided, touching her chin and catching her by the waist before she could escape. "And no, I was not listening. I *heard* you as I was coming from the back corridor. I am just surprised you thought no one *would* hear; your voice carries rather far. Besides, anger strains the—"

Christine warmed instantly, and grasping his lapels, she nipped one of his tutorial chastisements in the bud. "Hmm. . ." he growled, "I much prefer this type of greeting, your fire on my lips, not across the indifferent, unappreciative walls." Another kiss alighted. "All right, I'm listening," he assured when she began to walk about, fueled by her vexation to the benefit of his amusement. He particularly enjoyed the drama and since it was a private performance, he felt to be most rapt.

It was a site to behold, indeed. Her complexion became saturated by the second, the intense avowal of commitment matching each word emphasized. Erik was grateful not to be on the receiving end, which brought an overall sense of deference; though, he was less successful in covering his untoward betrayal of thought, and discovering all at once to be unexpectedly forced against his wife's solemn disapprobation, his countenance lowered to a more sincere display of civility. On impulse, he stood and flat out kissed her in defense of hearing every word.

Gesturing for her to resume her seat, she resisted. "I prefer to stand."

"So I see, please." Rendered speechless, Erik's sight never left hers as they watched the other indirectly, his persevering finger guiding her to her reflection before he took up the line of pacing from behind. "Your feelings are similar to those experienced several months ago, which evoke a conflict of internal frustration and cause you to doubt your decision, in addition to the irritating individual *or individuals* who receive pleasure from stealing our joy by imposing their selfishness in writ. You derived immense satisfaction midst our travels about Italy, and should prefer those moments to the Pandora's box we have set loose." Erik had reiterated a concise summary beneath her unfair accusations, her bend taking a turn toward the intricacies of the pink, green, and grey of the floral carpeting at her feet. "Christine, my dear, I am on your side and join in the aggravation. The Persian is quietly investigating. Look at me, please." His grave tone dropped. "I, too, have resentments. Being relegated to my passageways, to retired habits, is wearing. But if there is someone intent on making my wife out to be a target, I would prefer to feed information and not be dictated to."

Her head lolled, and he could see the apology form just before her skin flashed white. "Chèver!"

"He is with Meg and Richard at Adèle's, since she lives nearby. I wish to keep him as far from the Opera House as possible, and everyone associated."

"Even Adèle?"

"She knows too much; I could not risk adding to her vow of silence. She has kept our private lives as such and discusses nothing. At the very least we owe her preclusion."

A knock roused them to the present and Christine's chest heaved in a sigh of resigned defeat. "Forgive me, Erik."

Taking her by the hands, he led her to fill his embrace. "Forgiven.

And your rings, they are in our chamber?"

"Yes."

"Make me proud. Sing for me and I shall take care of the rest. If something comes of the notes," an odd distance greyed his normally piercing eyes, "this old assassin has a few tricks left up his sleeve yet."

"That would be *older*, Monsieur." She smiled and turned serious. "Take care?"

"Always." Then glancing to the mirror he stated, "Hmm, damn handsome, am I not?"

She nodded, their mouths greeted once again in safety then parted in trust as Christine strode to her place on stage and Erik seeped into the shadows, to observe those who would watch her.

The days and weeks scheduled for Christine to appear became a blur, ending in an exasperating conclusion with nary a tip as to whom their quarry was. Indeed, concern heightened each time a new batch of notes and cards materialized. Most were harmless, but every so often one would be singled out and recognized by the peculiar style, despite inconsistencies. The situation intrigued the Persian and had Erik strung out with scenarios too numerous to count; too much variance, and too little congruency were available to develop a profile.

"We are chasing a ghost, Erik. I compare, re-sort and verify everything new, and still I find nothing of consequence." The Persian removed his glasses, pinched the bridge of his nose, and sighed. "None arrive in a timely fashion, all are by different modes and are thus far untraceable. . ." The late nights had caused the lines around his already distinguished eyes to deepen as he pressed the heels of both hands to each in relief. He glanced knowingly at Erik, who was sitting opposite him; the limited verbal expression meant his mind was also viciously engaged. "It is all circumstantial."

Erik glared pointedly, finally covering his face in an attempt to shut out all distraction. After some time he lowered his hands, exposing the pained look in his eyes. "Daroga, there has to be something. I feel that same nefarious sense of patience."

"I apologize for my inept abilities, but it sounds as though you are trying to apply human traits to these notes or that they are somehow tainted with a personal imprint, which I might add, only you are blessed to perceive."

Erik slid the chair out away from the table, angst filling his lungs. "I have a wife and child to consider, Daroga. I cannot lose. I will... not lose." His tone darkened. "And, I will not ignore what has required years to develop. My heightened sensitivity kept me alive—though, there were times I wished it had not—it made me wary and I know full well that when I disregard this, I come up short. If it were only me, Daroga, only me, then I would accept those consequences, but I will not afford myself the flippant luxury." He whirled around to confront the Persian, the lamp's glow diffusing his anger into the cold, calculated demeanor hinting to resurface.

"Promise me that you will not kill this person, if they are discovered. Promise me—" The Persian had not finished before Erik's clenched fist struck the table, shaking its contents and unsettling the lamp.

"In defense! Self-defense or protection! *That* is what I promised! Do you even comprehend what it is like to end lives as I did? I can taste the feeling and it is as bile now; I loathe it, but if I am ill-equipped," his voice caught, "the result could be devastating. I understand the tedious patience, Daroga. This is comprised of extensive planning and is being executed in so precise a manner that I find myself pathetically jealous, scared, in awe, and hateful all simultaneously... and distraught because I, of all people, cannot figure it out!" The tirade ended quickly. "Forgive my outburst."

The Persian eyed the reflexive correction in Erik's behavior with acceptance. "Then, we shall remain vigilant for as long as we must."

In gratitude, Erik extended his hands to enclose a set of kind, dark ones within his own, and withdrew his presence for the night.

After a while, the hour late, there came a soft rap upon a château door out west of the city; all was quiet upon these grounds.

"Sir?" The butler's eyes widened only a smidge beyond his stiff air.

Is the man live? Erik wondered. And how, with a rod of indifference shoved the length of his spine, was one able to cope?

"May I say—?"

"No need, Joseph, no need." Richard patted the man's back. "I shall escort him in, do not bother yourself." Then turning, "Erik!" he boomed, "Come, come in, please."

Erik strode through into the foyer, scrutinizing the whole before commenting. "I am impressed." He turned around, cloak swirling, to address his host. "I thank you for being willing to accommodate our needs."

"Ah, for that I shall accept your thanks, but the house, all in the family I confess, and one amongst several, though I feel this more ideally suited to me. But that is neither here nor there, ay Erik? Come, Meg and Christine are just through here, and I daresay you are most eager to be with one and I the other."

"That I am."

As the gentlemen entered, the women glanced their direction and smiled, Christine rising to greet her husband. Erik took her hands, closed his eyes and kissed each most amiably, as one would do in the presence of others.

Richard coughed. "Pardon me, but as brash as I am, and I freely admit to resembling if not adhering to the essence of the accusation, I at least give my wife a proper hello when distance has been the means of separation."

Erik's lips pursed thin. "I appreciate being given leave to do so, however, I am old fashioned and still prefer privacy."

"Well, yes, um. . . then I shall escort my wife, who, being six months with child, needs her rest, and in doing so, shall provide said privacy."

Christine's gaze never left Erik until Meg and Richard wished them "good night" then her sight slipped to the shut door and back, puzzled at Erik's raised hand. He indicated she must stay herself a moment longer, the gesture melting to one finger as he looked back over his shoulder toward the slight gap between panels, a latch click lacked. They heard a muted slap, astonishment, and Richard's attempt to feign innocence and pain, then the crevice diminished with a light trip of the knob.

"Twenty-eight and all the boldness of an immature lad one-third his age. He is as bad, no, he is worse than most because of his insufferable curiosity and is thereby a nagging plague."

Removing his masque and cloak, Christine reached to ease the determination in his forehead while he began fumbling with the bothersome ascot and stud. "Chèver has missed you and your time together, not to mention your voice singing him to sleep."

"I shall not disappoint tomorrow; we leave for home late morning."

"My last performance is tomorrow night," she protested.

"Your final performance just became last night. I am sorry, it cannot be helped, and is the reason for me being detained longer than usual."

"Your tone of finality scares me."

"Come, sit with me and I shall explain." He invited her into his soothing embrace upon the sofa and commenced. "I spent the better part of the evening engaged in hypothesis and came up empty, but returned to your dressing room undefeated, hoping I might discover something missed, which I did. There was an envelope lying close to the threshold. Perhaps it was pushed from the hall, though I suspect it had been left on the table, having fallen to the floor later, for it was upside down on the lip of the carpet, more on than off. If the former were true, it would require the paper to be smooth in order to slide and it was not, which leads me to believe this person has the means to move about, entering and exiting at their leisure, thus explaining the varied modes of delivery."

"That could be any number of people," she said concerned.

"Yes, and what has been put into motion shall carry on. This slow progressive plan must be played out to the end if we are to rid ourselves of the parasite."

Erik could feel that the intensity of the information had unnerved Christine, she was trembling, but he knew it would not deter the strength possessed from the question next put to him. "And, do you have it with you?"

He produced the caustic note and together before the firelight, they read.

> *Mademoiselle Daaé,*
>
> *Such an ever-present delight to have one's senses filled with your talent, though until now it was truly a perplexing matter as to why certain performances were riddled with diversions, which never bodes well upon the stage. A child? Not at all expected, but not to worry. Distractions might be just as easily eliminated as they are acquired.*

Gaining her feet rather suddenly, as though trying to leave the note hanging in midair, the ominous paper dropped to the floor with her heart. Erik scrutinized the reaction, unsure of what emotion might yet surface, and called her name apologetically. "Christine."

She rotated cleanly around, her hands wrapping herself in an endeavor to warm a certain numbness one could not willfully erase. "This is madness, it reeks of extortion," she expressed tersely. "So,

I am to sing unhindered or all outside attentions shall be rendered... silent. He threatens Chèver!"

Feeling his arms encircle, he enquired tentatively, "Do you trust me?"

A tear rolled down her face to absorb into his sleeve. "Why? Why would someone wish to harm an innocent child?"

"I assume Meg brought Chèver in the carriage to retrieve you last night?"

"She did, he had been inconsolable. Oh, Erik, I could never blame her."

"I do not, in fact, her sweetness of heart caused the menace to betray himself, for the writing tied in two others. Perhaps it was enough of an irritant to force him from latent comfort. Add our peevish manner, and he shall be annoyed tomorrow when he finds we have extinguished the starlet from his night sky." He kissed her head. "You must understand how well-suited I am to this sort of mentality, excluding children. Were it I, I would not permit anything to thwart my plans. Often, a particular situation mandates the use of one like mind to catch another, however twisted."

"Erik."

"Hush. We leave in the morning, which is all you need worry about. Everything else shall follow accordingly. But, I must know, do you trust me?" Did she? The reluctance shown was quite to the contrary.

"Yes, implicitly. You have protected when others could not. You own my confidence, though it cannot dissuade my dread of the unknown."

His mind cleared, as did his lungs. "Respect for what we are unable to control is a healthy reaction and I would have it no other way."

"I believe in you as well, Erik."

Her perception, honesty, valiance, and resilience of spirit were critical factors to this madness—labeled by her as such—and his contribution became dependant upon that faith and hope, that he could minimize their exposure to danger. There would soon be time allotted for familiarity of domain, its people, both old and new, and their habits. In short, the preparation to do battle for his family and their safety, liberation for them, as well as those who found the Opera home, had commenced.

Having the plan set in motion, it was established the very next evening that "management should like to express their most sincere regrets for the lead being indisposed preceding her final performance." Audible disappointment filtered through the house at the unexpected, then composure rose with the curtain and a pair of ink-laden orbs narrowed in the dim light. *Unforeseen, insupportable, and unfortunate indeed, but she returned. . . she cannot resist and shall return once more. Patience, patience shall determine much and reap rewards long desired.*

Chapter Forty-One

Three seasons succeeded in such thrifty order that one blink of an eye might have seemed to encompass the whole of each, and as much as excitement protracts that which is desirable, the same is said for like circumstances of those opposite. Summer passed in splendour and gracious respite well deserved; the fall had Christine performing during a special two-day event, to which no peculiarities could be attached and thereafter the holidays were quietly enjoyed among friends unaffiliated with anything opera. The inevitable crept tranquilly as well, lacing vines of gnawing persistence throughout, lying in wait for the impending date in February they would soon venture upon.

Christine sat at the table in the intimately situated breakfast-parlor, head resting across her folded arms amidst several letters of correspondence. The end of next week would be crowned as the beginning or the final bow. Erik's will was known; bringing home the past would not be repeated, it must be abandoned no matter the consequences, no matter the effort. And here she was, too tired to fight or to care, and wishing for him to be home, away from the influences he blended with.

"Maman?"

"Here, Chèver."

An audible scruff-thump foretold of his passage down the stairs. His afternoon nap finished, he was now ready to tackle the world again but would first peek around the double doors to check on the status of one absentee father. "Papa?"

"Come here, my sweet boy," she encouraged, and the tousled head of spun silk, glistening under a lingering ray of sun, came bounding up into her lap. "I am sorry, Papa has yet to arrive."

Chèver became quiet, perhaps focused in thought, when a steady smile broke out across his face. Christine drew back and gazed into his eyes, tilting her head slightly to one side; he followed likewise, simulating the action. She kissed the ruddy cheeks, setting him atop the papers, and then poked his nose to elicit a giggle.

"You know, you are everything to your father."

"Want Papa home," he pouted innocently.

"Who is it desiring me home?" The highly favored voice floated unerring from the entryway, lighting Chèver's eyes quicker than a match to a gas lamp. He scrambled to the floor only to be lifted up by the arms of his father. Erik beamed.

"I cannot imagine a finer welcome!" he exclaimed, tossing Chèver into the air; the boy filled the house with a solo of chortles while being held aloft above his father's head with one hand. "You are a joy in my life, and I am terribly grateful you no longer have the propensity to spit."

With her chin perched comfortably over her clasped hands, Christine's eyes became distant, her thoughts dreamy. *Oh, God in heaven*, she prayed, *see to what level of felicity this man has been raised. The challenges, sorrows, and responsibilities are being managed, and in return, all hopes exceeded. His horizons expand daily. Please protect him, give us strength to confront our uncertainties in the coming weeks and to joy in our time together now. . . that he may experience life to its fullest.*

"Christine?" Erik moved quietly before her. "Maman is wandering, Chèver... Christine." A light touch to her cheek brought her sojourn to him, he bid her rise as Chèver patted Erik's masque.

"Off, Papa."

Erik looked cautiously about.

"It's all right, no one is here," she reassured.

He removed the world's ideal, preferring his family's acceptance instead. Chèver nestled in at his father's shoulder to watch with interest the caress of his mother's hands and how her lips softly feathered, and then how his father's touch drew their faces close.

"Kiss," Chèver stated, pleased with the outcome of contact.

"Yes, my son, a kiss. Now, if you will excuse me while I make up for lost time," that said, Chèver found himself hastily lowered to the floor, waiting against his parents' legs.

THE BUSTLE AND stir of the evening routine had a peaceful effect over Erik; he was currently observing his bay mare, Neziah, out frolicking in the lea, and smiled. From the looks of Rossi's gait and clipped bursts breaking the air, she would soon be haltered, groomed, and warm if he had his way or, which was often the case, all would be turned to an exercise in perseverance. A few moments longer lent the conclusion that Rossi was to be the recipient of exercise. "Cesar, and Neziah, poor man."

Erik glanced below into the gardens; the stillness of winter bringing his loitering thoughts seamlessly into review bade his heart pound, usurping the desire for calm with this fresh barrage of hornets. Each day seemed fraught with a new swarm to eradicate, and it was no different upon his arrival home today. The letters Christine poured over were just such a mixture. One had tidings of fretful happiness to relate, for Meg was a bundle of queries about the propensities of infancy and motherhood, but wonderfully exhausted with their son, Alec, who was presently at the mobile age of eight months. Next became an echo to the previous intelligence and precursor to the latter of the three letters, this being from Grandmamma Giry or Adèle, depending on the topic addressed, and the last was a response to the schedule limitations and explanation of circumstances sent to Mercier. *Perturbed would put it mildly*—profusely vexed was better suited—though, Mercier's feelings were loath to dictation regarding their request, thinking himself rightly justified because of the minute, two-day event performed in lieu of a full opera, as was earlier agreed upon. Security was offered and would later be declined to avoid undue attention, but the schedule and listing of accommodations must be adhered to, per Monsieur Gautier's, *his*, stringent demand.

"To run free, unbound, unburdened. . ." the words passed in a sigh from Erik's lips. "I appreciate and value life, and am placed in a position of preservation. What if all I do is not enough?" His head bowed slowly to his forearms, weighted in doubt. "The only things I have yet to accurately play out are the variables of choice." *Confound that Opera!* An open hand jarred the rail of the balcony in silent encore to the unspoken rebuke. *Why did I ever encourage her to go back? I am on its grand buffet one way or another, consumed in this feast of characters, from the stage, to every dark corner therein, every needful role filled; we have villains, victims, and potential heroes.*

Covering his face ended the whirlwind detour and sensing movement, he rounded sharply, scaring Christine half to death with his reflexes. They looked at one another in surprise. "Chèver. . ." she said, finally inhaling evenly, "is waiting for a story and wishes you to sing tonight."

Erik's eyes sought the flooring then lunged to pick up her shawl, draping it thoughtfully across her shoulders as he passed without sound into their room. Astonished, she breathed deeply and went inside, closing the door to the frigid air; as the incident would most likely become topic for later, she took herself into the study that she might reread and correspond to the less caustic letters in a more isolated location.

Quiet consumed the whole of the estate within a mere hour, the dwindling embers encouraging Christine's preparation to hazard the upstairs. She first checked Chèver's room, and finding it unoccupied she tried theirs, discovering both men fast asleep, the smallest, though both most beloved, pressed endearingly to the chest of the other. She trod softly and leaned in to gently release Chèver from Erik's grasp. Never having laid a finger to either, her motion, being interpreted as too close, had both wrists deftly ensnared. Again, the eyes of both went wide and Erik let go, offering up Chèver in dismay.

He heard the chamber door close after a time and then her voice.

"Are you ill?" she asked, seeing him leaning heavily before the mantelpiece.

Erik's hand cupped the base of his neck. "Perhaps," he whispered, pivoting to slump into the nearest chair.

Christine was at his side instantly, examining him, lips testing for the ravages of fever. "You're cool," she said, raising his sight to hers.

"I cannot restrain the urge. . ." he began, and seeing Christine shift as though to move away, he grabbed onto her skirts, afraid to touch her. "No! No more distance, please." The urgency in his tone concerned them immensely in equal portions. Erik required her comfort.

"Tell me," she nudged, when he gathered her with him.

"I love you, you and Chèver." There was suddenly no want for proof that he had yet to wrest control over some issue. His palms sweat, and the unease pressed heavily about his chest. "I have noticed the difficulty, it has worsened. . . I cannot separate my preparations in Paris with our life here. My senses are dangerously heightened, to the point that whatever I do not have contact with becomes a threat, and I react accordingly, hence the two incidents tonight. Forgive me, my reflexes betray what is anchored deep in my heart."

"Of course I—"

"Did I injure your wrists?" he asked abruptly, his mind seizing upon the dreaded thought.

"No, your grip was gentle, just sudden and distrustful. But what of Chèver?" Christine stroked his chest and Erik drew her even closer.

"What, that he may learn to fear his father? No, he must not! And because it is imperative that it must not be, I earnestly strive to master all that now resides within me, both the loving warmth and icy cunning. I feel an onslaught of evil, and despite what I have gleaned from my regular visits to the Opera House, I lack one element for that cohesiveness to take hold. I have no endless well of hatred to tap, I cannot even bring myself to think and feel emotionally in the same manner. The abilities are all sound, but my motivation has changed."

"And this gives rise to concern because our phantom's advantage was based on something that no longer exists?"

"Yes, I feel my anger based on concern, but have never functioned under such extremes without... The results are undefined and there too, is a deep seeded fear that I will succeed in resurrecting the incarnate of what I once was. How far does one tempt sobriety of character?" His agitation and pulse raced in conflict.

Drawing his attention away from the mesmerizing obsession of the flame, she pressed her lips to his forehead. "You will never forget."

Erik's head sunk languidly to the safety of her bosom and tender caresses, wishing that all troubles were this easily dispelled. "There is more, Christine, much more." He shivered lightly and held on to her, thinking she might flee.

"I'm listening."

Erik drifted. "It never occurred to me that the foyer on an upper floor of the Credit Lyonnais would be the place of such a fateful meeting. It was like most gatherings in the pre-investment milieu of an aristocratic frenzy..."

THE RUMOR OF A substantial profit scented the interests of those with deep pockets and had most lining the area in small groups, all waiting to be ushered into an adjacent conference room. And such gentlemen, who chanced upon an early arrival, were provided a complimentary bit of afternoon refreshment to accompany their acquaintance of one another, the terms under which the shares were to be secured, and to give common ground to those who would do business during the course of the day. Erik stood thusly, with his back to the room and opposite to the Persian, while heavily engaged in conversation with Basile Trudeau and Corbin Menard, both of whom were regarded as most amiable and, having met upon other occasions, found the degree of pleasure and perspective shared to be astonishingly similar—which is often the case when relating intelligence between those of like minds playing to the tune of good fortune, of course.

There was a short duration of time remaining prior to the initial welcoming pleasantries, when advisor and escort, Monsieur LaCroix, entered. An interesting cachet, how station and money profess a will all their own, the heir and principle legatee of an estate, just on his heels. Having the honor of representing his client within the various groups assembled, M. LaCroix made a point of whispering a few particulars about certain men and their known, savvy affairs before and after acquaintance. And, since this diversion of property and goods was outside the young man's area of expertise, it could only make for a lucrative heads-up.

Erik caught the furtive glances of the Persian during these few minutes, the light arch of a brow and eventual narrowing of the eyes, and wondered what could be so bothersome as to repeatedly detour the attention of his friend.

M. LaCroix squeezed the elbow of his young charge. "Come, the meeting starts in another moment or two and I wish you to cross paths with one more of these gentleman. He is somewhat eccentric, the issue having something to do with privacy," to which a flaring gesture was made, "but he is quite genial when one is on good terms with him."

As they approached, the young man glanced at the set of four, could see the tall, rather slim figured gentleman and commented, "I know him" in return.

"Do you now?" M. LaCroix half stated, half queried.

The greeting was abrupt but warm, as an exuberant smile creased the young man's face along with the jutting offer of a hand. "Daroga!"

The Persian smirked at the brash recognition forcing the circle to widen for two more. "Chagny, Raoul de Chagny," he responded in reserved civility.

M. Chagny had not yet turned to the others until his escort patted him on the left shoulder. "Pardon me, Monsieur, but I had intended to introduce you specifically to this other gentleman, on your right, Monsieur Gautier."

All thought, capability of speech, and for that matter, motion altogether, arrested completely as he glanced to the right. Erik's stature portrayed a most majestic, alluring air with one arm cast to his lower back; dressed in a long, split signature tailcoat, the raven black giving brilliant company to the burgundy accent draped about his neck, he bowed.

"Monsieur Chagny."

"Monsieur Gautier?"

Seconds passed in a room full of awkward silence. In a room whose din of investors were moving with the current flow, they were alone again; alone within that hellish chamber so desperately far beneath the depths of any reasonable level, under the Opera House. Erik was the first to surface with his wits intact.

"I believe, Monsieur LaCroix, that we are," he smirked, "well enough acquainted. But as you can see, time and distance have robbed us of our ability to elucidate properly."

M. LaCroix nodded in understanding, though slightly befuddled at the reaction of his charge; he was instantly willing to divest himself from the personal side of the obvious past encounter and attend to the interests of the present. "When you are ready."

"Yes, yes, Monsieur LaCroix, thank you," M. Chagny replied.

The Persian laid a friendly hand to Erik's shoulder and motioned in the direction of *the boy* just before departing with the other gentlemen in their company. "In light of the situation, hmm?"

"Thank you, Daroga."

Gesturing for M. Chagny to accompany him, Erik led the way to a less public location to converse. "Please, if you would be so kind as to sit down, before I am required to heft you from the floor," he spoke gently, amused at the wavering gait.

M. Chagny opened his mouth in resistance, thought better of it and obeyed this master of intonation. He shook his head, rubbed both eyes, his face, and combed the fingers of each hand through his hair, obviously trying to blink back the likelihood of such a confrontation.

"You may be assured, I am quite real," Erik remarked against the dubious ritual observed.

"You. . . are living. . . above?"

"Yes, and quite comfortably, thank you."

"And. . ." M. Chagny gazed at the ring proudly seated on Erik's left hand. "You are married?"

"Yes, nearly four years, and you?" Erik asked, taking notice as well.

"Oh, relatively recently, January of last year."

The exchange, which was at the onset tedious and wearisome with pause, began to ease the tension for the benefit of both in its length, and had Erik pursuant of basic cordiality. "What is her name?"

"Whose?"

"Your wife. She has a name, does she not?"

"Certainly, it's Jacqueline." M. Chagny shot a brazen look of challenge toward Erik before asking for the same in return. "And yours?"

Erik watched a chance hope appear, knowing his reply would not be what M. Chagny's heart secretly knew. "I married Christine," he responded confidently, squaring his shoulders, suddenly grateful he had not taken a seat. The last thing he desired was to seem apologetic in any way, neither did he wish to be made out a charity case and would not demonstrate his union as such. He was loved for who he was, chosen to be first in the life of his companion, and she in his.

M. Chagny covered his face then retracted his hands. "I see, well. . ."

"Goatee and moustache, eh, Chagny?" Erik could think of nothing ideal and changed the topic according to the errant pulling of facial hair. "I tried a beard once, but the bottom of one's jaw and neck are lost without the proper contours of the face, and therefore an unwise option."

M. Chagny looked up in surprise. Taking a jab at his own disfigurement was, Erik supposed, a rather shameless act of pride, and cocked his head at the vacuous expression. It was almost amusing, in an eerie way, as if M. Chagny were searching for the right words but was caught several comments behind in awe of the obliging grace and alacrity of manner.

"Gautier?"

"Ah, good, finally found your voice. Yes, I associated myself with a person for whom I worked."

"You cannot possibly have continued that farce you started, thinking all you had to do was give her a last name," he accused.

"Consider keeping a civil tongue, Chagny. Everything, every last detail is legal. It has been for years, even before. . ." Erik strained for dignity himself. "You will kindly refrain from enquiring into my personal affairs."

"Forgive me, I have no right. I gave my word as a gentleman that I would remember no more."

Now it became Erik's turn to mentally unlatch a gaping mouth to the floor, and with his jaw clenched and hands plied tightly to his back, he persisted. "The letter you wrote. . . were your statements and feelings, genuine?"

"At the time," M. Chagny paused at the embedded insinuation and adjusted his position in the chair. "At the time, I believe I wrote more to convince myself that what I had experienced had come to an irretrievable end. When she and I parted, it was clear to me that in order for her to make an informed decision, one in which she could follow her heart, she would require time away from every influence. Unfortunately, she had already decided quite readily on my account." The young man's emotions returned so precipitously, Erik could not help but empathize. "I would not be a contender for her affections, whatever the outcome between the two of you. Time at sea helped to ease the disappointment, though for some unknown reason, even now, I exhibit tendencies, a latent wish to watch out for her well-being." M. Chagny shied. "You have nothing to fear from me and may tell her not to worry, not to worry in the least." Ashamed, M. Chagny closed his eyes and brought a fist to press against his mouth.

Erik could see the pain, but the phrase *not to worry* could not be undone in his mind; they were the very words lifted from that dreaded note. Erik's finesse allowed him to dance the situation a bit before relinquishing his hold. "What are your feelings toward both women, if I may ask."

"I love my wife, Monsieur, I love her passionately." M. Chagny became unexpectedly extreme in his articulation. "There is no doubt of that, I can assure you! When I returned two years back, hardened and better off for the experience, we met at an engagement through friends of my sister, and she erased all thought of Christine in that light."

Satisfied with the quantity of information, as well as the quality, and wishing to be about the purpose intended, Erik released a quiet sigh, and nodding with civility he placed closure to their personal lives, retaining the right to be suspicious and to alter his opinion based on the slightest development.

"Forgive me, I have detained us long enough. If you would join me in the arena of investments, I am sure Monsieur LaCroix has been left far too long to stew in his anxiety without his charge to counsel. You may even find the *mobility* of goods and property to your liking."

Giving a sweeping invitation, Erik reflected on the metamorphose of Fate as the two walked side by side into the meeting, neither settled on their judgment of the other nor inclination to distrust, for it seemed just as probable as not that either should improve upon further acquaintance, and notwithstanding a wary observation, parted with regard to the differences noticed and impatience to know more...

"Perhaps, our lone deficiency was that of common ground outside the female persuasion." Erik's lighthearted thought was meant to segue between Christine's stints of fleeting tension during the narrative and her current apprehensions, each time the name of Chagny was mentioned. "Christine?"

He felt gentle pressure from her cheek depress against his scalp and the softness of her voice filled the void. "Strange, the schemes of this master puppeteer as he sets his stage for a repeat casting." Drawing away, he looked into the burning warmth of her dark eyes and she smiled. "*You* are my husband. In the past, we were all caught in the designs of singularity, where as now, we stand together. I belong in your embrace, Erik; no one shall take me from you again, ever."

How joyous the moment of proclamation, the grace of desire, and the kiss, which was lengthy, beautifully simple, and sweetly performed as night's prelude to love.

Chapter Forty-Two

The successive week had come and gone entirely in a state of monotonous routine, with rain pervading the five days preceding departure to Paris. And though its petulant delivery was hardly welcome, the sun could do nothing above the clouds, hermetically fused and impervious to viscosity as they were—the nervous agitation below would have eclipsed the light, had it shone, so it may have been just as well.

Such a gloomy, drizzly mass, do I not have plenty to handle that the weather must turn against us, too? The thought, persistent as the moisture snaking down the carriage window, hammered without preference, leaving Erik to glower after the outdoor scene, and since it was next to impossible for Christine to be any less affected by the periodic glances toward her husband, a scowl took hold across the delicate skin of her forehead.

"Erik." His name had no effect, but the small gesture of affection attached, did; the frisson livening a sideways cast of attention, lit a shy smile to restlessly tug at the corner of his mouth. "With conditions, such as they are, there is no need for our love to suffer. I cannot allow the distance, wishing we would have, when we can." Sliding Chèver over, she retrieved Erik's hands and moved to sit next to him, helping him to center.

"I love you," Erik mouthed tenderly. "Kiss me, please?" Christine unseated the masque and laid it gently on the cushion across from her. Then, holding his face to hers, she kissed him. "You lift my spirit and strengthen me with a kind touch and expression of sentiment. The simplicity is what I yearn for."

"Chèver, same as Papa!" the innocent voice stated, his opinion loud above the rattle and clop of cab and horse upon the cobbled street.

Looking to where Christine had placed the masque, they discovered a prominently settled young man, arms folded and shoulders held back in pride with masque donned, having secured it to his perfect, child-like features the best he could. Erik leaned over and snatched the little scamp from his soft platform, chuckling in his appreciation for love and the brief humorous insight. *Hope remains near,* he breathed.

One moment of hope brightened the interior of the carriage with smiles all around, one brief respite, as they approached the monolith compressed into the pewter backdrop. Pulling up short, the carriage paused long enough for its passengers to exit, heaving one of many groups before the skirts of the Paris Opera. Mercier watched with interest as Erik gave Christine's shoulders a squeeze, then the trio dashed inside before the deluge wrung complete. Having collapsed the umbrella, Erik trailed in behind Christine and Chèver, and shaking the excess rain from his hat and cloak in one majestic swoop, he offered his hand to Mercier in greeting.

"Good, good to see *all* of you." Mercier seemed a shade surprised. "Your son?"

"Yes, Edouard," Erik replied.

"Hmm, handsome young man. And, may I also presume arrangements for his care to have been made?" He enquired in such an offhand way that the overbearing query give offense.

"No, we have not yet settled on specifics for the duration of our stay, but—"

Mercier ignored Erik and turned directly to a wide-eyed Christine. "Though your husband may not, you know well enough what distractions can do to a performance."

"Excuse me." Erik stepped out boldly between the two, buffering the attack to redeem the inflexible will thought to have been brought on by their refusal to do more in the fall, and by the schedule request Mercier was forced to comply with. He inclined his head and spoke in a tone meant to inconspicuously forewarn against further badgering. "Perhaps you forget yourself, Monsieur Mercier, and, as I presume this to be the case I shall provide a quick refresher for your benefit. Let us remember the conjoining circumstances under which she appears at all, by invitation and at our discretion. So far, it has been most unsavory, and with the situation as it stands, you should be a good deal more accommodating. Such a condescending manner is intolerable and has no place when one addresses my wife. Am I clear, Monsieur?"

"Quite. I beg pardon, from both of you." His behavior remained stern, yet a level of civility shone through. "I find myself stressed and stretched to my limits more often of late, and can empathize with the former management in some aspects. If you will excuse me, I am sure there is much to settle and arrange for." He made a halfhearted gesture toward Chèver then retracted it. "I'll just have to tell myself not to worry, excuse me," he tossed back, and walked away muttering to himself in consolation.

Erik watched after the man, took Chèver, and led Christine to her dressing room, his mind trying to wrap around the trend in speech, and while doing so, he nearly tripped over a piece of scenery being repaired. The stagehand apologized for having it there, explaining that most places were teeming with activity, and since this area saw little, he spread out, but told them "not to worry" that it would soon be gone.

Entering and shutting the door, Christine spun around. "You told

Edouard we had no arrangements for Chèver, why? You could see his agitation."

"He was not listening, Christine. Besides, no one is above reproach, especially when our family is at risk, not Edouard, not the Comte de Chagny, nor that stagehand who almost had me on my knees," he added. *I shall watch that one closely.*

"Maman?" Erik handed Chèver over, she kissed his round cheek and held him cradled to her shoulder then shuddered in recognition of the truth.

"Everyone is suspect."

"Yes."

Looking past Erik toward the desk, she gasped and stiffened. "Another one."

He picked up the envelope, opened and read it. "It is from Adèle, wishing you her best. . . here," he offered, "the flowers are from her as well."

Christine took the letter and sighed in relief. "She thought the room could use some life. I do believe having a grandchild has softened her, if just by a hint."

"I shall take care of Chèver's needs and return. Give Maman a love." The bleary-eyed boy complied then curled up in his father's arms. "I shall listen and watch over you, unseen."

"Thank you, Erik."

Exchanging knowing glances, Erik touched Christine's cheek then silently left. There was no denying the unnaturally quiet figure draped in black who, with a small child attached about the neck, floated through the main foyer as though invisibly suspended; no sound betrayed his departure and no public entrance bid welcome twice, as seen by eyes that were once again vigilant to a secreted cause. *Distractions removed.*

The evening performance concluded with applause given and bows taken, all in stride of another success, although, once the curtain came down so did the façade; broad smiles reduced themselves to exhaustion, exuberance in step, lowered to an amble through the corridors, and costumes were shed in favor of less tedious attire. And, as was usually the case, the first few shows were to come peppered with technical glitches that routine would resolve once everyone settled into their roles. No different than any other, Christine felt the pressure subside and glanced upward.

Erik saw the look and sighed. "Ah... her voice is precise, maturing in timbre by season, and her clarity resounds here perfectly." He laid his hand in deep reverence against his heart. "Thank you, Christine."

Moving to and from miscellaneous vantage points throughout the performance, both within the auditorium and without, he observed nothing extraordinary, as such became the customary pace of a fortnight, to squander precious moments, entering March in much the same way as February exited.

Frustrated, after days and hours of unproductive time, traveling about the seventeen stories—and most of them spent in the ten above ground—Erik headed for the roof and the solitude of Apollo's lyre.

How often have I gazed out over this city, the City of Light—electricity shall see to it that she retain her title now that it has begun to replace gas—I, content in my ways, a proud, esurient cur, mad with want. How I despise the waste of what satisfied me a mere five years back; it all feels so childish in comparison with my life at present. Christine has said, less frequently, that I am my greatest critic, embroiling guilt with fairness. I have recognized the magnitude and must unchain my soul then learn to forgive myself. Oh! Such glorious changes held true, except for the light of a candle at day's end.

The appeal of lingering held nothing to the desire of being with Christine, hence his hastened descent to walk the passageways one last time. He rounded the corner in the passage behind Christine's room and saw a strange flicker of light at the end of the darkened path. His pace increased, as did his intrigue because Christine was no longer on the premises. Acutely heightened, Erik's senses gave a hesitated lurch on his approach when the dim glow was snuffed without warning. By the time he reached the mirror, he could see a retreating shadow eclipse the faint line of light from under the door. He was too late, but for what or for whom, he was unsure.

CHRISTINE FLEW THROUGH the doors to her dressing room the very next night; she refused access to any who would attend her needs and forcefully shut and locked everyone out in her head-long rush for protection. She looked frightened. Her shallow breathing and chalky white complexion attested to some form of anomaly, the source pressing in her throat, as she leaned her forehead to the cool, unfeeling grain to stare blankly at the knobs. "Not again, Erik. Oh, please tell me it was not you," she murmured.

A gentle finger touched her neck, followed by several more brushing down the length of her spine. She froze.

"It was not." The rich voice melted her defenses and she instantly sought his embrace. "It was not I," he reaffirmed.

"I heard a few of the ballet girls talking, they were huddled behind a partition. One of them said that someone had seen a hooded figure dart from behind a backdrop late last night and disappear around a stage set. The others gasped, would titter and together postulate on theories of all sorts, but it was their parting comments of Opera Ghost, which unnerved me. Add to that, seeing Raoul speaking with Edouard outside the green room just now and my mind attached the inevitable."

Erik pulled her into his chest, her curves fit against him well. "Word of mouth. . . gossip by far, resembles fire when relaying communication—an inaccurate embellishment, but strikingly fast," he quipped. "Worked wonders for my mystical personification, not to mention my ego. . ." He stopped short the habitual reminiscence, realizing the callous degree of levity he displayed to be inopportune. He again reassured, "I have been religiously invisible, and a most well-behaved fellow. That aside, what of your earlier chat with Edouard,

I was not close enough to hear but imagine this also compounds the issue."

"No, surprisingly. He was quite polite. He expressed regret for his behavior on opening night and asked where you had been keeping yourself. I told him, among other things, you were seeing to the needs of our son, and that perhaps fortune would permit you to attend the opera late next week."

"I should just wear one of my old masques and go sit in Box 5," he said without inhibition, she glared. "Yes, shameful, I know. I've been a bit restless and with you privy to such stirrings, you know what shall soon keep me occupied. Promise me to leave quickly."

"I will."

"Your voice nourished my soul tonight." Erik sighed into her neck.

"I suppose it is the only nourishment taken."

"Ah. . . not true," he defended.

"Good." She seemed satisfied that he was not neglecting himself. "I, we both have missed you. Your shadow is not substantial enough for either of us."

"I know." His head bowed to hers. "It cannot be helped."

Christine nodded. "I'll go. . . just remember, we love you."

Erik remembered. He saw her leave in the carriage belonging to the Baron de Barbezac and could now breathe with the ever-increasing distance between them. Distance was best. Turning, he headed off to apprize the Persian of the most recent occurrence, prior to establishing a patient watch for what would most likely mark the crossroads in this game of fancy, however mentally insane.

Arriving back at the Opera in the course of an hour, Erik planned to take up vigilance where he hoped someone else would, and set his pace in accordance. Rounding into the familiar passage one would have thought it impossible to tread more secretive, but the lure of discovery brought him nearer than before, the anticipation palpable just as the light was doused, again. This time, however, he was within a few yards and crept to the reverse side of the mirror. The blackness shrouded the confines of the room in permanence, a curtain against the wisp of smoke still floating about, his ears attuned to sound as eyes were to movement. Erik saw nothing but an abyss of emptiness. His hand slid quietly to release the counterbalance then stopped; the void fluttered slightly. There, in the corner of the room's rich greys, stood a deep onyx shape pressed against the wall. Erik focused intently and gave a mournful sigh; again the flutter and a shift in location toward the door.

"Why?" Erik's voice echoed lightly, filling the room, surrounding the shape and quite unexpectedly, a hand shot to the knob, created a narrow opening for the blackened figure to escape, and then all was gone.

Not wishing to betray his place of hiding, Erik withdrew several steps, only to retrace them in disgust. "This is absurd, reduced to chasing. . ." He scratched his chin, thinking. "Whoever this is, they are certainly not a ghost and therefore, purposeful in action. Hmm. . . push them further and they may be forced into irretrievable mistakes."

Opening the mirror, he saw at once the stark white of an envelope and plucked it from the desk. His hand stayed, hovering above the doorknob for a ghastly duration. He wished to follow, though his better judgment exerted restraint and turned him instead, from whence he had come. Was the verdict based in wisdom merely attributed to fortune, that he had not ventured, or could it have been intuition? Neither would ever know, but a hooded figure, watching from the cover of the shadows, saw naught to raise hope more. *Patience has its rewards, indeed it does, yes indeed, and investments of great value are worth the effort to protect, are they not? All which has beset the mind shall discover its undoing, soon.*

Chapter Forty-Three

The Persian peered furtively from over top his glasses for the third time, breath held at the pausing interval taken by Erik. He seemed on the verge of speech, but as it had been preferred twice before, his air was freed and they continued on in their separateness of intelligence; the former, perusing the newest addition to the evidence, all the while being grateful to be seated a comfortable span of steps from the tightly strung instrument, and the latter, winding himself still further by the pace he kept, weaving back and forth in front of the open window in the Persian's study, strategizing.

"This is more assertive than the others, Erik, more personal."

The remark halted and disrupted all at the same time. "And you think I don't know this," came the stony retort. "Perhaps you would care to tell me that the sun is up, that it is nine in the morning or that winter is coming to an end, hmm? Considering I have spent so much time in the dark, *that* sort of enlightenment could have been useful last night to discern Christine's reaction, which became apparent only *after* I allowed her to read. . ." He exhaled repeatedly in his struggle to retain composure. "Still, I should not have permitted her to do so, despite her adamancy, and yet I could not refuse nor will I keep secrets from her, of that I am incapable. You would not have recognized her, Daroga, she transformed, aged in seconds before me. I know she sleeps very little and it is telling in the skin beneath her eyes, so dark and unseeing. . . Those words reduced her stellar form to such waif-like fragility, and I in turn experienced what defeat would eventually do to her spirit; it will crush her."

The Persian watched helplessly, as Erik too, was being ravaged from within. Here was a man, whose voracious intensity could rival that of any when fully immersed, but at present, there seemed only wan hunger. His heart had changed. He detested time away from the joys and pleasures derived from his simple life. This man, who could command the will of others by walking across a room, wished to quietly sit in his corner of the world, embracing love.

Standing, the Persian gently placed his hand to Erik's arm. "We can leave this as it is, and you and Christine could take Chèver and go—"

"No, my friend, I cannot. I shall not permit another to rule my life, to chase me from what I have worked so hard to establish. When I married Christine, I swore to myself that hatred and fear would never dominate again, in any form."

"I am glad to hear it. Come and look at what I have deduced from the evidence thus far. You see," he pointed, "none of them contain reference to first person, the use of *I* or *me* is never seen. In every instance the phrases are meticulously worded to slough responsibility." His gaze shifted from the table to Erik's examining focus, no recognition came.

"Meaning. . ." Erik prefaced the beginning of a summation. "It will be requisite to ensnare the culprit with enough proof to try and convict, no doubt must exist."

"That," the Persian motioned positively, "would be the meaning, yes."

"Use the notebook."

"Still too risky." The Persian's tone took on a hint of gravity. "If it is confiscated, you shall be the one at the end of a rope."

Beyond the Masque

Erik shrugged uncaring, mumbling something about drastic measures, then said, "I have already removed and destroyed certain sections. I do not refer to yours, the one you always go about making notes in, use that in conjunction with the one I give you if you wish; the information can only be pinned to the Opera Ghost." He spoke in such a reticent and detached manner, it suddenly became obvious the scheming side of Erik had begun to resurface in order to deal with the imposing circumstances. "The evidence will seem to be of a most spurious nature and improbable on numerous accounts, just as before."

"But still possible," countered the Persian.

Erik tilted his head at the curious inflection. "You have it all, Daroga. And yet, you make concessions, taunt me, threaten defamation of character but are constant in your desires to preserve by means of compassion. It is as though you have granted me absolution in some way, despite your conscience screaming at you all these years about moral ethics. Why?"

"And why is it that you cannot leave something inexplicable, in the past?" the Persian dodged.

"Because the chapter is not finished," was the innocent remark.

"Investments of great value," he cleared his throat, "are worth the effort to protect. I had always hoped you would vindicate my sacrifice." The Persian sniffed ever so quietly and coughed. "Sometimes you are extremely thick."

Erik choked on his own emotion at the blaring comment. "You sure know how to ruin a perfectly good moment... between friends," he said, swiftly regaining the solemn demeanor. "I owe you far too much."

Needing to say no more, they looked at one another in quiet understanding and stoic resolve. Erik took his leave, silently descending the worn stairway to commence anew the search for an odious entity.

For a great many hours after he had left the Persian's flat, along the Rue de Rivoli, Erik ruminated upon the facts availing his cause, and finding them limited, roamed the Opera at length in hopes of accumulating a good deal more. And, as there was always more to be had, it was only a matter of discernment as to the benefit of additional intelligence. However, seeing as he had failed miserably the previous evening, and being less likely to pick up random bits, since this day progressed like the others and was considered typical, he was not adverse to something falling into his lap. Where had he been when the blast of emotion erupted? Not far from the source, to be sure. Erik looked up and was astonished, but not above adopting any rite of illumination procured.

    There was Mme Giry vacillating, had ready, Mercier's door open only a sigh. . . should she or should she not, bother him. Indeed, Erik agreed that at the rate of his preoccupation, Edouard was fast becoming acquainted with the strange conduct of men utterly encased, shut away with the obsession of mystery. Managers, they assumed the ostensible conquest of a professional venture, envisioned the potential, and would stand tall when entering upon such a battlefield as a rock of confidence, venerated until grinding obligation and mishaps brought each one to their knees in concession. Affix to the aforementioned, frivolous babble among the ballet chits, who claimed to have seen some dark, gruesome apparition, and the mix was slowly fermenting toward a repeat of a tumultuous event. One that would be on the streets just as quickly as an overturned barrel of sewage down the palace steps, making news prior to its reaching the bottom.

    Mme Giry closed her eyes, her lips moving quietly. "Never have you allowed. . . you are far too clever to be seen, and for all your efforts. . . he would not dare to resurrect. . ."

    No madam, never, Erik thought, hearing her.

    She gave a series of distinct taps; there was a flurry of paper shuffling and the invitation to enter.

"Come, please... yes, Adèle, you still about?" Mercier asked, somewhat distracted.

"Yes," she replied flatly. "Thirty minutes ago... prearranged meeting with a Monsieur Louis Monteil," she led, trying to spark his memory.

Attempting to shove a set of nervous fingers deeper into the pocket of his waistcoat, Mercier fumbled to regain a hold on time, glancing to Mme Giry's calm face, and then to that of his retrieved watch. "You must forgive me, Adèle. I do not seem to be at my best these days. And Monteil?"

"Unable to stay."

"Reasonable." He gestured for her to sit, the two taking residence across the desk from one another, he erect, fidgety and tense, and she, dubious as to what excuse he could possibly muster. "Yes, he is timely when I am the one being driven to distraction. I have a superstitious bookkeeper, a twit of a man, who has informed me that he'll not return until I can guarantee a stable environment, which is one way or another related to the circulating rumors popping up. Ill-got amusement," he said, rubbing the scruff along his cheek, the meeting already forgotten. "Awful, engaging scandalous gossip to sell tickets, and at the expense of our diva, Christine Daaé. Then, there is some concern fretting her, which I have yet to figure out because she continually frustrates the public, and me, with her schedule changes, tonight being one of many—thank goodness I took to employ an understudy! Numbers are not my forte, Adèle... and now, to have my performers sighting a formidable reincarnation of our Opera Ghost... well, there it is!"

Mme Giry frowned at the exposition and blighted state of nerves. "I was not aware you knew of—"

"This is *my* theatre," he shot back, startling her with his intensity. "It is my business to know!"

"Forgive my ignorance, I had no idea."

Mercier's eyes glazed then cleared, causing a warm shiver to address the unease between them. Her hand clasped the hard pit forming in her stomach. "You once told me, here, in the presence of witnesses that you knew he no longer lived. Was that a cover-up, a lie?"

Incensed at this severe accusation, she protested with an open slap to the arm of the chair. "I do not lie, not now and not then. There is no Opera Ghost." Her voice was low, deliberate and menacing, fixed on each syllable. "How dare you insinuate, after these past few years, that my allegiance was fabricated. You remember, do you not, all the accusations flung in my direction simply because of the contact I had in Box 5?" Mme Giry's cheeks flushed with rage, the rosy accent highlighted against the burgundy of her dress. "How dare you doubt me, Edouard Mercier, how dare you!"

"I remember everything, Madame!" The distance of such an unfeeling honorific between them had her understanding exactly where they stood in reference to intimacy of any previous attachment. "I have been through just as much, if not more," came his stark rebut. "The confidences, secrets, deaths, reports. . . I could fill novels!" Mercier slammed his fist into the desk, upsetting its contents. "There was someone behind it all, I know it. Debienne and Poligny were both spineless, Richard and Moncharmin, bumbling dolts lost in the gregarious mix. It cannot be allowed, I will not allow it to tear down and undo what has been done." Amidst Mercier's half-crazed remarks, Mme Giry saw his arms twitch through the limp cotton sleeves; the stress seemed to have possessed him. "You. . ." he straightened and addressed her coolly, staring down at the hour revealed in his hand. "You should go, we both should."

"Yes," she sighed, mentally fatigued. A drought of callousness left by the death of her husband had faded, was erased by him, by this man. Could she withstand the buffeting? Mme Giry's heart had had an ocean to draw upon, but now the distrust quickly evaporated it all, the savor fouled in the wake of this revelation. Pulling back her shoulders, she rose, unsure of their relationship at this point, and quit Mercier's presence in stoic elegance, his acrid breath deepening with each of her steps, his eyes staring scathingly and unaffected after her.

Painful as truth often is, the voices of Mme Giry and Mercier flowed unheeded to Erik, and though he was not a customary eavesdropper by any conventional means, he had been obliged to carry on in the strictest of confidence until the imposed gape of the door signaled finality. Blending at once into the darkened recesses of the hallway, Erik waited, shoulders weary in thought of Mme Giry's plight; there was the sound of the latch come, solidly engaging behind her. *Caring for someone, and then to be mistreated when she could have betrayed me for love, to remain loyal in keeping the memory of one dead, so another might live; too great a sacrifice, done.* And live he would, most honorably, too. Suddenly, feeling the warm surge of a grateful heart, Erik smiled inwardly, to learn that others cared in return.

Again the door opened and closed, Mercier's keys now marking his departure, and Erik's, from this place of woe and solemn reflection.

Later that night, when the moon surpassed its zenith unnoticed, one figure lay in wait behind a thin barrier of plated glass, ready, to which patience and long suffering were granted just recompense by the wary presence of another. Entering under the cover of pitch, the hall light having been recently doused, Erik's eyes and body contracted in interest as a candle flared to life. Standing within reach, the cloaked form had their back to the mirror, hands gloved. There was a quick exhale and the room, in its entirety, plunged into darkness. *Ritualistic, eh? Well, we shall not disappoint.*

Erik allowed a few moments to elapse, riveting his eyes to the dense mass of black, prior to speaking. "Why?" his voice echoed softly. "Why do you torment her?" Surprised, the shape seemed to recede in magnitude preparatory to a rise in height. "Why?" Erik repeated.

The ebon fluttered with little regard to cover and rasped out in assured wonder. "They lied. . . you live."

"Only between worlds."

"No, you have returned."

A sigh of resignation and long silence ensued. *Damnable chink, devilish weight, when shall I be free?* "There is no life," Erik finally spoke, "I am mere spirit burning in unrest." He paused suddenly at the breath and disturbance of air heard. Though futile, it may have been a possible effort to locate or make contact with something tangible. Piqued, he went on undeterred. "Is it not enough that my spirit shall never attain peace?"

"You must pay for all you have taken. You are real enough; a fact that shall be proven in time," he stated, listening for a direction in which to focus. "Patient, eh? You can afford to wait I suppose, but your precious songbird cannot, she will be your undoing. Most unfortunate."

The parting words were malevolent and bitterly cool, but Erik had already moved from the passageway, his blood hot and resolve impassioned. *Yes*, he thought, his jaw taut upon the word. *It shall be most unfortunate. . . for you.* Erik knew the exchange would be useful yet brief, for now it was his turn to watch, though *his* eyes would see reward.

Leaving quickly from the dressing room, the man lingered in the shadows under Erik's scrutinizing blue as one moved to trail the other. Erik moved unrestrained around the deserted corridors, making the distance traversed extremely direct. *A spider is a most thrifty creature, but its prey, while often traveling two or three times as far to avoid capture, often runs headlong into an unsuspecting net. Come to me you pesky gnat. . . show yourself.*

The man slowly made his way to the administration section of the building. Lightly amused at the enigmatic potential of *this* route, Erik continued on, his mind undeviating. He had not utilized the office connections for some time, not needing to pad his accounts or roll in self-indulgence, but they were at the very least, concise.

These days his perspective was much altered, and he nodded at the conservative fact, believing that opulence should be checked and not flaunted arrogantly.

These considerations came to an abrupt halt when the insinuated path of said prey became all at once ludicrous. What was this? He observed the hooded figure stop at the manager's office door, Edouard Mercier's door. Intrigued, though shock fused, his fingers gripped the drapery fabric leaving an actual imprint crushed into the velvety fibers, mental resistance battling in denial of what his emotions knew to be true: that this person was connected to Mercier. *Such idiocy! Why implicate by association? Why not meet in another, disconnected location? You are either overly confident,* Erik smirked, *and Mercier will surely not warm to that, or there is a level of insanity about—foolhardy dolt. Argh! How utterly exasperating to be led by crumbs!*

They remained obscured to the other, aware and not, until the key tried effectively refused its mate. Fumbling beneath the cloak revealed a second set of keys, and this time, having met with success, in the positive sense of a correct fit, came at the cost of revelation. The figure had pushed the hood back in permitting a line of sight from which to see by, which was precisely enough to catch upon a betraying moustache.

"Edouard!" Erik mouthed in disbelief. *So, you are in the market to burn bridges, are you? Exchanging the cost of trust and relationships for an obsession with the past. Christine is your pawn, for it is O.G. whom you seek to destroy, but in a dangerous frame of mind; to use anyone or anything at your disposal is caution sufficient to the wise.*

Erik vanished.

IT WAS MORNING and Dawn began its rise all too soon, the oranges spraying an effervescent blush against skyward clouds, passionately erased the slated haze from their pale countenance. Absent too, were any signs significant to others that Erik had been there too, but he had, Christine felt it even before she woke, it was in the disruption of silence. Rotating left, she came nose to nose with an unexpected angel, his round face in peaceful slumber. Several pillows barricaded the far side of the bed, and nestled into the one closest to her and Chèver was a note, a beautiful iris on the verge of bloom, and a small morsel of chocolate.

> *My dearest love,*
> *Something as simple as a note should be enjoyed from those who innocently admire your talents, and from your most adoring husband. You believe in me and impart faith in my abilities to do more than I ever imagined.*
> *You and Chèver are my life.*

Laying the paper aside, Christine snuggled into Chèver, brushing his soft hair and face with her fingertips, just like her mother had done when she was young. His hand came up to rub the tickle from his eye and stayed, draped contentedly across his forehead.

"I wish it were that easy to keep away the protruding thorn from snagging us all upon its point," she quietly muttered. "And, I am sure I can do better than to give in to such frailty of spirit as I did last night. I imposed rather than lifted a burden."

Meg's shy knock parted Christine from these obstacles and prefaced an invite to enter.

"He's not here? I'm sorry."

"Don't be, he has had much to deal with."

"I'll bet. That is why I have come barging in so early, just look at the morning paper." Christine stared as Meg commenced reading from where she had it folded to the theatrical section. "*Déjà vu Spirits Away Paris Opera; Clever Ploy or Gossip?* Who would start such a lie?" she asked, sitting in a defiant huff on the bed. "Maman has said nothing, but I am sure such disreputable hype would not have spread unless—"

"It's not a lie, Meg. There is someone." Christine saw her friend's complexion whiten and the questioning doubt rise. "No, it's not him." Then, to the best of her knowledge, Christine conveyed all the events leading up to her latest engagement at the Opera; she lovingly touched Meg's chin to aid in closure of her slightly estranged lips.

"You're serious," she said, astonished. "And you've kept this to yourself? Does Richard know?"

"Yes, and yes. Erik would not have your family obligated without his consent."

"What can I do?"

"Nothing, nothing more than you have. Just knowing Liana has had a safe environment in which to watch after Chèver during our absence is relief enough. Sincerely, Meg, Erik trusts you and Richard, which is saying much at this time."

"I know our husbands see things differently, and that Erik does not always approve of Richard's antics—"

"But," Christine interrupted, "it is that difference which endears one to the other. Erik knows Richard has a kind heart."

"Where is Papa?" Chèver asked.

Christine smiled and squeezed Meg's hand, then glanced to the source of the little hand patting her back. The question was similar to those rising in hope each morning only to be broken in disappointment. Gathering him next to her, she offered honestly, "He is away at present, but has left you something, there, on the pillow." She pointed to the tiny gift among the downy nesting.

"He is so like his father, is he not? His rate of development leaves me speechless, and shall leave you in such a state one of these days, Christine."

"I'm not sure you understand the truth in what you just said, for it is Erik who makes up for the child in them both. When he experiences with Chèver, I occasionally catch a glimpse of what he was like as a boy." The two grinned at the chocolate smeared across the corners of Chèver's mouth, followed by looks to the smaller nugget pooling under examination. "Like I said."

"Messy, Maman," he said, displaying his hands as proof.

"Messy, but delicious, yes?"

He nodded, agreeing with his mother wholeheartedly.

Chapter Forty-Four

"Are you sure, absolutely positive it was he whom—"

"Yes, there is no mistake!" Erik shouted, interrupting the line of methodical reasoning put forth by the Persian. This fit of storming, however controlled it was, had provided the Persian with sudden clarity as to why he, Erik, took up residence away from societal norms; bouts of anger, along with the ruin witnessed below would have certainly elicited complaints and unwanted attention. *Attention.* His insides formed a rapid knot, his arms ached, he desired his family and must shut off. . . watching them sleep, holding Chèver, where was his peace now? *In distance* spoke the soothing voice of conscience. *In distance*, he repeated.

The Persian sighed inwardly. "I take it you have seen the morning paper?"

"Of course!" Erik exclaimed, throwing his arms up to acquiesce in disgust and seat himself by the fire. The pleasurable sensations evaporated. "Do you realize this whole outrageous mess could have been brought to a close just hours ago, or for that matter, twice before? Those editors would be printing retractions after the delivery of said parcel arrived neatly bound upon their doorstep," he stated regrettably. "Now that would be efficient, save us all a huge quantity of grief, but no!" He bolted upright in a sarcastic rage. "I must be the one to conform, above all, *I* must be conventional!" His hand waved aimlessly, while wandering over the Persian's flat.

Both had been so immersed in emotion that neither had paid heed to the persistence of a caller, for it was Darius who sharpened their hearing with a knock to the study doors. The visitor was announced and Erik rolled his eyes impatiently, nodding in deference to the Persian, who bade Darius see the gentleman in.

"I see I have been located. Welcome, Monsieur Chagny, to my home."

"I beg your pardon, to call at such an early hour is reprehensible, I know. . ." The Comte looked lightly shaken, his sight shifting furtively between the Persian and the well-dressed M. Gautier.

"As you see, there are others who think nothing of the time of day," the Persian's sarcasm quipped afresh.

"Go on, we are listening." Erik's disembodied voice set the Comte at naught. "Really, young man, did you come here to gawk or is there something of interest you wish to impart?" He continued to entertain for his own amusement.

"Erik." The Persian knew the signs ventriloquism had on the unprepared and the word "fine" came as if in answer to some alternate conversation.

Blinking, the Comte recovered himself, directing his comment to Erik. "Actually, I came looking for your whereabouts when I read the paper."

"Providence shines, what might I do for you?" Erik asked genially.

"On the contrary. Perhaps it is I who may be of assistance."

"How so?" the Persian asked, sitting forward. "Please."

The Comte took up the offer and sat opposite the Persian before the fire. The young man's face bore an undeniable innocence. "After the most recent of Mademoiselle Daaé's, of Madame's. . ." He was clumsy at his reference, obviously unsure of which form Erik would consider acceptable.

Seeing his struggle, Erik clarified, "Christine."

"Thank you, yes. When her performance that evening was finished, I had the fortune or misfortune, depending, of being affronted by Monsieur Mercier." The name drew interest. "He trifled little with courtesy, which left my mind to straw-grasping while he boldly asked what the current nature of my relationship was to Mademoiselle Daaé. I explained I was uncertain, as I had not seen her for years. He ventured supposition on the subject, cutting me off post haste. He wished to know if I had ever experienced a chance meeting with the Opera Ghost, and if so, would I recognize him upon meeting again."

Erik bowed in derision, drawing his arm across his body in open invitation. "See, how much more do you need, Daroga?"

"This is all hearsay, Erik, you know that." Then, turning back to the Comte he enquired, "And how did you reply?"

"I expressed regret at not having such a lone encounter and felt the whole idea of a ghost to be a preposterous hoax or at least a glorified prank gone too far."

"Interesting twist to your narrative, considering."

The Comte smirked at Erik's insinuation. "I took an oath of silence in regard to a man, a madman who, despite nearly torturing me to death with heat, water, and various affairs of the heart, had the decency to give up what he most desperately wished to possess in this world," he said, acquiring such esteem from his listeners that both countenance and assertion made poignant what he wished known. "You gave Christine the freedom to choose her own happiness. And, since our chance encounter at the Credit Lyonnais, I have pondered a great deal; I'm not so sure I would have done the same of my own accord. Similarly, if she deems you of worth, then no, I would not know the ghost who once claimed the Opera as his rightful domain, but distinguish instead, the difference in the gentleman before me."

Erik fought against the well of emotion threatening, surprised that he could be so taken in by honesty. *The boy*, as he had once labeled the then, Vicomte de Chagny, had risen to more, was himself more, and knew more than he had presently divulged, but because of Christine's decision, was willing to leave the past where it belonged.

"Your kindness is overwhelming," Erik whispered humbly.

"I guess I am not singular in thinking your damnable hide is in some way, valuable."

"If you could possibly see your way to leaving my looks out of this!"

The men chuckled at the Persian's comment and Erik's wry wit, releasing at last the awkward tension from the room.

Finishing, to some degree with the restraint of formality, the Comte quickly desired understanding of what he had been an unknowing participant. He had recently placed the odd incidents as unimportant until seeing concurrent circumstances in print. As the generalities came to light, other questions became relevant, but were dispelled and put to rest, the most critical being the demise of a beloved brother. He had had his answer from the moment he learned of Christine's choice; it was the tacit charge of implied good-will that made the direction in which confidence was to be taken up, quite plain. And the Comte, he was glad of such an outcome.

Erik departed within the hour, leaving the Persian to distinguish the mettle of the young Comte de Chagny, and to which side his allegiance would now rest, prior to being entrusted with a beneficent link of solidity; and Erik, having more persuasive engagements pressing on his time, though dreadfully monotonous during earlier phases, had his attentions duly reinstated.

MERCIER ENTERED HIS gloomy office with all the punctuality of a regulated chronometer and headed straight for the drapes, throwing them wide to the sun as if in summons to bask in self-pride. Pleased, he stepped boldly to the desk and set out his coffee and paper, but thinking twice, he grabbed up the paper to go stand at the window. Erik watched, viewing each movement, strategically. *Hmm, most men would skim the first page or two, but then again, this being opera...* he went instead for what Erik supposed was the theatrical section, eager for reviews and gossip or the more likely reason, to check upon the accuracy of an item purposely submitted. In no doubt of the self-satisfaction seen, Erik decided to see how much rope Mercier would require to vertically suspend himself, as this was fast becoming a game of mental acumen, which seemed to suit the ostensible perpetrator most keenly.

Erik applied a mournful sigh to dance in and out of Mercier's mind as he sauntered back to his chair, though the sound did not register as anything other than his own until voice was given. "You seem to be well liked, despite being wretchedly shoddy in your impersonation."

Taken completely by surprise, Mercier sprayed a light mist of coffee across his desk. Owning to the fact it could not possibly be, he glanced around instinctively and finding no one there, promptly decided it was nothing, swore, and began dabbing at the mess with his handkerchief.

"Was it not enough that my death left you without debt? Humph, and with a profit from Box 5, no less."

Starting a second time, without tangible provocation, proved immediate grounds for Mercier to seek a more public area to deduce probability and, feeling rightfully on edge, he gathered his keys and scurried away in denial from a brush with his rifting sanity. Part of him laid blame for this brief lapse to recall, for he had been obsessed with specific facts opened by the case in question. Then again, it could be sleep deprivation and stress or confirmation that his speculations were indeed, correct.

"What if it truly is a ghost? My efforts would all be for naught, a waste. . . what of Adèle?" Allocating that sort of thought to a forbidden lobe, he shook himself sufficiently then returned to merge with the industrious flurry of duties and reality beyond the office. He stopped and took a long look at the closed door. "Nonsense," he said, and while glancing back over his shoulder to where he had left the voice, he ran directly into Raoul Comte de Chagny.

"Oomph! In a hurry are we?" The Comte steadied Mercier.

"Oh, forgive me, you must forgive me. My mind, as well as my sight, is preoccupied," he replied, relieved there was no coffee in the mix.

"Late night diversions never bode well, an unfortunate distraction." Erik filled Mercier's ear complete.

"I am most sorry, did you say something, Monsieur le Comte?"

"No, but after our chat I have had time to reflect, to do some mental research if you will, and thought I might lend a hand to quashing the wicked rumors rising from the dead."

"Rumors, from the dead, did you say?" Mercier repeated the Comte's words as absently as he fingered the end of his moustache.

"Is there aught amiss, Monsieur?"

"No, no, I'm sure it's just lack of sleep. . . stress. Come, shall we find a place to talk?"

Mercier nervously patted the Comte's shoulder while guiding him to one of the vacant offices nearby. The door closed and both were seated. "So, you remembered. . ." he began, at once feeling that familiar ease of confidence.

"Yes, well, it is most likely incidental, but I confirmed the image just this morning when I went to call on the Persian gentleman that often lurks about."

"Yes, yes. . ." Intrigue suddenly motivating Mercier's thoughts to the extreme.

"He was less prominent several years back... I remembered he made reference to the Opera Ghost and was always taking notes, writing in some leather-bound book. Perhaps the answers you seek reside within those pages, for I believe it was he who claimed the walls of this edifice had ears, and that *business*," the Comte sniffed his disdain, "was best left to those who were experienced. Unusual sort of traveler really, interested in the mechanisms behind the scenes, he seemed extremely forthright. I surmised my thoughts were of little consequence until I saw him writing in that same book I speak of now, during my unannounced visit this very morning. Certainly the paper has the attention of many, and most especially his!"

"This is enlightening and quite possibly the very particular needed, and all along, so close. Yes, I too recollect a similar volume on his person." Mercier spoke more to himself than to the Comte, and then as though something of urgency spurred him, he asked to be excused, murmuring oddly about a bookkeeping nightmare.

Shrugging, the Comte de Chagny smiled and indicated he was capable of finding his way out, though he very well suspected not a word to have been heard by the other.

"You would make a formidable enemy, my dear Comte." After nearly exiting his skin at the incorporeal compliment, the young man shuddered heavily and started anew when Erik stepped up behind him. "Are you unwell?"

"Has anyone ever commented on the unnerving mystery in which you conduct yourself, your wife perhaps?" The Comte's brows suspended all belief that he was much more than astonished, though the brazen query spoke otherwise.

"Her senses are very acute, oft times more precise than I would wish, but I am an acquired taste, what of it?" Erik felt he had been unnecessarily offended.

"Forgive me. You—"

"Unnerved your tongue, as well?"

"Yes, frankly speaking."

"Apology accepted. You should go." Erik doused the irritation.

"I will, but should like to know, since I am in the thick of memory. I suppose you remember a certain invincible, impetuous, head-strong young fool who shot at you one night?"

Erik smiled. "I do. You may label your intentions passionate and marksmanship deplorable."

The Comte laughed alone at the description, as Erik dissolved back into the shadows, leaving the young man glancing around in a state of boyish wonder. "How ridiculous." He flushed, and within seconds of one quitting his company another came, a maid, and as it was their tendency to maintain a level of anonymity, she grinned at the display, covering her mouth directly, which forced him to remark in consequence on the opulence of the building. He took his leave hastily and did not look back.

Erik's grin faded severely in relation to the next unfolding event. It was like watching greased clockwork, the doors shutting on one scene to open onto another, with each step purposely set. The Persian entered unhurried, possessing in full view the worn leather book tucked beneath one arm, protected until the precise moment when history would avail itself of the choice intelligence held; there were the Comte, maids, and various employees passing about attuned for the latest news, Daroga in a state of inconsistency, and Mercier seeing M. Gabion out. From Erik's secreted position, it was quite obvious to attest to the comings and goings in the foyer as a bazaar spectator sport—everyone staring after someone else under some vast magnification of distrust or pique of interest, which left one spirit taking it all in at his leisure. Yes, this was more to his liking.

Here, stopping at the base of the grand staircase, the Persian's foot came to rest, hesitantly at first, and then more decisive as he retracted the motion, sight transfixed to the opaque tiers, fingers heedlessly raised to the deeply lined forehead in thought.

"Are you all right?" Mercier asked attentively.

"Oh, quite well, Monsieur. Forgive the trouble."

"No trouble, you seemed distant, that's all."

The Persian straightened and readjusted the book more securely. "I was making notes while reading an article from the morning paper... I thought I brought them along, but find my assumption in err." He tossed a hand up lightly. "I am trying to recall where I may have set them in my apartment... strange."

"What sort of notes, if you don't mind my prying."

"Not at all. You see, in addition to my business investments, and occasional dabbling into certain legal situations, I've developed a fascination for controversy in unsolved cases." He hunched inwardly as if sharing a personal confidence. "In the paper, this very morning, rumor has once again turned up in the theatrical section in favor of our infamous Opera Ghost, but with you being so busy I am sure—"

"Yes, yes!" Mercier chimed in, lightly perturbed. "But no, I am not too busy to learn of the gossip floating about. Reckless blather is all it is, someone requiring attention, though it makes for excellent publicity."

"Ah, not a superstitious man then."

"I put up my best front and willingly admit, infrequently however, to being charmed into the alluring probability. Adds a bit of mystery to the place, and one can never get enough of that."

"Exactly, and I suppose the highly elusive creature shall remain so, without substantial proof. Fortunate for you and your business and for permitting my interest to continue, Monsieur. I shall return shortly."

"Very good. Oh, and if you turn up some clue of worth, come find me, I should be glad to hear of it. Put the gossip columnists out on their ears, touché!" he said with a stab to the air.

"Naturally," murmured the Persian, bowing curtly.

Mercier's mind must have worked overtime for a moment, trying to digest the auspicious nature of these informational tidbits, his conceit gorging wildly while watching for the Persian to reappear, and so he did, true to his word and quite rapidly, but was no better for the excursion home.

"I assume you have met with success?" Mercier was descending the stairs and paused to enquire.

"No, I must be getting old," he said, pinching the bridge of his nose. "I have arrived with the notes I jotted down. . . left my book, and my. . . ah, eyeglasses." He felt his pockets and retrieved them. "Humph, two out of three."

"Would you care to send someone in your stead for the third?"

"Thank you, perhaps later. I shall focus on other matters of business for now."

"Of course, good day to you," replied Mercier graciously.

Mercier had not known what to make of the Persian or how to get hold of the book he had seen, but looked to have his mind quite made up from that moment about the steps which might be used to gain the necessary item, and he rushed away to set them in motion.

Several messengers were summoned and dispatched during the noon hours and, with their orders delivered, Mercier awaited the response of favorable replies. The first came from the Barbezac Château in confirmation of Madame's performance as stated in the schedule, no deviations mentioned; next, a young page with a parcel intended for delivery to *le Manager, Paris Opera*. For this, Mercier thanked the young man and escorted him from the office, locking the door upon exit.

"Notes are wonderfully convenient, keeping one's thoughts until required at a later date." Sitting down, he could hardly contain the excitement he felt. Rubbing his hands together, Mercier prepared to open the cover, not daring to touch the delicate information without warmth to caress its vital pages. "Now we shall see whether or not your Persian skills have met with success, as I shall hold my opinions in reserve."

Mercier's eyes widened, as did the Persian's while elsewhere in the Opera House; he was perusing the vacant galleries, rehearsing the details he was to execute, when Erik discovered him.

"Surprised to see me?"

"A little, yes. I assumed you would be watching Mercier."

"He is consumed with the notes, so there is no need for me to be bored with his churlishness; the fawning he does over each page began to make me ill. He'll finish in good time. . ." Erik flicked his wrist.

"I would think your arrogance to have been removed, the haughty, foolish. . ." The Persian could not bring himself to end the sentence. He struggled to ease the stiffened posture, then let go of the matter somewhere between angered concern and indifference. He became grave and sullen, confined in speech as well as manner, which roused Erik to learn what troubled him.

"Distractions?"

"Just tired."

"A commonality spread upon everyone's plate today."

"Erik, please."

"What? You are offended by my levity, is that it? Keep in mind that it is the one tie binding me to sanity, Daroga. It is the only option blocking—"

"Say no more, I understand, but I feel you assume too much and do not give Mercier credit."

"Credit? I shall give him credit, my friend, for causing unrest in the life of my family during the past year. He may have it all." Erik's temper flared. "But I am sure he feels retribution a fair exchange, as do you from the look on your face."

The Persian swore mentally at Erik's discriminating sensitivity, the room was dim and yet he could distinguish the features upon a darkened face. Choosing to cock an eyebrow at the wrong time had been his demise, however misconstrued, and now he would have to wait to set things right between them, for Erik was not to be stopped at present.

"You're tired, of what, your association with me? I daresay I am quite the burden. I never asked you to be a part of my life, Daroga, but you found your way into it despite every effort I made to avail you of the responsibility and now, when I have requested your assistance, when I have come to depend upon our relationship, you..." Erik could not go on, and instead turned sharply, desperately pained. An antagonist was an exigency unaffordable; without the ethical anchor that that ebon skinned man proffered him he would be adrift.

"Erik, I am on your side." This sounded vaguely familiar, feeling the Persian grasp his shoulders. "Forgive my reaction, the concept of *unrest* struck me inappropriately, but for the agitation caused it may have been a beneficial release of tension. Come, it is time we were focused on this foray we are about to cut loose."

"Yes," was Erik's level response. "It needs to come to an end, for I am nearing exhaustion, *the leitmotif*[12] *tiresome*."

"Indeed, repetitive dying has that effect on one's soul," the Persian said.

Chapter Forty-Five

The day began to retire and sank low behind the clouds drawn to the forefront, leaving only theoretical remnants in prediction for the morrow. Erik was likewise drawn in place long before Mercier ever made to detach himself from the contents he was so thoroughly engrossed within, which gave the former an opportunity to calm and recenter in the relevancy afflicting his position.

I sense too many emotions, see too much of what may cohabitate within the hearts of others—the clip of revenge impartially serves. Darkness hides the confusion of sight and relies on instinct alone, the balance of grey releasing the boundaries created by society; one's physiognomy, physical traits, character, and status totally disintegrate, leaving us all vulnerable to some extent. The slap of a book closing brought Erik swiftly to attention.

Mercier sat there, eyes narrowed, his mind clinging to the wealth of knowledge greedily devoured. His eye twitched, then crinkled under the force of a maniacal grin. "There are no words," he expressed aloud. "A chronological record of the Opera House, and it lays at my fingertips... everything. The story is fantastic, a tale woven in glorious virtue about O.G. Too much, I suppose, for our dear examining-magistrate Faure, so sad." Mercier's tone spilled forth a measure of satirical sentimentality while his thoughts simmered for a time, then a gasping intake was heard, altering the quiet to still that gradual ideation process. "It all makes sense," he breathed, placing his hand firmly over the tattered leather jacket. "I should have connected it... the face, his marriage, the name. Oh, clever are you and, Adèle." Vexed at her deception and his recognition of being infallibly right, so unfortunately right, he bemoaned their attachment and rose, distancing himself from the book.

How Erik wished to do away with these hurdles, as the gaps—though filling—were not doing so at a pace conducive to foresight, embittering him against the last possible moment he would have to act.

Mercier cursed, then walked to the window and stared out at the dusky sky, his piteous expression on the verge of believable. "Patience, confirmation, and an accessory or two." His hands came together in a congratulatory clasp, massaged the other and immediately his countenance lifted to a sneer, resultant in a fit of raucous laughter. "What, you've not got much to say, Monsieur O.G.? Quite grave and silent when another has the upper hand, eh? You may be interested to know that my next move is already in progress. A pawn of insignificant worth shall entice the strategy to life and bring about the final checkmate." His gaze suddenly met with a premeditated vision of what was most likely taking place at that moment, and he grinned in wonder...

THE UNEVEN SYNCOPATION of wheels to ground swayed heedlessly the pair of individuals kept within the carriage, their primary destination an upscale neighborhood befitting those more well-to-do. And, as commissary of police, Monsieur Mifroid sat restlessly weighing risk and worth.

"Mercier knows where a man's heart bleeds: it is in his pride," he muttered.

Several years, unsolved cases—two dead ends, to be exact—and no promotion could wound this vital characteristic. And for these disappointments, he was not about to miss an opportunity to rectify a sore spot between himself and the retiring, examining-magistrate Faure. "The incessant persecution. . ." *I did my best and the Opera House did me one better. . . I believed when others would not and investigated every avenue without aid.* "The façade of appearance," he scoffed. *How many were placated, how much was explained away, and who shall be exposed?*

A nimble flip of the cap and he scrambled the thick mane with a good scratch to the crown of his head, sighing heavily at the past. Mifroid's roll of dialogue between verbal and mental had his mind busy, hoping there would be something to show for all his late nights skulking about in the cellars with Mercier. Oh, there were clues, hearsay, and leads, but a great deal of their time brought up items too circumstantial to mention, and there would be no end to the barrage of torment if proof came lacking in accompaniment. *Mercier said he conversed with him. Him? I cannot arrest a voice, so I shall be wary, prepare to cover my back and shift loyalty where necessary.*

Mifroid was shaken from his thoughts by a rough section of road, which rearranged the seating, and had him struggling to help re-situate his companion. He thumped the underside of the cab's roof and yelled, "What the devil are you doing up there, Chenault, trying to dismantle our transportation before we've gone an' reached our half way mark?"

"No, Monsieur! My apologies," the driver called back.

At length, they arrived in one piece at the Barbezac Château, and making a hasty exit, Mifroid summoned one of his armed men to accompany him. The crisp air chilled Mifroid—or perhaps it was his nerves sending some faint tremor through to the pit of his gut—but whatever the origin, conveying any portion of shocking news always made him cold. He held up his fist, paused, breathed deeply, and pounded his presence known. Reward greeted him in the face of a surprised footman, who enquired as to the business of M. le

Commissaire. As it was stated, he had come to call upon Mme Gautier, in a matter of imperative urgency. There was a nod to acknowledge the given information, and then the door was promptly shut, their forward expectation upon being shown into the interior of the house to await response, highly evident. Taken aback by the gauche reception, Mifroid waited impatiently without word, and shortly, as his temper was thus becoming, the door was reopened to invite them into the foyer before a fantastically dressed gentleman.

The gaily-clad Richard was quite a picture to behold, coming in his rich-colored robes and hat to address the men before him, but neither seemed particularly astute in their use of multiple senses, evidently their sight was overtly dominant to that of hearing. Richard apologized for the outrageous attire, explaining that such was a necessity when storytelling for young children, and repeated himself in query regarding the legal nature of their call.

"Yes, I come in search of Madame Gautier. If you don't mind, I should like to speak with her and dispense with the pleasantries," Mifroid replied curtly.

"You may leave your message with me and I shall impart the information when she is available."

"Please understand, I am here on official business, and engaged under time constraints as well. I should think it preferable to cooperate and not interfere." A rifle was raised within a most unfriendly range to this remark and regrettably, the tone being implied had the opposite affect in Richard's home, which gave rise to indignance rather than compliance.

"And *I* should think a man in your position would assume a different stance." Richard signaled, and several pistols were heard to cock. "You see. . . threats do not bode well here, for I have been commissioned to look after those in my care."

"Richard, I will hear him out." The men started; Christine stood just to their side of the drawing room doors.

"Very well."

It was obvious to the newly disgruntled Mifroid that Richard took staying as a contemptuous presumption and made concessions, instead of objecting: the sake of privacy for speed. "I come here on behalf of a Monsieur Edouard Mercier, and one Persian gentleman. These men are known to you?" She nodded. "We have a suspect in custody."

The clot of tension lessened. "What do you require of me?"

"Madame, as no one seems to know, I have come to you for recognition. It is most feasible that he is to blame for the menace that he is, in addition to the charge of attempted murder on Madame Giry—" There was a gasp. "… which was wholly unsuccessful… too many people, too close."

The complexions of both Richard and Christine drained white at the name strategically dropped.

"Is Adèle hurt?" Richard asked, pushing his hand across the surface of his hair.

"A minor injury is all. She said she was on her way to your dressing room, Madame; she had taken some of your things from a maid. She entered, startled the man there and was attacked, nearly strangled. Madame Giry has expressed a desire to return home soon."

"Richard, I'll go."

"I shall escort you," he insisted.

"What about Meg?" Christine's voice lowered instinctively.

"I would rather not upset her. I'll go to assess the situation and bring Mother Giry back here. I'll tell her that I am to accompany you." Then in a whisper, "You cannot accompany them alone." Christine nodded. "Monsieur le Commissaire, we shall require a moment," he declared, turning from Christine to summon their coats. Guns were lowered in check as Mifroid pressed his desire to be gone at once and would *wait* only a few moments. He and his guard departed. Richard retreated into the drawing room to come again just as quick.

Carriage and men were prepared by the time the two left the château minutes later, heading toward the open door and M. le Commissaire. Mifroid offered his hand upon Christine's approach, but taking one look inside, she became akin to a cat being put to bath. There was little struggle—the white cloth over mouth and nose had performed like a charm—and Richard ceased to be any trouble; his motionless body, now prostrate in the soft, moist dirt, blood seeping freely from the back of his skull, made discretionary collection requisite for a random deposit soon after.

Pleased with himself, and how well the eventual scene played out, considering the initial hostility of manners, Mifroid folded the limp woman nearly in half, and taking great care not to harm Mercier's treasure, placed her neatly into the corner. The door closed and they were gone, no one the wiser. A note, detailing the information meriting script, was penned and sent on ahead, during which time a natural course of silence prevailed. . .

GENEROUS AS THE time had seemed, it was fleeting. Mercier's head jerked to one side as an object came sailing from beneath the office door.

"Ah! Splendid, splendid," he commented, bending over to retrieve the fibrous raft, and hastily shedding the envelope, he studied the enclosed correspondence with open satisfaction. He peered around, centering his vision at various points while contemplating which to address, and finally deciding upon exclusivity of the whole, he imparted, "Apparently, while you kept me under surveillance, I managed to ensnare quite a lovely songbird among the briars; it was too tempting."

Erik seethed speechless as his hands convulsed in turn with the other, imagining the pleasure derived from snapping Mercier's neck under such a design; each vice clamping down upon the brittle pipe, compressing, watching. But the Persian's piercing words came, faintly at first, then the jarring shock of, *evidence, no doubt, and conviction*, all blared unmercifully to supplant this vengeful dream with a form of equanimity.

Another round of vile laughter echoed; Mercier calmed and listened, perhaps for some forthcoming retort? When none prevailed upon his hearing, Erik took note of the slight confusion. He was a man of few words and Mercier, totally mistaken if he felt sparring to be among Erik's traits. Patience of the inane was another. When would the man vacate the room?

Presumed alone in the end, Mercier slid the drapery to one side, revealing a small section of tile raised no more than one-eighth inch; it was here that Mercier removed the flooring and sub panel to access a safe below. His treasure stowed and securely at rest, he was able to extinguish the lights and leave, confident among the numbers of subscribers mingling prior to the evening ballet. Things were nearly in place; Mercier grinned, foreknowledge tickling his fancy that this night would bring more rewards than could have ever been hoped for.

To assume is to err, Mercier. Nothing is absolute nor as it seems, but shall be as it once was.

IT WAS BUT A tolerable duration, and for several it was interminably so; the curtains fell to applause as the general populace commenced their post-performance ogling at the who's who, for the event had been well attended. Mercier was at his best in manner and pride—too much in Erik's opinion; every feature was on the verge of wearing their impression thin, and the interruptions. . . well, there were too many.

Erik's interminable stride broke pattern for a second time in as many minutes, being industriously engaged about elsewhere as he was, and most fortunately so—he took notice of a pair of ungainly males when they exited through a rarely used stage door. It was not that the departure was of a strange nature itself, after all, this was theatre, and one had to learn to receive such rampant peculiarities; even the crowds made it difficult to take on such individualized interests, but it was the rag doll appearance of a dark haired woman slung over the shoulder of the larger. This would not raise an eyebrow either, if they had been going in the opposite direction toward the dormitories; nonetheless, the sight annoyed Erik, if only for the coincidence alone, and his light mental tug-of-war elected favorably in tailing the oddity.

"Do you know where you're going, Chenault?"

"Of course!" the man shot back. "I was called on several occasions to accompany le Commissaire, except, this has been quite out of the ordinary. That gentleman, the one you laid out flat?"

"Yeah, he'll have one devil of an ache if there's any skull left."

"Well, you better hope he's alive, no sense in coming up with an excuse if we don't have to, eh?" No answer came. Chenault made an abrupt rotation. "Jantot? I am not amused, Jantot. You know I can't do this on my own." There came a hush of irritation.

"Perhaps I may be of some assistance." The obliging tone had Chenault rounding to find generosity of space.

"All right, Jantot, you've gone far enough. I read the papers, an' if this is your way of leaving me to take the blame. . ." Nervous, Chenault lessened in severity. "Look, we have a job to do."

An object that was cool, thin, and lithe in its rapid application, wrapped about his neck, and a warm voice filled his mind before darkness triumphed. "I shall relieve you of your burden. . . not to worry."

Erik was alert once again, and with the loose ends tidied and out of the way, he went to go make contact with the Persian, who, having kept a discreet profile these months past, had been a regular visitor to the office of M. Faure. To trounce upon the threshold of this skeptical humbug of a man was to tread into the realm of an aloof dilettante—personally speaking—and therefore required much preparation before setting forth such palettes to induce him to partake, considering the happenstance of the story years ago proposed, sans proof. Incrementally, the whole mystery had literally opened the door for the examining-magistrate to willingly consider the situation with added evidence.

"Daroga." Erik reached out and grasped the Persian's shoulder, lessening the lurch of internal substances. "You shall find physical proof lying in wait along the corridors near the singers' foyer; two men, Chenault and Jantot, and one inebriated female, I believe she was a decoy. All are bound and alive. I feel it prudent to hasten your legal witness as the whole of this game will erupt when Mercier sees things beginning to unravel."

"You have kept your word and now, you shall have mine."

Erik's hand dropped away. "Two others are witnesses as well; Richard, if he is not too severely injured and," he struggled during the audible pause, "Christine. The commissary of police has her, or has knowledge of her whereabouts."

"I will do everything in my power to assist in locating her, Erik."

Before he had finished speaking, Erik had disappeared, but he heard the weary gratitude accompanying a distant "thank you."

"Let us hope you will be as generous when all is done," the Persian said. "Many aspects of this are yet uncertain, especially when there are distractions of the heart."

Yes, diversions and distractions were fast becoming inseparable as Mifroid made a direct advance at Mercier, and fastidious as he was regarding attire, he was able to blend in to avoid any undue attention.

"They are not where you instructed them—"

Mercier held up a finger, interposing the confidence while bidding the last of the faithful subscribers farewell. He then locked the final door and pivoted with flowing alacrity to walk back up the stairs, pondering while being obediently trailed by Mifroid. Suddenly, Mercier spun around to confront Mifroid, causing le Commissaire to side step in order to prevent colliding head on.

"What do you mean, not there?"

"Exactly that—my men are not in place." Mifroid watched an odd vacancy steal across Mercier's face; being sole observer of some vision checked into, post registration. His eye twitched, producing a shiver through Mifroid's torso. "I don't like this, Mercier." Mifroid's tone grated against Mercier's plan. "You say you have facts substantiating this *ghost* to be a flesh and blood human being, that he spoke to you, more than once. Well, so far all I have is air, missing men, and nothing to show for it except guilt. I will not be played the fool again." Mifroid's eyes burned through the fog, evaporating Mercier's visage.

"Fine time for your scruples to appear," he mocked.

"Well at least I have some," Mifroid maintained.

"I heard him! I have a book documenting everything I told you about, it is painstakingly exact; there are names." The din in his expression slapped the commissary with fiendish declaration. "He must pay, he must not be permitted to slip into the shadows. He has wreaked havoc, killed, caused mental anguish and instability. No, Mifroid, this is not a reckless scheme—it is justice for many."

"Justice?" repeated the curious echo.

Mercier's eyes came alive. "Listen, do you hear?"

Mifroid concentrated. Nothing.

Well-placed seed, that one, "I would call it a blind vendetta, hmm? And did you think me ignorant, that I would not recognize my genuine songbird from your cheap mockery?" Erik's smooth, modulating tone raised the hair on the back of Mercier's neck, taking the man to near boiling.

"All pawns are expended!" he cried, grabbing the commissary. Mifroid looked to the empty halls, the vestibules close by, and thought for sure he would live to regret every moment of the convoluted plot reversing upon itself. He stared at the raving lunatic clamping down on his forearm and backed up, swallowing hard.

"No one is here, Edouard. . . only I."

The shock of hearing his name had reestablished a rhythmic connection with sanity and he let go. "Forgive the behavior," Mercier said evenly. "I have been dealing with demons from my own past and often forget myself."

"Well, get hold then, this is no time to fall apart," Mifroid warned.

Standing within one of the conversation balconies, Mercier again reached for Mifroid's arm; the motion produced mild fear with resulting consistence, despite being civilly garnered.

"The Paris Opera has seen much, yet she keeps graciously silent, suffering, but I cannot, and wish to see all at peace, to release the scourge inflicted." Their eyes met and Mercier dropped his gaze. "Bring her. It is time we raised the stakes." His voice had resumed its cold edge. Nodding, Mifroid left to access the anteroom within the side doors of an upper gallery.

Mercier turned slowly, moving along the sumptuous corridor to pause at the head of the grand staircase. "Peaceful," he mumbled. Looking out over the magnificent foyer, he seemed to be contemplating its striking welcome and beneficent impression of creative genius housed therein, when the lights on the main level went out.

"Confound gas-man!" he swore under his breath. "I shall be glad to have electricity installed throughout the building and not just the gasoliers in the theatre."

"Afraid of the dark, are we?" The whisper came from behind Mercier and he froze. The chandeliers were next, bringing the chill of that opulent space into balance with the night, leaving the wall sconces to endure in either direction from where Mercier's feet were hopelessly fused.

"I know all, hear all that transpires within my world." The voice lured Mercier's gaze to the left. Did he dare turn around? Dare to see if his accursed presumption were true? He threw an elbow back and his body followed, nothing, nothing but dense emptiness. He stumbled slightly and groped to right his awkward stance.

"Show yourself, *Opera Ghost*," Mercier jeered, his breath coming in short spasms. "Show yourself and accept your dues."

The darkness shifted, flooding the reflecting marble below with liquid pitch, which solidified unseen to the wanton challenge.

"There is no Opera Ghost, Monsieur." Each word came as distracting thought, preventing Mercier from seeing a flanked figure emerge beneath the stairway, and as the shadows gradually betrayed their covert forms into the gloom from the expected direction, his eyes darted.

"Mifroid?" he hoped. Squinting, and counting no less than half a dozen unrecognizable shapes, Mercier hissed, "What is this?"

"I invited a few of my own guests to this midnight tryst. You see," Erik said, as his calm, dignified presence gestured in acquiescence before the awe of Mercier, "I must now rely on the impartiality of others."

The slam of each iron door filled Mercier's head, his options closing off, swirling copiously amidst the doubt, but he would not be denied, would not concede to the arbitrary credence surrounding him, and with violence of character, Mercier glared defiantly.

"Where is my wife, Mercier?" Erik growled.

"Safe, which is more than I can say for you." Then he professed louder, "I have written proof substantiating the identity of the nefarious Opera Ghost, the one who maintains such an alias, to be this man."

"I suppose you believe yourself immune to any incurred legalities pursuant to this cause," the Persian stated upon hearing the declaration, his whereabouts now clearly discernable.

Erik glanced left, to see a pistol trained on the commissary of police and a shaken Christine within the Persian's charge; there was a sign of tacit confirmation between them. The Persian relinquished control of the bound Mifroid to a guard securing the area from behind, who had one hand settled on his captive, directing him down the stairs, when Mercier turned the attention back toward himself.

"Mifroid, you. . ."

Weaponry cocked as the nearest guard shoved Mifroid to his knees and leveled a rifle to Mercier's chest, keeping *him* stationary as well.

"Somehow your allegiance is misaligned," Mercier said, confronting the guard. "A man of questionable character and ethics, one whose connection to this circumstance is all but assured, and you set your sights on me!"

The guard was undeterred.

"He does nothing unless it is by my order, Monsieur," Faure calmly explained, climbing within view to the first landing below. "Daroga?"

"Monsieur Faure?"

"This information, to which you gave deposition, would it be the same information upon which we have depended and added to these twelve months past? It would be the same information resident in *this* notebook, correct?" Faure held up a worn leather book. Mercier gasped in disbelief.

"One should make sure of what he has if he wishes to inculpate another. There are no barriers impervious," stated the muted conviction.

"If that is indeed my notebook, then yes, although I cannot vouch for said information, but what I do know is that it was obtained under false pretense from my manservant, taken from my home to be delivered to me here, at the Opera House, presumably at my request."

"Edouard, what have you done?" Mifroid shouted. "If Faure already knew, then—"

"He didn't know! That's what I'm trying to make clear."

"There shall be plenty of time for both you and Mifroid to explain—"

"No!" Mercier interrupted. "This is not how it was meant to happen!"

"You'll be put away for a sizable duration." Erik's voice penetrated again into Mercier's thoughts.

"Stop!" he yelled, pressing his hands to his ears in an attempt to ward off more. "Stop the voice! I don't know how." Mercier staggered, pointing to Erik. "He. . ."

The whole of the situation, as it was and had thus far been methodically played out, was deemed prudent in order to reasonably guarantee the safety of all involved, and to obtain a verifiable acknowledgment of guilt. Erik knew Mercier, who was cresting a loss on reality, would not endure the unfavorable turns, and had carefully positioned himself away from the Persian and Christine. How often could he have produced a conclusion, but resisted, his shame and strength of principle easily censuring habit, having wished his past contained, but *it* resisted? In some form, tonight would see cessation to it all. Was he willing to sacrifice all? He glanced at Christine; her face was pale and overspread in shock, eyes dull. How his arms ached to hold her, longed for her closeness, but it was not to be risked, and so he stood, separate and distant. It was time. Erik pushed.

"Unfortunate."

That word was the last in a dam ready to spew. Christine's vision distorted; she blinked, fighting the lightheadedness, only to succumb as her eyes flew up to lock with the animalistic rage unleashed, her legs slowly giving way beneath her. Keeping his pistol aimed at Mercier, the Persian abandoned his hold and let her slide to the floor unceremoniously, where she settled upright. Erik went instantly to one knee, which turned him to face her full on. Mifroid could see Mercier reach for something along his belt, knowing it was the motion of Erik's withdrawal alone that liberated *his* howl of repressed anger.

Mifroid twisted away and dove forward. At that moment, patience ceased, exploding fury into mayhem. Christine's scream rotated Erik toward the oncoming Mercier, and a shot pierced the air, locating its target as a glint of steel plunged into Erik's back. The finely honed instrument ripped flesh and sinew as it blunted against his shoulder blade, which deflected the course downward, cleaving Erik's right side. Pain went unheeded and Erik whirled on Mercier. Grasping him by the neck, he lifted, stared momentarily then heaved, rending his own wound in the exertion.

All went still.

Mercier laid in a crumpled heap at the feet of Faure, battered and broken, while higher up, a different scene, one filled with anguish and compassion, found closure. Christine was draped over Erik's collapsed body, weeping quietly as the Persian knelt close, his hand compressed, observing the slowly expanding pool of crimson.

Erik coughed lightly, placed his hand on Christine's wet cheek, and softly whispered, "Care for them, Soheil."

The Persian bowed his head reverently to a gruesome prospect without reply; here, three men lay for the price of justice, for the price of freedom.

Chapter Forty-Six

I stand at the edge of a vast expanse, for a duration yet unknown, at peace, experiencing a type of rest in which my soul takes the lead, and though my gaze carries outward to no significant point in the outlying depth of numb repose, I must wonder... surely, Death would not be so cruel as to leave me secluded, waiting, and alone. This element, however calming, does in no wise sate one's comprehension with its abrupt singular quality. I had always imagined that others would welcome me to a life in the hereafter, at least I had hoped as much. Then again, perhaps I should consider myself fortunate not to have necessitated the imposition of hell: where the person I am meets the person I might have become... I should have liked additional time for improvement. Here, pain is nonexistent, as well as sound and variance of light, wherein lies nothing and no one. It seems incomplete and, not unlike most decisions in life, I sense a choice looming nearby, one to which I feel my subconscious strangely drawn.

Where was his paradise? Was it where the sun set upon the eve of serenity, inherent in this state of no inclination, or was it achieved through happiness and love shared with another through challenges? Erik had decided that it would be the latter, and turning, he gracefully shied from the deception of ease to search his heart, and breathed in deeply. His hand gently stirred and the infusing breath gave way to pain in an airy groan.

Christine leaned by the open window, looking out upon everything fresh. Rain had come again to the thawing ground, giving rise to the life-blood of nature; trees were awash in plump buds, distant hills richly tinged in verdant veils, mist lifting from valleys, their earthen roads being sun baked hard as birds flitted like arrows through the sky; her white muslin dress shone brilliant, held aloft in motion by the breeze against the lightly-parted blue sheers. Hearing a familiar restlessness, she looked sideways to her left, half expecting the sound to be as the other, involuntary reactions, and was met with a thinly separated lid, which closed tightly thereafter against the harsh intrusion of light. Moving to sit at the bedside, Christine took his free hand and stroked the long fingers, tempting them to curl about the base of her thumb and wrist.

"Try again," she encouraged.

He felt her, heard her, and desired to clasp the dreamlike nymph, hold her to his breast, but could not for want of strength. Despair heightened, his calm deserting until she lightly rested her forehead to his, placed his left hand to her cheek and pressed. He nestled into her soft skin as tears streamed; they burned his parched throat, igniting an intense flush of emotion. "Christine."

"Hush, I'm here."

Erik could feel the gentleness of her lips and moaned. "Hurts..." he finally rasped out in his struggle for breath.

Withdrawing to inventory by sight, Christine realized the pain to be more from his existing condition than from the injury recently sustained; the limitation of motion, and constriction from the bandages wrapped about his chest and right arm, had induced near panic when coupled with the uncontrolled sentiments and initial lack of mental clarity. Slowly, she raised Erik's left arm above his head, removed the pillow, and rolled him somewhat prone. Distracted by the movement, which permitted an easier resolution to all affects, Erik sank, exhausted in the process until later that morning when he made to repeat the attempt at resurfacing. He listened now, detecting whispers, to which gender could barely be placed.

"Christine?" Erik's voice searched. "Christine?" he entreated a second time, thinking her gone when she did not appear.

"Here, I'm here, Erik."

The touch of her lips found the ravages of his face, and he reached for hers in earnest. "Again." To his request came answer enough, swelling the demand of his heart twofold, for the tender caresses roused life and gratitude through pain, though there was a timid reserve shown on her behalf. He heard a muffled chuckle and stiffened, winced, and gasped for air. Plainly understanding Christine's reluctance, worry now etched his features.

"Do not trouble your mind, Erik. Christine and I would not subject you to prying eyes, and that son of yours. . ." the Persian chuckled again. "He is quite determined that his father has no need for such veneer while in his presence."

Their dark friend moved over where Erik could see him at Christine's side, and the Persian's hand settled upon her shoulder. *Nowhere to go!* In seconds, Erik could bear the Persian's unflinching gaze no longer and looked away.

The Persian saw the distress in Erik's eyes. "You should give me more credit. . . friend," the Persian hit the last purposely.

Yes, you should, chided Erik's inner voice. . . *abysmal feeling to be cornered.* The man had seen him, more in this circumstance than any other, he supposed. . . *Don't push away, face him and relax.*

"You are unique, nothing will change that, Erik, but you are loved for who you are." Then, bending to Christine's ear, he accented the comment of sincerity with a lighthearted observation. "Can you believe it? He wakes, and the first things to plague him are love and vanity." He smiled broadly and placed his hand atop theirs. "We shall talk. Heal and absorb your wife's love."

Christine grinned as the Persian righted himself, took hold of and kissed her other hand, and quit the room.

Erik sighed languidly. "I care deeply for that man."

Christine nodded and glanced wistfully to the closed door. "We could not have had a more vigilant guardian, Erik. You were never out of his sight nor did he permit the physician to probe. But I see it in his countenance, when he thinks no one is aware of him watching from the shadows. . . he blames himself."

Erik was solemn, then quite suddenly, lucid as his hand compressed hers to his cheek. "I wish you close, to lay within your embrace."

"What of your—"

"I desire it, please. The pain will subside when I feel your hands apply their ministering balm and hear your heart beat close to mine."

Panting and cursing, sting or no, Erik was able to resettle and nestle in, head tucked securely at Christine's breast. He was satisfied, gently drifting while she brushed those delicate fingers in a light rhythm across his face, scalp, neck and shoulder, mumbling replies to her comments as his body tensed and unwound. Soon, what was once a cognizant exchange, lapsed to become an incoherent jumble of whispers, some of which were his most private feelings floating unguarded from his lips. Several drew tears, but the one eliciting a sweetness of heart came as he muttered, "over. . . just Erik."

"Yes, it is over, and you are now free to be. . . just Erik."

THOSE MOMENTS OF wakefulness increased over the next three days, but it was a week added in its entirety before Erik requested the details from that wretched night. Other matters ordered his attention, especially those of the estate. Word had been sent and received that all was well, and continued to be so under Rossi's competent watch, his management of property and the selective breeding previously arranged, left Erik to convalesce in town untroubled, his abilities later reported on by clients as exemplifying that of Monsieur Gautier.

The evening routine had been well under way this night, the Persian's nervous fashion making an itch seem a welcome distraction as he paced the upstairs hallway, waiting his turn to address both Erik and Christine in release of burden.

"If it were not for the gravity of the pending situation and deterioration of the accused. . ." Christine passed, interrupting his quiet discussion with a sleeping Chèver cradled in her arms. He bowed, the sight softening the memory of their first few nights there in the Barbezac Château. Chèver had been witness to the arrival of his father's unconscious form, but was denied access, understandably; Liana's strength was repeatedly tested while keeping him from the room, trying to soothe the young child's cries for his papa. After all the commotion died away, and the physician felt his patient to be reasonably stable, Christine brought Chèver into the room to see. She gave a brief explanation of the occurrences, relative to his age, and talked about the meaning of hurt and pain. Much to the Persian's astonishment, the child assumed an astute level of comprehension amidst the calming stutter of his small frame. When he quieted sufficiently, and this to the stipulation that the masque be removed, Christine laid him carefully alongside his father, where he remained, listening to his mother sing, and once asleep, he was transferred to a bed of his own.

Strange, the tranquility of rituals, and unfortunate that such a young life need be tainted by grim travesty. "If only Mercier would have left well enough alone," the Persian lamented. "Ah, to have the gift of a talisman conferred at birth would be a blessing indeed, a protection against evil trumping sweet innocence. Oh, little one, your father could have used. . ." He grinned, pausing mid thought. "Then again, my dear friend, perhaps the masque you wear, has been yours."

There was a gentle touch upon his arm, rousing him. "I am ready,"

Christine said. He nodded, both entering one after the other to discover Erik gazing steadily at the ceiling, his fist clenched, seething in pain.

"Erik?"

"Help me. . . please?" His voice was faint, and tears rolled, dripping into his ears.

"How ever did you manage this in ten minutes?" she asked, working together with the Persian to quickly prop him back to his left; newspapers lay strewn about, tenting wherever they had come to rest.

"I. . . ugh. . . wished to read, became irritated with the cushions and had issues keeping the paper from closing, then ended up flat, *damn*."

Christine grinned as she and the Persian gathered the sheets of newsprint. "You could have called out, Soheil was just beyond the door."

"Could not!" came the indignant reply. "Inhalation is near impossible, and if I exhale too far, the weight of my right arm presses unmercifully. Any muscle I attempt to use is an instant reminder, come to me with its manners sharp that I can do nothing unless it is assisted—an ugly fish cast to the shore, environmentally inept, complete with side ventilation. Arrrgh! And pain. Pain is now my constant companion! I cannot sit, stand, or lay without being in its grasp. Additionally, I am bored past what is—"

Christine touched his mouth and he stopped. "I had not expected the complaining to commence so soon." He looked sheepishly at the quelling glare she dispensed. "You are much improved, considering, but if you have chosen the role of martyr for selfish purposes you shall not gain my support nor pity, so think carefully. And if you are in such a rage to disparage this symbiotic relationship with Pain, one request would set you at ease and spare us the remarks."

Erik clasped her fingers; pressing them to his lips, his eyes begged forgiveness.

"Hmm, the justice of tough love inflicted soundly," the Persian said pointedly, as he rounded the foot of the bed.

Erik's forehead contracted, speaking while stretching out for his masque. "Better hers than having to endure the ramifications of yours, though I find myself suddenly mistaken as I have overlooked a twofold advantage, for I am favored equally with both."

"Convenient, taking refuge when the conversation heats up, eh?"

Appalled by the conduct of each, and confused beyond reason why they were so quick to loose their tongues, as neither seemed able to resist needling where it would hurt most, the assumed pardon was retracted in the same motion along with Christine's hand, much to Erik's dismay under observation of the Persian. Quite a drawback too, to the credit of one's ability to hear was surely being subjected to unprofitable adolescence in mixed company. So, with hands crossed in her lap, the foolhardy repartee would be waited out.

They took the hint from her vehement silence and while the Persian had seated himself with his head lowered, Erik, whose options to demonstrate his penance were limited, patiently fingered the tasseled bedding nearest his reach.

"All right..." she breathed evenly, directing her formality toward the Persian. "Would you kindly explain the nature of the crime, if indeed there is one with which we are to be concerned?"

The Persian looked to Erik's show of indifference and back to Christine before proceeding. "Erik, you are exonerated, there is no charge. In behalf of your family, the action of self-defense in order to preserve life, yours as well as your wife's, is permissible and recognized legally. However, Edouard Mercier is not so fortunate. Faure waits to indict him with attempted murder, then together with Mifroid and *his* men, the additional accusations mount from conspiracy, kidnapping, and assault in their varying degrees to other more individualized sins of commission. The two men you intercepted are alive, although one has several unexplained marks about his neck." The Persian glanced furtively at Erik, the pursed lips and eyes bent in attention, his hand once again being entwined with Christine's, were indicative of no forthcoming elaboration. "The woman slept off her stupor and was released, unharmed."

"And what of. . . Mercier? You said Faure waits to indict him," Erik urged.

"Mercier is not expected to live. I believe with the injuries sustained and the information given him, regarding the final outcome and charges, that it was altogether too climactic; he has lost all will to go on."

"Are you saying he knows what he did. . . to Erik?" Christine questioned delicately.

"Yes, he was apprized yesterday."

"Yet he has said nothing. . ." Erik's agitation deepened.

"He has confided in no one but Adèle; Faure will allow time its natural course."

"Where are the notebooks?"

The Persian grinned wide, edging a bit closer as if confiding in secret. "Providence must have specific purpose in mind for you, my friend."

Christine was astonished and puzzled to say the least, for the mischievous tone had Erik's interest fueled outright.

"Faure ended up with both; they were admissible as evidence, but my guess is that he never perused either. I went to see him after you were conscious and Faure handed them over into my possession for verification, then he tossed them into the fire before me, there in his office. I stood mouth agape—I know, not very becoming—then I recalled the discussion between the two of us, about the information and how it was possible, but highly improbable it would be used to charge you. Faure believes now, as he did when I first presented my testimony for deposition, that the whole of the affair surrounding the Opera House was and is, a sensational hoax." He grinned. "Personally, I say his career was tidy, and his disinterest in reopening such a case prior to retiring teetered on imperious, and he knew it. The new evidence gave him the out he was looking for and is what finally convinced him to take action."

"Gone, nothing remains?" Erik asked.

"Ashes," the Persian returned.

"It has ended then," he said, looking at the relief staining Christine's complexion. "And now I lack one thing more, your narrative to the segments my memory is devoid of; I remember only anger and pain."

"Yes, the scene. It is one that continues to solicit a headshake, for it could not have unfolded in the way it did any more than if it had been intentionally choreographed. You remember kneeling, facing Christine?"

"Vaguely."

"Her scream turned your body, angling your back away from Mercier, so when the knife entered, it was deflected down, fracturing the shoulder blade as it ripped your side nearly to the waist." Christine shuddered, not yet having seen the wound. "Mifroid must have noticed Mercier go for the knife because he lunged toward you at the same time you began to rise. Faure and I supposed his intent was to intercept in some way, but he never succeeded. Two shots discharged as one: I fired, simultaneously grazing your left arm while hitting Mifroid square in the shoulder, and the second was from another of Faure's men, who had his sights locked on Mercier; the lead caught him in the back, shattering the base of his spine. The guard closest to us was under strict orders not to fire his weapon, which was a wise move considering his proximity as one too close for speed and accuracy, except for backup. Your wound tore when you heaved Mercier. . . then you collapsed and struck the floor."

Erik winced. "Hence the lump."

"Yes."

"Such a waste." Christine sniffed, staring blankly across the room. Her tears had not the power of cessation and therefore went on. Erik kissed the one hand he held captive, leaving her the other to wipe and stifle the torrent. "Where is Adèle?"

"From what I understand, she stays at Mercier's bedside night and day. He has no family. She felt it only right that he not be alone," replied the Persian. "She knows."

"She would never forgive herself," Christine agreed.

The Persian leaned over as he had done once before and pressed his hand to theirs. "I feel my stewardship is at an end and shall take my leave." The twinkle in his eye gave rise for suspicion. "Christine, perhaps the time is right for you to impart the positive aspects which have come from this sordid ordeal. It is only proper that we end with a beginning. Good night."

Christine stood to embrace the Persian, kissing the softly aged cheek before he moved quietly away.

"Come," Erik, gestured, "tell me." His disappointment registered as she sat facing him.

"Trust me, it is best that we are able to see the other's eyes."

"Cryptic suspense. . . hmm, even better," he said, propping his head comically in the palm of his hand.

"Will you be serious?"

"Not if I can help it, Christine. Severity has dominated and overshadowed the past year and I shall not allow the emotion to control us one iota longer than is necessary."

"Then you are not to be swayed?"

"Depends on the bribe." Her eyes narrowed at that statement and flew wide in surprise.

"Erik!" She moved to fend off his hand as he made to grab hold of her thigh, just above the knee where she was most vulnerable; he snared both wrists. "Ugh! Injured you most definitely are not and you are far more ticklish than I!"

He let go, somewhat unsure of the outcome. "Idle threats, humph! You would never take advantage of me. You would not dare to. . . try?"

"I'm not sure, depends on the inducement."

"Extortionist!" he blurted, to which she produced her best frown. "Fine, fine."

Erik knew she found his behavior rather endearing, but there was always a shade of forced complaisance on his end, which tried her constancy. Usually a swift look away and polite cough behind the back of her hand was more than enough to aid in regaining her composure—the ultimate tongue or lip bite to save face was kept safe for other, more severe inflictions of humor. At the moment, he was all civility and deference, arm tucked up demurely beneath his head, his chin sporting a most undeniable thrust forward in the form of a pout. She was keen, no doubt she knew that he was mentally exploring the challenges of defense and weighing the merits of having use of both appendages; such thought, when placed in a personal light, invariably gave an empathetic rise toward Chanler.

She exhaled softly and reached to retrieve his hand, resting it in her lap. He watched then submitted as the masque was taken; he was listening.

"When we went to Sweden, your experience there made a solemn impression on your understanding about the worth of one soul to another. This week has been just such a manifestation. While you were yet unable to receive visitors for the greater part, many came to enquire, men who are your friends and acquaintances in various investment circles, members of the construction crew, those who worked for you here, and several of Chanler's, and Raoul, they all came to wish you well."

"There are no words," he choked out.

"Part of humanity cares for Erik Gautier." She smiled and cradled his face, drawing close to his ear with her lips. "You have made a difference, you are important, but most especially to me. Without you, *us* would not exist nor would our Chèver. Without you, the child I carry would not be blessing our family at summer's end."

Christine felt him seize her at the hip, her waist, arm, and neck, as though desperate to encompass and embrace every particle to him. He wished to know how long she had kept all a secret, and if it were deemed too long, he would not be accountable for his jealousy. She laughed at his stern attempt and told him that his covetousness was unfounded, for it was revelation to her as well. The Persian had judiciously divulged certain symptoms to the physician, who in turn suggested she undergo a precautionary exam. It was a practical request, yielding sweet results, none of which she would have desired to hide had she known sooner than late that very afternoon.

Erik kissed her tenderly and agreed; it was certainly a beginning well-suited if not well deserved.

Chapter Forty-Seven

The Paris newspaper clamored for no less than a week in hot pursuit, spilling into the next with their scandalous theories and tales; interviews and misquoted sources were prevalent, but there was never a paper left unsold. Most reports detailed Mercier's ravaged, war-scarred life, leaving the Gautier's privacy intact, and the time required in which to heal.

Mercier lost his family during the heartless shelling of the German confederation upon Paris. Upheaval within the city carried to those who had no means of defense, as places of refuge became mausoleums of hell—the only warmth lay among what remained in the blazing streets; ashen skies loomed, consuming the once confident political unit with relentless, belching smoke, and its people, with starvation. Mercier mourned bitterly the treachery displayed in the loss of wife and child, then he picked up the pieces to go on alone. Four years later, as the acting-manager in the newly opened Paris Opera, Mercier found a second opportunity to care again, a passion to encourage, but the tragic deception of it all—in which he permitted himself indulgence—was thinking that the building and business as a whole, were worth more than the people providing the life and soul of opera.

"*Opera Manager Snaps, Attempted Murder—Drama Unfolds Off Stage*. Periodicals filled with grandiose speculation and hype." Erik tossed another paper into the chair and sighed. "The price was too high Edouard, unfortunately high."

"'Unfortunately high'?"

Erik was surprised by the repetition of his words. "Ah, Richard, please."

"Forgive the intrusion on your privacy, the door was open."

"Certainly, I was making a worthy effort to read. Nothing but old news. . . not my preference of literary material, due in part to the situation. . ."

"Yes, yes, tedious and unreliable, completely unethical in their tactics for obtaining information, are they not? They cornered Adèle, poor thing," Richard volunteered quietly, making his way to where Erik had a more direct line of sight.

"Poor, in regard to her ability to stand her own, she is most definitely not."

"Perhaps under normal circumstances. . . Edouard passed away this morning." An uncomfortable moment elapsed and Richard added, "I know it is of no consequence to you—he is better off where we are all concerned actually, but Adèle formed some sort of attachment to him, and a bit of sensitivity from us might ease her heart."

"I feel more for the man than you are obviously aware; he was genuine, to a point. It was the over-extension of that boundary which changed him. Edouard opened Adèle's soul, gave her cheeks color and lightened her years, and for that I would not dream of condemning her compassion."

"Good to hear, because she is downstairs in the drawing room waiting to see you."

Erik coughed, his jaw tensing from the convulsion it evoked.

"May I get you something for the pain?" Richard asked.

"Thank you, no. But I should like to detain you a moment longer if I may. Would you mind?" Erik gestured to the chair next to the bed.

"Not at all," Richard responded nonchalantly.

Richard's ease was false. Perhaps sitting in his presence, and in such close proximity. . . Erik could not help but wonder: did he intimidate him? Here he was, practically laid out flat, and for the better part immobile, and he still maintained quiet nobility, someone that commanded respect; he did not mean to, and leastwise here, it was just. . . Erik sent the thought away.

"I must thank you, the hospitality, opening your home to our family, and your gallantry to ensure the safety of my wife, has not gone unappreciated. I apologize, too, for the injury sustained in the process."

"There is no need to apologize for a situation out of our control. Those men will be justly served, and as for accompanying Christine," Richard shifted his gaze to the newspapers he had set atop the night table, "my mistake was in lowering my guard, in trusting that man's word, and the consequence was being duped by the butt of a rifle." Richard folded his arms and rubbed his face as if an unseen beard were askew.

"It is regrettable when trust is rewarded with deception. You are improved then?" Erik lightened the atmosphere.

"Quite, the only ill effect thus far, in addition to fleeting headaches, is instability. In this case, I find the walls and balustrade work well enough to keep me in line." The two chuckled at the double meaning. "And your stay," Richard subjoined, "it is I who am indebted. Our wives are as sisters, in every sense they have been a support for the other; Christine's nurturing instincts exemplify what a mother ought to be, which in turn teaches Meg, inspires her with Alec, so she feels more at ease. You see, my elder brother, my sisters and I were raised by a nanny and taught by itinerant governesses, only to be thrown in the path of our parents when the formality of a suitable event arose." Richard shook his head in disgust and gnawed on the end of his thumb, speaking next as though a desire of his might yet be realized. "I do not wish my son, or any of my children for that matter, to be a stranger to me or their mother, to be intimidated by expectations, or thought of as failures if standards are not met. . ." He looked like he might say more while his conscience dictated he had said too much, all of which made Richard's character suddenly clear to Erik: no matter the circumstance, no one may claim immunity to hardships.

"As well they should not," Erik reassured.

"Yes, yes. . . well, ay Erik?" Richard stood too quickly, clumsily reaching to steady himself at the bedside, his color heightened as he nodded his leave. "Shall I inform Adèle you are ready to receive her?"

Erik affirmed by returning the nod, thinking silence best, and within minutes Christine was escorting Mme Giry into the room.

"I asked Christine to join me because what I have to say," Mme Giry prefaced, "shall lend closure to our experiences." She closed the door while Christine sat against the headboard, her lap obviously beckoning to Erik. He watched Mme Giry sit before them, a tight-lipped politeness about her emotionally worn face, at once peaceful.

"I apologize for not coming sooner, but knew your welfare was sufficiently tended to. Edouard. . . he had few friends, understandably." Then, looking directly at Erik, she said, "You were fortunate he was not able to inflict more; he meant to end your life even though his intent began with a desire to expose your past to the authorities. You became an obsession, one he was unwilling to surrender." She cried lightly. "Near the end, he shed his insane determination and asked me to convey his apologies; he seemed truly relieved you were alive and recovering."

Mme Giry averted her eyes, her vision blurring again. "He said, 'if the Opera Ghost is sincerely dead then I shall rejoice, hoping beyond hope that the Gautiers may find mercy in their hearts to forgive.' Then," she covered her mouth quickly to stifle a sob and Christine reached out to soothe the distress, which was gratefully met, caught and kissed. Courageously she was able to pronounce the next few words before succumbing fully. "He, he said. . . he loved me."

The room fell to a hush but for the soft weeping, the moving sentiments were observed in unspeakable astonishment until at length it was Erik who wished contact. Christine aligned their hands and he applied gentle pressure, speaking her name.

Her head rose. The grip relayed much, his warmth, sincere empathy and support, and that, coupled with the tenderness in his eyes, expressed remorse. His eyes spoke volumes to her and yet there was calm resolve and quiet.

"I must go, there are arrangements," she said, using the excuse to segue from the unfamiliar emotions in regaining her composure. Mme Giry had distanced herself abruptly by several steps, relinquishing the connection after so short a conveyance; she stopped and turned around to face them, ashamed. "I was mistaken in predicting ruin. To see you suffer devastation and remain so steadfast and devoted. . . If Edouard's death has taught me anything, it would be to let others know I care, before destiny forces reflection and constricts action. I exult in your wise step of faith and the joy your commitment brings. I love you, both of you." She smiled. At this time it was all she could offer in restitution. Looking hastily to the couple, her poise promptly solidified to one of obligation, and she departed.

"Nice to glimpse the vulnerability upon occasion, and although she hides it well, I still sense her disapproval and believe her a bit more severe than need be." Erik pushed up, bracing himself on his forearm.

"I've seen that trait running about in epidemic proportions." Christine stated.

"Have you?"

"I have. Those afflicted are very concise about when and where it is to be seen, and by whom, but by the looks of you, my care shall soon be an unwelcome bother unless I mandate a wife's prerogative to selfishness."

"By all means." Erik was quite ready to comply.

"I am tired of tripping over extra people and dislike being waited upon when I am perfectly able. I sent Liana back to Amiens just so

I might have more to do; she deserves time away from this house of drama, and I am sure Cerise has greatly desired her assistance," she talked on, dislodging his support to pull him close, which Erik did not mind in the least, as he took to nuzzling within the crook of her neck.

Musing at her ferocity, he let his mind wander back to Mme Giry, thinking that she might harbor resentment toward him for the secrecy she felt compelled to uphold, and for living while another did not. Loyalty was hard to come by, notwithstanding tests made even more arduous in the face of a challenge, as he knew only too well.

Erik resurfaced somewhere in the swirl of Christine's linguistic vent, "… dealing with Richard and his fancies, not to mention this malady of balance, poor soul; he saw me watching him make his way into the breakfast-parlor from the foot of the stairs. I suppose he thought I was staring when I was really waiting to see if I could offer assistance. His face told all and I dared not say a word after that for fear of wounding his pride or vanity or male ego, whichever was most applicable at the time."

"The minds of some men… their fixations upon a standard, the pettiness, all might appear to have no ground for expression, but to them it is real. Do not judge him too harshly, my dear. He could do with a bit of patience in his struggles."

Declaring surprise, Christine said, "You have discovered something."

"I have, yes. Interesting what happens when one listens to another who has shared in the same experience."

"Oh, how I love you… and wish to take you home, care for you."

"Persuasion is wholly unnecessary. I shall be at your side, that you may lend your able shoulder for use to the gentleman who loves she who avows her sentiments most ardently."

She hugged and kissed him in earnest.

Chapter Forty-Eight

Not a week more went by and Erik was able to sit and stand for extensive periods, stretching his newfound ability to the limits, and occasionally to exhaustion in order that he might grant his wife's desire to be home. Luckily, persistence won out prior to the evaporation of patience, and the Barbezacs sent the small party of three on their way from Paris to the Minot's waiting arms there at the Amiens train station, prepared to greet them all, hear of their immediate welfare, and to commence with the narrative. This had been Chanler's operative agenda, but it was preempted on the spot when Cerise laid hold of Chèver. All that mattered were present and uplifting subjects—anything else could wait until young ears were asleep. Naturally, the men made concessions up front then turned right around to sate curiosity. Erik was free and almost too happy to go against the grain and share openly, in hushed tones away from Grand-mère, of course.

Rain was as copious an element here as it had been in the east, the roads being abused worst by the unnatural combination of man, animal, and transportation. Although, however quintessential the upcoming carriage ride was, it would become an experience and exercise in how one might be disposed to the rank of mute. It could hardly be expected that Erik would not have some mild form of complaint. He lay over several cushions, and Christine's lap, hoping to mitigate the roughness. . . to no avail; groans were met with apologies, and a light gripe with disregard, but it was the threat of getting out to walk because it would be less jarring, which turned Cerise to disagreeable. She was ready to accommodate the whining with a kick to Erik's backside, and was about to make known something to that effect when Chèver, who had been keeping a most diligent watch, beat her to it.

"Trains don't hurt. Sorry, Papa."

Erik glanced up, kissed his finger, and held it out for his son to grasp. "You are correct, thank you, Chèver."

Cerise checked her temper and recovered unknown to the rest, clearly chastened by the compassion of an understanding child.

When the distance closed to a solid half-mile from the estate, Erik could tolerate the carriage no longer and wished to stretch his legs. "A stroll in appreciation of life," he said, enlisting his bones to task and, as Christine was to accompany him, Erik charged Chèver with seeing his *grands-parents* safely home, and after his walk with Maman, the two of them would see to the horses, together.

Chèver sulked bravely, agreeable as the idea was.

"He shall be fine," Cerise mouthed.

Erik cast a sideways glance with an idea in mind, and taking up Christine's hand in earnest, led her away amongst the trees. His gait was slow, halting but intent, the design set, as Erik pushed ahead, exerting himself; the sudden freedom from oppressed confinement, mentally and as nearly physically as could be, had delighted his senses. A keen impression of liberation was equally shared, and not knowing—for this escape met with his design only—whether it was sheer happenstance or will that she ensue this flight, both were duly charmed at the prospect of solitude.

Seeing the object recalled from a time before, Erik circled about, coming face to face with Christine as he moved backward to position himself within the barreled folds of a large, old oak. Panting lightly he leaned in to his left and drew her close, but not yet unto himself. She looked up at the magnificent tree and her countenance brightened; the branches spread close to twice its height and were covered in the feathery adolescence of spring, a freshness paralleled only in wonder by that of creating life. They inhaled, drinking in the affect without visual aid, to reopen jointly, their gaze affixed to the other in convential admiration. Both searched without benefit of word's confirmation, the depth to which either experienced the calming pleasure of being at last, content; but for Erik, it meant more.

Ever so quietly, he lifted her hand and pressed her palm softly to his lips, his eyes closing against the flow of quick, hot tears. Here, in the presence of his wife, it felt cleansing to permit the concluding release; he just stood there and wept openly. Despite the previous weeks of recuperation, to a point where he could travel, he was thoroughly tired out, both in mind and body, and had not found the privacy availed him to feel otherwise. So much feeling begged its turn that he had no wish to beleaguer such with speech, to hasten from that security upon which his soul relied, nor did he wish it from Christine, who was solemnly resolute and attuned to him. There was also the encumbrance the use of one arm afforded, and for her hand to linger as he embraced her lovingly, attached her to him all the more.

"Hold me tight, no. . . masque." His faltering request met with such warmth that he at once gave in to a second escape of emotion. Composing himself, he drew apart just enough, leaving his cheek touching hers. "I am home."

"And well loved."

To this simple avowal his breath shortened, the moist air caressing her ear renewed each time he swallowed until he could no longer curb the flare, then hesitantly, with mind alight, he claimed her lips for a gentle, impassioned kiss, and trembled. *Oh. . . she feels as I. Our responses mirror the other; the pleasure in loving and being loved. The control she has, to which I relinquish all sentiments and power. I do not feel it a threat, nor is it shameful or humiliating, but a refuge in which to place my trust; I love her, desire her. . .*

Indeed he did, and he told her most passionately, quickly sending her complexion into a feverish bloom, and he rejoiced. Those few precious moments were appreciated by both and fervently cherished, being a right of passage between husband and wife, for if they did not set aside time then, to allow the insecurities and relief some measure of safety, a compounding of assumptions may be misconstrued as content. The affair was over and neither would speak to it again. *En fin de compte, à la fin!*

The two ambled along arm in arm, and what remained of the intervening distance to the estate was soon diminished, placing them within sight of Chèver. Sniffling, he wriggled free from Grand-mère Cerise and padded thoughtfully to his parents, holding his arms out to be hoisted up by his mother.

"By the looks of things we have all had our share of tears, hmm?" Erik asked, observing the stains down Chèver's face.

Chèver nodded and held out his scraped hands for his father to inspect, and Erik, putting on his most distinguishable expression of severity, gave them a good once over. "Ah, took a tumble, did we?"

"I don't like hurt, Papa."

"Neither do I, Chèver. It will heal, Maman shall make it better, she makes Papa's pain go away." Erik winked, kissing them both. There was a ray of sunshine backlighting his smallish grin and tilt of the head as Chèver's brow furrowed in thought, ending the process with a swift, hard blink. Erik smirked at the attempt and pointed to Grand-père Chanler. "Grab his hand and we'll go see to the horses."

Christine and Cerise stood encircling the other, and together watched after their men, Chèver acting as malleable bond as they walked toward the stables.

Christine sighed. "Quite a picture, the three of them."

"That they are. Any clue as to who might be the wisest?" Cerise asked. "My best guess would be the one in the middle."

Laughing, Christine added, "They all have their moments, respectively."

More laughter came, and when they had quieted they heard Chanler's unmistakable bellow, followed by another equally as hearty, and the light giggle of the youngest. Christine moved to see if she could catch a glimpse of them, but was quickly prevented.

"It is best if we do not monitor their carefree moments and better for our sanity that we remain ignorant; we might live longer." Cerise was peremptory, it was a standing trait of hers that Christine had long since considered natural when professional duties arose, but found it decidedly odd that she did not mind its appearance in this instance; the tone of escort was anything but overbearing and was alternately in jest. She mused inwardly at Cerise and the momentary change of stripes, for no one would be denied that right, least of all anyone who set foot across the Gautier threshold.

And so it was that Peace began her refrain.

THE THREE QUARTERS of an hour, in which Chanler sat comfortably before the chessmen of opposing color, was beneficently spent. Heat filled the room on that uncommonly cold evening; the source crackled and popped merrily, its sound colliding with an angelic harmony drifting from the upstairs loft to engulf the willing listener.

"They construct brilliance; vocally raise mansions in homage to deity." He sunk into the rich confines of the chair relishing each note, and no sooner had he availed his full attention did the lyrical sedative take its course and cast him into a state of abandon.

Stepping up near Chanler, Erik whispered without mandate of bending, handkerchief in hand. "You're drooling like a babe, my friend." Chanler started, tossing his aim outward, narrowly missing all inanimate objects as cause. "Here," Erik offered. "Fortunate for me to be out of reach."

Gaining his head about him, Chanler tended to the errant spittle in haste. "Ugh! Thank you." His countenance kindled from the light surrender. "Such an exhibit and you, I daresay, are amused but shall abstain from laughter that I might save face, at least until I can make my getaway. Chess?" he interjected.

Erik rotated the chair opposite and seated himself firmly. "Of course... but I should laugh now; by the time you are gone from here I shall forget."

"That I should never believe."

"Agnostic that you are, reformation pleads at your feet. Your move."

"I know, don't push. One-armed men need more time to think."

"They're pawns, Chanler. It is a one-handed game and has naught to do with the quantity of limbs possessed. Besides, we are evenly matched, no excuses."

"You ascribe such candid fact to my one imperfection, and with ready wit and ease too... hmm, there."

"One?" Erik's query wounded swift the failing pride, salvaging it prior to unrecoverable collapse. "I mean—I figured our lineage converged somewhere... the intelligence and good looks, but *I* have more than one flaw."

"All right, I shall admit to it, I have more than one as well, though we shall not allude to more," Chanler stipulated on the sly. "Yes, we are a fine-looking pair of gentlemen."

Cerise caught the last phrase as she entered with tea, and knowing her husband well enough, she understood the comment and raise of conversational tone to be for her benefit. "Fine pair of gentlemen, the two of you?"

Erik could tell she was prepared to interpose as advocate, but in whose favor she would make this supporting intercession for, was as yet undecided.

"That was, fine-*looking* pair, my dear," Chanler clarified.

She set the tray on the side table and turned to scrutinize with a grin. "Fine-looking, yes, a pair, no... a mismatched set of bookends, *that* would better describe the likes of what I see," she said cheerily.

Christine's brief punctuation of laughter unexpectedly betrayed her presence to the occupants of the room and they all glanced up in her direction. "Forgive me, I. . ." She covered her mouth, self-conscious that her initial outburst was quickly becoming an irrepressible force, which suddenly turned her from their gaze to take hold of the rail. She gambled another look, and tears streamed in place of the jovial response as she tried to stifle the hilarity resounding in the sight and phrase. She required a few more moments, and thinking to have recovered herself sufficiently, wiped the tears from both cheeks while coming around once again. It was dizzying, the *fou rire*[13] which seized her. She fought, but succumbed, it was of no use confronting the visage of "bookends" when viewed in such a humorous light.

Cerise was first to join in, with the men tagging immediately after, as the purpose of such a reckless emancipation soon redirected itself toward Christine. There was now no way of bypassing her as center attraction; what with her soundless gesticulations, writhing and gasping, it was the typical circumstance of a damsel in distress, compelling Erik to leave his post and mount the stairs to enable a passage of rescue. Christine was by this time half seated, half sprawled between the head step and baluster.

Erik bowed royally, making a rolling motion with his left hand in greeting. "As representative, I can say we are well pleased in having provided your evening's dose of comedy, and if you are quite finished, I shall be delighted to escort you down."

She breathed deeply, which was a good omen, stood, and took

her husband's arm, to make a successful descent, void of recurrence. Chanler held out his hand to which she eagerly clasped hers. "Very entertaining, dear, perhaps your next audition should take place at the Comique Theatre, a different genre?"

"Thank you, no." Christine seemed almost amused, wiping away a residual drop near her eye. "I appreciate your tolerance, it felt refreshing to laugh, but the stage shall not be entertaining my attention as I have other, more engaging interests, and am entering a more private season in life." She patted Chanler's shoulder as Erik embraced her from behind, his hand giving her stomach a thoughtful touch.

"Come with me," Erik encouraged, leading her to the sofa.

Cerise glanced at Chanler, who had just begun sipping his tea. "Bring your cup. Let's you and I clean up."

"Clean up?" He followed her lead to whisper. "I just settled in! Fickle, that's what you are, we were—"

She nudged him, hushing the completion of his sentence with an incisive motion to heed the indications all around him.

"Ah, good night," Chanler called softly.

Christine looked their way and smiled, but Erik did not, making a believer of the agnostic, who was all but forsaken at present, and rightly so.

Her face glows, shines as it once did. She had been complacent, busy, and unsatisfied, but this is how I wish to see her. . . bright. Erik knelt before her, sat back on his heels and gazed steadily, suspending the moment to full. *I adore how she passionately reddens when caught off guard, how her lashes hold the last bit of moisture as dew; the starburst of crinkles that gather at the bridge of her nose when she expresses her tender sentiments. Her figure, as she leaned in at the doorway to Chèver's room tonight, I could envision the small life in blossom within her womb. . . strange how obvious it is to me now.*

Christine's eyes closed to mere slits, Erik had withdrawn into some sort of trance-like form of humility. "Care to enlighten me?" Her tone beguiling him, he grinned broadly, gained his footing and without utterance, caused her to be at his side.

Upstairs, their door slid shut. Erik checked her hand as he raised it close to his lips, and seemed to consider whether the atmosphere met with his approval; her hand finished its rise, was kissed and discarded. Leaving her standing, he walked to the mantelpiece, bent carefully to stoke the fire, rose up and pivoted to begin shoving furniture from off the circumference of the rug; he then tossed blankets and pillows to the floor in a heap and returned for her.

"Such an enigmatic demonstration." Again, the impish grin shone wide, only now, she had but to piece her visuals together. Erik watched the blaze increase in the reflection of Christine's eyes, marvel dancing from those volcanic pools. He pressed close and courted her descent to kneel with him, finally gliding to sit left of the other, foreheads touching.

"I feel..." he spoke tentatively, "I feel I love you more than I did four years ago, even more than when we first married, or when Chèver was born, if it is possible." His fingers caressed the skin along her neck. "You have given me life, in so many ways, Christine, and most recently by shifting my attention at such a crucial moment. There is no one I would rather be indebted to, than my wife."

Dislodging the hindrances to the enjoyment of delicacy, Christine's fingers massaged his scalp and stroked the tawny waves as he slumped against her. "I love you, Erik."

"But, are you happy?"

There seemed a thick apprehension on the verge of supplanting his already established felicity and she dared not hesitate upon a reply. "Yes, you brought me freedom this evening, and I let go the past and forgot." He relaxed, the answer easing that edgy trigger of doubt to remain inert, then she expounded, "I am blessed to share a life with someone who is concerned for my well-being. When I have the occasion to hear others deride the flaws of their spouses, I refrain from participation and rejoice inside. Marriage is the blending of two incompletes into an uncircumscribed whole and I experience joy in *all* that that encompasses. . . *all*."

"Would you tell me if you were not?"

"You are sensitive enough you would feel it on a more profound level."

He thought on that concept and followed through. "I do not recall sensing unhappiness from you, perhaps distaste for a specific position or circumstance and probable behavior, but never regarding our relationship, at least not after a certain point."

"Trust that, and know I am indeed, happiest of women." Erik's heart swelled, his lungs too, and he flinched in pain. "Someone exceeded their limits?"

"I might have," he grimaced.

"What would you have me do?" she asked, looking at him directly, as another of his devilish smiles played overtly about the corner of his mouth. She blushed. "Truly, Erik."

"Removing these cloth coils would be a start."

"You're sure?"

"Yes, please. I should like to examine the wound myself. Until we left Paris, I was in too much pain when the physician changed dressings to care; curiosity has gotten the better of me since."

Erik unfastened his shirt while Christine retrieved a few supplies for cleansing his skin, and included one hand mirror. Returning, she reclaimed the bandages from his torso and rolled them neatly for reuse. The familiar proximity was immensely enjoyed as Christine's arms circled his body at each revolution, and as the constriction began to subside he stretched his lungs in accordance.

"Better, hmm. . . much improved."

"You know, there are others who share in the preservation of your life," she commented, holding up the mirror so her fingers could be seen tracing the scar and stitches.

"I disagree. Any action occurring post injury would not have had any bearing upon my personal outcome."

"What about the part Soheil accepts?"

Erik's eyes were drawn to hers in an instant, his gaze disappointed. She was testing his tolerance for the topic he refused to acknowledge, and was sure she had received her answer; it was sorely fresh.

"Must we spoil our homecoming with talk of him?" He adjusted the mirror.

"I have been trying to understand the impasse on my own. Look at you, I mention his name and you tense. I also find the situation rather disturbing that we have had no contact since he relinquished his obligation and took leave of us." Her ambush was unjust, almost traitorous, talking of trust, joy and terms of endearment then serving it right back at him when he was most vulnerable. "I do not mean to interfere, I'm just worried for you both."

"I cannot take responsibility for the guilt he brings to the table between us; we shall deal with it in time. Our friendship has survived far worse." Then as a quiet afterthought, "I only hope it may come out unscathed."

"Has it?"

"What, been through worse?" he clarified, turning from his reflection. She nodded, muttering a soft "yes" while setting the mirror down out of the way.

Directly, there came a deafening silence, intrusive as the urgency of a knock from a trespassing interloper having stolen upon their evening; it was a relative of Past, arriving with baggage as if expecting to impose itself for an undisclosed time. Erik was agitated at his inability to manage longer intervals without such an intrusion from History, but it had come and meant to stay unless other, more fitting arrangements could be secured.

"You know this is highly unfair of you, to derail my tranquility."

"Meaning I am fortunate not to have brought out your resentment in full and there is hope for realignment?" Christine kissed his right hand, having commenced her ministrations upon the confining stiffness in his joints.

"Beguiling creature, using your feminine trickery to wheedle from me the knowledge you wish."

"You would prevent it if you did not think it wise to discuss. The tears we shed earlier today were the physical release for our emotions; the harbored thoughts have yet to be expressed, and they are those most specifically affecting the void Soheil leaves."

"Void." He nursed the connotation carefully. "I never desired his presence in my life. At first, he was someone who tolerated me, someone I felt remotely connected to because he made the effort to know the *why* behind who I was. Comprehending any sacrifice given me, by him, was as a gnat in the scheme of significance; I seemed invincible, and he didn't matter, not until you awakened in me the minute intimation that I might be loved." Erik stared into the flames. "You said he blames himself."

"By his looks, if not in word."

"You do not understand the poignant depth to which that observation bleeds. He and I spoke the morning we had set aside for his joint visit with us. He sat before me and confessed as though I were ecclesiastically endowed; his meeting with Faure after you and Chagny had disappeared, the written documentation detailing everything for the papers before I graced his doorstep, everything in the open... there was a slue of facts he never saw the need to disclose because he thought I was going to die. And when I did not, his skepticism aroused twofold; he wished to believe and put up an excellent front, kept his evidence as backup, adding tidbits to it continuously. What I had not foreseen was Soheil's use of the notebooks; he gave the more concise version to Mercier and the one

I reconfigured, *it* was provided openly to Faure. I knew, to some extent, of what Soheil hid away and did not fault him for it, I told him so, thanked him even, for his faith in me. I never questioned, only trusted his word when he said he believed there was good beneath my heinous exterior.

"His struggles heightened when this whole mess with Mercier started. I denied the tedious exhaustion playing about his efforts because I required assistance and he, halfheartedly, thought it might be another one of my elaborate, two-faced ploys. I could see it, sensed it when we met together, even when all came crashing down, but it was not until then that I finally realized the breach in our trust, and it pained me." Erik vacillated before prefacing the subsequent section of the account, for it would portray that which was most grievous to his heart.

"Soheil now blames himself for behaving similarly to Mercier, for being tempted to collaborate against me; I tormented him as well." Erik exhaled wistfully. "He is an excellent marksman, Christine. He was positioned at Faure's command and left up to his own volition, he would not have missed had I given him just cause, but his heart believed when he saw I put your life above that of my own, when I turned my back to all else."

Christine looked at Erik tearfully. "Why? He has always been there for you, so kind to me."

"And he always will, only now, our friendship shall subsist from sincerity and not from a sense of duty. There has always been a difference garnering his professional and individual ethics—the letter verses the spirit of the law—it was his reluctance to trust which made the dictates of a rigid penalty easier to uphold. What was most difficult for him were the days following my injury, when he was able to watch you and Chèver; he is ashamed, and condemns himself for not living up to the expectations of his given name. Soheil means star."

Lightly tarnished guide, she thought. "Your friendship. . . so you hold no enmity for what he has done." Her words were a sigh of calm fact as well as great consternation, for *her* ideal of a friend was not in the aforementioned description.

"How can I, Christine? In a state of double-mindedness, I could have carried off the farce with ease. Soheil is not my enemy, he has received my forgiveness and I his trust. I believe the burning of the notebooks, his care of us, and his suspicion of you being with child, to be a means of recompense. We shall see him, in time."

"But the way you two carried on. . . the banter, his undermining remarks of censure!"

"To assess, challenge, and try my worth."

"And the ostracism, he wishes this?"

"It is his burden of choice. Similarly, I would expect your feelings for him to remain unchanged. He cares most profoundly for those placed under his stewardship, and as complex an issue as this is for either of us to resolve, he must know of our love for him."

Never had Christine heard such tender compassion; he was demonstrating a side of meekness which she, until now, would not have dreamed existed toward anyone other than their family. The wise, forgiving counsel was beautiful. "Thank you for confiding in me. I care for him as well and shall not falter," she said softly.

Erik raised the determined focus away from his arm to him; her face bore moist streaks, which she suddenly found caressed by two hands. "I wished to be selfish with my joy, was lightly perturbed when I discovered our playfulness to be veering from the course envisioned, but I am grateful for the detour. The reverence feels right."

With the uninvited guest left desolate of narrative material, Love flourished in the governing hours, warming souls with appreciation for the intricacies of compassion and beauties that intrigued the senses to a level of keen perception, all of which were made possible by the underscore of sweet esteem.

Chapter Forty-Nine

An icy chill needled Erik through the drug-induced haze; he tried resisting the sojourn to consciousness, but the departure seemed imminent. There was a relentless cold buffeting the once anchored reef of blankets, which had gradually given way to nocturnal currents, exposing just enough skin to the elements that the discomfort could no longer be ignored and would now require effort. He shifted, fidgeted, and at last, sent his hands in reconnaissance for heat. Christine was nestled into, and a firm grasp placed across her abdomen, ensuring the satisfaction of the bow, but left the stern set wide.

Christine rolled in the tight embrace and rose up on her forearm to cover his shoulders, an instinctive response to a single moan and shiver. "Erik, the balcony door is open," she said, having spied the reason for his symptoms.

Still lightly groggy, Erik began to lift his ironclad lids and remarked, "Pleasant view."

She thumped his chest with the back of her hand. "Be serious."

Tucking his right arm in, he pushed with his left, elevating himself to sit as Christine moved gingerly from their earthen bed upon the floor, quickly donning her dressing gown as a second layer against the bitterness of the morning. Erik sensed nothing amiss—then again, he could not sense much of anything through the fog—and decided Christine would be quite capable of shouting her appeal, if one were absolutely necessary. Deeming the latter as the correct assumption, for it was entirely based on the smile now having captured every particular in his sight, and thinking his heroism to be unwarranted, he headed straight for the covers. Regrettably, he was not quick enough to evade the summons that came for him to silently join her.

"Look, the offender remains at the scene." Erik's eyes strayed beyond her gesture as he stepped up from behind.

The doors framed a precious first, with Chèver meagerly wrapped in a light blanket. He was squatting, one foot curled atop the other while examining the phenomenon presented before him. Holding out one hand, a delicate flake of snow would settle in his palm then disappear to nothing more than a droplet of water, and yet he could put his finger beneath a few inches of the peculiar substance already amassed and lift up, catching another on its descent, this one remained. His parents watched as an obvious thought deterred his young focus, and he glared at his feet, bothered; he was standing in a puddle. His face contorted into full pout before stating sadly, "Stars all gone."

Erik smiled proudly at the unique assumption. "I guess astronomy lessons to be in order."

"Is this how you were?" Christine wondered softly.

"Most likely. I know I grasped language early, same as he. My comprehension and musical skills together seemed to spur an insatiable voracity for learning, and I soon became an avid reader. I loved to draw and tinker, *detested* writing, and was most stubborn."

"We shall see which traits he tends toward," Christine murmured, stroking his cheek. Moving from Erik, she opened the door a bit wider and stooped next to Chèver. "Good morning, sweet boy."

"Morning," he said without turning to acknowledge her, his sullen reply indicative of the withdrawal from his revelry in nature. "Why do they fall?"

"Their beauty makes them seem like stars, come to shed their brilliance up close, does it not?"

He looked at his mother's face, unsure of the turn in her phrase. "Yes, but the sky is empty, I do not want them to go 'way."

"Chèver." The large blue eyes shifted to his father. "These are snowflakes, each a mere droplet of water, like rain, until cold air touches it, then it bursts and drifts gently to the ground. We'll gather some in a little while and take them downstairs for a look through Papa's microscope, what do you say?"

To this explanation, Chèver brightened and immediately went back to his evaluation of the frozen miracles, receiving a light tap to regain his attention.

"It's cold. Come, Chèver, come inside," Christine encouraged.

"Not yet."

"They are fascinating," she agreed, tugging at his blanket. "And if we hurry, you and Papa can collect them before the sun breaks across the horizon."

"No! I want to stay here," he exclaimed emphatically.

"Careful your tone, now come. . ."

"No!" Chèver refused abruptly. He spun sharply and flung his hand out toward his mother, but a larger, more agile hand intercepted, lifting the young man from the distraction and into the room to sit squarely on his parents' bed.

Erik was incensed at this behavior, his own manner a reflection of the inner rage, though he calmed just as quickly, moving a chair close to sit at eye level in front of Chèver. This, Erik presumed, would constitute another first: an encounter of wills, patience, and love in the face of discipline.

The two sat quietly, Father observing Son, the silent tears

streaming down the soft curves. "You made an attempt to strike your mother—why? She was kind and reasonable in her request of you."

His father's tone was very gentle, but the gaze was not so forgiving. Chèver could not bring himself to look fully upon the disappointed expression, it was new to him and unfavorable, yet he understood its meaning.

"Did you understand me, Chèver?" There was a quick bob. "Then, why?"

"I wanted to stay and Maman," his eyes flicked to his mother closing the door, then bent again on the rug, "wanted different."

"Yes, different," his father echoed. "The way you have chosen to express yourself is not acceptable, and shall not be tolerated as such. A woman, whether it is Tante Meg, a sister, a young girl, or someone older, and especially your mother, should be given honor and respected at all times. Has Maman ever struck you?"

"No."

"Has she ever moved to strike me or I her?"

"No."

"But you have seen this occur."

Chèver raised his head sorrowfully. "Oncle Richard."

Blast it! Erik's face pained, and taking offense at the name he looked away, momentarily unable to bear what his son had uttered in evidence of impressionable innocence. *Not only that, but I most likely compounded the issue by using Tante Meg as an example.* Christine was instantly there, her fingers wrapping supportively across Erik's shoulder providing the exemplar he needed most, and taking hold, he kissed her hand tenderly.

"Chèver, I should like you to follow our examples. Hands have the ability to bring joy and do so much good." He sighed before refocusing, genuinely amazed. "The unsavory behavior is not to be mimicked, not to happen again, are we clear upon this?"

"Yes," he replied, glad that his father's face had softened.

"All right, I wish you to think about your conduct, in your room, and when you have decided how to make amends, you come tell me."

Erik dismissed Chèver with a curt bow of his head, and scampering down from the bed, the child was off through his mother's dressing chamber, his blanket trailing directly behind.

Christine gave Erik's neck a light kiss. "What's that for?"

"For treating me well," her eyes went teary, meeting his enquiry straight on by sitting in the void left by Chèver. "And for your wise counsel to our son."

"I intend to teach him how to control his anger, seeing as my recently touted traits have come to light. Chèver shall learn what it means to be a gentleman as well." Erik huffed at the thought of what his son must have been witness to. "I may also have a few words to exchange with Richard. . . how dare he abuse Meg, and in front of our son."

"We do not know that, perhaps they thought themselves alone."

"Regardless!"

"Of what," she broke in gently. "This is the perspective of a young boy whose perception is based on inexperience."

"I won't go bursting in to accuse Richard, if that is what you imply. I just feel raising a hand against a woman, for any reason, to be inexcusable."

"I agree."

Presumptions might have continued on but for the exuberant distraction bounding through from the hall, which turned instantly and sunk. "Maman in trouble?" It was an obvious conclusion, grave faces, tears, low even tones, and his mother sitting where he had once been.

"No, of course not, leastwise this morning she is most amiable!" A glint brightened Erik's eye as he patted the spot next to Christine, her brow arching as Chèver climbed up. Chèver glanced to his mother to confirm and his father's brow rose, the emotional confusion being served in rather rich portions.

"Sometimes, Chèver, happiness overflows the bounds of the heart." She kissed his forehead and smiled.

"Well, you have come back quite speedily, and with a solution?"

"Yes, Papa," he responded, turning to look up at his mother. "I 'pologize Maman, I love you."

"Thank you, Chèver, I accept your apology." Upon this confirmation, he reached to hug her about the neck then slid to the floor, took her hand, and gave a pronounced kiss to the back of her fingers. The loud *smack* caused Erik's eyes to widen in surprise, but in order to conceal the smile, and near betrayal of a laugh at Chèver's sincere ovation, his hand flew up to a gruff throat clearing.

"Papa?" Chèver pulled on his father's sleeve. "May I see?"

Without a word, Erik lifted Chèver back up on the bed and sat next to Christine himself. The little features went through a myriad of contortions while his eyes traced the outline of his father's wound along with his fingers, gently caressing the extensive bruising full length. Questions were plied until satisfaction was met, and a kiss administered to make well the colorfully hued skin.

"I do not want you to hurt," came Chèver's guileless plea. The slim arms encircled, stretching as far as they could. "I should like you. . . better, Papa."

Erik held him tight against his chest. "In time," he said, cherishing the virtue, wishing he could protect the ingenuousness from the conflicting values of the world, and knowing all would resolve in the trusting arms of his child.

Chapter Fifty

Four months passed peacefully enough, till it was time once again to interface—on a larger scale—with humanity. Christine's confinement neared term, and Erik's injury had served to heal their family in several different respects. There was the ongoing, physical mending, Erik's range of motion being the current blight of frustration to which he must suffer patience, for *in time* it too would improve, and second; familial, the reclusive, self-indulgency had securely knit their reliance to one another. Erik flourished under his wife's attention and readily acknowledged the level of spoilage to which he had become accustomed, and Chèver's development increased, astounding even his father with his capacity to discern concepts. The two inseparable males would descend the stairs into the studio from the study, only to reemerge later, to seek out Christine and share a portion of their excitement from all the wondrous delicacies they had partaken. Already, Chèver had shown a preference, an inclination toward the whys of science and in turn, their daily routine included a healthy portion of play and attention to the arts. They basked in the intensity each had to offer the other; for one it was genius, and from the other, a childhood.

"Maman, may I have an apple?" Chèver asked, skip-hopping into the kitchen.

"Would you like it cut up?"

"Oh no, my horse prefers it whole."

"*Your* horse, and naught for yourself, hmm? Perhaps I should consider later as acceptable for a few slices?" He nodded. "So, which one is to be the recipient of such favoritism?"

"The one I caught." He was confident enough, but puzzling all the same.

Christine's heart began to race. "With a regular rope or lasso?" she asked, hoping the answer would be the former.

"A rope."

"I see." She breathed, now more intent on the informant. "Does your father know of this horse?"

"Naturally."

"And where is he. . . your father?"

Chèver looked up inquisitively at his mother, not understanding what could possibly be ascertained from asking so many questions. "Tied up at the moment."

Christine handed him the apple and he turned, thanking her as he went.

"Hold up there, my little man. You should wait for Papa, should you not?"

"Wait? No," he said flatly and rounded the doors.

Wiping her hands, Christine quickly shed the apron to tail after this mystery, which seemed a perfectly normal occurrence to the sandy blonde lad. She followed him right through the doors into the study and came so near to spurting an impulsive, unladylike guffaw of laughter that she had to employ both hands to muffle the callous fit.

Perched in front of the hearth was Erik, much as a turtle with his underside exposed, wrists and ankles bound.

"Are you ready, Papa?"

Erik glanced up at the subjoining movement into the room, embarrassment flashing hot at the predicament in which he found himself unavoidably stuck.

"Hello. . . Maman." *I'll not live this one down.* There was a brief pause. *Christine's journals, blast!. . . Generations, too!*

"Hello yourself, Papa." She looked at Erik, enigmatically amused, her eyes asking how he managed to get into this one, and then she promptly seated herself at arm's length from the spectacle. "Chèver, if you would elaborate upon your good fortune and how you came to ensnare such a fine specimen, I would be most obliged. As things stand, I am quite unfamiliar with the origin of this breed." Erik grimaced, she was playing right along.

"Glad to," he said, sitting in her lap. "This is a black 'rabian stallion, his bloodlines go way back to desert bred. . . he is very rare. . . because black gets hot." The gleam in Christine's eyes deepened; hot could not begin to describe it. "He should do nicely here in Europe with more shade."

Erik stared at the ceiling as Christine gave him the once over, eyeing his black riding trousers and the polished sheen of his boots. "You are enjoying this," he voiced within her ear, which invoked the response of a nose wrinkle and the mouthing of, "I believe so."

"Papa promised if I could tie the knots correct, he would show me how to eat an apple without any hands."

"No hands, I may be interested in this feat of trickery. I believe the knots are properly executed?" she posed, the wry query flattering.

"Yes, Chèver figured them out." He sighed in resignation, suddenly wishing he had not let his pride get the better of him, but he was a man of his word, and as he created the bed, so must he lie in it.

"Chèver, I should think your horse to be famished and amply tortured."

Carefully, Chèver placed the apple between his father's chin and shoulder, and without delay, the rosy orb began to disappear until only a thin core was left.

"Amazing," Christine gasped. Chèver clapped and removed the core, dangling the remains as though he had never before seen the innermost portions and what was contained therein, then handed it over to his mother for inspection. "Loosen your steed's bindings, Chèver."

Erik sat up to a more dignified position, wiping the sticky juice from his chin as Christine passed the core back to Chèver and asked him to deposit it in the basin, prior to devouring his own treat on the kitchen counter. Appreciation was expressed beforehand as he vanished through the doorway, exulting the marvels of his prize Arabian.

Head her off. She'll know it's not just a stunt and want to know the whys of ever having learned such a thing. All humor diminishing Erik began instantly to answer the forming questions. "When I was young, I discovered myself in quite a few disobliging circumstances, which required I become either adept at eating without hands or starve." He shrugged. "I had not expected an audience."

"You made your son happy by keeping your word. He was unaware of anything deeper."

"Yes, but—" Erik was silenced by an appreciative kiss.

"I understand."

Yes, she did. Her eyes told him she did. He loved her, their life. . . he sighed, relieved.

"No regrets, besides, I found you very appealing."

"Vulnerable," he countered, lifting her into his arms and walking through to the lounge in the great room. "Oh, and material aplenty, for some mortifying piece to be entered in that journal of yours." *However uncomfortable I was, the fact is, I am passionate about her opinion of me, and have ceased to allow the pessimist a dwelling.*

"Surely you could have extricated yourself at any time." His features rose; he neither gave opposition nor hint of confirmation to her inference—the furtive look was enough. "I take it you have not ventured out past our private sector of the house today?"

He shook his head and set her down, sliding in next to her. "I have been with Chèver, as you know. Why do you ask?"

"Such a beautifully telling indicator." She beamed, for he was quite innocent of the finding.

"Indicator of what? You are quite taciturn in your simplistic phrases, with some alternate meaning couched in its depth, no doubt. While I, on the other hand, am left floundering in want."

She smoothed the obstinate waves dislodged, bearing notice of a few grey strands, and drew him in for a pleasantry afforded in her embrace.

"Oh, that," he acknowledged. "And, how is baby?" The focus skirted the subject of liberties enjoyed without certain, limiting barriers, and was left.

Christine grinned. "Here, feel for yourself," she said, guiding him to the side of her stomach. His palms hovered then compressed gently, his lids making their descent to filter any visual distractions.

"I adore this sensation. Wherever I apply pressure there seems to be a force contrary to mine, as if. . ." He bit his lower lip in concentration and pressed again. "As if she were mirroring my positions, magnetically."

"You said, she."

Erik smiled. "Wishful thinking. I fancy myself being a recipient of the tenderness received from you, only on a smaller scale." Opening his eyes, Erik continued his motions, mesmerized by Christine's belly, the flash of hope welcoming those thoughts presented to be highly practicable. "The way in which you have always spoken so fondly of your father, of his stories and music, your love for him. . . I should like the opportunity to cultivate those same experiences and memories, with a daughter of my own."

Christine's knuckles met with three days' downy growth, stroking his neck against the nap to his chin. He gravitated closer, so close that if either were to stretch forward a hair's breadth, lips would touch. Right cheeks lovingly brushed and Erik's lips engaged across her jaw, sweeping back. She embraced his upper arm and pressed her head briefly to his shoulder. "You possess such refined sensitivity, Erik, and appreciate the facets suited to enrich our relationship at every turn." Her caresses lightened, tickling his throat, which necessitated pause upon occasion when a tacky site came up for redress, most of them unerringly near his mouth.

"It shall come off tomorrow; I must relent and attend to business in Paris the day after." Erik groaned at the enchanting feeling of being petted.

"Too bad, I rather like the texture." She nuzzled up under his chin, her lips latching onto a sweet spot. Erik made a perceivable swallow and gasped.

"Then, I shall wait one day more. Ugh! Do not taunt, Christine." Gruff frustration had seen reward in vain, twice having missed the location of her mouth full on, but when his persistence realized its sought after goal, an audible sigh of deep, resonating satisfaction burned from the innermost portions of his soul, down into the sanctifying union of an impassioned kiss.

"Papa?" Their lids flew open, eyes dancing upon the face of the other in wide surprise, neither moving a muscle. Chèver stood at the foot of the stairs in solemn observation.

"Yes, Chèver?" His tone gentle in its address, though his mind was reeling for a firm grip.

"You like kissing Maman," the youth stated blatantly.

"Very much so." Erik's mouth twitched in delight to admit this, his sight roaming about the face he wished to receive his affection.

Chèver nodded and pursed his lips in absent thought as his parents listened for what might possibly be voiced next. Some profound comment to be sure, but whatever the ascription appropriated to this situation, it would come directly, and the perspective more than likely would have Erik's intellect and emotions clamoring for shelter.

"I can tell," he spoke respectfully, patting his chest, "because I feel warm in here when you do."

Erik blinked hard to stave off the foreseeable and looked away, that he might compose himself after such an honest response. *Blast, not now!* He knew instantly that his choice had been a poor one; a negligible rise of feelings, though palpable, made air suddenly difficult to come by. The episode was brief, gone under Christine's calming touch before Chèver noted anything amiss.

Erik rested his forehead to Christine's. "Curse this frailty; sweet words and I have to struggle." He gave her a brief kiss and pulled away, gesturing for Chèver to join them.

"We seem to possess you at a disadvantage this morning, coming and going like we have," Christine whispered apologetically.

"I shan't argue there, my dear, the emotional ride has been quite invigorating, to say the least." Erik patted the cushion. "Come, Chèver," he encouraged, "let us see if our sweet babe will move." He proceeded to take each of Chèver's hands beneath his own, pressing them symmetrically to Christine's abdomen. The shiny blue eyes watched in earnest as his father's deft motions produced an awareness of life and a soft, "oh," emanated from his rounded mouth. Leaning over, Chèver placed his cheek atop the shifting mound and giggled, then much to his parents' astonishment, he began to hum. The melody was somewhat broken in phrase but discernable as an old Scandinavian tune sung to him while he was yet in his mother's womb, and most recently, during the nights immediately following his father's injury.

Erik grinned, contemplation ensued, and life moved on.

HOW GRATEFUL I AM *to be witness to the beauty of a child's sincere designs. I shall treasure up those times as precious jewels in remembrance; for all the wealth the world could offer, it would never approach the lasting happiness a family provides. The blessings come as a result of obedience and choice, this I have learned from bending my will to that which is good and right, to sacrifice for something better. . . it nearly cost me my life. Our dear Persian brought great insight; from an end, there most certainly has been a joyous beginning, for us all.*

I often ponder upon the reign of mortality. If we were able to plot a life course from birth through death, what we would include, and what we might choose to shun for fear of not living up to some expectation. I am most clear on the diversions I should have arranged for myself, had that been an option. But of greater interest is how my perspective has sharpened with the lens Christine has given me, all the knowledge gained and exchanged between us; life is in vain if not for the depth people contribute, and I have decided that we are here to rub souls with those who cross our path, however incremental the encounter, positive or negative. I believe this is what my Persian friend meant for me to discover, that interaction benefits us, and that it is most definitely all right not to expect perfection from others or from ourselves in every avenue traveled. We are fallible, commit mistakes, err in judgment, and share flaws in character. . . and this, which was highly difficult to admit for such an interminable length of time, has applied wholly to me! I am fallible, a man with limits, and must therefore permit the occurrence in others.

Erik crossed his arms, a frown creasing the well-hidden features while the mental lecture wore on. *My Persian brother Soheil, and I, have trudged through the muck of reconciliation and are stronger, more dedicated to the other; he forgave me, per my request, though I did not expect so keen a zealot in absolution and now, not ten days hence, I shall make to cross and weave the lives of the Comte and Comtesse de Chagny with that of the Gautiers. Peradventure when experiences are such that paths join twice, as I understand the phenomenon thus far, they are usually come to stay.*

"Our host has not expressed more than a dozen words since our departure from Amiens, which leaves me no alternative but to prod for my unease," he said to his wife without rise from the object of comment. "Erik?" The Comte leaned in, the movement deterring the appropriate attention.

"Beg pardon, you were saying?" Erik rallied.

"If I didn't know better I would surmise indecision to be about your mind on whether or not to follow through; your brooding does nothing for one's confidence."

"No, I suppose not."

"Care to enlighten? Surprises are not to my liking when I am not in the know."

Erik straightened then spoke. "It was my intention to leave business unfinished when I was last in Paris, to have a reason for a prospective client to visit. It is common for me to do—an occasional one-day stint to finish out, to extend invitations, or both. Christine knew the possibility of guests in the interim of my quarterly commutes. I mentioned at week's onset that I'd had word of the situation meeting with approbation and that I expected *them* to accompany me today upon my return. She is prepared." Then, almost as an apology, he said, "There was no mention of names, neither was there a connection made with persons to business."

"Marvelous conditions!" The Comte cast his eyes up in premeditated defeat. "I hope for all our sakes that your choice of scheme does not implode."

"It was the only way I could see to bring us all together; at least the situation improves for you," Erik defended.

The two glared, agitated at the implications they could gall the other with, and the Comtesse, unable to constrain herself longer remarked, "Not having the pleasure of Madame Gautier's acquaintance, but the advantage of hearsay, for whatever that is worth, I might presume her to be a gracious woman, despite the controversial forces of male insecurity working before me."

"Jacqueline, you can hardly place such contemptuous blame to the sanguine intent of a husband for his wife."

"Nor friend to friend?" she quipped euphemistically.

Erik smirked behind his hand and looked back and forth between the couple, finding the sudden remonstrance in his behalf to be on the verge of winning him over to the sincerity of heart possessed; yes, it was quite probable.

Meanwhile, the carriage had pulled up alongside the estate, giving the Comtesse an escape from sitting any longer in the mix of attitude stirred.

"Such a well-suited location," she said, exiting the carriage at the hand of her husband. "Oh, the trees. . . I like it already!"

"Your praise is appreciated, insomuch that my male insecurities are thus bolstered," Erik whispered, playing her retort in reverse.

She colored directly, setting the creamy whiteness of her skin to sun-kissed at the height of her cheeks; she then turned to feel the glowing rays of noonday extend across her face, her embarrassment impossible to overcome. The wind kicked up, and her hand flew to secure her hat from rising aloft, wrinkling the pert nose betwixt the hazel gems under the brim. Her wheaten curls framed the live portrait and were enhanced accordingly by the tenuous figure flush with impending signs of motherhood.

Making a grand motion, Erik bowed, parting the large, double doors to the guest wing. "Welcome."

No sooner had the voice bade enter to the estate than a buoyant lad leapt for the arms of his father.

"Well, if that is the greeting one has to encounter upon an arrival home, I am sure to enjoy my returns," the Comte exclaimed warmly.

"Papa, I missed you."

"And I you, Chèver. Here, we have guests," Erik explained, gesturing with an upturned palm. "This is the Comte and Comtesse de Chagny."

The little face brightened, his cheery disposition in line with a quick bow of the head. "Pleased to make your 'quaintance."

The Comte laughed. "Perfect replica of a gentleman! Thank you, young man." And he responded in kind.

"Monsieur?" came the noted reminder that the round-faced butler had appeared to receive his master's bidding.

Erik turned, his tone respectful, obviously at ease with those in his employ. "Yes, Ashton, avail yourself to direct the Chagnys' staff to their quarters, acquaint them with the appropriate rooms and interface our schedules, if you please."

"With pleasure, Monsieur." Ashton bowed, the additional responsibility putting a light pop in his step as he strode out-of-doors.

Then, tending to his guests, "I shall meet you in the drawing room once you are refreshed. Nañon, waiting there at the height of the stairs," the Chagnys glanced up quickly, "will see to your needs until all are settled. Excuse me." He almost leapt after his departing bow, carrying Chèver through to the breakfast-parlor. "Where is Maman?"

"Resting. Nañon said I was to let her alone and see to you first."

"Fine choice, and Liana?"

"In the kitchen."

"All right, would you stay with her while I wake Maman?" Chèver gladly complied with the sweet lure of smells he was experiencing. Erik straightened his attire, giving his waistcoat a jerk in preparation to accept whatever chastisement awaited him.

He entered through his dressing chamber to maintain the constancy of quiet. The room was peaceful and cool, despite the summer's heat wearing on, unbeknownst to the woman lying on his side of the bed—which was something she often did when he was away. Her hair fanned across the pillow, breast rising and falling in an even rhythm as she cradled their unborn child with her arm. Clinging to the headboard with his right hand, Erik placed his left upon the baby and kissed Christine. She stirred lightly, her lids fluttering open.

"Hmm, dreams do come true," she sighed, making space for a smiling Erik to sit. "You, Monsieur, must be the finest looking man in all of France."

"Not shy in your opinion, however biased it may be."

"Erik." He glanced to the baby at that weary tone, other things weighing heavy his concern. "Did you finish your business?"

"I did."

"And what of Soheil?"

"We shall see him in one week," he said absently.

"I'm glad. . . Richard?"

How many ticks left? "Richard. . ." he responded slowly, "apologized, said there was a misunderstanding between he and Meg. . . swore it was an isolated incident and promised me it had not, and would not, happen again. He seemed glad to be answerable." Which was more than he could say for himself at that precise second.

"Unfortunate that it happened at all." Christine could see something waiting, undisclosed. She touched his face. "Are you all right?"

"Tired."

"Is it your shoulder?"

"Partly."

"Do we have guests?" she wondered innocently.

Erik looked grave; he knew the brief patent upon these one-word turns had expired. His sight suddenly avoidant, he exhaled, and stood to pace. "I made arrangements. . . weeks ago." The speech began haltingly in an attempt to protract the consequences into some vacant arena he could close off and deal with later, when he might be more amply equipped, mentally. "I omitted mention and gave only vague. . ." Somehow, the sentence was amiss and he stepped up to Christine, holding out both hands. "If you must be upset with me, would you postpone until later?"

"We knew in advance of the likelihood, why should I be upset?"

"Right, answering with a question, yes. Well, it was not merely the act of invitation but to whom it was extended." Erik was closer, just not judiciously concise.

With Erik's support, she gained her feet and maneuvered into his embrace, pressing her lips to his. "You know, you really do make things much harder than they are. But, you are endearing in this state of confession. Perhaps we should see what might be done to loosen your tongue."

Erik pulled at the discomfiture of his shirt collar. "To enrapture, how you penetrate beneath. . . hmm, again," he mumbled incoherently.

"Now," Christine motioned, a finger of patience raised. "Permit me to make myself presentable, as I am sure you may wish to do the same after your dusty ride, and I should be glad for a formal introduction to the Chagnys."

His whole countenance contracted in such severity that he turned in haste and dropped unceremoniously into the nearest chair. There was a moment of silence before he supposed himself able to promote a calm enquiry. "Why do you torment me as you do, arrest my emotions?"

"Forgive me but for my deception of facts only as my sentiments bear no fabrication." She folded her arms, genuine in every move. "This you know."

"I do," he replied, lightly subdued. "When did you become aware?"

"I was in the nursery, having rested undisturbed for a bit, and heard your arrival, closely followed by Raoul's voice and laughter. Make no mistake about the upset and hurt caused by your need to force a confrontation. I did not understand your motive, especially since we agreed not to press the issue."

"Then, why the charade?" he asked, completely irritated with himself, his sight presently infatuated with the dense weave of his trousers.

"The charade. . . it allowed me time to study out your intentions. You did not toss me into the winds of surprise, but desired to explain privately, and your scruples regarding the origin of the situation, as I observed, were of personal annoyance, notwithstanding the strong sense of right that must have driven you on in my behalf." She knelt to divert his eyes to her. "I also discovered you would not have contrived such a plan if it were not for some degree of stability felt in our marriage. I do love you. I am proud to be your wife."

"I too, require forgiveness," his tone softened. "I care, and would in absolute honesty, not know what to do if you were not a part of my life, Christine, even amidst the rough spots."

"Does that imply my offense is pardonable?"

Solemnly, Erik rose and proffered his assistance, encircling her, his presentiment of conscience soon giving way to speech. "If mine are deemed as such, we shall endeavor upon mutual expiation, later."

"And welcome guests now?"

"If you please."

HAVING SETTLED INTO their rooms, the Chagnys were at leisure to partake and assess their various surroundings, eventually seeing their way into the drawing room.

"What do you think thus far, Jacqueline?"

"Of what or whom?" She gazed at her husband blankly.

"Of everything."

"I think my husband is nervous." Grinning impatiently, he gestured for her to bypass the obvious. "All right. I like Monsieur Gautier, he is witty, debonair, and every bit a gentleman, as is their precocious son, charming, too. Their estate evokes elegant simplicity and commands without pretension." Her voice lowered as if to conceal the next portion and then resumed light, "In some ways it makes ours feel overbearing and gaudy, but then I must take into account the venue in which each is situated. Beyond our window is a magnificent garden, and to its south, stables of reputable dimension." She beamed coquettishly. "So, if you are satisfied with the report, you may continue in your anxious indulgence, poor man."

"Do not pet me, Jacqueline. Are these indeed, your true findings?"

"Yes, Raoul, I have no doubt whatsoever that the change shall do us both some good." His shoulders relaxed as Jacqueline's eyes cautiously washed over him. "Raoul, are you concerned?"

"After the given foundation upon which our acquaintance is to occur, and the passing of. . ." he checked his pocket watch to the timepiece on a nearby stand, "three quarters of an hour, I am surprised you are not more so."

"As I understand it," she said politely, "we left the rush of Paris at the train station, and as I rather like the looks of my husband with a goatee, I should like to remind him that he has set a path toward complete erasure if the stroking recommences."

Taking up her hand, Raoul addressed it affectionately, proceeding afterwards with a jolt to attention, disconnecting them entirely. Jacqueline almost laughed at this response to the Gautiers' entrance; it resembled an unchaperoned lover caught during a superfluous display of ardor. *Oh dearest, Raoul,* she thought.

"Please, forgive our delay," Erik requested of their guests.

"Really," Christine broke in, "Erik cannot share in the blame, for it is I who was resting. Try as one might, the rate of absorption is a far cry from the expenditures."

"The voice of experience is well noted." Jacqueline smiled.

"My wife, Christine Gautier," Erik said proudly; there was a pause, and awkward as it was, Erik stepped in to finish out the introduction. "Christine, the Comtesse—"

"Oh, please don't, no titles. I'm Jacqueline."

Christine took both Jacqueline's outstretched hands and leaned in for a brief hug of greeting, touching stomachs in the process. They laughed. "Nothing like introductions all around." Then she turned to Raoul and with a playful grin extended her hands. "Dear Raoul, goatee and moustache, hmm? It is quite becoming on you." The best he could do was nod, and suddenly feeling quite warm, he squeezed her hands in return and let go. Christine glanced at Jacqueline. "How ever did you manage the silence?" Raoul's cheeks went several shades before they flamed their current deep, ruddy salmon.

"I think I shall take a great liking to you, Christine. I have not seen him this flustered since—"

"That is quite enough," Erik demanded, feeling Raoul in a similar position to his own from earlier. "Leave the man's pride intact, if you would, at least while in his presence."

"I appreciate your gallant efforts, Erik, but between them, I fear being at their mercy in more ways than even I am able to fathom."

"Yes, we men usually are," came Erik's retort, *and loving every moment.*

Taking their seats, spouses facing respectively, they began the pleasantries one would expect of becoming better acquainted. Tea was served, a tour of the estate followed and in succession, the evening meal; candles were lit, but only as a last recourse in continuation of what was naturally sustained through the summer months.

A RESTFUL NIGHT passed as a welcome to Eve's sister lay in wait during the early morning, for Dawn had yet to grace the calm with a rise of her crown from an earthen cradle. And, having infrequent occasion to greet the day, Christine made useful just such an escape, for it was an opportunity held in passionate reserve, a time most forsaken by humanity in ignorance to the faithful rotations.

Erik had stolen away for a jaunt with Chèver about the countryside, leaving her to partake of the cleansing effects on the senses. Each breath opened the mind to endless possibilities in thought as a tonic to her system, the changes in scenery, the warmth of its current season, and the diversion of associations.

She smiled, letting the shawl gently hung about her shoulders wilt according to the heat of first light. *I suspect it is all too easy to take up the habit of solitude, so simple to please and do for one's self, to see indisputably what is best for another, and remain altogether blind in the process. Here I upbraid the effort of my sweet companion because he had the strength to reach for what I did not: a resolution in fear of the unknown. Paralyzing and liberating by turns this. . . when holding out your hand to another, it is often as equally if not eagerly desired.*

Christine moved to lean against the smooth, immature wood of a young chestnut. "Too few years with you, Maman," she muttered, touching the diamond about her neck, a piece of heaven given her by Erik. "But, I remember your gentleness, your comfort." *I would also cherish a daughter. I just wish I could share thoughts and loving advice from you.* Her eyes floated shut to the gurgle of the stream behind. No breeze came on the stillness of air, but her heart wavered at the rustling of grass, eyes snapped alert, seeing Raoul coming toward her. He slowed when he realized she was aware of his presence, and their eyes met.

When he came close enough, Christine erased any feeling of disquiet with salutation. "Good morning." He gave a light bow of the head in address. "What brings you out so prematurely?"

"You."

The response struck her revelry with such pointed aim, had caused her composure to intimate everything and hold in confidence, nothing. And, as her conscience was now infused with a greater level of dread, she was instantly apprehensive and wary, thinking there would be a forthcoming reason to repent and rue the company of her former attachment.

"Please," he held up his hands as though staying a colt from flight. "I didn't mean to set you on edge, forgive me. I saw you walking the garden. . ."

"Restless?"

"Yes, I find that I'm even more so than Jacqueline these days."

"The condition seems to merit some tolerance for abruptness and strange twists of habit, on all fronts?"

Raoul suppressed the rush of a grin. "It does."

Grinning herself, she commented, "I sense reserve where boldness once dictated."

"You are too kind in your words, Christine. I was brash and violent in opinion and now claim a sober character, of sorts." Raoul rubbed the back of his neck and continued with purpose. "I have experienced going through second-hand filters and would like to have done with them altogether, to obtain some measure of closure between us. It is my reason for seeking a moment of your time."

"Of course, come," she suggested, "we can talk while we make our way to the stables."

There was an abiding patience as they walked in contemplation those few yards from the dense tree line, Raoul taking up speech when he was able to be at Christine's side. "I might enquire as to whether you actually received the letter I sent."

"I did, several days before I wed. Adèle staged a rather tactless delivery in front of Erik, but then, she had not the slightest idea of ever seeing me again and seized the moment, however inopportune."

"When Erik mentioned its contents, I feared—though I know

now it was completely unfounded—that he may have kept it from you."

"Perhaps it would have crossed his mind months before, but no, our relationship is built on trust. I felt it best to share the letter openly with him. It was beautiful; the freedom given me to decide for myself meant the world to us."

"I believe the letter was more therapeutic for myself than it was a confirmation of having relinquished my attachment to you. I still had hope, were you permitted to see things without your current influences bombarding you, that in time you would return my feelings. When my correspondence was not favored with a reply, for whatever reason, I knew you had decided otherwise." He breathed deeply, a weight lifted. "And now, I guess all I would wish to know. . . Does Erik bring you the happiness you so desired, and deserve, is he good to you, Christine?"

She touched his arm, arresting his step with the soft warmth of connection, and meeting his gaze with an application from which he could not break, she answered, "I have discovered a joy I never knew existed, Raoul, as his companion I am complete. He holds my heart to his, cherishes our life together, and places my well-being above his own. I love him."

When she removed her hand, his body surged cold, but the feeling was replenished by an inward peace. "I told Erik, prior. . ." he quickly stopped himself from further reference to the Opera House incident, and edited ahead. "I said that if you deemed him worthy, then I too, could feel no other way. I just wanted to hear affirmation from you. I'm glad," he sighed.

"Since we are about having curiosities sated, I should be in want of mine being justly served."

"All right, fair is fair," Raoul remarked.

"Do you truly love Jacqueline?"

His mouth broadened favorably, felicity bursting at the seams that he could profess his devotion. "At first, I found the preliminary hint of her affections flattering, but I avoided her at all cost and for any intimate circumstance, I made myself scarce. In all honesty," he whispered, "I was afraid of her advances and what I might feel for her in return. With you it was different—familiarity bred conceit, comfort, and a stern self-assurance; it was natural and safe. When confronted by Jacqui. . . oh! There was no net for my poor reluctant heart, entreating me to spare it another trampling. Fortunate for me, she was kind, patient, and showed me a passion for life I never imagined, and in the process somewhere, I know not when, my soul became attached. I fell in love, plunging headfirst without regret. In every way, I have you to thank. Neither of us would be as committed to our loves if it were not for your courage to follow your heart. I love Jacqui."

Raoul looked out over the southern meadows, which lay bathed in their rich cloak of emerald just beyond the stables, and seeing a dark shape gaining form and detail, he gestured in the general direction; what radiance it evoked.

"Erik deserves the delight you bring to his life."

"Thank you, Raoul."

Chapter Fifty-One

Five days of blissful interaction made fast friends of the intimate company of four, and upon the sixth came the Persian to reacquaint and overlap several days of his visit with those previously housed. The Chagnys were bid a fond farewell before a fortnight was complete, with profound exhortation that they would return, if no sooner, than the first of the year at winter's end; the prospect of several foals during the latter frame of time, a ready guarantee.

And too, their stay opened possibilities and secured a witness that laid Erik's soul astir to recall. So much of his life had been a mass of decay and rotting sores left untreated that to glance across such a field of hopeless desolation, one would cry out *War!* at the picture drawn. How to heal it? Where to begin? A fetid tome, compiled into so overwhelming a prospect that to continue forward, in postscript, would be the only way to cope. Erik kept upon this course from a young age, unable see how to go about its alteration, so he never looked back. Once begun, the degenerative tack beckoned ease, and it was only through the combination of determination, desire, and support that he could settle on a point with Destiny. Now, when he dared rummage about his past, the field had fewer wounds to dress, more scars closed over, more direction, purpose and forgiveness.

Erik embraced Christine from the back and together, watched the extravagance of carriage become blackened specks beneath the boughs littering the horizon; he heaved a sigh of content.

"Happy?" she asked.

"I believe so. Since that first morning I saw you and Raoul engaged in discussion, I felt empowered by the trust we share, no jealousy roused, and since you have come to terms with him in your own way, there is ease of spirit."

"Oh, to know the thoughts of another. You are essential to all that I am." She peered back over her right shoulder. "Yes, we agreed that salt water has great medicinal qualities."

Erik chuckled. "What else did he purport?"

"That our lives are as they should be."

"Ah, introspection from the wise," Erik praised. He gathered Christine and swept her into the house. "Yes indeed, as they should be. . . joyful."

Not able to stretch another three weeks, splendor of the most exquisite magnitude filled the Gautier household with an early debut on August 24, 1882. Emili Catherine was pronounced a healthy addition to the family, and how fitting that the Persian was able to be included amongst the glories.

He and Chèver had occupied the better part of the afternoon making company of the other, and thinking it best to be out from under foot, the two took a meal upstream—a meal it was not, merely bread and apples, but it would sustain them. The Persian was taken in as he watched the young boy turn up rocks with one hand and munch the juicy flesh of his apple with the other. The little one had soared under the constant tutelage of his father—the Persian's conversations were proof alone—yet he indulged in simple amusement and retained childish wonder; it was fascinating. The Persian's delight these last few days had been to utilize Chèver as a way to see into Erik's life, to demarcate aspects of time that would have encoded certain attributes, then predict at what time they might have been turned around during the maturation process. It was a speculative curiosity to think on.

"O'el?"

The Persian chuckled at the accent. "What is it, Chèver?"

"Papa says you are his brother." He looked steadily at the Persian.

"Did he now, well. . . I suppose we are, despite looks, and we certainly pose challenges to the betterment of one another."

"Why then, does he not use your name?"

"You must be referring to Daroga?" Chèver nodded once. "Perhaps it is habit from the years we spent together in the Middle East, where one usually is called by their title. Sometimes, the title becomes the man and visa versa, they become interconnected, so much so that a division is. . ." he paused to reflect a moment on the rationale, "impossible. I am glad you and your mother use my given name; it is enough." *Leave it to a child. I appoint myself principle guardian to maintain a hold over a man, praying my influence will somehow incite scruples to engage prior to action, and neither of us could ever make a distinction between man and occupation. Erik's use of my name, in my presence, was the first phase of that separation.*

The Persian started, Chèver was standing at his side, studying him; his small hand reached out, gently grasped the larger, darker hued one, and then rotated it front to back.

"We are the same, yet different."

"As humans, our journey in life begins similarly the world over, and it is from that point that we distinguish individuality."

"Is that critical?"

"*Critical?* I believe I would not wish to be a mindless replication of another."

"Papa said it is important to learn of others' ways, to understand."

"I agree. We are all basically the same, Chèver, but it is in acceptance of those aspects, which set us apart as unique, where we are most content."

"Like your skin and Papa's face?"

"Yes—*you are almost too perceptive*—you are correct."

"I like different, and I love Papa."

"It is well that you do. Come, I should think a good deal of joy at the house by now. What do you say we return for a look around, then you and I can go for a ride?"

"Can we ride Rakkas?"

"Ah, *dancer*, we shall take a celebration dance upon the wind!" The Persian laughed, casting the boy high into the air, much to a hearty consent as they tread back to make their enquiries.

LATE THAT AFTERNOON, during Chèver's initial introduction with the tiny nymph, he gave her a thorough once over and checked every particular: hands and feet, fingers and toes, in comparison to his own. Her lusty cries, though shocked at first that such a wail could emanate from something so small, decided it was a good alarm, and from one end to the other seemed pleased, his only criticism was in judgment of her little, pinkish form being 'quite skinny.'

When everyone had turned in, Erik sealed off the bedchamber for time alone and picked up his restless daughter from the cradle to soothe her. While Christine rested, he consoled near the lenient glow of the fire. *Oh, the wafer thin softness of a baby's skin upon my face, the clasp of such perfectly carved ivory around my thumb, and how she can curl herself so iron tight that it necessitates firm prying to disengage limbs from torso! Skinny?* He gave an amused snort. *You shall soon fill out, Maman will see to that, though I am astonished by each fine detail, not unlike your brother. Is it not amazing as well, that such an interest of sentiment may be awakened and raised to so grand a level by one as ignorant of their impact as the melted snow upon the mountain crag; all done unbeknownst to the heart until passion is woven, entwined with life's very pulse.*

Emili coughed then gave a stout sneeze, colliding fist and nose, which startled the poor infant into flailing for a hold on some unseen presence. Erik cinched her blanket and placed the end of his small finger into her mouth to pacify a possible cry, though such actions cannot confound an unsettled whimper nor deter maternal instinct; Christine heard.

"Erik, you may bring her, I'm awake." She motioned and gingerly shifted to permit them space beside her on the bed. There was a quick downward clamp on an already swollen lip, as disappointment raged that she could not obviate any outward sign of pain.

"Christine, must I remind that it was you who wished to inform me of your tolerance? If you resist until it becomes overpowering, I cannot maintain your comfort." He had been enchanted with the babe for a moment and looked up unprepared into a belligerent, pithy glare, intimating vehemently, *do not preach to me, I already know!* "Ah, loud and clear, my darling. We shall keep our distance until the tide stems." Erik removed himself from the vicinity with Emili.

"Erik!" She reached out; exasperated that he would, as a vane, move so easily in the direction blown. "Bring her back."

"Not until you yield the stubborn attitude and allow me to care for you," he snipped, turning his back while he swayed.

Christine crossed her arms in child-like defiance, the antipathy being a sizeable enough barrier to diverge their positions that he furtively watched the contrast in shadows cheating from her, her normally sweet complexion. A pillow thumped him squarely in the back of the head.

"Perfect, she is under siege and retaliates with an interposing projectile, beware my sweet," he cooed, "for your mother is skilled in such defensive arts."

"Erik! If I could gain my feet at once you would not stand so smug when wrestled to the floor, you ornery tease!"

"Hmm, the proverbial pot and kettle, neither of which is exempt from being called black," his tone mirroring Christine's justly called label.

Grabbing another pillow, she hid her face and tipped to one side, muffling the forlorn despair and wetness spilling freely. "Don't do this to me now, Erik!" came the entreaty, when she could account perceptively for speech. "I know I'm not pleasant, that I resist. . . I hurt, but I need you to dispense with further prescriptions, just overlook what I cannot control, please?"

Erik was already there, pulling both girls safely into his arms. "Forgive me?" he asked, kissing her in an appeal of caresses. "Too quickly I have forgotten the fragile state of emotions after such physical exertion."

"But I was not like this before, I don't understand why everything is in conflict." Christine clung to his linen shirt, eyes glistening, threatening their limits. "In my heart I wish to comply, then my mind screams bitterly to rebel. . . I'm scared, frustrated, and I hurt."

She would hold together not one moment more and broke down, sobbing in such violence of feeling that uncontrollable spasms betook her weakened form, and Erik could do nor say more in the passing of several minutes set together than their daughter did to bond their hearts; Emili cried. The imploring summoned and Erik encouraged Christine to feed, to attend to the needs of their child. Christine accepted, caressed, and stroked the beloved infant as if the tangible expiation would indeed assist in recompense for some unknown wrong committed. Reversing his position, Erik seated himself close, leaning in such a way over the two that he could soothe, dashing from Christine's eyes each wet bead upon appearance, at the same time searching the recesses of his understanding. Soon, the tears grew less in quantity and finally abated altogether as she inclined toward his touch; their gaze held transfixed to the other when his fingers began to massage at the base of her neck. Christine petitioned Erik to forgive her, but he motioned it was unnecessary then kissed his finger and set it to Emili's palm while he caressed the mother of his children, the woman he loved.

The written word... I have not sought proficiency in the literary genre simply because I prefer music over the other for expression, but I do comprehend that while I see the emotive well tapped, my legacy in score is insufficient, and so I place pen to paper and endeavor once again. We are close on the heels of passing out a month since Emili was born—my sweet pea (she has a dainty, light pink birthmark at the base of her neck that looks like butterfly wings when folded shut, similar to those of the flower; a whimsical prerogative of a father to pronounce such a sentiment). Our daughter's birth was difficult for Christine to bear, and while not breach, the rotation of skull to pelvic bone was painful and nearly as bad physically. She has struggled to reestablish balance all this time, and though her emotions are less divergent, and bouts of melancholy plague less, I believe that her system shall align itself completely in time.

Dr. Dubois assured me that all would heal; being in his profession, he has been privy to the capricious nature of numerous females. 'Give her support, patience, and attention,' was his prescription, to which I have most religiously adhered. I began leaving notes again, and left one most recently atop a bath full of fallen ginkgo leaves; it was a joyful sound to hear her laugh so loudly; little did I know, it was Chèver who took complete advantage of the situation—and the credit—to jump right in. Now that Christine is mobile, walks are on the rise and taken during the warmest segment at midday, and whether we are alone together or with our children, it is a glorious activity, one to liberate us before the cold of winter confines.

The unexplained, undefined wonder of the human mind and body to chemically right itself prodded Erik to further his intelligence upon the matter. He knew of instances incapable of reparation on their own, yet some defied all logic; to tip the scale in favor of unforeseen intervention, the years with and without Christine evinced in his mind that God existed for those who would believe.

Chapter Fifty-Two

There was never a repeat of this spectacle, not even when the Gautier's third and final child, a son, Étienne Valar, slipped into the world on March 9, 1886, to signal a marked understanding of enough.

Time obliged the wearing on of years in a most pleasant habit, lingering in the best of moments, when curiosities gave way to delight, when family and friends colored the halls of the guest wing, and during quiet opportunities of reflection. The latter, finding a hallowed partition set aside within Erik's memory, to replay in an instant if the mood jostled a similar frame of reference.

It was early in the summer of 1891, clearly one superb model of seasons, having opened the way with the precise amount of rainfall during spring, to create the lush display of velvety hills; each individual blade spanned thick its potential, vibrating as refined strings under the skilled hands of an angelic wind. Morning lessons had ceased, for the contagion of daydreaming set its sights on being released in continual doses, tempting those indoors to bask in the sunshine and have bleached, the rigidity of staleness from their bones. Erik sat on the front porch, reading the compositions penned by Chèver and Emili on the topic of the French Revolution; a stack of books lay in wait to his left and business ledgers in queue thereafter. The children, however burdened with education, had quite successfully shed any hint of academics and were absorbed in an assortment of occupations: swinging, searching the watery locks for treasures to capture, or perched high within a few protective boughs in leisure.

The front door remained ajar when, with arms loaded, Christine came bearing rations for unrelenting appetites in the morning air. "You are every pupil's dream," she complemented, setting the tray down and taking a place at her husband's side. Erik smirked, paying little heed otherwise. "But, you should seize upon their example." Her hand gently rested on his, forcing the papers to lower from his scrutinizing gaze.

"I detect a commonality between this and another time you came betwixt work and my intended goal," he chided.

"That was thirteen years ago!" her voice rose in protest. "And I happen to know of others."

The words replayed on his tongue in silence as the meaning took on a poignant flavor. *Thirteen years! So different, ones full in every way with purpose.* He glanced at Christine then looked away, clearing his heavily teemed throat of emotion while tucking the papers beneath his ledgers. Touching the cheek farthest from her, Christine was able to guide his eyes back. Those melted flecks of sun sparkled in the rippling pools before over-spilling their banks.

Kissing the underside of her wrist he stared at the calloused palm, the strength of its lithe form, and how the lily-white complexion had begun to glow with highlights from the changed season. Erik entwined his fingers with hers. "Every so often, something hits me, deeply. . . this is one of those moments." He tenderly bussed the skin of her hand and held it lovingly to his heart. "Thirteen years ago, you allowed a hateful, half-crazed man to blindly whisk you away, from everything and everyone meaningful in your life, to this." He gestured to the estate. "You turned from it all and gave your undivided patience and affection to me. You have willingly worked by my side, played, cried, laughed, have given birth to three extraordinary children. . . and have loved. . ." Erik's voice trailed off. He was thinking—it was what he always thought and marveled on peaceably.

He set one of her knuckles to his lips while in observance of Étienne's antics then looked up to where Chèver was splayed across the tree branch above Emili. "Christine, do you realize," he breathed out, "I was younger than Chèver when I left my father's house, on my own to survive in the world? I could not fathom such a thing for him. It shall be an arduous enough task as it is just sending him away to school in a year."

"Have you spoken with him on the subject?"

"Yes, he understands the benefits, verses the unconventional ways I attained my knowledge. I believe I may have to miss him; his intellect is remarkable."

"Are you sure there's not more? Chèver is most like you."

He fidgeted. "But, the temperance with which he is bound comes from you, my dear." He brightened, to think that his son would explore more in depth the matters of science in conjunction with anatomy. "Perhaps he will choose Edinburgh."

Gently patting his leg, Christine asked, "And what of our other two; do you have predictions for them as well?"

"Étienne is still young; at five he shows most promise with equations and drawing." He coughed lightly. "Excuse me. Then there is Emili. I was reading one of her most recent compositions and find her ability to string language together, utterly amazing. Her two-dimensional descriptions capture an astounding vivacity to project the vision she wishes to share, and the complexity. . ."

"Emili is mistress of observation and meaning," Christine added.

"That too, yes." Erik shrugged as if his next bit of intelligence were of little interest. "Musical preference is variant."

"You know you *cannot* compare."

"I do." His brevity testified of the disappointment he felt. "While the boys play the piano fairly well, with Chèver being quite accomplished, I fear it to be more of a pastime diversion, and Emili," he griped, "adamant girl, no amount of convincing can get her to even touch the keyboard. She would rather lose limbs if she could not play the violin."

"When you and Emili have some father-daughter time, I would suggest asking her why; you may be surprised by her insight."

"You know something," he stated.

"Perhaps."

Erik swung Christine up into his arms and she playfully screamed. "*You* are the balance in my life, Christine Daaé, soar with me!" he invited.

"Are you providing our means of flight?"

"But of course, Madame."

Their words became a long, impassioned kiss at the base of the stairs, at which time his addresses of affection lightened appropriately to be seen, prior to walking out beneath the huge trees along the stream.

"Father, must you?" Chèver rolled his eyes and let out such a distinguishable sigh that his father could not resist momentary indulgence, much to the disparaging gaze of his oldest son.

"Yes, son, I must." The action, coupled with their father's remarks, caused a small stir of laughter from Chèver's siblings. "One day you shall comprehend why I cherish the love of such an exceptional woman as your mother. Now," directing his focus toward Emili, "would you mind if Maman has a ride in your stead?"

"Not at all." She smiled.

"Bread and cheese on the porch, off you go, all of you," Erik said, catching Emili to allow his *ladies* an exchange of place as she slowly came to a stop. "What do you think, Christine, shall it be Emili who will one day write our story?"

Beyond the Masque

Emili heard her father's soft comment and looked back over her shoulder to the joyful faces of her parents, then to the gluttony of her brothers. What was it that compelled the behavior of people and motivated decisions? Her investigation based on reasons would be conducted during the next few days, but knowing her mother to be a tremendous resource, she would look for an opportunity to corner her in the kitchen, before unleashing the barrage of queries she had queued.

PREPARATIONS HAD BEEN well under way for a summer reunion; it was to be a phenomenal gathering of comings and goings, each party to arrive and depart as was deemed suitable to family schedules, and figuring there was no more preferential time than the present, Emili moved to seat herself at the kitchen worktable.

"Maman, would you help me?"

"I shall do my utmost, what is it you need?" her mother asked, brushing her hands of flour.

"Well, the other day Papa and Chèver were discussing a school for young men. . ." She saw her mother's brow arch. "It was during lessons and not at all secret," she defended. "But Chèver did not seem enthused when I asked him about it. He said that the topic was one he wished unopened between us because he could do without my pity."

"It sounds as though Chèver would rather you not feel badly on his account."

"That's just it, I would not. I think it a grand opportunity. Besides, I feel his reason more likely a poor façade for his true thoughts and feelings."

"Which are?" Christine was impressed with her daughter's general perception and wished to hear more.

"He just likes to be with Papa."

"Ah."

"I would no sooner pity Chèver than my own father."

Christine washed her hands of pastry dough. Seeing as how this conversation was becoming more than was first assumed, she took a seat opposite her daughter. Liana excused herself to attend in preparation elsewhere. "You are quick to utilize new vocabulary, Emili."

"Papa makes similar comments as well, thank you." The dissertation stopped abruptly while she organized her thoughts, seconds, the only requirement. "If I do not pity them, what do I call it?"

"Seems to me you have much on your mind, so. . . you feel pity inappropriate."

"Yes."

"Did you think Chèver might tie in sarcasm to its expression and wished to spare himself?

"Oh," she frowned remorsefully. "I had not. . . truthfully, Maman."

"All right, what of sympathy? Having regret for someone and/or their plight."

"No, it still sounds like pity."

"All right, can you empathize?"

Emily shook her head. "I cannot because I lack his experience and perspective."

"Then let us consider compassion." Christine grinned at the radiant face beaming with interest. "Compassion is active, often encompassing the other definitions as their physical expression. . . you do something to lessen the burden of another. With the others, it tends to be in word or thought only."

"Have people pitied Papa?" Emili's question was direct, taking Christine by surprise.

"I can tell you, that while young, his parents could not tolerate his looks, very few took pity, and most preferred to take advantage.

They shunned him, hated..." She had to pause, recalling the various narratives given her by Erik throughout their marriage. The tears welled, blurring vision and constricting voice. "I love him, Emili."

"Emili?" Her name burned warm from her left, and turning, she saw her father standing in the doorway to the great room, refolding several letters of correspondence. "Some people exhibited a shy version of compassion, those who have seen beneath my masque, but no one has made a greater difference in my life than your mother, your brothers and you."

"I love you, too, Papa."

"Come." Erik knelt down to pick up his daughter, arms outstretched.

Gently, Emili raised her hands up to remove the masque, and staring into the emotionally worn features, she pronounced her opinion, "Maman is right."

Quite often, he thought. "And in what light?" He must know.

"You *are* ruggedly handsome!"

Erik burst out laughing. Emili kissed him tenderly between the eyes and replaced the necessary cover. She was so matter-of-fact that the trait made her even more endearing and he could not bear to let go; a hug set her free. "We shall talk more about this later on, if you wish," he whispered, "but for now, why don't you run down to the stables and assist in the feeding. Dezi needs grooming as well, and I believe she actually prefers your touch to that of the new groom."

Emili bounded out the back door, honey-brown waves flying behind. Christine dried her cheeks and untied her apron, eyeing warily the keen gentleman sauntering toward her.

"Now, it is your turn." He motioned to her, summoning with only a finger and throaty inference.

"My turn?"

"Tell me," he demanded passionately, "Do you think God will

smite me for sullying the wings of his most beloved angel?"

"No, I am quite confident He shan't," she cooed, as Erik circled his arms around her waist and she, his neck. "Not as long as I am escorted back to His presence by you. Fortunately, the merit of worth comes with work, and if that means the acquisition of a smudge or two, so be it."

Erik grinned and nestled in close, laying his lips to descend the porcelain slope. "I have never heard. . . a more beautiful explanation. . . than yours to Emili."

Christine tilted her head to invite his persistent attentions and, being that there were no children near to decry *this* display of passion—not that it was of consequence within the appropriate context—he commandeered such leeway as availed the immediate situation. She, meanwhile, addressed the sensitive spot below his ear, which held him stable in anticipation of a follow through.

"Sometimes I wonder if my veins will continue to withstand. . . ah!" Erik gasped sharply when she caught his lobe, "the heat you induce."

"Would you wish otherwise?" Her tone was strangely provoking.

"Oh, heaven help me! Damn my veins, let them fuse!" he sputtered.

"Interesting choice of words," Christine murmured. "Now, kiss me."

Erik read her mind, both becoming ardently entangled in the other's embrace only to be interrupted by an unsuspecting "Oh, I beg your pardon!" and hasty footfalls ensuing the close of a door. They laughed. It had been Rossi, though somewhat early, he had come to meet with Erik upon matters occurring over the subsequent weeks—relating to guests and clients. The circumstance was embarrassing to say the least and gratifying at best, to know that one's employer cherished his wife. It was as it should be.

"I think he means for us to carry on. See? Doors shut, kitchen devoid of—"

"Guest rooms soon to be full and business with a mortified Taylor," she defied him, pushing away laughing. "Oh, heavens, who did you learn that from, Étienne?"

"Our son can certainly produce a better pout, but this is the best I can manage *under* these conditions," Erik growled sulkily from beneath the edge of his masque.

"All right, my love. Shed your shield that I may kiss you well, then it will be off with you."

The encounter was as genial a recognition as tipping one's hat, only the response was more than a batting of lashes and retrieved handkerchief; it was a prelude to memorable days.

Chapter Fifty-Three

*O*rchestrated chaos! Erik shook his head in awe, surveying the evening lull in the gardens while breathing greedily of the night air, *such a fitting vantage from atop a tree*. He wished he might have remembered earlier—adding it to the sealing off of his bedchamber against the excitable commotion, and riding, as a just means of separation. But despite the prolific attendance, and his tendency toward discomfort among lingering crowds, it was requisite to admit the execution superb. The laughter and joy became as an external tribute to the capable trio of Christine, Meg, and Jacqui, and their coordination of combined staff, which made the flow smooth for even the most basic of needs to occur without burden.

People—there were people wherever Erik ventured about the estate: adults, servants, and a plethora of children, which, if not directed in their exuberance at any given time, as a whole, frequently necessitated these certain designs of escape. Certainly, the ideal way to deal with them all was by cluster, eyes open and mouths shut. Then, each evening when it came time for staff and guests alike to retire, Erik sought his haven; Christine flattered, showered compliments to nourish areas depleted and in turn, he massaged the fatigue from her successful role as hostess.

Indeed, the evenings were a time for Erik to revel in his specialty of inspired magnificence, and as much as he would vehemently deny the obvious, he would never own up to his love of astonishing people; it was the power of suspense and unquenchable intrigue which could bind an audience within the master's palm.

"Christine," Richard whispered softly. "Erik is positively exceptional in his ability to rivet his listeners; these stories are amazing. I am there; transported mentally, often finding my mouth beyond normal range before regaining composure. Oh, and that slight of hand. . . I would do well to learn enough to discover what my competition had up their sleeves. Fascinating!"

Christine saw that he had slipped back beneath the spell and meandered laterally to better watch the captive faces. The adults would usually manage a showing after their tea or evening cordial, slipping into the drawing room when Erik was in the throes of some incredible encounter or at the height of producing items from thin air, having arrived in such a way that one would think guilt needled their minds for the enjoyment derived. They never tired of the marvels.

Large gatherings were not a common predilection where the Persian was concerned either, but he relented and came for a few days, if for no other reason than to ride the splendid Arabians on site. He and Erik went out in regularity before daybreak, during the reverent portrayal of homage nature bestows at dawn.

"These are truly majestic animals, Erik. . . fine creatures," he commented, stroking his mount's beauty. "Each visit stirs sentiments and legend from my homeland. . . I appreciate the peace in which it affords me recollection."

Erik only grinned. They had ridden south this particular day, and were now headed back to the estate at a slow, easy pace, grateful for the company and abiding friendship.

"The rosy hues have mellowed over time, have they?" Erik's glib remark unsettled the Persian.

"And yours are contrary?"

"I have vivid recall or do you forget? Especially when I recreate such grand tales for the children."

"You are a performer, my friend," the Persian croaked out, uniting the declaration with a faint chuckle. "It feeds your childish self-conceit, and to do it well, one requires a vast library of experience to draw from," he shrugged and added, "… however colorful it may be."

Erik snorted in disgust. "Childish self-conceit? You have become extremely bold in your old age, accusing me more now than you ever did back then."

"My assurance was clouded, I could not hazard more than I did."

"And your excuse now?" came the tease of indignation.

"I am tired and wish to leave this life without regret of never having fully expressed myself; I still enjoy testing the stability I've seen evolve." The Persian, having succeeded in goading his friend, backed down. "But, it is as you said, I am getting older."

Erik studied the dark gentleman. "In consideration of the volatile wretch you chose to manage, I cannot repudiate any form of standard you wish to hold me to. Our renewed trust shall stand as foundation and testament, but your comment on age I can hardly grant as valid—you are not much older than I, Soheil."

"Humph, no." He replied quickly. Emotion rose to prick the surface; that precise and cherished articulation of name warmed the Persian's heart, to hear the impeccable accent fall upon his ear. He revived. "However, I feel my quiet, sedentary nature, stress of profession, and weight of conscience to be a catalyst for age enhancement." Erik laughed outright, his eyes traveling over the peppered grey. "Ah, you laugh, but have you looked at yourself lately?"

"You know as well as I that I do not pursue an obsession of vanity," *at least, not in the same mode as others.*

"Well, then allow me to tell you, since my perspective has the advantage of infrequency. Except for the few creases related to happiness, you look to match your wife in youthfulness and shall most likely outlive every one of us!" he exclaimed, as each stared at the other in regard.

"While I appreciate your thoughts on longevity, despite what you see," Erik sighed, resuming his masque, "you must remember I started life with one foot in the grave, so if the rest of me bestows virtues of youth, I shall accept."

Nodding in light acknowledgment, the Persian smirked, and being much amused, gave a kick to his horse's flank. "Come! I should like some competition other than the wind in my face!"

Henceforth, the Persian made his person a familiar recurrence to the estate for the sole purpose of exercising the bay mare, which Erik labeled "a sound stirring" for the gift he had seen fit to present that self-same afternoon. Seeing an opportunity for an earlier than planned for departure had the Persian asking to be seen off personally by Erik, providing him leave to ride once again into Amiens. Dismounting with his few possessions, the Persian offered his hand and Erik pressed the reins to his palm, embracing the man with whom he shared a treasured relationship. The Persian was left without recourse to brush futilely at the escaping drops. This was a gift of honor bearing unspoken symbolism; the Arabian mare represented unfaltering support, pride, secrecy, and courage in the face of confrontation, but mostly, she bespoke an indemnification of loyalty.

As they parted, Erik found himself so much the better, his quality of life improved because of the persistent intrusion made upon his existence. "You are welcome, Soheil, always welcome."

The Persian smiled wearily, replacing the token under the vigilant care Erik would provide, then turned and left.

Chapter Fifty-Four

Where there are children, conflict and unplanned mishaps shall arise, and since age is not to be the monopolizing factor left to any generation, it often drops in unannounced then flees just as quickly. Such was the case awaiting Erik midst a small patch of grass and violet-colored statis upon his return, the nuclei of the scene tucked, knees under chin. He beat the dust from his gloves across the leg of his trousers and wandered along the more sheltered edge of the gravel path, the shade permitting him a view unhindered by the bite of the sun. *Just like Christine.* He had seen her, approached cautiously, and taking care not to startle his daughter, called to her. No answer came, though he knew she heard from the way she shifted at the mention of her name. Erik moved in to recline in the grass alongside her. Emili's eyes were closed, but the tell tale signs she had been crying left both cheeks stained as they had emptied into the fabric of her blue dress.

"How can I make it better?" he asked, the tenderness of his voice parting her lashes for eyes to meet. The soft skin furrowed painfully. "Come, tell me." He gestured and she scrambled into the comfort of his arms, tears bursting to rewet the arid tracks.

"Jeanette and I were upstairs playing in my room when she expressed a wish to hear the tunes from my music box collection; she especially liked the crystal butterfly inside the glass ball. I was real careful, Papa, we only listened to one at a time," her verbal urgency expanded, "then Maman called me away. I was gone for just a few minutes, and when I returned, she was gone, having left the box inoperable."

Inoperable, she is all about words. . . "Have you spoken with Jeanette?"

"I have not, I was unable to locate her so I assumed she had already started out toward the lea with the boys."

"Yes, all the horses are stabled," he murmured, "and this is where our guests have wandered, leaving my girl alone?"

"They went for a picnic, but it was my decision to remain behind. You were not home."

"I see." Erik kissed her head. "Your thoughtfulness warms me, thank you. Well, shall we take up an examination of the music box to ascertain what might be done?"

"Please." Emili brightened.

With a bit of prodding, and little violation to the mechanism, the trouble was soon found out, revealing itself to be nothing more than an over rotated turnkey, one which could be repaired at a later date. Most of the shadowed complexion had deserted the youth, despite the fact Jeanette had yet to acknowledge the incident; it was noted as being the very piece gnawing at Emili. She expressed how it was beyond comprehension as to why her friend would not wish to inform her of the misfortune; it was not done maliciously, that she knew, but the avoidance flashed all manner of despicable thought for review. Erik explained the importance and value of people over possessions, and how the sting of loss may seem great when unexpectedly dished, regardless of the longer lasting repercussions to the heart if action was sought before intent was learned, which would necessitate the implementation of a fastidious remedial plan.

Father stood apart from daughter, across one corner of the studio workbench, and as he lifted her chin, so too, was the weight of presumption eased. Then as promised, she would speak of her concerns with her friend, for she could not deny the vast pit of miscommunication to be waded through.

Erik's stomach suddenly gave a rousing protest that it had been kept from nourishment; having lost its patience among the many detours without courtesy of a morning meal, it grumbled contemptuously. Emili bit her lip to keep from laughing outright, both at the growl and the invitation proffered upon the arm of her father, but it was the gentlemanly bow which put the dimple back in her right cheek as the two quit the house and strolled out to dine.

After pleasure in partaking of the outstanding fare, Erik's body was ready to oblige the mind acquiesce the absence of anything more than facile thought, or none at all, as he lay fast asleep in Christine's lap.

There was the sound of light panting and a brush of hands to announce the approach of one in search of a place to hide, but was as yet enduring the irritation without success.

"This is your idea of fair, to be so plain?" Christine quietly teased Raoul, as he stumbled from the undergrowth into view. "Chèver shall not take kindly to the insult."

"I, insult him? I have thrown in the towel, for I cannot conceal myself well enough to escape his designs of revenge for tripping *him* at the edge of the pond; an accident, and I pay by becoming first sought and pegged. And," he alluded to the cozy arrangement, "how fair is it that he should reap paradise under the hands of a goddess, and I am left to fend off the cunning of a jackal?"

"Quite fair," Erik said under his breath. "I have entertained plenty and now claim no more than is right."

"Where is Jacqueline?" Raoul demanded passionately.

"Just past the clearing on the other side, near those rocks. I believe there to be some trove sought within the bowels of a rotted tree."

Raoul spun to gain his bearings at Christine's gesture. "Philippe and Alec have taken her in search of insects."

"Insects? My wife?" he said, disbelieving, as he went in the general direction of disenchanted groans.

"To see and hear before being seen and heard," Erik snickered, "Raoul would not know what to do with himself if he had to go to ground, now would he?"

"Behave."

"Christine," he bemoaned, having recoiled to one side from a jab to his ribs. "Now I shall have to relax all over again." He located her hand and lifted his masque, hinting that it resume from where it had taken leave, when the ministrations were so rudely called away. *Fair indeed, the little enjoyment I dare attempt for the sake of relief.* He gave a terse inhale.

"Too much heat and not enough liberation?" Christine put forth upon examination.

"How bad is it?" he asked, angling his head so she could see.

"Chaffed, but no broken skin, I am sorry."

"I have no regrets," he countered. "It is a small price to pay for connection."

"Yes, and did you and Emili do well?"

"We did, a few tears because of an over rotated key on a music box I made her, and a presumption, to which she will seek clarification, nothing more."

"It means more than you think, Erik, when you make time for her."

"And for you." His hand rose to caress her skin. "I also enquired about the whys of violin and no piano; I was amazed by her answer. After apologizing for not liking both equally, she confessed her reason to be of a purely logistical nature, and selfish: 'pianos are hardly portable,' was her argument in favoring one above the other. As for the violin, she is able to carry the instrument herself to quiet places, places where sound and word may blend to create pictures in her mind. When I told her she was not unlike your father, I immediately had the tables turned on me. She said *I* was to blame for the inspiration!"

"Ah, the tree."

"Yes, 'the tree.' Seems there have been a few tales shared amongst my quixotic females."

"Emili asked which memory I savored most, regarding our courtship, and I could hardly lie. No matter how romanticized the perspective, there is something to be said for a change in scenery. Did you eat enough?"

"Or topic, and yes, for now." Erik stretched his frame, weaving an arm around Christine's lower back to facilitate a resettlement of his bones. "I should like to petition for this to occur as regularly as it did prior to marriage. What do you say, my love?"

"Regarding my concern for your well-being? Oh, I can safely say that that has not diminished, but increased." She received a poke of her own for parrying.

"Try again."

"All right. I say. . . there are an abundance of joys one profits from by marriage, most health promoting, and for some reason you seem to think yourself able to secure them all uniformly."

He nodded emphatically to the alluding of *all*. "I may not glut myself as some men do," giving quick reference to his stomach with a rub, "but I will indulge in your attentions."

Christine's finger took a tender sojourn around the perimeter of Erik's masque, seating the barricade in place. It was not his desire, but one he must often give in to for the sake of others, as the *others* were to be the featured misfortune to disjoint his respite in their ignorance during those very next moments. The finger, in return, received a kiss to convey a gift of gratitude back; there was an exchange of smiles, a wink. . .

"I suppose we shall have Monsieur Gautier to thank for our current summons!"

"Can that woman never resist?" Erik exclaimed, with a smidge of asperity to Christine, declaring next, in a fit of open passion, "Ah, the voice of an angel! Welcome, *all* of you, to my piece of heaven."

"Yes, and now all these men are clamoring for a section of their own." Cerise stood before Erik's supine form, her mouth and flare of her nostrils, a grim punctuation to her rather haughty apparition. "Such an example! I suspect it will become some sort of ongoing ritual I am to perform."

Could this be? Cerise paving the way for such a beautiful comeback, and he, in command of the perfect one! Damn lucky! An example? Ha! Surely his time had come to squeeze the pit from its soft bed; he inhaled, felt Christine's fingers latch on to his ear, and observed the fanciful inclination all but vanish under her caress. She knew all too well what he contemplated, how he wished to torment the woman. He wanted to spear her harsh exterior with the knowledge of how often it reoccurred between the two of them, and to watch that callous temper burn. The time had gone.

"I shall do anything in my power to obtain preferential treatment for that good husband of yours, that is all." These words said, the benign attack receded in truce of a pleasant afternoon; no breeze blew, which brought a stifling reminder of the season and further motivation for each couple to curtail activities and plant themselves along the meadow's edge, the conversations affording, in those few hours of leisure, a realignment of marital priorities and appreciative bonds of friendship forged.

Children, notwithstanding their level of energy to be so tirelessly enduring, continued on in their endeavors and would not be swayed as their mature counterparts, but came and went from the central hub of repose. Emili and Jeanette had since solved their confusion, and being fast friends again, searched to make everything right with the world, as it could possibly be for two young ladies nearing the age of nine. Hand in hand they approached, determination etched to have their thoughts turned out, first to Father Chagny, and meeting with the appropriate direction, they came to Father Gautier. Erik was sound asleep, for the second time, not unlike several in their company, off in exploration of dreams. Christine motioned for the girls' silence, bidding them wait until later and both faces sank, perturbed.

"But, Maman," Emili pleaded, "the boys switched games and are playing war because there are more of them. They said that we *girls* were not permitted to enlist, so we are sticking together, as Tante Valery's Celeste is not yet old enough, at three, to count. I have come as Jen's ally, for she wishes to ask Papa a question."

Just then, an exuberant, but seemingly worn out soldier came and flopped down beside his mother, rifle (a stick) errantly discarded in a huff of irritation for the safety of a familiar embrace. Étienne said not a thing as he sidled up to watch and listen.

"Please?"

The intense whisper clashed when made upon unyielding ears. "Emili, your father is tired, you must be patient."

Christine felt a gentle pat and light pressure as Erik stirred, rolling up to his forearm. "It's all right. Come you two, what have you to ask?"

"Oncle Erik. . ." The reaction Emili's father had to the title of endearment stopped Jeanette; it was his eyes, and how they were suddenly riveted to hers, sincerely attentive, as though she mattered most at that moment.

"Yes, Jeanette."

She took a deep breath, her bravery spurred ahead by a squeeze from Emili. "Oncle Erik, my father said that if I would like to know something, I should ask the person most knowledgeable about the subject."

"He gives wise advice." Erik glanced over at Raoul, who was content not to be heard.

"I asked him if he knew why you wore a masque and he affirmed that he did, in a way, but that it would be more appropriate to ask you than for him to mislead me."

From the mouths of babes and female at that! The issue had not been raised for years, there was no need, but seeing this to be more than he anticipated, he gave the query the respect it deserved and sat upright, directing the girls to have a seat in front of him as he leaned into Christine.

"Has Emili told you. . . anything?" He plied the subject with sensitivity, looking straight at his daughter. Emili bit her lip.

"No, she claimed bias."

Erik winked at her, and then focused directly at Jeanette. "Before I was born, there was every reason to expect my birth would be as most, for there were no signs leading one to believe otherwise. I suspect that some genetic mishap occurred during the developmental process and so, there is a substantial portion of my face and skull which are not as well formed as yours. You can see that my right eye is not quite level with my left, yes?"

Jeanette dropped her chin slightly and repeated with a sullen, "yes."

Both girls seemed to feel quite consciously the discomfort of the question, but Erik was kind, and brought Jeanette's gaze back up with a touch to her cheek.

"I wear this masque so those who are not familiar with my situation do not become shocked or afraid. And," he poked her little nose, "as long as you are sincere, do not ever be concerned when asking about what is not understood. I would rather it be the case, personally." He checked to see if Richard was applying himself against this bit of intelligence, but alas, there was too great a strong hold over his lids. Meg smiled.

"That hardly seems fair," Jeanette protested indignantly. "Why must you take on the responsibility to yield?"

"Because, Jeanette, the world's perception of normal or even that of beauty, does not include what I choose to cover."

Christine linked her hand within the crook of Erik's arm and kissed his shoulder. The girls smiled at the loving gesture. "Emili, do you think you could see your way to convincing all those young *military men* that it is time for rations back at the house?"

"Certainly, Maman," she replied, standing up with Jeanette in tow.

There was a suspicious glare at the eagerness before Christine looked about to rejoin, "We may be enlisting a measure of aid in the rousting of these high ranking administrators, too."

Emili giggled at the inference made, in relation to what she knew from studying real conflicts of war, and stooped to kiss her father on the forehead, which was joined and dispensed by the second as they merrily went to task—a flash of brown and gold, to carry out their orders.

After the parting, Erik at once gave heed to the tugging of his shirtsleeve. "What is it, Étienne?"

"When shall it be just you and I?"

"Are you at your wits' end?" The young boy stayed his tongue, but could not staunch the prick of heat in his throat or ripples blurring his vision as he instinctively reached out to be held. "The woes and endless frustrations of being the youngest midst the tyranny of certain *cousins* and elder brother, hmm?"

Étienne sniffed and situated into his father's neck, finding his voice when his mother kissed her finger for him to grasp. "I dislike Sean and Daniel Minot today; they are ornery, selfish, and unfair. They said Grand-mère was not mine, only theirs."

"Indeed, there is plenty of impetus to fuel one's take on the meaning of the last, and deductions to make of the other two. I am sorry, son."

"Erik, take him home," Christine urged. "I shall look to the rest." He nodded and set out quietly.

Trying to initiate movement among the more sedentary fixtures proved more of a challenge. Several had become adhered to their location as a century's old stone, rooted to the very earth by sheer mass, but it was never said that persistence did not reap effect, and they migrated victoriously after prying. The march proved vindicating as Valery informed Christine of hearing Étienne's disappointment, and assured her that the boys would mend the hurt from such remarks. It pained her deeply, for she wished the conclusion of their stay to be cheerfully based, their presence not dreaded in its coming, to be tolerated, and then turned out knowing relief was attained only by absence.

Having been raised herself without the benefit of generational interaction, from either maternal or paternal relations, Valery empathized, glad for the encounter both sets of children had with Cerise and Chanler, and she was adamant it should remain; no child need be starved of affection when there was plenty to be had. Christine could see that Valery expected no real response as they walked on, which was just as well, for Christine would have righted the ignorance had she not been strangled in sentiment, caught by no fault of her own nor that of her now quiet friend.

In a matter of hours the Minots, both young and old with entailment of children, bid farewell for Amiens; being close enough to arrive by sunset they felt it best after the apologies came, not to tempt providence by staying to week's end of one day more. Those who stayed were to take their leave the next morning, and so it happened, that withdrawal shook the estate in its fist for a few days longer. . . then all was calm.

Experiences left valuable thoughts to ponder on in the evenings, done whilst Erik and Christine observed their children playing together, as they listened to the laughter, and the squeals and teases each mingled with the simplicity of their surroundings; it was a testimony, counterpoint to the harmonics of love that would at long last be played to completion.

Chapter Fifty-Five

What does one say when there has been more life lived than there is yet to be acquainted? If it is mandatory to bequeath some profound exhortation to bind up my past, then I shall remain silent, for no amount of expression will ever do justice to the sacred honor reserved for the woman who has held captive, my heart and soul. I remain in awe over the impact one may have in altering the path of another, and so it is here that I sit, deeply consumed with the events she has so faithfully penned, in quiet contemplation at her side. Each journal, a volume of blessings and lessons. . . I have learned to care nothing for the opinions of men, finally! For it is what Christine thinks, what God may think, which have set the standards I live by.

Since those first years with her, when I sought to undermine any quality of light or beneficence of good, due to the then-unmitigated factors I could never change (and still cannot), she had the foresight to make me stand, and pushed back when I thwarted. Humph, perhaps I was tired of pushing alone in the wrong direction and was ready to accept the force of another. A coincidence? Not in the least! I believe our choices govern much of what is labeled as Destiny and Fate, nothing "just" happens; my heart is an evolutionary unit under this conversion. My whole life has been constructed around music and yet I sang a cappella for decades, and what good did it do me? None save stroking the pride and power achieved from triumph over mere vocal inflection. I proved I could go life alone; it was dissatisfying, but to share with the support of accompaniment. . . infinitely gratifying.

And, how regularly had I tempted the gates of death to swing, gaping in their anticipatory celebration, to have rid my ever-pressing summons? I suppose I could never submit to entry by my own hand, but it is as it always is when the petition lies dormant—the appeal is rarely heeded, especially later, in the cause of one so dear. "I've changed my mind," say I, and yet God answers mercifully, "I know." I understood occasionally, and now, more readily than I wish to admit.

Erik could concentrate no longer and pressed the black threads softly together, those within the journal detailing *their* history, his and Christine's, and rested his mouth upon the top edge. He stared at her, unable to avert his fixation from her face, remembering the softness of their first touch, the gentleness of voice and sweet caress when lips brushed flesh. Not having expected the sensation that such an innocent memory could evoke, he gasped and shut his eyes tight. *I love her touch; how shall I endure?* His jaw clenched and sight burned as he compressed his fist from whence the journal was removed. He knew the instant he suppressed his emotion that it was a mistake, the one offense most often repeated but never wholly regretted to correctly amend, so he seized, tensing in resistance to the constricting pain in his chest.

"Erik, come here." She had the covers turned down, waiting.

"It. . . Christine. . . Arrrgh!" He struggled to sit forward. "It hurts."

"When has pain ever occurred that it does not draw upon its synonym?" she chided, as he knew she would. He deserved the rebuke and nestled in against her warmth, uncaring if his ear were to be filled by the simmering indignation. "Going without sleep is not a suitable habit for you to resume, nor are the missives of sentiment when you forget to correspond with she who is attached to your heart."

"I cannot help myself. Forgive me?" he entreated, managing to rasp out the few words while melting under the douse of caresses, but it appeared to him she was taking her sweet time to respond. Could it be that the more dispassionate side of her personality had seriously been taken under advisement?

"I always do," she replied, when he had managed to draw a sustaining breath for her. "Tell me, how am I to continue when your aberrant actions continue to reoccur? Your vigilance does me no good if it runs you into the ground."

Erik pulled back, shocked, as another long, uncomfortable pause ensued in which he chose to rise and sit with his back to her. "Your morbid reference is offensive," he said, his voice sullenly tinged.

"So is yours," her tone flattened.

He cringed, realizing this was to be another of those experiences, where right and wrong did not exist among the prevalent feelings displaced from content. His long-denied anger, tempered beneath gentle regard, flared, as fists prepared to pound upon the downward force of their swing—but strike they did not; they forbore and slowly opened to release their hostility. He sat panting, then clasped one hand to the other, shuddered, and retreated soundlessly into a numbing calm. Being unsure how to stay the course of a man, limited and subject to mortal laws, Erik averted his eyes upward.

"If you must cry," she quivered vocally, "would you at least do me the courtesy of sharing?" Her brave front had diminished and she was just as lost as he.

"I don't know what to do anymore, Christine."

"Love me." There was an inner gleam magnified by the shine in her eyes. She smiled, touching his hand. "Love me and laugh with me. We cannot waste our moments pining and wondering when our tomorrows will become the yesterdays for those we leave behind. Erik, I wish to use every precious now, and if that means we are in the arms of the other, just being near, just touching, it will be enough."

"Enough? More than half my life, Christine Daaé, more than half," he emphasized, "… have I been loved by you."

"It feels good to be loved, does it not?"

Erik looked away, presently distressed, and buried his hands in the now thinning silver, to sigh in thought, which was all the encouragement Christine required for the delivery of a light thump to the back of his head.

"Ah," she winked at his dubious glare. "Though my strength is not what it once was, it is a good thing you were not far from my reach or my aim may have been less accurate."

"You're so damn. . ."

"What? Impertinent, irreverent, spontaneous, mischievous, feisty, romantic. . ." She paused and gave Erik a fleeting smirk, holding up a second pillow. "You might stop me, you know, before I reach the nasty traits."

"There are none." He scowled. *How does she do this? When one sees the path from which they can no longer detour, she chases the despondency away with hope. Beautiful woman.*

"There is always hope, Erik."

"You amaze me," he whispered, his countenance having at last been raised, if only by a dim flicker.

It has been more than five years, I know there cannot possibly be much remaining. . . all I can do, is love her. . .

AFTER THE HEATED blush from the whispering spring, the smooth stone floor was cool to the touch that fall evening of 1913. Christine had lingered again, but what did it matter? There was a point in everyone's life when time and priorities must give way to the importance of a moment, and knowing the penetrating warmth came highly recommended for the weariness maturity brings, no other choice existed. Stretching, she resumed her dressing gown and walked through into their chamber. Erik had yet to return, meaning, if she dispensed with the more tedious portions of the coiffure she had determined upon, there would be time enough.

Settling in front of the vanity, she commenced the satisfying task of brushing through her thick waves; once a lush auburn, she noted the strands were gradually spinning themselves silver as age intertwined with the richness of youth. Her mind drifted through the memories with the blending of each stroke, those savored and irreplaceable. On the darkened backdrops played well-logged vignettes, only now, there were silhouettes of those beloved who had gone missing from the chapters she had composed, and a sense of melancholy swept in. She, but more particularly Erik, had been ill prepared for the heart wrenching turn of events over such a closed span of time.

Chanler passed away after a lingering illness in 1910, devastating Cerise, as they had been the staple of each other's life for so long. She remained in Amiens for more than a year, discovering she needed the comfort that only blood-ties could provide, and we could never impose our sincerest claim to her as friend and grand-mère, though Étienne tried. So, she left for America to be with her son and his family. The adjustment was culturally 'interesting,' I believe is the word she used in one of her letters when expounding upon the intensity of living, and though there was much discomfiture during the outset, the benefit since has outweighed all to a fine level of contentment.

Sorrowfully, Adèle preceded the departure of the Minots and has been missed terribly by Meg. We miss her too, but the culmination of deaths has had a different impact on each of us. For the children, it was losing one grandparent after another, so to speak, and therefore a deeper ache, despite the letters written to America. Erik revered each woman—in his own way—and esteemed Chanler as friend, mentor, and father figure in a cherished and fulfilling relationship. I, on the other hand, am grateful to correspond with Cerise; I hold dear the bond first established, which in turn has diminished the hurt and circumstance of distance.

At these junctures we are permitted introspection, if grasped, but I was uncertain regarding the state of mind Erik would assume, when Soheil's life met the horizon just over a year ago. Among his last requests were that he be allowed to live out his remaining days at the estate, close to nature, before being committed to a final place of repose—similar to what he would be granted in his own country. The location, one chosen while "riding the wind," was where eventide kissed the twilight of dawn. Darius prepared, washed, and shrouded his master's body in accordance with tradition, then he and Erik rode to the site in quiet and took care of Soheil, peacefully. Given a sobering dose of liberation, Darius decided a journey home to be the first option availed him, knowing he could return if there were no prospects to attach him permanently within the East. Erik managed the personal effects and disbursements of Soheil's will, which he later expressed to be a very cleansing process in putting another's house in order, what little there was; the fastidious man had left minimal to deal with in his absence.

While making contact with those who had yet to be made aware of the Persian's death, Erik used Soheil's appointment book as an aid and, as was to be expected, there were meetings with business associates to cancel: one with the new manager of the Opera, Monsieur Gabion, a few literary acquaintances, and his attorney, but one in particular caught Erik's eye longer than the rest, as a hybrid mix. It seemed Soheil had agreed to confer with some legal journalist, at M. Gabion's urging, early on in 1911. Said person was unnamed, but the entry had the following notation inscribed below it—*interest in mysterious deaths and unsolved cases for literary intent*. Nothing was ever mentioned.[14]

And with death comes renewal... Christine's complexion lightened at this poignant bit, countering the block of gloom upon which she had been focused. Each of their children, had in turn, chosen sweet companions, and were receiving additions into their own families, soothing the void greatly felt.

Having finished her hair, Christine became attentive again to the reasons for her current state. "More than thirty-five years Erik... Grand-père." *They are all dear to his heart, but none like his Emili. If ever a bond were more pure between father and daughter... I see so much of myself and equal portions of all that is good in him.*

ACROSS THE ROOM, Erik found his arms in sudden want as he entered the chamber. Not that they had been deprived before, but what they held could not compare to what might be had.

Christine looked up, visibly shaken by Erik's appearance in the mirror. "Why do you do that to me?"

Erik stood directly behind her in his evening attire, staring, his lips pursed thin in concern to her accusation. *To her? To me!* His mind labored over the habit. Then, bending close to her ear he whispered, "Because, when I see fluid beauty, I wish to leave it undisturbed for as long as possible, in its natural state of grace."

Christine watched his reflection, attended his subtleties, and was drawn to him. His eyes were inescapable, they sensed beyond the surface into her soul. Gloves dropped to the floor, and a quick release of the cloak had it joining its counterparts in a heap of black. Her chest rose and fell in anticipation of his touch, eyes trained upon reverse images; he delicately caressed her throat, losing himself in its softness; so light, so slow were his ministrations that it was the embodiment of being bathed in the scent of love. His voice held her aloft, sustaining every desire.

"Erik." His name, elongated on her tongue gave rise to his pulse; he descended to bent knee, subject and willing hostage before her.

"Please, I do not wish to share you with anyone tonight. No eyes to see you, no other words to imbue your ear's delight but mine." Erik kissed her hand in accent to his proposal.

"And who shall be guest in our place for Otello?"

"Already arranged." He smirked mischievously. "Étienne and Annica said they have friends who have not yet been to the Opera, and I affirmed the opportunity as one not to be missed."

Christine's eyes roved the still features while the playful anticipation livened his from the divesting of masque and pretense. "This leads me to believe there is another plan in mind?"

"Always," he murmured. "Come, my love."

Erik escorted her to the spring, where she gladly sat along the edge. He adored the way he could tease her thoughts with the mysteriousness of his designs. He was scarcely gone from her side when he reappeared mystically, arms filled by several parcels, and what looked to be the lower portion of a lantern. In brief, a creamy confection was melted into which they could dip an array of cakes and fruit. The evening was one of pleasurable indulgence, if not a great deal messy, while they tested, mixed, and delightfully combined.

"What an absolutely delicious interlude," Christine remarked, rather impressed.

"Hmm, it is not my doing, but Annica's; she sends her best to us for a surreptitious celebration. I believe her wishes are sarcastic in nature, considering she and Étienne never know our location when we visit. It frustrates her, especially when she is relegated intentionally to ignorance by my refusal to *hear* the meaning of her comments."

"Perhaps I should clue her in, such torment is intolerable," Christine exclaimed with a mouth full, her hand covering the contents in as lady-like a manner as was possible.

"Is it?" Erik defended.

"No," she complied instantly. "I would never betray your confidence."

"What about to Emili?" he asked. The idea had made a strange exit, he realized, almost before the thought was even perceivable.

"Never. Not even to her, Erik. This place has been a gift, one shared, but not owned by me. I cannot share with another what is not mine to give, without consent from you."

He caught her off guard, saw the hesitance and probed, "There is more; come, out with it."

"All right. If we *were* to take anyone into our confidence, to divulge what we have kept private, it would be she because I trust her, and Miykael."

"Yes. I feel the same," he said in a fashion more reserved than he meant, so much so that Christine made an extra effort to dismiss the matter altogether.

"Quite the dress standard."

Erik cocked his head at the topic, confused. "I missed the segue in conversation."

"Sorry, we are at opposite ends of the spectrum and mismatched in every way. I, hopelessly intimate and you, pleasing to the extreme of society."

"I took no notice," although his attention quickly fixated.

"Really? You did our first night at the estate."

A gentle parting of his mouth was normally anticipatory to the proceeds of mind, but nothing witty loosed his tongue, his inability to articulate figuring him most likely to take a stance of denial.

"I did n—"

"You did!" she finished, adding a chocolate-slathered berry to the lure. Their mouths connected jointly to contend with the sweetness, spilling from all corners unheeded.

"Perhaps." He chuckled, separating to assess the damage. "So much for a white dress shirt."

"Oh, it was doomed from the start, look." Christine gazed at a place he could not have possibly noticed himself, and pulled on his tie.

"Don't tell me I have reached the age of requiring assistance to accomplish such a menial task as feeding myself?" She laughed, but remained otherwise mute to the dreaded question while attempting a stealth assault from under his chin. "Stop!"

The tone and tumble of disapprobation shocked Christine, but no more than the frantic shove as Erik steadied and bolted upright, contorting and straining to unfasten the unbearable constriction of tie and collar in haste for relief.

"Is it your chest, what did I do?" She rose quickly to her feet.

"No, no," he wheezed. "Forgive me, I had not intended to be so brash." Erik held up his hand and bent over at the waist, providing the space needed to gain control and hazard several deep, unhindered breaths. He waved Christine close and grasped her hand. "We shall need more light. Come, I shall explain while changing." Still feeling half strangled, he led her into the alcove, unfastening buttons as he went, and after seating her on the bed tipped his head back to enquire on appearance. "How does it look?"

Unsure of what she was to be looking for, Christine answered topically. "Red, but what is its cause?" she asked, motioning toward his throat.

"No! Please, don't touch it." She drew away and helped to remove his cuff links while Erik made a thorough exam by testing various sections for soreness, relating in his process the tale, but only when a certain stipulation was adhered to. "Promise not to laugh?"

"Why would I?"

"Promise! Please." He rounded at the armoire.

"You have my word."

Throwing on his dressing gown he moved next to Christine. "While I was busy gathering up the items for our sweet encounter this evening, saying my good-byes and so forth, Jean expressed his wish for a hug. I was distracted, not watching, and he leapt just as I leaned over to pick him up. His head caught me hard, nearly causing me to pass out and collapse to the floor."

Christine lifted his chin, checking gently, now that she knew to what degree his neck was tender.

"I was at the mercy of a three-year-old boy and most successful in scaring us all from our wits with my violent gasping and panting for air; it was all I could do to keep from ripping my masque off, I was that desperate. Annica grabbed a chair and Étienne held me upright from an embarrassing sprawl. I was quite a spectacle, having to explain what happened to Jean before he would come near me, poor child. But, upon my return here, I was so taken, so utterly enthralled by you, and busy in mind at each point, that I forgot completely about the incident until the pressure triggered a relapse. Ugh. . . I fear it to be quite bruised."

"Jean clipped you a good one, I'm sorry."

"What a damper I have gone and placed on our evening." Erik took a deep shuddering breath and his ears colored in the youthful confession. "I was enjoying our direction."

Keenly aware of this, Christine rose, caressing the soft spot between his thumb and index. "To be reminded we are no longer invincible has served to keep us grateful. Do not give up hope; there remains plausible cause for such goals. Stay."

"Enigmatic imp!" he declared of her when she vanished. *That smile! Always so jovial in its display, she has loved far beyond. . .* his trusting grin lessened. *I have noticed the years, how they creep beautifully upon her. It is true, we have both slowed and take advantage of this new pace; my accounts require less time and Christine more, our focus has reverted back, full circle. Growing seasoned can be a tremendous blessing, being alone with her, my companion. . . it fills my existence.*

Christine was with him once more and he sighed inwardly, noting the linen-draped parcel she brought with interest and dismay in glaring interchange. "I thought we agreed there was to be only time between us, no gifts."

She shrugged. "Shall we abide by the letter or spirit? Pleasure is sure to be had by both, and the endeavor required several years, multiplied by two because Emili was my accomplice in acquisition. Your verdict?"

"I shall withhold until further evidence proves more convincingly, one way or the other. At this moment, I am undecided."

"I see how it is," she smiled suggestively, "you desire a visual. Well, these were too special to be prettied by modern vanity, so, I wrapped them in something more honored, more simple."

"What have you been up to?" It was indeed an inviting bit of proposition she transferred into his lap, and a heavy one at that. "Clearly, a formidable task on my behalf, especially when it leaves in its wake aches and pains on delivery."

The behavior, one that had been on the rise during the past few months, had Erik eyeing the massage to the upper chest, near each shoulder. Her symptoms were limited, and surfaced only when her physical abilities were taxed or when exhaustion loomed.

Her brow furrowed. "Would you just enjoy?" she lashed out with the light reprimand.

The kiss planted upon his forehead pushed the clouds from his features as she moved to kneel behind him on the left. A deft flick of the wrist removed the linen to reveal a graduated tower of books tied up neatly with string; one pull brought the volumes their freedom, and they spilled across the covers.

"Hugo," he whispered, his sight blanketing the prize in recognition.

"Yes. Emili and I were able to locate a significant number of his novels and poetry, some are even first editions." Christine stroked the back of his head down to his neck, smoothing his lightly greyed temple in place.

Erik's hand curved around her thigh to give it an appreciative squeeze, the other traced the titles as he read them quietly aloud, "*Odes et Poésis Diverses, Notre-Dame de Paris, Les Châtiments. . .*"

"That," she announced proudly, "is the ever popular forbidden book of poetry."

Leave it to my wife. Erik grinned and went on, "*Les Travailleurs de la Mer, Les Misérables.*" He chuckled as he held up *L'Art d'être grand-père.* "How to be a grandfather? This, from a man who was in voluntary exile for twenty years."

They laughed at the odd paradox and stored each text in an orderly fashion for their return trip, leaving the first compilation of Hugo's poems available, as requested by Christine.

"Now it is my turn." He looked at her attentively to see the reaction his words would imbue.

"Guilty! Shame on you, taking me to task!"

"Oh, you shall not pin that on me, chastising so sharp without due course."

"You just. . ."

"I was not specific, but now I shall be. I bear a gift from our son, with strict instructions that it be opened while standing in your embrace. Étienne recommends the position for optimal affect."

"He is as hopeless a romantic as his father, no? Such instructions. . . were they his or issued by your design?" she taunted, sauntering along behind him, barely out of reach and dubious to his intent when she saw him pivot and quit the alcove.

"What, you think I require a ploy from my own son to incline your affections toward me? Nonsense! Come," he encouraged passionately.

Erik retrieved a rather large framed, art shaped item from between the doors leading into their chamber and laid it atop the bed, held onto Christine, and with one hand apiece, they removed the paper sheath.

"Oh, Erik." Her hand rested over her mouth in awe. Stunned, he could say little more and therefore remained speechless, neither seeming to draw enough breath to substantiate the existence of the other. Christine was first to comment.

"After all these years, and such exquisite detail." There was a faint "yes" and she glanced from the portrait to Erik's face.

Contorted in wretched anguish, he could hardly stand to look upon the likeness, but would not tear his gaze from it, fearing the visage to feign reality at his expense. She kissed his cheek.

"He sees, he possess a talent I shall never understand, it is so. . . alive, so true. Wish that it were, my. . ." Erik could not bring himself to finish and curtailed any hope of furthering the sentence.

"You know it has always bothered him."

"What has?"

"That you created works of art to portray others and never made any attempt or would allow for yourself."

"For reasons unfailingly obvious."

"To whom?" No reply came. "When Étienne was about ten, he asked me if you had ever drawn anything, had ever given semblance to how you saw yourself in your own mind's eye."

"What did you tell him?"

"That your masques were the expression and illusion in unison, except for one other, to my knowledge at that time."

"One other. . ." he led on, somewhat intrigued.

"We went upstairs and I showed him the angel carved into the footboard of our bed. He smiled and seemed genuinely pleased."

"You and I have never discussed *that* angel, the poor forgotten soul." He hugged her.

"Forgotten? No, he is the undeclared token of a destiny no longer forsaken. And our son, thoughtful in his esteem for you."

The family portrait was discussed, admired, and appreciated for some time; done in the medium of oil—one talent in which Erik openly professed to having none—there was a quality the artist was able to capture, something which, in his opinion, lacked in all other two-dimensional genres: the accuracy of emotion as related to an understanding of what was considered real. Colors, layered in just the right way, were able to give such opulent depth and perception of inner-self that one felt they could touch and raise from the canvas a tangible measure of life. Étienne had a remarkable sense for the skill and an eye for naturally filling the canvas to facilitate a smooth line. He had positioned his parents, Father sitting astride the bench upon which Mother sat, brothers standing, one on either side of their father, and sister, adoringly set at the foot of their parents, skirts flowing, a vertical feast for any onlooker to behold.

Leaning into Erik's chest, Christine asked if he might read at that time, so they arranged and situated for comfort then he commenced with a preface. "The inconsistencies in Hugo's life are abundant, his perspectives, morals and beliefs alike, give the impression they were all subject to a mere page turn. Brilliant writer," Erik muttered, whilst searching for a place to begin. "I believe he once wrote: 'Romanticism is the liberalism of literature.' I suppose emotion to be as subjective as faith, myself, and hope you will take from his works as much pleasure as I."

Together, they roamed the vivid imagination of this author, stopping upon occasion to express a concept of their own, and for the purpose of resettling. When the adjusting persisted, past what Erik deemed sufficient, he remarked once more upon the subject. Christine spoke diminutively, placing the source to hefting books, along with age, then bid him to go on reading. But as much as he appreciated her flattery, regarding the fluidity of his voice, he detested the flippant attitude; it did not bode well, the explanation nor the excuse, and as neither was viable in his mind, they left more unrest than resolve. Riding on a regular basis, gardening, hikes, and any multitude of estate affairs had created a wonderfully fit, handsomely robust woman. No, it refused to add up.

Sitting forward, he twisted around to face her as the descriptions of her prowess dried in his throat upon evaluation. His probing fingers ran across each shoulder, her upper chest, underarms. . . the glands were swollen, nodules of the left more prominent than those of the right; he kissed her forehead, cheeks, and lips dispassionately, hoping for a sign of a low-grade fever, but there was none. Christine jested sarcastically that it was a stroke of luck he did not engage in the field of medicine, for his manner of concern was demonstratively inept.

"Christine," Erik cupped her face in his hands, the tone of his voice severe. "I have enough background to know when something is not right. I shall make the necessary arrangements with Chèver; we can leave for London by way of home."

She gripped his wrists, and with tears filling her eyes pulled Erik's hands away. "No! I do not wish it, nor do I wish to leave, not now!"

"Humor me. I do not trust the physicians here." Erik hesitated. "And, we can visit *le petits-enfants*, perhaps there will even be a new one."

A bit of light flashed beneath the stormy rage and she assented. Her hands dropped into her lap allowing Erik's to return, his fingers twining themselves in the silvery-brown. "While it may be nothing, I would rather make sure. You are too precious for me to ignore. I love you far too much to sit idle when I can do something, when there are resources at my disposal."

Christine closed her eyes to the overwhelming alarm compounding his frustration. "Look at me, please," he begged, and her lids parted. "You are my life, do you understand? My life!"

The intensity flared and spoke greatly of desperation. Fear seized at his heart, branding its deepest, most sincere confession across their vitals. He was telling her soul that if something were to happen to her, he would be totally and unequivocally lost. The emotions mortality fraught upon this sensitive man beat at her stiff-necked tenacity, forcing her to realize he had begun to tread on unfamiliar ground, and it frightened him. He fought valiantly against the surge, to constrain, but thought better of it and permitted the release.

"Do you comprehend my love for you?" Erik swallowed, trying to alleviate the pain constricting in his sore throat and chest.

"Yes." Her answer was soft and comforting to his ears.

It was but a tender signal, ever so light, drawing her nearer. His breathing labored on as Christine embraced his neck then lips touched and parted. "Never let me go Christine, hold me tight, love me, need me."

WITHIN A SPAN OF two weeks Erik and Christine traveled to London, where Chèver and Michele welcomed them with warmth and open arms. Their son had done well for himself, taking it into his mind to refuse at the first opportunity any acceptance of monetary support when he could manage independently. While finishing his schooling at the university in Scotland, Chèver took on an internship there, in Edinburgh, and later began the arduous task of deciding whether to become a general practitioner or to seek out an area in which to specialize. Eventually, post research and additional education, he took a position in London as a surgical physician, amidst the splendid opportunities developing in the field of medicine and all that centered about the fast pace of the city. Leisure had not been in the young man's vocabulary for some time, but music saw its way to becoming a release and the ideal diversion, as the one effectively procured the attentions of a pretty face, and tipped the scale in favor of a worthy second. He could not seem to get his fill of those bright, challenging eyes, silken tresses, and uncommonly smooth skin, and though she seemed reserved, there came a fiery buoyancy, which never played false nor the least bit coquettish. She dazzled Chèver with her originality of intellect and won his heart. His father had been correct, he understood, he cherished Michele. Chèver and Michele were married the summer of 1908, and were now expecting their second child in the next few weeks.

The appointment was set—one of Chèver's colleagues had agreed to come at week's end, following the completion of rounds, and so, all was conditionally granted by Christine; and as such, Chèver was to lay hold upon his father if an attempt were made to enter the room in which the physical was to be administered, the stipulation: strict and abiding.

"I wish my findings were more conclusive than your initial detection, Mrs. Gautier, but I would not postpone the biopsy. Chèver can arrange for a day next week." The physician looked to her stoic posture as he cleansed in the washbasin, unsure about her frame of mind. "Your symptoms suggest several possibilities, though I would prefer to know what we are dealing with before I make my diagnosis, then we can proceed with a course of action befitting."

"Would my son attend the procedure?" Christine asked, looking back over her shoulder.

"Only if you wish him there, Ma'am."

Drying his hands, the physician gathered his instruments and stood, watching for some acknowledgment before taking his leave.

When Christine realized he wished a response, she obliged, "Thank you for your time. I shall be in touch soon, to let you know what is decided."

He nodded. "Shall I inform your husband?"

"No, if you please, I will speak with him, but I should like a few moments first."

"Certainly," he acquiesced, bowing gently. "I shall see myself out."

He quit the room, quietly slipping through the door as she calmly walked to the window. The gold-fringed drapes hung in sullen reverence, penitent in their shortcoming to block out the anger and embittered pleas echoing the corridors, unable to deliver tranquility from the clutches of fear.

"Oh, God in heaven," she prayed, "my strength cannot bear this, I cannot manage his *and* mine," she whispered to the empty room. "I don't know what to do next."

"What do you mean. . . cannot?" Erik raged, dogging the man down the stairs and into the entry. "Cannot or won't? Damn! Let go of me, Chèver!" Erik jerked his arm from his son's grasp and stared menacingly at the man before him, the man labeled physician. Suddenly, London's doctors were not as they were touted, despite his son's esteemed devotion.

"Sir, it is her wish, please understand." Chèver waved the servant off and dispensed his friend's coat and hat that he might depart the situation without suffering a longer interface with his father's temper. "Now, if you will excuse me. Chèver." He nodded curtly and exited while he was still in one piece, the acknowledgment made in haste.

"Father!" he exclaimed, upon securing the door.

"She is my wife, Chèver!"

"Paul knows that, I know that, but his obligation is to Mother," he said evenly, taking hold of his father's shoulder.

The two stood eye to eye at roughly the same height, and though one was more aged, he would have, without doubt, made a formidable match for the younger.

"Chèver, remove your hand, please." The tone dripped of ire beneath the rapid gain of control, surprising Chèver, but he was not to be fooled.

"Why, so you may storm upstairs and compound Mother's turmoil? I should think not."

"As you wish."

The glib complaisance was unexpected and worked precisely in getting Chèver to relax his grip. Erik was already part way up the stairs when Chèver discovered him gone, mandating he mount the steps by twos to apprehend the weasel.

"You smug old man!" Chèver nabbed Erik from behind.

"Damn you, Chèver!" he yelled. Every muscle flexed and the blood boiled to near explosive levels as years of suppression flooded his veins. He wanted answers!

"This is exactly why she wants time! Look at how irrational you are!" Erik's body deflated at the blame placed. "I inherited your sharp temper, remember, hmm? You taught me control. Now, let it go."

At that moment, when he desired otherwise, Erik found out just how successful he had been in his instruction. Observing the set jaw, tense and unwilling to yield, the irregular pattern of intake, retention and exhales of air. . . Chèver remained steadfast, and when he was convinced of his father's composure, he released him.

Erik rotated slowly to face his son, tears glistening. "Forgive me. I am an old fool, seething antipathy with nowhere to direct it, blinded by the unknown because I don't know what lies ahead. I don't know if I can handle what is to come, Chèver."

A large, solid arm embraced the opulent frailty and the affection was duly returned. "You also gave me the capacity to love, Father, and with that came a huge well, which overflows regularly." They drew apart, giving rise to better visibility of the tears cascading to Chèver's shirt. "I shall be at your side," he declared passionately.

The sight lessened the burden, but nearly broke her resolve as Christine opened the door to Erik and Chèver locked in the other's arms.

"Erik?" He wheeled obediently to her summons and was there. Christine raised her thumb to erase the wet trail down his masque.

"I love you," she said, smiling. "I need you. One step at a time."

"One step at a time," he repeated.

Chapter Fifty-Six

*M*edical facilities. . ." Erik scoffed aloud. *Not foremost on a list of places where one's senses are soothed with pleasantries. The first to go is that of smell, the stark pungency of ether and carbolic acid has filled any and all vacancies allotted; there is just no plausible means to prevent the stench—much as one would like to capture the scent of a rose that it may be relegated to memory for the feelings evoked—this odor expunges everything, and leaves its noxious remnants for me to remember in taste as well, putrid. Next to be assaulted is visual acuity; white, nothing but a barren void attributed to a claim of sterility, highly impersonal; the halls where Chèver accumulated his knowledge were far more colorful, and alight with faces inclined in wonder! But this, this depresses me greatly; to think that healing occurs in such an environment. Touch, caring, the concern. . . some thing, or rather some aspect, has to go despite the progress and zest igniting that contagion of extrapolation.*

I feel as Christine did all those years ago, prior to Chèver's birth, as part of an intricate lab experiment being watched under glass. While I wait for the biopsy to conclude, my determination to whisk her away from here has increased, and yes, my masque has been an unwavering source for every pair of eyes to weld themselves. Good heavens, not even in investment meetings or with clients at the stables, have I ever experienced a sensation such as this—it is unnerving at best. In the medical profession there is a strong compulsion to "fix" what is somehow deemed abnormal, and I must pose an unquenchable challenge.

Obviously, my impatient wandering of the hallways led me back midst the reclusive four walls of Christine's room. I fretted and stewed the whole of a weekend, but ultimately knew she would be guarded well. She was explicit; come to think of it. . . Chèver was to advocate on her behalf—all decisions to be made jointly, consciously, not by those wielding the knife under the premise of silent consent.

Erik continued to dull the finish from the floor with his incessant habit of pacing, pausing only briefly to look out upon the constantly shrouded city. "White inside and grey without, how does Chèver cope?" He caught himself, amused by the contrast. *And I, underground, what a dreary time.*

"Father?" Chèver gave credence to appearing out of thin air, as he now stood directly facing his father. Erik drew back. "Forgive me, when you did not respond. . ."

"Never mind," Erik stifled the apology. "Your mother. . . how is Mother?"

"She is recovering and shall be here shortly."

"Do you know anything?" The last word was a halting slur, insipid in nature.

"The results should be available soon; when they are, I shall confer with the attending physician." Erik's hand came down softly on his son's arm. Nothing was said, but its meaning was rejoined in a coarse tone of emotion. "Your suspicions. . . shall most likely be confirmed. . . as to the severity. . ." Chèver's gaze dropped to one side.

"There is a summation, based on what was observed, am I correct?"

"Father, I would prefer to speak with you both."

Erik patted his son's arm and erased the urgency in his voice. "I can accept that."

Neither was required to wait interminably long. Once Christine was brought back to the room, and Erik had scoured the place for enough pillows to satisfy himself of her comfort, Chèver was again with them. The door was closed; an entombing decree, as Chèver took a seat at the foot of the bed. Erik settled against Christine, his arm curved about her neck and shoulder, his thumb caressing her cheek. Watching them connect with the other, one would be remiss to deny the inspiration derived from their example, a deep and abiding love could be felt by others in their presence.

Eyes met, and Chèver began. "During the procedure, biopsies were taken from several locations, and not just from the original site." He could see the information give rise to a hint of distress in his mother, but pressed on. "I concurred because I knew the additional intelligence would aid our final diagnosis. Maman," Chèver defined his regard for his mother by the tender address, "you have breast cancer."

His father's hand arrested its motions, surprising Chèver slightly that neither of them reacted adversely; they seemed to take the news in stride, being anxious for more.

"The cancer has spread and will continue to do so. What we do not know is how aggressive it is. You are already acquainted with varying degrees of soreness." A nod of assent confirmed this. "The surgeon found several small tumors and was able to retrace a probable path from some of the lymph nodes, back to their origin. He was convinced as to the direction to take; I was the one to stay his hand."

"Thank you, Chèver." He pursed his lips into a weak grin at her appreciation.

"Chèver, what are Mother's options?"

An unmistakable and unrelenting gaze passed directly between mother and son. "I believe I shall allow her to explain because she has known about this far longer than she is willing to admit." He saw the hurt his betrayal caused, but he would not be compelled to feel guilt. Being obliged to secrecy for the sake of ethics had him bound, to a point, but he would not permit the deception out of love for his father. The man had a right to know. He rose and bent low to kiss his mother, and as his father slid from the bedside he whispered, "I shall leave for now, Mother, but do not underestimate my love. If you do not tell him, I will."

This forced tears to brim, the fear etching indelibly into her forehead as that click announced their privacy secure.

"How. . . long?" Erik asked numbly.

"I have suspected, more. . . than a year." The confession already pained her heart.

"A. . . my. . ." There was some profession in vain that he could not force from his lips while standing defeated at the window, eyes unseeing. "You concealed this from me, intentionally, deliberately said nothing, and never even. . . complained? Pushed me away, and forbade my love, my comfort?" *Why?* Screamed his heart.

"I wrote to Cerise."

He writhed in anguish, and recalled the intimacy she had with the woman on the subject of "all things feminine." This was to be a most excruciating road chosen.

"She. . . contacted the John Hopkins University in Baltimore, where a Doctor Halsted had been performing what was, *is* termed, a mastectomy. She related a list of possible symptoms and options then warned me against some of the hideous outcomes. I…"

Erik had removed his masque and was now helplessly deep in grief, head bent and pressed, cradled into the protective crook of his elbow, quietly weeping upon the sill. The others—Chanler, Adèle, Soheil—were they a precursor, come to inoculate his heart? Whatever the intent, it was failing miserably. Immune, he was not. Not now, not after. . . *why must I hurt again?*

Obviously unable to meet the display caused, her vision was gone as well, the twisted sheet becoming a neutral default for the mounds of self-reproach. "Despite the joys we have experienced in our life,

I saw an emptiness left from the passing of Chanler, and then Soheil's weighted your heart, and... I could not bear to add to that hurt!" Her voice rang out. "I'm sorry, I'm so sorry, I just couldn't!"

After sorrow prevailed for some undetermined length, a gentle touch at Erik's waist necessitated his deprived lungs take in air, and slowly he responded to her as his hand lowered, fingers trembling in a blind search for hers; it was a fruitful pursuit.

"Look at me." She encased his hand.

He had heard that entreaty before. So hard to do! *No! I cannot. Yes, you can.* His mind swung and held. *You ought not to withhold, she has been without solace, turn and face her!* He circled, damp paths shinned down his face, his eyes red and swollen, breathing labored and ragged as he tried to reclaim some level of composure; fingers raking his hair and a handkerchief to wipe their eyes had to suffice initially. Erik's arm hung tenderly down her back, pulling her close.

"Come, back to bed with you," he ordered, gesturing weakly with a lift of his chin.

"And you will accompany me?"

"I will." Thusly spoken, but harder to follow through, he found the difficulty to be centered in those brown orbs—each time they became transfixed to his the strain of tears poured melodically.

"Tell me what you have learned, the options you would like to consider."

Christine burst into tears.

"What?" His eyes widened in horror, thinking the worst and wishing to be of comfort.

"I cannot lift my arms up far enough to touch your face; it hurts."

"Hush, it is easily remedied." And he took refuge in his favorite lap, admitting it was possibly the most ideal position in which to attain reception. "Whenever you are ready." Christine paused and he looked up. "There should not be debate, spare nothing, the covert expedition must end."

Her head bowed wearily. "I asked. . . for Chèver's assistance in gathering facts, three months ago." Erik tensed. "Between what he was able to impart, and the letters I received from Cerise, I knew." Christine began to shake involuntarily and Erik wrapped his arms about her lower back to communicate his support; he was there for her.

"A mastectomy will leave me with nothing but pain, loss of movement, emotional and physical damage, and mental anguish. There is no guarantee and it is not a cure. The medical profession considers this a standard procedure, according to Cerise, but what she was able to glean in her research is that this mastectomy, or complete breast removal, has become a dominating treatment. A woman could agree to a probing biopsy, as I did, and never know whether she would wake up whole or mutilated. Had I submitted in ignorance, my right to decide would have been forfeited. That was my reason for requesting Chèver's presence." Erik nestled tighter.

"I know what I might experience post surgery. . . that I will have increasing pain throughout my body if the procedure is declined. I may have five years, more or less; the uncertainties are great, but one thing I am sure about, I would prefer to live complete, without the disfigurement. It is not worth the risk nor the outcome."

"You know I love you, will accept you. How could I not after all you have seen beyond?" he consoled, and a drop graced his cheek then another as she cried once more.

"I want to go home, Erik, to be with you."

He rose up and sat at her side, their tears mingling as he kissed her face in accord with his avowal of phrase. "In the morning, I shall take you home, home to our fresh air, to the color and peaceful surroundings and, home to my heart."

There was a light knock on the door and no time to resume the masque, which lay on a table across the room. Was such inconvenience to become an habitual trademark and diminutive consideration for privacy? Erik rolled his eyes and sighed, ready to turn away as the door parted.

"Father?"

Erik breathed in relief. "Come in, Chèver."

Much improved—his parents were smiling, a good omen indeed. And, standing stock still in place, he too smiled, almost forgetting his mission. "Oh, yes!" He bowed, as if he had been in preparatory contemplation. "I just received word to return home, Michele has begun labor. So, if you could postpone *your* flight home, from our dreary little English countryside, I should like Grandma-mère—as Charles calls Mother—to convalesce with my wife and infant, and I could not possibly tolerate a *no* from either of you!"

Christine squeezed Erik, and glancing from the exuberance of one to the hope of the other, he answered, "Then we shall stay. . . for as long as your mother wishes."

"I'll consider it settled and shall have a carriage sent round tomorrow. I must go," he said, almost darting through the door save for a quick afterthought, "Oh, and Father?"

"Yes?"

"You might don the masque, you never know when one of the nurses will show up; they tend to do that rather unexpectedly." Chèver winked and quit the room altogether.

Celebration flowed in the subsequent days as a tiny girl made her entry into the world, a most boisterous occasion, lungs unforgiving, when Maria Deahn was expelled against her will, or so it was thus presumed; proud parents and those grand alike, reveled in the newness, the purity of spirit, and all felt right.

Continuing on, the ravages of war came with blessings of safe return for their family, and the cyclical rounds spoke their truth of renewal come spring and each in succession thereafter; marked yearly with a token of Christine's strength by the planting of a white rose bush, on the hill just behind the ridge. Rarely were Erik and Christine seen apart or far from the other's sight during the first few years of her illness, but as her seasons became increasingly difficult to manage, they adjusted; there were days when Erik would just hold her in his arms and read, and others where Christine rallied, coping and stretching the limits forever more. When she began to decline they were inseparable, appreciating moment to moment. . .

ERIK LAY FAST ASLEEP, exhausted past comprehension as Christine's eyes blinked open. He slept, her knight. . . so sweet and vigilant, ever by her side. She looked sideways to his post and their journey in verse. The journals each brought solace and joy to the changes, which made him the gentle man he was now, and as her stamina permitted, she would again take to writing. She must, for he would need an indelible witness to rely upon when the memory faded under that oppressive well of emotion.

"You are awake," Erik said, his eyes still closed.

"I am," she affirmed, placing the palm side of her fingers to his mouth. "This morning, I should love to have you ask me something different, anything other than how I feel. Your intuition serves you well enough that you know of any deficiency before I make mention, not even fatigue inhibits your ability to detect the slightest differentiation in my breathing."

"Fair enough. . ." He paused in thought, kissing her wrist then enquired, "When did you know, for certain, that you could look past my face, past my hatred of the world and my heinous crimes, and truly love me?"

Christine placed a simple kiss upon his lips and he froze into submission. Again her mouth drew him in, moist and soft. He was blind to all other senses, soaking in that passionate spring, their lips moving in unison, accepting.

"Hmm, you confuse me. Summoning strength from some hidden resource in lieu of an answer."

"It was a loaded question, but more time with me should remedy the befuddled glaze in your eyes." She shivered and poked his chest.

"The fire... I should—"

"You should do nothing. Stay close, your warmth is all I need, worry about rekindling the fire later. Now, I believe I was in love with you from the moment you nearly lifted the door from its hinges. Such abuse!" she exclaimed in sarcasm. "I can only imagine how many objects... wait, I need not imagine, I *have* seen all that lay at the mercy of your fiery temper."

"Really?" He sounded incredulous, disregarding the reference to his flat below the Opera House. "Prior to disgorging my history at your feet? That cannot be right. I would have placed it much later... after I was recovered or, that day you desired to know about my masque."

"I made a commitment, Erik, to follow my heart, despite the hardships. And yes... I struggled that first afternoon, but my heart won. Each time I doubted my ability to go on, God spoke peace to my soul that it would be worth my time to endure."

His chest gave a blunt heave. "Christine, those initial twenty-four hours were so revealing."

"Yes, and you *wrapped* your mind around every sensation!" Her emphasis lightened the mood.

"I am afraid you had a highly attentive pupil. Never having been given the opportunity to experience so much affection inspired me to learn quickly, though I applied it incrementally." There was a minute of intense quiet. "The door, hmm? If I would have known—"

"What? What would you have changed?" she asked outright.

"Nothing," he sighed. "Nothing. I required those months to convince myself I could be loved."

"Are you convinced?"

"I am, and each day I have been reminded. Would you have changed... do *you* regret, anything?" he reworded.

"Only one—"

"That you married an older man?" Erik chimed in. Christine rose up sharply and plastered him with a crusty glare, causing him to wish a recapture of haste. "My apologies, sorry."

She soon lowered herself again and expressed completely. "I regret a fact that was not mine to control. My desire to have known you sooner, so I could love you longer, was thwarted by birth in the wrong decade."

All the reminiscing began to oblige and engage the mind to thoughts of *if only*. Erik knew he was quite fortunate to spend these precious times in conversation, discovering, as a great quantity of people are lost to abrupt tragedy, and those who are left, must recall alone. Returning from London, Christine went multiple rounds with him in regard to the torment he insisted he inflict on his tender conscience; the selfishness felt in his inability to recognize and interpret what he saw in perfect hindsight. That day at the window, he had wept because of her sacrifice for him, and now a reverent "oh" proclaimed it all.

The day warmed and Christine made a request, which had a palpable undertone. One moment they were reading together and the next, her hand gravitated to the book and closed the pages, right along with Erik's sentence. "We need to talk," she said in a low murmur, while removing the volume to the table, "on the ridge."

Her eyes stared distantly ahead to a revelation discernable only to her, then turning her gaze to Erik, she smiled and relieved the urgency she had so blatantly seeded. He marveled at how she could reach for the vibrancy she so prudently employed, as though it came from some never ending reservoir, and he granted her desire by kiss.

"What is it commanding such prompt attention?" Erik dared trust, putting voice to thought, but Christine never gave a response. It was rhetorical in nature, for the port was nearing empty as she prepared to soar one last time. . . he knew.

He set her down in front of the roses they had cultivated together, recalling the choice and painstaking search for each until success was met. He cherished walking with her clasped to his side as she examined the already emerging blooms for the precise hue of white; not ecru, not one yellowed or a vague pretense would do. Those were, in her mind, a mockery of what it meant to be pure, and the result stood firm beneath her hands in a tribute of light.

Erik watched her fingers move lovingly over the floral display, and when she took a few unsteady steps to look out past the ridge, the expanse that fell away at her feet somehow forced a satisfying determination to her lips, and she straightened. Erik walked up to support her small frame against the subtle breeze; he was patient and tender in the silence they shared, their memories flashing in a collage of scenes.

"When my father died. . ." she began, pausing instantly at the taut ripple flexed in denial from behind her. Christine extended her hand up slowly until Erik leaned in for her caress. "When he died, I remember listening to odd bits and pieces of conversation, finding safety as I clung to the skirts of Mamma Valerius. Comments floated above me, but there was something the priest said which comforted me then, and proves little more than an annoyance now. He said that my father lay reposed in hallowed ground, ground sanctified by God for such a purpose."

While Christine spoke, Erik felt the silkiness of her hair flit across his face; those strings seemed to sweep a fleeting thought of when his skin first made contact with the fascinating sensation, the clean scent, and the tingle. . .

Christine pulled him back. "Erik, why do priests use guilt and fear to instill obedience? They make the place one is buried sound more important for the salvation of the soul than any deed performed while alive. I refuse to believe it."

"If that were the case, all manner of sin could be enjoyed if one were guaranteed absolution from a consecrated resting place. No, merit comes from our choices. You are talking to one who has experienced both sides, and I much prefer the joy a conscience affords."

"What about sanctified ground? The earth is God's creation, all of it."

"Feeling a tad rebellious?" He adored the fire in her and the provoking questions.

"Yes."

"Well. . . perhaps those who are characterized as pious in their beliefs wish to provide a sense of peace for the families left behind, that their loved ones are safe, protected."

"But, Erik. . ." her hand felt leaden and rested on the strength surrounding her waist. "I feel safe here. I do not wish bars or a cage, only this. . . this, is where I want to be, close to all I hold dear."

"Christine, don't. . . please." She looked to the side to see his tear-soaked face.

"We both know that my time nears." He trembled at the serenity of fact. "I attribute my blessed extension of time to your unwavering love. Your research and knowledge of natural properties has fortified me, but you can see what our hearts wish to deny. I'm tired, Erik."

"I know."

Erik swung her up into his arms, damning his own vitality that had yet to do more than slow, though he did feel a twinge in his chest more regularly, whenever his emotions rendered him vocally mute.

Christine was correct—she did not return to the ridge again, like they had that afternoon. Their sons and their families were summoned home to join their daughter and her family, that each might partake of the precious time, individually. Every so often, Christine would request that they all gather upstairs to laugh and share stories, to hear of their lives through the challenges and joys they all faced, but above all, she remained open with her condition; questions were always soothed and frustrations balanced, so that death could be met with understanding. When Erik and Christine were alone, one could hear the mix of laughter and tears; it was bittersweet.

"Christine, may I share these journals with the children and their spouses?" Erik asked. "The nuances. . . I believe they would take comfort in knowing."

"Give them to Emili, she will know how best to share. The wonderful tales shall be a narrative of awe when they learn the stories to be true, but some lie unknown. I trust Emili will. . . understand." Her breath came in short uneven spurts, the searing darkness gripped her lungs and she sobbed in desperation.

Erik gently scooped her up and took her out into the warmth on the balcony. The heat from the fall sun permeated the coldness of her skin and she relaxed into his neck.

"Let me. . ." he prefaced, "ease the torment for you. I know you do not wish for the haze of mind or dulling of emotion. It will only be. . ."

"Later, for now it is enough to be in your embrace; *you* are my comfort."

"Let me, Christine, please."

"I want to feel, not go. . . numb. . . ugh. . ." Another breath wracked her frail body. "Forgive me." Her tears wet his chest, pooling beneath her cheek until they spilled forth from the shallow cavity at the base of his throat.

"Whatever for?"

"For," her thought trailed slightly, "leaving you. I promised."

"Hush," came Erik's soothing tone. It wrapped her mind and body in soft velvet as the melodic whisper caressed her ear. "You are not leaving me for long, nor are you leaving where I cannot follow." He hugged her, lingering until the shadows began to lengthen and ease with her breathing.

Placing her tenderly against the pillow, Erik covered her failing limbs and carefully closed the door to the world.

Time hastened.

Erik leaned at the balcony railing as the next morning burst its rays upward, away from a horizontal sleep. Closing his eyes, he listened to the strange veil of quiet. A soft touch startled him.

"Papa, she is asking for you." Erik embraced Emili and kissed her on the head, moving to follow her back inside; the children had had their time: it was well spent.

The panel slid into the frame and Erik sat beside Christine; her breathing was languid, barely noticeable as she fought to keep her eyes open.

"I'm here," he reassured, laying her hand along his arm for more contact.

"Stay close."

He brushed the softness of her cheek. "As close as you wish."

"Your embrace?"

Erik slid carefully alongside her, held her and caressed the diminishing light of her face then she touched his. "I love you, Christine Daaé. You saved me from myself."

"I will be here, in your heart."

"It will hurt."

"For a time, and then you shall pick up and go on. Emili, Chèver and Étienne. . ."

"It won't be the same. . . I ache when I see you in their eyes, their faces."

"It shall also be of comfort, my love."

Christine passed silently and peacefully that day, and her body was laid to rest on the ridge, before their symbolic triumph to courage.

The ceremony was simple, a few friends and family, then all were left to thoughts singular in belief and faith after paying their respects to Erik. Most everyone had begun the trek back toward the estate, but he wished to remain, understandably. Dressed in black, save the burgundy ascot about his neck, the tails of his overcoat flitted gingerly on an occasional breeze, his majestic shape, unmoved from the place he had last shared with Christine, hands atop the head of his cane. He gazed out, far into the distance, but there was no future; to pivot around only brought what was past, and so he would adhere to the present. *How composed I am, is it shock? No, death is inevitable; it is only the when which takes our breath away, and I breathe yet. The exchanges with people these few days. . . the people, it is just as I remember in Sweden, but the outpouring of joy has been far greater.*

"Erik." He felt a hand clamp slowly upon his shoulder. Raoul had waited, protracted his remarks until now. "I, we—Jacqueline and I..." he fumbled momentarily before gaining a fluid leash on what he wished to convey, though the words would not be enough to quell the rising knot. "We are grateful for the inclusion you so selflessly granted us in your lives, especially these, so close to..." He coughed, deeply moved, voice tenuous. "Our children have developed ties which prove steadfast and are stronger than I could have ever foreseen. When I think of what I might have denied you... I would have never forgiven myself. Christine had tremendous foresight to pursue her heart, and for that, I shall be forever grateful. You deserved love, her love..."

Erik listened intently and gave a nod of deference, shaking loose a distinguished strand of grey. Raoul squeezed lightly and moved off, leaving Erik, his lone, dark figure against the night.

As Erik smoothed his hair back into place, his demeanor broke, walking to the foot of Christine's grave. "You would have done that." Sorrow gripped his features and the first of numerous tears streamed. "Blast you, Soheil! You and your infernal predictions! Guardian! You inadvertently condemned me to watch over everyone. . . and now, I am without my companion, without her and alone again!"

His sobs pressed him humbly, trembling into the freshly turned soil. He drew a handkerchief to stifle the uncontrollable urge to scream and ripped his masque away, then knelt for what seemed like hours with a mind beating against the peace he wanted for his heart, until at long last, the tears ceased altogether.

"You said you wouldn't leave me, Christine, you promised." He spoke as a dejected child, searching for home. "You. . . promised. . ."

All was silent.

It commenced, and was no more than a spark in a blackened room, no less than a flicker compelling attention inward. Erik's hand sought out the smoldering sensation burning in his chest; it warmed and traveled through his very existence as though he had been blessed with some ethereal infusion. His eyes drifted shut, desiring the feeling to replace the numbing cold of abandon, never to flee or to dissipate, then it came stronger, forcing its heat straight to his heart; golden ministrations, desolation fed by sweet remembrance of souls.

He sensed, her. "Christine. . ."

"I am here. . . this, this is where our love continues."

Chapter Fifty-Seven

Two months have come and gone since Chèver and Étienne discovered my weakened, paralyzed body in a crumpled heap atop Christine's grave. When I did not return by dark, Emili sent the boys to search and retrieve 'for my own good' then Chèver consigned me into the capable hands of his sister, and the bed, for he knew I had been deprived of sleep, and was physically and mentally void of rationale. The emotional side wishes he would have just let me be, but that is the physician in him—preservation of life be damned!

Those first days I floated in a stupor between where I wished to be and where I did not want to wake up. What made the delirium easy to bask in was the fact that I lay where Christine had been, to pass the anniversary of our union in self-imposed isolation. It was rather simple; I said nothing, appeased no one, and made little effort to interact until they granted me a reprieve from their good intentions and went away to some other interest. I felt and smelled her very essence, and would curl up to indulge as a child would at the loss of some precious treasure. I wept.

I laid in seclusion, in similar fashion for nearly a fortnight, moping and wallowing until le petits-enfants—all of them—from the oldest, which would be Emili's son, Braeton, at thirteen, right down to Chèver's little Aimee, at one; they pestered me for attention, bless them. Not even Soheil could have matched the tenacity and relentless entreaties. By then, Chèver had pronounced me fit in body, though as stubborn in mind as an ox, and twice as thick, but his diagnosis was perplexing; a seizure, brought about by stress on the heart, and due in part to some loss of blood flow, repressed anxiety... an amusing speculation, which sounded utterly contradictory. I smiled civilly, and graciously accepted his wisdom, but there was then and is now, no denying what I felt pierce my breast and root deep within my soul. The heat, which burns from that experience, fuels my life, and is what carries me through these mundane toils of routine giving structure to my daily sojourn. Right now, it is all I have to move me forward.

My... hmm, "our" sons, were soon required to take up their own lives again, and so departed back to London and Paris, respectively. Emili and her husband Miykael have made this their home for the past three years. His wish to continue on with the breeding of our Arabians is to his credit, as he has since broadened our clientele through his intelligence of thoroughbred racing and profession in veterinary medicine. And Emili, she is like Christine in so many ways, especially the intractable side to her disposition. I am not to be left to 'rot' and so each of her children, the three of them, have been assigned on a rotating basis to Grand-père or Opa time (Miykael's mother was German)... smart woman!

Erik chuckled to himself and took a deep breath of air. He was in his usual place on the ridge, no matter the weather, convinced there was always a moment to make his daily pilgrimage, and to ponder. "Emili knows how I lose myself when teaching, well executed, my dear." A tip of his hat acknowledged his daughter, a hand laid to the warmth in his chest for his wife, and he was ready to head back. I have heard said that "old" is a state of mind imposed upon the heart. If this is indeed the case, it would explain why I suddenly feel my age. The natural color of my hair is a silvery white, though no one but Christine and I were privy to the swift transformation. Perhaps it is a physical display of suppression. Strange, how the deep scar has become lighter to bear and my strength wanes, almost as if I willingly trade a part of myself to have the serenity I need.

EMILI WATCHED FROM the balcony, anxious for her father to return, worried for him. When he left on horseback each day she thought the worst if he was too long, but constrained herself faithfully, as all women do when those they love are beyond their safe-keeping. A deep sigh rushed past her lips, seeing him ride toward the stables, which signaled the end of another watch.

"He and Miykael will soon be at the back door, and hungry," she muttered gladly, bounding down to the kitchen to make ready. It was an interesting conundrum, living married beneath the roof of one's parents in an attempt to create the delicate balance autonomy mandates between the roles of wife, mother, and daughter—the bounding was just one of those traits she refused denotation to any one category in her life, for it was an aspect to all.

"Emili?"

"I'm here, Miykael," she answered, rounding from the breakfast-parlor.

Emili's husband, though not quite as tall as her father or brothers, made an excellent presence whenever he entered a room. His features were subtle, not overly sharp, and were a compliment to his square jaw, well-groomed fair shock of hair, blue-green eyes, and broad build. She could hardly keep from staring as both men entered the preparation area.

Shedding hat and coat, Erik pointed, being keen to the hypnotic gaze before the youth had noticed. "Guard up, Kael, her target has been sighted."

"Oh, Papa! Must you be so obvious?" Emili scoffed.

"Forgive me, was I not supposed to warn your prey? *I am all for an amorous exchange, but why not make the most of it instead of flooding the air to pit hope against frustration, hmm?*" She flushed to hear such things emanate from her own father and grateful too, that the advice was heard by her alone.

"It is all right, Erik, after what. . ." Miykael paused for a quick calculation, "fifteen years?" his eyes met hers and Emili nodded, "… one becomes accustomed to the alluring stares."

"Depends on the origin," Erik offered, light concern creasing his tone for the dismissal. "That is to say, I trust you do not take them for granted?"

"Never! Not to mention—"

"Perhaps I should leave and come back later, seeing as my sex is the subject of conversation and not a participant?" Stunned and appalled, Emili untied her apron and shot them both a look of distaste then made to vacate the area by way of the nearest door to the great room.

Erik shoved Miykael. "Go catch her," he urged, watching Miykael make it past the counter to Emili, successfully arresting her effort just before she slid the panels wide enough to walk through.

"Don't go, please," he pleaded, snaring her waist from behind and kissing her neck, oblivious to others present. "Emi, I should like to settle my account, if I may."

She adored when he shortened her name by holding onto the accents with his rough, German élan, but now was not the time. "Kael, my father!" she whispered, struggling to maintain some propriety on the intent while reminding her husband of their resolve.

"Oh, I. . ." Miykael tripped over his forgetfulness and dropped his hands, making them look even more sheepish.

"Spare me, would you?" Erik spat ill-tempered, eyes lowered in disappointment that he had yet to dislodge their embedded guilt. "The taboo placed on your natural regard for the other is a mistake, and it has begun to wear on my nerves. All the skulking about and avoidance of affection. . . making it a curse hurts far more."

"We were—"

"I know, Kael, but if you have learned nothing more from living under our roof than how to hide feelings, then *we* have failed. Please, honor us by showing your affection as we did." Erik winced at the tense and approached the couple. "I always openly expressed my love for your mother at an appropriate level, when in the company of immediate family, always."

"I remember." Emili's throat thickened at the disservice she had done her parents and the pain caused. She was appreciative for the gingerly administered rebuke and walked into her father's embrace.

"Your capacity to love is endless; do not barricade its source, it is imperative for the children to see. Show it to Kael as you did prior to Mother's passing," he wished softly, kissing Emili's forehead.

"I will, Papa."

"And, I am most thankful for a caring daughter but should mention that relocation from the balcony merits some looking into, if you wish to continue your stationary reconnaissance. You are about as surreptitious as your beloved Dezi was in a field of white."

"Good thing I do not claim the occupation to be more than a hobby."

The men chuckled at her expense.

"All right, now, if you two will excuse me, I shall be in my study, reading and waiting," he looked at his pocket watch, "for Evan to join me at nine o'clock."

"What of breakfast, Papa?" she asked, her voice animating to a troublesome pitch.

"I shall forego the repast until later, if that meets with your approbation, my dear."

"It does not, though I respect it nonetheless and shall bring in some tea."

Erik made no reply and smiled weakly, striding through into the next room to retire within the pages of a good book.

When he had gone, the footsteps diminishing to silence, Emili put her arms around Miykael. "His illusion is a brave one, Kael. I know he misses her something fierce. She was everything to him and I'm afraid he won't be able to make it here alone. His eyes, I can see it, I'm going to lose them both and there is nothing I can do."

Miykael folded his hands about his wife's slender form and pulled close. "Emili, would you really want to prevent them from being together?"

She shook her head. "Since we have been back, there are things I never pieced together in my youth. . . when I was young, music, both instrumental and voice alike, would fill the halls upon occasion to an almost obsessive height. . . sometimes I resented the way it filtered and saturated my mind, happy that I could take my violin to some distant corner or out to the stables to play in Dezi's stall, but it gave me purpose and direction. I miss it. I miss it because he has not lifted a finger to that keyboard for over a year."

"The boys play, as do your brothers when they come, so there is no lack. I am sure he just wished more time with Mother."

"You do not understand," Emili exclaimed passionately, gesturing through the framed doorway to the piano, patient in its unmastered silence. "Music is what brought them together, it is how they celebrated life. You have heard them together."

"I have. Do you not suspect, that after all these years, they just discovered a more unique way to express that music?"

"I don't know. . ."

"Oh, my dearest Emi, I think you do." She looked up into the eyes of her wise, soft-spoken husband, smiling through the gathering storm, and as Miykael deflected the single drops peering too far out over the edge, she sought to press near.

"It will hurt again and reopen my sore heart, I know. . . I know all too well."

Emili knew, however, the days succeeding that fair morning gave a vague impression of hope, as if her father could read the couched print she left lingering in the shadow of her words and actions, and she rather liked the anticipation that would spirit her doubts from those impinging, sable clouds of tomorrow.

All through the winter, Erik imbued the personification of one content and industrious to the point of self-belief; the curiosities his *petits-enfants* saw, and the delight he gained while instructing, validated an ongoing inkling that despite sorrow and resilience, upon which the human will could draw, purpose was indeed, a life sustaining and empowering advocate.

ONE NIGHT, AT the close of January, the moon being near on three-quarters and fine enough in shape that it shone as if its potential were full, Erik awoke with a light cough, one prohibiting any continuance of sleep. Annoyed from within and from without, he set about to quell the tickle and wound up in the kitchen rummaging for some tea, which was an unsuccessful endeavor; he settled for steaming water and honey, unable to scare up more, and walked back into the great room to take a seat within the recess of the window. There had been one cold snap after another, but the glorious veil of stars blanketing the ground attested to him of God's desire in maintaining wonder for generations to come; it also served as a caveat that the insulation would recede and he, exposed among the grand spring of things, would not endure much past its burst.

Sporting an earnest desire to conjure sweetness from the old familiar habit of past, he deposited his cup and saucer upon the writing desk and moved over, to sit in quiet alongside his beloved instrument, exile of heart silencing them both. Erik fingered the case and pushed up on the cover; revealing the keyboard, he touched each key to reacquaint, hearing the individual sounds without depression. *All is here, awaiting emotion to unite passion to the keys. . . for you, Christine. It is time to give our past an anchor, allowing knowledge of my history to roll forth so our children may comprehend the bearing their mother had on my life. To love and to be loved, has indeed, enriched my soul.*

Erik's hands soon buried themselves in a remarkable pleasantry, yielding to the fervor pounding its truth for no other, and when his hands lifted their guiding weight, he felt the yearning succor, quenched.

"Thank you." Erik looked up from whence the voice came and sighed at the visage standing against the wall. "I could not rest and heard the music."

"Come," he encouraged her to join him.

"It was so delicate; did you compose it for Mother?"

"Yes, for our first anniversary; it is entitled *When Angels Kiss*. I am glad you listened and, you are welcome."

They sat, side-by-side, Father and Daughter consoling the dull ache when the moment was disrupted by a brief refraction, catching Erik's eye to direct his glance left. Emili was wearing her mother's necklace; he raised his finger up, kissed it, and touched the diamond. "Did she ever tell you about the smiles of heaven, and the gifts she gave me when we first wed?"

Emili nodded, fondly recalling the stories. "She did."

"And do you believe?"

"Yes." Her bottom lip quivered.

"The violins are yours, Emili. Cherish the one from Grand-père Daaé." She had lost her voice and could only press her lips to the hand she clasped within her own. "I should like today for myself, if I may, and would enjoy the company of both you and Miykael later, when the children are asleep. Will you come?"

"Yes, I'll inform Kael."

"Trust me, Emili," he said, placing his forehead to hers. "It will be all right."

Chapter Fifty-Eight

The knock came at nine-thirty that night, somewhat earlier than expected. Erik called for a moment more while stoking the fire in preparation for a time ill-determined in its length. So, his guests waited and he paced in those few minutes' intermission, organizing his thoughts upon what might be judged a confessional. Of course, there was a part of him wishing to let all secrets go with him to his grave, though, for some odd reason he felt, as did Christine, that Emili should be told. Having a less than exemplary life is always a concern when confronting antecedents with one's progeny, and altogether frightening when one is faced with divulging blatant hypocrisy. But, it would be better for them to know, no sense in setting them up for an untimely haunt because their father was less than forthright.

"Kael, Emili, please. . . come in," he invited, opening the panel. Escorting his daughter to the threesome of chairs arranged before the fireside, he turned, gesturing back toward his son-in-law and the door. "Kael, would you mind?"

"Oh, not at all."

Once the two were seated, Erik settled in against the mantle and began. "I have much to say and not knowing for sure how this will play out, I desire your questions, and shall do my utmost to answer in a clear and concise manner."

Miykael and Emili chanced a look at each other; puzzled, but committed in whatever capacity they were needed, they made assent.

"Kael, you are a talented man, have good business sense, knowledge of veterinary medicine, and share the same loves as I: a good woman, your children, and horses, though Emili shall endeavor to assist your balance in the arts." The two grinned. "You treat them well, respect and cherish them. . . no father could ask more for his only daughter. Love them," Erik demanded passionately.

"I will, Monsieur."

Erik nodded in satisfaction. "What I am about to share with you is—was—only known in its entirety by your mother. Others, knew pieces, have been involved in circumstances surrounding my existence, but never knew the full extent to which my life bore humanity." *Although,* he mused inwardly, *my Persian brother Soheil, guessed far more than he ever let on.* "I shall begin where all life does, at birth. . ."

Those wee hours of the morning, which only ever share their time with daylight, once in every twenty-four, were creeping on as the intimate trio drew their encounter to a close. Miykael had enquired heartily at first and now showed no comprehensive expression in his current state of ambiguity, sitting with fingers poised together and sight locked to the few embers left neglected. Erik had given up the floor and stood, leaning weary and careworn, his head propped against the mantle, wishing there were some gauge for measuring thought to duration of silence, however tumultuous or calm the inner workings.

Emili was the first to move, and gathering her feet she rose, gliding to her father's side. He was prepared, and knew to expect repulsion and pity, and probable rejection, but what did it matter? His companion loved him. Erik shut his eyes tight and waited.

"Papa. . ." Erik turned toward the warm touch at his shoulder, it beckoned him to circle and face his daughter, eyes transfixed. Her hands moved slowly to either side of his masque, rendering him motionless as she gently removed the covering to the small table.

The descriptions her father gave were nothing in comparison, leaving Miykael to gaze upon the scene as a whole. Even after all these years, to know and behold what actually lay behind Erik's masque had never been a priority. He felt that if it were of consequence, it would have been made known in more depth, but all was answered in that sweet moment.

Erik bent his head in shame, only to have Emili raise it for a light kiss. "You have done nothing of which to be ashamed; nothing you have shared tonight could ever alter who you are to me, Papa, to Chèver or to Étienne. I love you... you are my father, no matter your doubts, Maman *is* right, that man no longer exists. He ceased to exist when he chose integrity and trust over deceit, and has since raised his family to uphold those qualities among many others."

"My voice of endearing reason." He reached for his masque.

"No, please." She stayed his hand.

"You and Chèver always despised my masques."

"I still do, but it was Maman and Étienne who could see much more."

Erik and Emili suddenly realized that Miykael was standing near them, tears freely descending from reddened eyes. He touched Emili and she moved to one side. This was the first time Erik had afforded any of his children's spouses the experience of his exposed flesh. Looking his father-in-law straight in the eye, Miykael embraced him lovingly, and softly said, "You are a phenomenal human being, Erik, and clearly a testimony to Christine's life."

Beauty is judged from soul to soul, not from whence it is encased.

Erik relished that peaceful acceptance and made no disclosure or reference thereafter, as if biding time. Sometimes, Emili would find him staring at their family portrait during all hours of the day and evening—she supposed night visits to be part and ventured upon occasion, but never found him out, if it were indeed the case.

SPRING WOKE IN AN unusual fashion of haste, bud and leaf alike, to pay deference to one whose mission was fast coming to an end. Emili noticed a marked change the day her father departed for the ridge to plant a red rose bush at the crown of the grave site, central to where he would lay his mortal body to rest at his beloved's side. He touched his heart and pronounced all to be finished returning, strangely enough, beneath a cloud of melancholy, a singular mood of will bent toward what was to finally be granted him. Erik's health diminished steadily. He was not alone; friends and family arrived as well as acquaintances, until he became too weak and could summon naught. Emili sat by her father as she had done the previous fall with her mother, savoring one difference; it was in the absence of sorrow; this had become a trading of journeys.

"Emili, read the journals. I have left things for you, instructions. . ."

"I will, Papa." She took his hand in hers and looked at the frailness etched. Those hands loved her mother with tender regard, caressed tear stained faces, and blessed her marriage; they were hands that brought forth beauty in so many magnificent ways. She felt a squeeze.

"No masque, Emili. I wish to greet Mother with the face she helped me see, through her eyes." Tenderly, it was removed and with a sigh of relief he called her name. "Christine."

Erik felt the same burning in his chest grow more intense until a radiant light filled the room, its glory brighter than that of the sun. In the midst of the whiteness approached an image, which diffused the severity within which he was caught, until he recognized the visage he had missed.

"Christine."

"Yes," she acknowledged.

"*I was not alone.*"

"*I am glad,*" she said knowingly. "*And neither are you to experience that here. Come, there are those who wish to greet you, those who have prepared the way.*"

"But. . ."

"*Tell Emili it is time, she will understand.*"

Erik glanced to his daughter and smiled. "I must go, I. . ."

"I know, Papa. I can feel her too. Go now, go with her."

"*Come, Erik.*"

And, as he reached out, her name slowly eased past his lips. He was at peace and never looked back.

How exquisite she was to him. They touched, their hands meeting beneath an ethereal sensation; it was light and weightless, his earthly chains at last shed.

Christine smiled. "Place your hands. . . here." She guided, taking each of his under her gentle grasp, settling them upon either side of his face. Expecting to trace the forever-familiar curse of a temporal shell, he winced. It was smooth and had semblance of feature, whole and complete. Christine pressed close to his heart.

"This, my dearest Erik, is who I saw for so many years. . . beyond the masque."

Epilogue

Often, it is the foresight of another which sees when we cannot, and thus was the prediction of Emili's father established for fulfillment: that of becoming the family journalist or historian, depending on one's perception; a process remarkably cleansing when one indulges in the properties of pen and paper.

I was intrigued by the seamless passing of my father from this life to the next, and feeling immediately seized upon to loose thought on record—as time would permit of course—I set out on a journey of my own. The relating of my experience between his death and Mother's is now entwined, and appropriately so. Chèver and Étienne attended to Father's burial clothing, as I had for Mother: both were laid in white, hands crossed atop the other over their heart, the left prominently displaying their rings. Father was specific when he placed a red rose in with Mother, to supplant the removal of her jewelry, just prior to her body being committed to ground. Étienne did the same for Father, but we felt white to be a more fitting color—especially after what he had entrusted to me. The three of us stood for a long time at the feet of our parents. We were and are living proof of their passionate love and devotion for each other. Our hearts ached that day, to lose them both within months, but we knew they were together at last. No earthly ties to bind a love, which transcends death, as their spirits shall continue together what their mortal bodies could not, apart.

As Emili and Miykael bid farewell to guests and family they decided to set aside a margin of time each evening to sift through the books and information left under their stewardship. Prior to the journals, Emili experienced an awe-inspiring moment when she came across a rather large envelope addressed specifically to her. She looked at Miykael and he encouraged her to open it because, "staring would certainly not see the contents into light." He joined her on the floor and together they broke the waxen seal. Inside, was a letter, which read...

My dearest Emili,

You may recall that portion of my life I spent in reclusive, albeit a humbugged subsistence—if my life then can even be referred to in such a manner—below the Opera House in Paris. As I mentioned, everything is sealed up, every room, and was done based on a mutual decision because the legacy, in that sense alone, could not be perpetuated; it had to end. But, there is one item, one in which your mother was not even remotely aware, and such had remained lost to me for a time as well, the composition of Don Juan Triumphant.

Before I stole Mother away, I had planned for it to be quite finished, so I might take it with me to my grave, unheard. You see, I could not risk the consumption of soul or condemn another being to be tainted by such a brilliant hatred, as those red notes did in proclaiming justice; however, I never finished it. I left the last three measures unwritten. I believed that in doing so, I prolonged hope—though deep down I knew it to be a futile cause at the time—as I remembered what Mother had said to me when I explained my idea of "growing accustomed" to eternity and to the inevitable. She said, 'You must work at it as seldom as you can.' Well, that morning I could not sleep, the morning you heard me play? I played for Mother, and suddenly realized I had yet to erase the one aspect I could make right.

I finished the composition and have herein, included an uplifting arrangement devoid of hate, and one I can be proud to leave with my other compositions (its predecessor met with a just consumption by flame). The music is a transposed version for the violin. Enjoy my gift, Emili. I've trusted you as no other, and will love you forever alongside Maman.

Yours dearly, Papa

The music tumbled forth in sheets, as did the gratitude and tears.

We look forward to celebrating the glorious change in seasons each fall and spring, as I sit in my favorite place upon the rocky precipice our parents once enjoyed, listening to the teases and laughter in appreciation. Chèver came home that first fall, after speaking with Étienne and Annica, to propose our family gatherings be commemorative, and we all agreed. But it was the sight greeting us upon our visit the following spring that shall be etched and unchanged in my mind.

Just prior to sunrise we began our walk, intent on breaking our fast with the rising of the morning, remembering to bring our tools, that we might attend to a bit of pruning, as was needful. The children were running and dancing about, the adults engrossed in various bits of conversation, when Jean came to hasten us to our destination. He had been there and back already, on a mission of being "first" and now wished his discovery to be had by all before he could no longer constrain tongue and voice. It was a marvel indeed, beheld by our fresh eyes. The roses had set to bloom early on, though instead of their singular colors being displayed amongst their own, they now carried the traits of the other in varying degrees of either white or red.

I thought, how poignant... their love was an example to all of the barriers one can overcome if we set aside the obvious and see beyond, to the potential of the heart.

Endnotes

1. (p. 32) *do ut des*: Latin, meaning tit for tat, a principle of reciprocity.

2. (p. 41) *Comte de Chagny*: Comte/Vicomte are the titles of a European nobleman. Comte is from the Latin *comes*, meaning imperial companion or delegate to the emperor. French nobility was a legal characteristic, usually acquired from the father, but was later accepted from the mother's lines as well, and is based on possession of land. In this instance, the eldest son, Philippe, inherited his parents' entire estate—his brother and sisters waiving claim to their shares, respectively—though, when the sisters married, a dowry for each was provided. Upon the death of Philippe, all rights, privileges, and management became those of Raoul, whose courtesy title of vicomte elevated as sole heir.

3. (p. 59) *Borage flower*: echium amoenum (also known as 'starflower' in Persian), is an annual herb found throughout the Mediterranean region, Europe, North Africa, and Iran. As a whole, borage has properties useful to both medicinal and culinary professions. The leaves have a flavor similar to that of a cucumber and are used in salads and when ingested hot, in the form of tea, aids in the reduction of fever. As a diaphoretic, borage induces sweating, thus lowers the fever and restores *joie de vivre* (energy) during convalescence. Though prolonged use is not advisable.

4. (p. 101) *arrondissement*: a major subdivision within an administrative area in France, which is most often referred to as a neighborhood (written: 10ème).

5. (p. 109) *Bretagne*: French pronunciation of Brittany, the northwest region or province of the country, occupying a large peninsula.

6. (p. 249) *Bois de Boulogne*: a park of substantial size, being larger than Central Park in New York, and Hyde Park in London.

7. (p. 261) *Parian marble*: white, semi-transparent stone used for sculptures and construction; found on the island of Páros, Greece and highly prized by the ancient Greeks.

8. (p. 271) *cadeau*: a present/gift.

9. (p. 329) *faux pas*: an indiscretion that breaks some form of social convention and is embarrassing.

10. (p. 344) . . . *previously prolonged governmental intermission*: a reference to the untimely hold placed on the construction of the Opera House. The unveiling of the outer façade came in 1867, six years after the work began, but due to financial shortfalls the government reined in its support. Another interruption came by way of the Franco-Prussian war (July 1870 through May 1871), thus beleaguering completion—the building, while boasting triumph upon its inaugural Gala with full attendance on January 5, 1875, was as yet unfinished.

11. (p. 436) *tête-à-tête*: a private conversation between two people.

12. (p. 536) *leitmotif*: a recurring theme, which may be musical, literary, or historical in nature.

13. (p. 577) *fou rire*: fit of laughter, usually uncontrollable upon the onset.

14. (p. 650) '*Nothing was ever mentioned*': the gentleman, with whom the Persian had met, was none other than Gaston Leroux, author of *Le Fantôme de l'Opèra*.

Characters

(In order of relative appearance)

Erik (er-EEK) Gautier (gōt-YAY): aka... Phantom of the Opera, Opera Ghost (O.G.)... was born in a small town just outside Rouen, France; he is an artistic genius, architect, musical prodigy—both vocal and instrumental—and lays claim to a myriad of other skills in addition to his superior intelligence. He has done extensive traveling throughout Europe, the Middle East, and Asia. Owner of Arabian stud farm *Gautier Winds,* and resides in Amiens, France with his wife.

Christine (krees-TEEN) Daaé (dī-YAY): born in Sweden on a farm northeast of Upsala. At a young age she showed an inclination toward singing, her voice angelic, and was given an opportunity by the Valeriuses to go to school and then on to the Conservatoire in Paris. Father Daaé had sold his land to go searching for fame and fortune, but finding nothing save poverty and a soul filled with stories and music, they accepted the generosity of their patrons. She is married to Monsieur Gautier and mother of three children.

Adèle (a-DEL) Giry (zhr-REE): mother of Meg and widow of Jules Giry, was portress of the Opera in earlier times and always held herself before others with dignity, knowing she could defend her innocence as a martyr in the cause of truth. She only knew the Opera

Ghost's voice and ability to succeed in bringing about change to comply with his will, but was glad for her own fortune and rising employment at the Opera, and never happier when silence reigned.

Meg Giry de Castelot-Barbezac (Baroness): leader of a row in the corps de ballet and great gossip in her youth, who has since sobered to loyal confidant of Christine. Easing sore feet and the long hours dancing requires, she gave up theatre for the love of a British baronet.

Daroga of Mazanderan—Soheil (Ō-ayl): chief of police in Persia beneath the Shah. He searched out fairs and followed the reputation of a fantastical man, as retold by those in caravans returning to Asia, and brought him back to be employed in Persia. And, as one repays services when in another's debt, the daroga, in his kindness, provided Erik with a way to escape death.

Edouard (ay-DWAR) Mercier (mer-CYAY): widower and long-time employee of the Opera House, one could never remark that he was not earnest in providing Paris with the best place for society to gather.

Chanler (shaw^n-LER) Minot (MEE-nyō): rough, bear-like man who is altogether personable and nonjudgmental. Owner of a construction company based out of Amiens, France, he is possessed of a forthright nature and hefty dose of common sense.

Cerise (sĕ-REEZ) Minot: married to Chanler and is the refiner's fire for all that cross her path. As a nurse of obstetrics under Dr. Dubois, she maintains her ability to think quickly and act concisely in any given medical situation. She and Chanler have one son, Nicolas.

Richard James de Castelot-Barbezac (Baronet): favored by a childless uncle on his mother's side, he was bequeathed his title in a state of gratitude to be self-sustaining—being the second of two sons his elder brother would be heir, leaving him to make his own living. He enjoyed the freedoms, took care of his responsibilities autonomous of relations, but was mindful of certain obligations to family and proved himself quite capable.

Liana (LEE-an-a): young maid in the Gautier household who aspires to gain recognition in the field of obstetrics; she is mentored by Mme Minot.

Taylor Rossi (Roh-SEE): was discovered while in the employment of another and later came to work for the Gautiers as head stable master. He has learned from the foundation up what is required to make the breeding of Arabians a success.

Chèver (shë-vair) Matieu (ma-TYU) Gautier: Gautier's eldest son. Born 12 May 1880.

Comte Raoul (Ra-ool) de Chagny (shĕh-NEE): youngest child of one of the most distinguished families in France. He and Mlle Daaé had two portions of time allotted them in their early acquaintance: once when he took lessons from her father, and again when he chanced to find her visiting Perros three years later. Enjoying a furlough from the navy, they met a third time in Paris and he at once became a contender for her love.

Commissary of Police—Mifroid: heavily involved in the initial investigation of one O.G. when several people went missing in the Opera House, he was again taken up when others would have nothing to do with the case.

Comtesse Jacqueline (zhak-LEEN) de Chagny: married to the Comte de Chagny, they have two children. Her fiery wit endeared her to the-then shy Raoul and brought them together.

Emili (ay-mee-LEE) Catherine Gautier: Gautier's only daughter. Born 24 August 1882.

Étienne (ay-TYEN) Valar Gautier: Gautier's youngest son. Born 9 March, 1886.

Jeanette (zha-NET) Maryn (MAR-en) Chagny: Best friend to Emili Gautier. Born 14 November 1882.

Alec (a-lek) Jérôme (zhay-ROM) de Castelot-Barbezac: Born 10, June 1881.

René (re-NAY) Laurent (lo-RAW^n) de Castelot-Barbezac: Born 21 March 1885.

Philippe (fee-LEEP) Roche (RAW-sh) Chagny: named for his deceased oncle and an ancestor, a naval admiral. Born 27 February 1885.

Nicolas (nee-ko-LA) Minot: Minot's only son.
Valery (va-lay-REE) Minot: married to Nicolas Minot, they have three children.
Daniel (dan-YEL) Minot
Sean (ZYAN) Minot
Céleste (say-LEST) Minot
Annica (ahn-EEKA): married to Étienne Gautier.
Michele (mee-SHEL): married to Chèver Gautier.
Miykael (mee-KAYL): married to Emili Gautier.

Author's Note

I pondered often, and figured there had to be more to such an encounter, much more . . . Gaston Leroux's *Le Fantôme de l'Opèra* ends with such guarded hints of mystery and possibility, that intrigue told me it was highly probable. And so it was determined, the conclusion of this book could end with nothing less than closure and appreciation for the journey taken. I would be remiss if acknowledgments were not duly appropriated to the inspiration I attained from reading, listening, and researching until I discovered who the phantom was to me, of the beauty one may impart to another of self.

I began by reading the original work of Leroux, and then moved to the music and familiarity of Andrew Lloyd Webber, shifting to the different visual portrayals on film and returning full circle to Leroux. I experienced such fluidity of historical element as my search unearthed delicacy at every turn to entwine the lives of Erik and Christine. At first, I believed the lives mentioned belonged to those of whom I wrote, but time showed the introspection of one more, and I treasured the inclusion . . . I was there, and am now extending the invitation to others.

There is a word, which expresses the concept of *feeling into*, and is termed, *einfühlung*. It is a state of being, of listening to one's internal emotion, and describes a person's capacity to identify creatively with, and to participate in, the feelings as they are evoked by a work of art (Henderson & Brown, 1997. Glossary of Literary Theory).

Little did Gaston Leroux know that his zest for observation would bring fame, fascination, and creative interpretation posthumously, and he shall continue to do so unfailingly, as generations discover and rekindle their interest in the original novel through reintroduction. I am a firm believer that people can be profoundly touched by connection with past experiences; where humans identify and claim hold upon historical mediums. We desire trust and thusly, make a passionate connection, some of which are intrinsically felt from those carefully cultivated relationships, and most especially for those which took shape before me when it all came alive to ignite the pages.

There was more . . .
Kae D. Jacobs
December 2006

Contacts and interviews welcome, visit KaeDJacobs@gmail.com

The Last Word

There is an enormous amount of effort behind every work
of the heart.

Many thanks to:
The team at Granite Publishing & Distribution
And to my editor Lorie Humpherys
... because they believed.